THE AMERICAN READER

FROM COLUMBUS TO TODAY

*Being a Compilation or Collection
of the Personal Narratives, Relatives
and Journals Concerning the Society,
Economy, Politics, Life and Times
of Our Great and Many-Tongued
Nation —* BY THOSE WHO WERE THERE

by Paul M. Angle

RAND McNALLY & COMPANY

New York   •   Chicago   •   San Francisco

CONTENTS

vi

viii

CHAPTER XVI: NATION IN FERMENT, 1862 – 1913

CHAPTER XVII: ENJOYING LIFE — AND LEARNING,
                1865 – 1906

⟨ *A Union officer lies behind a low stone wall near Gettysburg, Pennsylvania, and watches the Confederate lines approach. How can he and his comrades withstand these men in gray who come on relentlessly even though their ranks are ripped by shrapnel, canister, and finally, musket balls? Somehow he and they do, and the officer lives to write a vivid account of the charge and its repulse a few weeks later. . . .*

The military aide of President Theodore Roosevelt, and after him, of William Howard Taft, liked to write long letters to his mother and sister, describing the habits, the characteristics, the foibles of his superiors. . . .

An old cowhand whiles away the last years of his life by putting down the recollections of his sturdy youth on range and trail. . . .

The Allied Commander in World War II tells the story of his experience at the center of civilization's greatest convulsion. . . .

Of these narratives, and hundreds like them, this book is made.

I do not pretend that this collection, or any other like it, is history in its final, balanced form. The personal narrative, the diary entry, the contemporary record of a traveler—these are too subjective, too near the event, often too prejudiced to be an adequate substitute for more formal history. Yet they have qualities that textbooks and monographs and general histories rarely achieve: they make the past real, they make it vivid, and they prove that our heritage springs from millions of ordinary people no less than from the few whose names are perpetuated in the school books.

I do not pretend, either, that these are the best selections that could be made. The firsthand literature of American history is so vast that no person can become familiar with it in a lifetime. A few years ago Wright Howes, an erudite bookseller of fifty years' experience, listed 11,450 titles, largely personal narratives or the records of contemporary observers, relating to that part of North America which, in 1776, became the United States.[1] But Mr. Howes restricted his list to books so difficult to obtain that they sell at several times their original price. Certainly the common books outnumber the rare ones ten to one. Add to the books the thousands of personal accounts that have been published by historical societies in the last one hundred and fifty years, and to those the other thousands which remain unpublished in the nation's libraries, and one acquires some notion of the enormous scope of the field.

I can only say, of the selections offered here, that they are representative in the sense that they cover many phases of human activity and that they originated with all kinds of people. I have included such subjects as industry, sports, and literature as well as politics and wars. I have tried to let the common soldiers speak as often as the generals, and when the subject permitted—the Civil War, for example, and capital and labor—each side has been given a chance to make its case.

In one respect I have departed in some measure from the strict meaning of my title. Canadians and Mexicans complain, and with justice, that we of the United States are presumptuous when we use the term "American" as applying only to our own country. But brevity and euphony dictated the old usage, and I hope that I will be forgiven for it by our neighbors north and south.

I should be remiss if I did not acknowledge the very effective help I received from my son, John E. Angle, in selecting material for this book.

PAUL M. ANGLE

---

[1] *U. S.-Iana (1700-1950)* (New York; R. R. Bowker Company, 1954.)

CHAPTER I

A NEW CONTINENT

1492 – 1692

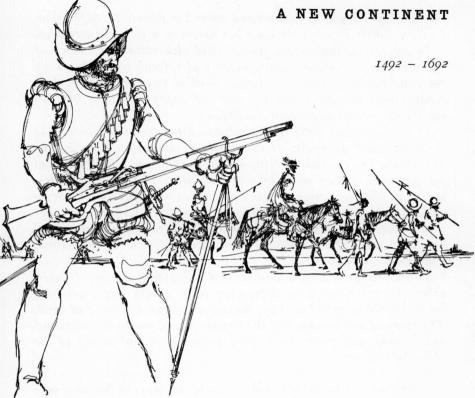

1. *1492*—COLUMBUS DISCOVERS AMERICA

❮ *By the year 1491 a native of the Italian city of Genoa had become a familiar figure at the court of Spain. For seven years Cristoforo Columbo, whom we know as Christopher Columbus, had been begging Ferdinand and Isabella to sponsor a voyage of discovery beyond the western horizon.*

Columbus was a zealot, but not an ignorant one. He had spent years at sea, and he had lived in Portugal, whose sailors were extending the map by their voyages along the western coast of Africa. He was convinced, like many informed men of his time, that the earth was round, and that one could reach the fabulous East, with its silks and spices and jewels, by sailing to the west. The Spanish monarchs were skeptical and several times rejected his proposals. But finally, in the fall of 1491, the Queen yielded to the determina-

"The Voyages of Columbus and John Cabot," in Edward Gaylord Bourne, *The Northmen, Columbus and Cabot* (New York, 1906), 90–91, 106–10, 113.

1

tion and sincerity of Columbus and agreed to finance an expedition. In the following spring she gave her assent in a formal agreement.

If successful, the voyage would yield rich returns. Cargoes of "pearls, precious stones, gold, silver and spices" would build up the royal treasury, while Columbus, entitled to a tenth of the proceeds, would become a wealthy man and enjoy the honor of governing the newly discovered dominions.

In the spring of 1492 the expedition fitted out at Palos on the southern coast of Spain. It consisted of three ships—the SANTA MARIA, the PINTA, and the NINA—all low in the waist, high fore and aft, and ridiculously small by our standards. The SANTA MARIA, largest of the three, may have been a ship of 100 tons with an overall length of 100 feet. (The QUEEN ELIZABETH, largest passenger ship afloat today, has a gross tonnage of 83,673 and an overall length of 1,031 feet.) Each ship had its complement of sailors and gentleman adventurers.

After leaving Palos, Columbus refitted at the Canary Islands, where he remained until September 6. A month later, with his crews on the verge of mutiny, he saw unmistakable signs of land. The story of the last days of the voyage is told partly in Columbus' own words, and partly by a third person who had access to the Admiral's account.

I left the city of Granada on the 12th day of May, in the same year of 1492, being Saturday, and came to the town of Palos, which is a seaport; where I equipped three vessels well suited for such service; and departed from that port, well supplied with provisions and with many sailors, on the 3d day of August of the same year, being Friday, half an hour before sunrise, taking the route to the islands of Canaria, belonging to your Highnesses, which are in the said Ocean Sea, that I might thence take my departure for navigating until I should arrive at the Indies, and give the letters of your Highnesses to those princes, so as to comply with my orders. As part of my duty I thought it well to write an account of all the voyage very punctually, noting from day to day all that I should do and see, and that should happen, as will be seen further on. Also, Lords Princes, I resolved to describe each night what passed in the day, and to note each day how I navigated at night. I propose to construct a new chart for navigating, on which I shall delineate all the sea and lands of the Ocean in their proper positions under their bearings; and further, I propose to prepare a book, and to put down all as it were in a picture, by latitude from the equator, and western longitude. Above all, I shall have accomplished much, for I shall forget sleep, and shall work at the business of navigation, that so the service may be performed; all of which will entail great labor.

Friday, 3d of August

We departed on Friday, the 3d of August, in the year 1492, from the bar of Saltes, at 8 o'clock, and proceeded with a strong sea breeze until sunset, towards the south, for 60 miles, equal to 15 leagues;[1] afterwards S.W. and W.S.W., which was the course for the Canaries. . . .

Sunday, 7th of October

. . . This day, at sunrise, the caravel *Niña,* which went ahead, being the best sailer, and pushed forward as much as possible to sight the land first, so as to enjoy the reward which the Sovereigns had promised to whoever should see it first, hoisted a flag at the mast-head and fired a gun, as a signal that she had sighted land, for such was the Admiral's order. He had also ordered that, at sunrise and sunset, all the ships should join him; because those two times are most proper for seeing the greatest distance, the haze clearing away. No land was seen during the afternoon, as reported by the caravel *Niña,* and they passed a great number of birds flying from N. to S.W. This gave rise to the belief that the birds were either going to sleep on land, or were flying from the winter which might be supposed to be near in the land whence they were coming. The Admiral was aware that most of the islands held by the Portuguese were discovered by the flight of birds. For this reason he resolved to give up the west course, and to shape a course W.S.W. for the two following days. He began the new course one hour before sunset. They made good, during the night, about 5 leagues, and 23 in the day, altogether 28 leagues.

Monday, 8th of October

The course was W.S.W., and 11½ or 12 leagues were made good in the day and night; and at times it appears that they went at the rate of 15 miles an hour during the night. . . . The sea was like the river at Seville. "Thanks be to God," says the Admiral, "the air is very soft like the April at Seville; and it is a pleasure to be here, so balmy are the breezes." The weed seemed to be very fresh. There were many landbirds, and they took one that was flying to the S.W. Terns, ducks, and a booby were also seen.

Tuesday, 9th of October

The course was S.W., and they made 5 leagues. The wind then changed, and the Admiral steered W. by N. 4 leagues. Altogether, in day and night, they made 11 leagues by day and 20½ leagues by night; counted as 17 leagues altogether. Throughout the night birds were heard passing.

---

[1] The Spanish league was approximately three nautical miles. The nautical miles measures 6,067.1 feet; the U.S. statute mile 5,280 feet.

Wednesday, 10th of October

The course was W.S.W., and they went at the rate of 10 miles an hour, occasionally 12 miles, and sometimes 7. During the day and night they made 59 leagues, counted as no more than 44. Here the people could endure no longer. They complained of the length of the voyage. But the Admiral cheered them up in the best way he could, giving them good hopes of the advantages they might gain from it. He added that, however much they might complain, he had to go to the Indies, and that he would go on until he found them, with the help of our Lord.

Thursday, 11th of October

The course was W.S.W., and there was more sea than there had been during the whole of the voyage. They saw sandpipers, and a green reed near the ship. Those of the caravel *Pinta* saw a cane and a pole, and they took up another small pole which appeared to have been worked with iron; also another bit of cane, a land-plant, and a small board. The crew of the caravel *Niña* also saw signs of land, and a small branch covered with berries. Every one breathed afresh and rejoiced at these signs. The run until sunset was 27 leagues.

After sunset the Admiral returned to his original west course, and they went along at the rate of 12 miles an hour. Up to two hours after midnight they had gone 90 miles, equal to 22½ leagues. As the caravel *Pinta* was a better sailer, and went ahead of the Admiral, she found the land, and made the signals ordered by the Admiral. The land was first seen by a sailor named Rodrigo de Triana. But the Admiral, at ten o'clock, being on the castle of the poop, saw a light, though it was so uncertain that he could not affirm it was land. He called Pero Gutierrez, a gentleman of the King's bed-chamber, and said that there seemed to be a light, and that he should look at it. He did so, and saw it. The Admiral said the same to Rodrigo Sanchez of Segovia, whom the King and Queen had sent with the fleet as inspector, but he could see nothing, because he was not in a place whence anything could be seen. After the Admiral had spoken he saw the light once or twice, and it was like a wax candle rising and falling. It seemed to few to be an indication of land; but the Admiral made certain that land was close. When they said the *Salve*, which all the sailors were accustomed to sing in their way, the Admiral asked and admonished the men to keep a good look-out on the forecastle, and to watch well for land; and to him who should first cry out that he saw land, he would give a silk doublet, besides the other rewards promised by the Sovereigns. . . . At two hours after midnight the land was sighted at a distance of two leagues. They shortened sail, and lay by under the mainsail without the bonnets.

Friday, 12th of October

The vessels were hove to, waiting for daylight; and on Friday they arrived at a small island of the Lucayos, called, in the language of the Indians, Guanahani.[2] Presently they saw naked people. The Admiral went on shore in the armed boat, and Martin Alonso Pinzon, and Vicente Yañez, his brother, who was the captain of the *Niña*. The Admiral took the royal standard, and the captains went with two banners of the green cross, which the Admiral took in all the ships as a sign, with an F and a Y[3] and a crown over each letter, one on one side of the cross and the other on the other. Having landed, they saw trees very green, and much water, and fruits of diverse kinds. The Admiral called to the two captains, and to the others who leaped on shore, and to Rodrigo Escovedo, secretary of the whole fleet, and to Rodrigo Sanchez of Segovia, and said that they should bear faithful testimony that he, in presence of all, had taken, as he now took, possession of the said island for the King and for the Queen his Lords, making the declarations that are required, as is now largely set forth in the testimonies which were then made in writing. . . .

This island is rather large and very flat, with bright green trees, much water, and a very large lake in the centre, without any mountain, and the whole land so green that it is a pleasure to look on it. The people are very docile, and for the longing to possess our things, and not having anything to give in return, they take what they can get, and presently swim away. Still, they give away all they have got, for whatever may be given to them, down to broken bits of crockery and glass. I saw one give 16 skeins of cotton for three *ceotis*[4] of Portugal, equal to one *blanca* of Spain, the skeins being as much as an *arroba* of cotton thread. I shall keep it, and shall allow no one to take it, preserving it all for your Highnesses, for it may be obtained in abundance. It is grown in this island, though the short time did not admit of my ascertaining this for a certainty. Here also is found the gold they wear fastened in their noses. But, in order not to lose time, I intend to go and see if I can find the island of Cipango.[5]

2.   *1541*—CORONADO FINDS STRAW HUTS INSTEAD OF GOLD

⟨ *Columbus never found Cipango, or Cathay, or any of the other lands of the Far East. After four voyages he died unaware of the fact that he had discovered a new world. His countrymen, how-*

George Parker Winship, *The Journey of Coronado, 1540–1542* (New York, 1922), 213–20.

[2] Watling Island in the Bahamas, British West Indies.
[3] For Ferdinand and Ysabel.
[4] Small coins of the time.
[5] Japan. On this first voyage Columbus progressed no farther than the island of Hispaniola, now occupied by Haiti and the Dominican Republic.

5

ever, soon realized that new lands lay before them—lands which
offered wealth, places of power, and souls to be saved for the glory
of God. In conquests marked by incredible bravery and equal
cruelty, Cortés took Mexico from the Aztecs, Pizarro seized Peru
from the Incas.

The Spanish wanted more gold, even, than these conquests af-
forded. When reports reached Coronado, governor of one of the
northern districts of Mexico, that seven glittering cities stood in a
region called Cíbola far to the north, he organized an expedition
to conquer them. In early July, 1540, after months of arduous
marching, he reached his destination, only to find that the fabled
cities were adobe pueblos in what is now north central New Mexico.

But no Spaniard of Coronado's time could resist the lure of gold.
When Indians told the Spanish commander of a rich city, called
Quivira, far to the east, he decided that it might make up for the
riches he had failed to find at Cíbola. On April 23, 1541, he set out
from his camp near the present city of Albuquerque. Six months
later he wrote a report of his expedition to Charles I of Spain.

Although Coronado had penetrated a new country as far, perhaps,
as central Kansas, and had added much to geographical knowledge,
he returned to Mexico a failure in his own eyes and in the view
of the Spanish officials.

After nine days' march I reached some plains, so vast that I did not
find their limit anywhere that I went, although I traveled over them for
more than 300 leagues. And I found such a quantity of cows[6] in these,
of the kind that I wrote Your Majesty about, which they have in this
country, that it is impossible to number them, for while I was journey-
ing through these plains, until I returned to where I first found them,
there was not a day that I lost sight of them. And after seventeen days'
march I came to a settlement of Indians who are called Querechos, who
travel around with these cows, who do not plant, and who eat the raw
flesh and drink the blood of the cows they kill, and they tan the skins
of the cows, with which all the people of this country dress themselves
here. They have little field tents made of the hides of the cows, tanned
and greased, very well made, in which they live while they travel
around near the cows, moving with these. They have dogs which they
load, which carry their tents and poles and belongings. These people
have the best figures of any that I have seen in the Indies. They could
not give me any account of the country where the guides were taking
me. I traveled five days more as the guides wished to lead me, until I
reached some plains, with no more landmarks than as if we had been

---

[6] Buffaloes.

swallowed up in the sea, where they strayed about, because there was not a stone, nor a bit of rising ground, nor a tree, nor a shrub, nor anything to go by. There is much very fine pasture land, with good grass. And while we were lost in these plains, some horsemen who went off to hunt cows fell in with some Indians who also were out hunting, who are enemies of those that I had seen in the last settlement, and of another sort of people who are called Teyas; they have their bodies and faces all painted, are a large people like the others, of a very good build; they eat the raw flesh just like the Querechos, and live and travel round with the cows in the same way as these. I obtained from these an account of the country where the guides were taking me, which was not like what they had told me, because these made out that the houses there were not built of stones, with stories, as my guides had described it, but of straw and skins, and a small supply of corn there.

This news troubled me greatly, to find myself on these limitless plains, where I was in great need of water, and often had to drink it so poor that it was more mud than water. Here the guides confessed to me that they had not told the truth in regard to the size of the houses, because these were of straw, but that they had done so regarding the large number of inhabitants and the other things about their habits. . . . It seemed to me best, in order to see if there was anything there of service to Your Majesty, to go forward with only 30 horsemen until I should be able to see the country, so as to give Your Majesty a true account of what was to be found in it. I sent all the rest of the force I had with me to this province, with Don Tristan de Arellano in command, because it would have been impossible to prevent the loss of many men, if all had gone on, owing to the lack of water and because they also had to kill bulls and cows on which to sustain themselves. And with only the 30 horsemen whom I took for my escort, I traveled forty-two days after I left the force, living all this while solely on the flesh of the bulls and cows which we killed, at the cost of several of our horses which they killed, because, as I wrote Your Majesty, they are very brave and fierce animals; and going many days without water, and cooking the food with cow dung, because there is not any kind of wood in all these plains, away from the gullies and rivers, which are very few.

It was the Lord's pleasure that, after having journeyed across these deserts seventy-seven days, I arrived at the province they call Quivira, to which the guides were conducting me, and where they had described to me houses of stone, with many stories; and not only are they not of stone, but of straw, but the people in them are as barbarous as all those whom I have seen and passed before this; they do not have cloaks, nor cotton of which to make these, but use the skins of the cattle they kill, which they tan, because they are settled among these on a very large river. They eat the raw flesh like the Querechos and Teyas; they are enemies of one another, but are all of the same sort of people, and these at Quivira have the advantage in the houses they build and in planting corn. In this province of which the guides who brought me are natives, they received me peaceably, and although they told me when I set out for it that I could not succeed in seeing it all in two months, there are not more than 25 villages of straw houses there and in all the rest of the country that I saw and learned about, which gave their obedience to Your Majesty and placed themselves under your royal overlordship.

The province of Quivira is 950 leagues from Mexico. Where I reached it, it is in the fortieth degree. The country itself is the best I have ever seen for producing all the products of Spain, for besides the land itself being very fat and black and being very well watered by the rivulets and springs and rivers, I found prunes like those of Spain and nuts and very good sweet grapes and mulberries. I have treated the natives of this province, and all the others whom I found wherever I went, as well as was possible, agreeably to what Your Majesty had commanded, and they have received no harm in any way from me or from those who went in my company. I remained twenty-five days in this province of Quivira, so as to see and explore the country and also to find out whether there was anything beyond which could be of service to Your Majesty, because the guides who had brought me had given me an account of other provinces beyond this. And what I am sure of is that there is not any gold nor any other metal in all that country, and the other things of which they had told me are nothing but little villages, and in many of these they do not plant anything and do not have any houses except of skins and sticks, and they wander around with the cows; so that the account they gave me was false, because they wanted to persuade me to go there with the whole force, believing that as the way was through such uninhabited deserts, and from the lack of water, they would get us where we and our horses would die of hunger. And the guides confessed this, and said they had done it by the advice and orders of the natives of these provinces. At this, after having heard the account of what was beyond, which I have given above, I returned to these provinces to provide for the force I had sent back here and to give Your Majesty an account of what this country amounts to, because I wrote Your Majesty that I would do so when I went there.

3. *1541*—DE SOTO DISCOVERS THE MISSISSIPPI

❲ *While Coronado chased a will-o'-the-wisp in the Southwest, another Spaniard was engaged in the same vain search several hundred miles to the east and north.*

"The Narrative of the Expedition of Hernando de Soto by the Gentleman of Elvas," *Spanish Explorers in the Southern United States, 1528–1534* (New York, 1907), 201–04.

Hernando De Soto had served with Pizarro in the conquest of Peru. Concluding that Florida held as much wealth as the land of the Incas, De Soto returned to Spain and obtained from the king permission to undertake the conquest. In the mother country and in Cuba, of which he was made governor, he raised a small army. In the late spring of 1539 the expedition landed on the shore of Charlotte Bay on the west coast of Florida.

De Soto marched north, then west, zigzagging back and forth over much of what is now the southeastern section of the United States. Always hunting the elusive gold, his men fought with the Indians, suffered casualties continuously, underwent constant hardships. In April, 1541, they came to the Mississippi River some thirty or thirty-five miles below the present city of Memphis, Tennessee.

In this account by "The Gentleman of Elvas," a member of the expedition, the Mississippi is not named, nor is it given much prominence in the narrative. The explorers, as so often happens, did not realize the importance of their discovery.

Three days having gone by since some maize had been sought after, and but little found in comparison with the great want there was of it, the Governor[7] became obliged to move at once, notwithstanding the wounded had need of repose, to where there should be abundance. He accordingly set out for Quizquiz,[8] and marched seven days through a wilderness, having many pondy places, with thick forests, all fordable, however, on horseback, except some basins or lakes that were swum. He arrived at a town of Quizquiz without being descried, and seized all the people before they could come out of their houses. . . .

There was little maize in the place, and the Governor moved to another town, half a league from the great river,[9] where it was found in sufficiency. He went to look at the river, and saw that near it there was much timber of which piraguas[10] might be made, and a good situation in which the camp might be placed. He directly moved, built houses, and settled on a plain a crossbow-shot from the water, bringing together there all the maize of the towns behind, that at once they might go to work and cut down trees for sawing out planks to build barges. The Indians soon came from up the stream, jumped on shore, and told the Governor that they were the vassals of a great lord, named Aquixo, who was the suzerain of many towns and people on the other shore; and they made known from him, that he would come the day after, with all his people, to hear what his lordship would command him.

---

[7] De Soto.
[8] Roughly, what is now western Tennessee.
[9] The Mississippi.
[10] Long narrow canoes hollowed from the trunks of trees.

The next day the cacique[11] arrived, with two hundred canoes filled with men, having weapons. They were painted with ochre, wearing great bunches of white and other plumes of many colors, having feathered shields in their hands, with which they sheltered the oarsmen on either side, the warriors standing erect from bow to stern, holding bows and arrows. The barge in which the cacique came had an awning at the poop, under which he sate; and the like had the barges of the other chiefs; and there, from under the canopy, where the chief man was, the course was directed and orders issued to the rest. All came down together, and arrived within a stone's cast of the ravine, whence the cacique said to the Governor, who was walking along the river-bank, with others who bore him company, that he had come to visit, serve, and obey him; for he had heard that he was the greatest of lords, the most powerful on all the earth, and that he must see what he would have him do. The Governor expressed his pleasure, and besought him to land, that they might the better confer; but the chief gave no reply, ordering three barges to draw near, wherein was great quantity of fish, and loaves like bricks, made of the pulp of plums (persimmons), which Soto receiving, gave him thanks and again entreated him to land.

Making the gift had been a pretext, to discover if any harm might be done; but, finding the Governor and his people on their guard, the cacique began to draw off from the shore, when the crossbowmen who were in readiness, with loud cries shot at the Indians, and struck down five or six of them. They retired with great order, not one leaving the oar, even though the one next to him might have fallen, and covering themselves, they withdrew. Afterwards they came many times and landed; when approached, they would go back to their barges. These were fine-looking men, very large and well formed; and what with the awnings, the plumes, and the shields, the pennons, and the number of people in the fleet, it appeared like a famous armada of galleys.

During the thirty days that were passed there, four piraguas were built, into three of which, one morning, three hours before daybreak, the Governor ordered twelve cavalry to enter, four in each, men in whom he had confidence that they would gain the land notwithstanding the Indians, and secure the passage, or die: he also sent some cross-bowmen of foot with them, and in the other piragua, oarsmen, to take them to the opposite shore. He ordered Juan de Guzman to cross with the infantry, of which he had remained captain in the place of Francisco Maldonado; and because the current was stiff, they went up along the side of the river a quarter of a league, and in passing over they were carried down, so as to land opposite the camp; but, before arriving there, at twice the distance of a stone's cast, the horsemen

---

[11] Chief.

rode out from the piraguas to an open area of hard and even ground, which they all reached without accident.

So soon as they had come to shore the piraguas returned; and when the sun was up two hours high, the people had all got over. The distance was near half a league: a man standing on the shore could not be told, whether he were a man or something else, from the other side. The stream was swift, and very deep; the water, always flowing turbidly, brought along from above many trees and much timber, driven onward by its force. There were many fish of several sorts, the greater part differing from those of the fresh waters of Spain.

4. *1542*—DEATH COMES TO THE EXPLORER

❨ *After crossing the Mississippi, De Soto's men made their way through what is now Arkansas and then turned south. At a place called Autiamque on the Ouachita River they spent the bitter winter of 1541–42. With spring they took up their march again, this time in a southeasterly direction. Mid-April found them on the west bank of the Mississippi. The lack of canoes and the hostility of the Indians kept them from crossing. There, on May 21, the intrepid Governor came to his end.*

De Moscoso led the 320 survivors of the expedition to Panuco in Mexico, which they did not reach until the fall of 1543.

The Governor, conscious that the hour approached in which he should depart this life, commanded that all the King's officers should be called before him, the captains and the principal personages, to whom he made a speech. He said that he was about to go into the presence of God, to give account of all his past life; and since He had been pleased to take him away at such a time, and when he could recognize the moment of his death, he, His most unworthy servant, rendered Him hearty thanks. He confessed his deep obligations to them all, whether present or absent, for their great qualities, their love and loyalty to his person, well tried in the sufferance of hardship, which he ever wished to honor, and had designed to reward, when the Almighty should be pleased to give him repose from labor with greater prosperity to his fortune. He begged that they would pray for him, that through mercy he might be pardoned his sins, and his soul be received in glory: he asked that they would relieve him of the charge he held over them, as well of the indebtedness he was under to them all, as to forgive him any wrongs they might have received at his hands. To prevent any divisions that might arise, as to who should command, he asked that

"The Narrative of . . . the Gentleman of Elvas," *Spanish Explorers in the Southern United States, 1528–1534*, 232–34.

they would be pleased to elect a principal and able person to be governor, one with whom they should all be satisfied, and, being chosen, they would swear before him to obey: that this would greatly satisfy him, abate somewhat the pains he suffered, and moderate the anxiety of leaving them in a country, they knew not where.

Baltasar de Gallegos responded in behalf of all, consoling him with remarks on the shortness of the life of this world, attended as it was by so many toils and afflictions, saying that whom God earliest called away, He showed particular favor; with many other things appropriate to such an occasion: And finally, since it pleased the Almighty to take him to Himself, amid the deep sorrow they not unreasonably felt, it was necessary and becoming in him, as in them, to conform to the Divine Will: that as respected the election of a governor, which he ordered, whomsoever his Excellency should name to the command, him would they obey. Thereupon the Governor nominated Luys Moscoso de Alvarado to be his captain-general; when by all those present was he straightway chosen and sworn Governor.

The next day, the twenty-first of May, departed this life the magnanimous, the virtuous, the intrepid captain, Don Hernando de Soto, Governor of Cuba and Adelantado of Florida. He was advanced by fortune, in the way she is wont to lead others, that he might fall the greater depth: he died in a land, and at a time, that could afford him little comfort in his illness, when the danger of being no more heard from stared his companions in the face, each one himself having need of sympathy, which was the cause why they neither gave him their companionship nor visited him, as otherwise they would have done.

Luys de Moscoso determined to conceal what had happened from the Indians; for Soto had given them to understand that the Christians were immortal; besides, they held him to be vigilant, sagacious, brave; and, although they were at peace, should they know him to be dead, they, being of their nature inconstant, might venture on making an attack; and they were credulous of all that he had told them, for he made them believe that some things which went on among them privately, he had discovered without their being able to see how, or by what means; and that the figure which appeared in a mirror he showed, told him whatsoever they might be about, or desired to do; whence neither by word nor deed did they dare undertake any thing to his injury.

So soon as the death had taken place, Luys de Moscoso directed the body to be put secretly into a house, where it remained three days; and thence it was taken at night, by his order, to a gate of the town, and buried within. The Indians, who had seen him ill, finding him no longer, suspected the reason; and passing by where he lay, they observed the ground loose, and, looking about, talked among themselves. This coming to the knowledge of Luys de Moscoso, he ordered the corpse to be taken up at night, and among the shawls that enshrouded it having cast abundance of sand, it was taken out in a canoe and committed to the middle of the stream. The cacique of Guachoya asked for him, saying: "What has been done with my brother and lord, the Governor?" Luys de Moscoso told him that he had ascended into the skies, as he had done on many other occasions; but as he would have to be detained there some time, he had left him in his stead. The chief, thinking within himself that he was dead, ordered two well-proportioned young men to be brought, saying, that it was the usage of the country, when any lord died, to kill some persons, who should accompany and serve him on the way, on which account they were brought; and he told him to command their heads to be struck off, that they might go accordingly to attend his friend and master. Luys de Moscoso replied to him, that the Governor was not dead, but only gone into the heavens, having taken with him of his soldiers sufficient number for his need, and he besought him to let those Indians go, and from that time forward not to follow so evil a practice. They were presently ordered to be let loose, that they might return to their houses; but one of them refused to leave, alleging that he did not wish to remain in the power of one who, without cause, condemned him to die, and that he who had saved his life he desired to serve as long as he should live.

5. *1534*—CARTIER STAKES A CLAIM FOR FRANCE

⟨ *While the Spanish were hunting for gold in the southern part of the newly discovered continent, and incidentally exploring it, the French were at work thousands of miles farther north. In the spring of 1534 Jacques Cartier, an experienced navigator, sailed from St. Malo for the new world with the blessing and financial support of the French king, Francis I. The expedition, consisting of two ships, each of sixty tons burthen, made its way across the north Atlantic to the east coast of Newfoundland, and then through Belle Isle Strait to the Gulf of St. Lawrence. By mid-July the explorers were in Gaspé Bay. Delayed there, Cartier made a point of observing the Indians, undoubtedly the Hurons and Iroquois, and took possession of the country for his king.*

We lay at the entrance until the 16th,[12] hoping to have good weather to go out. And the said day, the 16th, which was Thursday, the wind increased so much that one of our ships lost an anchor, and it behooved us to enter seven or eight leagues farther up this stream, in a good and

James Phinney Baxter, *A Memoir of Jacques Cartier* (New York, 1906), 108–12.
[12] July 16, 1534.

safe harbor that we had been to see with our boats. And owing to the evil weather, the storm and obscurity that it caused, we were in this harbor and stream until the 25th day of the said month, without being able to go out, during the which time we saw a great number of savages, who had come into the said stream to fish for mackerel, of which there is great abundance; and there were men, women, and children as well, more than two hundred persons, who had about forty boats, who, after having been a little on land with them, came freely with their boats close alongside our ships. We gave them knives, paternosters of glass, combs, and other articles of little worth, for which they made many signs of joy, raising their hands to the sky while singing and dancing in their boats. These people can well be called savages, because they are the poorest folks that there may be in the world, for altogether they have not the value of five sous, their boats and their fishing-nets excepted. They are wholly naked, except a little skin with which they cover their private parts, and some old skins of beasts which they throw over them scarf-wise. They are not by nature nor tongue like the first we found. They have their heads shorn close all about, except a tuft on the top of the head, which they leave long like a horse's tail, which they tie and bind upon their heads in a lump with thongs of leather. They have no other lodgings but under their said boats, which they turn over before lying down on the ground. Under these they eat their flesh almost raw after being a little warmed on coals, and likewise their fish. We went on Magdalen Day with our boats to the place where they were on the shore of the stream, and landed freely among them; for which they showed great joy, and all the men began to sing and dance in two or three bands, making great signs of joy of our coming. But they had caused all the young women to flee into the woods, save two or three who remained, to whom we gave each a comb, and to each a little tin bell, wherefore they showed great joy, thanking the captain by stroking his arms and breast with their hands. And seeing what he had given to those who had remained, they made those return who had fled to the woods, in order to get from him as much as the others, who were quite a score, who gathered about the said captain, while stroking him with their hands, which is their style of endearment; and he gave them each her little tin bell of small value, and immediately they assembled together to chatter and sing a number of songs. We found a great quantity of mackerel that they had caught near the shore with the nets which they have for fishing, which are of hemp that grows in their country where they ordinarily abide; for they only come to the sea in the season of fishing, as far as I have learned and understood. Likewise there grows a large millet like peas, the same as in Brazil, which they eat in place of bread, of which they have full plenty with them, which they name in their language

Kagaige.[13] . . . If one shows them anything of which they may not have and which they do not know what it is, they shake their heads and say, "Nouda," which is to say that there is not any of it and they know not what it is. Of the things which they have they showed us by signs in what manner it grows, and how they dress it. They never eat a thing wherein there may be a taste of salt. They are to a marvelous degree thieves of all that they can steal.

The 24th day of the said month we caused a cross to be made thirty feet in height, which was made before a number of them on the point at the entrance of the said harbor, on the cross-bar of which we put a shield embossed with three fleurs-de-lis, and above where it was an inscription graven in wood in letters of large form, "VIVE LE ROY DE FRANCE." And this cross we planted on the said point before them, the which they beheld us make and plant; and after it was raised in the air we all fell on our knees, with hands joined, while adoring it before them, and made them signs, looking up and showing them the sky, that by it was our redemption, for which they showed much admiration, turning and beholding the cross.

6. *1535*—CARTIER DISCOVERS THE ST. LAWRENCE AND GIVES MOUNT ROYAL ITS NAME

❮ *A few days after planting the cross at Gaspé Bay, Cartier set sail for France. The following summer he returned, this time with three ships. At Blanc Sablon on Belle Isle Strait, the place of rendezvous for his little fleet, he heard for the first time of the great river of Canada and a populous town called Hochelaga on an island in the river hundreds of miles inland. He decided to ascend that far, even though he had learned enough about the river to be sure that it was not the coveted passage to the Far East.*

About September 12, 1535, Cartier entered the broad St. Lawrence. Two weeks later he found a good harbor at the site of the present city of Quebec. There he left his ships and continued the journey in small boats. On October 2 the party reached its destination, the future city of Montreal.

We navigated with weather at will until the second day of October, when we arrived at the said Hochelaga, which is about forty-five leagues distant from the place where the said pinnace was left, during which time and on the way we found many folks of the country, the which brought us fish and other victuals, dancing and showing great joy at our coming. And to attract and hold them in amity with us, the

Baxter, *A Memoir of Jacques Cartier*, 161–71.
[13] Maize, or Indian corn.

said captain gave them for recompense some knives, paternosters, and other trivial goods, with which they were much content. And we having arrived at the said Hochelaga, more than a thousand persons presented themselves before us, men, women, and children alike, the which gave us as good reception as ever father did to child, showing marvelous joy; for the men in one band danced, the women on their side and the children on the other, the which brought us store of fish and of their bread made of coarse millet, which they cast into our said boats in a way that it seemed as if it tumbled from the air. Seeing this, our said captain landed with a number of his men, and as soon as he was landed they gathered all about him, and about all the others, giving them an unrestrained welcome. And the women brought their children in their arms to make them touch the said captain and others, making a rejoicing which lasted more than half an hour. And our captain, witnessing their liberality and good will, caused all the women to be seated and ranged in order, and gave them certain paternosters of tin and other trifling things, and to a part of the men knives. Then he retired on board the said boats to sup and pass the night, while these people remained on the shore of the said river nearest the said boats all night, making fires and dancing, crying all the time "Aguyaze!" which is their expression of mirth and joy.

The next day, in the early morning, the captain attired himself and had his men put in order to go to see the town and habitation of the said people, and a mountain that is adjacent to their said town, whither the gentlemen and twenty mariners went with the said captain, and left the rest for the guard of the boats, and took three men of the said town of Hochelaga to bring and conduct them to the said place. And we, being on the road, found it as well beaten as it might be possible to behold, and the fairest and best land, all full of oaks as fine as there may be in a forest of France, under the which all the ground was covered with acorns. And we, having marched about a league and a half, found on the way one of the chief lords of the said town of Hochelaga, accompanied by a number of persons, the which made us a sign that we should rest at the said place near a fire that they had made by the said road, which we did, and then the said lord began to make a discourse and oration, as heretofore is said to be their custom of showing joy and familiarity, this lord thereby showing welcome to the said captain and his company; the which captain gave him a couple of hatchets and a couple of knives, with a cross and memorial of the crucifixion, which he made him kiss, and hung it on his neck, for which he rendered thanks to the said captain. This done, we marched farther on, and about a half-league from there we began to find the land cultivated, and fair, large fields full of grain of their country, which is like Brazil millet, as big or bigger than peas, on which they live just as we do on wheat; and in the midst of these fields is located and seated the town of Hochelaga, near to and adjoining a mountain, which is cultivated round about it and highly fertile, from the summit of which one sees a very great distance. We named the said mountain Mont Royal. The said town is quite round and inclosed with timbers in three rows in the style of a pyramid, crossed at the top, having the middle row in the style of a perpendicular line; then ranged with timbers laid along, well joined and tied in their manner, and is in height about two pikes. There is in this town but one gate and entrance, which fastens with bars, upon which and in many places of the said inclosure there are kinds of galleries and ladders to mount to them, which are furnished with rocks and stones for the guard and defense of it. There are within this town about fifty long houses of about fifty paces or more each, and twelve or fifteen paces wide, and all made of timbers covered and garnished with great pieces of bark and strips of the said timber, as broad as tables, well tied artificially according to their manner. And within these there are many lodgings and chambers, and in the middle of these houses there is a great room on the ground where they make their fire and live in common; after that the men retire with their wives and children to their said chambers.

When we had arrived near the town, a great number of the inhabitants of it presented themselves before us, who, after their fashion of doing, gave us a good reception; and by our guides and conductors we were brought to the middle of the town, where there was a place between the houses the extent of a stone's throw or about in a square, who made us a sign that we should stop at the said place, which we did. And suddenly all the women and girls of the said town assembled together, a part of whom were burdened with children in their arms, and who came to us to stroke our faces, arms, and other places upon our bodies that they could touch; weeping with joy to see us; giving us the best welcome that was possible to them, and making signs to us that it might please us to touch their said children. After the which things the men made the women retire, and seated themselves on the ground about us, as if we might wish to play a mystery. And, suddenly, a number of men came again, who brought each a square mat in the fashion of a carpet, and spread them out upon the ground in the middle of the said place and made us rest upon them. After which things were thus done there was brought by nine or ten men the king and lord of the country, whom they call in their language Agohanna, who was seated upon a great skin of a stag; and they came to set him down in the said place upon the said mats beside our captain, making us a sign that he was their king and lord. This Agohanna was about the age of fifty years, and was not better appareled than the others, save that he had about his head a kind of red band for his crown, made of the quills of porcupines; and this lord was wholly impotent and diseased in his limbs. After he had made his sign of salutation to the said captain and to his folks, making them evident signs that they should make them very welcome, he showed his arms and legs to the said captain, praying that he would touch them, as though he would beg healing and health from him; and then the captain began to stroke his arms and legs with his hands; whereupon the said Agohanna took the band and crown that he had upon his head and gave it to our captain; and immediately there were brought to the said captain many sick ones, as blind, one-eyed, lame, impotent, and folks so very old that the lids of their eyes hung down even upon their cheeks, setting and laying them down nigh to our said captain for him to touch them, so that it seemed as if God had descended there in order to cure them.

Our said captain, seeing the misery and faith of this said people, recited the Gospel of St. John: to wit, the *In principio,* making the sign of the cross on the poor sick ones, praying God that he might give them knowledge of our holy faith and the passion of our Saviour, and grace to receive Christianity and baptism. Then our said captain took a prayer-book and read full loudly, word by word, the passion of our Lord, so that all the bystanders could hear it, while all these poor people kept a great silence and were marvelously good hearers, looking up to heaven and making the same ceremonies that they saw us make; after which the captain made all the men range themselves on one side, the women on another, and the children another, and gave to the chiefs hatchets, to the others knives, and the women paternosters and other trifling articles; then he threw into the midst of the place among the little children some small rings and Agnus Dei of tin, at which they showed a marvelous joy. This done, the said captain commanded the trumpets and other instruments of music to sound, with which the said people were greatly delighted; after which things we took leave of them and withdrew. Seeing this, the women put themselves before us for to stop us, and brought us of their victuals, which they had prepared for us, as fish, stews, beans, and other things, thinking to make us eat and dine at the said place; and because their victuals were not to our taste and had no savor of salt, we thanked them, making them a sign that we did not need to eat.

After we had issued from the said town many men and women came to conduct us upon the mountain aforesaid, which was by us named Mont Royal, distant from the said place some quarter of a league; and we, being upon this mountain, had sight and observance for more than thirty leagues round about it. Toward the north of which is a range of mountains which stretches east and west, and toward the south as well; between which mountains the land is the fairest that it may be possible to see, smooth, level, and tillable; and in the middle of the said lands we saw the said river beyond the place where our boats were left, where there is a waterfall, the most impetuous that it may be possible to see, and which it was impossible for us to pass. And we saw this river as far as one could discern, grand, broad, and extensive, which flowed toward the southwest and passed near three fair, round mountains which we saw and estimated that they were about fifteen leagues from us. And we were told and shown by signs by our said three men of the country who had conducted us that there were three such falls of water on the said river like that where our said boats were, but we could not understand what the distance was between the one and the other. Then they showed us by signs that, the said falls being passed, one could navigate more than three moons by the said river; and beyond they showed us that along the said mountains, being toward the north, there is a great stream, which descends from the west like the said river. We reckoned that this is the stream which passes by the realm and province of Saguenay, and, without having made them any request or sign, they took the chain from the captain's whistle, which was of silver, and the haft of a poniard, the which was of copper, yellow like gold, which hung at the side of one of our mariners, and showed that it came from above the said river, and that there were Agojuda, which is to say evil folks, the which are armed even to the fingers, showing us the style of their armor, which is of cords and of wood laced and woven together, giving us to understand that the said Agojuda carried on continual war against one another; but by default of speech we could not learn how far it was to the said country. Our captain showed them some red copper, which they call *caignetdaze,* pointing them toward the said place, and asking by signs if it came from there, and they began to shake their heads, saying no, and showing that it came from Saguenay, which is to the contrary of the preceding. After which things thus seen and understood, we withdrew to our boats, which was not without being conducted by a great number of the said people, of which part of them, when they saw our folk weary, loaded them upon themselves, as upon horses, and carried them. And we, having arrived at our said boats, made sail to return to our pinnace, for doubt that there might be some hindrance; which departure was not made without great regret of the said people, for as far as they could follow us down the said river they would follow us, and we accomplished so much that we arrived at our said pinnace Monday, the fourth day of October.

7. *1565*—PEDRO MENENDEZ FOUNDS ST. AUGUSTINE

❲ *The European nations exploring the North American continent and founding colonies there would sooner or later clash. The French*

"Memoir of Francisco Lopez de Mendoza Grajales," in *Historical Collections of Louisiana and Florida,* Second Series (New York, 1875), II, 215–21.

*were secure enough while they remained in the valley of the St.
Lawrence, but when they attempted to plant settlements of Huguenots on the east coast of Florida they invited trouble. One such
colony, called Fort Caroline, was located near the mouth of the St.
Johns River. This move the Spanish countered by establishing St.
Augustine, now the oldest city in the United States. The account
that follows was written at the time by one of the men from the
fleet of the Spanish commander, Pedro Menéndez de Avilés.*

*In the fall of 1565 a storm wrecked the French fleet protecting
Fort Caroline. Soon afterward the fort fell to the Spanish, and most
of the Huguenots, being heretics as well as Frenchmen, were massacred. Thus ended France's attempt to break the hold of Spain
on the lands which the conquistadors had discovered.*

On Thursday, just as day appeared, we sailed towards the vessel
at anchor, passed very close to her, and would certainly have captured
her, when we saw another vessel appear on the open sea, which we
thought was one of ours. At the same moment, however, we thought
we recognized the French admiral's ship. We perceived the ship on the
open sea; it was the French galley of which we had been in pursuit.
Finding ourselves between these two vessels, we decided to direct our
course toward the galley, for the sake of deceiving them and preventing
them from attacking us, so as not to give them any time to wait. This
bold maneuver having succeeded, we sought the river *Seloy* and port,
of which I have spoken, where we had the good fortune to find our
galley, and another vessel which had planned the same thing we had.
Two companies of infantry now disembarked; that of Captain Andres
Soyez Patino, and that of Captain Juan de San Vincente, who is a very
distinguished gentleman. They were well received by the Indians, who
gave them a large house belonging to a chief, and situated near the
shore of the river. Immediately Captain Patino and Captain San
Vincente, both men of talent and energy, ordered an intrenchment to
be built around this house, with a slope of earth and fascines, these
being the only means of defense possible in that country, where stones
are nowhere to be found. Up to to-day we have disembarked twenty-
four pieces of bronze guns of different calibers, of which the least
weighed fifteen hundredweight. *Our fort is at a distance of about
fifteen leagues from that of the enemy (Fort Carolin). The energy and
talents of those two brave captains, joined to the efforts of their brave
soldiers, who had no tools with which to work the earth, accomplished
the construction of this fortress of defense; and when the general
disembarked, he was quite surprised with what had been done.*
On Saturday, the 8th, the general landed with many banners spread,
to the sound of trumpets and salutes of artillery. As I had gone ashore

the evening before, I took a cross and went to meet him, singing the hymn *Te Deum laudamus*. The general marched up to the cross, followed by all who accompanied him, and there they all kneeled and embraced the cross. A large number of Indians watched these proceedings and imitated all they saw done. The same day the general took formal *possession of the country in the name of his Majesty, and all the captains took the oath of allegiance to him, as their general and governor of the country.* When this ceremony was ended, he offered to do everything in his power for them, especially for Captain Patino, who during the whole voyage had ardently served the cause of God and of the King; and, I think, will be rewarded for his assiduity and talents in constructing a fort in which to defend ourselves until the arrival of help from *St. Domingo* and *Havana*. The French number about as many as we do, and perhaps more. My advice to the general was not to attack the enemy, but to let the troops rest all winter and wait for the assistance daily expected; and then we may hope to make a successful attack.

God and the holy Virgin have performed another great miracle in our favor.

8. *1607—*CAPTAIN JOHN SMITH DESCRIBES THE FOUNDING OF JAMESTOWN

❪ *In the century that followed the discovery of the new world the Spanish established themselves in the southeastern part of the present United States and in Mexico; the French penetrated the valley of the St. Lawrence. The English lagged far behind their continental rivals. Not until 1585 did they attempt to plant a colony in North America. In that year Sir Walter Raleigh, a favorite of Queen Elizabeth, sent a group of 108 men to Roanoke Island off the coast of North Carolina, which had been explored by an expedition the preceding year. In the spring of 1586 all but fifteen returned to England. When Raleigh sent a second group of colonists the next year, the newcomers found only bones and the ruins of a fort and houses. They themselves were to meet the same fate as their predecessors. No English ship visited Roanoke Island until 1591. By that time no trace of the settlement remained.*

Fifteen years passed before the English made another attempt. In 1606 the Virginia Company of London sent out three ships. On May 13, 1607, the captains cast anchor at an island in the broad James River. The site, a poor one, pleased the majority of the colonists; there they would stay.

"A True Relation," in Lyon G. Tyler, *Narratives of Early Virginia, 1606–1625* (New York, 1907), 32–38.

Among the leaders of the group was Captain John Smith, who appears to have spent most of his adult life—he was only twenty-eight—as a soldier of fortune. A year after the landing Smith sent back to England a "True Relation" in which he described the founding of Jamestown, the first contacts with the Indians, and the quarreling and hardships that marked the colony's first year.

Kinde Sir, commendations remembred, &c. You shall understand that after many crosses in the downes by tempests, wee arrived safely uppon the Southwest part of the great Canaries: within foure or five daies after we set saile for Dominica, the 26. of Aprill: the first land we made, wee fell with Cape Henry, the verie mouth of the Bay of Chissiapiacke, which at that present we little expected, having by a cruell storme bene put to the Northward. Anchoring in this Bay twentie or thirtie went a shore with the Captain,[14] and in coming aboard, they were assalted with certaine Indians which charged them within Pistoll shot: in which conflict, Captaine Archer and Mathew Morton were shot: wherupon Captaine Newport seconding them, made a shot at them, which the Indians little respected, but having spent their arrowes retyred without harme. And in that place was the Box opened, wherein the Counsell for Virginia was nominated:[15] and arriving at the place where wee are now seated, the Counsel was sworn, and the President elected, which for that yeare was Maister Edm. Maria Wingfield, where was made choice for our scituation, a verie fit place for the erecting of a great cittie, about which some contention passed betwixt Captaine Wingfield and Captaine Gosnold: notwithstanding, all our provision was brought a shore, and with as much speede as might bee wee went about our fortification. . . .

Captaine Newport having set things in order, set saile for England the 22d of June, leaving provision for 13. or 14 weeks. The day before the Ships departure, the King of Pamaunke sent the Indian that had met us before in our discoverie, to assure us peace; our fort being then palisadoed round, and all our men in good health and comfort, albeit, that through some discontented humors, it did not so long continue, for the President and Captaine Gosnold, with the rest of the Counsell, being for the moste part discontented with one another, in so much, that things were neither carried with that discretion nor any busines effected in such good sort as wisdome would, nor our owne good and safetie required, whereby, and through the hard dealing of our President, the rest of the counsell beeing diverslie affected through his au-

---

[14] Captain Christopher Newport, who commanded the *Susan Constant* (100 tons) and the entire expedition. The other ships were the *Godspeed* (40 tons), Captain Bartholomew Gosnold; and the *Discovery* (20 tons), Captain John Ratcliffe. The three ships carried 144 persons.
[15] The colonists had been given a box which was not to be opened until they had reached their destination. It contained the names of the councilors who were to govern the colony.

dacious commaund; and for Captaine Martin, albeit verie honest, and wishing the best good, yet so sicke and weake; and my selfe so disgrac'd through others mallice: through which disorder God (being angrie with us) plagued us with such famin and sicknes, that the living were scarce able to bury the dead: our want of sufficient and good victualls, with continuall watching, foure or five each night at three Bulwarkes, being the chiefe cause: onely of Sturgion wee had great store, whereon our men would so greedily surfet, as it cost manye their lives: the Sack, Aquavitie, and other preservatives for our health, being kept onely in the Presidents hands, for his owne diet, and his few associates. Shortly after Captaine Gosnold fell sicke, and within three weekes died, Captaine Ratcliffe being then also verie sicke and weake, and my selfe having also tasted of the extremitie therof, but by Gods assistance being well recovered, Kendall about this time, for divers reasons deposed from being of the Councell: and shortly after it pleased God (in our extremity) to move the Indians to bring us Corne, ere it was halfe ripe, to refresh us, when we rather expected when they would destroy us: about the tenth of September there was about 46. of our men dead, at which time Captaine Wingefield having ordred the affaires in such sort that he was generally hated of all, in which respect with one consent he was deposed from his presidencie, and Captaine Ratcliffe according to his course was elected.

Our provision being now within twentie dayes spent, the Indians brought us great store both of Corne and bread ready made: and also there came such aboundance of Fowles into the Rivers, as greatly refreshed our weake estates, whereuppon many of our weake men were presently able to goe abroad. As yet we had no houses to cover us, our Tents were rotten and our Cabbins worse then nought: our best commoditie was Yron which we made into little chissels. The president and Captaine Martins sicknes, constrayned me to be Cape Marchant, and yet to spare no paines in making houses for the company; who notwithstanding our misery, little ceased their mallice, grudging, and muttering. As at this time were most of our chiefest men either sicke or discontented, the rest being in such dispaire, as they would rather starve and rot with idlenes, then be perswaded to do any thing for their owne reliefe without constraint: our victualles being now within eighteene dayes spent, and the Indians trade decreasing, I was sent to the mouth of the river, to Kegquouhtan an Indian Towne, to trade for Corne, and try the River for Fish, but our fishing we could not effect by reason of the stormy weather. The Indians thinking us neare famished, with carelesse kindnes, offred us little pieces of bread and small handfulls of beanes or wheat, for a hatchet or a piece of copper: In like maner I entertained their kindnes, and in like scorne offered them like commodities, but the Children, or any that shewed extraordinary kindnes, I liberally contented with free gifte, such trifles as wel contented them. Finding this colde comfort, I anchored before the Towne, and the next day returned to trade, but God (the absolute disposer of all heartes) altered their conceits, for now they were no lesse desirous of our commodities then we of their Corne: under colour to fetch fresh water, I sent a man to discover the Towne, their Corne, and force, to trie their intent, in that they desired me up to their houses: which well understanding, with foure shot I visited them. With fish, oysters, bread, and deere, they kindly traded with me and my men, beeing no lesse in doubt of my intent, then I of theirs; for well I might with twentie men have fraighted a Shippe with Corne. The Towne conteineth eighteene houses, pleasantly seated upon three acres of ground, uppon a plaine, halfe invironed with a great Bay of the great River, the other parte with a Baye of the other River falling into the great Baye, with a little Ile fit for a Castle in the mouth thereof, the Towne adjoyning to the maine by a necke of Land of sixtie yardes. With sixteene bushells of Corne I returned towards our Forte: by the way I encountered with two Canowes of Indians, who came aboord me, being the inhabitants of Waroskoyack, a kingdome on the south side of the river, which is in breadth 5. miles and 20 mile or neare from the mouth: With these I traded, who having but their hunting provision, requested me to returne to their Towne, where I should load my boat with corne: and with near thirtie bushells I returned to the fort, the very name wherof gave great comfort to our desparing company.

9. *1608*—POCAHONTAS SAVES THE LIFE OF CAPTAIN JOHN SMITH

❴ *Everyone knows the story of Pocahontas, the Indian princess who saved John Smith's life by throwing herself over him as he lay on the ground with warriors about to club him to death. Smith himself told the tale, which may or may not be true—the Captain was sometimes free with his facts—in his* GENERALL HISTORIE OF VIRGINIA.

If ingratitude be a deadly poyson to all honest vertues, I must bee guiltie of that crime if I should omit any meanes to bee thankful. So it is, that some ten yeeres agoe being in Virginia, and taken prisoner by the power of Powhatan their chiefe King, I received from this great Salvage exceeding great courtesie, especially from his sonne Nanta-quaus, the most manliest, comeliest, boldest spirit, I ever saw in a Salvage, and his sister Pocahontas, the Kings most deare and wel-

---

In Tyler, *Narratives of Early Virginia*, 326–27.

beloved daughter, being but a childe of twelve or thirteene yeeres of age, whose compassionate pitifull heart, of my desperate estate, gave me much cause to respect her: I being the first Christian this proud King and his grim attendants ever saw: and thus enthralled in their barbarous power, I cannot say I felt the least occasion of want that was in the power of those my mortall foes to prevent, notwithstanding al their threats. After some six weeks fatting amongst those Salvage Courtiers, at the minute of my execution, she hazarded the beating out of her owne braines to save mine; and not onely that, but so prevailed with her father, that I was safely conducted to James towne: where I found about eight and thirtie miserable poore and sicke creatures, to keepe possession of all those large territories of Virginia; such was the weaknesse of this poore Commonwealth, as had the Salvages not fed us, we directly had starved.

And this reliefe, most gracious Queene, was commonly brought us by this Lady Pocahontas. Notwithstanding all these passages, when inconstant Fortune turned our peace to warre, this tender Virgin would still not spare to dare to visit us, and by her our jarres have beene oft appeased, and our wants still supplyed; were it the policie of her father thus to imploy her, or the ordinance of God thus to make her his instrument, or her extraordinarie affection to our Nation, I know not: but of this I am sure; when her father with the utmost of his policie and power, sought to surprize mee, having but eighteene with mee, the darke night could not affright her from comming through the irkesome woods, and with watered eies gave me intelligence, with her best advice to escape his furie; which had hee knowne, hee had surely slaine her. James towne with her wild traine she as freely frequented, as her fathers habitation; and during the time of two or three yeeres, she next under God, was still the instrument to preserve this Colonie from death, famine and utter confusion; which if in those times, had once beene dissolved, Virginia might have line as it was at our first arrivall to this day. Since then, this businesse having beene turned and varied by many accidents from that I left it at: it is most certaine, after a long and troublesome warre after my departure, betwixt her father and our Colonie; all which time shee was not heard of. About two yeeres after shee her selfe was taken prisoner, being so detained neere two yeeres longer, the Colonie by that meanes was relieved, peace concluded; and at last rejecting her barbarous condition, was maried to an English Gentleman[16], with whom at this present she is in England; the first Christian ever of that Nation, the first Virginian ever spake English, or had a childe in mariage by an Englishman: a matter surely,

---

[16] John Rolfe, a Jamestown colonist, fell in love with Pocahontas, and married her in April, 1614. In 1616 he took her to England, where she died a year later.

if my meaning bee truly considered and well understood, worthy a Princes understanding.

10. *1620*—THE PURITANS LAND AT PLYMOUTH

❨ *Thirteen years after the founding of Jamestown another group of English colonists set out for North America. They were mostly Puritans, so dissatisfied with the Church of England that they had lived for eleven years in Holland, where they could worship as they chose. Yet above all they were Englishmen, and unwilling to see their sons and daughters become citizens of a foreign land. So they chose to found a colony in Virginia.*

The Puritans left Holland in the summer of 1620 for England. There, at Plymouth, they boarded the MAYFLOWER *along with a considerable number of adventurers more interested in finding wealth than the peace of God. The voyage began on September 6. Two months and a few days later the little ship dropped anchor off the coast of Cape Cod, hundreds of miles north of its destination.*

The story of the voyage, an anxious one, is told in the words of William Bradford, who would be elected governor of Plymouth Colony within a few months.

Septr. 6. These troubles being blowne over, and now all being compacte togeather in one shipe, they put to sea againe with a prosperus winde, which continued diverce days togeather, which was some incouragmente unto them; yet according to the usuall maner many were afflicted with sea-sicknes. And I may not omite hear a spetiall worke of Gods providence. Ther was a proud and very profane yonge man, one of the sea-men, of a lustie, able body, which made him the more hauty; he would allway be contemning the poore people in their sicknes, and cursing them dayly with gree[v]ous execrations, and did not let to tell them, that he hoped to help to cast halfe of them over board before they came to their jurneys end, and to make mery with what they had; and if he were by any gently reproved, he would curse and swear most bitterly. But it pl[e]ased God before they came halfe seas over, to smite this yong man with a greeveous disease, of which he dyed in a desperate maner, and so was him selfe the first that was throwne overbord. Thus his curses light on his owne head; and it was an astonishmente to all his fellows, for they noted it to be the just hand of God upon him.

After they had injoyed faire winds and weather for a season, they were incountred many times with crosse winds, and mette with many

---

William Bradford, *History of the Plymouth Plantation, 1620–1647* (Boston, 1912), I, 149–55.

feirce stormes, with which the shipe was shroudly shaken, and her
upper works made very leakie; and one of the maine beames in the
midd ships was bowed and craked, which put them in some fear that
the shipe could not be able to performe the vioage. So some of the
cheefe of the company, perceiveing the mariners to feare the suffisiencie
of the shipe, as appeared by their mutterings, they entred into serious
consulltation with the m[aste]r and other officers of the ship, to consider in time of the danger; and rather to returne then to cast them
selves into a desperate and inevitable perill. And truly ther was great
distraction and differance of oppinion amongst the mariners them
selves; faine would they doe what could be done for their wages sake,
(being now halfe the seas over,) and on the other hand they were loath
to hazard their lives too desperatly. But in examening of all oppinions,
the m[aste]r and others affirmed they knew the ship to be stronge and
firme underwater; and for the buckling of the maine beame, ther was
a great iron scrue the passengers brought out of Holland, which would
raise the beame into his place; the which being done, the carpenter
and m[aste]r affirmed that with a post put under it, set firme in the
lower deck, and otherways bounde, he would make it sufficiente. And
as for the decks and uper workes they would calke them as well as
they could, and though with the workeing of the ship they would not
longe keepe stanch, yet ther would otherwise be no great danger, if
they did not overpress her with sails. So they commited them selves
to the will of God, and resolved to proseede. In sundrie of these stormes
the winds were so feirce, and the seas so high, as they could not beare a
knote of saile, but were forced to hull, for diverce days togither. And
in one of them, as they thus lay at hull, in a mighty storme, a lustie
yonge man (called John Howland) coming upon some occasion above
the grattings, was, with a seele of the shipe throwne into [the] sea; but
it pleased God that he caught hould of the top-saile halliards, which
hunge over board, and rane out at length; yet he held his hould (though
he was sundrie fadomes under water) till he was hald up by the same
rope to the brime of the water, and then with a boathooke and other
means got into the shipe againe, and his life saved; and though he was
something ill with it, yet he lived many years after, and became a
profitable member both in church and commone wealthe. In all this
viage ther died but one of the passengers, which was William Butten,
a youth, servant to Samuell Fuller, when they drew near the coast. But
to omite other things, (that I may be breefe,) after longe beating at sea
they fell with that land which is called Cape Cod; the which being
made and certainly knowne to be it, they were not a litle joyfull. After
some deliberation had amongst them selves and with the m[aste]r of
the ship, they tacked aboute and resolved to stande for the southward
(the wind and weather being faire) to finde some place aboute Hudsons

river for their habitation. But after they had sailed that course aboute halfe the day, they fell amongst deangerous shoulds and roring breakers, and they were so farr intangled ther with as they conceived them selves in great danger; and the wind shrinking upon them withall, they resolved to bear up againe for the Cape, and thought them selves hapy to gett out of those dangers before night overtooke them, as by Gods good providence they did. And the next day they gott into the Cape-harbor wher they ridd in saftie. A word or too by the way of this cape; it was thus first named by Capten Gosnole and his company, Anno: 1602, and after by Capten Smith was caled Cape James; but it retains the former name amongst sea-men. Also that pointe which first shewed those dangerous shoulds unto them, they called Pointe Care, and Tuckers Terrour; but the French and Dutch to this day call it Malabarr, by reason of those perilous shoulds, and the losses they have suffered their.

Being thus arived in a good harbor and brought safe to land, they fell upon their knees and blessed the God of heaven, who had brought them over the vast and furious ocean, and delivered them from all the periles and miseries therof, againe to set their feete on the firme and stable earth, their proper elemente. And no marvell if they were thus joyefull, seeing wise Seneca was so affected with sailing a few miles on the coast of his owne Italy; as he affirmed, that he had rather remaine twentie years on his way by land, then pass by sea to any place in a short time; so tedious and dreadfull was the same unto him.

11. *1620*—THE PLYMOUTH SETTLERS MAKE A COMPACT

❨ *Before the* MAYFLOWER *passengers had left England the Virginia Company had given them a patent granting them certain rights of self-government, but the document would have no standing in the far-off region where they had chosen to settle. The "strangers"—the fortune-hunters who had joined the group from other than religious motives—were already threatening to go their own way as soon as the colony was established. How the Pilgrims met this crisis, planted the seed of democracy by forming the Mayflower Compact, and survived their first few months in the harsh surroundings of New England, is related by Governor Bradford.*

I shall a litle returne backe and begine with a combination made by them before they came a shore, being the first foundation of their govermente in this place; occasioned partly by the discontented and mutinous speeches that some of the strangers amongst them had let fall

---

History of the Plymouth Plantation, I, 189–96.

from them in the ship; That when they came a shore they would use their owne libertie; for none had power to command them, the patente they had being for Virginia, and not for New england, which belonged to an other Goverment, with which the Virginia Company had nothing to doe. And partly that shuch an acte by them done (this their condition considered) might be as firme as any patent, and in some respects more sure.

The forme was as followeth.

"In the name of God, Amen. We whose names are underwriten, the loyall subjects of our dread soveraigne Lord, King James, by the grace of God, of Great Britaine, Franc, and Ireland king, defender of the faith, etc.

"Haveing undertaken, for the glorie of God, and advancemente of the Christian faith, and honour of our king and countrie, a voyage to plant the first colonie in the Northerne parts of Virginia, doe by these presents solemnly and mutualy in the presence of God, and one of another, covenant and combine our selves togeather into a civill body politick, for our better ordering and preservation and furtherance of the ends aforesaid; and by vertue hearof to enacte, constitute, and frame shuch just and equall lawes, ordinances, acts, constitutions, and offices, from time to time, as shall be thought most meete and convenient for the generall good of the Colonie, unto which we promise all due submission and obedience. In witnes wherof we have hereunder subscribed our names at Cap-Codd the ·11· of November, in the year of the raigne of our soveraigne lord, King James, of England, France, and Ireland, the eighteenth, and of Scotland the fiftie fourth. Anno Dom. 1620."

After this they chose, or rather confirmed, Mr. John Carver (a man godly and well approved amongst them) their Governour for that year. And after they had provided a place for their goods, or comone store, (which were long in unlading for want of boats, foulnes of the winter weather, and sicknes of diverce,) and begune some small cottages for their habitation, as time would admitte, they mette and consulted of lawes and orders, both for their civill and military Govermente, as the necessitie of their condition did require, still adding therunto as urgent occasion in severall times, and as cases did require.

In these hard and difficulte beginings they found some discontents and murmurings arise amongst some, and mutinous speeches and carriages in other; but they were soone quelled and overcome by the wisdome, patience, and just and equall carrage of things by the Gov[erno]r and better part, which clave faithfully togeather in the maine. But that which was most sadd and lamentable was, that in ·2· or ·3· moneths time halfe of their company dyed, espetialy in Jan: and

February, being the depth of winter, and wanting houses and other comforts; being infected with the scurvie and other diseases, which this long voiage and their inacomodate condition had brought upon them; so as ther dyed some times ·2· or ·3· of a day, in the aforesaid time; that of ·100· and odd persons, scarce ·50· remained. And of these in the time of most distres, ther was but ·6· or ·7· sound persons, who, to their great comendations be it spoken, spared no pains, night nor day, but with abundance of toyle and hazard of their owne health, fetched them woode, made them fires, drest them meat, made their beads, washed their lothsome cloaths, cloathed and uncloathed them; in a word, did all the homly and necessarie offices for them which dainty and quesie stomacks cannot endure to hear named; and all this willingly and cherfully, without any grudging in the least, shewing herein their true love unto their friends and bretheren. A rare example and worthy to be remembred. Tow of these ·7· were Mr. William Brewster, ther reverend Elder, and Myles Standish, ther Captein and military comander, unto whom my selfe, and many others, were much beholden in our low and sicke condition. And yet the Lord so upheld these persons, as in this generall calamity they were not at all infected either with sicknes, or lamnes. And what I have said of these, I may say of many others who dyed in this generall vissitation, and others yet living, that whilst they had health, yea, or any strength continuing, they were not wanting to any that had need of them. And I doute not but their recompence is with the Lord.

12. 1637—THE CONNECTICUT SETTLERS WIPE OUT THE PEQUOTS

❡ *In spite of poor soil and harsh winters New England attracted settlers in ever-growing numbers. Between 1629 and 1640 so many discontented Englishmen left the home country that historians have labelled this period the years of the "Great Migration." Perhaps 20,000 found their way to the newly established colonies of Massachusetts Bay, Connecticut, and Rhode Island.*

Sooner or later a clash with the Indians was inevitable. The Pequots, a warlike tribe which lived in the southeastern part of Connecticut, had given trouble for several years, but no serious attempt was made to punish them until the spring of 1637, when the Indians murdered nine settlers. The colonists raised a force of ninety men, placed them under the command of Captain John Mason, and, with the aid of several hundred Mohegans and Narragansetts, set out to teach their enemies a lesson. In the conflict

John Mason, "A Brief History of the Pequot War," in Charles Orr, *History of the Pequot War* (Cleveland, 1897), 25–29, 36–40.

that followed, the Pequots were practically exterminated.

This account of early Indian warfare was written by Captain Mason himself, a Connecticut colonist who had served with English troops in the Low Countries before emigrating in 1633.

On the Thursday about eight of the Clock in the Morning, we Marched thence towards Pequot, with about five hundred Indians: But through the Heat of the Weather and want of Provisions some of our Men fainted: And having Marched about twelve Miles, we came to Pawcatuck River, at a Ford where our Indians told us the Pequots did usually Fish; there making an Alta, we stayed some small time. . . .

And after we had refreshed our selves with our mean Commons, we Marched about three Miles, and came to a Field which had lately been planted with Indian Corn: There we made another Alt, and called our Council, supposing we drew near to the Enemy: and being informed by the Indians that the Enemy had two Forts almost impregnable; but we were not at all Discouraged, but rather Animated, in so much that we were resolved to Assault both their Forts at once. But understanding that one of them was so remote that we could not come up with it before Midnight, though we Marched hard; whereat we were much grieved, chiefly because the greatest and bloodiest Sachem there resided, whose name was Sassacous: We were then constrained, being exceedingly spent in our March with extream Heat and want of Necessaries, to accept of the nearest. . . .

In the Morning, we awaking and seeing it very light, supposing it had been day, and so we might have lost our Opportunity, having purposed to make our Assault before Day; rowsed the Men with all expedition, and briefly commended ourselves and Design to God, thinking immediately to go to the Assault; the Indians shewing us a Path, told us that it led directly to the Fort. We held on our March about two Miles, wondering that we came not to the Fort, and fearing we might be deluded: But seeing Corn newly planted at the Foot of a great Hill, supposing the Fort was not far off, a Champion Country being round about us; then making a stand, gave the Word for some of the Indians to come up: At length Onkos and one Wequash appeared; We demanded of them, Where was the Fort? They answered On the Top of that Hill: Then we demanded, Where were the Rest of the Indians? They answered, Behind, exceedingly afraid: We wished them to tell the rest of their Fellows, That they should by no means Fly, but stand at what distance they pleased, and see whether English Men would now Fight or not. Then Capt. Underhill came up, who Marched in the Rear; and commending ourselves to God, divided our Men: There being two Entrances into the Fort, intending to enter both at once: Captain Mason leading up to that on the North East Side; who approaching within one Rod, heard a Dog bark and an Indian crying Owanux! Owanux! which is Englishmen! Englishmen! We called up our Forces with all expedition, gave Fire upon them through the Pallizado; the Indians being in a dead indeed their last Sleep: Then we wheeling off fell upon the main Entrance, which was blocked up with Bushes about Breast high, over which the Captain passed, intending to make good the Entrance, ecouraging the rest to follow. Lieutenant Seeley endeavoured to enter; but being somewhat cumbred, stepped back and pulled out the Bushes and so entred, and with him about sixteen Men: We had formerly concluded to destroy them by the Sword and save the Plunder.

Whereupon Captain Mason seeing no Indians, entred a Wigwam; where he was beset with many Indians, waiting all opportunities to lay Hands on him, but could not prevail. At length William Heydon espying the Breach in the Wigwam, supposing some English might be there, entred; but in his Entrance fell over a dead Indian; but speedily recovering himself, the Indians some fled, others crept under their Beds: The Captain going out of the Wigwam saw many Indians in the Lane or Street; he making towards them, they fled, were pursued to the End of the Lane, where they were met by Edward Pattison, Thomas Barber, with some others; where seven of them were Slain, as they said. The Captain facing about, Marched a slow Pace up the Lane he came down, perceiving himself very much out of Breath; and coming to the other End near the Place where he first entred, saw two Soldiers standing close to the Pallizado with their Swords pointed to the Ground: The Captain told them that We should never kill them after that manner: The Captain also said, We must Burn them; and immediately stepping into the Wigwam where he had been before, brought out a Firebrand, and putting it into the Matts with which they were covered, set the Wigwams on Fire. Lieutenant Thomas Bull and Nicholas Omsted beholding, came up; and when it was thoroughly kindled, the Indians ran as Men most dreadfully Amazed.

And indeed such a dreadful Terror did the Almighty let fall upon their Spirits, that they would fly from us and run into the very Flames, where many of them perished. And when the Fort was thoroughly Fired, Command was given, that all should fall off and surround the Fort; which was readily attended by all; only one Arthur Smith being so wounded that he could not move out of the Place, who was happily espied by Lieutenant Bull, and by him rescued.

The Fire was kindled on the North East Side to windward; which did swiftly over-run the Fort, to the extream Amazement of the Enemy, and great Rejoycing of our selves. Some of them climbing to the Top of the Pallizado; others of them running into the very Flames; many of them gathering to windward, lay pelting at us with their Arrows;

and we repayed them with our small Shot: Others of the Stoutest issued forth, as we did guess, to the Number of Forty, who perished by the Sword. . . .

About a Fortnight after our Return home, which was about one Month after the Fight at Mistick, there Arrived in Pequot River several Vessels from the Massachusetts, Captain Israel Stoughton being Commander in Chief; and with him about One hundred and twenty Men; being sent by that Colony to pursue the War against the Pequots: The Enemy being all fled before they came, except some few Straglers, who were surprised by the Moheags and others of the Indians, and by them delivered to the Massachusetts Soldiers.

Connecticut Colony being informed hereof, sent forthwith forty Men, Captain Mason being Chief Commander; with some other Gent, to meet those of the Massachusetts, to consider what was necessary to be attended respecting the future. . . .

We then hastened our march towards the Place where the Enemy was: And coming into a Corn Field, several of the English espyed some Indians, who fled from them: They pursued them; and coming to the Top of an Hill, saw several Wigwams just opposite, only a Swamp intervening, which was almost divided in two Parts. Sergeant Palmer hastening with about twelve Men who were under his Command to surround the smaller Part of the Swamp, that so He might prevent the Indians flying; Ensign Danport, Sergeant Jeffries &c, entering the Swamp, intended to have gone to the Wigwams, were there set upon by several Indians, who in all probability were deterred by Sergeant Palmer. In this Skirmish the English slew but few; two or three of themselves were Wounded: The rest of the English coming up, the Swamp was surrounded.

Our Council being called, and the Question propounded, How we should proceed, Captain Patrick advised that we should cut down the Swamp; there being many Indian Hatchets taken, Captain Traske concurring with him; but was opposed by others: Then we must pallizado the Swamp; which was also opposed: Then they would have a Hedge made like those of Gotham; all which was judged by some almost impossible, and to no purpose, and that for several Reasons, and therefore strongly opposed. But some others advised to force the Swamp, having time enough, it being about three of the Clock in the Afternoon: But that being opposed, it was then propounded to draw up our Men close to the Swamp, which would much have lessened the Circumference; and with all to fill up the open Passages with Bushes, that so we might secure them until the Morning, and then we might consider further about it. But neither of these would pass; so different were our Apprehensions; which was very grievous to some of us, who concluded the Indians would make an Escape in the Night, as easily they might

33

and did: We keeping at a great distance, what better could be expected? Yet Captain Mason took Order that the Narrow in the Swamp should be cut through; which did much shorten our Leaguer. It was resolutely performed by Serjeant Davis.

We being loth to destroy Women and Children, as also the Indians belonging to that Place; whereupon Mr. Tho. Stanton a Man well acquainted with Indian Language and Manners, offered his Service to go into the Swamp and treat with them: To which we were somewhat backward, by reason of some Hazard and Danger he might be exposed unto: But his importunity prevailed: Who going to them, did in a short time return to us, with near Two Hundred old Men, Women and Children; who delivered themselves, to the Mercy of the English. And so Night drawing on, we beleaguered them as strongly as we could. About half an Hour before Day, the Indians that were in the Swamp attempted to break through Captain Patrick's Quarters; but were beaten back several times; they making a great Noise, as their Manner is at such Times, it sounded round about our Leaguer: Whereupon Captain Mason sent Sergeant Stares to inquire into the Cause, and also to assist if need required; Capt. Traske coming also in to their Assistance: But the Tumult growing to a very great Heighth, we raised our Siege; and Marching up to the Place, at a Turning of the Swamp the Indians were forcing out upon us; but we sent them back by our small Shot.

We waiting a little for a second Attempt; the Indians in the mean time facing about, pressed violently upon Captain Patrick, breaking through his Quarters, and so escaped. There were about sixty or seventy as we were informed. We afterwards searched the Swamp, and found but few Slain. The Captives we took were about One Hundred and Eighty; whom we divided, intending to keep them as Servants, but they could not endure that Yoke; few of them continuing any considerable time with their masters.

Thus did the Lord scatter his Enemies with his strong Arm!

13. *1692*—THE DEVIL IN MASSACHUSETTS

❪ *The New England colonists were godly people, but their strict faith admitted a large element of superstition. Many of them believed in the existence of witches: women who, with the aid of the devil or other evil spirits, could do harm by supernatural means. Suddenly, in 1692, strange events began to take place in Salem Village, now Danvers, Massachusetts. Young women fell down in fits and claimed to feel pains like those caused by invisible pins. The*

Thomas Hutchinson, *The Witchcraft Delusion of 1692* (Boston, 1870), 26–29.

work of witches, the clergymen cried. Between May and September several hundred persons were accused of witchcraft, many were convicted, nineteen were hanged. Eventually the people came to their senses, and most of them regretted having lost their heads.

When the hysteria was at its height, Mary Lacey, under examination, confessed that she had practiced witchcraft. So did many other women, only to take back their confessions when they believed themselves to be out of danger.

Mary Lacey was brought in, and Mary Warren in a violent fit.

Question (to Mary Lacey): "How dare you to come in here, and bring the Devil with you, to afflict these poor creatures?"

Answer: "I know nothing of it."

Lacey laying her hand on Warren's arm, she recovered from her fit.

Q. "You are here accused for practising witchcraft upon Goody Ballard; which way do you do it?"

A. "I cannot tell. Where is my mother that made me a witch, and I knew it not?"

Q. "Can you look upon that maid, Mary Warren, and not hurt her? Look upon her in a friendly way."

She trying so to do, struck her down with her eyes.

Q. "Do you acknowledge now you are a witch?"

A. "Yes."

Q. "How long have you been a witch?"

A. "Not above a week."

Q. "Did the Devil appear to you?"

A. "Yes."

Q. "In what shape?"

A. "In the shape of a horse."

Q. "What did he say to you?"

A. "He bid me not to be afraid of any thing, and he would not bring me out; but he has proved a liar from the beginning."

Q. "When was this?"

A. "I know not; above a week."

Q. "Did you set your hand to the book?"

A. "No."

Q. "Did he bid you worship him?"

A. "Yes; he bid me also to afflict persons."

Q. "You are now in the way to obtain mercy if you will confess and repent. Do not you desire to be saved by Christ?"

A. "Yes."

The judges: "Then you must confess freely what you know in this matter."

Mary Lacey: "I was in bed, and the Devil came to me, and bid me obey him and I should want for nothing, and he would not bring me out."

Q. "But how long ago?"

A. "A little more than a year."

Q. "Was that the first time?"

A. "Yes."

Q. "How long was you gone from your father, when you run away?"

A. "Two days."

Q. "Where had you your food?"

A. "At John Stone's."

Q. "Did the Devil appear to you then, when you was abroad?"

A. "No, but he put such thoughts in my mind as not to obey my parents."

Q. "Who did the Devil bid you afflict?"

A. "Timothy Swan. Richard Carrier comes often a-nights and has me to afflict persons."

Q. "Where do ye go?"

A. "To Goody Ballard's sometimes."

Q. "How many of you were there at a time?"

A. "Richard Carrier and his mother, and my mother and grand-mother."

Upon reading over the confession so far, Goody Lacey, the mother, owned this last particular.

Q. "How many more witches are there in Andover?"

A. "I know no more, but Richard Carrier."

Q. "Tell all the truth."

A. "I cannot yet."

Q. "Did you use at any time to ride upon a stick or pole?"

A. "Yes."

Q. "How high?"

A. "Sometimes above the trees."

Q. "Your mother struck down these afflicted persons, and she con-fessed so far, till at last she could shake hands with them freely and do them no hurt. Be you also free and tell the truth. What sort of worship did you do the devil?"

A. "He bid me pray to him and serve him and said he was a god and lord to me."

Q. "What meetings have you been at, at the village?"

A. "I was once there and Richard Carrier rode with me on a pole, and the Devil carried us."

Q. "Did not some speak to you to afflict the people there?"

A. "Yes, the Devil."

Q. "Was there not a man also among you there?"

A. "None but the Devil."

Q. "What shape was the Devil in then?"

A. "He was a black man, and had a high crowned hat."

Q. "Your mother and your grandmother say there was a minister there. How many men did you see there?"

A. "I saw none but Richard Carrier."

Q. "Did you see none else?"

A. "There was a minister there, and I think he is now in prison."

Q. "Were there not two ministers there?"

A. "I cannot tell."

Q. "Was there not one Mr. Burroughs there?"

A. "Yes."

We whose names are underwritten, inhabitants of Andover; when as that horrible and tremendous judgment beginning at Salem village in the year 1692, by some called witchcraft, first breaking forth at Mr. Paris's house, several young persons, being seemingly afflicted, did accuse several persons for afflicting them, and many there believing it so to be, we being informed that, if a person was sick, the afflicted persons could tell what or who was the cause of that sickness: Joseph Ballard, of Andover, his wife being sick at the same time, he either from himself or from the advice of others, fetched two of the persons, called the afflicted persons, from Salem village to Andover, which was the beginning of that dreadful calamity that befel us in Andover, believing the said accusations to be true, sent for the said persons to come together to the meeting house in Andover, the afflicted persons being there. After Mr. Barnard had been at prayer, we were blindfolded, and our hands were laid upon the afflicted persons, they being in their fits and falling into their fits at our coming into their presence, as they said; and some led us and laid our hands upon them, and then they said they were well, and that we were guilty of afflicting of them; whereupon we were all seized, as prisoners, by a warrant from the justice of the peace, and forthwith carried to Salem. And by reason of that sudden surprisal, we knowing ourselves altogether innocent of that crime, we were all exceedingly astonished and amazed, and consternated and affrighted even out of our reason; and our nearest and dearest relations, seeing us in that dreadful condition, and knowing our great danger, apprehending that there was no other way to save our lives, as the case was then circumstanced, but by our confessing ourselves to be such and such persons as the afflicted represented us to be, they, out of tender love and pity, persuaded us to confess what we did confess. And indeed that confession, that it is said we made, was no other than what was suggested to us by some gentlemen, they telling us that we were witches, and they knew it, and we knew it, and they knew that we knew it, which made us think that it was so; and our understanding, our reason, our faculties almost gone, we were not capable of judging our condition; as also the hard measures they used with us rendered us incapable of making our defence, but said any thing and every thing which they desired, and most of what we said was but in effect a consenting to what they said. Some time after, when we were better composed, they telling us of what we had confessed, we did profess that we were innocent and ignorant of such things; and we hearing that Samuel Wardwell had renounced his confession, and quickly after condemned and executed, some of us were told that we were going after Wardwell.

MARY OSGOOD
MARY TILER
DELIVERANCE DANE
ABIGAIL BARKER
SARAH WILSON
HANNAH TILER.

14. *1673*—MARQUETTE AND JOLIET EXPLORE THE MISSISSIPPI

⟪ *While the English colonies on the Atlantic coast grew strong, the French pushed westward steadily. First went the explorers, then the missionaries. In 1668 the Jesuits established a mission at Sault Ste. Marie on the St. Mary's River, which connects Lake Superior with Lake Huron. Two years later they founded St. Ignace on Mackinac Island; in 1671 they established themselves at Green Bay, where the Fox River of Wisconsin empties into Lake Michigan.*

One of the priests who served both at Sault Ste. Marie and St. Ignace was Jacques Marquette, who had come to Canada from France in 1666. In the missions the Indians told him of a great river to the west. While at St. Ignace in the winter of 1672–73 he learned that he was to join a young explorer and map-maker of Quebec, Louis Joliet, in finding and exploring the river of which the Indians spoke.

Priest and explorer left St. Ignace in mid-May, 1673. They traveled in two canoes, with five voyageurs, or boatmen. Their route took them to Green Bay, then to the headwaters of the Fox River where they portaged to the Wisconsin, flowing westward. On June 17 they found themselves on the Mississippi.

In a "Relation" to his superiors Marquette told the story of the

John Gilmary Shea, *Discovery and Exploration of the Mississippi Valley* (Albany, 1903), 18, 21–25.

first week on the river, marveled at the fish and the buffalo, and described the visit the little party of Frenchmen made to a village of Illinois Indians on the west bank of the stream.

Here then we are on this renowned river, of which I have endeavored to remark attentively all the peculiarities. The Mississippi river has its source in several lakes in the country of the nations to the north; it is narrow at the mouth of the Miskousing; its current, which runs south, is slow and gentle; on the right is a considerable chain of very high mountains, and on the left fine lands; it is in many places studded with islands. On sounding, we have found ten fathoms of water. Its breadth is very unequal: it is sometimes three quarters of a league, and sometimes narrows in to three *arpents* (220 yards). We gently follow its course, which bears south and southeast till the forty-second degree. Here we perceive that the whole face is changed; there is now almost no wood or mountain, the islands are more beautiful and covered with finer trees; we see nothing but deer and moose, bustards and wingless swans, for they shed their plumes in this country. From time to time we meet monstrous fish, one of which struck so violently against our canoe, that I took it for a large tree about to knock us to pieces. . . .

We advanced constantly, but as we did not know where we were going, having already made more than a hundred leagues without having discovered anything but beasts and birds, we kept well on our guard. Accordingly we make only a little fire on the shore at night to prepare our meal, and after supper keep as far off from it as possible, passing the night in our canoes, which we anchor in the river pretty far from the bank. Even this did not prevent one of us being always as a sentinel for fear of a surprise. . . .

At last, on the 25th of June, we perceived footprints of men by the water-side, and a beaten path entering a beautiful prairie. We stopped to examine it, and concluding that it was a path leading to some Indian village, we resolved to go and reconnoitre; we accordingly left our two canoes in charge of our people, cautioning them strictly to beware of a surprise; then M. Jollyet and I undertook this rather hazardous discovery for two single men, who thus put themselves at the discretion of an unknown and barbarous people. We followed the little path in silence, and having advanced about two leagues, we discovered a village on the banks of the river, and two others on a hill, half a league from the former. Then, indeed, we recommended ourselves to God, with all our hearts; and having implored his help, we passed on undiscovered, and came so near that we even heard the Indians talking. We then deemed it time to announce ourselves, as we did by a cry, which we raised with all our strength, and then halted without advancing any further. At this cry the Indians rushed out of their cabins, and having probably recognised us as French, especially seeing a black gown, or at least having no reason to distrust us, seeing we were but two, and had made known our coming, they deputed four old men to come and speak with us. Two carried tobacco-pipes well-adorned, and trimmed with many kinds of feathers. They marched slowly, lifting their pipes toward the sun, as if offering them to him to smoke, but yet without uttering a single word. They were a long time coming the little way from the village to us. Having reached us at last, they stopped to consider us attentively. I now took courage, seeing these ceremonies, which are used by them only with friends, and still more on seeing them covered with stuffs, which made me judge them to be allies. I, therefore, spoke to them first, and asked them, who they were; they answered that they were Ilinois and, in token of peace, they presented their pipes to smoke. They then invited us to their village where all the tribe awaited us with impatience. These pipes for smoking are called in the country calumets, a word that is so much in use, that I shall be obliged to employ it in order to be understood, as I shall have to speak of it frequently.

At the door of the cabin in which we were to be received, was an old man awaiting us in a very remarkable posture; which is their usual ceremony in receiving strangers. This man was standing, perfectly naked, with his hands stretched out and raised toward the sun, as if he wished to screen himself from its rays, which nevertheless passed through his fingers to his face. When we came near him, he paid us this compliment: "How beautiful is the sun, O Frenchman, when thou comest to visit us! All our town awaits thee, and thou shalt enter all our cabins in peace." He then took us into his, where there was a crowd of people, who devoured us with their eyes, but kept a profound silence. We heard, however, these words occasionally addressed to us: "Well done, brothers, to visit us!"

As soon as we had taken our places, they showed us the usual civility of the country, which is to present the calumet. You must not refuse it, unless you would pass for an enemy, or at least for being impolite. It is, however, enough to pretend to smoke. While all the old men smoked after us to honor us, some came to invite us on behalf of the great sachem of all the Ilinois to proceed to his town, where he wished to hold a council with us. We went with a good retinue, for all the people who had never seen a Frenchman among them could not tire looking at us: they threw themselves on the grass by the wayside, they ran ahead, then turned and walked back to see us again. All this was done without noise, and with marks of a great respect entertained for us.

Having arrived at the great sachem's town, we espied him at his cabin-door, between two old men, all three standing naked, with their calumet turned to the sun. He harangued us in few words, to congratulate us on our arrival, and then presented us his calumet and made us smoke; at the same time we entered his cabin, where we received all their usual greetings. Seeing all assembled and in silence, I spoke to them by four presents which I made: by the first, I said that we marched in peace to visit the nations on the river to the sea: by the second, I declared to them that God their Creator had pity on them, since, after their having been so long ignorant of him, he wished to become known to all nations; that I was sent on his behalf with this design; that it was for them to acknowledge and obey him: by the third, that the great chief of the French informed them that he spread peace everywhere, and had overcome the Iroquois. Lastly, by the fourth, we begged them to give us all the information they had of the sea, and of the nations through which we should have to pass to reach it.

When I had finished my speech, the sachem rose, and laying his hand on the head of a little slave, whom he was about to give us, spoke thus: "I thank thee, Blackgown, and thee, Frenchman," addressing M. Jollyet, "for taking so much pains to come and visit us; never has the earth been so beautiful, nor the sun so bright, as to-day; never has our river been so calm, nor so free from rocks, which your canoes have removed as they passed; never has our tobacco had so fine a flavor, nor our corn appeared so beautiful as we behold it to-day. Here is my son, that I give thee, that thou mayst know my heart. I pray thee to take pity on me and all my nation. Thou knowest the Great Spirit who has made us all; thou speakest to him and hearest his word: ask him to give me life and health, and come and dwell with us, that we may know him." Saying this, he placed the little slave near us and made us a second present, an all-mysterious calumet, which they value more than a slave; by this present he showed us his esteem for our governor, after the account we had given of him; by the third, he begged us, on behalf of his whole nation, not to proceed further, on account of the great dangers to which we exposed ourselves.

I replied, that I did not fear death, and that I esteemed no happiness greater than that of losing my life for the glory of Him who made all. But this these poor people could not understand.

The council was followed by a great feast which consisted of four courses, which we had to take with all their ways; the first course was a great wooden dish full of sagamity, that is to say, of Indian meal boiled in water and seasoned with grease. The master of ceremonies, with a spoonful of sagamity, presented it three or four times to my mouth, as we would do with a little child; he did the same to M. Jollyet. For the second course, he brought in a second dish containing three fish; he took some pains to remove the bones, and having blown upon it to cool it, put it in my mouth, as we would food to a bird; for the third course, they produced a large dog, which they had just killed, but

41

learning that we did not eat it, it was withdrawn. Finally, the fourth course was a piece of wild ox, the fattest portions of which were put into our mouths.

After this feast we had to visit the whole village, which consists of full three hundred cabins. While we marched through the streets, an orator was constantly haranguing, to oblige all to see us without being troublesome; we were everywhere presented with belts, garters, and other articles made of the hair of the bear and wild cattle, dyed red, yellow, and gray. These are their rareties; but not being of consequence, we did not burthen ourselves with them.

We slept in the sachem's cabin, and the next day took leave of him, promising to pass back through his town in four moons. He escorted us to our canoes with nearly six hundred persons, who saw us embark, evincing in every possible way the pleasure our visit had given them.

15. *1673*—MARQUETTE AND JOLIET VISIT THE SITE OF CHICAGO

❪ *Marquette and Joliet descended the Mississippi to the mouth of the Arkansas (Akamsea), then turned back. On their return they shortened their route by ascending the Illinois River and the Des Plaines, portaging their canoes to the Chicago River and thence to Lake Michigan, the "lake of the Illinois." Thus they became the first white men to visit the site of the future city of Chicago.*

We embarked next morning with our interpreter, preceded by ten Indians in a canoe. Having arrived about half a league from Akamsea (Arkansas), we saw two canoes coming toward us. The commander was standing up holding in his hand the calumet, with which he made signs according to the custom of the country; he approached us, singing quite agreeably, and invited us to smoke, after which he presented us some sagamity and bread made of Indian corn, of which we ate a little. He now took the lead, making us signs to follow slowly. Meanwhile they had prepared us a place under the war-chief's scaffold; it was neat and carpeted with fine rush mats, on which they made us sit down, having around us immediately the sachems, then the braves, and last of all, the people in crowds. We fortunately found among them a young man who understood Ilinois much better than the interpreter whom we had brought from Mitchigamea. By means of him I first spoke to the assembly by the ordinary presents; they admired what I told them of God, and the mysteries of our holy faith, and showed a great desire to keep me with them to instruct them.

Shea, *Discovery and Exploration of the Mississippi Valley,* 49–55.

We then asked them what they knew of the sea; they replied that we were only ten days' journey from it (we could have made this distance in five days); that they did not know the nations who inhabited it, because their enemies prevented their commerce with those Europeans; that the hatchets, knives, and beads, which we saw, were sold them, partly by the nations to the east, and partly by an Ilinois town four days' journey to the west; that the Indians with fire-arms whom we had met, were their enemies who cut off their passage to the sea, and prevented their making the acquaintance of the Europeans, or having any commerce with them; that, besides, we should expose ourselves greatly by passing on, in consequence of the continual war-parties that their enemies sent out on the river; since being armed and used to war, we could not, without evident danger, advance on that river which they constantly occupy.

During this converse, they kept continually bringing us in wooden dishes of sagamity, Indian corn whole, or pieces of dog-flesh; the whole day was spent in feasting.

These Indians are very courteous and liberal of what they have, but they are very poorly off for food, not daring to go and hunt the wild-cattle, for fear of their enemies. It is true, they have Indian corn in abundance, which they sow at all seasons; we saw some ripe; more just sprouting, and more just in the ear, so that they sow three crops a year. They cook it in large earthen pots, which are very well made; they have also plates of baked earth, which they employ for various purposes. The men go naked, and wear their hair short; they have the nose and ears pierced, and beads hanging from them. The women are dressed in wretched skins; they braid their hair in two plaits, which fall behind their ears; they have no ornaments to decorate their persons. Their banquets are without any ceremonies; they serve their meats in large dishes, and every one eats as much as he pleases, and they give the rest to one another. Their language is extremely difficult and with all my efforts, I could not succeed in pronouncing some words. Their cabins, which are long and wide, are made of bark; they sleep at the two extremities, which are raised about two feet from the ground. They keep their corn in large baskets, made of cane, or in gourds, as large as half barrels. They do not know what a beaver is; their riches consisting in the hides of wild cattle. They never see snow, and know the winter only by the rain which falls oftener than in summer. We eat no fruit there but watermelons; if they knew how to cultivate their ground, they might have plenty of all kinds.

In the evening the sachems held a secret council on the design of some to kill us for plunder, but the chief broke up all these schemes, and sending for us, danced the calumet in our presence, in the manner

I have described above, as a mark of perfect assurance; and then, to remove all fears, presented it to me.

M. Jollyet and I held another council to deliberate on what we should do, whether we should push on, or rest satisfied with the discovery that we had made. After having attentively considered that we were not far from the gulf of Mexico, the basin of which is 31° 40′ north, and we at 33° 40′, so that we could not be more than two or three days journey off; that the Missisipi undoubtedly had its mouth in Florida or the gulf of Mexico, and not on the east, in Virginia, whose seacoast is at 34° north, which we had passed, without having as yet reached the sea, nor on the western side in California, because that would require a west, or west-southwest course, and we had always been going south. We considered, moreover, that we risked losing the fruit of this voyage, of which we could give no information, if we should throw ourselves into the hands of the Spaniards, who would undoubtedly, at least, hold us as prisoners. Besides, it was clear, that we were not in a condition to resist Indians allied to Europeans, numerous and expert in the use of fire-arms, who continually infested the lower part of the river. Lastly, we had gathered all the information that could be desired from the expedition. All these reasons induced us to resolve to return; this we announced to the Indians, and after a day's rest, prepared for it.

. . . We left the village of Akamsea on the 17th of July, to retrace our steps. We accordingly ascended the Mississippi, which gave us great trouble to stem its currents. We left it indeed, about the 38th degree, to enter another river, which greatly shortened our way, and brought us, with little trouble, to the lake of the Ilinois.[17]

We had seen nothing like this river for the fertility of the land, its prairies, woods, wild cattle, stag, deer, wild-cats, bustards, swans, ducks, parrots, and even beaver; its many little lakes and rivers. That on which we sailed, is broad, deep, and gentle for sixty-five leagues. During the spring and part of the summer, the only portage is half a league.

We found there an Ilinois town called Kaskaskia,[18] composed of seventy-four cabins; they received us well, and compelled me to promise to return and instruct them. One of the chiefs of this tribe with his young men, escorted us to the Ilinois lake, whence at last we returned in the close of September to the bay of the Fetid, whence we had set out in the beginning of June.

Had all this voyage caused but the salvation of a single soul, I should deem all my fatigue well repaid, and this I have reason to think, for, when I was returning, I passed by the Indians of Peoria. I was

---

[17] The original name of Lake Michigan. The river was the Illinois.

[18] Kaskaskia, or the Great Village of the Illinois, was located about midway between the present cities of La Salle and Ottawa.

three days announcing the faith in all their cabins, after which as we were embarking, they brought me on the water's edge a dying child, which I baptized a little before it expired, by an admirable Providence for the salvation of that innocent soul.

16.   *1682*—LA SALLE CLAIMS THE MISSISSIPPI VALLEY FOR FRANCE

❨ *Other Frenchmen soon followed up the discoveries of Marquette and Joliet. One of the greatest was Robert Cavelier, Sieur de la Salle, who was determined to establish a great trading empire in the Mississippi Valley. In 1680 he built Fort Crevecoeur near the site of the present city of Peoria, Illinois, only to have the post attacked by the Indians and destroyed within three months. Two years later La Salle, with Henry de Tonty, descended the Mississippi to its mouth. There, on April 9, 1682, he formally took possession of the great valley in the name of the King of France.*

The description of the ceremony is from the official record kept by Jaques de la Metairie, who accompanied the expedition as its notary.

We continued our voyage till the 6th, when we discovered three channels by which the River Colbert discharges itself into the sea. We landed on the bank of the most western channel, about three leagues from its mouth. On the 7th, M. de la Salle went to reconnoitre the shores of the neighboring sea, and M. de Tonty likewise examined the great middle channel. They found these two outlets beautiful, large and deep. On the 8th, we reascended the river, a little above its confluence with the sea, to find a dry place, beyond the reach of inundations. The elevation of the North Pole was here about 27 degrees. Here we prepared a column and a cross, and to the said column were affixed the arms of France, with this inscription:

LOUIS LE GRAND, ROI DE FRANCE ET DE NAVARRE, REGNE; LE NEUVIEME, AVRIL, 1682

The whole party, under arms, chanted the Te Deum, the Exaudiat, the Domine salvum fac Regem; and then, after a salute of firearms and cries of Vive le Roi, the column was erected by M. de la Salle, who, standing near it, said, with a loud voice, in French: "In the name of the most high, mighty, invincible, and victorious Prince, Louis the Great, by the Grace of God, King of France and of Navarre, Fourteenth of that name, this ninth day of April, one thousand six hundred

Collections of the Illinois State Historical Library, Volume One (Springfield, 1903), 110-13.

and eighty-two, I, in virtue of the commission of his Majesty which I hold in my hand, and which may be seen by all whom it may concern, have taken, and do now take, in the name of his Majesty and of his successors to the crown, possession of this country of Louisiana, the seas, harbours, ports, bays, adjacent straits; and all the nations, people, provinces, cities, towns, villages, mines, minerals, fisheries, streams, and rivers, comprised in the extent of the said Louisiana, from the mouth of the great river St. Louis on the eastern side, otherwise called Ohio, Alighin, Sipore, or Chikachas, and this with the consent of the Chaouanons, Chikachas, and other people dwelling therein, with whom we have made alliance; as also along the River Colbert, or Mississipi, and rivers which discharge themselves therein, from its source beyond the country of the Kious or Nadouessious, and this with their consent, and with the consent of the Motantees, Ilinois, Mesigameas, Natches, Koroas, which are the most considerable nations dwelling therein, with whom also we have made alliance, either by ourselves or by others in our behalf; as far as its mouth at the sea, or Gulf of Mexico, about the 27th degree of the elevation of the North Pole, and also to the mouth of River of Palms; upon the assurance which we have received from all these nations, that we are the first Europeans who have descended or ascended the said River Colbert; hereby protesting against all those who may in future undertake to invade any or all of these countries, people, or lands, above described, to the prejudice of the right of his Majesty, acquired by the consent of the nations herein named. Of which, and of all that can be needed, I hereby take to witness those who hear me, and demand an act of the Notary, as required by law."

To which the whole assembly responded with shouts of Vive le Roi, and with salutes of firearms. Moreover, the said Sieur de la Salle caused to be buried at the foot of the tree, to which the cross was attached, a leaden plate, on one side of which were engraved the arms of France, and the following Latin inscription:

LVDOVICVS MAGNVS REGAT. NONO APRILIS CIƆ IƆC LXXXII. ROBERTVS CAVE-
LIER, CVM DOMINO DE TONTY, LEGATO, R. P. ZENOBIO MEMBRE, RECOL-
LECTO, ET VIGINTI GALLIS, PRIMVS HOC FLVMEN, INDE AB ILINEORVM
PAGO, ENAVIGAVIT, EJVSQVE OSTIVM FECIT PERVIVM, NONO APRILIS
ANNI CIƆ IƆC LXXXII.

After which the Sieur de la Salle said, that his Majesty, as eldest son of the Church, would annex no country to his crown, without making it his chief care to establish the Christian religion therein, and that its symbol must now be planted; which was accordingly done at once by erecting a cross, before which the Vexilla and the Domine salvum fac Regem were sung. Whereupon the ceremony was concluded with cries of Vive le Roi.

Of all and every of the above, the said Sieur de la Salle having re-quired of us an instrument, we have delivered to him the same, signed by us, and by the undersigned witnesses, this ninth day of April, one thousand six hundred and eighty-two.

La Metairie,
Notary.

De la Salle.
P. Zenobe, Recollet Missionary.
Henry de Tonty.
Francois de Boisrondet.
Jean Bourdon.
Sieur d'Autry.
Jaques Cauchois.
Pierre You.
Gilles Meucret.
Jean Michel, Surgeon.
Jean Mas.
Jean Dulignon.
Nicolas de la Salle.

CHAPTER II

LIFE IN COLONIAL AMERICA

1730 – 1778

1.   *1730*—NEW ORLEANS, OUTPOST OF FRANCE

❦ *By the beginning of the eighteenth century the little European outposts in North America had become firmly established colonies with customs and characteristics different from each other and from the mother countries. One of the most distinctive was Louisiana, which France held under the claim first asserted by La Salle. New Orleans, founded by Bienville in 1718 as a trading post, was the metropolis of the colony. We see it through the eyes of a pioneer planter, Le Page du Pratz, who watched it grow from a single cabin to a thriving town.*

New Orleans, the Capital of the Colony, is situated to the East, on the banks of the *Missisippi,* in 30° of North Latitude. At my first arrival in *Louisiana,* it existed only in name; for on my landing I under-

Le Page du Pratz, *The History of Louisiana* (London, 1763), I, 89–93.

stood, M. *de Biainville,* Commandant General, was only gone to mark out the spot; whence he returned three days after our arrival at *Isle Dauphine.*

He pitched upon this spot in preference to many others, more agreeable and commodious; but for that time this was a place proper enough: Besides, it is not every man who can see so far as some others. As the principal settlement was then at *Mobile,* it was proper to have the Capital fixed at a place from which there could be an easy communication with this Post: And thus a better choice could not have been made, as the town being on the banks of the *Missisipi,* vessels, tho' of a thousand ton, may lay their sides close to the shore, even at low water; or at most, need only lay a small bridge, with two of their yards, in order to load or unload, to roll barrels and bales, &c. without fatiguing the ship's crew. This town is only a league from *St. John's Creek,* where passengers take water for *Mobile,* in going to which they pass Lake *St. Louis,* and from thence all along the coast; a communication which was necessary at that time. . . .

The place of arms is in the middle of that part of the town which faces the river; in the middle of the ground of the place of arms stands the parish-church, called *St. Louis,* where the *Capuchins* officiate, whose house is to the left of the Church. To the right stand the prison, or jail, and the guard-house: Both sides of the place of arms are taken up with two bodies or rows of barracks. The place stands all open to the river.

All the streets are laid out both in length and breadth by the line, and intersect and cross each other at right angles. The streets divide the town into sixty-six *Isles;* eleven along the river lengthwise, or in front, and six in depth: Each of those *Isles* is fifty square toises, and each again divided into twelve *Emplacements,* or compartments, for lodging as many families. The *Intendant's* house stands behind the barracks on the left; and the magazine, or warehouse-general behind the barracks on the right, on viewing the town from the river side. The *Governor's* house stands in the middle of that part of the town, from which we go from the place of arms to the habitation of the *Jesuits,* which is near the town. The house of the *Ursilin* Nuns is quite at the end of the town, to the right; as is also the hospital of the sick, of which the Nuns have the inspection. What I have just described faces the river.

On the banks of the river runs a causey, or mole, as well on the side of the town as on the opposite side, from the *English Reach* quite to the town, and about ten leagues beyond it; which makes about fifteen or sixteen leagues on each side the river; and which may be travelled in a coach or on horse-back, on a bottom as smooth as a table.

The greatest part of the houses is of brick: the rest are of timber and brick.

2. *1766—DETROIT, OUTPOST OF ENGLAND*

❲ *Hundreds of miles to the north of New Orleans stood another village established by the French. Fort Pontchartrain du Detroit, built in 1701, became the nucleus of a settlement known simply as Detroit. Jonathan Carver, a Connecticut explorer, described the town as he saw it in 1766, six years after the English had captured it in the French and Indian War. No prophet could have seen in the neat little village, with its small British garrison, the seed of the great industrial city of today.*

The river that runs from Lake St. Claire to Lake Erie (or rather the Straight, for thus might be termed from its name) is called Detroit, which is in French, the Straight. It runs nearly south, has a gentle current, and depth of water sufficient for ships of considerable burthen. The town of Detroit is situated on the western banks of this river, about nine miles below Lake St. Claire.

Almost opposite, on the eastern shore, is the village of the ancient Hurons: a tribe of Indians which has been treated of by so many writers, that . . . I shall omit giving a description of them. A missionary of the order of Carthusian Friars, by permission of the bishop of Canada, resides among them.

The banks of the River Detroit, both above and below these towns, are covered with settlements that extend more than twenty miles; the country being exceedingly fruitful, and proper for the cultivation of wheat, Indian corn, oats, and peas. It has also many spots of fine pasturage; but as the inhabitants, who are chiefly French that submitted to the English government after the conquest of these parts by General Amherst, are more attentive to the Indian trade than to farming, it is but badly cultivated.

The town of Detroit contains upwards of one hundred houses. The streets are somewhat regular, and have a range of very convenient and handsome barracks, with a spacious parade at the south end. On the west side lies the king's garden belonging to the governor, which is very well laid out and kept in good order. The fortifications of the town consist of a strong stockade made of round piles, fixed firmly in the ground, and lined with palisades. These are defended by some small bastions, on which are mounted a few indifferent cannon of an inconsiderable size, just sufficient for its defence against the Indians, or an enemy not provided with artillery.

The garrison, in time of peace, consists of two hundred men commanded by a field officer, who acts as chief magistrate under the governor of Canada.

J. Carver, *Travels Through The Interior Parts of North-America* (London, 1778), 150–52.

3. *1766–68*—THE ORIGINAL AMERICANS

❲ *From New Orleans to Detroit and beyond eastward to the Alleghenies, and westward to the Pacific, the Indians occupied the continent with little disturbance from the white man. Carver describes customs and characteristics of the tribes he encountered in traveling through the region that would soon become the northern section of the United States.*

The Indian nations . . . are in general slight made, rather tall and strait, and you seldom see any among them deformed; their skin is of a reddish or copper colour; their eyes are large and black, and their hair is of the same hue, but very rarely is it curled; they have good teeth, and their breath is as sweet as the air they draw in; their cheek-bones rather raised, but more so in the women than the men, the former are not quite so tall as the European women, however you frequently meet with good faces and agreeable persons among them, although they are more inclined to be fat than the other sex. . . .

The men of every nation differ in their dress very little from each other, except those who trade with the Europeans; these exchange their furs for blankets, shirts, and other apparel, which they wear as much for ornament as necessity. The latter fasten by a girdle around their waists about half a yard of broadcloth, which covers the middle parts of their bodies. Those who wear shirts never make them fast either at the wrist or collar; this would be a most insufferable confinement to them. They throw their blanket loose upon their shoulders, and holding the upper side of it by the two corners, with a knife in one hand, and a tobacco-pouch, pipe, &c. in the other, thus accoutred they walk about in their villages or camps: but in their dances they seldom wear this covering. . . .

They paint their faces red and black, which they esteem as greatly ornamental. They also paint themselves when they go to war; but the method they make use of on this occasion differs from that wherein they use it merely as a decoration. . . .

The women wear a covering of some kind or other from the neck to the knees. Those who trade with the Europeans wear a linen garment the same as that used by the men; the flaps of which hang over the petticoat. Such as dress after their ancient manner, make a kind of shirt with leather, which covers the body but not the arms. Their petticoats are made either of leather or cloth, and reach from the waist to the knee. . . .

The Indians, in general, pay a greater attention to their dress and to

---

Carver, *Travels Through The Interior Parts of North-America,* 223–26, 229–33, 243–45.

the ornaments with which they decorate their persons, than to the accommodations of their huts or tents. They construct the latter in the following simple, and expeditious manner.

Being provided with poles of a proper length, they fasten two of them across, near their ends, with bands made of bark. Having done this, they raise them up, and extend the bottom of each as wide as they purpose to make the area of the tent: they then erect others of an equal height, and fix them so as to support the two principal ones. On the whole they lay skins of the elk or deer, sewed together, in quantity sufficient to cover the poles, and by lapping over to form the door. A great number of skins are sometimes required for this purpose, as some of their tents are very capacious. That of the chief-warrior of the Naudowessies was at least forty feet in circumference, and very commodious. . . .

The huts also, which those who use not tents, erect when they travel, for very few tribes have fixed abodes or regular towns or villages, are equally simple and almost as soon constructed.

They fix small pliable poles in the ground, and bending them till they meet at the top and form a semi-circle, then lash them together. These they cover with mats made of rushes platted, or with birch bark, which they carry with them in their canoes for this purpose.

These cabins have neither chimnies nor windows; there is only a small aperture left in the middle of the roof, through which the smoke is discharged, but as this is obliged to be stopped up when it rains or snows violently, the smoke then proves exceedingly troublesome.

They lie on skins, generally those of the bear, which are placed in rows on the ground; and if the floor is not large enough to contain beds sufficient for the accommodation of the whole family, a frame is erected about four or five feet from the ground, in which the younger part of it sleep. . . .

Every nation pays a great respect to old age. The advice of a father will seldom meet with any extraordinary attention from the young Indians, probably they receive it with only a bare assent; but they will tremble before a grandfather, and submit to his injunctions with the utmost alacrity. The words of the ancient part of their community are esteemed by the young as oracles. If they take during their hunting parties any game that is reckoned by them uncommonly delicious, it is immediately presented to the oldest of their relations.

They never suffer themselves to be overburdened with care, but live in a state of perfect tranquillity and contentment. Being naturally indolent, if provision just sufficient for their subsistence can be procured with little trouble, and near at hand, they will not go far, or take any extraordinary pains for it, though by so doing they might acquire greater plenty, and of a more estimable kind.

Having much leisure time they indulge this indolence to which they are so prone, by eating, drinking, or sleeping, and rambling about in their towns or camps. But when necessity obliges them to take the field, either to oppose an enemy, or to procure themselves food, they are alert and indefatigable. . . .

The infatuating spirit of gaming is not confined to Europe; the Indians also feel the bewitching impulse, and often lose their arms, their apparel, and every thing they are possessed of. In this case, however, they do not follow the example of more refined gamesters, for they neither murmur nor repine; not a fretful word escapes them, but they bear the frowns of fortune with a philosophic composure.

The greatest blemish in their character is that savage disposition which impels them to treat their enemies with a severity every other nation shudders at. But if they are thus barbarous to those with whom they are at war, they are friendly, hospitable, and humane in peace. It may with truth be said of them, that they are the worst enemies, and the best friends, of any people in the whole world.

4. *1759*—VIRGINIA AFTER A CENTURY AND A HALF

❲ *By the middle of the eighteenth century the English colonies were firmly established along the Atlantic seaboard from Georgia to New Hampshire. Long before the American Revolution most of them had achieved a settled way of life. Towns, often of considerable size, had grown up and were beginning to exhibit, in colleges, libraries, and music halls, the graces of civilization.*

The English colonies attracted many travelers from abroad. One of these, with a flair for description, was Andrew Burnaby, a young man recently graduated from Cambridge. Burnaby spent two years in Virginia, the middle settlements, and New England, and then went home to write a book about his experiences. In his pages we see what the passage of a hundred and fifty years had meant to England's first outpost in North America.

Williamsburg is the capital of Virginia: it is situated between two creeks; one falling into James, the other into York river; and is built nearly due east and west. The distance of each landing-place is something more than a mile from the town; which, with the disadvantage of not being able to bring up large vessels, is the reason of its not having increased so fast as might have been expected. It consists of about two hundred houses, does not contain more than one thousand souls, whites and negroes; and is far from being a place of any consequence. It is

Andrew Burnaby, *Travels Through The Middle Settlements in North America* (London, 1775), 6–7, 19–22, 31–32.

regularly laid out in parallel streets, intersected by others at right angles; has a handsome square in the center, through which runs the
principal street, one of the most spacious in North-America, three quarters of a mile in length, and above a hundred feet wide. At the ends of
this street are two public buildings, the college and the capitol: and
although the houses are of wood, covered with shingles, and but indif-
ferently built, the whole makes a handsome appearance. There are few
public edifices that deserve to be taken notice of; those, which I have
mentioned, are the principal; and they are far from being magnificent.
The governor's palace, indeed, is tolerably good, one of the best upon
the continent; but the church, the prison, and the other buildings, are
all of them extremely indifferent. The streets are not paved, and are
consequently very dusty, the soil hereabout consisting chiefly of sand:
however, the situation of Williamsburg has one advantage, which few
or no places in these lower parts have; that of being free from mos-
quitoes. Upon the whole, it is an agreeable residence; there are ten or
twelve gentlemen's families constantly residing in it, besides merchants
and tradesmen: and at the time of the assemblies, and general courts,
it is crowded with the gentry of the country: on those occasions there
are balls and other amusements; but as soon as the business is finished,
they return to their plantations; and the town is in a manner deserted.

Viewed and considered as a settlement, Virginia is far from being
arrived at that degree of perfection which it is capable of. Not a
tenth of the land is yet cultivated: and that which is cultivated, is far
from being so in the most advantageous manner. It produces, however,
considerable quantities of grain and cattle, and fruit of many kinds.
The Virginian pork is said to be superior in flavour to any in the
world, but the sheep and horned cattle being small and lean, the meat
of them is inferior to that of Great Britain, or indeed, of most parts
of Europe. The horses are fleet and beautiful; and the gentlemen of
Virginia, who are exceedingly fond of horse-racing, have spared no expense or trouble to improve the breed of them by importing great
numbers from England. . . .

The inhabitants are supposed to be in number between two and
three hundred thousand. There are a hundred and five thousand tythe-
ables, under which denomination are included all white males from
fifteen to sixty; and all negroes whatsoever within the same age. The
former are obliged to serve in the militia, and amount to forty thousand.

The trade of this colony is large and extensive. Tobacco is the principal article of it. Of this they export annually between fifty and sixty
thousand hogsheads, each hoghead weighing eight hundred or a thousand weight: some years they export much more. They ship also for
the Madeiras, the Streights, and the West-Indies, several articles, such
as grain, pork, lumber, and cyder: to Great Britain, bar-iron, indigo, and

a small quantity of ginseng, tho' of an inferior quality; and they clear out one year with another about————tons of shipping.

Their manufactures are very inconsiderable. They make a kind of cotton-cloth, which they clothe themselves with in common, and call after the name of their country; and some inconsiderable quantities of linen, hose, and other trifling articles: but nothing to deserve attention. . . .

From what has been said of this colony, it will not be difficult to form an idea of the character of its inhabitants. The climate and external appearance of the country conspire to make them indolent, easy, and good-natured; extremely fond of society, and much given to convivial pleasures. In consequence of this, they seldom show any spirit of enterprize, or expose themselves willingly to fatigue. Their authority over their slaves renders them vain and imperious, and intire strangers to that elegance of sentiment, which is so peculiarly characteristic of refined and polished nations. Their ignorance of mankind and of learning, exposes them to many errors and prejudices, especially in regard to Indians and Negroes, whom they scarcely consider as of the human species; so that it is almost impossible, in cases of violence, or even murder, committed on those unhappy people by any of the planters, to have the delinquents brought to justice. . . .

The public or political character of the Virginians, corresponds with their private one: they are haughty and jealous of their liberties, impatient of restraint, and can scarcely bear the thought of being controuled by any superior power. Many of them consider the colonies as independent states, not connected with Great Britain, otherwise than by having the same common king, and being bound to her with natural affection. There are but few of them that have a turn for business, and even those are by no means adroit at it. . . . In matters of commerce they are ignorant of the necessary principles that must prevail between a colony and the mother country; they think it a hardship not to have an unlimited trade to every part of the world. They consider the duties upon their staple as injurious only to themselves; and it is utterly impossible to persuade them that they affect the consumer also. Upon the whole, however, to do them justice, the same spirit of generosity prevails here which does in their private character; they never refuse any necessary supplies for the support of government when called upon, and are generous and loyal people.

5. *1774—*AMUSEMENTS OF THE CAVALIERS

❆ *The large plantation, owned by a man of wealth and worked by*

John Rogers Williams, Ed., *Philip Vickers Fithian Journal and Letters, 1767–1774* (Princeton, N.J., 1900), 94–97.

Negro slaves, was a feature of life in Virginia and the other South-
ern colonies. The plantation owner could afford gay and luxurious
amusements. Through the diary of Philip Vickers Fithian, a young
man from New Jersey who had attended Princeton College and was
now (1774) employed as a tutor at Nomini Hall, the estate of
Robert Carter, we look in on one of the lively evenings beloved by
the Virginia gentry.

[January 18, 1774]

Mrs. Carter, & the young Ladies came Home last Night from the
Ball, & brought with them Mrs. *Lane,* they tell us there were upwards
of Seventy at the Ball; forty-one Ladies; that the company was genteel;
& that Colonel *Harry Lee,* from *Dumfries,* & his Son *Harry* who was
with me at College, were also there; Mrs. Carter made this an argument, and it was a strong one indeed, that to-day I must dress & go
with her to the Ball. She added also that She desired my Company
in the Evening when we should come Home as it would be late. After
considering a while I consented to go, & was dressed. We set away
from Mr. Carters at two; Mrs. *Carter* & the young Ladies in the
Chariot, Mrs. Lane in a Chair, & myself on Horseback. As soon as I
had handed the Ladies out, I was saluted by Parson *Smith;* I was
introduced into a small Room where a number of Gentlemen were
playing Cards (the first game I have seen since I left Home) to lay
off my Boots Riding-Coat &c. Next I was directed into the Dining-
Room to see young Mr. *Lee;* He introduced me to his Father. With
them I conversed til Dinner, which came in at half after four. The
Ladies dined first, when some Good Order was preserved; when they
rose, each nimblest Fellow dined first. The Dinner was as elegant as
could well be expected when so great an Assembly were to be kept
for so long a time. For Drink, there were several sorts of Wine, good
Lemon Punch, Toddy, Cyder, Porter &c. About Seven the Ladies and
Gentlemen begun to dance in the Ball-Room—first Minuets one Round;
Second Giggs; third Reels; And last of All Country-Dances; tho' they
struck several Marches occasionally. The Music was a French-Horn
and two Violins. The Ladies were Dressed Gay, and splendid, & when
dancing, their Skirts & Brocades rustled and trailed behind them! But
all did not join in the Dance for there were parties in Rooms made
up, some at Cards; some drinking for Pleasure; some toasting the
Sons of america; some singing "Liberty Songs" as they call'd them;
in which six, eight, ten or more would put their Heads near together
and roar, & for the most part as unharmonious as an affronted———.
Among the first of the Vociferators was a young Scotch-Man, Mr.
Jack Cunningham; he was nimis bibendo appotus; noisy, droll, wag-

gish, yet civil in his way & wholly inoffensive. I was solicited to dance
by several, Captain Chelton, Colonel Lee, Harry Lee, and others; But
George Lee, with great Rudeness as tho' half drunk, asked me why
I would come to the Ball & neither dance nor play Cards? I answered
him shortly (for his Impudence moved my resentment) that my Invitation to the Ball would Justify my Presence; & that he was ill qualified to direct my Behaviour who made so indifferent a Figure himself.
Parson Smiths, & Parson Gibberns Wives danced, but I saw neither
of the Clergymen dance or game. At Eleven Mrs. Carter call'd upon
me to go, I listened with gladness to the summons & with Mrs. Lane
in the Chariot we rode Home, the Evening sharp and cold! I handed
the Ladies out, waited on them to a warm Fire, then ran over to my
own Room, which was warm and had a good Fire; oh how welcome!
Better this than to be at the Ball in some corner nodding, and awakened
now & then with a midnight Yell! In my Room by half after twelve;
& exceeding happy that I could break away with Reputation.

6.   1778—SLAVERY

*[Plantation life and Negro slavery were inseparable. As early as
1619 a Dutch vessel landed captured Negroes in Virginia and sold
them to the colonists. Later, slaves were bought and sold in all the
English colonies, north as well as south. Their number, however,
did not increase rapidly until the latter half of the eighteenth century, when the Southern planters began to produce tobacco, rice,
cotton, and sugar—crops which required many hands—on large
plantations.*

*An English soldier gives us one of the best concise descriptions
of slavery as it existed at the end of the colonial period. Among the
officers in the army of General John Burgoyne, who surrendered to
the Americans in the fall of 1777, was Thomas Anburey, Lieutenant
in the Twenty-Ninth Regiment of Foot. Anburey, with the other
prisoners of war, was marched to Boston and thence to Charlottes-
ville, Virginia, where he was held until the end of the war. He kept
a shrewd and entertaining record of his observations, which he
published after his return to England. Like all foreigners, and many
Americans, Anburey was affronted by the spectacle of men holding
other men in bondage.*

The whole management of the plantation is left to the overseer, who
as an encouragement to make the most of the crops, has a certain
portion as his wages, but not having any interest in the negroes, any

Thomas Anburey, *Travels Through The Interior Parts of America* (Boston, 1923), II, 191–94.

further than their labour, he drives and whips them about, and works them beyond their strength, and sometimes till they expire; he feels no loss in their death, he knows the plantation must be supplied, and his humanity is estimated by his interest, which rises always above freezing point.

It is the poor negroes who alone work hard, and I am sorry to say, fare hard. Incredible is the fatigue which the poor wretches undergo, and that nature should be able to support it; there certainly must be something in their constitutions, as well as their color, different from us, that enables them to endure it.

They are called up at day break, and seldom allowed to swallow a mouthful of homminy, or hoe cake, but are drawn out into the field immediately, where they continue at hard labour, without intermission, till noon, when they go to their dinners, and are seldom allowed an hour for that purpose; their meals consist of homminy and salt [pork], and if their master is a man of humanity, touched by the finer feelings of love and sensibility, he allows them twice a week a little fat, skimmed milk, rusty bacon, or salt herring, to relish this miserable and scanty fare. The man at this plantation, in lieu of these, grants his negroes an acre of ground, and all Saturday afternoon to raise grain and poultry for themselves. After they have dined, they return to labour in the field, until dusk in the evening; here one naturally imagines the daily labour of these poor creatures was over, not so, they repair to the tobacco houses, where each has a task of stripping allotted which takes them up some hours, or else they have such a quantity of Indian corn to husk, and if they neglect it, are tied up in the morning, and receive a number of lashes from those unfeeling monsters, the overseers, whose masters suffer them to exercise their brutal authority without constraint. Thus by their night task, it is late in the evening before these poor creatures return to their second scanty meal, and the time taken up at it encroaches upon their hours of sleep, which for refreshment of food and sleep together can never be reckoned to exceed eight.

When they lay themselves down to rest, their comforts are equally miserable and limited, for they sleep on a bench, or on the ground, with an old scanty blanket, which serves them at once for bed and covering, their cloathing is not less wretched, consisting of a shirt and trowsers of coarse, thin, hard, hempen stuff, in the Summer, with an addition of a very coarse woollen jacket, breeches and shoes in Winter. But since the war, their masters, for they cannot get the cloathing as usual, suffer them to go in rags, and many in a state of nudity.

The female slaves share labour and repose just in the same manner, except a few who are term'd house negroes, and are employed in household drudgery.

These poor creatures are all submission to injuries and insults, and are obliged to be passive, nor dare they resist or defend themselves if attacked, without the smallest provocation, by a white person, as the law directs the negroe's arm to be cut off who raises it against a white person, should it be only in defence against wanton barbarity and outrage.

Notwithstanding this humiliating state and rigid treatment to which this wretched race are subject, they are devoid of care, and appear jovial, contented and happy. It is a fortunate circumstance that they possess, and are blessed with such an easy satisfied disposition, otherwise they must inevitably sink under such a complication of misery and wretchedness.

7.   1760—THE THRIVING REALM OF THE PURITANS

❬ *The second English colony, founded in 1620, had grown equally with Virginia. But its people and institutions were different.*

Boston, the metropolis of Massachusets-Bay, in New England, is one of the largest and most flourishing towns in North America. It is situated upon a peninsula, or rather an island joined to the continent by an isthmus or narrow neck of land half a mile in length, at the bottom of a spacious and noble harbour, defended from the sea by a number of small islands. The length of it is nearly two miles, and the breadth of it half a one; and it is supposed to contain 3000 houses, and 18 or 20,000 inhabitants. At the entrance of the harbour stands a very good light-house; and upon an island, about a league from the town, a considerable castle, mounting near 150 cannon: there are several good batteries about it, and one in particular very strong, built by Mr. Shirley. There are also two batteries in the town, for 16 or 20 guns each; but they are not, I believe, of any force. The buildings in Boston are in general good; the streets are open and spacious, and well-paved; and the whole has much the air of some of our best county towns in England.—The country round about it is exceedingly delightful; and from a hill, which stands close to the town, where there is a beacon erected to alarm the neighbourhood in case of any surprize, is one of the finest prospects, the most beautifully variegated, and richly grouped, of any without exception that I have ever seen.

The chief public buildings are, three churches; thirteen or fourteen meeting-houses; the governor's palace; the courthouse, or exchange; Faneuils-hall; a linen-manufacturing-house; a work-house; a bridewell; a public granary; and a very fine wharf, at least half a mile long, undertaken at the expence of a number of private gentlemen, for the

---

Andrew Burnaby, *Travels,* 133–37, 141–45.

advantage of unloading and loading vessels. Most of these buildings are handsome: the church, called King's Chapel, is exceedingly elegant; and fitted up in the Corinthian taste. There is also an elegant private concert-room, highly finished in the Ionic manner.—I had reason to think the situation of Boston unhealthy, at least in this season of the year; as there were frequent funerals every night during my stay there.

The number of souls in this province is supposed to amount to 200,000; and 40,000 of them to be capable of bearing arms. They carry on a considerable traffick, chiefly in the manner of the Rhode-Islanders; but have some material articles for exportation, which the Rhode-Islanders have not, except in a very trifling degree: these are salt fish, and vessels. Of the latter they build annually a great number, and send them, laden with cargoes of the former, to Great Britain, where they sell them. They clear out from Boston, Salem, Marblehead, and the different ports in this province, yearly, about———tons of shipping. Exclusive of these articles, their manufactures are not large; those of spirits, fish oil, and iron, are, I believe, the most considerable. They fabricate beaver-hats, which they sell for a moidore[1] a piece; and some years ago they erected a manufactory, with a design to encourage the Irish settlers to make linens; but at the breaking out of the war the price of labour was inhanced so much, that it was impossible to carry it on. Like the rest of the colonies they also endeavour to make woollens, but they have not yet been able to bring them to any degree of perfection; indeed it is an article in which I think they will not easily succeed; for the American wool is not only coarse, but, in comparison of the English, exceedingly short. . . .

Arts and Sciences seem to have made a greater progress here, than in any other part of America. Harvard college has been founded above a hundred years; and although it is not upon a perfect plan, yet it has produced a very good effect. The arts are undeniably forwarder in Massachusetts-Bay, than either in Pensylvania or New York. The public buildings are more elegant; and there is a more general turn for music, painting, and the belles lettres.

The character of the inhabitants of this province is much improved, in comparison of what it was: but puritanism and a spirit of persecution is not yet totally extinguished. The gentry of both sexes are hospitable, and good-natured; there is an air of civility in their behaviour, but it is constrained by formality and preciseness. Even the women, though easiness of carriage is peculiarly characteristic of their nature, appear here with more stiffness and reserve than in the other colonies. They are formed with symmetry, are handsome, and have fair and

---

[1] An old English coin worth twenty-seven shillings.

delicate complexions; but are said universally, and even proverbially, to have very indifferent teeth. . . .

Singular situations and manners will be productive of singular customs; but frequently such as upon slight examination may appear to be the effects of mere grossness of character, will, upon deeper research, be found to proceed from simplicity and innocence. A very extraordinary method of courtship, which is sometimes practised amongst the lower people of this province, and is called Tarrying, has given occasion to this reflection. When a man is enamoured of a young woman, and wishes to marry her, he proposes the affair to her parents, (without whose consent no marriage in this colony can take place); if they have no objection, they allow him to tarry with her one night, in order to make his court to her. At their usual time the old couple retire to bed, leaving the young ones to settle matters as they can; who, after having sate up as long as they think proper, get into bed together also, but without pulling off their under-garments, in order to prevent scandal. If the parties agree, it is all very well; the banns are published, and they are married without delay. If not, they part, and possibly never see each other again; unless, which is an accident that seldom happens, the forsaken fair-one prove pregnant, and then the man is obliged to marry her, under pain of excommunication.

8.   1760—WHAT OF THE FUTURE?

❨ *What of the future of the English colonies, now restless under the rule of a mother country which could not quite bring itself to believe that the offspring had grown up?*

Andrew Burnaby's forecast shows how easy it is for common sense to be wrong. What he wrote of the handicaps and jealousies of the Americans was all true. What he predicted on the basis of his knowledge was all wrong.

Having travelled over so large a tract of this vast continent, before I bid a final farewell to it, I must beg the reader's indulgence, while I stop for a moment, and as it were from the top of a high eminence, take one general retrospective look at the whole.—An idea, strange as it is visionary, has entered into the minds of the generality of mankind, that empire is travelling westward; and every one is looking forward with eager and impatient expectation to that destined moment, when America is to give law to the rest of the world. But if ever an idea was illusory and fallacious, I will venture to predict, that this will be so.

America is formed for happiness, but not for empire: in a course

---

Andrew Burnaby, *Travels*, 154–62.

of 1200 miles I did not see a single object that sollicited charity; but I saw insuperable causes of weakness, which will necessarily prevent its being a potent state.

Our colonies may be distinguished into the southern and northern; separated from each other by the Susquehannah and that imaginary line which divides Maryland from Pensylvania.

The southern colonies have so many inherent causes of weakness, that they can never possess any real strength.—The climate operates very powerfully upon them, and renders them indolent, inactive, and unenterprizing; this is visible in every line of their character. I myself have been a spectator, and it is not an uncommon sight, of a man in the vigour of life, lying upon a couch, and a female slave standing over him, wafting off the flies, and fanning him, while he took his repose.

The southern colonies (Maryland, which is the smallest and most inconsiderable, alone excepted) will never be thickly seated: for as they are not confined within determinate limits, but extend to the westward indefinitely, men, sooner than apply to laborious occupations, occupations militating with their dispositions, and generally considered too as the inheritance and badge of slavery, will gradually retire westward, and settle upon fresh lands, which are said also to be more fertile; where, by the servitude of a Negroe or two, they may enjoy all the satisfaction of an easy and indolent independency: hence the lands upon the coast will of course remain thin of inhabitants.

The mode of cultivation by slavery, is another insurmountable cause of weakness. The number of Negroes in the southern colonies is upon the whole nearly equal, if not superior, to that of the white men; and they propagate and increase even faster.—Their condition is truly pitiable; their labour excessively hard, their diet poor and scanty, their treatment cruel and oppressive: they cannot therefore but be a subject of terror to those who so inhumanly tyrannize over them.

The Indians near the frontiers are a still farther formidable cause of subjection. The southern Indians are numerous, and are governed by a sounder policy than formerly: experience has taught them wisdom. They never make war with the colonists without carrying terror and devastation along with them. They sometimes break up intire counties together.—Such is the state of the southern colonies.—

The northern colonies are of stronger stamina, but they have other difficulties and disadvantages to struggle with, not less arduous, or more easy to be surmounted, than what have been already mentioned. Their limits being defined, they will undoubtedly become exceedingly populous: for though men will readily retire back towards the frontiers of their own colony, yet they will not so easily be induced to settle beyond them, where different laws and policies prevail, and where, in short, they are a different people: but in proportion to want of territory, if we consider the proposition in a general and abstract light, will be want of power.—But the northern colonies have still more positive and real disadvantages to contend with. They are composed of people of different nations, different manners, different religions, and different languages. They have a mutual jealousy of each other, fomented by considerations of interest, power, and ascendency. Religious zeal too, like a smothered fire, is secretly burning in the hearts of the different sectaries that inhabit them, and were it not restrained by laws and superior authority, would soon burst out into a flame of universal persecution. Even the peaceable Quakers struggle hard for preeminence, and evince in a very striking manner, that the passions of mankind are much stronger than any principles of religion.

The colonies, therefore, separately considered, are internally weak; but it may be supposed, that, by an union or coalition, they would become strong and formidable: but an union seems almost impossible: one founded in dominion or power is morally so: for, were not England to interfere, the colonies themselves so well understand the policy of preserving a balance, that, I think, they would not be idle spectators, were any one of them to endeavour to subjugate its next neighbour. Indeed, it appears to me a very doubtful point, even supposing all the colonies of America to be united under one head, whether it would be possible to keep in due order and government so wide and extended an empire; the difficulties of communication, of intercourse, of correspondence, and all other circumstances considered.

A voluntary association or coalition, at least a permanent one, is almost as difficult to be supposed: for fire and water are not more heterogeneous than the different colonies in North-America. Nothing can exceed the jealousy and emulation, which they possess in regard to each other. The inhabitants of Pensylvania and New York have an inexhaustible source of animosity, in their jealousy for the trade of the Jerseys. Massachusetts Bay and Rhode Island, are not less interested in that of Connecticut. The West Indies are a common subject of emulation to them all. Even the limits and boundaries of each colony, are a constant source of litigation. In short, such is the difference of character, of manners, of religion, of interest, of the different colonies, that I think, if I am not wholly ignorant of the human mind, were they left to themselves, there would soon be a civil war, from one end of the continent to the other; while the Indians and Negroes would, with better reason, impatiently watch the opportunity of exterminating them all together.

After all, however, supposing what I firmly believe will never take place, a permanent union or alliance of all the colonies, yet it could not be effectual, or productive of the event supposed; for such is the extent of coast settled by the American colonies, that it can never be defended but by a maritime power: America must first be mistress of the sea, before she can be independent, or mistress of herself. Suppose the colonies ever so populous; suppose them capable of maintaining 100,000 men constantly in arms (a supposition in the highest degree extravagant), yet half a dozen frigates would, with ease, ravage and lay waste the whole country from end to end, without a possibility of their being able to prevent it; the country is so intersected by rivers, rivers of such magnitude as to render it impossible to build bridges over them, that all communication is in a manner cut off. An army under such circumstances could never act to any purpose or effect; its operations would be totally frustrated.

Further, a great part of the opulence and power of America depends upon her fisheries, and her commerce with the West Indies; she cannot subsist without them; but these would be intirely at the mercy of that power, which might have the sovereignty of the seas. I conclude therefore, that England, so long as she maintains her superiority in that respect, will also possess a superiority in America; but the moment she loses the empire of the one, she will be deprived of the sovereignty of the other: for were that empire to be held by France, Holland, or any other power, America, I will venture to foretell, will be annexed to it.—New establishments formed in the interior parts of America, will not come under this predicament. I should therefore think it the best policy to enlarge the present colonies, but not to establish fresh ones; for to suppose interior colonies to be of use to the mother country, by being a check upon those already settled, is to suppose what is contrary to experience, and the nature of things, viz., that men removed from the reach of power will be subordinate to it.

CHAPTER III

FRANCE LOSES AN EMPIRE

1745 – 1763

1.   *1745*—ROGER WOLCOTT DESCRIBES THE CAPTURE OF LOUISBOURG

❬ *In the middle years of the eighteenth century the longstanding rivalry between England and France burst into worldwide war. Human nature being what it is, conflict between the two nations was inevitable. As world powers, no other countries approached them. Each, through alliances, sought to dominate Europe, or at least to prevent the other from dominating it. Each had a thriving world trade with many ships on the sea lanes, and each had colonial outposts in North America, the West Indies, India, and other far-away regions.*

In 1740 both England and France became involved, on opposite sides, in a war over the succession to the Austrian throne. The con-

"Journal of Roger Wolcott at the Siege of Louisbourg in 1745," *Collections of the Connecticut Historical Society*, Volume One (Hartford, 1860), 149–53.

65

flict spread to America, where it was known as King George's War. At Louisbourg (now known as Cape Breton Island, immediately north of Nova Scotia) the French held a post that was supposed to be able to resist any attack. New Englanders, suspecting that the strength of Louisbourg was overrated, decided to assault it. What followed is described by Roger Wolcott, who headed the Connecticut volunteers and served as second in command under Sir William Pepperrell. Wolcott attributed the surprising success of the New Englanders to the fact that "our soldiers were freeholders and freeholders' sons, while the men within the walls were mercenary troops."

Massachusetts and New Hampshire sent 3,250 land forces into the service, with what ships of force they had and needful transports. Connecticut sent 500 land forces in transports, with Capt. Prentis in the Defense Sloop with 100 men for the sea service. Rhode Island sent Capt. Fones in the Tartar with 90 men. Gov. Clinton sent ten eighteen pounders from New York.

These forces all met at Canso April 25th 1745, and left 100 men with eight cannon to fortify that place; 400 men, under the command of Col. Moulton, were ordered to reduce St. Peters; and on the 29th day the fleet set sail from Canso for Cape Breton, and on the 30th, about one of the clock P.M. they arrived in Chapeaurouge Bay, near Flat Point. We are now ready for landing 3250 men for the land service furnished with sixteen eighteen-pounders, two nine-pounders, three mortars, 1 thirteen, 1 eleven, and 1 nine inch diameter, and a suitable number of shot and shell, with about 500 barrels of powder.

Altho' commonly the surf runs so high that there is no landing, yet now it was favourable to a wonder, and as soon as the whale boats were let down our men flew to shore like eagles to the quarry; the enemy soon advanced to meet the first that landed, at whose appearance our men made no stop but prest on upon the enemy, and at our first discharge the enemy fled, some of them were killed, some wounded and some taken prisoners; in the encounter we lost none but had two or three slightly wounded; the landing continued with utmost dispatch, and the men as soon as on shore prest forward thro' the forest to the town, being about three miles; in their passing they gave and received several shot from the enemy, in which none were lost on our side.

Our resolute landing and beating the enemy back to the town, struck such a terror on them that they abandoned the grand battery with the cannon, great shot and shells that were there; they burnt several of their houses without the town, and retired within their walls. This night our men lay in the forest without any regular encampment.

The next morning Sergt. Leeds with some Indians entered the royal battery, and about sixteen of our men drove back about eighty of the enemy who were returning from the town to the royal battery, and upon Brigadier Waldo's desire, his regiment was put into it.

We now spent several days in landing our tents and stores, fixing our camp, setting up our store-houses and hospitals, sending out advanced parties to meet any of the enemy that might be patrolling about and reduce the adjacent settlements. Workmen were employed to drill the cannon at the grand battery, which the enemy had plugged up, others were employed to view the ground where we might erect our batteries to the best advantage. As soon as the cannon were freed, they began a very brisk fire upon the town to the great annoyance of the enemy.

Our advanced parties met parties of the enemy which they constantly beat, and from the adjacent settlements brought in many prisoners, and things being settled respecting our camp and store-houses, &c., it was agreed to erect a battery at the green hill, being about 1760 yards west of the town. To this place from the landing, being about a mile and quarter, we drew our mortars, cannon, and carried our powder, ball and shells, over stony hills and deep morasses; all done in the night because the way was exposed to the shot from the walls. From hence we played upon the town without any great success, unless by the shells from our great mortar, which fell within the walls, and here we constantly received the great shot and shells from the town. Upon further consideration it was resolved to remove the cannon from the green hill to the cohorn battery, standing about 880 yards westward of the town, which was accomplished accordingly, and from thence we played with better success upon the town, but unhappily split our great mortar by a shell bursting within it. We also erected the advanced battery about 200 yards distance from the north-west gate, and the two-gun battery, being about 880 yards north of the town; these two batteries were furnisht with cannon from the royal battery. The advanced battery beat down the west gate and the walls near it, and dismounted several cannon on the walls, the shot passing through the houses in the town; the two-gun battery dismounted the cannon on the circular battery and raked the town from end to end, driving the inhabitants out [of] their houses into their casemates, where many of them sickened and died.

Notwithstanding, it was feared the town could not be taken unless the ships came in and a general storm was given by land and sea, and some of the ship captains thought the king's ships ought not [to] be so exposed to the enemy until the island battery was reduced, therefore the reduction of that battery became the matter of our greatest attention. It was resolved to attempt it in the night, by landing men in whale boats; four times this was attempted but failed without landing a man, but on the night after the 26th of May, about 400 volunteers undertook it and chose Capt. Brooks for their leader, a number of them landed, but 'tis uncertain how many—as soon as they were perceived by the garrison the battery was in a blaze from their cannon, swivells and small arms, their langrell cutting boats and men to pieces as they were landing, yet those who landed maintained a desperate fight for two hours and a half to the amazement of the enemy—at length some few of them got back into their boats and returned, 189 were left behind, 120 of which were found prisoners when the town was taken, and 69 perished in the attempt.

Col. Gorham's regiment had for some time been stationed on the light-house side in order to erect a battery there to annoy the island battery, and upon this defeat that battery was hastened, the perfecting of it was attended with much difficulty and delay, but by the 14th of June with the large mortar that came from Annapolis and five eighteen-pounders he played successfully on the island battery, breaking down some of the embrazures and driving the French out of the battery into the sea. Our fire from the grand battery and other batteries had greatly distrest the enemy in the town and island battery, and time was very precious with us; we had now been encamped 47 days in an enemy's country, far from any English settlements that might give us relief, the French and Indians in the adjacent parts were numerous, we were in danger of a surprize from them, especially those that were gone off from Annapolis, who we heard were advancing towards us; our stores were far spent, and the weather (though favorable to a wonder hitherto) was much to be feared, the climate being usually covered with palpable fogs and much rain, in which case no business could be done, and we must suffer very much in our camp and trenches.

But now, in this difficult and critical hour, the Sunderland, Canterbury, and Lark, having joined the fleet, the captains of the ships agreed to the commodore to bring in the ships before the town and storm it by land and sea, and on the 15th of June the honble. commodore came on shore and informed us of his resolution to come in with his ships, and that from his broadsides he could discharge 364 guns on the town at once; it was then agreed in council to storm the town by land and sea the first fair wind to bring the ships into the harbour, but this was happily prevented by a flag of truce coming out the same day towards night, proposing to enter into a capitulation for surrendering the town; the capitulation was finisht the next day, the town &c. surrendered to his Britannic majesty, and on the 17th we took possession of the town and island battery and advanced the union flag upon the walls. By this the effusion of much Christian blood was prevented, as also much damage that would likely have been done to the ships and town, now all belonging to the King of Great Britain.

2. *1755*—THE FRENCH AND INDIANS SMASH BRADDOCK'S REGULARS

❨ *To the disgust of the colonists, England returned Louisbourg to France when peace was made in 1748. But her loss of the fortress, even though temporary, served as a warning. France would strengthen her hold on North America, for next time the British might not be so lenient. Forts were either built or reinforced along the whole vast line of her settlements and influence: the valley of the St. Lawrence, the region of the Great Lakes, the entire length of the Mississippi.*

The English colonists watched this activity with fear and dismay. A truly strong ring of French fortifications would set limits to expansion from the seaboard. Settlers were already spreading out beyond the Alleghenies; they wanted no Frenchmen stopping them. Besides, the French had Indian allies whom they would not always restrain from attacking the outlying settlements. Men who had ventured beyond the mountains knew well the meaning of the war whoop when heard from a cabin in a lonely clearing.

A peace made uneasy by such fears and tensions could not last. It neared its end in 1753, when the Marquis Duquesne, governor of New France, began the erection of a chain of forts in the upper Ohio valley, closer than ever before to the Atlantic colonies. The governor of Virginia sent George Washington, then only twenty-one years old, to demand that the intruders withdraw. Meanwhile, local militia built a small fort at the forks of the Ohio (where Pittsburgh now stands) which the French promptly captured, strengthened, and renamed Fort Duquesne.

The English government decided that the time for action had come. The War Office sent General Braddock, with two regiments of regulars, to Virginia with orders to drive the French from the Ohio valley. As the expedition, consisting of colonial troops as well as the regulars, neared its goal, the officers became overconfident and careless. On July 9 the advance guard marched into an ambush of French and Indians. An officer of the Coldstream Guards describes the battle that followed.

ORDERS AT THE CAMP NEAR THE MONONGAHELA.

All the men are to draw and clean their pieces, and the whole are to load to-morrow on the beating of the General with fresh cartridges.

Winthrop Sargent, "Captain Orme's Journal," in *The History of an Expedition against Fort Du Quesne in 1755* (Philadelphia, 1856), 353–57.

No tents or baggage are to be taken with Lieutenant Colonel Gage's party.

July 9th. The whole marched agreeably to the Orders before mentioned, and about 8 in the morning the General made the first crossing of the Monongahela by passing over about one hundred and fifty men in the front, to whom followed half the carriages. Another party of one hundred and fifty men headed the second division; the horses and cattle then passed, and after all the baggage was over, the remaining troops, which till then possessed the heights, marched over in good order.

The General ordered a halt, and the whole formed in their proper line of march.

When we had moved about a mile, the General received a note from Lieutenant Colonel Gage acquainting him with his having passed the river without any interruption, and having posted himself agreeably to his orders.

When we got to the other crossing, the bank on the opposite side not being yet made passable, the artillery and baggage drew up along the beach, and halted 'till one, when the General passed over the detachment of the 44th, with the pickets of the right. The artillery waggons and carrying horses followed; and then the detachment of the 48th, with the left pickets, which had been posted during the halt upon the heights.

When the whole had passed, the General again halted, till they formed according to the annexed plan.

It was now near two o'clock, and the advanced party under Lieutenant Colonel Gage and the working party under Sr John St Clair were ordered to march on 'till three. No sooner were the pickets upon their respective flanks, and the word given to march, but we heard an excessive quick and heavy firing in the front. The General imagining the advanced parties were very warmly attacked, and being willing to free himself from the incumbrance of the baggage, order'd Lieutenant Colonel Burton to reinforce them with the vanguard, and the line to halt. According to this disposition, eight hundred men were detached from the line, free from all embarrassments, and four hundred were left for the defence of the Artillery and baggage, posted in such a manner as to secure them from any attack or insults.

The General sent forward an Aid de Camp to bring him an account of the nature of attack, but the fire continuing, he moved forward himself, leaving Sr Peter Halket with the command of the baggage. The advanced detachments soon gave way and fell back upon Lieutenant Colonel Burton's detachment, who was forming his men to face a rising ground upon the right. The whole were now got together in great confusion. The colours were advanced in different places, to separate the men of the two regiments. The General ordered the officers to endeavour to form the men, and to tell them off into small divisions and to advance with them; but neither entreaties nor threats could prevail.

The advanced flank parties, which were left for the security of the baggage, all but one ran in. The baggage was then warmly attacked; a great many horses, and some drivers were killed; the rest escaped by flight. Two of the cannon flanked the baggage, and for some time kept the Indians off: the other cannon, which were disposed of in the best manner and fired away most of their ammunition, were of some service, but the spot being so woody, they could do little or no execution.

The enemy had spread themselves in such a manner, that they extended from front to rear, and fired upon every part.

The place of action was covered with large trees, and much underwood upon the left, without any opening but the road, which was about twelve foot wide. At the distance of about two hundred yards in front and upon the right were two rising grounds covered with trees.

When the General found it impossible to persuade them to advance, and no enemy appeared in view; and nevertheless a vast number of officers were killed, by exposing themselves before the men; he endeavoured to retreat them in good order; but the panick was so great that he could not succeed. During this time they were loading as fast as possible and firing in the air. At last Lieutenant Colonel Burton got together about one hundred of the 48th regiment, and prevailed upon them, by the General's order, to follow him towards the rising ground on the right, but he being disabled by his wounds, they faced about to the right, and returned.

When the men had fired away all their ammunition and the General and most of the officers were wounded, they by one common consent left the field, running off with the greatest precipitation. About fifty Indians pursued us to the river, and killed several men in the passage. The officers used all possible endeavours to stop the men, and to prevail upon them to rally; but a great number of them threw away their arms and ammunition, and even their cloaths, to escape the faster.

About a quarter of a mile on the other side the river, we prevailed upon near one hundred of them to take post upon a very advantageous spot, about two hundred yards from the road. Lieutenant Colonel Burton posted some small parties and centinels. We intended to have kept possession of that ground, 'till we could have been reinforced. The General and some wounded officers remained there about an hour, 'till most of the men run off. From that place, the General sent Mr Washington to Colonel Dunbar with orders to send waggons for the wounded, some provision, and hospital stores; to be escorted by two youngest Grenadier companies, to meet him at Gist's plantation, or nearer, if possible. It was found impracticable to remain here, as the General and officers were left almost alone; we therefore retreated in the best manner we were able. After we had passed the Monongahela the second time, we were joined by Lieutenant Colonel Gage, who had rallied near 80 men. We marched all that night, and the next day, and about ten o'clock that night we got to Gist's plantation.

July 11th. Some waggons, provisions, and hospital stores arrived. As soon as the wounded were dressed, and the men had refreshed themselves, we retreated to Colonel Dunbar's Camp, which was near Rock Fort. The General sent a serjeant's party back with provision to be left on the road on the other side of the Yoxhio Geni for the refreshment of any men who might have lost their way in the woods. Upon our arrival at Colonel Dunbar's camp, we found it in the greatest confusion. Some of his men had gone off upon hearing of our defeat, and the rest seemed to have forgot all discipline. Several of our detachment had not stopped 'till they had reached this camp.

It was found necessary to clear some waggons for the wounded, many of whom were in a desperate situation; and as it was impossible to remove the stores, the Howitzer shells, some twelve pound shot, powder, and provision, were destroyed or buried.

July 13th. We marched from hence to the Camp, near the great Meadows, where the General died.

3. *1763*—ALEXANDER HENRY ESCAPES AN INDIAN MASSACRE

❡ *Braddock's defeat, which marked the beginning of the French and Indian War (in Europe, the Seven Years' War), was a British disaster. Yet it was not a mortal one. In aggressive campaigns British and colonial troops took Louisbourg again, captured Quebec, and broke the French line of forts leading into the Ohio valley. On the sea and in India the British won equally decisive victories. France, thoroughly defeated, was forced to relinquish all her North America colonies to Britain.*

In the American West the Indians smarted at the French defeat. They disliked the new British officials, resented the greediness of the traders, and feared the advance of white settlers. Loosely organized by Pontiac, a remarkable chief, the Indians attacked in the spring of 1763. At almost the same time they struck at British posts scattered over a thousand miles. At Michilimackinac, on the uppermost tip of lower Michigan, they achieved surprise under the cover

Milo M. Quaife, *Alexander Henry's Travels and Adventures* (Chicago, R. R. Donnelley & Sons Co., 1921), 78–94.

of a game of lacrosse. Alexander Henry, a young trader at the post, was lucky enough to escape the massacre. Taken prisoner, he was treated not unkindly, and lived with the Indians for almost a year before resuming his trading activities.

The morning was sultry. A Chipewa came to tell me that his nation was going to play at baggatiway with the Sacs or Saäkies, another Indian nation, for a high wager. He invited me to witness the sport, adding that the commandant was to be there, and would bet on the side of the Chipewa. In consequence of this information I went to the commandant and expostulated with him a little, representing that the Indians might possibly have some sinister end in view; but the commandant only smiled at my suspicions.

Baggatiway, called by the Canadians *le jeu de la crosse,* is played with a bat and ball. The bat is about four feet in length, curved, and terminating in a sort of racket. Two posts are planted in the ground at a considerable distance from each other, as a mile or more. Each party has its post, and the game consists in throwing the ball up to the post of the adversary. The ball, at the beginning, is placed in the middle of the course and each party endeavors as well to throw the ball out of the direction of its own post as into that of the adversary's.

I did not go myself to see the match which was now to be played without the fort, because there being a canoe prepared to depart on the following day for Montreal I employed myself in writing letters to my friends; and even when a fellow trader, Mr. Tracy, happened to call upon me, saying that another canoe had just arrived from Detroit, and proposing that I should go with him to the beach to inquire the news, it so happened that I still remained to finish my letters, promising to follow Mr. Tracy in the course of a few minutes. Mr. Tracy had not gone more than twenty paces from my door when I heard an Indian war cry and a noise of general confusion.

Going instantly to my window I saw a crowd of Indians within the fort furiously cutting down and scalping every Englishman they found. In particular I witnessed the fate of Lieutenant Jemette.

I had in the room in which I was a fowling piece, loaded with swan-shot. This I immediately seized and held it for a few minutes, waiting to hear the drum beat to arms. In this dreadful interval I saw several of my countrymen fall, and more than one struggling between the knees of an Indian, who, holding him in this manner, scalped him while yet living.

At length, disappointed in the hope of seeing resistance made to the enemy, and sensible, of course, that no effort of my own unassisted arm could avail against four hundred Indians, I thought only of seeking shelter. Amid the slaughter which was raging I observed many of the Canadian inhabitants of the fort calmly looking on, neither opposing the Indians, nor suffering injury; and from this circumstance I conceived a hope of finding security in their houses.

Between the yard door of my own house and that of M. Langlade, my next neighbor, there was only a low fence, over which I easily climbed. At my entrance I found the whole family at the windows, gazing at the scene of blood before them. I addressed myself immediately to M. Langlade, begging that he would put me into some place of safety until the heat of the affair should be over; an act of charity by which he might perhaps preserve me from the general massacre; but while I uttered my petition M. Langlade, who had looked for a moment at me, turned again to the window, shrugging his shoulders and intimating that he could do nothing for me:—"Que voudriez-vous que j'en ferais?"

This was a moment for despair; but the next a Pani woman, a slave of M. Langlade's, beckoned me to follow her. She brought me to a door which she opened, desiring me to enter, and telling me that it led to the garret, where I must go and conceal myself. I joyfully obeyed her directions; and she, having followed me up to the garret door, locked it after me and with great presence of mind took away the key.

This shelter obtained, if shelter I could hope to find it, I was naturally anxious to know what might still be passing without. Through an aperture which afforded me a view of the area of the fort I beheld, in shapes the foulest and most terrible, the ferocious triumphs of barbarian conquerors. The dead were scalped and mangled; the dying were writhing and shrieking under the unsatiated knife and tomahawk; and from the bodies of some, ripped open, their butchers were drinking the blood, scooped up in the hollow of joined hands and quaffed amid shouts of rage and victory. I was shaken not only with horror, but with fear. The sufferings which I witnessed I seemed on the point of experiencing. No long time elapsed before every one being destroyed who could be found, there was a general cry of "All is finished!" At the same instant I heard some of the Indians enter the house in which I was.

The garret was separated from the room below only by a layer of single boards, at once the flooring of the one and the ceiling of the other. I could therefore hear everything that passed; and the Indians no sooner came in than they inquired whether or not any Englishman were in the house. M. Langlade replied that he could not say—he did not know of any—answers in which he did not exceed the truth, for the Pani woman had not only hidden me by stealth, but kept my secret and her own. M. Langlade was therefore, as I presume, as far from a wish to destroy me as he was careless about saving me, when he added to these answers that they might examine for themselves, and would soon be satisfied as to the object of their question. Saying this, he brought them to the garret door.

The state of my mind will be imagined. Arrived at the door some delay was occasioned by the absence of the key and a few moments were thus allowed me in which to look around for a hiding place. In one corner of the garret was a heap of those vessels of birch bark used in maple sugar making. . . .

The door was unlocked, and opening, and the Indians ascending the stairs, before I had completely crept into a small opening, which presented itself at one end of the heap. An instant after four Indians entered the room, all armed with tomahawks, and all besmeared with blood upon every part of their bodies.

The die appeared to be cast. I could scarcely breathe; but I thought that the throbbing of my heart occasioned a noise loud enough to betray me. The Indians walked in every direction about the garret, and one of them approached me so closely that at a particular moment, had he put forth his hand, he must have touched me. Still I remained undiscovered, a circumstance to which the dark color of my clothes and the want of light in a room which had no window, and in the corner in which I was, must have contributed. In a word, after taking several turns in the room, during which they told M. Langlade how many they had killed and how many scalps they had taken, they returned down stairs, and I with sensations not to be expressed, heard the door, which was the barrier between me and my fate, locked for the second time.

There was a feather bed on the floor, and on this, exhausted as I was by the agitation of my mind, I threw myself down and fell asleep. In this state I remained till the dusk of the evening, when I was awakened by a second opening of the door. The person that now entered was M. Langlade's wife, who was much surprised at finding me, but advised me not to be uneasy, observing that the Indians had killed most of the English, but that she hoped I might myself escape. A shower of rain having begun to fall, she had come to stop a hole in the roof. On her going away, I begged her to send me a little water to drink, which she did.

As night was now advancing I continued to lie on the bed, ruminating on my condition, but unable to discover a resource from which I could hope for life. A flight to Detroit had no probable chance of success. The distance from Michilimackinac was four hundred miles; I was without provisions; and the whole length of the road lay through Indian countries, countries of an enemy in arms, where the first man whom I should meet would kill me. To stay where I was threatened nearly the same issue. As before, fatigue of mind, and not tranquillity, suspended my cares and procured me further sleep. . . .

The respite which sleep afforded me during the night was put an end to by the return of morning. I was again on the rack of apprehension. At sunrise I heard the family stirring, and presently after, Indian voices informing M. Langlade they had not found my hapless self among the dead, and that they supposed me to be somewhere concealed. M. Langlade appeared from what followed to be by this time acquainted with the place of my retreat, of which no doubt he had been informed by his wife. The poor woman, as soon as the Indians mentioned me, declared to her husband in the French tongue that he should no longer keep me in his house, but deliver me up to my pursuers, giving as a reason for this measure that should the Indians discover his instrumentality in my concealment, they might revenge it on her children, and that it was better that I should die than they. M. Langlade resisted at first this sentence of his wife's; but soon suffered her to prevail, informing the Indians that he had been told I was in his house, that I had come there without his knowledge, and that he would put me into their hands. This was no sooner expressed than he began to ascend the stairs, the Indians following upon his heels.

I now resigned myself to the fate with which I was menaced; and regarding every attempt at concealment as vain, I arose from the bed and presented myself full in view to the Indians who were entering the room. They were all in a state of intoxication, and entirely naked, except about the middle. One of them, named Wenniway, whom I had previously known, and who was upward of six feet in height, had his entire face and body covered with charcoal and grease, only that a white spot of two inches in diameter encircled either eye. This man, walking up to me, seized me with one hand by the collar of the coat, while in the other he held a large carving knife, as if to plunge it into my breast; his eyes, meanwhile, were fixed steadfastly on mine. At length, after some seconds of the most anxious suspense, he dropped his arm, saying, "I won't kill you!" To this he added that he had been frequently engaged in wars against the English, and had brought away many scalps; that on a certain occasion he had lost a brother whose name was Musinigon, and that I should be called after him.

A reprieve upon any terms placed me among the living, and gave me back the sustaining voice of hope; but Wenniway ordered me downstairs, and there informing me that I was to be taken to his cabin, where, and indeed everywhere else, the Indians were all mad with liquor, death again was threatened, and not as possible only, but as certain. I mentioned my fears on this subject to M. Langlade, begging him to represent the danger to my master. M. Langlade in this instance did not withhold his compassion, and Wenniway immediately consented that I should remain where I was until he found another opportunity to take me away.

Thus far secure I reascended my garret stairs in order to place myself the furthest possible out of the reach of insult from drunken Indians; but I had not remained there more than an hour, when I was called to the room below in which was an Indian who said that I must go with him out of the fort, Wenniway having sent him to fetch me. This man, as well as Wenniway himself, I had seen before. In the preceding year I had allowed him to take goods on credit, for which he was still in my debt; and some short time previous to the surprise of the fort he had said upon my upbraiding him with want of honesty that he would pay me before long. This speech now came fresh into my memory and led me to suspect that the fellow had formed a design against my life. I communicated the suspicion to M. Langlade; but he gave for answer that I was not now my own master, and must do as I was ordered.

The Indian on his part directed that before I left the house I should undress myself, declaring that my coat and shirt would become him better than they did me. His pleasure in this respect being complied with, no other alternative was left me than either to go out naked, or to put on the clothes of the Indian, which he freely gave me in exchange. His motive for thus stripping me of my own apparel was no other as I afterward learned than this, that it might not be stained with blood when he should kill me.

I was now told to proceed; and my driver followed me close until I had passed the gate of the fort, when I turned toward the spot where I knew the Indians to be encamped. This, however, did not suit the purpose of my enemy, who seized me by the arm and drew me violently in the opposite direction to the distance of fifty yards above the fort. Here, finding that I was approaching the bushes and sand hills, I determined to proceed no farther, but told the Indian that I believed he meant to murder me, and that if so he might as well strike where I was as at any greater distance. He replied with coolness that my suspicions were just, and that he meant to pay me in this manner for my goods. At the same time he produced a knife and held me in a position to receive the intended blow. Both this and that which followed were necessarily the affair of a moment. By some effort, too sudden and too little dependent on thought to be explained or remembered, I was enabled to arrest his arm and give him a sudden push by which I turned him from me and released myself from his grasp. This was no sooner done than I ran toward the fort with all the swiftness in my power, the Indian following me, and I expecting every moment to feel his knife. I succeeded in my flight; and on entering the fort I saw Wenniway standing in the midst of the area, and to him I hastened for protection. Wenniway desired the Indian to desist; but the latter pursued me round him, making several strokes at me with his knife, and foaming at the mouth with rage at the repeated failure of his purpose. At length

77

Wenniway drew near to M. Langlade's house; and, the door being open, I ran into it. The Indian followed me; but on my entering the house he voluntarily abandoned the pursuit.

Preserved so often and so unexpectedly as it had now been my lot to be, I returned to my garret with a strong inclination to believe that through the will of an overruling power no Indian enemy could do me hurt; but new trials, as I believed, were at hand when at ten o'clock in the evening I was roused from sleep and once more desired to descend the stairs. Not less, however, to my satisfaction than surprise, I was summoned only to meet Major Etherington, Mr. Bostwick, and Lieutenant Lesslie, who were in the room below.

These gentlemen had been taken prisoners while looking at the game without the fort and immediately stripped of all their clothes. They were now sent into the fort under the charge of Canadians, because, the Indians having resolved on getting drunk, the chiefs were apprehensive that they would be murdered if they continued in the camp. Lieutenant Jemette and seventy soldiers had been killed; and but twenty Englishmen, including soldiers, were still alive. These were all within the fort, together with nearly three hundred Canadians.

These being our numbers, myself and others proposed to Major Etherington to make an effort for regaining possession of the fort and maintaining it against the Indians. The Jesuit missionary was consulted on the project; but he discouraged us by his representations, not only of the merciless treatment which we must expect from the Indians should they regain their superiority, but of the little dependence which was to be placed upon our Canadian auxiliaries. Thus the fort and prisoners remained in the hands of the Indians, though through the whole night the prisoners and whites were in actual possession, and they were without the gates.

That whole night, or the greater part of it, was passed in mutual condolence, and my fellow prisoners shared my garret. In the morning, being again called down, I found my master, Wenniway, and was desired to follow him. He led me to a small house within the fort, where in a narrow room and almost dark I found Mr. Ezekiel Solomons, an Englishman from Detroit, and a soldier, all prisoners. With these I remained in painful suspense as to the scene that was next to present itself till ten o'clock in the forenoon, when an Indian arrived, and presently marched us to the lakeside where a canoe appeared ready for departure, and in which we found that we were to embark.

Our voyage, full of doubt as it was, would have commenced immediately, but that one of the Indians who was to be of the party was absent. His arrival was to be waited for; and this occasioned a very long delay during which we were exposed to a keen northeast wind. An old shirt was all that covered me; I suffered much from the cold;

and in this extremity M. Langlade coming down to the beach, I asked him for a blanket, promising if I lived to pay him for it at any price he pleased; but the answer I received was this, that he could let me have no blanket unless there were some one to be security for the payment. For myself, he observed, I had no longer any property in that country. I had no more to say to M. Langlade; but presently seeing another Canadian, named John Cuchoise, I addressed to him a similar request and was not refused. Naked as I was, and rigorous as was the weather, but for the blanket I must have perished. At noon our party was all collected, the prisoners all embarked, and we steered for the Isles du Castor in Lake Michigan.

CHAPTER IV

TOWARD REVOLUTION

1765 – 1775

1. *1765*—THE VIRGINIANS TAKE CARE OF A STAMP DISTRIBUTOR

❡ *Great Britain emerged from the Seven Years' War with her empire strong as never before. She was mistress of the seas, of North America, of India. She could not see at the time that her victory had been too sweeping. Her American colonists had played their own part in the defeat of the French. In their campaigns they had gained self-reliance at the same time that they had lost some of their respect for the fighting qualities of the British regular. Moreover, they no longer had an enemy at their back door to drive them to the mother country for support.*

The cost of the war had been heavy, and the cost of defending the empire would continue. Pontiac's conspiracy had shown that even in North America colonial boundaries would have to be protected. From this expenditure the colonies would benefit, as they

---

Journals of the House of Burgesses, 1762–65, lxviii-lxxi.

had benefited from the war just ended. What could be fairer than that they should bear a share of the burden? So the British ministers reasoned. To that end the enforcement of various revenue acts—the Navigation Act, the Sugar Act—was tightened. The Americans, used to trading as they pleased regardless of laws to the contrary, were annoyed, but limited themselves to grumbling. But when the Stamp Act was passed early in 1765 grumbling changed to forcible resistance.

The Stamp Act required that revenue stamps be placed on all legal and commercial papers, pamphlets, newspapers, cards, and dice. It was not a burdensome measure, but it was Parliament's first attempt to lay a direct tax on the colonists, and it could not be evaded. The Americans reacted with fury. In a letter to the Lords of Trade, Francis Fauquier, acting governor of Virginia, described what happened when the newly appointed stamp distributor arrived at Williamsburg.

WILLIAMSBURG Nov. 3d 1765.

MY LORDS,

The present unhappy state of this Colony, will, to my great concern, oblige me to trouble Your Lordships with a long and very disagreeable letter. We were for some time in almost daily expectations of the arrival of Colonel Mercer with the Stamps for the use of this Colony, and rumours were industriously thrown out that at the time of the General Court parties would come down from most parts of the country to seize on and destroy all Stamped Papers. . . .

Very unluckily, Colonel Mercer arrived at the time this town was the fullest of Strangers. On Wednesday the 30th October he came up to town. I then thought proper to go to the Coffee house . . . that I might be an eye witness of what did really pass, and not receive it by relation from others. The mercantile people were all assembled as usual. The first word I heard was "One and all"; upon which, as at a word agreed on before between themselves, they all quitted the place to find Colonel Mercer at his Father's lodgings where it was known he was. This concourse of people I should call a mob, did I not know that *it was chiefly if not altogether composed of gentlemen of property* in the Colony, some of them at the head of their respective Counties, *and the merchants of the country,* whether English, Scotch or Virginian; for few absented themselves. They met Colonel Mercer on the way, just at the Capitol: there they stopped and demanded of him an answer whether he would resign or act in this office as Distributor of the Stamps. He said it was an affair of great moment to him; he must consult his friends; and promised to give them an answer at 10 o'clock on Friday morning at that place. This did not satisfy them; and they followed him to the Coffee house, in the porch of which I had seated myself with many of the Council and the Speaker, who had posted himself between the crowd and myself. We all received him with the greatest marks of welcome; with which, if one may be allowed to judge by their countenances, they [the "mob"] were not well pleased, tho' they remained quiet and were silent. Now and then a voice was heard from the crowd that Friday was too late; the Act would take place, they would have an answer tomorrow. Several messages were brought to Mr. Mercer by the leading men of the crowd, to whom he constantly answered he had already given an answer and he would have no other extorted from him. After some little time a cry was heard, "let us rush in." Upon this we that were at the top of the [steps], knowing the advantage our situation gave us to repell those who should attempt to mount them, advanced to the edge of the Steps, of which number I was one. I immediately heard a cry, "See the Governor, take care of him." Those who before were pushing up the steps, immediately fell back, and left a small space between me and them. If your Lordships will not accuse me of vanity I would say that I believe this to be partly owing to the respect they bore to my character and partly to the love they bore to my person. After much entreaty of some of his friends, Mr. Mercer was, against his own inclination, prevailed upon to promise them an answer at the Capitol the next evening at five. The crowd did not yet disperse; it was growing dark, and I did not think it safe to have to leave Mr. Mercer behind me, so I again advanced to the edge of the steps and said aloud I believed no man there would do me any hurt, and turned to Mr. Mercer and told him if he would walk with me through the people I believed I could conduct him safe to my house; and we accordingly walked side by side through the thickest of the people, who did not molest us, tho' there was some little murmurs. By me thus taking him under my protection, I believe I saved him from being insulted at least. When we got home we had much discourse on the subject. . . . He left me that night in a state of uncertainty what part he should act.

Accordingly Mr. Mercer appeared at the Capitol at 5, as he had promised. The number of people assembled there was much increased, by messengers having been sent into the neighborhood for that purpose. Colonel Mercer then read to them the answer [his resignation] which is printed in the Supplement of the Gazette, of which I enclose your Lordships a copy, to which I beg leave to refer. . . .

If I accepted the resignation, I must appoint another, and I was well convinced I could not find one to accept of it, in those circumstances, which would render the office cheap. Besides if I left Mr. Mercer in possession of the place he would be always ready to distribute the Stamped papers, whenever peoples eyes should be opened and they should come to their senses, so as to receive them. . . .

FRANCIS FAUQUIER.

Colonel Mercer has informed me that he proposes to apply to the Commanders of His Majesty's ships of War, to take the Stamped Papers on board their ships for His Majesty's service: it being the place of the greatest if not the only security for them: for I am convinced, as well as himself, that it would be extremely dangerous to attempt to land them during the present fermented state of the Colony. If these Gentlemen should refuse to take charge of them, and Mr. Mercer should apply to me, I will do my duty to His Majesty and save them from being destroyed, to the best of my power, tho' I can by no means answer for the success of my endeavours. . . .

I am with the greatest respect and esteem, my Lords
Your Lordships most obedient
and devoted Servant.

FRANCIS FAUQUIER.

2. 1765—JOHN ADAMS ACCLAIMS THE SPIRIT OF LIBERTY

❨ *In faraway Massachusetts, John Adams, a thirty-four-year-old lawyer from whom more would be heard in the future, recorded year-end reflections in his diary. His view of the Stamp Act differed from that of Governor Fauquier.*

Braintree, December 18, Wednesday. . . . The year 1765 has been the most remarkable year of my life. That enormous engine, fabricated by the British Parliament, for battering down all the rights and liberties of America, I mean the Stamp Act, has raised and spread through the whole continent a spirit that will be recorded to our honor with all future generations. In every colony, from Georgia to New Hampshire inclusively, the stamp distributers and inspectors have been compelled by the unconquerable rage of the people to renounce their offices. Such and so universal has been the resentment of the people, that every man who has dared to speak in favor of the stamps, or to soften the detestation in which they are held, how great soever his abilities and virtues had been esteemed before, or whatever his fortune, connections, and influence had been, has been seen to sink into universal contempt and ignominy.

The people, even to the lowest ranks, have become more attentive to their liberties, more inquisitive about them, and more determined to defend them, than they were ever before known or had occasion to be; innumerable have been the monuments of wit, humor, sense, learning, spirit, patriotism, and heroism, erected in the several colonies and provinces in the course of this year. Our presses have groaned, our pulpits have thundered, our legislatures have resolved, our towns have voted;

Charles Francis Adams, Ed., *The Works of John Adams* (Boston, 1850), II, 154, 173.

the crown officers have everywhere trembled, and all their little tools and creatures been afraid to speak and ashamed to be seen. . . .

[January 2, 1766.] At Philadelphia, the Heart-and-Hand Fire Company has expelled Mr. Hughes, the stamp man for that colony. The freemen of Talbot county, in Maryland, have erected a gibbet before the door of the court-house, twenty feet high, and have hanged on it the effigies of a stamp informer in chains, *in terrorem* till the Stamp Act shall be repealed; and have resolved, unanimously, to hold in utter contempt and abhorrence every stamp officer, and every favorer of the Stamp Act, and to "have no communication with any such person, not even to speak to him, unless to upbraid him with his baseness." So triumphant is the spirit of liberty everywhere. Such a union was never before known in America.

3. *1772*—RHODE ISLANDERS BURN THE GASPÉE

❬ *In the face of united opposition the British government retreated. In March, 1766, Parliament repealed the Stamp Act. But it had no intention of allowing the colonists to escape taxation permanently. In 1767 it passed the Townshend Acts, levying certain customs duties in addition to those already in force, only to repeal the Acts when the Americans refused to import British goods. Repealed them, that is, except for the tax on tea, which a stubborn monarch, George III, insisted on retaining as a mark of Parliamentary authority. At the same time, the British strengthened the customs patrol in American waters. By this time, smuggling had become a patriotic duty. When the* Gaspée, *a British revenue cutter, ran aground in Narragansett Bay, she offered an opportunity too tempting to be neglected. Ephraim Bowen tells what happened.*

In the year 1772, the British government had stationed at Newport, Rhode Island, the schooner called the Gaspee, of eight guns, commanded by Wm. Duddingston, a Lieutenant in the British Navy, for the purpose of preventing the clandestine landing of articles, subject to the payment of duty. The Captain of this schooner made it his practice to stop and board all vessels entering or leaving the ports of Rhode Island, or leaving Newport for Providence.

On the 10th day of June, 1772, Capt. Thomas Lindsey left Newport in his packet for Providence, about noon, with the wind at North; and soon after, the Gaspee was under sail, in pursuit of Lindsey, and continued the chase as far as Namquit Point, which runs off from the farm in Warwick about seven miles below Providence, now owned by Mr.

William R. Staples, Ed., *Documentary History of the Burning of the Gaspée* (Providence, 1845), 8–9.

John Brown Francis, our late Governor.—Lindsey was standing easterly, with the tide on ebb about two hours, when he hove about, at the
end of Namquit Point, and stood to the westward, and Duddingston in
close chase, changed his course and ran on the Point, near its end, and
grounded. Lindsey continued on his course up the river, and arrived at
Providence about sunset, when he immediately informed Mr. John
Brown, one of our first and most respectable merchants, of the situation
of the Gaspee. He immediately concluded that she would remain im-
movable until after midnight, and that now an opportunity offered of
putting an end to the trouble and vexation she daily caused. Mr. Brown
immediately resolved on her destruction, and he forthwith directed one
of his trusty shipmasters to collect eight of the largest long-boats in the
harbor, with five oars to each, to have the oars and row-locks well
muffled, to prevent noise, and to place them at Fenner's wharf, directly
opposite to the dwelling of Mr. James Sabin, who kept a house of
board and entertainment for gentlemen, being the same house purchased
a few years after by the late Welcome Arnold, and is now owned by
and is the residence of Colonel Richard J. Arnold, his son.

About the time of the shutting up of the shops soon after sunset, a
man passed along the Main street beating a drum and informing the
inhabitants of the fact, that the Gaspee was aground on Namquit Point,
and would not float off until 3 o'clock the next morning, and inviting
those persons who felt a disposition to go and destroy that troublesome
vessel, to repair in the evening to Mr. James Sabin's house. About
9 o'clock, I took my father's gun and my powder horn and bullets and
went to Mr. Sabin's, and found the southeast room full of people, where
I loaded my gun, and all remained there till about 10 o'clock, some casting bullets in the kitchen, and others making arrangements for departure, when orders were given to cross the street to Fenner's wharf and
embark; which soon took place, and a sea captain acted as steersman of
each boat, of whom I recollect Capt. Abraham Whipple, Capt. John B.
Hopkins, (with whom I embarked,) and Capt. Benjamin Dunn. A line
from right to left was soon formed, with Capt. Whipple on the right
and Capt. Hopkins on the right of the left wing.

The party thus proceeded till within about sixty yards of the Gaspee,
when a sentinel hailed, "Who comes there?" No answer.—He hailed
again and no answer. In about a minute Duddingston mounted the starboard gunwale in his shirt and hailed, "Who comes there?" No answer. He hailed again, when Capt. Whipple answered as follows—"I
am the sheriff of the county of Kent, G—d d—n you. I have got a warrant to apprehend you, G—d d—n you; so surrender, G—d d—n you."
I took my seat on the main thwart, near the larboard row-lock, with my
gun by my right side, facing forwards. As soon as Duddingston began
to hail, Joseph Bucklin, who was standing on the main thwart by my

right side, said to me, "Ephe, reach me your gun and I can kill that fellow." I reached it to him accordingly, when, during Capt. Whipple's replying, Bucklin fired and Duddingston fell, and Bucklin exclaimed, "I have killed the rascal." In less than a minute after Capt. Whipple's answer, the boats were alongside of the Gaspee, and boarded without opposition. The men on deck retreated below as Duddingston entered the cabin.

As it was discovered that he was wounded, John Mawney, who had for two or three years been studying physic and surgery, was ordered to go into the cabin and dress Duddingston's wound, and I was directed to assist him. On examination, it was found the ball took effect about five inches directly below the navel. Duddingston called for Mr. Dickinson to produce bandages and other necessaries for the dressing of the wound, and when finished, orders were given to the schooner's company to collect their clothing and everything belonging to them and put them into their boats, as all of them were to be sent on shore. All were soon collected and put on board of the boats, including one of our boats. They departed and landed Duddingston at the old still-house wharf, at Pawtuxet, and put the chief into the house of Joseph Rhodes. Soon after, all the party were ordered to depart, leaving one boat for the leaders of the expedition, who soon set the vessel on fire, which consumed her to the waters' edge.

4.   *1775*—MINUTEMEN PUNISH THE BRITISH IN MASSACHUSETTS

❲ *Relations between England and the colonies steadily became worse. Bostonians pitched a cargo of tea into the harbor. The British retaliated by closing the Massachusetts port to shipping and stationing troops there. Minutemen, pledged to spring to arms at a minute's warning, drilled on village greens. In mid-April, 1775, the British commander in Boston heard a report that arms were being collected at Concord, some twenty miles northwest of the city. On the evening of the 18th he dispatched a force of 700 regulars to destroy the stores. Warned by Paul Revere and William Dawes, the militia assembled under arms at Lexington, five miles east of Concord. This account of the day's events comes from the Rev. Jonas Clark, a Lexington minister in the forefront of the revolutionary movement.*

Between the hours of twelve and one, on the morning of the nineteenth of April, we received intelligence, by express, from the Honor-

Jonas Clark, *Opening of the War of the Revolution, 19th of April, 1775: A Brief Narrative of the Principal Transaction of That Day* (Boston, 1875), 5–8.

able Joseph Warren Esq; at Boston, "that a large body of the king's troops (supposed to be a brigade of about 12, or 1500) were embarked in boats from Boston, and gone over to land on Lechmere's-Point (so called) in Cambridge: And that it was shrewdly suspected, that they were ordered to seize and destroy the stores, belonging to the colony, then deposited at Concord," in consequence of General Gage's unjustifiable seizure of the provincial magazine of powder at Medford, and other colony stores in several other places.

Upon this intelligence, as also upon information of the conduct of the officers as above-mentioned, the militia of this town were alarmed, and ordered to meet on the usual place of parade; not with any design of commencing hostilities upon the king's troops, but to consult what might be done for our own and the people's safety: And also to be ready for whatever service providence might call us out to, upon this alarming occasion, in case overt acts of violence, or open hostilities should be committed by this mercenary band of armed and bloodthirsty oppressors.

About the same time, two persons were sent express to Cambridge, if possible, to gain intelligence of the motions of the troops, and what route they took.

The militia met according to order; and waited the return of the messengers, that they might order their measures as occasion should require. Between 3 and 4 o'clock, one of the expresses returned, informing, that there was no appearance of the troops, on the roads, either from Cambridge or Charlestown; and that it was supposed that the movements in the army the evening before, were only a feint to alarm the people. Upon this, therefore, the militia company were dismissed for the present, but with orders to be within call of the drum,—waiting the return of the other messenger, who was expected in about an hour, or sooner, if any discovery should be made of the motions of the troops.—But he was prevented by their silent and sudden arrival at the place where he was, waiting for intelligence. So that, after all this precaution, we had no notice of their approach, 'till the brigade was actually in the town, and upon a quick march within about a mile and a quarter of the meeting house and place of parade.

However, the commanding officer thought best to call the company together,—not with any design of opposing so superior a force, much less of commencing hostilities; but only with a view to determine what to do, when and where to meet, and to dismiss and disperse.

Accordingly, about half an hour after four o'clock, alarm guns were fired, and the drums beat to arms; and the militia were collecting together.—Some, to the number of about 50, or 60, or possibly more, were on the parade, others were coming towards it.—In the mean time, the troops, having thus stolen a march upon us, and to prevent any intelligence of their approach, having seized and held prisoners several persons whom they met unarmed upon the road, seemed to come determined for murder and bloodshed; and that whether provoked to it, or not!—When within about half a quarter of a mile of the meeting-house, they halted, and the command was given to prime and load; which being done, they marched on 'till they came up to the east end of said meeting-house, in sight of our militia (collecting as aforesaid) who were about 12, or 13 rods distant.—Immediately upon their appearing so suddenly, and so nigh, Capt. Parker, who commanded the militia company, ordered the men to disperse, and take care of themselves; and not to fire.—Upon this, our men dispersed;—but, many of them, not so speedily as they might have done, not having the most distant idea of such brutal barbarity and more than savage cruelty, from the troops of a British king, as they immediately experienced!-!—For, no sooner did they come in sight of our company, but one of them, supposed to be an officer of rank, was heard to say to the troops, "Damn them; we will have them!"—Upon which the troops shouted aloud, huzza'd, and rushed furiously towards our men.—About the same time, three officers (supposed to be Col. Smith, Major Pitcairn and another officer) advanced, on horse back, to the front of the body, and coming within 5 or 6 rods of the militia, one of them cried out, "ye villains, ye Rebels, disperse; Damn you, disperse!"—or words to this effect. One of them (whether the same, or not, is not easily determined) said, "Lay down your arms; Damn you, why don't you lay down your arms!"—The second of these officers, about this time, fired a pistol towards the militia, as they were dispersing.—The foremost, who was within a few yards of our men, brandishing his sword, and then pointing towards them, with a loud voice said, to the troops, "Fire!—By God, fire!"—which was instantly followed by a discharge of arms from the said troops, succeeded by a very heavy and close fire upon our party, dispersing, so long as any of them were within reach.—Eight were left dead upon the ground! Ten were wounded.—The rest of the company, through divine goodness, were (to a miracle) preserved unhurt in this murderous action!

. . . Having thus vanquished the party in Lexington, the troops marched on for Concord, to execute their orders, in destroying the stores belonging to the colony, deposited there.—They met with no interruption in their march to Concord.—But by some means or other, the people of Concord had notice of their approach and designs, and were alarmed about break of day; and collecting as soon, and as many as possible, improved the time they had before the troops came upon them, to the best advantage, both for concealing and securing as many of the public stores as they could, and in preparing for defence.—By the stop of the troops at Lexington, many thousands were saved to the colony, and they were, in a great measure, frustrated in their design.

When the troops made their approach to the easterly part of the town, the provincials of Concord and some neighbouring towns, were collected. and collecting in an advantageous post, on a hill, a little distance from the meeting-house, north of the road, to the number of about 150, or 200: but finding the troops to be more than three times as many, they wisely retreated, first to a hill about 80 rods further north, and then over the north-bridge (so called) about a mile from the town: and there they waited the coming of the militia of the towns adjacent, to their assistance.

In the mean time, the British detachment marched into the center of the town. A party of about 200, was ordered to take possession of said bridge, other parties were dispatched to various parts of the town, in search of public stores, while the remainder were employed in seizing and destroying, whatever they could find in the town-house, and other places, where stores had been lodged.—But before they had accomplished their design, they were interrupted by a discharge of arms, at said bridge.

It seems, that of the party above-mentioned, as ordered to take possession of the bridge, one half were marched on about two miles, in search of stores, at Col. Barret's and that part of the town: while the other half, consisting of towards 100 men, under Capt. Lawrie, were left to guard the bridge. The provincials, who were in sight of the bridge, observing the troops attempting to take up the planks of said bridge, thought it necessary to dislodge them, and gain possession of the bridge.—They accordingly marched, but with express orders not to fire, unless first fired upon by the king's troops. Upon their approach towards the bridge, Capt. Lawrie's party fired upon them, killed Capt. Davis and another man dead upon the spot, and wounded several others. Upon this our militia rushed on, with a spirit becoming free-born Americans, returned the fire upon the enemy, killed 2, wounded several and drove them from the bridge, and pursued them towards the town, 'till they were covered by a reinforcement from the main body. The provincials then took post on a hill, at some distance, north of the town: and as their numbers were continually increasing, they were preparing to give the troops a proper discharge, on their departure from the town.

In the mean time, the king's troops collected; and having dressed their wounded, destroyed what stores they could find, and insulted and plundered a number of the inhabitants, prepared for a retreat.

While at Concord, the troops disabled two 24 pounders; destroyed their 2 carriages, and seven wheels for the same, with their limbers. Sixteen wheels for brass 3 pounders, and 2 carriages with limber and wheels for two 4 pounders. They threw into the river, wells, &c. about

500 weight of ball: and stove about 60 barrels of flour; but not having time to perfect their work, one half of the flour was afterwards saved.

The troops began a hasty retreat about the middle of the day: and were no sooner out of the town, but they began to meet the effects of the just resentments of this injured people. The provincials fired upon them from various quarters, and pursued them (though without any military order) with a firmness and intrepidity, beyond what could have been expected, on the first onset, and in such a day of confusion and distress!—The fire was returned, for a time, with great fury, by the troops as they retreated, though (through divine goodness) with but little execution.—This scene continued, with but little intermission, till they returned to Lexington; when it was evident, that, having lost numbers in killed, wounded, and prisoners that fell into our hands, they began to be, not only fatigued, but greatly disheartened. And it is supposed they must have soon surrendered at discretion, had they not been reinforced.—But Lord Percy's arrival with another brigade, of about 1000 men, and 2 field pieces, about half a mile from Lexington meeting-house, towards Cambridge, gave them a seasonable respite.

The coming of the reinforcement, with the cannon, (which our people were not so well acquainted with then, as they have been since) put the provincials also to a pause, for a time.—But no sooner were the king's troops in motion, but our men renewed the pursuit with equal, and even greater ardor and intrepidity than before, and the firing on both sides continued, with but little intermission, to the close of the day, when the troops entered Charlestown, where the provincials could not follow them, without exposing the worthy inhabitants of that truly patriotic town, to their rage and revenge.—That night and the next day, they were conveyed in boats, over Charles-River to Boston, glad to secure themselves, under the cover of the shipping, and by strengthening and perfecting the fortifications, at every part, against the further attacks of a justly incensed people, who, upon intelligence of the murderous transactions of this fatal day, were collecting in arms, round the town, in great numbers, and from every quarter.

In the retreat of the king's troops from Concord to Lexington, they ravaged and plundered, as they had opportunity, more or less, in most of the houses that were upon the road.—But after they were joined by Percy's brigade, in Lexington, it seemed as if all the little remains of humanity had left them; and rage and revenge had taken the reins, and knew no bounds!—Cloathing, furniture, provisions, goods, plundered, broken, carried off, or destroyed!—Buildings (especially dwelling houses) abused, defaced, battered, shattered and almost ruined!—And as if this had not been enough, numbers of them doomed to the flames! —Three dwelling houses, two shops and a barn, were laid in ashes, in Lexington!—Many others were set on fire, in this town, in Cambridge,

&c. and all must have shared the same fate, had not the close pursuit of the provincials prevented, and the flames been seasonably quenched! —Add to all this; the unarmed, the aged and infirm, who were unable to flee, are inhumanly stabbed and murdered in their habitations! Yea, even women in child-bed, with their helpless babes in their arms, do not escape the horrid alternative, of being either cruelly murdered in their beds, burnt in their habitations, or turned into the streets to perish with cold, nakedness and distress!

. . . Our loss, in the several actions of that day, was 49 killed, 34 wounded and 5 missing, who were taken prisoners, and have since been exchanged. The enemy's loss, according to the best accounts, in killed, wounded and missing, about 300.

5.   *1775*—ETHAN ALLEN TAKES TICONDEROGA

❲ *Word of Lexington and Concord spread fast. Ethan Allen, commandant of the Green Mountain Boys, heard it in Vermont. On the heels of the news came instructions from Connecticut that he attack Fort Ticonderoga, a British outpost on Lake Champlain. To the hot-tempered, impulsive, courageous commander no order could have been more welcome. Allen himself describes the way he carried it out.*

Ever since I arrived to a state of manhood, and acquainted myself with the general history of mankind, I have felt a sincere passion for liberty. The history of nations, doomed to perpetual slavery, in consequence of yielding up to tyrants their natural-born liberties, I read with a sort of philosophical horror; so that the first systematical and bloody attempt, at Lexington, to enslave America, thoroughly electrified my mind, and fully determined me to take part with my country: And, while I was wishing for an opportunity to signalize myself in its behalf, directions were privately sent to me from the then colony (now state) of Connecticut, to raise the Green Mountain Boys, and, if possible, with them surprise and take the fortress, Ticonderoga. This enterprise I cheerfully undertook; and, after first guarding all the several passes that led thither, to cut off all intelligence between the garrison and the country, made a forced march from Bennington, and arrived at the lake opposite to Ticonderoga, on the evening of the ninth day of May, 1775, with two hundred and thirty valiant Green Mountain Boys; and it was with the utmost difficulty that I procured boats to cross the lake. However, I landed eighty-three men near the garrison, and sent the boats back for the rear guard, commanded by Col. Seth Warner; but

A Narrative of Col. Ethan Allen's Captivity . . . *Written by Himself* (Walpole, N. H., 1807), 13–20.

the day began to dawn, and I found myself under a necessity to attack the fort, before the rear could cross the lake; and, as it was viewed hazardous, I harrangued the officers and soldiers in the manner following:

"Friends and fellow soldiers: You have, for a number of years past, been a scourge and terror to arbitrary power. Your valor has been famed abroad, and acknowledged, as appears by the advice and orders to me, from the General Assembly of Connecticut, to surprise and take the garrison now before us. I now propose to advance before you, and, in person, conduct you through the wicket-gate; for we must this morning either quit our pretensions to valor, or possess ourselves of this fortress in a few minutes; and, inasmuch as it is a desperate attempt, which none but the bravest of men dare undertake, I do not urge it on any contrary to his will. You that will undertake voluntarily, poise your firelocks."

The men being, at this time, drawn up in three ranks, each poised his firelock. I ordered them to face to the right; and, at the head of the centre file, marched them immediately to the wicket gate aforesaid, where I found a sentry posted, who instantly snapped his fusee at me: I ran immediately towards him, and he retreated through the covered way into the parade in such manner as to face the two barracks which faced each other. The garrison being asleep, except the sentries, we gave three huzzas which greatly surprised them. One of the sentries made a pass at one of my officers with a charged bayonet, and slightly wounded him: my first thought was to kill him with my sword; but, in an instant, I altered the design and fury of the blow to a slight cut on the side of the head; upon which he dropped his gun, and asked quarter, which I readily granted him, and demanded of him the place where the commanding officer kept; he shewed me a pair of stairs in front of a barrack, on the west part of the garrison, which led up to a second story in said barrack, to which I immediately repaired, and ordered the commander, Capt. Delaplace, to come forth instantly, or I would sacrifice the whole garrison; at which the Capt. came immediately to the door, with his breeches in his hand; when I ordered him to deliver to me the fort instantly, he asked me by what authority I demanded it: I answered him, "In the name of the great Jehovah, and the Continental Congress." The authority of the Congress being very little known at that time, he began to speak again; but I interrupted him, and, with my drawn sword over his head, again demanded an immediate surrender of the garrison; with which he then complied, and ordered his men to be forthwith paraded without arms, as he had given up the garrison.

In the meantime some of my officers had given orders, and, in consequence thereof, sundry of the barrack doors were beat down, and about one-third of the garrison imprisoned, which consisted of the said commander, a Lieut. Feltham, a conductor of artillery, a gunner, two serjeants, and forty-four rank and file; about one hundred pieces of cannon, one thirteen inch mortar, and a number of swivels. This surprise was carried into execution in the gray of the morning of the tenth day of May, 1775. The sun seemed to rise that morning with a superior lustre; and Ticonderoga and its dependencies smiled on its conquerors, who tossed about the flowing bowl, and wished success to Congress, and the liberty and freedom of America.

6. *1775*—BUNKER HILL

❮ *Concord, Lexington, Ticonderoga—these were war, though the colonists were subjects of Great Britain and many, perhaps most of them, still rejected the idea of independence. But sentiment did not prevent the New Englanders from laying siege to Boston, to which the British had retired after their disastrous expedition to Lexington and Concord. The siege dragged on into June. On the 15th of that month the Americans learned that General Gage, commanding the King's troops, intended to occupy Dorchester Heights outside of the city. The next day the Americans, to checkmate Gage, moved into position on Breed's Hill, from which they could throw shot into the city itself. The British had no real choice: either they drove the American forces from their new position, a strong one, or Boston would be battered down around them.*

A colonial officer described the action, known in history as Bunker Hill though it actually was fought on Breed's Hill.

Finding the zeal of the troops so great . . . it was resolved to force General Gage to an action; with this view it was determined to seize possession of the height on the peninsula of Charles-Town, which General Gage had occupied before the 19th of April, and erect some batteries on Banhin-hill [Bunker-hill], to batter down the town and General Gage's camp on the common and his entrenchment on Boston neck (which you know is only about three fourths of a mile across); 4000 men commanded by General Putnam, and led on by Dr. Warren, having prepared every thing for the operation as well as could be contrived or collected were stationed under a half unfinished breastwork and some palisadoes fix'd in a hurry. When the enemy were landed, to the number of 2500, as we are since informed, being the light infantry and the grenadiers of the army with a compleat train of artillery, howitzers and field pieces, drawn by 200 sailors, and commanded by

Margaret Wheeler Willard, *Letters on the American Revolution* (Boston: Houghton Mifflin, 1925), 150–52.

93

the most gallant and experienced officers of the last war; they marched to engage 3000 provincials, arrayed in red worsted caps and blue great coats, with guns of different sizes, few of which had bayonets, ill-served artillery, but of invincible courage! The fire from the ships and artillery of the enemy was horrid and amazing; the first onset of the soldiers was bold and fierce, but they were received with equal courage; at length the 38th regiment gave way, and the rest recoiled. The King's troops were commanded by General Howe, brother to that gallant Lord Howe to whose memory the province of Massachusett's Bay erected a statue; he marched with undaunted spirit at the head of his men; most of his followers were killed round his own person. The King's troops about this time got into much confusion and retreated; they were rallied by the reproaches of General Howe, and the activity of General Clinton who then joined the battle. The King's troops again made their push against Charles-Town, which was then set on fire by them, our right flank being then uncovered, two floating batteries coming in by the mill dam to take us in the rear, more troops coming from Boston, and our ammunition being almost expended, General Putnam ordered the troops on the left to retreat; the confusion was great for twenty minutes, but in less than half an hour we fell into compleat order; the regulars were so mauled they durst not pursue us 200 yards; almost the last shot they fired they killed good Dr. Warren, who had dressed himself like Lord Falkland, in his wedding suit, and distinguished himself by unparalleled acts of bravery during the whole action, but particularly in covering the retreat; he was a man of great courage, universal learning, and much humanity. It may well be said he is the greatest loss we have sustained. General Putnam, at the age of 60, was as active as the youngest officer in the field. We have lost 104 killed, and 306 wounded; a Lieutenant Colonel and 30 men are prisoners; we anxiously wait their fate; if there are any severity used the war will become most horrid.—We lost before the action began 18 men by the fire of the ships and the battery from Boston; these were burried before the assault. The number of the King's troops killed and wounded are three times our loss. A sailor belonging to one of the transports, who was busy with many of his companions in rifling the dead, and who has since deserted, assured me the ground was covered with officers. The cannon was dreadful. The King's troops began firing at a great distance, being scarce of ammunition deferred our fire. It was impossible to send troops from Roxburgh, because we expected an attack there, or at Dorchester neck. I am well informed many of the old English officers are since dead.

CHAPTER V

1. *1774*—JOHN ADAMS DESCRIBES THE GATHERING OF THE FIRST CONTINENTAL CONGRESS

❡ *In the summer of 1774 the American colonists came to the conclusion that if they were to make their protests against the course of the mother country effective they would have to act together. Accordingly a Congress—later known as the First Continental Congress—was called to meet at Philadelphia in early September. All the colonies except Georgia sent delegates.*

John Adams, from Massachusetts, reached Philadelphia at the end of August. Each night he recorded the events of the day in his diary. His entries afford a vivid picture of the leading men of the colonies, most of whom were meeting each other for the first time. Their attitudes, as Adams reported them, reflected the public opinion of the colonists: resistance, in the name of liberty but as loyal British subjects, to what they considered invasions of their rights by the

Edmund C. Burnett, *Letters of Members of the Continental Congress* (Washington, 1921), I, 1–4.

King and his ministers. The delegates, Adams makes clear, were not old fogies; they saw no reason for not having a good time even though they were considering problems as grave as men have ever faced.

[August 29–September 3, 1774.]

29. Monday. . . . A number of carriages and gentlemen came out of Philadelphia to meet us—Mr. Thomas Mifflin, Mr. McKean, of the lower counties, one of their delegates, Mr. Rutledge of Carolina, and a number of gentlemen from Philadelphia, Mr. Folsom and Mr. Sullivan, the New Hampshire delegates. We were introduced to all these gentlemen, and most cordially welcomed to Philadelphia. We then rode into town, and dirty, dusty, and fatigued as we were, we could not resist the importunity to go to the tavern, the most genteel one in America. There we were introduced to a number of other gentlemen of the city: Dr. Shippen, Dr. Knox, Mr. Smith, and a multitude of others, and to Mr. Lynch and Mr. Gadsden of South Carolina. Here we had a fresh welcome to the city of Philadelphia, and after some time spent in conversation, a curtain was drawn, and in the other half of the chamber a supper appeared as elegant as ever was laid upon a table. About eleven o'clock we retired.

By a computation made this evening by Mr. McKean, there will be at the Congress about fifty-six members, twenty-two of them lawyers. . . .

30. Tuesday. Walked a little about town; visited the market, the State House, the Carpenters' Hall, where the Congress is to sit, etc.; then called at Mr. Mifflin's; a grand, spacious, and elegant house. Here we had much conversation with Mr. Charles Thomson, who is, it seems, about marrying a lady, a relation of Mr. Dickinson's, with five thousand pounds sterling. This Charles Thomson is the Sam Adams of Philadelphia, the life of the cause of liberty, they say. A Friend, Collins, came to see us, and invited us to dine on Thursday. We returned to our lodgings, and Mr. Lynch, Mr. Gadsden, Mr. Middleton, and young Mr. Rutledge came to visit us. Mr. Lynch introduced Mr. Middleton to us; Mr. Middleton was silent and reserved; young Rutledge was high enough. A promise of the King was mentioned. He started! "I should have no regard to his word; his promises are not worth any thing", etc. This is a young, smart, spirited body. . . .

31. Wednesday. Breakfasted at Mr. Bayard's, of Philadelphia, with Mr. Sprout, a Presbyterian minister.

Made a visit to Governor Ward, of Rhode Island, at his lodgings. There we were introduced to several gentlemen. Mr. Dickinson, the farmer of Pennsylvania, came in his coach with four beautiful horses to Mr. Ward's lodgings, to see us. He was introduced to us, and very politely said he was exceeding glad to have the pleasure of seeing these gentlemen. . . . We dined with Mr. Lynch, his lady and daughter, at their lodgings, Mrs. McKenzie's; and a very agreeable dinner and afternoon we had, notwithstanding the violent heat. We were all vastly pleased with Mr. Lynch. He is a solid, firm, judicious man. He told us that Colonel Washington made the most eloquent speech at the Virginia Convention that ever was made. Says he, "I will raise one thousand men, subsist them at my own expense, and march myself at their head for the relief of Boston." . . .

September 1. Thursday. This day we breakfasted at Mr. Mifflin's. Mr. C. Thomson came in, and soon after, Dr. Smith, the famous Dr. Smith, the provost of the college. He appears a plain man, tall and rather awkward; there is an appearance of art. We then went to return visits to the gentlemen who had visited us. We visited a Mr. Cadwallader, a gentleman of large fortune, a grand and elegant house and furniture. We then visited Mr. Powell, another splendid seat. We then visited the gentlemen from South Carolina, and, about twelve, were introduced to Mr. Galloway, the Speaker of the House in Pennsylvania.

We dined at Friend Collins's, Stephen Collins's, with Governor Hopkins, Governor Ward, Mr. Galloway, Mr. Rhoades, etc. In the evening, all the gentlemen of the Congress who were arrived in town, met at Smith's, the new city tavern, and spent the evening together. Twenty-five members were come. Virginia, North Carolina, Maryland, and the city of New York, were not arrived. Mr. William Livingston, from the Jerseys, lately of New York, was there. He is a plain man, tall, black, wears his hair; nothing elegant or genteel about him. They say he is no public speaker, but very sensible and learned, and a ready writer. Mr. Rutledge, the elder, was there, but his appearance is not very promising. There is no keenness in his eye, no depth in his countenance; nothing of the profound, sagacious, brilliant, or sparkling, in his first appearance. . . .

2. Friday. Dined at Mr. Thomas Mifflin's, with Mr. Lynch, Mr. Middleton, and the two Rutledges with their ladies. The two Rutledges are good lawyers. Governor Hopkins and Governor Ward were in company. Mr. Lynch gave us a sentiment: "The brave Dantzickers, who declare they will be free in the face of the greatest monarch in Europe." We were very sociable and happy. After coffee, we went to the tavern, where we were introduced to Peyton Randolph, Esquire, Speaker of Virginia, Colonel Harrison, Richard Henry Lee, Esquire, and Colonel Bland. Randolph is a large, well looking man; Lee is a tall, spare man; Bland is a learned, bookish man.

These gentlemen from Virginia appear to be the most spirited and consistent of any. Harrison said he would have come on foot rather than not come. Bland said he would have gone, upon this occasion, if it had been to Jericho.

3. Saturday. Breakfasted at Dr. Shippen's; Dr. Witherspoon was there. Col. R. H. Lee lodges there; he is a masterly man. This Mr. Lee is a brother of the sheriff of London, and of Dr. Arthur Lee, and of Mrs. Shippen; they are all sensible and deep thinkers. Lee is for making the repeal of every revenue law—the Boston Port Bill, the bill for altering the Massachusetts constitution, and the Quebec Bill, and the removal of all the troops, the end of the Congress, and an abstinence from all dutied articles, the means—rum, molasses, sugar, tea, wine, fruits, etc. He is absolutely certain that the same ship which carries home the resolution will bring back the redress. If we were to suppose that any time would intervene, he should be for exceptions. He thinks we should inform his Majesty that we never can be happy, while the Lords Bute, Mansfield, and North, are his confidants and counsellors. He took his pen and attempted a calculation of the numbers of people represented by the Congress, which he made about two millions two hundred thousand; and of the revenue, now actually raised, which he made eighty thousand pounds sterling. He would not allow Lord North to have great abilities; he had seen no symptoms of them; his whole administration had been blunder. He said the opposition had been so feeble and incompetent hitherto, that it was time to make vigorous exertions. . . .

Mr. Lee thinks that to strike at the Navigation Acts would unite every man in Britain against us, because the kingdom could not exist without them, and the advantages they derive from these regulations and restrictions of our trade are an ample compensation for all the protection they have afforded us, or will afford us. Dr. Witherspoon enters with great spirit into the American cause. He seems as hearty a friend as any of the natives, an animated Son of Liberty. This forenoon, Mr. Caesar Rodney of the lower counties on Delaware River, two Mr. Tilghmans from Maryland, were introduced to us. We went with Mr. William Barrell to his store, and drank punch, and eat dried smoked sprats with him; read the papers and our letters from Boston; dined with Mr. Joseph Reed, the lawyer, with Mrs. Deberdt and Mrs. Reed, Mr. Willing, Mr. Thomas Smith, Mr. Dehart, etc.; spent the evening at Mr. Mifflin's, with Lee and Harrison from Virginia, the two Rutledges, Dr. Witherspoon, Dr. Shippen, Dr. Steptoe, and another gentleman; an elegant supper, and we drank sentiments till eleven o'clock. Lee and Harrison were very high. Lee had dined with Mr. Dickinson, and drank Burgundy the whole afternoon.

Harrison gave us for a sentiment, "A constitutional death to the Lords Bute, Mansfield, and North." Paine gave us, "May the collision of British flint and American steel produce that spark of liberty which shall illumine the latest posterity." "Wisdom to Britain, and firmness to the Colonies; may Britain be wise, and America free." "The friends of America throughout the world." "Union of the Colonies." "Unanimity to the Congress." "May the result of the Congress answer the expectations of the people." "Union of Britain and the Colonies on a constitutional foundation," and many other such toasts. Young Rutledge told me he studied three years at the Temple. He thinks this a great distinction; says he took a volume of notes which J. Quincy transcribed; says that young gentlemen ought to travel early, because that freedom and ease of behavior which is so necessary cannot be acquired but in early life. This Rutledge is young, sprightly, but not deep; he has the most indistinct, inarticulate way of speaking; speaks through his nose; a wretched speaker in conversation. How he will shine in public, I don't yet know. He seems good-natured, though conceited. His lady is with him, in bad health. His brother still maintains the air of reserve, design, and cunning, like Duane and Galloway and Bob Auchmuty. Caesar Rodney is the oddest looking man in the world; he is tall, thin and slender as a reed, pale; his face is not bigger than a large apple, yet there is sense and fire, spirit, wit, and humor in his countenance. He made himself very merry with Ruggles and his pretended scruples and timidities at the last Congress. Mr. Reed told us, at dinner, that he never saw greater joy than he saw in London when the news arrived that the non-importation agreement was broke. They were universally shaking hands and congratulating each other. He says that George Hayley is the worst enemy to America that he knew there. Swore to him that he would stand by government in all its measures, and was always censuring and cursing America. . . .

2. *1775*—GEORGE WASHINGTON IS PLACED IN COMMAND OF THE CONTINENTAL ARMY

❰ *The First Continental Congress adopted a Declaration of Rights and a series of agreements by which the colonists pledged themselves neither to import from nor to export to Great Britain. Before adjourning, the delegates resolved to meet again on May 10, 1775, if by that time their grievances had not been redressed.*

At the appointed time the delegates were back in Philadelphia. They knew that an army of New Englanders had laid Boston under siege. Should that army be declared the military force of the united colonies under a commander chosen by the Continental Congress? John Adams related in his Autobiography how George Washington, the forty-three-year-old Virginia planter whom he described elsewhere as "modest and virtuous, amiable, generous, and brave," was chosen in the face of considerable opposition.

Charles Francis Adams, Ed., *The Life and Works of John Adams* (Boston, 1850), II, 416–18.

In several conversations, I found more than one very cool about the appointment of Washington, and particularly Mr. Pendleton was very clear and full against it. Full of anxieties concerning these confusions, and apprehending daily that we should hear very distressing news from Boston, I walked with Mr. Samuel Adams in the State House yard, for a little exercise and fresh air, before the hour of Congress, and there represented to him the various dangers that surrounded us. He agreed to them all, but said, "What shall we do?" I answered him, that he knew I had taken great pains to get our colleagues to agree upon some plan, that we might be unanimous; but he knew that they would pledge themselves to nothing; but I was determined to take a step which should compel them and all the other members of Congress to declare themselves for or against something. "I am determined this morning to make a direct motion that Congress should adopt the army before Boston, and appoint Colonel Washington commander of it." Mr. Adams seemed to think very seriously of it, but said nothing.

Accordingly, when Congress had assembled, I rose in my place, and in as short a speech as the subject would admit, represented the state of the Colonies, the uncertainty in the minds of the people, their great expectation and anxiety, the distresses of the army, the danger of its dissolution, the difficulty of collecting another, and the probability that the British army would take advantage of our delays, march out of Boston, and spread desolation as far as they could go. I concluded with a motion, in form, that Congress would adopt the army at Cambridge, and appoint a General; that though this was not the proper time to nominate a General, yet, as I had reason to believe this was a point of the greatest difficulty, I had no hesitation to declare that I had but one gentleman in my mind for that important command, and that was a gentleman from Virginia who was among us and very well known to all of us, a gentleman whose skill and experience as an officer, whose independent fortune, great talents, and excellent universal character, would command the approbation of all America, and unite the cordial exertions of all the Colonies better than any other person in the Union. Mr. Washington, who happened to sit near the door, as soon as he heard me allude to him, from his usual modesty, darted into the library-room. Mr. Hancock,—who was our President, which gave me an opportunity to observe his countenance while I was speaking on the state of the Colonies, the army at Cambridge, and the enemy,—heard me with visible pleasure; but when I came to describe Washington for the commander, I never remarked a more sudden and striking change of countenance. Mortification and resentment were expressed as forcibly as his face could exhibit them. Mr. Samuel Adams seconded the motion, and that did not soften the President's physiognomy at all. The subject came under debate, and several gentlemen declared themselves against the appointment of Mr. Washington, not on account of any personal objection against him, but because the army were all from New England, had a General of their own, appeared to be satisfied with him, and had proved themselves able to imprison the British army in Boston, which was all they expected or desired at that time. Mr. Pendleton, of Virginia, Mr. Sherman, of Connecticut, were very explicit in declaring this opinion; Mr. Cushing and several others more faintly expressed their opposition, and their fears of discontents in the army and in New England. Mr. Paine expressed a great opinion of General Ward and a strong friendship for him, having been his classmate at college, or at least his contemporary; but gave no opinion upon the question. The subject was postponed to a future day. In the mean time, pains were taken out of doors to obtain a unanimity, and the voices were generally so clearly in favor of Washington, that the dissentient members were persuaded to withdraw their opposition, and Mr. Washington was nominated, I believe by Mr. Thomas Johnson of Maryland, unanimously elected, and the army adopted.

3.   1776—THE COLONIES PROCLAIM THEIR INDEPENDENCE

❡ *As months passed, the colonies and Great Britain moved toward an open, final break with what seemed to be the inevitability of fate. The Continental Congress petitioned the King for the redress of grievances and expressed the hope that harmony would be restored; the stubborn monarch refused even to receive the petition and began hiring German troops—"Hessians"—to strengthen the army. An American force invaded Canada, took Montreal, and held Quebec under siege for several months. Thomas Paine won thousands of converts to the idea of independence through his vigorous pamphlet,* COMMON SENSE. *The colonies adopted constitutions and began to govern themselves. By the early summer of 1776 the Congress was ready to act. On June 7 Richard Henry Lee of Virginia offered a resolution that the united colonies "are, and of right ought to be, free and independent States." Action on the resolution was deferred until July 1, but meanwhile a committee consisting of Thomas Jefferson, Benjamin Franklin, John Adams, Robert Livingston, and Roger Sherman was charged with preparing a Declaration of Independence. The draft, largely Jefferson's work, was presented to Congress on June 28 and adopted by it on July 4. Independence, however, was declared on July 2, which would be our national holiday if posterity had regard for historical accuracy.*

Christopher Marshall, Pennsylvania delegate, recorded the stirring events of early July in his "Remembrancer," or diary.

William Duane, Ed., *Extracts from the Diary of Christopher Marshall* (Albany, 1877), 81–83.

July 2, 1776 . . . Past seven, to [the] Committee Room at Philosophical [Hall] ; none been there ; went to John Lynn's ; stayed till near
eight ; then returned ; broke up past ten. At this meeting, six besides
myself, were appointed a Committee of Secrecy to examine all inimical
and suspected persons that come to their knowledge. . . . This day, the
Continental Congress declared the United States Free and Independent
States. . . .

July 6. . . . Near eight, went to committee, Philosophical Hall,
where eight members were voted for and carried by majority, some
of whom I have no objection to, but would not rise, nor agree to support at the election some others. Agreed that the Declaration of Independence be declared at the State House next Second Day. At same
time, the King's arms there are to be taken down by nine Associators,
here appointed, who are to convey it to a pile of casks erected upon
the commons, for the purpose of a bonfire, and the arms placed on
the top. . . .

July 8. Warm sunshine morning. At eleven, went and met [the]
Committee of Inspection at Philosophical Hall ; went from there in a
body to the lodge ; joined the Committee of Safety (as called) ; went
in a body to [the] State House Yard, where, in the presence of a
great concourse of people, the Declaration of Independence was read
by John Nixon. The company declared their approbation by three
repeated huzzas. The King's Arms were taken down in the Court
Room, State House same time. From there, some of us went to B.
Armitage's tavern ; stayed till one. I went and dined at Paul Fooks's ;
lay down there after dinner till five. Then he and the French Engineer
went with me on the commons, where the same was proclaimed at each
of the five Battalions. . . . Fine starlight, pleasant evening. There were
bonfires, ringing bells, with other great demonstrations of joy upon the
unanimity and agreement of the declaration.

4.   *1776*—"AND ALL THE PEOPLE SHALL SAY AMEN"

❴ *Throughout the colonies, the Declaration of Independence was
received with unbounded enthusiasm. Mrs. John Adams wrote her
husband of the rejoicing in Boston. Similar celebrations took place
everywhere.*

Boston, 21 July, 1776.

Last Thursday, after hearing a very good sermon, I went with the
multitude into King Street to hear the Proclamation for Independence
read and proclaimed. Some field-pieces with the train were brought

Charles Francis Adams, Ed., *Familiar Letters of John Adams and His Wife, Abigail Adams,
During the Revolution* (New York, 1876), 204.

there. The troops appeared under arms, and all the inhabitants assembled there (the small-pox prevented many thousands from the country), when Colonel Crafts read from the balcony of the State House the proclamation. Great attention was given to every word. As soon as he ended, the cry from the balcony was, "God save our American States," and then three cheers which rent the air. The bells rang, the privateers fired, the forts and batteries, the cannon were discharged, the platoons followed, and every face appeared joyful. Mr. Bowdoin then gave a sentiment, "Stability and perpetuity to American independence." After dinner, the King's Arms were taken down from the State House, and every vestige of him from every place in which it appeared, and burnt in King Street. Thus ends royal authority in this State. And all the people shall say Amen.

THE WAR FOR INDEPENDENCE

1776 – 1782

1.   *1776*—ALEXANDER GRAYDON HAS RECRUITING TROUBLES

❨ *Shouting for independence was one thing; fighting for it another. A young Philadelphian, Alexander Graydon, discovered this disconcerting fact when he set out to raise a company of volunteers in the spring of 1776.*

The object now was to raise my company, and as the streets of the city had been pretty well swept by the preceding and contemporary levies, it was necessary to have recourse to the country. My recruiting party was therefore sent out in various directions; and each of my officers as well as myself, exerted himself in the business. Among the many unpleasant peculiarities of the American service, it was not the least that the drudgery, which in old military establishments belong to sergeants and corporals, here devolved on the commissioned officers; and that the whole business of recruiting, drilling, &c., required their

Alexander Graydon, *Memoirs of His Own Time with Reminiscences of the Men and Events of the Revolution* (Philadelphia, 1846), 133–35.

unremitted personal attention. This was more emphatically the case in recruiting; since the common opinion was, that the men and the officers were never to be separated, and hence, to see the persons who were to command them, and above all, the captain, was deemed of vast importance by those inclining to enlist: for this reason I found it necessary, in common with my brother officers, to put my feelings most cruelly to the rack; and in an excursion I once made to Frankford, they were tried to the utmost. A number of fellows at the tavern, at which my party rendezvoused, indicated a desire to enlist, but although they drank freely of our liquor, they still held off. I soon perceived that the object was to amuse themselves at our expense, and that if there might be one or two among them really disposed to engage, the others would prevent them. One fellow in particular, who had made the greatest show of taking the bounty, presuming on the weakness of our party, consisting only of a drummer, corporal, my second lieutenant and myself, began to grow insolent, and manifested an intention to begin a quarrel, in the issue of which, he no doubt calculated on giving us a drubbing. The disgrace of such a circumstance, presented itself to my mind in colours the most dismal, and I resolved, that if a scuffle should be unavoidable, it should, at least, be as serious as the hangers which my lieutenant and myself carried by our sides, could make it. Our endeavour, however, was to guard against a contest; but the moderation we testified, was attributed to fear. At length the arrogance of the principal ruffian, rose to such a height, that he squared himself for battle and advanced towards me in an attitude of defiance. I put him by, with an admonition to be quiet, though with a secret determination, that, if he repeated the insult to begin the war, whatever might be the consequence. The occasion was soon presented; when taking excellent aim, I struck him with my utmost force between the eyes and sent him staggering to the other end of the room. Then instantly drawing our hangers, and receiving the manful co-operation of the corporal and drummer, we were fortunate enough to put a stop to any farther hostilities. It was some time before the fellow I had struck, recovered from the blow, but when he did, he was quite an altered man. He was as submissive as could be wished, begging my pardon for what he had done, and although he would not enlist, he hired himself to me for a few weeks as a fifer, in which capacity he had acted in the militia; and during the time he was in this employ, he bore about the effects of his insolence, in a pair of black eyes. This incident would be little worthy of relating, did it not serve in some degree to correct the error of those who seem to conceive the year 1776 to have been a season of almost universal patriotic enthusiasm. It was far from prevalent in my opinion, among the lower ranks of the people, at least in Pennsylvania. At all times, indeed, licentious, levelling principles are much to the general taste, and were of course popular with us; but the true merits of the contest, were little understood or regarded. The opposition to the claims of Britain originated with the better sort: it was truly aristocratic in its commencement; and as the oppression to be apprehended, had not been felt, no grounds existed for general enthusiasm. The cause of liberty, it is true, was fashionable, and there were great preparations to fight for it; but a zeal proportioned to the magnitude of the question, was only to be looked for in the minds of those sagacious politicians, who inferred effects from causes, and who, as Mr. Burke expresses it, "snuffed the approach of tyranny in every tainted breeze."

2. *1776*—WASHINGTON EVACUATES NEW YORK

❨ *The Revolutionary troops had behaved valorously at Concord and Lexington, Ticonderoga and Bunker Hill. But when Washington, in the middle of September, 1776, decided to withdraw from New York rather than run the risk of being trapped on lower Manhattan Island—the British held Staten Island and Brooklyn—many of his men fought so badly that the General lost his always-touchy temper.*

Lt. Col. George Weedon of the First Virginia Regiment described the battle—and Washington's unbounded disgust—in a letter to John Page, President of the Virginia Council of Public Safety.

HEAD QUARTERS AT MORIS'S HEIGHTS
10 MILES ABOVE YORK
SEPR. 20TH 1776

MY DEAR SIR,

Since my last we have evacuated N. York, a step that was found absolutely necessary for the preservation of the Army, as we held it on very precarious Terms, and might have been attended with the worst of consequences at this time, the General not having an Army that he could depend upon, and so circumstanced from the situation of the place, that a safe retreat could not be made had the enemy have landed above us, which was easy to effect. We should have got off all the stores & Troops on Sunday night, but believe the Enemy suspected a thing of the sort, and early on Sunday morning sent several Frigates up the East & North Rivers, and landed two considerable Armies near the same time on the shores of each. Genl. Putnam commanded in York, and had time to bring the troops out whilst our Batteries amused the shipping. Two Brigades of Northern Troops were to oppose their landing, and engage them. They run off without firing a gun, tho' Genl.

Original letter in the Weedon Papers, Chicago Historical Society.

Washington was himself present, and [in spite of] all he, his Aide-de-Camps, & other Genl. Officers could do, they were not to be rally'd till they had got some miles. The General was so exasperated that he struck several officers in their flight, three times dashed his hat on the ground, and at last exclaimed "Good God, have I got such troops as those!" It was with difficulty his friends could get him to quit the field, so great was his emotions. He himself got off safe, and all the Troops as you may think. Nothing was left in York but about 700 Barrels of flour & some old cannon of little consequence.

The Enemy, elated at this piece of success, formed next morning and advanced in three columns. A disposition was made at this place to check them, in which your 3d Virginia Regiment made part. I was ordered to defend a pass at a valley that divides those heights from N. York and the country below. The brave Major Lietch (?) was detached with the 3 Rifle companies commanded by Captains Thornton, West, and Ashby to flank the Enemy that was then making for it. I soon got engaged, as did the Major & his party. How we behaved it does not become me to say. Let it suffice to tell you that we had the General's thanks in publick Orders for our conduct. We were reinforced by some Maryland Troops & others who behaved well. The poor Major received three Balls through his body before he quitted the field, and so lucky are their direction that I am in hopes he will do well. At present he is in a fair way. I lost with his party and my own, three killed & 12 wounded. The other cores [corps] that joined us, lost in proportion. The enemies loss was at first supposed to be 97 but a Deserter that came in today makes them to have lost between 2 & 3 hundred. . . . Upon the whole they got cursedly thrashed, and have since declared they did not think the Virginians had get-up.

We are now very near neighbours, and view each other every hour in the day. The two armies lay within two miles of each other and a general action is every hour expected. . . .

Believe me to be my Dear Sir
Yrs affectionately
G Weedon

3.   1776—Washington crosses the Delaware and takes Trenton

⟨ *But the Revolutionary Army was made of good material. The men needed discipline, arms, and an understanding of the fact that war is a grim business, and not a summer holiday. These requisites they soon acquired. When Washington decided to surprise the Hes-*

Original letter in the Weedon Papers, Chicago Historical Society.

sian garrison at Trenton, New Jersey, seasoned veterans could not have behaved better. The same Colonel Weedon who reported disgraceful conduct in the evacuation of New York was high in his praise of the men who braved the icy Delaware on Christmas night.

NEW TOWN Decr. 29th 1776

MY DEAR SIR,

I can now sit down with some satisfaction to write to my Countrymen, having spent my Xmas this far, with more real enjoyment than I ever did one, and the frolick not yet over as another Expedition into the Jerseys is this night set on foot. You will have seen the event of that on the 26th before this reaches you, but I know you want the particulars, & as I am at present unfit for duty, shall endeavour to give them to you.

Know then, that on the 25th part of our Army was ordered to cross the Delaware at a place call'd McConkeys Ferry, the embarcation to begin after dark. Agreeable to order, the Troops assembld. It took us till three in the morning to finnish our crossing. We had then 12 miles to Trenton, where three Regiments of Hessians lay, viz. Cols. Lassburgs, Kniphausens, & Ralls. The weather set in extremely bad, however it did not check the ardour of our Troops. The noble example set by our General made all other difficulties & hardships vannish. We got up by Eight next morning, and in so private a manner that the Enemy never suspected our approach till their outguards were attack'd by our advance, commanded by Captain Wm Washington of the 3d Regt. of Virginia, who drove all before him till he, and his Lt. Jas. Monroe got wounds. The main body of our Troops soon after entered the Town in two different places as was first directed. The Enemy were put into confusion, and tho' they made several attempts to form, never could. Our men entered the Town in a trot, & pursued so close that in less than one hour we made ourselves masters of all their Field pcs (six in number), Baggage &c, and 919 Prisoners, amongst them Thirty Officers, none of higher rank than Cols. The whole loss on our side I believe sustained, which was not more than three privts killed & these two brave officers wounded. The Enemies loss, killd, was also inconsiderable, not more than 30 or 40, their wounded not so many, which is something extraordinary.

I was honored with his Excellencies Orders to take charge of the prisoners with my Regt. and that night returned to our old Quarters. The behaviour of our people in general, far exceeded anything I ever saw. It's worth remarking that not one officer or privt was known that day to turn his back. Should our prest Expedition prove equally successful, we shall have these Robbers that have so long lived upon the fat of the Jersey Farms, once more over the Hudsons river. As a particular Acct. of Prisoners, Arms, &c, will be published shant trouble you with them, but conclude in wishing you the Compliments of the season with respects to all friends.

Am Dr. Sir

Your Most Obt. Servt.

G WEEDON

4. *1777*—BURGOYNE SURRENDERS AT SARATOGA

⟨ *The year 1776 slipped into 1777. British and American troops clashed in battles that went one way or another—Princeton, Oriskany, Bennington, Brandywine—but never so decisively as to eliminate the defeated side as a military force. Then, in the fall, a major movement came to its climax. The British General Burgoyne, who had started from Canada with a strong force to join Clinton at Albany, found himself in trouble. Clinton had not stirred from New York, Burgoyne's supplies were low, his army shrinking daily. On September 19, 1777, at Freeman's Farm in eastern New York, he suffered a costly repulse when he attacked a well placed American force. Three weeks later Benedict Arnold led a smashing assault at Bemis Heights. Burgoyne retreated to Saratoga, took stock, decided that his situation was helpless, and asked for terms.*

Lieutenant William Digby of the 53rd or Shropshire Regiment of Foot describes the surrender.

Gen Burgoyne desired a meeting of all the officers early that morning [October 17], at which he entered into a detail of his manner of acting since he had the honour of commanding the army; but he was too full to speak; heaven only could tell his feelings at the time. He dwelled much on his orders to make the wished for junction with General Clinton, and as to how his proceedings had turned out, we must (he said), be as good judges as himself. He then read over the Articles of Convention, and informed us the terms were even easier than we could have expected from our situation, and concluded with assuring us, he would never have accepted any terms, had we provisions enough, or the least hopes of our extricating ourselves any other way.

About 10 o'clock, we marched out, according to treaty, with drums beating & the honours of war, but the drums seemed to have lost their former inspiriting sounds, and though we beat the Grenadiers march, which not long before was so animating, yet then it seemed by its last feeble effort, as if almost ashamed to be heard on such an occasion. As

"The Journal of Lieutenant William Digby," in James Phinney Baxter, Ed., *The British Invasion from the North* (Albany, 1887), 317–21.

to my own feelings, I cannot express them. Tears (though unmanly) forced their way, and if alone, I should have burst to give myself vent. I shall never forget the appearance of their troops on our marching past them; a dead silence universally reigned through their numerous columns, and even then, they seemed struck with our situation and dare scarce lift up their eyes to view British Troops in such a situation. I must say their decent behaviour during the time, (to us so greatly fallen) meritted the utmost approbation and praise. The meeting between Burgoyne and Gates was well worth seeing. He paid Burgoyne about as much respect as if he was the conqueror, indeed, his noble air, tho prisoner, seemed to command attention and respect from every person. A party of Light dragoons were ordered as his guard, rather to protect his person from insults than any other cause. Thus ended all our hopes of victory, honour, glory &c. &c. &c.

5. 1777–78—FIRE CAKE AND WATER AT VALLEY FORGE

⟨ *In late September, 1777, the British defeated Washington's army at Brandywine Creek, then occupied Philadelphia. The American army struck the enemy at Germantown, ten miles north of the city, on October 4, but was again defeated. Washington drew off his troops to the west, and a few weeks later went into winter quarters at Valley Forge. The site was admirably chosen for defensive purposes, and its high ground should have made it well drained and healthful. But winter came early, and both the commissary department and the transport service broke down. The men went hungry, shivered in ragged uniforms, tossed with fevers, and died by the hundreds. Surgeon Albigence Waldo of the Connecticut Line described the sufferings of the men during the first weeks of winter. After his departure, conditions became even worse. Only determination and patriotism kept the army intact.*

December 16 [1777].—Cold Rainy Day, Baggage ordered over the Gulph of our Division, which were to march at Ten, but the baggage was order'd back and for the first time since we have been here the Tents were pitch'd, to keep the men more comfortable. Good morning Brother Soldier (says one to another) how are you? All wet I thank'e, hope you are so (says the other). The Enemy have been at Chestnut Hill Opposite to us near our last encampment the other side Schuylkill, made some Ravages, kill'd two of our Horsemen, taken some prisoners. We have done the like by them. . . .

"Diary of Surgeon Albigence Waldo, of the Connecticut Line," *The Pennsylvania Magazine of History and Biography*, Vol. XXI, No. 3, 299–322, passim.

December 18.—Rank & Precedence make a good deal of disturbance & confusion in the American Army. The Army are poorly supplied with Provision, occasioned it is said by the Neglect of the Commissary of Purchases. Much talk among Officers about discharges. Money has become of too little consequence. The Congress have not made their Commissions valuable Enough. Heaven avert the bad consequences of these things! . . .

December 21.—[Valley Forge.] Preparations made for hutts. Provisions Scarce. . . . Heartily wish myself at home, my Skin & eyes are almost spoil'd with continual smoke. A general cry thro' the Camp this Evening among the Soldiers, "No Meat! No Meat!" Immitating the noise of Crows & Owls, also, made a part of the confused Musick.

What have you for your Dinners Boys? "Nothing but Fire Cake & Water, Sir." At night, "Gentlemen the Supper is ready." What is your Supper Lads? "Fire Cake & Water, Sir." Very poor beef has been drawn in our Camp the greater part of this season. A Butcher bringing a Quarter of this kind of Beef into Camp one day who had white Buttons on the knees of his breeches, a Soldier cries out—"There, there Tom is some more of your fat Beef, by my soul I can see the Butcher's breeches buttons through it."

December 22.—Lay excessive Cold & uncomfortable last Night— my eyes are started out from their Orbits like a Rabbit's eyes, occasion'd by a great Cold & Smoke.

What have you got for Breakfast, Lads? "Fire Cake & Water, Sir." The Lord send that our Commissary of Purchases may live on Fire Cake & Water, 'till their glutted Gutts are turned to Pasteboard. . . .

December 24.—. . . Hutts go on Slowly—Cold & Smoke make us fret. . . . I don't know of any thing that vexes a man's Soul more than hot smoke continually blowing into his Eyes, & when he attempts to avoid it, is met by a cold and piercing Wind.

December 25, Christmas.—We are still in Tents—when we ought to be in huts—the poor Sick, suffer much in Tents this cold Weather. But we now treat them differently from what they used to be at home, under the inspection of Old Women and Doct. Bolus Linctus. We give them Mutton & Grogg and a Capital Medicine once in a While, to start the disease from its foundation at once. We avoid Piddling Pills, Bolus's Linctus's Cordials and all such insignificant matters whose powers are Only render'd important by causing the Patient to vomit up his money instead of his disease. . . .

December 28.—Building our Hutts.

December 29.—Continued the Work. Snow'd all day pretty briskly. —The party of the 22d return'd—lost 18 men who were taken prisoners by being decoyed by the Enemies Light Horse who brought up the

Rear, as they Repass'd the Schuylkill to the City. Our party took 13 or 14 of their Horsemen. The Enemy came out to plunder—& have strip'd the Town of Derby of even all its Household furniture. Our party were several times mixed with the Enemy's horse—not knowing them from our Connecticut Light Horse—their Cloaks being alike.

So much talk about discharges among the Officers—& so many are discharged—his Excellency lately expressed his fears of being left Alone with the Soldiers only. Strange that our Country will not exert themselves for his support, and save so good—so great a Man from entertaining the least anxious doubt of their Virtue and perseverance in supporting a Cause of such unparallel'd importance !!. . . .

December 31.—We got some Spirits and finish'd the Year with a good Drink & thankfull hearts in our new Hutt, which stands on an Eminence that overlooks the Brigade, & in sight of the Front Line. . . .

January 6, 1778.—We have got our Hutts to be very comfortable, and feel ourselves happy in them—I only want my family and I should be as happy here as anywhere, except in the Article of food, which is sometimes pretty scanty. . . .

January 8.—Unexpectedly got a Furlow. Set out for home. . . .

6.   *1778*—GEORGE ROGERS CLARK CAPTURES KASKASKIA

⟨ *In Pennsylvania, Washington began to put new life into the men who had come through Valley Forge, while the Baron von Steuben, Prussian drillmaster, gave them discipline and morale. At the end of June, when the Continental Army met the British retiring from Philadelphia, it gave a good account of itself in the Battle of Monmouth. Meanwhile, nearly a thousand miles to the west, a young frontiersman who held a colonel's commission from Patrick Henry, Governor of Virginia, came to the climax of a daring adventure.*

In the spring of 1778 George Rogers Clark enlisted 175 men at Louisville, Kentucky. Their objective, known only to Clark, was the capture of Kaskaskia, a British outpost in southwestern Illinois on the Kaskaskia River near its juncture with the Mississippi. The inhabitants of the town, which had been under French rule until 1765, could be counted on to be friendly; even the commandant was a Frenchman in the British service.

On June 28, 1778, Clark's force struck out from Fort Massac, on the north bank of the Ohio River where the Illinois city of Metropolis now stands. Six days later the men looked down from the hills on the unsuspecting village. Clark himself tells the story of its capture.

Milo M. Quaife, Ed., *The Capture of Old Vincennes: The Original Narratives of George Rogers Clark and of His Opponent Gov. Henry Hamilton* (Indianapolis; Bobbs Merrill, 1927), 57–58.

On the evening of July fourth we arrived within a few miles of the town, where we threw out scouts in advance and lay until nearly dark. We then resumed our march and took possession of a house on the bank of the Kaskaskia River, about three-quarters of a mile above the town, occupied by a large family. We learned from the inmates that the people had been under arms a few days before but had concluded the alarm to be groundless and at present all was quiet, and that there was a large number of men in town, although the Indians were for the most part absent. We obtained from the man boats enough to convey us across the river, where I formed my force in three divisions. I felt confident the inhabitants could not now obtain knowledge of our approach in time to enable them to make any resistance. My object was now to get possession of the place with as little confusion as possible, but to have it if necessary at the loss of the whole town. I did not entirely credit the information given us at the house, as the man seemed to contradict himself, informing us among other things that a noise we heard in the town was caused by the negroes at a dance. I set out for the fort with one division, ordering the other two to proceed to different quarters of the town. If I met with no resistance, at a certain signal a general shout was to be given and a certain part of the town was to be seized immediately, while men from each detachment who were able to talk French were to run through the streets proclaiming what had happened and informing the townsmen to remain in their houses on pain of being shot down.

These arrangements produced the desired effect, and within a very short time we were in complete possession of the place, with every avenue guarded to prevent any one from escaping and giving the alarm to the other villages. Various orders not worth mentioning had been issued for the guidance of the men in the event of opposition. Greater silence, I suppose, never reigned among the inhabitants of a town than in Kaskaskia at this juncture; not a person was to be seen or a word to be heard from them for some time. Meanwhile our troops purposely kept up the greatest possible noise throughout every quarter of the town, while patrols moved around it continually throughout the night, as it was a capital object to intercept any message that might be sent out. In about two hours all the inhabitants were disarmed, and informed that any one who should be taken while attempting to escape from the place would immediately be put to death. Mr. Rochblave was secured, but some time elapsed before he could be got out of his room. I suppose he delayed to tell his wife what disposition to make of his public papers, but a few of which were secured by us. Since his chamber was not entered during the night, she had ample opportunity to dispose of them, but how she did it we could never learn.

7.   *1779—*CLARK RETAKES VINCENNES

❦ *After the fall of Kaskaskia the other villages of the Illinois Coun-*
try—Cahokia, Prairie du Rocher, Vincennes—quickly proclaimed
their allegiance to the Americans. The British, however, had no
intention of giving up this vast territory without a struggle. Lieu-
tenant Governor Henry Hamilton of Detroit led the counter-attack.
In December, 1778, at the head of a force of militia and Indians,
he easily took Vincennes.

From Kaskaskia, one hundred and eighty miles to the west, Clark
saw the seriousness of the threat. Hamilton was strong enough to
retake the entire Illinois Country; with the spring, he would do it.
The only chance of the Americans was an attack before the British
would be expecting one. On February 6, 1779, Clark, with 130 men
—half of them French volunteers—left Kaskaskia. Seldom has a
military march been made under greater hardships. The prairies froze
by night, thawed into slippery mud by day. As the men approached
the Wabash River they found streams out of their banks; often they
marched waist-high in icy water. But on the 23rd of the month
Vincennes lay before them. As at Kaskaskia, they had achieved
surprise.

Again, Clark is the narrator.

23rd Feby. Sett off very early, waded better than three miles on a
stretch, our people prodigious, yet they keep up a good heart in hopes
of a speedy sight of our enemy. At last about two o'clock we came in
sight of this long sought town and enemy, all quiet, the spirits of my
men seemed to revive. We marched up under cover of a wood called
the Warriours Island where we lay concealed untill sunset, several of
the inhabitants were out a shooting by which was assur'd they had no
intelligence of us yet. I sent out two men to bring in one who came and
I sent him to town to inform the inhabitants I was near them ordering
all those attached to the King of England to enter the Fort and defend
it, those who desired to be friends to keep in their houses. I order'd the
march in the first division Capt. Williams, Capt. Worthington's Company and the Cascaskia Volunteers, in the 2nd commanded by Capt.
Bowman his own Company and the Cohos Volunteers. At sun down I
put the divisions in motion to march in the greatest order and regularity and observe the orders of their officers—above all to be silent—
the 5 men we took in the canoes were our guides; we entered the town
on the upper part having detached Lt. Bayley and 15 riflemen to attack
the Fort and keep up a fire to harrass them until we took possession of

---

James Alton James, Ed., *George Rogers Clark Papers, 1771–1781* (Springfield, Ill., 1912), 164–68.

the town and they were to remain on that duty untill relieved by another party, the two divisions marched into the town and took possession of the main street, put guards &c without the least molestation. I continued all night sending parties out to annoy the enemy and caused a trench to be thrown up across the main street about 200 yds from the Fort Gate—we had intelligence that Capt. Lamotte and 30 men were sent out about 3 hours before our arrival to reconnoitre, as it seems they had some suspicion of a party being near them. One Maisonville and a party of Indians coming up the Ouabache with 2 prisoners made on the Ohio had discover'd our fires and they arrived here a few hours before us. I order'd out a party immediately to intercept them and took sᵈ Maisonville and one man—they gave us no intelligence worth mentioning.

24th. As soon as daylight appeared the enemy perceived our works and began a very smart fire of small arms at it, but could not bring their cannon to bear on them. About 8 o'clock I sent a flag of truce with a letter desiring Lt. Gov. Hamilton in order to save the impending storm that hung over his head immediately to surrender up the Garrison, Fort, Stores &ᶜ &ᶜ and at his peril not to destroy any one article now in the said Garrison—or to hurt any house &ᶜ belonging to the Inhabitants for if he did by Heaven, he might expect no mercy—his answer was Gov. H. begs leave to acquaint Col. C. that he and his Garrison were not disposed to be awed into any action unworthy of British subjects—I then ordered out parties to attack the Fort and the firing began very smartly on both sides. One of my men thro' a bravery known but to Americans walking carlesly up the main street was slightly wounded over the left eye but no ways dangerous—About 12 o'clock the firing from the Fort suspended. A Flag coming out I order'd my people to stop firing till further orders. I soon perceived it was Capt. Helm who after salutations inform'd me that the purport of his commission was, that Lt. Gov. Hamilton was willing to surrender up the Fort and Garrison provided Col. Clarke would grant him honourable terms and that he beg'd Col. Clarke to come into the Fort to confer with him, first I desired Capt. Helm not to give any inteligence of G. H.'s strength &ᶜ he being on his Parole, second my answer to Gov. H was that I should not agree to any other terms than that Lt. Gov. H should immediately surrender at discretion and allowed him half an hour to consider thereof—as to entering the Fort my offʳˢ and men would not allow of it, for it was with difficulty I restrained them from storming the Garrison. I dismissed Capt. Helm, with my answer. At the time allowed Capt. Helm came back with Lieut. Gov. H's second proposals which were—Lt Govʳ Hamilton proposes to Col. Clarke a truce for three days, during which time there shall no defensive works be carried on in the Garrison provided Col. Clarke shall observe the like cessation on his part—he further proposes that whatever may pass between them two and any person mutually agreed upon to be present shall remain secret untill matters be finally determined. As he wishes that whatever the result of this conference may be —the Honor and credit of each may be considered—so he wishes he may confer with Col. Clarke as soon as may be—as Col. Clarke makes a difficulty of coming into the Fort, Lt Gov. H will speak to him before the Gate.

24 Feby 1779 (sign'd) H. H.

This moment received intelligence that a party of Indians were coming up from the falls with Pris^{rs} or Scalps, which party was sent out by G. Hamilton for that purpose, my people were so enraged they immediately intercepted the party which consisted of 8 Indians and a french man of the Garrison. They killed three on the spot and brought 4 in who were tomahawkd in the street oposite the Fort Gate and thrown into the river—the frenchman we shewd mercy as his aged father had behaved so well in my party—I relieved the two poor Pris^{rs} who were French hunters on the Ohio, after which Lt Helm carried my answer thus—Col. Clarks comp^{ts} to G. H. and begs leave to inform him that Col. Clark will not agree to any other terms than of G. H. surrendering himself and Garrison prisoners at discretion—if G. H. desires a conference with Col. Clarke, he will meet him at the church with Capt. Helm.

24 Feb^{ry} 1779 (signd) G. R. CLARK.

I immediately repaired there to confer with G. Hamilton where I met with him and Capt. Helm.

Gov. Hamilton then begd I would consider the situation of both parties that he was willing to surrender the Garrison but was in hopes that Col. Clark would let him do it with Honour—I answered him I have been informed that he had 800 men—I have not that number but I came to fight that number. G. H. then replied who could give you this false information? I am Sir (replied I) well acquainted with your strength and force and am able to take your Fort, therefore I will give no other terms but to submit yourself and Garrison to my discretion and mercy—he reply'd Sir my men are brave and willing to stand by me to the last, if I can't surrender upon Honble terms I'll fight it out to the last—Answered, Sir this will give my men infinite satisfaction and pleasure for it is their desire. He left me and went a few pays aloof, I told Capt Helm Sir you are a prisoner on your parole, I desire you to reconduct G. H. into the Fort and there remain till I retake you. Lt Gov. Hamilton then returned saying, Col. Clarke why will you force me to dishonour myself when you cannot acquire more honour by it— I told him could I look on you Sir as a Gentlemen I would do to the utmost of my power, but on you Sir who have embrued your hands in the blood of our women and children, Honour, my country, everything

116

calls on me alloud for Vengeance. G. H. I know my character has been staind but not deservedly for I have alwaise endeavour'd to instill Humanity as much as in my power to the Indians whom the orders of my superiours obliged me to employ. C. C. Sir I speak no more on this subject. My blood glows within my veins to think on the crueltys your Indian parties have committed, therefore repair to your Fort and prepare for battle on which I turned off and the Gov and C^t Helm towards the Fort—when Capt Helm says Gentlemen don't be warm, strive to save many lives which may be useful to their country which will unavoidably fall in case you don't agree on which we again conferd —G Hamilton said, is there nothing to be done but fighting—Yes, Sir, I will send you such articles as [I] think proper to allow, if you accept them, well—I will allow you half an hour to consider on them on which C^t Helm came with me to take them to G.H.—having assembled my officers I sent the following articles viz.:

1st Lt. Gov. Hamilton engages to deliver up to Col. Clark Fort Sackville as it is at present with all the stores, ammunition, provisions, &^{c}.

2nd. The Garrison will deliver themselves up Pris^{rs} of War to march out with their arms accoutrements, Knapsacks &^{c}.

3. The Garrison to be delivered up tomorrow morning at 10 o'clock.

4th. Three days to be allowed to the Garrison to settle their accounts with the traders of this place and inhabitants.

5. The officers of the Garrison to be allowed their necessary baggage &^{c}.

(signed) Post Vincents 24th Feby 1779 G. R. CLARK.

Within the limited time Capt. Helm returned with the articles signed thus, viz

Agreed to for the following reasons, remoteness from succours, the state and quantity of Provisions &^{c} the unanimity of officers and men on its expediency, the Honble terms allow^d and lastly the confidence in a generous Enemy.

(signed) H. HAMILTON Lt Gov & Superintend^t

8. *1780*—ANDRÉ PAYS FOR ARNOLD'S TREASON

(*No event of the war shook the Americans more than the treason of Benedict Arnold. This proud, impetuous Connecticut soldier had fought with outstanding bravery at Ticonderoga and Saratoga. Then he began to brood over wrongs: the failure of Congress to recognize his services, a court-martial by Pennsylvania authorities for alleged illegal acts while he commanded the American forces in*

James Thacher, *A Military Journal During the American Revolutionary War from 1775 to 1783* (Boston, 1823), 272–74.

Philadelphia. Moreover, he lived extravagantly and needed money. In 1779 he started to sell military information to the British. The following year he obtained command of West Point, the key to the American positions north of New York. Soon he was deep in negotiations to turn that post over to the enemy in return for a large sum of money. At the last minute Major John André, the British officer who had been assigned to deal with Arnold, was captured. The plot was discovered. Arnold, warned in time, escaped to the British lines, but within a week André was tried by a court-martial, convicted of being a spy, and sentenced to be hanged. James Thacher, surgeon in a Massachusetts regiment, watched the young officer meet death.

October 2d.—Major Andre is no more among the living. I have just witnessed his exit. It was a tragical scene of the deepest interest. During his confinement and trial, he exhibited those proud and elevated sensibilities which designate greatness and dignity of mind. Not a murmur or a sigh ever escaped him, and the civilities and attentions bestowed on him were politely acknowledged. Having left a mother and two sisters in England, he was heard to mention them in terms of the tenderest affection, and in his letter to Sir Henry Clinton, he recommends them to his particular attention.

The principal guard officer who was constantly in the room with the prisoner, relates that when the hour of his execution was announced to him in the morning, he received it without emotion, and while all present were affected with silent gloom, he retained a firm countenance, with calmness and composure of mind. Observing his servant enter the room in tears, he exclaimed, "leave me till you can show yourself more manly." His breakfast being sent to him from the table of General Washington, which had been done every day of his confinement, he partook of it as usual, and having shaved and dressed himself, he placed his hat on the table, and cheerfully said to the guard officers, "I am ready at any moment, gentlemen, to wait on you." The fatal hour having arrived, a large detachment of troops was paraded, and an immense concourse of people assembled; almost all our general and field officers, excepting his Excellency and his staff, were present on horseback; melancholy and gloom pervaded all ranks, and the scene was affectingly awful. I was so near during the solemn march to the fatal spot, as to observe every movement, and participate in every emotion which the melancholy scene was calculated to produce. Major Andre walked from the stone house, in which he had been confined, between two of our subaltern officers, arm in arm; the eyes of the immense multitude were fixed on him, who, rising superior to the fears of death, appeared as if conscious of the dignified deportment which he displayed. He betrayed no want of fortitude, but retained a complacent smile on his countenance, and politely bowed to several gentlemen whom he knew, which was respectfully returned. It was his earnest desire to be shot, as being the mode of death most conformable to the feelings of a military man, and he had indulged the hope that his request would be granted. At the moment, therefore, when suddenly he came in view of the gallows, he involuntarily started backward, and made a pause. "Why this emotion, Sir," said an officer by his side? Instantly recovering his composure, he said, "I am reconciled to my death, but I detest the mode." While waiting and standing near the gallows, I observed some degree of trepidation; placing his foot on a stone, and rolling it over and choking in his throat, as if attempting to swallow. So soon, however, as he perceived that things were in readiness, he stepped quickly into the wagon, and at this moment he appeared to shrink, but instantly elevating his head with firmness, he said, "It will be but a momentary pang," and taking from his pocket two white handkerchiefs, the provost marshal with one, loosely pinioned his arms, and with the other, the victim, after taking off his hat and stock, bandaged his own eyes with perfect firmness, which melted the hearts, and moistened the cheeks, not only of his servant, but of the throng of spectators. The rope being appended to the gallows, he slipped the noose over his head and adjusted it to his neck, without the assistance of the awkward executioner. Colonel Scammel now informed him that he had an opportunity to speak, if he desired it; he raised the handkerchief from his eyes and said, "I pray you to bear me witness that I meet my fate like a brave man." The wagon being now removed from under him, he was suspended and instantly expired; it proved indeed "but a momentary pang." He was dressed in his royal regimentals and boots, and his remains, in the same dress, were placed in an ordinary coffin, and interred at the foot of the gallows; and the spot was consecrated by the tears of thousands. Thus died in the bloom of life, the accomplished Major Andre, the pride of the royal army, and the valued friend of Sir Henry Clinton.

9. *1779*—BONHOMME RICHARD DEFEATS THE SERAPIS

❮ *Soon after the Continental Congress took over the patriot army it set about creating a navy. With their slender resources the Americans could never hope to overthrow Great Britain as a sea power, but with luck, valor, and skill they could harass her merchantmen and now and then corner a man-of-war. That is what happened on September 23, 1779, when John Paul Jones, in the* BONHOMME

John S. Barnes, Ed., *Fanning's Narrative, Being the Memoirs of Nathaniel Fanning . . . 1778–1783* (New York, 1912), 38–48.

RICHARD, *sighted the British* SERAPIS *conveying cargo vessels off the east coast of England. The* BONHOMME RICHARD *was an ancient, unseaworthy, converted merchantman, but she mounted forty-two guns, and her commander knew no fear.*

Nathaniel Fanning, captain of the maintop in the RICHARD, *describes one of the most memorable of American naval victories.*

I shall now proceed to give a circumstantial account of this famous BATTLE, fought on the night of the 22d day of September, 1779, between the GOOD MAN RICHARD, an American ship of war commanded by John Paul Jones; and the SERAPIS, an English ship of war, commanded by Captain Parsons, off Flamborough Head, upon the German Ocean. . . .

The two ships were nearly within hail of each other, when captain Jones ordered the yards slung with chains, and our courses hauled up. By this time the Serapis had tacked ship, and bore down to engage us; and at quarter past 8, just as the moon was rising with majestic appearance, the weather being clear, the surface of the great deep perfectly smooth, even as in a mill pond, the enemy hailed thus: "What ship is that?" (in true *bombastic English stile,* it being hoarse and hardly intelligible.) The answer from our ship was, "Come a little nearer, and I will tell you." The next question was, by the enemy, in a contemptuous manner, "What are you laden with?" The answer returned was, if my recollection does not deceive me, "Round, grape, and double-headed shot." And instantly, the Serapis poured her range of upper and quarter-deck guns into us; as she did not shew her lower-deck guns till about ten minutes after the action commenced. The reason of this, I could not learn but suppose they intended to have taken us without the aid of their lower-deck guns. We returned the enemies fire, and thus the battle began. At this first fire, three of our starboard lower-deck guns burst, and killed the most of the men stationed at them. As soon as captain Jones heard of this circumstance, he gave orders not to fire the other three eighteen pounders mounted upon that deck; but that the men stationed to them, should abandon them. Soon after this we perceived the enemy, by their lanthorns, busy in running out their guns between decks, which convinced us the Serapis was a two decker, and more than our match. She had by this time got under our stern, which we could not prevent. And now she raked us with whole broadsides, and showers of musketry. Several of her eighteen pound shot having gone through and through our ship, on board of which, she made a dreadful havock among our crew. The wind was now very light, and our ship not under proper command, and the Serapis out-sailing us by *two feet to one;* which advantage the enemy discovered, and improved it, by keeping under our stern, and raking us fore and aft; till at length the poor French colonel, who was stationed upon the poop, finding almost all his men slain, quit that station with his surviving men, and retired upon the quarter-deck. All this time our tops kept up an incessant and well-directed fire into the enemies' tops which did great execution. The Serapis continued to take a position, either under our stern, or athwart our bow; gauled us in such a manner that our men fell in all parts of the ship by *scores*. At this juncture, it became necessary on the part of our commander, to give some orders to extricate us from this scene of bloody carnage; for, had it lasted one half an hour longer, in all human probability the enemy would have slain nearly all our officers and men; consequently we should have been compelled to strike our colours and yield to superior force. Accordingly, captain Jones ordered the sailing master, *a true blooded yankee,* whose name was Stacy, to lay the enemies' ship on board; and as the Serapis soon after passed across our fore foot, our helm was put hard aweather, the main and mizzen topsails, then braced aback, were filled away, a fresh flaw of wind swelling them at that instant, which shot our ship quick ahead, and she ran her jib boom between the enemies star-board mizzen shrouds and mizzen vang. Jones at the same time cried out, "Well done, my brave lads, we have got her now; throw on board the grappling irons, and stand by for boarding": which was done, and the enemy soon cut away the chains, which were affixed to the grappling-irons; more were thrown on board, and often repeated. And as we now hauled the enemies' ship snug along side of ours, with the tailings to our grappling-irons; her jib-stay was cut away aloft and fell upon our ship's poop, where Jones was at the time, and where he assisted Mr. Stacy in making fast the end of the enemies' jib-stay to our mizzenmast. The former here checked the latter for swearing, by saying, "Mr. Stacy, it is no time for swearing now, you may by the next moment be in eternity; but let us do our duty." A strong current was now setting in towards Scarborough, the wind ceased to blow, and the sea became as smooth as glass. By this time, the enemy finding that they could not easily extricate themselves from us let go one of their anchors, expecting that if they could cut us adrift, the current would set us away out of their reach, at least for some time. The action had now lasted about forty minutes, and the fire from our tops having been kept up without intermission, with musketry, blunderbusses, cowhorns, swivels, and pistols, directed into their tops, that these last at this time, became silent, except one man in her foretop, who would once in a while peep out from behind the head of the enemies' foremast and fire into our tops. As soon as I perceived this fellow, I ordered the marines in the main-top to reserve their next fire, and the moment they got sight of him to level their pieces at him and fire; which they did, and we soon saw this skulking tar, or marine, fall out of the top upon the enemies' fore-castle. Our ensign-staff was shot away, and both that and the thirteen stripes fell into the sea. . . .[1]

About this time the enemy's light sails, which were filled onto the Serapis's cranes over her quarter-deck sails caught fire; this communicated itself to her rigging and from thence to ours; thus were both ships on fire at one and the same time; therefore the firing on both sides ceased till it was extinguished by the contending parties, after which the action was renewed again. By this time, the top-men in our tops had taken possession of the enemy's tops, which was done by reason of the Serapis's yards being locked together with ours, that we could with ease go from our main top into the enemy's fore top, and so on from our fore top into the Serapis's main top. Having knowledge of this, we transported from our own into the enemy's tops, stink pots, flasks, hand grenadoes, &c. which we threw in among the enemy whenever they made their appearance. The battle had now continued about three hours, and as we, in fact, had possession of the Serapis's top, which commanded her quarter-deck, upper gun-deck and forecastle, we were well assured that the enemy could not hold out much longer, and were momentarily expecting that they would strike to us, when the following farcical piece was acted on board our ship.

It seems that a report was at this time, circulated among our crew between decks, and was credited among them, that captain Jones and all his principal officers were slain; the gunners were now the commanders of our ship; that the ship had four or five feet of water in her hold; and that she was then sinking: they therefore advised the gunner to go upon deck, together with the carpenter, and master at arms, and beg of the enemy quarters, in order, as they said, to save their lives. These three men being thus delegated, mounted the quarter-deck, and bawled out as loud as they could, "Quarters, quarters, for God's sake, quarters! our ship is sinking!" and immediately got upon the ship's poop with a view of hauling down our colours. Hearing this in the top, I told my men that the enemy had struck and was crying out for quarters, for I actually thought that the voices of these men sounded as if on board of the enemy; but in this I was soon undeceived. The three poltroons, finding the ensign, and ensign-staff gone, they proceeded upon the quarter-deck, and were in the act of hauling down our pendant, still bawling for "quarters!" when I heard our commodore say, in a loud voice, "what d——d rascals are them—shoot them— kill them!" He was upon the forecastle when these fellows first made their appearance upon the quarter-deck where he had just discharged his pistols at some of the enemy. The carpenter, and the master-at-arms, hearing Jones's voice, sculked below, and the gunner was at-

---

[1] John Paul Jones, in this action, was the first American commander to fly the Stars and Stripes in approximately the flag's present form.

tempting to do the same, when Jones threw both of his pistols at his head, one of which struck him in the head, fractured his scull, and knocked him down, at the foot of the gang-way ladder, where he lay till the battle was over. Both ships now took fire again; and on board of our ship it communicated to, and set our main top on fire, which threw us into the greatest consternation imaginable for some time, and it was not without some exertions and difficulty that it was overcome. The water which we had in a tub, in the fore part on the top, was expended without extinguishing the fire. We next had recourse to our clothes, by pulling off our coats and jackets, and then throwing them upon the fire, and stamping upon them, which in a short time, smothered it. Both crews were also now, as before, busily employed in stopping the progress of the flames, and the firing on both sides ceased. The enemy now demanded of us if we had struck, as they had heard the three poltroons halloo for quarters. "If you have," said they, "why don't you haul down your pendant"; as they saw our ensign was gone. "Ay, ay," said Jones, "We'll do that when we can fight no longer, but we shall see yours come down the first; for you must know, that Yankees do not haul down their colours till they are fairly beaten." The combat now recommenced again with more fury if possible than before, on the part of both, and continued for a few minutes, when the cry of fire was again heard on board of both ships. The firing ceased, and both crews were once more employed in extinguishing it, which was soon effected, when the battle was renewed again with redoubled vigour, with what cannon we could manage: hand grenados, stink pots, &c., but principally, towards the closing scene, with lances and boarding pikes. . . .

At thirty-five minutes past 12 at night, a single hand grenado having been thrown by one of our men out of the main top of the enemy, . . . it took a direction and fell between their decks, where it communicated to a quantity of loose powder scattered about the enemy's cannon; and the hand grenado bursting at the same time, made a dreadful explosion, and blew up about twenty of the enemy. This closed the scene, and the enemy now in their turn, (notwithstanding the gasconading of capt. Parsons) bawled out "Quarters, quarters, quarters, for God's sake!" It was, however, some time before the enemy's colours were struck. The captain of the Serapis gave repeated orders for one of his crew to ascend the quarter-deck and haul down the English flag, but no one would stir to do it. They told the Captain they were afraid of our rifle-men; believing that all our men who were seen with muskets were of that description. The captain of the Serapis therefore ascended the quarter-deck, and hauled down the very flag which he had nailed to the flagstaff a little before the commencement of the battle; and which flag he had at that time, in the presence of his principal officers, swore he never would strike to that infamous pirate J. P. Jones. The enemy's flag being struck, captain Jones ordered Richard Dale, his first lieutenant, to select out of our crew a number of men, and take possession of the prize, which was immediately put in execution. Several of our men, (I believe three) were killed by the English on board of the Serapis after she had struck to us, for which they afterwards apologized, by saying, that the men who were guilty of this breach of honour, did not know at the time, that their own ship had struck her colours. Thus ended this ever memorable battle, after a continuance of a few minutes over *four hours*. The officers, headed by the captain of the Serapis, now came on board of our ship; the latter, (captain Parsons) enquired for captain Jones, to whom he was introduced by Mr. Mase, our purser. They met, and the former accosted the latter, in presenting his sword, in this manner: "It is with the greatest reluctance that I am now obliged to resign you this, for it is painful to me, more particularly at this time, when compelled to deliver up my sword to a man, who may be said to fight *with a halter around his neck!*" Jones, after receiving his sword, made this reply: "Sir, you have fought like a hero, and I make no doubt but your sovereign will reward you in a most ample manner for it."

10.   *1782*—ABOARD THE JERSEY PRISON SHIP

⟨ *The real naval strength of the Americans during the Revolution lay not in the tiny regular navy but in the privateers. These armed vessels, owned and officered by private persons but operated under the authority of one of the states or the Continental Congress, captured 600 British ships, including sixteen men-of-war, before hostilities ended.*

Yet the service was a hazardous one, and often as not the venturesome seaman ended up in a British prison ship. The worst of these floating dungeons was the JERSEY, *a dismantled man-of-war moored in New York harbor. The horrors she held, Thomas Dring discovered, had to be experienced to be believed.*

In the month of May, 1782, I sailed from Providence, Rhode Island, as Master's-mate, on board a privateer called the *Chance*. This was a new vessel, on her first cruise. . . . She was commanded by Captain Daniel Aborn, mounted twelve six-pound cannon, and sailed with a complement of about sixty-five men. . . .

Our cruise was but a short one; for in a few days after sailing, we were captured by the British ship-of-war *Belisarius*, Captain Graves, of twenty-six guns. We were captured in the night; and our crew,

---

Thomas Dring, *Recollections of the Jersey Prison Ship* (Providence, 1829), 23-27, 33-36, 48-50.

having been conveyed on board the enemy's ship, were put in irons the next morning. . . . The *Belisarius* soon made her way for New York. . . .

The ship dropped her anchor abreast of the city, and signals were immediately made that she had prisoners on board. Soon after, two large gondolas or boats came alongside, in one of which was seated the notorious David Sproat, the Commissary of Prisoners. This man was an American refugee, universally detested for the cruelty of his conduct, and the insolence of his manners.

We were then called on deck, and having been released from our irons, were ordered into the boats. This being accomplished, we put off from the ship, under a guard of marines, and proceeded towards our much dreaded place of confinement, which was not then in sight. As we passed along the Long Island shore, against the tide, our progress was very slow. The prisoners were ordered by Sproat to apply themselves to the oars; but not feeling any particular anxiety to expedite our progress, we declined obeying the command. His only reply was, "I'll soon fix you, my lads."

We at length doubled a point, and came in view of . . . the black hulk of the *Old Jersey,* with her satellites, the three Hospital-ships; to which Sproat pointed, in an exulting manner, and said: "There, Rebels, *there* is the *cage* for you." Oh! how I wished to be standing alone with that inhuman wretch upon the green turf at that moment!

As he spoke, my eye was instantly turned from the dreaded hulk; but a single glance had shown us a multitude of human beings moving upon her upper deck. . . .

It was then nearly sunset, and before we were alongside, every man, except the sentinels on the gangway, had disappeared. Previous to their being sent below, some of the prisoners, seeing us approaching, waved their hats, as if they would say, "Approach us not," and we soon found fearful reason for the warning. . . .

After passing the weary and tedious night . . . I was permitted to ascend to the upper deck. . . . I found myself surrounded by a motley crew of wretches, with tattered garments and pallid visages, who had hurried from below for the luxury of a little fresh air. . . .

In the wretched groups around me, I saw but too faithful a picture of our own almost certain fate; and found that all which we had been taught to fear of this terrible place of abode was more than realized.

During the night, in addition to my other sufferings, I had been tormented with what I supposed to be vermin; and on coming upon deck, I found that a black silk handkerchief, which I wore around my neck, was completely spotted with them. Although this had often been mentioned as one of the miseries of the place, yet, as I had never before been in a situation to witness any thing of the kind, the sight made me shudder; as I knew, at once, that so long as I should remain on board, these loathsome creatures would be my constant companions and unceasing tormentors.

The next disgusting object which met my sight was a man suffering with the small-pox; and in a few minutes I found myself surrounded by many others laboring under the same disease, in every stage of its progress.

As I had never had the small-pox, it became necessary that I should be inoculated; and there being no proper person on board to perform the operation, I concluded to act as my own physician. On looking about me, I soon found a man in the proper stage of the disease, and desired him to favor me with some of the matter for the purpose. He readily complied; observing that it was a necessary precaution on my part, and that my situation was an excellent one in regard to *diet,* as I might depend upon finding that *extremely moderate.*

The only instrument which I could procure, for the purpose of inoculation, was a common pin. With this, having scarified the skin of my hand, between the thumb and forefinger, I applied the matter and bound up my hand. The next morning, I found that the wound had begun to fester; a sure sympton that the application had taken effect.

Many of my former shipmates took the same precaution, and were inoculated during the day. In my case the disorder came on but lightly, and its progress was favorable; and without the least medical advice or attention, by the blessing of Divine Providence, I soon recovered. . . .

The prisoners . . . were confined on the two main decks below. My usual place of abode being in the Gun-room, on the centre deck, I was never under the necessity of descending to the lower dungeon; and during my confinement, I had no disposition to visit it. It was inhabited by the most wretched in appearance of all our miserable company. From the disgusting and squalid appearance of the groups which I saw ascending the stairs which led to it, it must have been more dismal, if possible, than that part of the hulk where I resided. Its occupants appeared to be mostly foreigners, who had seen and survived every variety of human suffering. The faces of many of them were covered with dirt and filth; their long hair and beards matted and foul; clothed in rags, and with scarcely a sufficient supply of these to cover their disgusting bodies. Many among them possessed no clothing except the remnants of those garments which they wore when first brought on board; and were unable to procure even any materials for patching these together, when they had been worn to tatters by constant use; and had this been in their power, they had not the means of procuring a piece of thread, or even a needle. Some, and indeed many of them, had not the means of procuring a razor or an ounce of soap.

Their beards were occasionally reduced by each other with a pair of shears or scissors; but this operation, though conducing to cleanliness, was not productive of much improvement in their personal appearance. The skins of many of them were discolored by continual washing in salt water, added to the circumstance that it was impossible for them to wash their linen in any other manner than by laying it on the deck, and stamping on it with their feet, after it had been immersed in salt water, their bodies remaining naked during the operation. . . .

As soon as the gratings had been fastened over the hatchways for the night, we generally went to our sleeping-places. It was, of course, always desirable to obtain a station as near as possible to the side of the ship, and, if practicable, in the immediate vicinity of one of the air-ports, as this not only afforded us a better air, but also rendered us less liable to be trodden upon by those who were moving about the decks during the night.

But silence was a stranger to our dark abode. There were continual noises during the night. The groans of the sick and the dying; the curses poured out by the weary and exhausted upon our inhuman keepers; the restlessness caused by the suffocating heat and the confined and poisoned air, mingled with the wild and incoherent ravings of delirium, were the sounds which every night were raised around us in all directions. Such was our ordinary situation; but, at times, the consequences of our crowded condition were still more terrible, and proved fatal to many of our number in a single night.

11.   *1781*—THE BRITISH SURRENDER AT YORKTOWN

⟨ *Before Dring and his fellow-prisoners fell into the hands of the British, the fighting on land had ended.*

In the early summer of 1781 Lafayette forced Cornwallis, the British commander, into the Peninsula between the York and James rivers southeast of Richmond, Virginia. In August, Cornwallis settled himself at Yorktown. Washington, in a daring move, brought his own army and the French troops of Rochambeau down from New York, thus confronting the British army with an overwhelming force. For the first two weeks of October, Americans and French battered at the enemy fortifications, taking one redoubt after another. On the 17th Cornwallis, his situation hopeless, asked for terms. Surgeon James Thacher described the formal surrender, which took place on October 19.

Although two years would pass before the signing of a treaty of peace, the surrender of Yorktown marked the end of the war. There

---

Thacher, *A Military Journal*, 346–47.

was a kind of grim appropriateness in the fact that Great Britain should lose most of her North American empire within a few miles of the spot where the first tiny colony had been established.

At about twelve o'clock, the combined army was arranged and drawn up in two lines extending more than a mile in length. The Americans were drawn up in a line on the right side of the road, and the French occupied the left. At the head of the former the great American commander, mounted on his noble courser, took his station, attended by his aids. At the head of the latter was posted the excellent Count Rochambeau and his suite. The French troops, in complete uniform, displayed a martial and noble appearance, their band of music, of which the timbrel formed a part, is a delightful novelty, and produced while marching to the ground, a most enchanting effect. The Americans though not all in uniform nor their dress so neat, yet exhibited an erect soldierly air, and every countenance beamed with satisfaction and joy. The concourse of spectators from the country was prodigious, in point of numbers probably equal to the military, but universal silence and order prevailed. It was about two o'clock when the captive army advanced through the line formed for their reception. Every eye was prepared to gaze on Lord Cornwallis, the object of peculiar interest and solicitude; but he disappointed our anxious expectations; pretending indisposition, he made General O'Harra his substitute as the leader of his army. This officer was followed by the conquered troops in a slow and solemn step, with shouldered arms, colors cased and drums beating a British march. Having arrived at the head of the line, General O'Harra, elegantly mounted, advanced to his Excellency the Commander in Chief, taking off his hat, and apologized for the non appearance of Earl Cornwallis. With his usual dignity and politeness his Excellency pointed to Major General Lincoln for directions, by whom the British army was conducted into a spacious field where it was intended they should ground their arms. The royal troops, while marching through the line formed by the allied army, exhibited a decent and neat appearance, as respects arms and clothing, for their commander opened his store and directed every soldier to be furnished with a new suit complete, prior to the capitulation. But in their line of march we remarked a disorderly and unsoldierly conduct, their step was irregular, and their ranks frequently broken. But it was in the field when they came to the last act of the drama, that the spirit and pride of the British soldier was put to the severest test, here their mortification could not be concealed. Some of the platoon officers appeared to be exceedingly chagrined when giving the word *"ground arms,"* and I am a witness that they performed this duty in a very unofficer like manner, and that many of the soldiers manifested a *sullen temper,* throwing their arms on the pile with violence, as if determined to render them useless. This irregularity, however, was checked by the authority of General Lincoln. After having grounded their arms and divested themselves of their accoutrements, the captive troops were conducted back to Yorktown and guarded by our troops till they could be removed to the place of their destination.

CHAPTER VII

THE NEW NATION

1787 – 1807

1.   *1787*—BENJAMIN FRANKLIN URGES THE ADOPTION OF THE CONSTITUTION

❨ *During the Revolution, the Continental Congress managed the affairs of the young United States fairly effectively. But with the close of the war, a permanent form of government became imperative. That was provided for by the Articles of Confederation, which went into effect in 1781. The next six years proved that however admirable the Articles might be on paper, they simply did not work in practice. Under them, the Congress had no power to levy taxes; it could only ask the states to contribute to the central government. It could not regulate interstate commerce. And, since the states voted as units, with many decisions requiring nine votes, five small states could thwart the will of a large majority of the people. In short, the country had to have a stronger central government if it were not to fall into anarchy.*

Henry D. Gilpin, Ed., *The Papers of James Madison* (New York, 1841), III, 1596–98, 1605, 1624.

In 1786 James Madison, Alexander Hamilton, and a few other leaders who faced the seriousness of the situation succeeded in having a convention called at Annapolis for the purpose of giving the Congress power to regulate commerce. The convention decided that any piecemeal amending of the Articles of Confederation would be futile. What was needed was an entirely new framework of government. To that end, it called a constitutional convention to meet at Philadelphia in May, 1787.

The delegates included many of the leading men of the country. Foremost among them was George Washington, who was elected to preside. Benjamin Franklin, revered for his ripe wisdom, was present; so were James Madison and Alexander Hamilton. Notably absent were Thomas Jefferson, abroad as Minister to France, and John Adams, in London as Minister to England.

In four months the delegates framed the Constitution of the United States, which the English statesman William E. Gladstone described as "the most wonderful work ever struck off at a given time by the brain and purpose of men." By the 17th of September, 1787, the document had reached its final form. Would the delegates adopt it? James Madison, keeping his own notes—there was no official reporter—described the scene.

In Convention,—The engrossed Constitution being read,—

Doctor FRANKLIN rose with a speech in his hand, which he had reduced to writing for his own convenience, and which Mr. WILSON read in the words following:—

"Mr. PRESIDENT:

"I confess that there are several parts of this Constitution which I do not at present approve, but I am not sure I shall never approve them. For having lived long, I have experienced many instances of being obliged by better information, or fuller consideration, to change opinions even on important subjects, which I once thought right, but found to be otherwise. It is therefore that, the older I grow, the more apt I am to doubt my own judgment, and to pay more respect to the judgment of others. Most men, indeed, as well as most sects in religion, think themselves in possession of all truth, and that where-ever others differ from them, it is so far error. Steele, a Protestant, in a dedication, tells the Pope, that the only difference between our churches, in their opinions of the certainty of their doctrines, is, 'the Church of Rome is infallible, and the Church of England is never in the wrong.' But though many private persons think almost as highly of their own infallibility as of that of their sect, few express it so naturally as a certain

131

French lady, who, in a dispute with her sister, said, 'I don't know how it happens, sister, but I meet with nobody but myself, that is always in the right—*il n'y a que moi qui a toujours raison.*'

"In these sentiments, sir, I agree to this Constitution, with all its faults, if they are such; because I think a General Government necessary for us, and there is no form of government, but what may be a blessing to the people if well administered; and believe further, that this is likely to be well administered for a course of years, and can only end in despotism, as other forms have done before it, when the people shall become so corrupted as to need despotic government, being incapable of any other. I doubt, too, whether any other Convention we can obtain may be able to make a better Constitution. For when you assemble a number of men to have the advantage of their joint wisdom, you inevitably assemble with those men all their prejudices, their passions, their errors of opinion, their local interests and their selfish views. From such an assembly can a perfect production be expected? It therefore astonishes me, sir, to find this system approaching so near to perfection as it does; and I think it will astonish our enemies, who are waiting with confidence to hear that our councils are confounded, like those of the builders of Babel; and that our States are on the point of separation, only to meet hereafter for the purpose of cutting one another's throats. Thus I consent, sir, to this Constitution, because I expect no better, and because I am not sure, that it is not the best. The opinions I have had of its errors I sacrifice to the public good. I have never whispered a syllable of them abroad. Within these walls they were born, and here they shall die. If every one of us, in returning to our constituents, were to report the objections he has had to it, and endeavour to gain partizans in support of them, we might prevent its being generally received, and thereby lose all the salutary effects and great advantages resulting naturally in our favor among foreign nations as well as among ourselves, from our real or apparent unanimity. Much of the strength and efficiency of any government, in procuring and securing happiness to the people, depends on opinion—on the general opinion of the goodness of the government, as well as of the wisdom and integrity of its governors. I hope, therefore, that for our own sakes, as a part of the people, and for the sake of posterity, we shall act heartily and unanimously in recommending this Constitution (if approved by Congress and confirmed by the Conventions) wherever our influence may extend, and turn our future thoughts and endeavours to the means of having it well administered.

"On the whole, sir, I cannot help expressing a wish that every member of the Convention, who may still have objections to it, would with me, on this occasion, doubt a little of his own infallibility, and to make manifest our unanimity, put his name to this instrument."

. . . . The members then proceeded to sign the Constitution, as finally amended, as follows:

We, the people of the United States, in order to form a more perfect union, establish justice, insure domestic tranquillity, provide for the common defence, promote the general welfare, and secure the blessings of liberty to ourselves and our posterity, do ordain and establish this Constitution for the United States of America. . . .

Whilst the last members were signing, Doctor FRANKLIN, looking towards the President's chair, at the back of which a rising sun happened to be painted, observed to a few members near him, that painters had found it difficult to distinguish in their art, a rising, from a setting, sun. I have, said he, often and often, in the course of the session, and the vicissitudes of my hopes and fears as to its issue, looked at that behind the President, without being able to tell whether it was rising or setting: but now at length, I have the happiness to know, that it is a rising, and not a setting sun.

2.   *1789*—A DUTCH DIPLOMAT SEES WASHINGTON INAUGURATED

❰ *In spite of strong opposition, eleven states had ratified the Constitution by the summer of 1788. On March 4, 1789, it would go into effect. In the young nation one man—George Washington—stood out from all others. He had led the armies of the Revolution to victory, and he had presided over the convention which had devised the new framework of government. When the electors met in February, 1789, Washington was their only choice for the Presidency. Reluctantly, he left his beloved Mount Vernon and made his way to New York, then the seat of government.*

Rudolph Van Dorsten, the United Netherlands Secretary of Legation, described Washington's arrival in New York and his inauguration in a report to the head of the Netherlands foreign office.

NEW YORK, May 4, 1789

YOUR RIGHT NOBLE WORSHIP:

Since I wrote to you, on April 7th, both the President and Vice-President arrived here and took charge of their respective offices. Mr. Vice-President John Adams entered this city on the 20th of April, and was received fifteen miles from the city by Brigadier-General Malcom and the officers of the brigade, besides a company of uniformed citizens on horseback, and sundry notable personages in coaches, as well as

Clarence Winthrop Bowen, Ed., *The History of the Centennial Celebration of the Inauguration of George Washington as First President of the United States* (New York, 1892), 49–50.

gentlemen of Congress and residents of New York. They accompanied his Excellency to the residence of Mr. Jay, where he alighted. When passing the Battery, thirteen shots were fired as a salute. Immediately after his Excellency received the congratulations of the gentlemen of the committee of Congress on his safe arrival. The next day, April 21st, the gentlemen of the committee of Congress escorted his Excellency to the Senate-chamber, and, after being seated in the presidential chair, his Excellency delivered a speech, of which I enclose a copy.

President George Washington made his entry into New York on Thursday, April 23d. On the previous day a barge left this city. The barge was built expressly by the citizens of New York, and was rowed by thirteen pilots, all dressed in white. A committee of three Senators and five Representatives on behalf of Congress, and three of the first officers on behalf of New York, went to Elizabethtown in New Jersey, to welcome the President, and to await his arrival there. His Excellency was also accompanied by some well-equipped sloops and by a multitude of small craft with citizens of New Jersey and New York on board. A Spanish royal packet-boat, happening to be anchored at the entrance of the harbor, at sight of the barge, on board of which was the President, fired a signal-shot, whereupon that vessel was dressed at once with the flags of all nations. When the presidential barge passed, the Spanish vessel saluted his Excellency by firing thirteen guns, which was repeated by the Battery, and again thirteen guns were fired by the fort when the President landed. His Excellency was received by Governor George Clinton, the mayor of the city and other officers, and, after a procession had formed, consisting of some companies of uniformed citizens and the merchants and other citizens of the city, the President walked with his escort, and Governor Clinton at his side, to the house prepared by Congress for his use. Shortly afterward his Excellency was called for in a coach by Governor Clinton, without any ceremony. At Governor Clinton's residence he took a midday meal, though a magnificent dinner had been prepared for his Excellency at his own residence. Both these personages were on that day dressed very plainly in civilian clothes, without any display.

The rush of the people to see their beloved General Washington was amazing, and their delight and joy were truly universal and cordial. At night the whole city was illuminated. No accident occurred, and everything passed off well and quietly.

On Thursday, April 30th, General Washington was inaugurated President of the United States. New York was represented by the same companies of citizens under arms as on his arrival. . . . After the President, pursuant to the new Constitution, had publicly taken the oath of office, in presence of an innumerable crowd of people, his Excellency was led into the Senate-chamber and there delivered an oration. . . . By this address this admirable man made himself all the more beloved. The coaches, in which were seated gentlemen of Congress, were drawn by two horses and the presidential coach by four. His Excellency was dressed in plain brown clothes, which had been presented to him by the mill at Hartford, Connecticut. At night there was a display of fire-works at the State-House. Moreover, the houses of the Comte de Moustier, the minister of France, and of Senor de Gardoqui, of Spain, were illuminated. The next day the President received congratulations. The President adopts no other title than simply President of the United States. He receives visits twice a week, Tuesdays and Fridays, from two to three o'clock, and not at other times. It is further stated that his Excellency returns no visits, nor will he accept invitations to attend banquets or other entertainments, for the reason that his Excellency, as head of the Executive Department of the new Government, has his time fully occupied. This gentleman alone, by his courteous and friendly demeanor and still more so by his frugal and simple mode of living, is able to unite the parties in America and to make the new Government effective and regular in execution, if such be possible.

3.   *1789*—THE DEAL FOR THE CAPITAL

❪ *With Washington and John Adams, Vice President, a new Congress was elected. One of its first duties was the selection of a permanent capital. After much jockeying and trading, a site on the Potomac River was chosen. The decision was a triumph for Alexander Hamilton, who thus won Virginia's support for his plan to have the Federal government assume the debts which the states had incurred in the Revolutionary War. Pennsylvania, with high hopes for Philadelphia, was consoled by the choice of that city as the seat of government until the new site should be ready.*

William Maclay, disgruntled Senator from Pennsylvania, confided his disappointment at the outcome of the capital negotiations, and some tart comments about the participants, to his diary.

June 30th.—The Vice-President gave us a long speech on the orderly conduct, decent behavior of the citizens of New York, especially in the gallery of the other House; said no people in the world could behave better. I really thought he meant this lavish praise as an indirect censure on the city of Philadelphia, for the papers have teemed with censorious charges of their rudeness to the members of public bodies. Be that, however, as it may, he declared he would go to Phila-

---

Edgar S. Maclay, Ed., *The Journal of William Maclay* (New York, 1890), 312–14, 328–29.

delphia without staying a single hour, and gave us his vote. I think it was well he did not know all, for, had he given this vote the other way, the whole would have been lost. The question on the passage to the third reading was carried: fourteen to twelve. . . .

I am fully convinced Pennsylvania could do no better. The matter could not be longer delayed. It is, in fact, the interest of the President of the United States that pushes the Potomac. He [Washington], by means of Jefferson, Madison, Carrol, and others, urged the business, and, if we had not closed with these terms, a bargain would have been made for the temporary residence in New York. They have offered to support the Potomac for three years' temporary residence (in New York, I presume), and I am very apprehensive they would have succeeded if it had not been for the Pennsylvania threats that were thrown out of stopping all business if an attempt was made to rob them of both temporary and permanent residence.

July 1st.—Knowing nothing of immediate consequence, I attended the Hall early. Took a seat in the committee-room. Began an examination of the journals of the old Congress touching some matters before us in committee. Had thus an opportunity at the members as they came in, but such rushing and caballing of the New England men and Yorkers!

When the minutes were read, King observed that the yeas and nays were not inserted on the motion for staying two years in New York. The Vice-President and Secretary of the Senate both denied that they were taken, but I believed they erred. This, however, I did not consider as much for them. We read the Rhode Island Enumeration [Census] bill. Committed the Settlement bill and one for the regulation of seamen.

And now came the residence. Elsworth moved that the extent of the Potomac should be thirty miles above and thirty below Hancocktown. Lost. Second motion, "To insert the first Monday in May, instead of first Monday in December, for removal." The yeas and nays equal. And now John Adams gave us one of his pretty speeches. He mentioned many of the arguments for removal, and concluded that justice, policy, and even necessity, called for it.

Now King took up his lamentations. He sobbed, wiped his eyes, and scolded and railed and accused, first everybody and then nobody, of bargaining, contracting arrangements and engagements that would dissolve the Union. He was called on sharply. He begged pardon, and, blackguard-like, railed again. Butler replied in a long, unmeaning talk; repeated that he was sure the honorable gentleman did not mean him; and yet, if there really was any person to whom King's mysterious hints would apply, Butler's strange conduct marked him as the most proper object for them. Talk followed talk. It was evident they meant to spend the day. Dr. Johnson cried, "Adjourn!" "Question! question!" re-echoed from different quarters of the House. Few begged leave to move an amendment. It was to restore the appropriation clause. It was lost, and at last we got the question on transmitting the bill to the Representative—yeas, fourteen; nays, twelve.

As I came from the chamber [Senate], King gave me a look. I replied, "King's Lamentations." "That won't do," said he. When we were down-stairs he turned on me, and said, "Let us now go and receive the congratulations of the city for what we have done." I had heard so much and so many allusions to the hospitality, etc., I thought it no bad time to give both him and them a wipe. "King, for a session of near six months I have passed the threshold of no citizen of New York; I have no wish to commence acquaintance now." He muttered some ejaculation and went off. In truth, I never was in so inhospitable a place. The above declaration I thought it not amiss to make, that they may know that I am not insensible of their rudeness; and, further, that I am quite clear of any obligations to them. . . .

July 15th.—The President of the United States has (in my opinion) had a great influence in this business. The game was played by him and his adherents of Virginia and Maryland, between New York and Philadelphia, to give one of those places the temporary residence, but the permanent residence on the Potomac. I found a demonstration that this was the case, and that [New] York would have accepted of the temporary residence if we did not. But I did not then see so clearly that the abominations of the funding system and the assumption were so intimately connected with it. Alas, that the affection—nay, almost adoration—of the people should meet so unworthy a return! Here are their best interests sacrificed to the vain whim of fixing Congress and a great commercial town (so opposite to the genius of the Southern planter) on the Potomac, and the President has become, in the hands of Hamilton, the dishclout of every dirty speculation, and his name goes to wipe away blame and silence all murmuring.

4. *1800*—MRS. JOHN ADAMS DESCRIBES THE NEW WHITE HOUSE

❲ *The government moved from Philadelphia to Washington in the summer of 1800. In the fall of that year Mrs. John Adams, wife of the President, described her new residence to her daughter.*

Washington, 21 November, 1800.

MY DEAR CHILD,

I ARRIVED here on Sunday last, and without meeting with any acci-

Charles Francis Adams, Ed., *Letters of Mrs. Adams, the Wife of John Adams* (Boston, 1848), 381–83.

dent worth noticing, except losing ourselves when we left Baltimore, and going eight or nine miles on the Frederick road, by which means we were obliged to go the other eight through woods, where we wandered two hours without finding a guide, or the path. Fortunately a straggling black came up with us, and we engaged him as a guide, to extricate us out of our difficulty; but woods are all you see, from Baltimore until you reach *the city,* which is only so in name. Here and there is a small cot, without a glass window, interspersed amongst the forests, through which you travel miles without seeing any human being. In the city there are buildings enough, if they were compact and finished, to accommodate Congress and those attached to it; but as they are, and scattered as they are, I see no great comfort for them. The river, which runs up to Alexandria, is in full view of my window, and I see the vessels as they pass and repass. The house is upon a grand and superb scale, requiring about thirty servants to attend and keep the apartments in proper order, and perform the ordinary business of the house and stables; an establishment very well proportioned to the President's salary. The lighting the apartments, from the kitchen to parlors and chambers, is a tax indeed; and the fires we are obliged to keep to secure us from daily agues is another very cheering comfort. To assist us in this great castle, and render less attendance necessary, bells are wholly wanting, not one single one being hung through the whole house, and promises are all you can obtain. This is so great an inconvenience, that I know not what to do, or how to do. The ladies from Georgetown and in the city have many of them visited me. Yesterday I returned fifteen visits,—but such a place as Georgetown appears,—why, our Milton is beautiful. But no comparisons;—if they will put me up some bells, and let me have wood enough to keep fires, I design to be pleased. I could content myself almost anywhere three months; but, surrounded with forests, can you believe that wood is not to be had, because people cannot be found to cut and cart it! Briesler entered into a contract with a man to supply him with wood. A small part, a few cords only, has he been able to get. Most of that was expended to dry the walls of the house before we came in, and yesterday the man told him it was impossible for him to procure it to be cut and carted. He has had recourse to coals; but we cannot get grates made and set. We have, indeed, come into *a new country.*

You must keep all this to yourself, and, when asked how I like it, say that I write you the situation is beautiful, which is true. The house is made habitable, but there is not a single apartment finished, and all withinside, except the plastering, has been done since Briesler came. We have not the least fence, yard, or other convenience, without, and the great unfinished audience-room I make a drying-room of, to hang up the clothes in. The principal stairs are not up, and will not be this winter. Six chambers are made comfortable; two are occupied by the President and Mr. Shaw; two lower rooms, one for a common parlor, and one for a levee-room. Up stairs there is the oval room, which is designed for the drawing-room, and has the crimson furniture in it. It is a very handsome room now; but, when completed, it will be beautiful. If the twelve years, in which this place has been considered as the future seat of government, had been improved, as they would have been if in New England, very many of the present inconveniences would have been removed. It is a beautiful spot, capable of every improvement, and, the more I view it, the more I am delighted with it.

Since I sat down to write, I have been called down to a servant from Mount Vernon, with a billet from Major Custis, and a haunch of venison, and a kind, congratulatory letter from Mrs. Lewis, upon my arrival in the city, with Mrs. Washington's love, inviting me to Mount Vernon, where, health permitting, I will go, before I leave this place.

5. *1801*—THE INAUGURATION OF THOMAS JEFFERSON

❨ *During the two administrations of George Washington the first political parties took shape: the Federalists, favoring a strong central government in the hands of the conservative propertied class, and the Republicans,[1] stressing states' rights and the welfare of the farmers, small merchants, and workingmen. With the election of Thomas Jefferson in 1800, the Republicans came to power. Jefferson's supporters looked on his inauguration as the beginning of a new era. Mrs. Samuel Harrison Smith, wife of the editor of the Washington* NATIONAL INTELLIGENCER, *described the event in a letter to her sister.*

March 4, 1801.

Let me write to you my dear Susan, e'er that glow of enthusiasm has fled, which now animates my feelings; let me congratulate not only you, but all my fellow citizens, on an event which will have so auspicious an influence on their political welfare. I have this morning witnessed one of the most interesting scenes, a free people can ever witness. The changes of administration, which in every government and in every age have most generally been epochs of confusion, villainy and bloodshed, in this our happy country take place without any species of distraction, or disorder. This day, has one of the most amiable and worthy men taken that seat to which he was called by the voice of his country. I cannot describe the agitation I felt, while I looked around on

Gaillard Hunt, Ed., *The First Forty Years of Washington Society, Portrayed in the Family Letters of Mrs. Samuel Harrison Smith* (New York, 1906), 25–27.
[1] Not to be confused with the present-day Republican Party, founded in 1854.

the various multitude and while I listened to an address, containing principles the most correct, sentiments the most liberal, and wishes the most benevolent, conveyed in the most appropriate and elegant language and in a manner mild as it was firm. If doubts of the integrity and talents of Mr. Jefferson ever existed in the minds of any one, methinks this address must forever eradicate them. The Senate chamber was so crowded that I believe not another creature could enter. On one side of the house the Senate sat, the other was resigned by the representatives to the ladies. The roof is arched, the room half circle, every inch of ground was occupied. It has been conjectured by several gentlemen whom I've asked, that there were near a thousand persons within the walls. The speech was delivered in so low a tone that few heard it. Mr. Jefferson had given your Brother a copy early in the morning, so that on coming out of the house, the paper was distributed immediately. Since then there has been a constant succession of persons coming for the papers. I have been interrupted several times in this letter by the gentlemen of Congress, who have been to bid us their adieus; since three o'clock there has been a constant succession. Mr. Claibourn, a most amiable and agreeable man, called the moment before his departure and there is no one whose society I shall more regret the loss of. You will smile when I tell you that Gouveneur Morris, Mr. Dayton and Bayard drank tea here; they have just gone after sitting near two hours.

Mr. Foster will be the bearer of this letter; he is a widower, looking out for a wife; he is a man of respectable talents, and most amiable disposition and comfortable fortune. What think you my good sister Mary of setting your cap for him? As for you, Susan, you are rather too young, and I have another in my eye for you.

6. *1801*—MANASSEH CUTLER DESCRIBES LIFE AS A CONGRESSMAN

❪ *Manasseh Cutler was a man of parts. In the course of a long life he taught school, practiced both law and medicine, served as a Congregational minister, and made scientific investigations in botany and astronomy. As an agent of the Ohio Company he had a part in securing the passage of the famous Ordinance of 1787 and obtained the grant of land on which Marietta, one of the first permanent settlements in the Northwest Territory, was located.*

In 1800 Cutler ran for Congress in the Essex district of Massachusetts, was elected as a Federalist, and took his seat in the new Capitol. A letter to his daughter reflects a pleasant way of life.

William Parker Cutler and Julia Perkins Cutler, *Life, Journals and Correspondence of Rev. Manasseh Cutler* (Cincinnati, 1888), II, 50–53.

WASHINGTON, *Dec.* 21, 1801.

My Dear Betsy: . . . It shall be the subject of this letter to give you some account of my present situation and of occurrences since I left home.

The city of Washington, in point of situation, is much more delightful than I expected to find it. The ground, in general, is elevated, mostly cleared, and commands a pleasing prospect of the Potomac River. The buildings are brick, and erected in what are called large blocks, that is, from two to five or six houses joined together, and appear like one long building. There is one block of seven, another of nine, and one of twenty houses, but they are scattered over a large extent of ground. The block in which I live contains six houses, four stories high, and very handsomely furnished. It is situated east of the Capitol, on the highest ground in the city. Mr. King, our landlord, occupies the south end, only one room in front, which is our parlor for receiving company and dining, and one room back, occupied by Mr. King's family, the kitchen is below. The four chambers are appropriated to the eight gentlemen who board in the family. In each chamber are two narrow field beds and field curtains, with every necessary convenience for the boarders. Mr. Read and myself have, I think, the pleasantest room in the house, or in the whole city. It is in the third story, commanding a delightful prospect of the Capitol, of the President's house, Georgetown, all the houses in the city, a long extent of the river, and the city of Alexandria.

The air is fine, and the weather, since I have been here, remarkably pleasant. I am not much pleased with the Capitol. It is a huge pile, built, indeed, with handsome stone, very heavy in its appearance without, and not very pleasant within. The President's house is superb, well proportioned and pleasingly situated.

But I will hasten to give you a more particular account of our family, which, I presume, will be more interesting to you than the Geography of this District. Mr. King's family consists only of himself, his lady and one daughter, besides the servants, all of whom are black. Mr. King was an officer in the late American Army, much of a gentleman in his manner, social and very obliging. I have seen few women more agreeable than Mrs. King. She almost daily brings to my mind Dr. Lakeman's first wife. She was the daughter of Mr. Harper, a very respectable merchant in Baltimore; has been favored with an excellent education, has been much in the first circles of society in this part of the country, and is in nothing more remarkable than her perfect freedom from stiffness, vanity, or ostentation. Their only daughter, Miss Anna, is about seventeen, well formed, rather tall, small featured, but is considered very handsome. She has been educated at the best schools in Baltimore and Alexandria. She does not converse much, but is very modest and agreeable. She plays with great skill on the Forte Piano, which she always accompanies with a most delightful voice, and is frequently joined in the vocal part by her mother. Mr. King has an excellent Forte Piano, which is connected with an organ placed under it, which she fills and plays with her foot, while her fingers are employed upon the Forte Piano.

The gentlemen, generally, spend a part of two or three evenings in a week in Mr. King's room, where Miss Anna entertains us with delightful music. After we have been fatigued with the harangues of the Hall in the day, and conversing on politics, in different circles (for we talk about nothing else), in the evening, an hour of this music is truly delightful. On Sunday evenings, she constantly plays Psalm tunes, in which her mother, who is a woman of real piety, always joins. We have three gentlemen in the family (General Mattoon, Mr. Smith, and Mr. Perkins) who are good singers and extravagantly fond of music, and always join in the Psalmody. Miss Anna plays Denmark remarkably well, and, when joined with the other singers, it exceeds what I have ever heard before. But the most of the Psalm tunes our gentlemen prefer are the old ones, such as Old Hundred, Canterbury, which you would be delighted to hear on the Forte-Piano, assisted by the organ and accompanied with the voice.

We breakfast at nine, dine between three and four. If we happen to be in the parlor in the first of the evening, at the time Mrs. King makes tea in her own room, she sends in a servant with a salver of tea and coffee and a plate of toast, but we never eat any supper.

I can not conclude without giving you some description of our fellow-lodgers, with whom I enjoy a happiness which I by no means expected. We have Mr. Hillhouse, of New Haven, and Judge Foster, of Brookfield, two of the most sensible and respectable members of the Senate; Mr. Davenport, of Connecticut, who is a deacon and a very pleasant, agreeable man; Mr. Smith, who is the son of a clergyman, of very sprightly and distinguished talents; Mr. Perkins, of New London, a man of very handsome abilities; General Mattoon, much of a gentleman, facetious; and Mr. Read and myself. It is remarkable that all these gentlemen are professors of religion, and members of the churches to which they respectively belong. An unbecoming word is never uttered by one of them, and the most perfect harmony and friendliness pervades the family.

Colonel Tallmadge came here with the hopes of boarding with us, and tarried two or three days, but, when the other gentlemen came, who had previously applied to Mr. King, he was obliged, much to his regret and mine, to take lodgings in another house.

I must add that I am exceedingly happy with Mr. Read. Were I to have made my choice among all the members of Congress for one to have lived in the same chamber with me, all things considered, I should have chosen Mr. Read. But, after all I have said to you, it is not home, it is not where I wish to be, and I long for the day when I shall set my face eastward, to return to our family.

Your affectionate parent,
M. Cutler.

7. 1804—Aaron Burr Kills Alexander Hamilton in a Duel

❨ *Aaron Burr had a fine mind, personal charm, and the knack of winning votes. These qualities carried him to the United States Senate, and almost to the Presidency. In 1800 the federal electors divided their votes equally between Burr and Jefferson for thirty-six ballots before they finally named Jefferson President and Burr Vice President.*

In his political activities Burr had incurred the enmity of Hamilton, although outwardly the two men were friends. In 1804, during the course of a hot campaign for the governorship of New York, the ill-feeling came to the surface. Hamilton, it was said, had asserted that Burr was a "dangerous man and one who ought not to be trusted with the reins of government." Burr demanded an explanation; Hamilton made an evasive reply. Burr issued a challenge; Hamilton accepted, though reluctantly. The duellists met at Weehawken, New Jersey, on July 11, 1804.

Matthew L. Davis, Burr's close friend, gives an eye-witness account of the encounter, in which Hamilton was mortally wounded.

Colonel Burr arrived first on the ground, as had been previously agreed. When General Hamilton arrived, the parties exchanged salutations, and the seconds proceeded to make their arrangements. They measured the distance, ten full paces, and cast lots for the choice of position, as also to determine by whom the word should be given, both of which fell to the second of General Hamilton. They then proceeded to load the pistols in each other's presence, after which the parties took their stations. The gentleman who was to give the word then explained to the parties the rules which were to govern them in firing, which were as follows: "The parties being placed at their stations, the second who gives the word shall ask them whether they are ready; being answered in the affirmative, he shall say—*present!* After this the parties shall present and fire *when they please.* If one fires before the other, the opposite second shall say *one, two, three, fire,* and he shall then fire or

Matthew L. Davis, *Memoirs of Aaron Burr, with Miscellaneous Selections from His Correspondence* (New York, 1837), 309–10.

lose his fire." He then asked if they were prepared; being answered in the affirmative, he gave the word *present,* as had been agreed on, and both parties presented and fired in succession. The intervening time is not expressed, as the seconds do not precisely agree on that point. The fire of Colonel Burr took effect, and General Hamilton almost instantly fell. Colonel Burr advanced towards General Hamilton with a manner and gesture that appeared to General Hamilton's friend to be expressive of regret; but, without speaking, turned about and withdrew, being urged from the field by his friend, as has been subsequently stated, with a view to prevent his being recognised [*sic*] by the surgeon and bargemen who were then approaching. No further communication took place between the principals, and the barge that carried Colonel Burr immediately returned to the city. We conceive it proper to add, that the conduct of the parties in this interview was perfectly proper, as suited the occasion.

In the interviews between Mr. Pendleton and Mr. Van Ness, they were not able to agree in two important facts that passed on the ground. Mr. Pendleton expressed a confident opinion that General Hamilton did not fire first, and that he did not fire at all at Colonel Burr. Mr. Van Ness seemed equally confident in opinion that General Hamilton did fire first; and, of course, that it must have been *at* his antagonist.

8. *1807*—BURR STANDS TRIAL FOR TREASON

❬ *After the duel with Hamilton, Burr determined to rebuild his fortune and his reputation, now badly damaged. Apparently he planned an expedition to seize Spanish territory west of the Mississippi, although scholars have never agreed on exactly what he intended. In his early scheming he had the secret support of General James Wilkinson, who commanded the American army on the Mississippi. But when Burr finally approached New Orleans, Wilkinson, a thorough scoundrel and an accomplished turncoat, arrested Burr and sent him east for trial.*

On May 22, 1807, Burr appeared before the grand jury in the United States Circuit Court at Richmond, with Chief Justice John Marshall presiding. On June 24 the grand jury returned an indictment for treason. Burr was tried on this charge between August 3 and September 1, when he was acquitted.

Washington Irving, just coming into his reputation as an author, spent several weeks in Richmond during the trial and described the proceedings in letters to his friends. His sympathies, he made clear, were all with Burr.

Pierre M. Irving, Ed., *The Life and Letters of Washington Irving* (New York, 1869), I, 142–43.

To Mrs. Hoffman

Richmond, June 4, 1807

. . . Day after day have we been disappointed by the non-arrival of the magnanimous Wilkinson; day after day have fresh murmurs and complaints been uttered; and day after day are we told that the next mail will probably bring his noble self, or at least some accounts when he may be expected. We are now enjoying a kind of suspension of hostilities; the grand jury having been dismissed the day before yesterday for five or six days, that they might go home, see their wives, get their clothes washed, and flog their negroes. As yet we are not even on the threshold of a trial; and, if the great hero of the South does not arrive, it is chance if we have any trial this term. I am told the Attorney-general talks of moving the Court next Tuesday, for a continuance and a special Court, by which means the present grand jury (the most enlightened, perhaps, that was ever assembled in this country) will be discharged; the witnesses will be dismissed; many of whom live such a distance off that it is a chance if half of them will ever be again collected. The Government will be again subjected to immense expense, and Colonel Burr, besides being harassed and detained for an additional space of time, will have to repeat the enormous expenditures which this trial has already caused him. I am very much mistaken, if the most underhand and ungenerous measures have not been observed towards him. He, however, retains his serenity and self-possession unshaken, and wears the same aspect in all times and situations. I am impatient for the arrival of this Wilkinson, that the whole matter may be put to rest; and I never was more mistaken in my calculations, if the whole will not have a most farcical termination as it respects the charges against Colonel Burr. . . .

To James K. Paulding

Richmond, June 22, 1807

. . . Wilkinson, you will observe, has arrived; the bets were against Burr that he would abscond, should W. come to Richmond; but he still maintains his ground, and still enters the Court every morning with the same serene and placid air that he would show were he brought there to plead another man's cause, and not his own.

The lawyers are continually entangling each other in law points, motions, and authorities, and have been so crusty to each other, that there is constant sparring going on. Wilkinson is now before the grand jury, and has such a mighty mass of *words* to deliver himself of, that he claims at least two days more to discharge the wondrous cargo. The jury are tired enough of his verbosity. The first interview between him and Burr was highly interesting, and I secured a good place to witness

145

it. Burr was seated with his back to the entrance, facing the judge, and conversing with one of his counsel. Wilkinson strutted into the Court, and took a stand on a parallel line with Burr on his right hand. Here he stood for a moment swelling like a turkey cock, and bracing himself up for the encounter of Burr's eye. The latter did not take any notice of him until the judge directed the clerk to swear General Wilkinson; at the mention of the name Burr turned his head, looked him full in the face with one of his piercing regards, swept his eye over his whole person from head to foot, as if to scan its dimensions, and then coolly resumed his former position, and went on conversing with his counsel as tranquilly as ever. The whole look was over in an instant; but it was an admirable one. There was no appearance of study or constraint in it; no affectation of disdain or defiance; a slight expression of contempt played over his countenance, such as you would show on regarding any person to whom you were indifferent, but whom you considered mean and contemptible. Wilkinson did not remain in Court many minutes. . . .

To Miss Mary Fairlie

Washington City, July 7, 1807

. . . The last time I saw Burr was the day before I left Richmond. He was then in the Penitentiary, a kind of State prison. . . . I found great difficulty in gaining admission to him, for a few moments. The keeper had orders to admit none but his counsel and his witnesses— strange measures these! That it is not sufficient that a man against whom no certainty of crime is proved, should be confined by bolts, and bars, and massy walls in a criminal prison; but he is likewise to be cut off from all intercourse with society, deprived of all the kind offices of friendship, and made to suffer all the penalties and deprivations of a condemned criminal. I was permitted to enter for a few moments, as a special favor, contrary to orders. Burr seemed in lower spirits than formerly; he was composed and collected as usual; but there was not the same cheerfulness that I have hitherto remarked. He said it was with difficulty his very servant was allowed occasionally to see him; he had a bad cold, which I suppose was occasioned by the dampness of his chamber, which had lately been whitewashed. I bid him farewell with a heavy heart, and he expressed with peculiar warmth and feeling his sense of the interest I had taken in his fate. I never felt in a more melancholy mood than when I rode from his solitary prison. . . .

1.   *1769*—DANIEL BOONE DISCOVERS A PARADISE

❮ *Even before the Revolution restless men in the colonies began to cross the Alleghenies, sometimes only to hunt, sometimes to clear little farms on virgin land that could be had for the taking. Though not the first to explore the western country, Daniel Boone has come to stand for the many men of his kind whose daring, skill in woodcraft, and willingness to endure hardship blazed trails for the millions of settlers who followed them.*

In his home on the Yadkin River in western North Carolina, Boone listened to tales of the country beyond the mountains and determined to see the region for himself. In the fall of 1767, with a companion or two, he made his first try, but only succeeded in reaching the forbidding hill country in the vicinity of the Big Sandy River. This was far from the gentle swells and thick carpets of blue grass that other explorers had described. In the spring of 1769

"The Adventures of Daniel Boone," in Gilbert Imlay, *A Topographical Description of the Western Territory of North America* (London, 1797), 339–43.

Boone set out again. His adventures are described in the following narrative—his own story, though dressed up, for publication, in words beyond the vocabulary of the hardy frontiersman.

It was on the 1st of May in the year 1769, that I resigned my domestic happiness for a time, and left my family and peaceable habitation on the Yadkin river, in North-Carolina, to wander through the wilderness of America, in quest of the country of Kentucky, in company with John Finley, John Stewart, Joseph Holden, James Monay, and William Cool. We proceeded successfully; and after a long and fatiguing journey, through a mountainous wilderness, in a westward direction, on the seventh day of June following we found ourselves on Red river, where John Finley had formerly been trading with the Indians, and, from the top of an eminence, saw with pleasure the beautiful level of Kentucky. Here let me observe, that for some time we had experienced the most uncomfortable weather as a prelibation of our future sufferings. At this place we encamped, and made a shelter to defend us from the inclement season, and began to hunt and to reconnoitre the country. We found everywhere abundance of wild beasts of all sorts, through this vast forest. The buffalo were more frequent than I have seen cattle in the settlements, browzing on the leaves of the cane, or cropping the herbage on those extensive plains, fearless, because ignorant, of the violence of man. Sometimes we saw hundreds in a drove, and the numbers about the salt springs were amazing. In this forest, the habitation of beasts of every kind natural to America, we practiced hunting with great success, until the 22d day of December following.

This day John Stewart and I had a pleasing ramble, but fortune changed the scene in the close of it. We had passed through a great forest, on which stood myriads of trees, some gay with blossoms, others rich with fruits. Nature was here a series of wonders, and a fund of delight. Here she displayed her ingenuity and industry in a variety of flowers and fruits, beautifully coloured, elegantly shaped, and charmingly flavoured; and we were diverted with innumerable animals presenting themselves perpetually to our view.—In the decline of the day, near Kentucky river, as we ascended the brow of a small hill, a number of Indians rushed out of a thick cane-brake upon us, and made us prisoners. The time of our sorrow was now arrived, and the scene fully opened. The Indians plundered us of what we had, and kept us in confinement 7 days, treating us with common savage usage. During this time we discovered no uneasiness or desire to escape, which made them less suspicious of us; but in the dead of the night, as we lay in a thick cane-brake by a large fire, when sleep had locked up their senses, my situation not disposing me for rest, I touched my companion, and gently awoke him. We improved this favourable opportunity, and departed, leaving them to take their rest, and speedily directed our course towards our old camp, but found it plundered, and the company dispersed and gone home. About this time, my brother, Squire Boon, with another adventurer, who came to explore the country shortly after us, was wandering through the forest, determined to find me if possible, and accidentally found our camp. Notwithstanding the unfortunate circumstances of our company, and our dangerous situation, as surrounded with hostile savages, our meeting so fortunately in the wilderness, made us reciprocally sensible of the utmost satisfaction. So much does friendship triumph over misfortune, that sorrows and sufferings vanish at the meeting not only of real friends, but of the most distant acquaintances, and substitute happiness in their room.

Soon after this, my companion in captivity, John Stewart, was killed by the savages, and the man that came with my brother returned home by himself. We were then in a dangerous, helpless situation, exposed daily to perils and death, amongst savages and wild beasts, not a white man in the country but ourselves.

Thus situated, many hundred miles from our families, in the howling wilderness, I believe few would have equally enjoyed the happiness we experienced. I often observed to my brother, You see now how little nature requires to be satisfied. Felicity, the companion of content, is rather found in our own breasts than in the enjoyment of external things: and I firmly believe it requires but a little philosophy to make a man happy in whatsoever state he is. This consists in a full resignation to the will of providence; and a resigned soul finds pleasure in a path strewed with briars and thorns.

We continued not in a state of indolence, but hunted every day, and prepared a little cottage to defend us from the winter storms. We remained there undisturbed during the winter; and on the first day of May 1770, my brother returned home to the settlement by himself, for a new recruit of horses and ammunition, leaving me by myself, without bread, salt, or sugar, without company of my fellow-creatures, or even a horse or dog. I confess I never before was under greater necessity of exercising philosophy and fortitude. A few days I passed uncomfortably. The idea of a beloved wife and family, and their anxiety upon the account of my absence and exposed situation, made sensible impressions on my heart. A thousand dreadful apprehensions presented themselves to my view, and had undoubtedly disposed me to melancholy, if further indulged.

One day I undertook a tour through the country, and the diversity and beauties of nature I met with in this charming season, expelled every gloomy and vexatious thought. Just at the close of day the gentle gales retired, and left the place to the disposal of a profound calm. Not a breeze shook the most tremulous leaf. I had gained the summit of a commanding ridge, and, looking round with astonishing delight, beheld the ample plains, the beauteous tracts below. On the other hand,

I surveyed the famous river Ohio, that rolled in silent dignity, marking the western boundary of Kentucky with inconceivable grandeur. At a vast distance I beheld the mountains lift their venerable brows, and penetrate the clouds. All things were still. I kindled a fire near a fountain of sweet water, and feasted on the loin of a buck, which a few hours before I had killed. The sullen shades of night soon overspread the whole hemisphere, and the earth seemed to gasp after the hovering moisture. My roving excursion this day had fatigued my body, and diverted my imagination. I laid me down to sleep, and I awoke not until the sun had chased away the night. I continued this tour, and in a few days explored a considerable part of the country, each day equally pleased as the first. I returned again to my old camp, which was not disturbed in my absence. I did not confine my lodging to it, but often reposed in thick cane-brakes, to avoid the savages, who, I believe, often visited my camp, but fortunately for me, in my absence. In this situation I was constantly exposed to danger and death. How unhappy such a situation for a man tormented with fear, which is vain if no danger comes, and if it does, only augments the pain! It was my happiness to be destitute of this afflicting passion, with which I had the greatest reason to be affected. The prowling wolves diverted my nocturnal hours with perpetual howlings; and the various species of animals in this vast forest, in the day-time, were continually in my view.

Thus I was surrounded with plenty in the midst of want. I was happy in the midst of dangers and inconveniences. In such a diversity it was impossible I should be disposed to melancholy. No populous city, with all the varieties of commerce and stately structures, could afford so much pleasure to my mind, as the beauties of nature I found here.

Thus, through an uninterrupted scene of sylvan pleasures, I spent the time until the 27th day of July following, when my brother, to my great felicity, met me, according to appointment, at our old camp. Shortly after, we left this place, not thinking it safe to stay there longer, and proceeded to Cumberland river, reconnoitring that part of the country until March 1771, and giving names to the different waters.

Soon after, I returned home to my family, with a determination to bring them as soon as possible to live in Kentucky, which I esteemed a second paradise, at the risk of my life and fortune.

2. *1788*—MARIETTA CELEBRATES ITS FIRST FOURTH OF JULY

❲ *As soon as the Ordinance of 1787 organized the Northwest Territory, groups of settlers moved to establish themselves there. First in the field was the Ohio Company of Associates, New England*

Richard S. Edes and William M. Darlington, Eds., *Journal and Letters of Col. John May, of Boston* (Cincinnati, 1873), 57–59.

veterans of the Revolution who obtained a federal grant of land in southeastern Ohio in return for a subscription of $1,000,000, payable in Continental currency. In the spring of 1788 the Company's advance parties chose a site at the juncture of the Ohio and Muskingum rivers and started to build the town of Marietta. A few weeks later Colonel John May, one of the Company members, arrived from Boston and commenced the first frame house to be erected in the new settlement. His diary describes life in this outpost of New England, not omitting an elaborate celebration of the Fourth of July.

Monday, May 26, 1788 . . . The sun rose beautifully on us this morning, and the prospect is as pleasant as the imagination can conceive. . . . We are passing by one lovely island after another, floating tranquilly, but majestically, at the rate of four and one-half miles an hour. Thus we moved on, constantly espying new wonders and beauties, till 3 o'clock, when we arrived safely on the banks of the delightful Muskingum.

Tuesday, 27th. Slept on board last night, and rose early this morning. Have spent the day in reconnoitering the spot where the city is to be laid out, and find it to answer the best descriptions I have ever heard of it. The situation delightfully agreeeable, and well calculated for an elegant city. . . .

As to our surveying, buildings, etc., they are in a very backward state. Little appears to be done, and a great deal of time and money misspent. There are now here about thirty Indians, who appear to be friendly enough; but they are a set of creatures not to be trusted. General Putnam tells me there have been several parties here since his arrival. For my part I am not fond of them, neither do I fear them. Dined today with General Harmer, by invitation. Had an elegant dinner. Amongst the variety was (beef) *à la mode,* boiled fish, bear-steaks, roast venison, etc., excellent succotash, salads, and cranberry sauce; grog and wine after dinner. . . .

Friday, 30th. Men employed in cutting timber for my house. . . .

Saturday, 31st. All hands at work on my *ten-acre lot.* Took hold of it with spirit. There are six of us in all, and we completely cleared an acre and a half by sunset. The land as good as any that can be found in the universe. . . .

Saturday, June 14th . . . A delightful morning. The river beginning to fall. At 2 o'clock completed my brew-house—and two barrels of beer, and one of vinegar. . . .

Sunday, 15th. This morning as delightful as ever shone in Eden; but from some mighty rains at a distance the rivers are taking a new start. I am still on board the ship, which gives me an opportunity to observe the rising and falling of the waters. A number of poor devils—five in all—took their departure homeward this morning. They came from home moneyless and brainless, and have returned as they came. . . .

Tuesday, 17th. All hands employed as usual. Great preparations are making at the garrison for the treaty. Two large keel-boats—one of which is eighty-five feet long, the other seventy-two—arrived here three days ago, from Pittsburg, laden with merchandise, for use in the treaty. The contractors are on board; and two days ago the boats went up the Muskingum to the forks, about sixty miles, to make preparations to build a council-house, etc. The catfish and perch make such a noise under my ship that they frequently keep me awake half the night. My garden-seeds came up finely; but insects are numerous, and destroy a great deal. . . .

This evening Judge Parsons' and General Varnum's commissions were read; also, regulations for the government of the people. In fact, by-laws were much wanted. Officers were named to command the militia; guards to be mounted every evening; all males more than fifteen years old to appear under arms every Sunday. . . .

Monday, 30th. All employed about the house. Poor Dr. M. out of provisions, and no money. Had pity on him, and took him into my family, although it was quite large enough before. I put powder-horn and shot-bag onto him, and a gun in his hand, with a bottle of grog by his side, and told him to live in my corn-field, and keep off squirrels and crows. . . .

Tuesday, July 1st . . . We were alarmed today by a letter from Major Doughty, at Pittsburg, stating that they had just received intelligence from Detroit, that two parties of Indian warriors, about forty in each party, were started on a hostile expedition against our settlement and Kentucky. Our people were called in from labor at 11 o'clock, and a guard consisting of a subaltern and thirty men sent to reconnoiter and scour the woods. They took a day's provisions with them. . . .

Thursday, 3d . . . All hands at work on the house. I returned from labor at sunset, and found hanging up in my cellar a pike that weighed twenty-one pounds, and a perch twenty-four and one-half pounds. This preparation in part for the entertainment of tomorrow. . . .

Friday, 4th. Warm, moist, and a brisk wind from southwest. At 11 o'clock it rained hard. The cloud, black and heavy, shakes the rain out easily. All labor comes to pause today in memory of the Declaration of Independence. Our long bowery is built on the east bank of the Muskingum; a table laid sixty feet long, in plain sight of the garrison, at one-quarter of a mile distance. At 1 o'clock General Harmer and his lady, Mrs. McCurders, and all the officers not on duty came over, and several other gentlemen. An excellent oration was delivered by Judge

Varnum, and the cannon fired a salute of fourteen guns. At 3 o'clock, just as dinner was on table, came on a heavy shower, which lasted for half an hour. However, the chief of our provisions were rescued from the deluge, but injured materially. When the rain ceased, the table was laid again; but before we had finished, it came on to rain a second time. On the whole, though, we had a handsome dinner: all kinds of wild meat, turkey, and other fowls of the woods; gammon, a variety of fish, and plenty of vegetables; a bowl of punch, also grog, wine, etc. Our toasts were as follows:

1. The United States.
2. Congress.
3. His Most Christian Majesty the King of France.
4. The United Netherlands.
5. The Friendly Powers throughout the World.
6. The New Federal Constitution.
7. General Washington and the Society of Cincinnati.
8. His Excellency Governor St. Clair and the Western Territory.
9. The Memory of Heroes.
10. Patriots.
11. Captain Pipes, and a Successful Treaty.
12. The Amiable Partners of our Lives.
13. All Mankind.

Pleased with the entertainment, we kept it up till after 12 at night, then went home and to bed, and slept sound till morning.

3.   *1802*—THE KENTUCKIAN

❪ *So many settlers followed the trails marked out by Daniel Boone and other pioneers that Kentucky, their favorite destination, entered the Union as a state in 1792. By 1800 it had a population of more than 200,000 and a local pride the equal of any of the older states. F. A. Michaux, a French botanist who spent several years in the United States, offered a sympathetic picture of the Kentuckian as he appeared after ten years of statehood.*

The inhabitants of Kentucky . . . are nearly all natives of Virginia, and particularly the remotest parts of that state; and exclusive of the gentlemen of the law, physicians, and a small number of citizens who have received an education suitable to their professions in the Atlantic states, they have preserved the manners of the Virginians. With them the passion for gaming and spirituous liquors is carried to excess, which frequently terminates in quarrels degrading to human nature.

F. A. Michaux, *Travels to the West of the Allegheny Mountains,* in Reuben Gold Thwaites, *Early Western Travels* (1904), III, 247–50.

The public-houses are always crowded, more especially during the sittings of the courts of justice. Horses and law-suits comprise the usual topic of their conversation. If a traveller happens to pass by, his horse is appreciated; if he stops, he is presented with a glass of whiskey, and then asked a thousand questions, such as, Where do you come from? where are you going? what is your name? where do you live? what profession? were there any fevers in the different parts of the country you came through? These questions, which are frequently repeated in the course of a journey, become tedious, but it is easy to give a check to their inquiries by a little address; their only object being the gratification of that curiosity so natural to people who live isolated in the woods, and seldom see a stranger. They are never dictated by mistrust; for from whatever part of the globe a person comes, he may visit all the ports and principal towns of the United States, stay there as long as he pleases, and travel in any part of the country without ever being interrogated by a public officer.

The inhabitants of Kentucky eagerly recommend to strangers the country they inhabit as the best part of the United States, as that where the soil is most fertile, the climate most salubrious, and where all the inhabitants were brought through the love of liberty and independence!

. . . Among the various sects that exist in Kentucky, those of the Methodists and Anabaptists are the most numerous. The spirit of religion has acquired a fresh degree of strength within these seven or eight years among the country inhabitants, since, independent of Sundays, which are scrupulously observed, they assemble, during the summer, in the course of the week, to hear sermons. These meetings, which frequently consist of two or three thousand persons who come from all parts of the country within fifteen or twenty miles, take place in the woods, and continue for several days. Each brings his provisions, and spends the night round a fire. The clergymen are very vehement in their discourses. Often in the midst of the sermons the heads are lifted up, the imaginations exalted, and the inspired fall backwards, exclaiming, "Glory! glory!" This species of infatuation happens chiefly among the women, who are carried out of the crowd, and put under a tree, where they lie a long time extended, heaving the most lamentable sighs.

There have been instances of two or three hundred of the congregation being thus affected during the performance of divine service; so that one-third of the hearers were engaged in recovering the rest. Whilst I was at Lexington I was present at one of these meetings. The better informed people do not share the opinion of the multitude with regard to this state of ecstacy, and on this account they are branded with the appellation of *bad folks*. Except during the continuance of this preaching, religion is very seldom the topic of conversation. Although divided into several sects, they live in the greatest harmony;

and whenever there is an alliance between the families, the difference of religion is never considered as an obstacle; the husband and wife pursue whatever kind of worship they like best, and their children, when they grow up, do just the same, without the interference of their parents.

4. *1802*—THE FRONTIERSMAN

❰ *The American frontiersman rarely became a settled citizen. He would push beyond the borders of civilization, clear a little land, and move west again when the advance guard of true settlers caught up with him. Michaux, traveling in the vicinity of the Ohio River, sketched the type.*

More than half of those who inhabit the borders of the Ohio, are again the first inhabitants, or as they are called in the United States, the *first settlers,* a kind of men who cannot settle upon the soil that they have cleared, and who under pretence of finding a better land, a more wholesome country, a greater abundance of game, push forward, incline perpetually towards the most distant points of the American population, and go and settle in the neighbourhood of the savage nations, whom they brave even in their own country. Their ungenerous mode of treating them stirs up frequent broils, and brings on bloody wars, in which they generally fall victims; rather on account of their being so few in number, than through defect of courage.

Prior to our arrival at Marietta, we met one of these *settlers,* an inhabitant of the environs of Wheeling, who accompanied us down the Ohio, and with whom we travelled for two days. Alone in a canoe from eighteen to twenty feet long, and from twelve to fifteen inches broad, he was going to survey the borders of the Missouri for a hundred and fifty miles above its *embouchure.* The excellent quality of the land that is reckoned to be more fertile than that on the borders of the Ohio . . ., the quantity of beavers, elks, and more especially bisons, were the motives that induced him to emigrate into this remote part of the country, whence after having determined on a suitable spot to settle there with his family, he was returning to fetch them from the borders of the Ohio, which obliged him to take a journey of fourteen or fifteen hundred miles. His costume, like that of all the American sportsmen, consisted of a waistcoat with sleeves, a pair of pantaloons, and a large red and yellow woolen sash. A carabine, a tomahawk or little axe, which the Indians make use of to cut wood and to terminate the existence of their enemies, two beaver-snares, and a large knife sus-

Michaux, *Travels to the West of the Allegheny Mountains,* in Thwaites, *Early Western Travels,* III, 192–93.

pended at his side, constituted his sporting dress. A rug comprised the whole of his luggage. Every evening he encamped on the banks of the river, where, after having made a fire, he passed the night; and whenever he conceived the place favourable for the chace, he remained in the woods for several days together, and with the produce of his sport, he gained the means of subsistence, and new ammunition with the skins of the animals he had killed.

Such were the first inhabitants of Kentucky and Tennessea, of whom there are now remaining but very few. . . . They have emigrated to more remote parts of the country, and formed new settlements. It will be the same with most of those who inhabit the borders of the Ohio.

5. *1802*—THE LOG CABIN

❮ *The pioneer's first dwelling was a log cabin, a kind of structure which had long since disappeared in the older communities. Michaux offers a good description.*

On the 27th of June I set out from Lancaster for Shippensburgh. There were only four of us in the stage, which was fitted up to hold twelve passengers. Columbia, situated upon the Susquehannah, is the first town that we arrived at; it is composed of about fifty houses, scattered here and there, and almost all built with wood; at this place ends the turnpike road.

It is not useless to observe here, that in the United States they give often the name of town to a group of seven or eight houses, and that the mode of constructing them is not the same everywhere. At Philadelphia the houses are built with brick. In the other towns and country places that surround them, the half, and even frequently the whole, is built with wood; but at places within seventy or eighty miles of the sea, in the central and southern states, and again more particularly in those situated to the Westward of the Alleghany Mountains, one third of the inhabitants reside in *log houses*. These dwellings are made with the trunks of trees, from twenty to thirty feet in length, about five inches diameter, placed one upon another, and kept up by notches cut at their extremities. The roof is formed with pieces of similar length to those that compose the body of the house, but not quite so thick, and gradually sloped on each side. Two doors, which often supply the place of windows, are made by sawing away a part of the trunks that form the body of the house; the chimney, always placed at one of the extremities, is likewise made with the trunks of trees of a suitable length; the back of the chimney is made of clay, about six inches thick, which sepa-

Michaux, *Travels to the West of the Allegheny Mountains,* in Thwaites, *Early Western Travels,* III, 136–37.

rates the fire from the wooden walls. Notwithstanding this want of precaution, fires very seldom happen in the country places. The space between these trunks of trees is filled up with clay, but so very carelessly,
that the light may be seen through in every part; in consequence of
which these huts are exceedingly cold in winter, notwithstanding the
amazing quantity of wood that is burnt. The doors move upon wooden
hinges, and the greater part of them have no locks. In the night time
they only push them to, or fasten them with a wooden peg. Four or
five days are sufficient for two men to finish one of these houses, in
which not a nail is used. Two great beds receive the whole family. It
frequently happens that in summer the children sleep upon the ground,
in a kind of rug. The floor is raised from one to two feet above the
surface of the ground, and boarded. They generally make use of feather
beds, or feathers alone, and not mattresses. Sheep being very scarce, the
wool is very dear; at the same time they reserve it to make stockings.
The clothes belonging to the family are hung up round the room, or
suspended upon a long pole.

6. 1807—HIGHWAYS THICK WITH TRAVELERS

⟨ *As the "western" country filled with people, the highways, poor
as they were, swarmed with humanity. Wagons and packhorses carried articles of commerce, movers sought new farms, judges and
lawyers traveled back and forth between courts. The ways of the
road were hard, manners rough. This was a new breed of people,
as the Irish-born New Yorker, Fortescue Cuming, discovered when
he went west in 1807 to inspect land in Ohio which he had recently
purchased.*

The travelling on these roads [in western Pennsylvania] in every
direction is truly astonishing, even at this inclement season, but in the
spring and fall, I am informed that it is beyond all conception.

Apropos of travelling—A European, who had not experienced it,
could form no proper idea of the manner of it in this country. The
travellers are, wagonners, carrying produce to, and bringing back foreign goods from the different shipping ports on the shores of the At-
lantick, particularly Philadelphia and Baltimore;—Packers with from
one to twenty horses, selling or trucking their wares through the country;—Countrymen, sometimes alone, sometimes in large companies,
carrying salt from M'Connelstown, and other points of navigation on
the Potomack and Susquehannah, for the curing of their beef, pork,
venison, &c.;—Families removing farther back into the country, some

F. Cuming, *Sketches of a Tour to the Western Country*, in Thwaites, *Early Western Travels*,
IV, 62–63.

with cows, oxen, horses, sheep, and hogs, and all their farming imple-
ments and domestick utensils, and some without; some with wagons,
some with carts and some on foot, according to their abilities:—The
residue, who make use of the best accommodations on the roads, are
country merchants, judges and lawyers attending the courts, members
of the legislature, and the better class of settlers removing back. All
the first four descriptions carry provisions for themselves and horses,
live most miserably, and wrapped in blankets, occupy the floor of the
bar rooms of the taverns where they stop each night, which the landlords give them the use of, with as much wood as they choose to burn,
in consideration of the money they pay them for whiskey, of which
they drink great quantities, expending foolishly, for that which poisons
them, as much money as would render them comfortable otherwise.—
So far do they carry this mania for whiskey, that to procure it, they in
the most niggardly manner deny themselves even the necessaries of
life; and, as I was informed by my landlord Fleming, an observing and
rational man, countrymen while attending the courts (for they are generally involved in litigation, of which they are very fond) occupy the
bar rooms of the taverns in the country towns, for several days together, making one meal serve them each day, and sometimes two, and
even three days—but drinking whiskey without bounds during the same
time. The latter description of travellers—the merchants, lawyers, &c.
travel as in other countries—making use of and paying for their regular meals, beds, &c.

7.   1807—FEDERALISTS AND DEMOCRATS

〖 *The intensity of political differences in the back country amazed
Cuming, the Easterner.*

Politicks, throughout the whole of this country [western Pennsyl-
vania], seems to be the most irritable subject which can be discussed.
There are two ruling or prevailing parties; one, which styles itself
Federal, founded originally on the federal league or constitution which
binds the states to each other; in contradistinction to a party which
attempted to prevent the concurrence of the states to the present constitution, and after it was agreed to, made some fruitless attempts to
disorganize it, and was called *Antifederal.* The opposite party is one
which has since sprung up and styles itself the Democratick Republican. Since the federal constitution has been established, the first party
exists no longer except *in name. That* which assumes it, stickles for the
offices of government being executed with a high hand, and is therefore accused of aristocratick and even of monarchick sentiments by its

Cuming, *Sketches of a Tour to the Western Country,* in Thwaites, *Early Western Travels,* IV,
71–72.

opponents, who in their turn are termed factious, and disorganizers, by the federalists. They nickname each other *Aristocrats* and *Democrats,* and it is astonishing to what a height their mutual animosity is carried. They are not content with declaiming against each other in congress, or in the state legislatures, but they introduce the subject even at the bars of the judicial courts, and in the pulpits of the places of religious worship. In some places, the males who might otherwise be on terms of friendship with each other, are, merely on account of their diversity of sentiment on politicks, avowed and illiberal enemies; and the females carry the spirit of party into their coteries, so far as to exclude every female whose husband is of a different political opinion, however amiable, and ornamental to society she may be. The most illiberal opinions are adopted by each party, and it is sufficient with a federalist that another man is a republican, to pronounce him capable of every crime; while the republican takes care not to allow the federalist the smallest of the attributes of virtue.—Their *general* difference of opinion, at last becomes *particular,* and a mistaken point of honour frequently hurries the one or the other maniack into a premature grave.—The political wheel is kept in constant motion by those two parties, who monopolize it to themselves, to the exclusion of the moderate, well disposed, and best informed part of the community; who quietly pursue their several avocations, lamenting at, yet amused by the bickerings, disputes and quarrels of the turbulent and ambitious leaders of the parties, and their ignorant, prejudiced and obstinate tools—satisfied with the unexampled prosperity they enjoy as a people and a nation—and equally watchful perhaps to guard against tyranny or licentiousness, with the violent and avowed opponents of both.

8. *1803*—THE STARS AND STRIPES REPLACE THE TRICOLOR

⟪ *As the eighteenth century gave way to the nineteenth, Americans looked with foreboding to the vast province of Louisiana, ostensibly held by Spain, but actually, as they suspected, a possession of France. New Orleans, capital of the province, was the outlet for the produce of the Ohio and Mississippi River valleys. When the Spanish, in 1802, prohibited American citizens from depositing their goods there for reshipment on ocean-going vessels, President Jefferson sent a special envoy, James Monroe, to France with instructions to assist Robert R. Livingston, the American Minister, in restoring the right of deposit. The upshot was the unexpected purchase, from a Napoleon hard pressed for money, of all Louisiana.*

Late in December, 1803, the French prefect at New Orleans, Pierre-Clement Laussat, formally transferred the province to the

C. C. Robin, *Voyages dans l'interieur de la Louisiane* (Paris, 1807), II, 137–39. My translation. P.M.A.

*United States. C. C. Robin, a French naturalist who had come to
explore the country in the interest of his science, described the
ceremony.*

On the morning of the day of the retrocession of Louisiana to the
United States I proceeded to the city hall, where the respective com-
missioners were to play their parts. During the preliminary arrangements I strolled with the Prefect Laussat on the gallery which looks
out over the square. Our conversation turned on the consequences of
what was about to take place. The Prefect was deeply moved, and so
was I; but when he proclaimed, in a voice broken by emotion, that all
the French inhabitants of Louisiana were freed from their oath of
allegiance to France, that they now became American citizens, that new
oaths would link them to a new country—then unlooked-for sentiments,
unsuspected until that moment, overwhelmed me. What! I said to myself: this country which I have loved so much, to whose fostering
bosom I have always been true, to which I hold all that I value, which
holds all that I cherish, kindred and friends; this country, whose name
alone caresses my ear and arouses in me feelings truly noble—could it
cease to be mine? Could I cut the ties which unite me to France? Could
I suddenly become indifferent, even make her my enemy? Could I take
up arms against her? Could I cease to address my prayers to her?

Meanwhile I watched the French flag drop slowly, and that of the
United States ascend little by little. A French soldier takes the former,
folds it, and carries it in silence to the ranks. The American flag stops
at half-mast in spite of efforts to raise it, as if ashamed to take the
place of the banner to which it owed its glorious independence. An uneasy silence fell on all the spectators who filled the square, who crowded
the galleries and balconies and windows, and it was not until the flag
reached the top of the pole that huzzas broke from one particular group
who at the same time raised their hats. The cheers and salute made all
the more dismal the silence of the rest of the spectators; these were
the French and the Spanish, all deeply moved, but suppressing their
sighs and their tears.

9. *1805*—MERIWETHER LEWIS RECORDS TWO NARROW ESCAPES

❬ *Even before Louisiana was acquired, Thomas Jefferson had determined to find out the extent and nature of the vast territory that
stretched from the Mississippi to the Pacific. At his urging, in 1803,*

Reuben Gold Thwaites, Ed., *Original Journals of the Lewis and Clark Expedition, 1804–1806*
(New York, 1904), Vol. II, Part I, 33–36. In the interest of readability, slight changes have
been made in punctuation and capitalization.

Congress authorized an expedition to search out a route across the plains and mountains, make scientific observations, and establish friendly relations with the Indians. The purchase of Louisiana made these objectives even more important, and at the same time removed the possibility of interference by a foreign power.

To lead the party, made up mainly of regular army soldiers, Jefferson chose his private secretary, Meriwether Lewis, who in turn selected William Clark, a younger brother of George Rogers Clark, as co-commander. The expedition outfitted at the mouth of Wood River, opposite St. Louis, in the winter of 1803–04, and started up the Missouri by flatboat and keelboat in mid-May, 1804. By fall it had reached the Mandan villages about 150 miles east of the junction of the Missouri and the Yellowstone. There the men wintered. Shortly after resuming their westward march in the spring of 1805 several members of the party narrowly escaped death in an encounter with a bear. On the same day the expedition came within seconds of losing indispensable equipment when a sudden squall upset one of their pirogues, or dugout canoes. Meriwether Lewis, more concerned with making a record than with the niceties of spelling, described both incidents in his journal.

Tuesday, May 14th, 1805.

Some fog on the river this morning, which is a very rare occurrence. The country much as it was yesterday with this difference that the bottoms are somewhat wider; passed some high black bluffs. Saw immence herds of buffaloe today also elk deer wolves and antelopes. Passed three large creeks one on the stard. and two others on the lard.[1] side, neither of which had any runing water. Capt Clark walked on shore and killed a very fine buffaloe cow. I felt an inclination to eat some veal and walked on shore and killed a very fine buffaloe calf and a large woolf, much the whitest I had seen, it was quite as white as the wool of the common sheep. One of the party wounded a brown bear very badly, but being alone did not think proper to pursue him. In the evening the men in two of the rear canoes discovered a large brown bear lying in the open grounds about 300 paces from the river, and six of them went out to attack him, all good hunters. They took the advantage of a small eminence which concealed them and got within 40 paces of him unperceived. Two of them reserved their fires as had been previously conscerted, the four others fired nearly at the same time and put each his bullet through him, two of the balls passed through the bulk of both lobes of his lungs. In an instant this monster ran at them with open mouth. The two who had reserved their fires discharged

---

[1] The starboard and larboard sides. In landlubber language, the right and left sides.

their pieces at him as he came towards them. Boath of them struck him, one only slightly and the other fortunately broke his shoulder. This however only retarded his motion for a moment. The men unable to reload their guns took to flight, the bear pursued and had very nearly overtaken them before they reached the river. Two of the party betook themselves to a canoe and the others seperated and concealed themselves among the willows, reloaded their pieces, each discharged his piece at him as they had an opportunity. They struck him several times again but the guns served only to direct the bear to them. In this manner he pursued two of them seperately so close that they were obliged to throw away their guns and pouches and throw themselves into the river altho' the bank was nearly twenty feet perpendicular. So enraged was this anamal that he plunged into the river only a few feet behind the second man he had compelled [to] take refuge in the water, when one of those who still remained on shore shot him through the head and finally killed him. They then took him on shore and butchered him when they found eight balls had passed through him in different directions. The bear being old the flesh was indifferent, they therefore only took the skin and fleece, the latter made us several gallons of oil.

It was after the sun had set before these men come up with us, where we had been halted by an occurrence, which I have now to recappitulate, and which altho' happily passed without ruinous injury, I cannot recollect but with the utmost trepidation and horror; this is the upseting and narrow escape of the white perogue. It happened unfortunately for us this evening that Charbono was at the helm of this perogue, instead of Drewyer, who had previously steered her. Charbono cannot swim and is perhaps the most timid waterman in the world. Perhaps it was equally unluckey that Capt. C. and myself were both on shore at that moment, a circumstance which rarely happened; and tho' we were on the shore opposite to the perogue, were too far distant to be heard or to do more than remain spectators of her fate. In this perogue were embarked our papers, instruments, books, medicine, a great part of our merchandize and in short almost every article indispensibly necessary to further the views, or insure the success of the enterprize in which we are now launched to the distance of 2200 miles. Surfice it to say, that the perogue was under sail when a sudon squawl of wind struck her obliquely, and turned her considerably. The steersman allarmed, instead of puting her before the wind, lufted her up into it. The wind was so violent that it drew the brace of the squarsail out of the hand of the man who was attending it, and instantly upset the perogue and would have turned her completely topsaturva, had it not have been for the resistance made by the oarning [awning] against the water. In this situation Capt. C. and myself both fired our guns to attract the attention if possible of the crew and ordered the halyards to be cut and the sail hawled in, but they did not hear us. Such was their confusion and consternation at this moment, that they suffered the perogue to lye on her side for half a minute before they took the sail in, the perogue then wrighted but had filled within an inch of the gunwals. Charbono still crying to his god for mercy, had not yet recollected the rudder, nor could the repeated orders of the bowsman, Cruzat, bring him to his recollection untill he threatened to shoot him instantly if he did not take hold of the rudder and do his duty. The waves by this time were runing very high, but the fortitude resolution and good conduct of Cruzat saved her. He ordered 2 of the men to throw out the water with some kettles that fortunately were convenient, while himself and two others rowed her ashore, where she arrived scarcely above the water. We now took every article out of her and lay them to drane as well as we could for the evening, baled out the canoe and secured her. There were two other men beside Charbono on board who could not swim, and who of course must also have perished had the perogue gone to the bottom. While the perogue lay on her side, finding I could not be heard, I for a moment forgot my own situation, and involluntarily droped my gun, threw aside my shot pouch and was in the act of unbuttoning my coat, before I recollected the folly of the attempt I was about to make, which was to throw myself into the river and indevour to swim to the perogue. The perogue was three hundred yards distant the waves so high that a perogue could scarcely live in any situation, the water excessively could, and the stream rappid; had I undertaken this project therefore, there was a hundred to one but what I should have paid the forfit of my life for the madness of my project, but this had the perogue been lost, I should have valued but little. After having all matters arranged for the evening as well as the nature of circumstances would permit, we thought it a proper occasion to console ourselves and cheer the sperits of our men and accordingly took a drink of grog and gave each man a gill of sperits.

10. *1805*—LEWIS AND CLARK REACH THE PACIFIC

⟨ *On November 7, 1805, Clark and a detachment of men reached the Pacific, or thought they did. They may have been mistaken, for the mouth of the Columbia River is wide and hard to distinguish from the ocean. They were entitled, however, to rejoice at the successful end of a great adventure, even though a few more days would pass before they camped on what was unquestionably the Pacific's shore.*

William Clark, with spelling even more uncertain than Lewis's,

---

Thwaites, *Original Journals of the Lewis and Clark Expedition,* Vol. III, Part 2, 208–10. Again, slight changes have been made in punctuation and capitalization.

described the emotions of the party when they heard the breakers for the first time.

Nov. 7, 1805. A cloudy foggey morning. Some rain. We set out early, proceeded under the stard. [starboard] side under high ruged hills with steep assent, the shore boalt and rockey, the fog so thick we could not see across the river. Two canos of Indians met and returned with us to their village which is situated on the stard. side behind a cluster of marshey islands, on a narrow chanl. of the river through which we passed to the village of 4 houses. They gave us to eate some fish, and sold us fish, *wap pa to* roots, three dogs and 2 otter skins for which we gave fish hooks principally, of which they were verry fond. . . .

After delaying at this village one hour and a half we set out piloted by an Indian dressed in a salors dress, to the main chanel of the river. The tide being in we should have found much dificuelty in passing into the main chanel from behind those islands, without a pilot. A large marshey island near the middle of the river near which several canoes came allong side with skins, roots, fish &c. to sell, and had a temporey residence on this island. Here we see great numbers of water fowls about those marshey islands. Here the high mountainous countrey approaches the river on the lard [larboard] side, a high mountn. to the s. w. about 20 miles, the high mountans' countrey continue on the stard. side. About 14 miles below the last village and 18 miles of this day we landed at a village of the same nation. . . . We proceeded on about 12 miles below the village under a high mountaneous countrey on the stard. side, shore boald and rockey, and encamped under a high hill on the stard. side opposit to a rock situated half a mile from the shore, about 50 feet high and 20 feet deamieter. We with dificuelty found a place clear of the tide and sufficiently large to lie on and the only place we could get was on round stones on which we lay our mats. . . .

Great joy in camp. We are in view of the ocian (in the morning when fog cleared off just below last village, first on leaving this village, of Warkiacum) this great Pacific Octean which we been so long anxious to see, and the roreing or noise made by the waves brakeing on the rockey shores (as I suppose) may be heard distictly.

11.   *1806—*PIKE DESCRIBES THE PEAK THAT BEARS HIS NAME

(*Before Lewis and Clark returned from the Pacific another expedition headed for the southwestern part of Louisiana. On July 15, 1806, Lieutenant Zebulon M. Pike started west with a small party*

Milo M. Quaife, Ed., *The Southwestern Expedition of Zebulon M. Pike* (Chicago, R. R. Donnelley & Sons Co., 1925), 70–79.

of U. S. Regulars. Four months later the explorers came within sight of the Rampart Range of the Rockies. Pike could only describe the magnificent peak that bears his name, although he did ascend nearby Cheyenne Mountain. This record of his experiences comes from his own journal.

15th November, Saturday: Marched early. Passed two deep creeks and many high points of the rocks, also large herds of buffalo. At two o'clock in the afternoon I thought I could distinguish a mountain to our right, which appeared like a small blue cloud. Viewed it with the spy glass and was still more confirmed in my conjecture, yet only communicated it to Doctor Robinson, who was in front with me, but in half an hour they appeared in full view before us. When our small party arrived on the hill they with one accord gave three cheers to the Mexican mountains. Their appearance can easily be imagined by those who have crossed the Alleghanies; but their sides were whiter, as if covered with snow or a white stone. . . . They appear to present a natural boundary between the provinces of Louisiana and New Mexico, and would be a defined and natural boundary. . . .

17th November, Monday: Marched at our usual hour. Pushed [on] with an idea of arriving at the mountains, but found at night no visible difference in their appearance, from what we did yesterday. . . .

23d November, Sunday: Marched at ten o'clock. At one o'clock came to the third fork on the south side and encamped at night in the point of the grand forks.[1] As the river appeared to be dividing itself into many small branches, and of course must be near its extreme source, I concluded to put the party in a defensible situation and ascend the north fork, to the high point[2] of the blue mountain, which we conceived would be one day's march, in order to be enabled from its pinnacle to lay down the various branches and position of the country. Distance nineteen miles. Killed five buffalo.

24th November, Monday: Early in the morning cut down fourteen logs and put up a breast work five feet high on three sides and the other was thrown on the river. After giving the men necessary orders for their government during my absence, in case of our not returning, we marched at one o'clock with an idea of arriving at the foot of the mountain, but found ourselves obliged to take up our night's lodging under a single cedar, which we found in the prairie, without water and extremely cold. . . .

25th November, Tuesday: Marched early, with an expectation of ascending the mountain, but were only able to encamp at its base, after passing over many small hills covered with cedars and pitch-pines. . . .

---

[1] The site of the present city of Pueblo, Colorado.
[2] Pike's Peak.

165

26th November, Wednesday: Expecting to return to our camp that evening, we left all our blankets and provisions at the foot of the mountain. Killed a deer of a new species and hung his skin on a tree with some meat. We commenced ascending but found it very difficult, being obliged to climb up rocks, sometimes almost perpendicular; after marching all day we encamped in a cave without blankets, victuals, or water. We had a fine clear sky whilst it was snowing at the bottom. On the side of the mountain we found only yellow and pitch-pine. . . .

27th November, Thursday: Arose hungry, dry, and extremely sore from the inequality of the rocks on which we had lain all night, but were amply compensated for toil by the sublimity of the prospect below. The unbounded prairie was overhung with clouds, which appeared like the ocean in a storm; wave piled on wave and foaming, whilst the sky was perfectly clear where we were. Commenced our march up the mountain and in about one hour arrived at the summit of this chain. Here we found the snow middle deep; no sign of beast or bird inhabiting this region. The thermometer, which stood at 9° above zero at the foot of the mountain, here fell to 4° below zero. The summit of the Grand Peak,[3] which was entirely bare of vegetation and covered with snow, now appeared at the distance of fifteen or sixteen miles from us, and as high again as what we had ascended, and would have taken a whole day's march to have arrived at its base, when I believe no human being could have ascended to its pinnacle. This, with the condition of my soldiers, who had only light overalls on and no stockings and every way ill provided to endure the inclemency of the region, the bad prospect of killing anything to subsist on, with the further detention of two or three days which it must occasion, determined us to return. The clouds from below had now ascended the mountain and entirely enveloped the summit, on which rests eternal snow. We descended by a long deep ravine with much less difficulty than contemplated. Found all our baggage safe, but the provisions all destroyed. It began to snow and we sought shelter under the side of a projecting rock, where we all four made a meal on one partridge and a piece of deer's ribs the ravens had left us, being the first we had eaten in that forty-eight hours.

12. *1820*—CASS AND SCHOOLCRAFT ON THE UPPER MISSISSIPPI

⟦ *The expeditions of Lewis and Clark and Zebulon M. Pike gathered much information about the territory west of the Mississippi,*

Henry R. Schoolcraft, *Narrative Journal of Travels Through the Northwestern Regions of the United States* (Albany, 1821), 238–55.

[3] Pike's Peak, which Pike and his companions did not climb. They ascended near-by but lower Cheyenne Mountain.

but many years would pass before the region would be fully explored. One of the geographical facts that stubbornly resisted discovery was the source of the Mississippi River. Where did it rise? Pike thought he had reached the headwaters when he ascended the river a year before he started for the Southwest. Henry R. Schoolcraft, the explorer and scientist who accompanied Governor Lewis Cass of Michigan Territory in the summer of 1820, was equally certain of success. Both men were wrong, although Schoolcraft, a dozen years later, would finally identify Lake Itasca as the place where the great river originated.

In 1820, nevertheless, the members of the Cass expedition enjoyed all the thrills of discovery, and Schoolcraft wrote an eloquent account that not only expressed their feelings but also afforded a description of a region still far removed from civilization.

July 17, 1820. We left the fort at half past nine in the morning, in three canoes, manned by nineteen voyageurs and Indians, and provisioned for twelve days. Our party now, exclusive of the working men, consisted of Governor Cass, Dr. Wolcott, Capt. Douglass, Lieut. Mackay, Maj. Forsyth, and myself. The balance of the expedition—men, baggage, and canoes, was left at the Company's establishment. A mile from the fort we entered the mouth of Sandy Lake River, which discharges into the Mississippi, two miles below. Its course is winding, and near its junction with the Mississippi, it has a rapid where the water descends three feet in sixty yards. On entering the Mississippi, we found a strong current—reddish water, a little turbid—some snags and drifts—and alluvial banks, elevated from four to eight feet, bearing a forest of elm, maple, oak, poplar, pine, and ash. The elm predominates; maple and oak are common—pine, ash, and poplar, sparing. The river has a width of sixty yards, and the shores are skirted with bull rushes, folle avoine,[4] and tufts of willow. . . .

We encamped twenty miles above the sixth rapid at eight o'clock in the evening, having been eleven hours in our canoes, and progressed forty-six miles. . . . The river has received no tributary streams; no islands have been encountered, nor have any hills been seen, but the country is low, and swampy at a short distance from the river. . . .

July 18th . . . We embarked at five—the weather remained cloudy and misty. On ascending one mile, we passed Swan River, which enters, by a mouth of twenty yards wide, on the right shore. Loose rocks appear in the water at its mouth. . . . Thirteen leagues above we passed Rapid No. 7, where the water falls three feet in a hundred and fifty yards. Trout River enters six miles higher, on the right side. It is about

---

[4] Wild oats.

thirty feet wide at its mouth, but deep, and widens above. It originates in Trout Lake, and is connected with Swan River near its source. Prairie River is four miles above, and enters on the same side. It is ninety feet wide at its mouth—has a considerable rapid three miles above, but may be ascended with canoes, through an open prairie country, ninety miles. . . . We encamped on a sand bank, five hundred yards above its entrance, having progressed fifty-one miles. The current of the Mississippi River, this day, has been strong, and a number of snags and drifts have been encountered. . . . The general course of the river is west of north; it is very serpentine, and the curves short, seldom exceeding a mile—the width of the river has been less than yesterday, and may be computed to average forty yards. Tufts of willow, grass, and wild rice, skirt the water's edge. . . .

July 19th. The night was so cold that water froze upon the bottoms of our canoes, and they were encrusted with a scale of ice of the thickness of a knife blade. The thermometer stood at 36 at sun-rise. There was a very heavy dew during the night, and a dense fog in the morning. The forenoon remained cloudy and chilly. Six miles above our encampment we passed the eighth Rapid, where the water falls two feet in a hundred yards; and half a mile above, the ninth Rapid, which consists of a series of small rapids, extending a thousand yards, in the course of which, there is an aggregate fall of sixteen feet. Four miles above the termination of the ninth Rapid, we landed at the foot of the falls of Peckagama, where the river has a descent of twenty feet in three hundred yards. This forms an interruption to the navigation, and there is a portage around the falls of two hundred and seventy-five yards. The Mississippi, at this fall is compressed to eighty feet in width, and precipitated over a rugged bed of sandstone, highly inclined towards the northeast. . . . After passing the falls of Peck-agama, a striking change is witnessed in the character of the country. We appear to have attained the summit level of waters. The forests of maple, elm, and oak, cease, and the river winds in the most devious manner through an extensive prairie, covered with tall grass, wild rice, and rushes. This prairie has a mean width of three miles, and is bounded by ridges of dry sand, of moderate elevation, and covered sparingly with yellow pine. Sometimes the river washes close against one of these sand ridges—then turns into the centre of the prairie, or crosses to the opposite side; but nothing can equal its sinuosities—we move towards all points of the compass in the same hour—and we appear to be winding about in an endless labyrinth, without approaching nearer to the object in view. In one instance, we rowed nine miles by the windings of the stream, and advanced but one mile in a direct line. While sitting in our canoes, in the centre of this prairie, the rank growth of grass, rushes, &c. completely hid the adjoining forests from view, and it appeared as if we were lost in a boundless field of waving grass. Nothing was to be seen but the sky above, and the lofty fields of nodding grass, oats, and reeds upon each side of the stream. The monotony of the view can only be conceived by those who have been at sea—and we turned away with the same kind of interest to admire the birds, and water fowl, who have chosen this region, for their abode. The current of the river is gentle, its velocity not exceeding one mile per hour:—its width is about eighty feet. . . .

July 20th . . . We embarked at half past five; our route lay through a prairie country, similar in every respect to that yesterday passed. At the distance of ten miles we passed the mouth of Leech River, entering on the left. This is the main southwestern fork of the Mississippi, and is ascended about fifty miles, to its source, in Leech Lake, where the American fur company have an establishment. . . .

At the distance of thirty-five miles above Leech River, we entered Little Lake Winnipec, which is about five miles long, and three in width. The water is clear. Its shores are low and marshy, covered with rushes, spear grass, and wild rice, which in some places extend quite across the lake, giving it rather the appearance of a marsh. On passing through this, the river again assumes the size and general appearance it had below, for a distance of ten miles, when it opens into a spacious bay, which is the northeastern extremity of the Upper Lake Winnepec. We proceeded through this, and encamped on the north shore of the lake, at the mouth of Turtle Portage River. . . .

On passing through Little Lake Winnipec, we met a couple of Indian women in a canoe, being the first natives seen on the river, of whom our interpreter made enquiry as to the course of the river, and the nature of the country above. They manifested no alarm on our approach, and communicated what they knew frankly and without reserve. They had come down the river for the purpose of observing the state of the wild rice, and at what places it could be most advantageously gathered. None, however, was yet sufficiently ripe to admit of harvesting, but this precaution evinces a degree of care and foresight, which is not always found among savages. . . .

July 21st. We continued our journey at half past four o'clock in the morning. . . . We steered northwest across the bay, and entered the mouth of the Mississippi inlet, which we pursued up fifty miles to its origin, in Upper Red Cedar or Cassina Lake,[5] where we arrived at three o'clock in the afternoon. This may be considered the true source of the Mississippi River, although the greatest body of water is said to come down the Leech Lake Branch. The river between Lake Winnipec and Cassina Lake winds through a prairie-valley, a mile in width,

---

[5] Schoolcraft's own designation in honor of Governor Cass.

which is bounded by ridges of sandy land covered with yellow and white pine. The river pursues the same devious course, and its banks are overgrown with oats, rushes, and grass. Cassina Lake is about eight miles long by six in width, and presents to the eye a beautiful sheet of transparent water. . . .

Cassina Lake, the source of the Mississippi, is situated seventeen degrees north of the Balize on the Gulf of Mexico, and two thousand nine hundred and seventy-eight miles, pursuing the course of the river. Estimating the distance to Lake La Beesh, its extreme northwestern inlet at sixty miles, which I conclude to be within bounds, we have a result of three thousand and thirty-eight miles, as the entire length of this wonderful river, which extends over the surface of the earth in a direct line, more than half the distance from the Arctic Circle to the Equator. It is also deserving of remark, that its sources lie in a region of almost continual winter, while it enters the Ocean under the latitude of almost perpetual verdure; and at last, as if disdaining to terminate its career at the usual point of embouchure of other large rivers, has protruded its banks into the Gulf of Mexico, more than a hundred miles beyond any other part of the main. To have visited both the sources and the mouth of this celebrated stream, falls to the lot of few, *and I believe there is no person living, beside myself, of whom the remark can now be made.* On the 10th of July, 1819, I passed out of the mouth of the Mississippi in a brig bound for New-York, after descending it in a steam-boat from St. Louis, and little thinking I should soon revisit its waters; yet, on the 21st of July of the following year, I found myself seated in an Indian canoe, upon its source.

CHAPTER IX

THE WAR OF 1812

1811 – 1815

1. *1811*—BLOOD FLOWS ON TIPPECANOE CREEK

❲ *By the Treaty of Paris, in 1783, Great Britain recognized the independence of her American colonies. But she gave them up reluctantly, and soon proved that she would yield no more than she was compelled to. In violation of the terms of the treaty she kept garrisons for a dozen years at several western outposts—notably Niagara, Detroit, and Michilimackinac—and incited the Indians to harass the settlers who were crossing the Alleghenies. (The Americans were far from blameless. We had refused to pay debts owed to British merchants or to compensate Loyalists for the loss of their property. We had agreed to do both.)*

After the western posts were surrendered to the United States in accordance with Jay's Treaty, made in 1795, British officers in

---

Adam Walker, "A Journal of Two Campaigns of the Fourth Regiment of U. S. Infantry," *Indiana Historical Collections*, Vol. VII (Indianapolis, 1922), 700–02.

Canada continued to play on the anti-American feelings of the Indians. One of those who needed little encouragement was Tecumseh, who, with his brother, the Prophet, lived on the Wabash River near the mouth of the Tippecanoe. Tecumseh, alarmed at the advancing tide of white settlers, set out to form a confederacy of tribes to resist further encroachments on Indian lands. His activities convinced William Henry Harrison, Governor of Indiana Territory, that war with the Indians was inevitable. Harrison decided to strike first. In the fall of 1811 he advanced from Fort Harrison, where Terre Haute now stands, to the vicinity of the Prophet's town with a force of 1,000 men. In the absence of Tecumseh, the Prophet stirred the Indians to frenzy. The Battle of Tippecanoe resulted.

A soldier of the Fourth Regiment, U. S. Infantry, tells the story.

November 6th. When our spies, who had ventured near the Indian village, returned, and informed the Governor we were within a few miles of the Prophet's town—we were ordered to throw off our knapsacks, and be in preparation for an attack. We advanced about four miles to the edge of a piece of woods, when we were ordered to break off by companies, and advance in single lines; keeping a convenient distance from each other to enable us to form a line of battle, should necessity require it;—this was frequently done in the course of our advance toward the town, in consequence of the unevenness of the land, and the appearance of many favorable places for the enemy to attack us. In this manner we advanced very cautiously, until we came in sight of the Indian village, when we halted. The Indians appeared much surprised and terrified at our sudden appearance before their town; we perceived them running in every direction about the village, apparently in great confusion; their object however, was to regain in season their different positions behind a breast work of logs which encircled the town from the bank of the Wabash. A chief came out to the Governor, begging of him not to proceed to open hostilities; but to encamp with the troops for that night, and in the morning they solemnly promised to come into camp and hold a council, and they would agree to almost any terms the Governor might propose; expressing their earnest desire for peace without bloodshed—but the treacherous villains merely made this promise to gain sufficient time to put their infernal scheme in execution. The Governor enquired of the chief where a situation suitable for encamping might be found; being informed, he dispatched three or four officers to examine the ground, who returned with a favorable report of the place—which was a piece of narrow rising ground, covered with heavy timber, running some length into a marshy prairie, and about three-quarters of a mile northwest of the town. Here we encamped for the night, as near the form of a hollow-square as the nature of the ground would admit. Being cool, cloudy weather, we built large fires in front of our tents, to dry our clothing, cook our provisions, etc. The signal for the field officers to collect at the Governors marque was given; we were soon after ordered to lay with our cartridge boxes on, and our guns at our sides—and in case of an attack (as was always the order, while on the march), each man stepped five paces in front of his tent, which formed the line of battle.

On the morning of the 7th November, a few minutes before 4 o'clock, while we were enjoying the sleep so necessary to the repose of our wearied limbs—the attack commenced—when only a single gun was fired by the guard, and instantly we were aroused by the horrid yells of the savages close upon our lines.

The dreadful attack was received first by a company of regulars, under the command of Capt. Barton, and a company of militia, commanded by Capt. Geiger,—their men had not the least notice of the approach of the Indians until they were aroused by a horrid yell and a discharge of rifles at the very door of their tents; considerable confusion ensued in these two companies before they could be formed in any regular order; but notwithstanding the disorder this sudden attack created, the men were not wanting in their duty—they sprang from their tents and discharged their pieces upon the enemy, with great execution, and kept their ground good until relief could be brought them. The attack soon extended round to the right line, where the troops were formed in complete order, and the assaults of the savages were returned in full measure. One company of Indiana militia fell back, in great disorder, but after some arduous exertions of their officers, they were again rallied and fought with a spirit that evinced a determination to escape the odium of cowardice. The battle had now become general, every musket and rifle contributed its share to the work of carnage. A few Indians had placed themselves in an advantageous situation on the left of the front line, and being screened from our fire by some large oak trees, did great execution in our ranks. The small company of U. S. Riflemen, commanded by Lieut. Hawkins, were stationed within two rods of these trees, and received the heaviest of their fire, but maintained the position in a most gallant manner, although the company of militia on their left were giving way in great disorder. Major Daviess, with a small detachment of dragoons attempted to dislodge them; but failed in the attempt, and was himself mortally wounded. Capt. Snelling, of the regulars, soon after made a desperate charge at the head of his company, with success, losing one man, who was tomahawked by a wounded Indian. The Indians fell back, and for a short time, continued the action at a distance—here was some sharp shooting, as they had greatly the advantage, by the light afforded them from our fires, which could not be entirely extinguished. We were well supplied with buck shot cartridges, which were admirably calculated for an engagement of this nature. The savages were severely galled by the steady and well directed fire of the troops. When near day-break they made their last desperate effort to break our lines, when three cheers were given, and charge made by the 4th Regt. and a detachment of dragoons—they were completely routed and the whole put to a precipitate flight. They fled in all directions leaving us masters of the field which was strewn with the bodies of the killed and wounded. Some sharp-shooters of the militia, harrassed them greatly in their retreat, across the marshy prairie. The day was appropriated to the mournful duties of dressing the wounds of our unfortunate comrades, and burying the dead. To attempt a full and detailed account of this action, or portray to the imagination of the reader the horrors attendant on this sanguinary conflict, far exceeds my power of description—the awful yell of the savages, seeming rather the shriek of despair, than the shouts of triumph—the tremendous roar of musquetry—the agonizing screams of the wounded and dying, added to the shouts of the victors, mingling in tumultuous uproar, formed a scene that can better be imagined than described.

2. *1812*—THE INDIANS MASSACRE THE GARRISON OF FORT DEARBORN

❪ *Tippecanoe, though an American victory, had been costly. The people of the West, knowing that the British had encouraged Tecumseh and supplied him with arms, clamored for war. If the Indians were ever to be held in check, the British must be expelled from Canada.*

There were other sources of friction. On the continent of Europe, Great Britain was engaged in a life-and-death struggle with Napoleon, and neither the British nor the French paid much attention to the rights of neutrals. The United States had legitimate grievances against both nations, but hostility toward Great Britain was intensified by her practice of seizing American seamen and forcing them to serve in the royal navy. Many Americans, moreover, coveted a chance to take the Floridas from Spain, Britain's ally in her war against France.

In November, 1811, President Madison called Congress in special session and recommended that it prepare the country for war. Not until June 18, 1812, did the members make up their minds and adopt a declaration. During the seven months they had spent in debate

Nelly Kinzie Gordon, Ed., *The Fort Dearborn Massacre* (Chicago, 1912), 15–23.

*they had done little to place the nation on a war footing. American
weakness was soon revealed. The first disaster came at Chicago,
where Fort Dearborn had stood for a dozen years. Lieutenant Linai
T. Helm, second in command, lived to tell the story.*

Capt. Heald got the information of War being declared, and on the
8th of August got Gen. Hull's order to evacuate the Post of Fort Dearborn by the route of Detroit, or Fort Wayne, if practicable. This letter
was brought by a Potowautemie Chief Winnemeg, and he informed
Capt. Heald, through Kenzie, to evacuate immediately the next day,
if possible, as the Indians were hostile and that the troops should change
the usual routes to go to Fort Wayne. On the 12th August, Capt.
William Wells arrived from Fort Wayne with 27 Miamis, and after
a council being held by him with the tribes there assembled to amount
of 500 warriors 179 women and children. He after council declared
them hostile and that his opinion was that they would interrupt us on
our route. Capt. Wells enquired into the State of the arms, ammunition
and provisions. We had 200 stand of arms, four pieces of artillery,
6,000 lbs. of powder and a sufficient quantity of shot lead, etc. 3 months
provisions taken in Indian corn and all this on the 12th of August,
having prior to this expended 3 months provisions at least in the interval between the 7th and 12th of August, exclusive of this we had at
our command 200 head of horned cattle and 27 barrels of salt. After
this survey, Wells demanded of Capt. Heald if he intended to evacuate.
His answer was he would. Kenzie then, with Lt. Helm, called on Wells
and requested him to call on Capt. Heald and cause the ammunition
and arms to be destroyed, but Capt. Wells insisted on Kenzie and Helm
to join with him. This being done, Capt. Heald hesitated and observed
that it was not sound policy to tell a lie to an Indian; that he had
received a positive order from Gen. Hull to deliver up to those Indians
all the public property of whatsoever nature particularly to those Indians that would take in the Troops and that he could not alter it, and
that it might irritate the Indians and be the means of the destruction
of his men. Kenzie volunteered to take the responsibility on himself,
provided Capt. Heald would consider the method he would point out
a safe one, he agreed. Kenzie wrote an order as if from Genl. Hull,
and gave it into Capt. Heald. It was supposed to answer and accordingly was carried into effect. The ammunition and muskets were all
destroyed the night of the 13th. The 15th, we evacuated the Garrison,
and about one and half mile from the Garrison we were informed
by Capt. Wells that we were surrounded and the attack by the Indians
began about 10 of the clock morning. The men in a few minutes were,
with the exception of 10, all killed and wounded. The Ensign and
Surgeons Mate were both killed. The Capt. and myself both badly

wounded during the battle. I fired my piece at an Indian and felt confident I killed him or wounded him badly. I immediately called to the men to follow me in the pirara, or we would be shot down before we could load our guns. We had proceeded under a heavy fire about an hundred and five paces when I made a wheel to the left to observe the motion of the Indians and avoid being shot in the back, which I had so far miraculously escaped. Just as I wheeled I received a ball through my coat pocket, which struck the barrel of my gun and fell in the lining of my coat. In a few seconds, I received a ball in my right foot, which lamed me considerably. The Indians happened immediately to stop firing and never more renewed it. I immediately ordered the men that were able to load their guns and commenced loading for them that were not able. I now discovered Capt. Heald for the first time to my knowledge during the battle. He was coming from towards the Indians and to my great surprise they never offered to fire on him. He came up and ordered the men to form; that his intentions were to charge the body of Indians that were on the bank of the Lake where we had just retreated from. They appeared to be about 300 strong. We were 27, including all the wounded. He advanced about 5 steps and not at all to my surprise was the first that halted. Some of the men fell back instead of advancing. We then gained the only high piece of ground there was near. We now had a little time to reflect and saw death in every direction. At this time an interpreter from the Indians advanced towards us and called for the Captain, who immediately went to meet him (the interpreter was a half Indian and had lived a long time within a few yards of the fort and bound to Mr. Kinzie; he was always very friendly with us all). A chief by the name of Blackbird advanced to the interpreter and met the Captain, who after a few words conversation delivered him his sword, and in a few minutes returned to us and informed me he had offered 100 dollars for every man that was then living. He said they were then deciding on what to do. They, however, in a few minutes, called him again and talked with him some time, when he returned and informed me they had agreed if I and the men would surrender by laying down our arms they would lay down theirs, meet us half way, shake us by the hand as friends and take us back to the fort. I asked him if he knew what they intended doing with us then. He said they did not inform him. He asked me if I would surrender. The men were at this time crowding to my back and began to beg me not to surrender. I told them not to be uneasy for I had already done my best for them and was determined not to surrender unless I saw better prospects of us all being saved and then not without they were willing. The Captain asked me the second time what I would do, without an answer. I discovered the interpreter at this time running from the Indians towards us, and when he came in about 20 steps the

Captain put the question the third time. The Interpreter called out, "Lieut. don't surrender for if you do they will kill you all, for there has been no general council held with them yet. You must wait, and I will go back and hold a general council with them and return and let you know what they will do." I told him to go, for I had no idea of surrender. He went and collected all the Indians and talked for some time, when he returned and told me the Indians said if I would surrender as before described they would not kill any, and said it was his opinion they would do as they said, for they had already saved Mr. Kinzie and some of the women and children. This enlivened me and the men, for we well knew Mr. Kinzie stood higher than any man in that country among the Indians, and he might be the means of saving us from utter destruction, which afterwards proved to be the case. We then surrendered, and after the Indians had fired off our guns they put the Captain and myself and some of the wounded men on horses and marched us to the bank of the lake, where the battle first commenced. When we arrived at the bank and looked down on the sand beach I was struck with horror at the sight of men, women and children lying naked with principally all their heads off, and in passing over the bodies I was confident I saw my wife with her head off about two feet from her shoulders. Tears for the first time rushed in my eyes, but I consoled myself with a firm belief that I should soon follow her. I now began to repent that I had ever surrendered, but it was too late to recall, and we had only to look up to Him who had first caused our existence. When we had arrived in half a mile of the Fort they halted us, made the men sit down, form a ring around them, began to take off their hats and strip the Captain. They attempted to strip me, but were prevented by a Chief who stuck close to me. I made signs to him that I wanted to drink, for the weather was very warm. He led me off towards the Fort and, to my great astonishment, saw my wife sitting among some squaws crying. Our feelings can be better judged than expressed. They brought some water and directed her to wash and dress my wound, which she did, and bound it up with her pocket handkerchief. They then brought up some of the men and tommyhawked one of them before us. They now took Mrs. Helm across the river (for we were nearly on its banks) to Mr. Kinzie's. We met again at my fathers in the State of New York, she having arrived seven days before me after being separated seven months and one week. She was taken in the direction of Detroit and I was taken down to Illinois River and was sold to Mr. Thomas Forsyth, half brother of Mr. Kinzie's, who, a short time after, effected my escape. This gentleman was the means of saving many lives on the warring frontier. I was taken on the 15th of August and arrived safe among the Americans at St. Louis on the 14th of October.

3. *1812*—A COWARDLY COMMANDER SURRENDERS DETROIT

❨ *The day after the Fort Dearborn massacre General William Hull surrendered Detroit to General Brock, the British commander. Hull's incompetence and cowardice were apparent even to the enemy. This account was written by Thomas Vercheres de Boucherville, a French Canadian serving in the British army.*

Quite late in the afternoon he [General Brock] left Amherstburg with his regular troops and militia. . . . We soon reached the outskirts of Sandwich, directly opposite Springwells on the American side, and here we bivouacked, waiting for the artillery, which came up but did not halt. . . .

We on our part were inspected by the General before crossing to the opposite shore. While this was going on, the savages arrived in their bark canoes to the number of three hundred. According to custom they had spent the preceding night at Amherstburg dancing the war dance. It was an extraordinary spectacle to see all these aborigines assembled together at one time, some covered with vermillion, others with blue clay, and still others tattooed in black and white from head to foot. Their single article of clothing was a breechcloth, always worn when going to war. An European witnessing this strange spectacle for the first time would have thought, I truly believe, that he was standing at the entrance to hell, with the gates thrown open to let the damned out for an hour's recreation on earth! It was frightful, horrifying beyond expression. Accustomed as I was to seeing them on such occasions I could not but feel overcome, as though under the influence of some kind of terror which I was powerless to control.

Between seven and eight in the evening the crossing was effected at Springwells, General Brock leading, then Tecumseh with his tribes, Shawnee, Potawatomi, Ottawa, Sauteau, Sacs, and Winnebagoes following him. From the shore it must have been an impressive sight to see all those boats drawing off in perfect order and landing together on the other side. The debarkment was made without any confusion and there we remained till dark, the Indians surrounding the American garrison from the wooded side, the orders being to scale the fort at midnight with the ladders we had brought for the purpose.

Soon the bombs of the British began to burst. The balls were fired by our artillery stationed opposite Detroit and they fell like hail upon the town. The bombardment became ever fiercer; not for a single instant did the explosion of shells above and within the fort cease. The

"The Journal of Thomas Vercheres de Boucherville," in Milo M. Quaife, Ed., *War on the Detroit* (Chicago, R. R. Donnelley & Sons Co., 1940), 106–11.

terrific din was increased by the howls of the savages, impatient to take part in the combat. It was the first time I had ever witnessed the firing and effect of a bomb and I was deeply impressed.

All this terrible noise had so frightened General Hull that he dared make no reply to our bombardment, although he had everything at hand for his defense. More than three thousand men were under his orders, and cannon of every caliber, including some 24 pounders, were mounted advantageously against us. To tell the truth he lacked the capacity for vigorous action.

General Brock remained at our head, ready to advance when the moment came for an assault on the fort at the point of the bayonet, in conjunction with the savages. Thus we passed the whole night under arms. What was our surprise to see at dawn a white flag floating over the fort, and soon General Brock opened negotiations with the American commander. Their garrison surrendered to the little British army, which entered by the gate on the forest side of the fort while the Americans marched out through the river gate. Cries of "Long live the King," were heard on all sides, even from the Sandwich shore across the river. The band played Rule Britannia and the British flag was raised. It was nearly seven in the morning when we took possession of Detroit.

The American militia from Virginia and Kentucky embarked on small vessels bound for Cleveland and thence to their respective homes on parole. The action terminated, the Indians rode through the streets of the town in the fine carriages of the American officers. Soon every savage among them was dead drunk, either stretched out in the carriages or lying full length in the dust of the streets. Their joy would not have been complete if they had not presented this disgusting spectacle.

We found four officers dead in the messroom, their brains scattered over the walls. They had been killed by the bursting of a bomb during the bombardment. A number of soldiers had also been killed by shells and grapeshot. It seemed apparent that if the attack had been deferred until the next day, our soup would have been much hotter, for the garrison was on the eve of being reinforced by a body of regular troops commanded by Colonel McArthur, who was even then at the gates. But on learning that the flag had just been lowered he hastily retreated, swearing that if he had been present at the moment of capitulation he himself would have put a bullet through General Hull, who was a coward and more fit to be a cowherd than the commander of an army. He considered the surrender disgraceful, the place being so well supplied with men, ammunition, and especially with cannon. He regretted most the brass cannon which had been captured from Burgoyne, a general who resembled Hull in more ways than one, and who had made such a costly sacrifice for the British.

4. *1814*—THE BRITISH BURN WASHINGTON

⁅ *The crowning disgrace of the War of 1812 came in August, 1814, when British forces under General Robert Ross and Admiral Sir George Cockburn captured and burned much of the city of Washington. The British landed on Chesapeake Bay, easily routed the poorly organized and badly led militia who opposed them at Bladensburg, Maryland, and made their way unhindered to the capital, from which President Madison and other government officials had fled in a hurry. A British officer, George R. Glieg, wrote a lively account of the bloodless and farcical conquest.*

While the two brigades which had been engaged, remained upon the field to recover their order, the third, which had formed the reserve, and was consequently unbroken, took the lead, and pushed forward at a rapid rate towards Washington.

As it was not the intention of the British government to attempt permanent conquests in this part of America; and as the General was well aware that, with a handful of men, he could not pretend to establish himself, for any length of time, in an enemy's capital, he determined to lay it under contribution, and to return quietly to the shipping. . . .

Such being the intention of General Ross, he did not march the troops immediately into the city, but halted them upon a plain in its immediate vicinity, whilst a flag of truce was sent in with terms. But whatever his proposal might have been, it was not so much as heard; for scarcely had the party bearing the flag entered the street, than they were fired upon from the windows of one of the houses, and the horse of the General himself, who accompanied them, killed. . . . All thoughts of accommodation were instantly laid aside; the troops advanced forthwith into the town, and having first put to the sword all who were found in the house from which the shots were fired, and reduced it to ashes, they proceeded, without a moment's delay, to burn and destroy every thing in the most distant degree connected with government. In this general devastation were included the Senate-house, the President's palace, an extensive dock-yard and arsenal, barracks for two or three thousand men, several large store-houses filled with naval and military stores, some hundreds of cannon of different descriptions, and nearly twenty thousand stand of small arms. There were also two or three public rope-works which shared the same fate, a fine frigate pierced for sixty guns, and just ready to be launched, several gun-brigs and armed schooners, with a variety of gun-boats and small craft.

George Robert Glieg, *The Campaigns of the British Army at Washington and New Orleans* (London, 1821), 124-32.

The powder magazines were of course set on fire, and exploded with a tremendous crash, throwing down many houses in their vicinity, partly by pieces of the walls striking them, and partly by the concussion of the air; whilst quantities of shot, shell, and hand-grenades, which could not otherwise be rendered useless, were thrown into the river. . . .

Had the arm of vengeance been extended no farther, there would not have been room given for so much as a whisper of disapprobation. But, unfortunately, it did not stop here; a noble library, several printing offices, and all the national archives were likewise committed to the flames, which, though no doubt the property of government, might better have been spared. . . .

While the third brigade was thus employed, the rest of the army, having recalled its stragglers, and removed the wounded into Bladensburg, began its march towards Washington. Though the battle was ended by four o'clock, the sun had set before the different regiments were in a condition to move, consequently this short journey was performed in the dark. The work of destruction had also begun in the city, before they quitted their ground; and the blazing of houses, ships, and stores, the report of exploding magazines, and the crash of falling roofs, informed them, as they proceeded, of what was going forward. You can conceive nothing finer than the sight which met them as they drew near to the town. The sky was brilliantly illumined by the different conflagrations; and a dark red light was thrown upon the road, sufficient to permit each man to view distinctly his comrade's face. . . .

I need scarcely observe, that the consternation of the inhabitants was complete, and that to them this was a night of terror. So confident had they been of the success of their troops, that few of them had dreamt of quitting their houses, or abandoning the city; nor was it till the fugitives from the battle began to rush in, filling every place as they came with dismay, that the President himself thought of providing for his safety. That gentleman, as I was credibly informed, had gone forth in the morning with the army, and had continued among his troops till the British forces began to make their appearance. Whether the sight of his enemies cooled his courage or not, I cannot say, but, according to my informer, no sooner was the glittering of our arms discernible, than he began to discover that his presence was more wanted in the senate than with the army; and having ridden through the ranks, and exhorted every man to do his duty, he hurried back to his own house, that he might prepare a feast for the entertainment of his officers, when they should return victorious. For the truth of these details, I will not be answerable; but this much I know, that the feast was actually prepared, though, instead of being devoured by American officers, it went to satisfy the less delicate appetites of a party of English soldiers. When the detachment, sent out to destroy Mr. Maddison's house, entered his dining parlour, they found a dinner-table spread, and covers laid for forty guests. Several kinds of wine, in handsome cut-glass decanters, were cooling on the side-board; plate-holders stood by the fire-place, filled with dishes and plates; knives, forks and spoons, were arranged for immediate use; in short, every thing was ready for the entertainment of a ceremonious party. Such were the arrangements in the dining-room, whilst in the kitchen were others answerable to them in every respect. Spits, loaded with joints of various sorts, turned before the fire; pots, saucepans, and other culinary utensils, stood upon the grate; and all the other requisites for an elegant and substantial repast, were exactly in a state which indicated that they had been lately and precipitately abandoned.

You will readily imagine, that these preparations were beheld, by a party of hungry soldiers, with no indifferent eye. An elegant dinner, even though considerably over-dressed, was a luxury to which few of them, at least for some time back, had been accustomed; and which, after the dangers and fatigues of the day, appeared peculiarly inviting. They sat down to it, therefore, not indeed in the most orderly manner, but with countenances which would not have disgraced a party of aldermen at a civic feast; and having satisfied their appetites with fewer complaints than would have probably escaped their rival *gourmands,* and partaken pretty freely of the wines, they finished by setting fire to the house which had so liberally entertained them. . . .

At day-break next morning, the light brigade moved into the city, while the reserve fell back to a height, about half a mile in the rear. Little, however, now remained to be done, because every thing marked out for destruction, was already consumed. Of the senate-house, the President's palace, the barracks, the dock-yard, &c. nothing could be seen, except heaps of smoking ruins; and even the bridge, a noble structure upwards of a mile in length, was almost wholly demolished. There was, therefore, no farther occasion to scatter the troops, and they were accordingly kept together as much as possible on the Capitol hill.

5. *1812*—THE CONSTITUTION VANQUISHES THE GUERRIÈRE

❲ *Fortunately for the country, the Americans were not always as inept as they were at Detroit and Washington. They recaptured Detroit, won the Battle of the Thames (on Canadian soil), and fought well at Chippewa, Lundy's Lane, and Fort Erie. But it was on the sea that they proved their prowess most clearly. None of the naval duels of the war aroused more patriotic fervor than the first one: the engagement between the* CONSTITUTION *and the* GUERRIÈRE,

Bruce Grant, *Isaac Hull, Captain of Old Ironsides* (Chicago, 1947), 394–97.

fought 750 miles off the coast of Massachusetts. Captain Isaac Hull,
reporting the victory to the Secretary of the Navy, did not mention
the incident that gave his ship immortality. That occurred when a
seaman, watching a shot from the GUERRIÈRE *bounce off the* CON-
STITUTION'S *stout oak hull, sang out: "Huzza, her sides are made*
of iron!" From that moment she became "Old Ironsides." A symbol
of national pride that the American people have never been willing
to part with, "Old Ironsides" rides today, as she has for more than
fifty years, in Boston harbor.

U. S. FRIGATE CONSTITUTION
OFF BOSTON LIGHT August 28th 1812

SIR,

I have the Honour to inform you that on the 19th inst. at 2 P.M.
being in Latitude 41 42 and Longitude 55 48 with wind from the Northward, and the Constitution under my command, Steering to the S.S.W.
a sail was discovered from the Mast head bearing E. by S. or E.S.E.
but at such a distance that we could not make out what she was. All
sail was immediately made in chace, and we soon found we came
fast up with the chace, so that at 3 P.M. we could make her out to be a
Ship on the Starboard tack close by the wind under easy sail. At ½
past 3 P.M. closing very fast with the chace could see that she was a
large Frigate. At ¾ past 3 the Chace backed her maintopsail, and lay
by on the Starboard tack. I immediately ordered the light sails taken
in, and the Royal yards sent down, took two reefs in the topsails, hauled
up the foresail and mainsail and got all clear for action. After all was
clear, the Ship was ordered to be kept away for the Enemy, on hearing
of which the Gallant crew gave three cheers, and requested to be laid
close alongside the chace. As we bore up she hoisted an English Ensign
at the Mizen Gaff, another in the Mizen Shrouds, and a Jack at the
Fore, and MizentopGallant Mast heads. At 5 Minutes past 5 P.M. as
we were running down on her weather quarter She fired a Broadside
but without effect the Shot all falling short. She then wore and gave
us a broadside from her Larboard Guns, two of which shot struck us
but without doing any injury. At this time finding we were within
gunshot, I ordered the Ensign hoisted at the Mizen Peak and a Jack at
the Fore and MizentopGallantmast head, and a Jack bent ready for
hoisting at the Main. The Enemy continued wearing, and manouvering
for about ¾ of an hour, to get the wind of us. At length finding that
she could not she bore up to bring the wind on the quarter and run
under her topsails, and Gib. Finding that we came up very slow, and
were receiving her shot without being able to return them with effect,
I ordered the Main top Gallant Sail set, to run up alongside of her.

At 5 Minutes past 6 P.M. being alongside, and within less than Pistol
Shot, we commenced a very heavy fire from all our Guns, loaded with

round, and grape, which done great Execution, so much so that in less than fifteen minutes from the time, we got alongside, his Mizen Mast went by the board, and his Main Yard in the slings and the Hull and Sails very much injured, which made it difficult for them to manage her. At this time the Constitution had received but little damage, and having more sail set than the Enemy She Shot ahead. On seeing this I determined to put the helm to Port, and oblige him to do the same, or suffer himself to be raked by our getting across his Bows. On our Helm being put to Port the Ship came to, and gave us an opportunity of pouring in upon his Larboard Bow several Broadsides, which made great havock amongst his men on the forecastle and did great injury to his forerigging and sails. The Enemy put his Helm to Port, at the time we did, but his Mizen Mast being over the Quarter, prevented her coming to, which brought us across his Bows, with his Bowsprit over our Stern. At this Moment I determined to board him, but the instant the Boarders were called for that purpose, his Foremast and Mainmast went by the board, and took with them the Gibboom, and every other Spar except the Bowsprit. On seeing the Enemy totally disabled, and the Constitution received but little injury, I ordered the Sails filled, to hawl off, and repair our damages and return again to the action, not Knowing whether the Enemy had struck, or not. We stood off for about half an hour, to repair our Braces, and such other rigging as had been shot away, and wore around to return to the Enemy. It being now dark, we could not see whether she had any colours flying or not, but could discover that she had raised a Small flag Staff or Jury Mast forward. I ordered a Boat hoisted out and sent Lieutenant Reed on board as a———to see whether she had surrendered or not, and if she had to see what assistance she wanted, as I believed she was sinking. Lieutenant Reed returned in about twenty minutes, and brought with him James Richard Dacres Esq. Commander of his Britannic Majesty's Frigate the Guerriere, which Ship had surrendered to the United States Frigate Constitution. Our Boats were immediately hoisted out, and sent for the Prisoners, and were kept at work bringing them and their Baggage on board, all night. At daylight we found the Enemy's Ship a perfect Wreck, having many shot holes between wind and water, and about Six feet of the Plank below the Bends taken out by our round Shot, and her upperworks so shattered to pieces, that I determined to take out the sick and wounded as fast as possible and set her on fire, as it would be impossible to get her into Port.

At 3 P.M. all the Prisoners being out, Mr. Reed was ordered to set fire to her in the Store Rooms, which he did, and in a very short time she blew up. I want words to convey to you the Bravery, and Gallant conduct, of the Officers and the crew under my command during the action. I can therefore only assure you, that so well directed was the fire of the Constitution, and so closely kept up, that in less than thirty minutes, from the time we got alongside of the Enemy (one of their finest Frigates) she was left without a Spar Standing, and the Hull cut to pieces, in such a manner as to make it difficult to keep her above water, and the Constitution in a State to be brought into action in two hours. Actions like these speak for themselves which makes it unnecessary for me to say any thing to Establish the Bravery and Gallant conduct of those that were engaged in it. Yet I cannot but make you acquainted with the very great assistance I received from that valuable Officer Lieutenant Morris in bringing the Ship into action, and in working her whilst alongside the Enemy, and I am extremely sorry to state that he is badly wounded, being shot through the Body. We have yet hopes of his recovery, when I am sure he will receive the thanks and gratitude of his Country, for this and the many Gallant acts he has done in its Service.

Were I to name any particular Officer as having been more useful than the rest, I should do them great injustice. They all fought bravely and gave me every possible assistance, that I could wish. I am extremely sorry to State to you the loss of Lieutenant Bush of Marines. He fell at the head of his men in getting ready to board the Enemy. In him our Country has lost a valuable and Brave Officer. After the fall of Mr. Bush, Lieut. Contee of the corps took command of the Marines, and I have pleasure in saying his conduct was that of a Brave, good Officer, and the Marines behaved with great coolness, and courage during the action, and annoyed the Enemy very much whilst she was under our Stern. Enclosed I have the Honour to forward you a list of Killed, and Wounded, on board the Constitution, and a list of Killed, and Wounded on board the Enemy, with a List of her crew and a Copy of her Quarter Bill, also a report of the damages the Constitution received in the Action.

> I have the honour to be
> With very great Respect,
> Sir, Your Obedient Servant,
> ISAAC HULL.

THE HONBLE. PAUL HAMILTON
Secretary of the Navy, Washington.

6. *1813*—"WE HAVE MET THE ENEMY; AND THEY ARE OURS!"

⟨ *On the morning of September 10, 1813, an indifferent little fleet under Oliver Hazard Perry met a British squadron off Put-in-Bay near the western tip of Lake Erie. The two fleets drew up in single*

The Naval Monument, Containing Official and Other Accounts of All the Battles between the Navies of the United States and Great Britain during the Late War (Boston, 1830), 84–86, 92–93.

lines and commenced firing shortly before noon. Three hours later the British, in spite of their advantage in having guns of longer range than the Americans, struck their colors.

Perry announced the victory in a historic message to General William Henry Harrison and in a longer report to the Secretary of the Navy; another officer supplied an account of Perry's conduct that the commander was too modest to include.

U. S. BRIG NIAGARA, OFF THE WESTERN SISTER,

DEAR GENERAL,   LAKE ERIE, Sept. 10, 1813.

We have met the enemy; and they are ours! 2 ships, 2 brigs, 1 schooner, and 1 sloop.

Yours with great respect and esteem,

Gen. HARRISON.   O. H. PERRY.

U. S. SCHOONER ARIEL, PUT-IN-BAY,

SIR,   September 13, 1813.

IN my last I informed you that we had captured the enemy's fleet on this lake. I have now the honour to give you the most important particulars of the action. On the morning of the 10th instant, at sunrise, they were discovered from Put-in-Bay, where I lay at anchor with the squadron under my command. We got under way, the wind light at S. W. and stood for them. At 10 A.M. the wind hauled to S. E. and brought us to windward: formed the line and bore up. At 15 minutes before 12, the enemy commenced firing; at 5 minutes before 12, the action commenced on our part. Finding their fire very destructive, owing to their long guns, and its being mostly directed at the *Lawrence,* I made sail and directed the other vessels to follow for the purpose of closing with the enemy. Every brace and bow-line being shot away, she became unmanageable, notwithstanding the great exertions of the sailing master. In this situation she sustained the action upwards of 2 hours within cannister distance, until every gun was rendered useless, and the greater part of her crew either killed or wounded. Finding she could no longer annoy the enemy, I left her in charge of Lieut. Yarnall, who I was convinced, from the bravery already displayed by him, would do what would comport with the honour of the flag. At half past two, the wind springing up, Capt. Elliott was enabled to bring his vessel, the *Niagara,* gallantly into close action: I immediately went on board of her, when he anticipated my wish by volunteering to bring the schooners which had been kept astern by the lightness of the wind, into close action. It was with unspeakable pain, that I saw, soon after I got on board the *Niagara,* the flag of the *Lawrence* came down, although I was perfectly sensible that she had been defended to the last, and that to have continued to make a show of resistance would have been a wanton sacrifice of the remains of her brave crew. But the enemy was not able to take possession of her, and circumstances soon permitted her flag again to be hoisted.

At 45 minutes past 2, the signal was made for "close action." The *Niagara* being very little injured, I determined to pass through the enemy's line, bore up and passed ahead of their two ships and a brig, giving a raking fire to them from the starboard guns, and to a large schooner and sloop from the larboard side at half pistol shot distance. The smaller vessels at this time having got within grape and cannister distance, under the direction of Capt. Elliott, and keeping up a well directed fire, the two ships, a brig and a schooner surrendered, a schooner and sloop making a vain attempt to escape. . . .

> Very respectfully, I have the honour to be,
> Sir, your obedient servant,

Hon. WILLIAM JONES,   O. H. PERRY.
   Sec'y of the navy.

October 7, 1813.

Had I been able, I should before now have sent you some particulars of the action of the memorable 10th of September. As we have not many letter writers in our squadron, the public will have to put up with the Commodore's 'round, unvarnished tale;' which however is very well told. All the fault I find with it is, that he himself is too much in the back ground.

In no action fought [in] this war has the conduct of the commanding officer been so conspicuous or so evidently decisive of the fate of the battle, as in this. When he discovered that nothing further could be done in the *Lawrence,* he wisely removed to the *Niagara,* and by one of the boldest and most judicious manœuvres ever practised, decided the contest at once. Had the *Niagara* shared the fate of the *Lawrence,* it was his intention to have removed to the next best vessel, and so on as long as one of his squadron continued to float. The enemy saw him put off, and acknowledge that they fired a broadside at him. With his usual gallantry he went off standing up in the stern of the boat; but the crew insisted on his sitting down. The enemy speak with admiration of the manner in which the *Lawrence* bore down upon them. She continued her course so long and so obstinately, that they thought we were going to board them. They had a great advantage in having long guns. Many of our men were killed on the birth deck and in the steerage, after they were taken below to be dressed—Midshipman Laub was of this number. One shot went through the light room, and knocked the snuff of the candle into the magazine—the gunner happened to see it immediately, and extinguished it with his hand: 2 shot passed through the magazine; 2 through the cabin; 3 or 4 came into the ward room—but I believe only one went quite through, and that passed a few inches over the surgeon's head as he sat in the cockpit. Our short guns lodged their shot in the bulwarks of the *Detroit;* where a number of them now remain. Her bulwarks however were vastly superiour to ours, being of oak and very thick. Many of their grape shot came through ours. They acknowledge that they threw combustible matter on board of us, which set our sails and rigging on fire in several places. I am clearly of opinion, that they were better manned than we were. They had a much greater number—they had veteran troops—their men were all well. We had as motley a crew as ever went into action; and our vessels looked like hospital ships.

During the whole of the action the most complete order prevailed on board the *Lawrence.* There was no noise, no bustle, no confusion. As fast as the men were wounded they were taken below and replaced by others. The dead remained where they fell until the action was over. Capt. Perry exhibited that cool, collected, dignified bravery, which those acquainted with him would have expected.—His countenance all the time was just as composed as if he had been engaged in ordinary duty. As soon as the action was over he gave all his attention to the securing of the prisoners and to the wounded on both sides. Capt. Barclay declared to one of our officers, several days after the action, that Capt. Perry had done himself immortal honour by his humanity and attention to the wounded prisoners. The action was fought on Friday— we got into harbour next day. On Sunday all the officers on both sides, who fell, were buried on South Bass Island, at Put-in-Bay, with the honours of war.

7. *1815*—JACKSON ROUTS THE BRITISH AT NEW ORLEANS

(*At New Orleans, on January 8, 1815, an American army under Andrew Jackson won the most complete victory of the war.*

In the fall of 1814 a British fleet brought a veteran army under Sir Edward Packenham to the mouth of the Mississippi. After defeating a small American naval force on Lake Borgne, the British marched overland to the Mississippi a few miles below New Orleans. There they faced a hastily assembled force consisting mainly of Louisiana militia and volunteers from Kentucky and Tennessee. The British attacked. In less than half an hour they lost more than 2,000 men; the Americans lost seventy-one.

"A Contemporary Account of the Battle of New Orleans," *The Louisiana Historical Quarterly,* Vol. IX, No. 1, January, 1926, 11–15.

Ironically, the battle was fought two weeks after a treaty ending the war had been signed at Ghent.

Col. Smiley, from Bardstown, was the first one who gave us orders to fire from our part of the line; and then, I reckon, there was a pretty considerable noise. There were also brass pieces on our right, the noisiest kind of varmints, that began blaring away as hard as they could, while the heavy iron cannon, toward the river, and some thousands of small arms, joined in the chorus and made the ground shake under our feet. Directly after the firing began, Capt. Patterson, I think he was from Knox County, Kentucky, but an Irishman born, came running along. He jumped upon the brestwork and stooping a moment to look through the darkness as well as he could, he shouted with a broad North of Ireland brogue, "shoot low, boys! shoot low! rake them— rake them! They're comin' on their all fours!"

The official report said the action lasted two hours and five minutes, but it did not seem half that length of time to me. It was so dark that little could be seen, until just about the time the battle ceased. The morning had dawned to be sure, but the smoke was so thick that every thing seemed to be covered up in it. Our men did not seem to apprehend any danger, but would load and fire as fast as they could, talking, swearing, and joking all the time. All ranks and sections were soon broken up. After the first shot, every one loaded and banged away on his own hook. Henry Spillman did not load and fire quite so often as some of the rest, but every time he did fire he would go up to the brestwork, look over until he could see something to shoot at, and then take deliberate aim and crack away. Lieut. Ashby was as busy as a nailor and it was evident that, the River Raisin was uppermost in his mind all the time. He kept dashing about and every now and then he would call out, with an oath, "We'll pay you now for the River Raisin! We'll give you something to remember the River Raisin!"[1] When the British had come up to the opposite side of the brestwork, having no gun, he picked up an empty barrel and flung it at them. Then finding an iron bar, he jumped up on the works and hove that at them.

At one time I noticed, a little on our right, a curious kind of a chap named Ambrose Odd, one of Captain Higdon's company, and known among the men by the nickname of "Sukey," standing coolly on the top of the brestworks and peering into the darkness for something to shoot at. The balls were whistling around him and over our heads, as thick as hail, and Col. Slaughter coming along, ordered him to come down. The Colonel told him there was policy in war, and that he was exposing

---

[1] An American defeat on the Raisin River in southeastern Michigan. After the battle, which took place on January 22, 1813, the defeated Americans were shamefully massacred by the Indian allies of the British.

himself too much. Sukey turned around, holding up the flap of his old broad brimmed hat with one hand, to see who was speaking to him, and replied: "Oh! never mind Colonel—here's Sukey—I don't want to waste my powder, and I'd like to know how I can shoot until I see something?" Pretty soon after, Sukey got his eye on a red coat, and, no doubt, made a hole through it, for he took deliberate aim, fired and then coolly came down to load again.

During the action, a number of the Tennessee men got mixed with ours. One of them was killed about five or six yards from where I stood. I did not know his name. A ball passed through his head and he fell against Ensign Weller. I always thought, as did many others who were standing near, that he must have been accidently shot by some of our own men. From the range of the British balls, they could hardly have passed over the brestwork without passing over our heads, unless we were standing very close to the works, which were a little over brest high, and five or six feet wide on the top. This man was standing a little back and rather behind Weller. After the battle, I could not see that any of the balls had struck the oak tree lower than ten or twelve feet from the ground. Above that height it was thickly peppered. This was the only man killed near where I was stationed.

It was near the close of the firing. About the time that I observed three or four men carrying his body away or directly after, there was a white flag raised on the opposite side of the brestwork and the firing ceased.

The white flag, before mentioned, was raised about ten or twelve feet from where I stood, close to the brestwork and a little to the right. It was a white handkerchief, or something of the kind, on a sword or stick. It was waved several times, and as soon as it was perceived, we ceased firing. Just then the wind got up a little and blew the smoke off, so that we could see the field. It then appeared that the flag had been raised by a British Officer wearing epaulets. It was told he was a Major. He stepped over the brestwork and came into our lines. Among the Tennesseeans who had got mixed with us during the fight, there was a little fellow whose name I do not know; but he was a cadaverous looking chap and went by that of Paleface. As the British Officer came in, Paleface demanded his sword. He hesitated about giving it to him, probably thinking it was derogatory to his dignity, to surrender to a private all over begrimed with dust and powder and that some Officer should show him the courtesy to receive it. Just at that moment, Col. Smiley came up and cried, with a harsh oath, "Give it up—give it up to him in a minute." The British Officer quickly handed his weapon to Paleface, holding it in both hands and making a very polite bow.

A good many others came in just about the same time. Among them I noticed a very neatly dressed young man, standing on the edge of the brestwork, and offering his hand, as if for some one to assist him. He appeared to be about nineteen or twenty years old, and, as I should judge from his appearance, was an Irishman. He held his musket in one hand, while he was offering the other. I took hold of his musket and set it down, and then giving him my hand, he jumped down quite lightly. As soon as he got down, he began trying to take off his cartouch box, and then I noticed a red spot of blood on his clean white under jacket. I asked him if he was wounded, he said that he was and he feared pretty badly. While he was trying to disengage his accouterments, Capt. Farmer came up, and said to him, "Let me help you my man!" The Captain and myself then assisted him to take them off. He begged us not to take his canteen, which contained his water. We told him we did not wish to take anything but what was in his way and cumbersome to him. Just then one of the Tennesseeans, who had run down to the river, as soon as the firing ceased, for water, came along with some in a tin coffee-pot. The wounded man observed him, asked if he would please give him a drop. "O! Yes," said the Tenneessean, "I will treat you to anything I've got." The young man took the coffee-pot and swallowed two or three mouthfuls out of the spout. He then handed back the pot, and in an instant we observed him sinking backward. We eased him down against the side of a tent, when he gave two or three gasps and was dead. He had been shot through the brest.

On the opposite side of the brestwork there was a ditch about ten feet wide, made by the excavation of the earth, of which the work was formed. In it, was about a foot or eighteen inches of water, and to make it the more difficult of passage, a quantity of thornbush had been cut and thrown into it. In this ditch a number of British soldiers were found at the close under the brestwork, as a shelter from our fire. These, of course, came in and surrendered.

When the smoke had cleared away and we could obtain a fair view of the field, it looked, at the first glance, like a sea of blood. It was not blood itself which gave it this appearance but the red coats in which the British soldiers were dressed. Straight out before our position, for about the width of space which we supposed had been occupied by the British column, the field was entirely covered with prostrate bodies. In some places they were laying in piles of several, one on the top of the other. On either side, there was an interval more thinly sprinkled with the slain; and then two other dense rows, one near the levee and the other towards the swamp. About two hundred yards off, directly in front of our position, lay a large dapple gray horse, which we understood to have been Packenham's.

Something about half way between the body of the horse and our brestwork there was a very large pile of dead, and at this spot, as I was afterward told, Packenham had been killed; his horse having staggered off to a considerable distance before he fell. I have no doubt that I could not have walked on the bodies from the edge of the ditch to where the horse was laying, without touching the ground. I did not notice any other horse on the field.

When we first got a fair view of the field in our front, individuals could be seen in every possible attitude. Some laying quite dead, others mortally wounded, pitching and tumbling about in the agonies of death. Some had their heads shot off, some their legs, some their arms. Some were laughing, some crying, some groaning, and some screaming. There was every variety of sight and sound. Among those that were on the ground, however, there were some that were neither dead nor wounded. A great many had thrown themselves down behind piles of slain, for protection. As the firing ceased, these men were every now and then jumping up and either running off or coming in and giving themselves up.

Among those that were running off, we observed one stout looking fellow, in a red coat, who would every now and then stop and display some gestures toward us, that were rather the opposite of complimentary. Perhaps fifty guns were fired at him, but as he was a good way off, without effect. "Hurra, Paleface! load quick and give him a shot. The infernal rascal is patting his butt at us!" Sure enough, Paleface rammed home his bullet, and taking a long sight, he let drive. The fellow, by this time, was from two to three hundred yards off, and somewhat to the left of Packenham's horse. Paleface said as he drew sight on him and then run it along up his back until the sight was lost over his head, to allow for the sinking of the ball in so great a distance, and then let go. As soon as the gun cracked, the fellow was seen to stagger. He ran forward a few steps, and then pitched down on his head, and moved no more. As soon as he fell, George Huffman, a big stout Dutchman, belonging to our Company, asked the Captain if he might go and see where Paleface hit him. The Captain said he didn't care and George jumping from the brestwork over the ditch, ran over the dead and wounded until he came to the place where the fellow was lying. George rolled the body over until he could see the face and then turning round to us, shouted at the top of his voice, "Mine Gott! he is a nagar!" He was a mulatto and he was quite dead. Paleface's ball had entered between the shoulders and passed out through his brest.

CHAPTER X

YOUNG AMERICA

1816 – 1850

1. *1816*—TIMOTHY FLINT'S KEELBOAT RIDES OUT A STORM

❰ *With the end of the War of 1812 the people of the United States moved westward as never before. New states came into the Union: Indiana in 1816, Illinois in 1818, Missouri in 1821. Settlers and travelers crowded the roads and floated down the rivers on any kind of craft that would carry them. Timothy Flint, a Congregational missionary from Massachusetts, chose a keelboat to take his family from Cincinnati to St. Charles, Missouri, in the spring of 1816. The trip did not lack excitement.*

Our keel-boat was between eighty and ninety feet in length, was fitted up with a small but comfortable cabin, and carried seventeen tons. It was an extremely sultry afternoon when we embarked. . . . Nothing

Timothy Flint, *Recollections of the Last Ten Years* (Boston, 1826), 80–82.

could exceed the grandeur of the vegetable kingdom on the banks of the broad and beautiful Ohio. The magnificent beeches, cotton-trees, and sycamores, had developed all the richness of their foliage. The shrubs and trees were enlivened with the glittering plumage of their feathered tenants, and were "prodigal of harmony." The river, full almost to the summit of its banks, swept along an immense volume of water, and its aspect had nothing in common with the clean and broad sand-bars and shallow waters of the channel down which we descended in autumn. We found the current, too, had more than twice the rapidity. We could not tire in extending our sight to the farthest stretch of vision, over a surface of forest, clothed with a depth of verdure, with a richness of foliage, and a grandeur of size and height, that characterize the forest bottoms at this point of the Ohio.

We commenced this trip, like that of our first embarkation on the Ohio, with the most cheering auspices. We experienced in a couple of hours, what has so often been said and sung of all earthly enjoyments, how near to each other are the limits of happiness and trouble. Banks of thunder-clouds lowered in the horizon, when we left Cincinnati. They gathered over us, and a violent thunder-storm ensued. We had not time to reach the shore before it burst upon us, attended with strong gusts of wind. The gale was too violent for us to think of landing on a bluff, and rock-bound shore. We secured, as well as we could, the open passage into midship, and made arrangements for scooping out the water, which the boat took in from the waves. We had some ladies passengers on board, whose screams added to the uproar without. I was exposed to the storm on the deck, ready occasionally to assist the "patron," as he is called, of the boat, whenever he found himself unable, from the violence of the wind, to manage the helm. The peals of thunder were incessant, and the air was in a blaze with the flashes of lightning. We frequently saw them apparently dart into the river. The storm continued to rage with unremitting fury, for more than an hour. Such storms, to a frail keel-boat, loaded like ours to the water's edge, are always dangerous, and sometimes fatal. The patron, who had been for many years in this employment, and who had been, as he said, boat-wrecked half a dozen times, kept, indeed, perfectly cool. But his countenance manifested great anxiety. We weathered the storm, however, with no other inconvenience than getting drenched with rain, and hearing the frequent and earnest assertions of our passengers, that they would never expose themselves to the danger of such a storm again. . . . But, as the atmosphere brightened, as happens to beings so dependent upon external nature for the tone of our minds, our thoughts began to brighten, and our strength and courage for pursuing our journey were renewed. We landed in the evening, near the mansion of General Harrison, and were most hospitably received by him.

2. 1836—"FIFTEEN MILES ON THE ERIE CANAL"

❡ *After 1825, when the Erie Canal was finished, the canal boats, slow as they were, carried thousands of passengers annually. Thomas S. Woodcock, a New York engraver, described the accommodations he enjoyed between Schenectady and Buffalo in the late spring of 1836.*

We arrived at this place [Schenectady, New York] at ½ past 10. From the cars we proceeded to enter our names for the Packet Boat. These boats are about 70 feet long, and with the exception of the Kitchen and bar, is occupied as a Cabin. The forward part being the ladies' Cabin, is seperated by a curtain, but at meal times this obstruction is removed, and the table is set the whole length of the boat. The table is supplied with every thing that is necessary and of the best quality with many of the luxuries of life. On finding we had so many passengers, I was at a loss to know how we should be accommodated with berths, as I saw no convenience for anything of the kind, but the Yankees, ever awake to contrivances, have managed to stow more in so small a space than I thought them capable of doing. The way they proceed is as follows—The Settees that go the whole length of the Boat on each side unfold and form a cot bed. The space between this bed and the ceiling is so divided as to make room for two more. The upper berths are merely frames with sacking bottoms, one side of which has two projecting pins, which fit into sockets in the side of the boat. The other side has two cords attached one to each corner. These are suspended from hooks in the ceiling. The bedding is then placed upon them, the space between the berths being barely sufficient for a man to crawl in, and presenting the appearance of so many shelves. Much apprehension is always entertained by passengers when first seeing them, lest the cords should break. Such fears are however groundless. The berths are allotted according to the way bill, the first on the list having his first choice, and in changing boats the old passengers have the preference. The first Night I tried an upper berth, but the air was so foul that I found myself sick when I awoke. Afterwards I chose an under berth and found no ill effects from the air. These Boats have *three* Horses, go at a quicker rate, and have the preference in going through the locks, carry no freight, are built extremely light, and have quite Genteel Men for their Captains, and use *silver* plate. The distance between Schenectady and Utica is 80 Miles, the passage is $3.50, which includes board. There are other Boats called Line Boats that carry at a cheaper rate, being found for ⅔ of the price mentioned. They are larger

Deoch Fulton, Ed., *New York to Niagara, 1836: The Journal of Thomas S. Woodcock* (New York, New York Public Library, 1938), 8–9.

Boats, carry freight, have only two horses, and consequently do not go as quickly, and moreover have not so select a company. Some boats go as low as 1 cent per Mile, the passengers finding themselves.

The Bridges on the Canal are very low, particularly the old ones. Indeed they are so low as to scarcely allow the baggage to clear, and in some cases actually rubbing against it. Every Bridge makes us bend double if seated on anything, and in many cases you have to lie on your back. The Man at the helm gives the word to the passengers: "Bridge," "*very* low Bridge," "the lowest in the Canal," as the case may be. Some serious accidents have happened for want of caution. A young English Woman met with her death a short time since, she having fallen asleep with her head upon a box, had her head crushed to pieces. Such things however do not often occur, and in general it affords amusement to the passengers who soon imitate the cry, and vary it with a command, such as "All Jackson men bow down." After such commands we find few aristocrats.

3. *1835*—ELLEN BIGELOW MAKES "A VERY GOOD TRIP" FROM BUFFALO TO CHICAGO

❲ *When the Great Lakes were open those who could afford the fare traveled to the West by ship rather than overland. Steamers had operated on the upper lakes since 1818, but sailing ships continued to draw full complements of passengers. They might not blow up, as the steamers had a habit of doing, but, as Ellen Bigelow discovered, they offered thrills of other kinds. Ellen was a young woman of nineteen on her way from Massachusetts to join her parents at Peoria, Illinois.*

At sunrise, Saturday, May 2nd, we entered Buffalo, and to our dismay, the lake was covered as far as the eye could see with solid ice. By the advice of Mr. L., we went to the "Mansion House," where Dr. Harding left us and sallied forth to determine what could be done. He returned with the news that he had secured a passage for us on board the Brig *Illinois,* Captain Wagstaff, which would be the first vessel out of port, and that we must establish ourselves on board in the afternoon. . . .

The *Illinois* is the largest vessel on the lake. . . . Freight was taken to the extent of what she would bear, consequently the deck was so crowded with bags, boxes and barrels of every description, that no rest could be found even for the sole of a foot. The cabin, if possible, was more disagreeable still. We were gathered together from every quarter

Ellen Smith to her aunt, June 27, 1835, in *Journal of the Illinois State Historical Society,* July, 1929, 335–53.

of the earth, men, women and children, talking, laughing, crying, screaming and scolding. Such a bedlam I am sure was never seen before. Persons applied for passage till the cabins and staterooms were completely filled, and room was then made among the freight in the hold, where about 30 people were stowed away. . . . Our vessel lay at the wharf for days from the time we entered it, and a more hateful scrape I never got into. . . .

Several steamboats were injured in the fruitless attempt to get through the ice. The *Ohio* tried it, broke both paddles and so damaged her engine that three days were required to repair it. The second effort was more successful. A channel was formed through which the vessels could pass. The steamers *Thomas Jefferson, Ohio, Gov. Marcy* and *Charles Townsend,* brigs *Illinois* and *Indiana,* schooners *Huron, Michigan* and *Barker* immediately hoisted sail, and Friday, May 8th, with a strong northeasterly wind we left Buffalo. Our brig was a first-rate sailor. She dashed gallantly through the ice, cleared it all before her, passed every vessel, and in one hour's time was fairly upon the broad bosom of the lake. The wind continued steady and the water smooth, till Saturday morning, when it commenced blowing very severely. The sea ran high and the vessel pitched and tossed incessantly. The consequence was, of course, that we were all dreadfully seasick. Captain Wagstaff persuaded us to leave our berths and go on deck, in the hope that the air would relieve us. About a dozen others were our companions in misery, and the different positions chosen with the peculiar expression which distinguished each face would have been a grand study for a painter.

We stayed on deck till it began to storm violently, when we retreated to our berths. Dr. H. had as much as he could do to go from one patient to another, administering ether, laudanum and divers other specifics for seasickness. Towards night, the wind lulled a little and we were all flattering ourselves with the hope of rest, when about 10 o'clock to our great horror, the vessel struck a rock. Great alarm was excited, but the waves were running high and soon took us off. All betook ourselves again to our beds, and save myself, were soon soundly sleeping. A fit of foreboding would not suffer me to close my eyes. My fears were shortly realized. About 12 o'clock all were awakened by a loud shout from the cook that we were going to the bottom, and sure enough, there was little doubt of it, for one moment sufficed to convince us that we were already there. The vessel had grounded upon a rocky shoal and every wave made her quiver and shake like one with the ague. We remained there about an hour, and an hour of greater confusion and fright I never passed.

The cabin was crowded with half dressed beings of every size, sex and color. Deputations were dispatched every few minutes to ascertain the state of things, but very little comfort could be obtained from their contradictory reports.

Thus we sat in fear and trembling till the deck load was thrown overboard, when the cheerful voice of an old Irish sailor apprized us that the vessel was off. Had the brig been an old one, she must have received much injury from the strain to which she was exposed, but being entirely new, the damage sustained was only a splintering of the keel beneath her bows. The accident resulted from no want of skill in our captain, who was a most perfect master of his profession. . . .

We reached Detroit Monday, and found it more of a place than I expected. We were obliged to anchor 20 miles from Detroit, as we were in the neighborhood of flats, which could be passed only by daylight. The only channel through which a vessel could pass was so narrow that it is requisite to point it out by stakes, and as its location varies with change of seasons, it is necessary that they should be often moved. This duty it seems was neglected by the revenue officers, and by following the channel of a former season, we were soon brought hard aground.

The schooner *Michigan* directly in our wake, went to windward of us, and stuck fast alongside, a circumstance at which we all rejoiced, wicked though it might be. We were less lonely in consequence of it than we should otherwise have been, and beside that our captain had laid a wager with the master of the *Michigan* that he would be in Chicago first, and we were all anxious he should win.

Much labor was required to heave the vessel off, by carrying out the anchor, but as all finite things have an end, it was at last accomplished.

We had hardly proceeded a mile before we were in the same scrape again, and by the time we had extricated ourselves, the wind died away and we were obliged to anchor.

Setting sail the next day, the vessel had proceeded a few miles, when a sudden blow of wind took the sails flat aback, whirled her off her course, and we were fast aground again. . . .

At the mouth of the River St. Claire, is the entrance to Lake Huron. The waters of Superior, Michigan and Huron have here their outlet, less than half a mile in width, and the current is consequently very rapid, seven and a half miles an hour. Very few vessels can pass without the aid of a steamboat unless they have a strong breeze. We had just given up all hopes of proceeding when a steamboat hove in sight, which proved to be the *General Gratiot,* coming out expressly to tow us up the Rapids. We were immediately lashed to their side, and the brig *Indiana,* with which we were in company, mate and exact counterpart of our vessel, was lashed to the other side. A wind very opportunely sprung up to aid us on the way, and we passed Fort Gratiot with all sails set and flying colors in compliment to the troops paraded in front of the barracks. Both vessels carried an unusual quantity of canvas in proportion to their burden, and filled as it was in addition to the steamboat, we stemmed the current most bravely and were soon separated from the *General Gratiot* and alone upon Lake Huron. . . .

We went speedily and prosperously through the Straits of Mackinaw, down Lake Michigan and anchored at Chicago Friday forenoon, May 24th, just 14 days from the time we left Buffalo, which, considering the divers perils we encountered and the delay occasioned by getting aground upon the flats, foul winds, etc., may be set down as a very good trip.

4. *1832*—"STEAMBOAT ROUND THE BEND"

❡ *Timothy Flint had foreseen in 1816 that the steamboat would soon drive all other forms of transportation from the rivers. When Charles J. Latrobe, an Englishman, went down the Ohio and up the Mississippi in 1832 the steamboat not only monopolized passenger traffic; it also had come to offer the most luxurious accommodations available to travelers anywhere. But even those accommodations, Latrobe found, did not include all comforts.*

State-rooms are not always to be had by gentlemen, as they are commonly found to be attached to the ladies' cabin alone—but in case they are unoccupied they may be secured, and your position is so far more than ordinarily a favoured one, as you have private access to them by the outward gallery. Otherwise it must be conceded that nothing is omitted that the known ingenuity of this people can contrive, to render the berths in the main cabin as tidy and ornamental in appearance by day, and as secluded and convenient by night as circumstances permit of. They are so arranged, that when you retire to rest, the thick curtains with their vallance can slide forward upon brass rods, two or three feet from the berth itself, and thus form a kind of draped dormitory for you and your companion.

About an hour before the time appointed for breakfast, after the broom has been heard performing its duty for some time,—a noisy bell rung vociferously at the very porches of your ear, as the domestic marches from one end of the cabin to the other, gives notice that the hour of rising has arrived, and it is expected that every one will obey it and be attired in such time as to allow the berths to be arranged, and the whole cabin put in its day-dress, before the breakfast, which like all the other meals is set out in the gentlemen's cabin, is laid upon the

Charles J. Latrobe, *The Rambler in North America* (London, 1836), I, 288–96.

table. In vain you wish to indulge in a morning doze and thus to cut short the day; every moment your position becomes more untenable. Noises of all kinds proceed from without. You persevere—shut your eyes from the bright light which glares upon you through the little square window which illumines your berth, and your ears to all manner of sounds. Suddenly your curtains are drawn unceremoniously back, the rings rattle along the rods, and you see your place of concealment annihilated and become a part of the common apartment, while the glistening face and bright teeth of the black steward are revealed, with eyes dilated with well-acted surprise, as he says, "Beg pardon! Colonel; thought him war up: breakfast almost incessantly on de table." He retrogrades with a bow, half-closing the curtains; but you have no choice, rise you must. Happy he, whose foresight has secured to him all the enjoyment of the luxury of his own clean towels, as none but the disagreeable alternative of drying his person by the heat of the stove, can be the fate of him who has not done this. As to making use of the common articles, hung up for the accommodation of some thirty citizens in rotation, no one need blush at being termed fantastically delicate in avoiding that. . . .

During the interval which elapses between your being thus unceremoniously ousted from your quarters and forced to begin the day, and the ringing of the breakfast-bell, you may walk forward to the boiler-deck, and satisfy yourself as to the progress which has been made during the hours of darkness; or, if you choose to follow the custom of the country, and the example of a great majority of the passengers, you may linger in the antichamber opposite the bar, and take the glass of wine and bitters, which the prevalence of that common complaint of the United States, dyspepsia, finds a bad apology for. . . .

But I have anticipated breakfast. . . . The table is spread with substantials, both in profusion and variety; and considerable impatience is generally observable to secure places, as it frequently happens that the number of cabin passengers is greater than can be seated with comfort at the table, however spacious. The Steward, or his assistant, after many a considerate glance at his preparations, to see that all is right, goes to the ladies' cabin, and announces breakfast—an announcement which is generally followed by their appearance. They take their places at the upper end of the table, and then, and not till then, the bell gives notice that individuals of the rougher sex may seat themselves. The meal I leave to your lively imagination to picture. . . . You might imagine that the beings engaged in it were for the time, part of the engine, which is sighing and working underneath at the rate of one hundred strokes in the minute, so little does their occupation admit of interruption. There is little or no conversation, excepting of the monosyllabic and ejaculatory kind which is absolutely necessary; and instead of the social hour, during which in other lands, the feast of the body is often found to be compatible with the feast of the soul,—you spend, in fact, an uneasy ten minutes, in which the necessary act of eating is certainly stript of all the graces. . . . Woe to the poor gentleman of habitually slow and careful mastication. . . . Woe to the epicure, whose eye might well else dilate at the sight of the well-covered board, and its crowd of western delicacies. Woe to the hungry gallant, whose chivalry cannot suffer him to enjoy a morsel till he has seen the ladies well-served and attended through the meal. Small credit gets the good-natured soul who deftly carves for all, and ever carves in vain. There is no quarter given. Many of the males will leave the table the moment they are satisfied—the ladies leave it as soon as they well can; —and then in come the bar-keepers, engineers, carpenter, pilot, and inferior officers of the boat: the table again groans with its load of plenty, and is again stripped and forsaken, to be a third time the scene of feasting for the black steward and coloured servants of both sexes. During these latter scenes of the same act of the same play, I need hardly press you to quit the cabin for the seats on the boiler-deck, or, still better, for the hurricane-deck above.

In fine warm weather, more especially during your first voyage in the West, both curiosity and comfort will lead you to spend by far the greater part of your time in the open air; where the gentle breeze, freshened by the rapid motion of the boat, and the magical manner in which scenes rise and disappear, will always cheer you, while with conversation and reading you while away the monotonous hours of a long morning. . . . It is possible that you may meet with a few well-bred, intelligent travellers—that you may be both in good health and good-humour—that the general run of the voyage may be prosperous and without accidents or detention. . . . But you may chance to fare otherwise, and for the sake of illustration we will suppose that the very contrary is the case in almost every particular; that heated in body and mind by confinement and disappointment, you are peevish as a peahen; that the society is decidedly ill-bred and vicious—that the boat jars so with every stroke of the piston that you cannot write a line—further that you have no books—the cabin is crowded—the machinery wants constant repair—the boilers want scraping. This hour you get upon a sand-bank, the next you are nearly snagged—drift-wood in the river breaks your paddles—the pilot is found to be a toper—the engineer an ignoramus—the steward an economist—the captain a gambler—the black firemen insurgent, and the deck passengers riotous. This moment you have too little steam, and hardly advance against the current; another, too much, and the boat trembles with the tremendous force exerted by the power that impels her. To complete your dismay, the captain agrees to take a disabled steamboat, or a couple of heavily-laden barges, in tow, for the next four or five hundred miles. Instead of accomplished females, such as at another time you might have as fellow-passengers, we will suppose the ladies' cabin to be tenanted by a few grotesque, shy, uninteresting beings, never seen but when marshalled in by the steward to their silent and hurried repast, and never heard, but, when shut up in their own apartment, a few sounds occasionally escape through the orifice of the stove-pipe, making up in strength for what they want in sweetness.

What are you to do in such cases? You may lounge in the anti-chamber, and watch the progress of stimulating at the bar—you may re-enter the cabin and strive to get possession of a chair and a gleam from the stove; or you may ascend to a small apartment found in some steamboats, called Social Hall, in other words a den of sharpers and blacklegs, where from morning to night the dirty pack of cards are passed from hand to hand. For the rest, you may study human nature in many forms, and one thing will not fail to strike you, and that is the marvellous rapidity with which the meals follow, and the world of important preparation which passes before your eyes for an end so little worthy of it.

5. *1833*—TRAVELING ON THE NATIONAL ROAD

❨ *The canals, rivers, and lakes might offer the traveler or settler the most comfortable means of reaching the West, but ice closed them for several months each year. Besides, they led to a limited number of destinations, and thousands of emigrants could not afford to pay fares. So the roads, too, were thick with men—and women and children also. Of all the roads, the most traveled was the National Road, which extended from Cumberland, Maryland, to Wheeling, and finally, through Columbus, Ohio, to Vandalia, Illinois.*

Charles Fenno Hoffman, one of the first of the country's professional men of letters, traveled over a stretch of the National Road in 1833, when he toured the Old Northwest on horseback.

About thirty miles from Wheeling we first struck the national road. It appears to have been originally constructed of large round stones, thrown without much arrangement on the surface of the soil, after the road was first levelled. These are now being ploughed up, and a thin layer of broken stones is in many places spread over the renovated surface. I hope the roadmakers have not the conscience to call this Macadamizing.[1] It yields like snow-drift to the heavy wheels which

Charles Fenno Hoffman, *A Winter in the West* (New York, 1835), I, 47–48, 42–46.
[1] A process of building crushed-stone roads, named for the Scotchman, John L. McAdam, who devised it about 1815.

traverse it, and the very best parts of the road that I saw are not to be compared with a Long Island turnpike. Two-thirds indeed of the extent traversed were worse than any artificial road I ever travelled, except perhaps the log causeways among the new settlements in northern New-York. The ruts are worn so broad and deep by heavy travel, that an army of pigmies might march into the bosom of the country under the cover they would afford. . . .

There is one feature, however, in this national work which is truly fine,—I allude to the massive stone bridges which form a part of it. They occur, as the road crosses a winding creek, a dozen times within twice as many miles. They consist either of one, two, or three arches; the centre arch being sprung a foot or two higher than those on either side. Their thick walls projecting above the road, their round stone buttresses, and carved key-stones combine to give them an air of Roman solidity and strength. They are monuments of taste and power that will speak well for the country when the brick towns they bind together shall have crumbled in the dust. . . .

Apropos of pedestrians, though your true western man generally journeys on horseback, yet one meets numbers of the former on this side [the western side] of the Alleghanies. They generally have a tow-cloth knapsack, or light leathern valise, hung across their backs, and are often very decently dressed in a blue coat, gray trousers, and round hat. They travel about forty miles a day.

The horsemen almost invariably wear a drab great-coat, fur cap, and green cloth leggins; and in addition to a pair of well-filled saddle-bags, very often have strapped to their crupper a convenience the last you would expect to find in the wardrobe of a backwoodsman, videlicit, an umbrella. The females of every rank, in this mountainous country, ride in short dresses. They are generally wholly unattended, and sometimes in large parties of their own sex. The saddles and housings of their horses are very gay; and I have repeatedly seen a party of four or five buxom damsels, mounted on sorry-looking beasts, whose rough hides, unconscious of a currycomb, contrasted oddly enough with saddles of purple velvet, reposing on scarlet saddle-cloths, worked with orange-coloured borders. I have examined the manufacture of these gorgeous trappings at the saddleries in some of the towns in passing. They much resemble those which are prepared in New-York for the South American market, and are of a much cheaper make, and far less durable, than those which a plainer taste would prefer. Still the effect of these gay colours, as you catch a glimpse of them afar off, fluttering through the woods, is by no means bad. They would show well in a picture, and be readily seized by a painter in relieving the shadows of a sombre landscape.

But by far the greatest portion of travellers one meets with, not to mention the ordinary stage-coach passengers, consists of teamsters and the emigrants. The former generally drive six horses before their enormous wagons—stout, heavy-looking beasts, descended, it is said, from the famous draught horses of Normandy. They go about twenty miles a day. The leading horses are often ornamented with a number of bells suspended from a square raised frame-work over their collars, originally adopted to warn these lumbering machines of each other's approach, and prevent their being brought up all standing in the narrow parts of the road.

As for the emigrants, it would astonish you to witness how they get along. A covered one-horse wagon generally contains the whole worldly substance of a family consisting not unfrequently of a dozen members. The tolls are so high along this western turnpike, and horses are comparatively so cheap in the region whither the emigrant is bound, that he rarely provides more than one miserable Rosinante to transport his whole family to the far west. The strength of the poor animal is of course half the time unequal to the demand upon it, and you will, therefore, unless it be raining very hard, rarely see anyone in the wagon, except perhaps some child overtaken by sickness, or a mother nursing a young infant. The head of the family walks by the horse, cheering and encouraging him on his way. The good woman, when not engaged as hinted above, either trudges along with her husband, or, leading some weary little traveller by the hand far behind, endeavours to keep the rest of her charge from loitering by the wayside. The old house-dog—if not chained beneath the wagon to prevent the half-starved brute from foraging too freely in a friendly country—brings up the rear. I made acquaintance with more than one of these faithful followers in passing, by throwing him a biscuit as I rode by, and my canine friend, when we met at an inn occasionally afterward, was sure to cultivate the intimacy. Sometimes these invaluable companions give out on the road, and in their broken-down condition are sold for a trifle by their masters. I saw several fine setters which I had reason to suspect came into the country in this way; and the owner of a superb brindled greyhound which I met among the mountains, told me that he had bought him from an English emigrant for a dollar. He used the animal with great success upon deer, and had already been offered fifty dollars for him.

The hardships of such a tour must form no bad preparatory school for the arduous life which the new settler has afterward to enter upon. Their horses, of course, frequently give out on the road; and in companies so numerous, sickness must frequently overtake some of the members. Nor should I wonder at serious accidents often occurring with those crank conveyances among the precipices and ravines of the mountains. At one place I saw a horse, but recently dead, lying beneath a steep, along the top of which the road led; and a little farther in advance, I picked up a pocketbook with some loose leaves floating near the edge of the precipice.

6. *1842—"LOOK OUT FOR THE LOCOMOTIVE!"*

《 *Before many years the locomotive would eclipse all other means of travel in popularity. In the beginning, however, it made slow progress. As late as 1842, when Charles Dickens toured the United States, railroads lacked the comforts one could find even on the slow-moving canal boats. Dickens' somewhat supercilious description—he made himself exceedingly unpopular on this American visit —applied to a trip from Boston to Lowell.*

There are no first and second class carriages as with us; but there is a gentlemen's car and a ladies' car: the main distinction between which is that in the first, everybody smokes; and in the second, nobody does. As a black man never travels with a white one, there is also a negro car; which is a great blundering clumsy chest, such as Gulliver put to sea in, from the kingdom of Brobdignag. There is a great deal of jolting, a great deal of noise, a great deal of wall, not much window, a locomotive engine, a shriek, and a bell.

The cars are like shabby omnibusses, but larger: holding thirty, forty, fifty, people. The seats, instead of stretching from end to end, are placed crosswise. Each seat holds two persons. There is a long row of them on each side of the caravan, a narrow passage up the middle, and a door at both ends. In the centre of the carriage there is usually a stove, fed with charcoal or anthracite coal; which is for the most part red-hot. It is insufferably close; and you see the hot air fluttering between yourself and any other object you may happen to look at, like the ghost of smoke.

In the ladies' car, there are a great many gentlemen who have ladies with them. There are also a great many ladies who have nobody with them: for any lady may travel alone, from one end of the United States to the other, and be certain of the most courteous and considerate treatment everywhere. The conductor or check-taker, or guard, or whatever he may be, wears no uniform. He walks up and down the car, and in and out of it, as his fancy dictates; leans against the door with his hands in his pockets and stares at you, if you chance to be a stranger; or enters into conversation with the passengers about him. A great many newspapers are pulled out, and a few of them are read. Everybody talks to you, or to anybody else who hits his fancy. If you are an Englishman, he expects that that railroad is pretty much like an English

Charles Dickens, *American Notes* (London, 1842), I, 145–52.

railroad. If you say "No," he says "Yes?" (interrogatively), and asks in what respect they differ. You enumerate the heads of difference, one by one, and he says "Yes?" (still interrogatively) to each. Then he guesses that you don't travel faster in England; and on your replying that you do, says "Yes?" again (still interrogatively), and, it is quite evident, don't believe it. After a long pause he remarks, partly to you, and partly to the knob on the top of his stick, that "Yankees are reckoned to be considerable of a go-ahead people too"; upon which *you* say "Yes," and then *he* says "Yes" again (affirmatively this time); and upon your looking out of the window, tells you that behind that hill, and some three miles from the next station, there is a clever town in a smart lo-ca-tion, where he expects you have con-cluded to stop. Your answer in the negative naturally leads to more questions in reference to your intended route (always pronounced rout); and wherever you are going, you invariably learn that you can't get there without immense difficulty and danger, and that all the great sights are somewhere else.

If a lady takes a fancy to any male passenger's seat, the gentleman who accompanies her gives him notice of the fact, and he immediately vacates it with great politeness. . . .

Except when a branch road joins the main one, there is seldom more than one track of rails; so that the road is very narrow, and the view, where there is a deep cutting, by no means extensive. When there is not, the character of the scenery is always the same. Mile after mile of stunted trees: some hewn down by the axe, some blown down by the wind, some half fallen and resting on their neighbours, many mere logs half hidden in the swamp, others moulded away to spongy chips. The very soil of the earth is made up of minute fragments such as these; each pool of stagnant water has its crust of vegetable rottenness; on every side there are the boughs, and trunks, and stumps of trees, in every possible stage of decay, decomposition, and neglect. Now you emerge for a few brief minutes on an open country, glittering with some bright lake or pool, broad as many an English river, but so small here that it scarcely has a name; now catch hasty glimpses of a distant town, with its clean white houses and their cool piazzas, its prim New England church and schoolhouse; when whir-r-r-r! almost before you have seen them, comes the same dark screen: the stunted trees, the stumps, the logs, the stagnant water—all so like the last that you seem to have been transported back again by magic.

The train calls at stations in the woods, where the wild impossibility of anybody having the smallest reason to get out, is only to be equalled by the apparently desperate hopelessness of there being anybody to get in. It rushes across the turnpike road, where there is no gate, no policeman, no signal: nothing but a rough wooden arch, on which is painted

"WHEN THE BELL RINGS, LOOK OUT FOR THE LOCO-
MOTIVE." On it whirls headlong, dives through the woods again,
emerges in the light, clatters over frail arches, rumbles upon the heavy
ground, shoots beneath a wooden bridge which intercepts the light for
a second like a wink, suddenly awakens all the slumbering echoes in the
main street of a large town, and dashes on haphazard, pell-mell, neck-
or-nothing, down the middle of the road. There—with mechanics working at their trades, and people leaning from their doors and windows,
and boys flying kites and playing marbles, and men smoking, and
women talking, and children crawling, and pigs burrowing, and un-
accustomed horses plunging and rearing, close to the very rails—there
—on, on on—tears the mad dragon of an engine with its train of cars;
scattering in all directions a shower of burning sparks from its wood
fire; screeching, hissing, yelling, panting; until at last the thirsty monster stops beneath a covered way to drink, the people cluster round, and
you have time to breathe again.

7. *1821*—PIONEERS TAKE ROOT: THE STORY OF ELIJAH ILES

⟦ *What happened to the pioneer, once he had made his way, by
whatever means, to the thinly settled West? The experience of
Elijah Iles was typical of many. Born in Kentucky in 1796, Iles
tired of the little "zig-zag" corn fields of his native state and determined to strike out for a region that would support fields large and
square. In 1818 he moved to Missouri, where he clerked in a store
and made a thousand dollars trading in land. After three years he
returned to Kentucky to visit his family. On his way back to Missouri he heard of a district in central Illinois called the Sangamon
valley where a new county had just been created and a county seat—
Springfield—staked out. A dozen settlers already lived in the vicinity.
The place would grow. Iles decided to turn his experience to advantage and found a store. His narrative recounts the beginnings of a
career that would lead to wealth and a position as one of the leading
citizens of the capital of Illinois.*

I hunted around and found the stake that had been stuck for the
beginning of a town named Springfield, and then bargained for the
erection of a store house, to be set near the stake, eighteen feet square,
with sheds on the sides for shelter. The house was to be of hewn logs,
covered with boards, with heavy poles laid on to keep the boards from
blowing off. . . .

I bought my goods at St. Louis, mostly at auction at very low prices,

---

Elijah Iles, *Sketches of Early Life and Times* (Springfield, Illinois, 1883), 28–35.

as many goods were then being forced to sale, but to complete the assortment had to buy some at private sale. I then chartered a boat . . . on which to ship my goods up the Illinois river to the mouth of the Sangamon, one hundred and fifty miles above St. Louis and within fifty miles of Springfield. The boat was towed up the river by five men walking on shore and pulling a tow line about three hundred feet long. One man on the boat acting as steersman, with myself as supercargo, completed the crew.

Just below the mouth of the Missouri river, where the current was very strong, a large cottonwood tree had fallen into the water, and the boat had to be steered out so as to clear it. As it struck the current, the bow was forced under the water. I calmly folded my arms with the thought that if it went down I would go too, as it held all that I had so far struggled for, together with four hundred dollars belonging to each of my brothers, William and Washington Iles, which my father had given me to invest for them; but, as the hatches were closed, only a few barrels of water got into the boat, and the bow soon raised and we pursued our upward course rejoicing—at least I did. The first house we came to above the mouth of the Missouri was the ferryman's, now the city of Alton. The next was at the mouth of the Illinois river. The next was a vacant cabin, with doors and windows cut out, but without shutters. This was at the mouth of the Sangamon river. . . .

At the vacant cabin the boatmen landed my goods on the beach and started down the river on their return to St. Louis. I took my seat on the head of a whisky barrel, or salt barrel, I don't know which, and watched the boat until it got out of sight, and I thought and thought. But as thinking would do no good, I went to the top of the bank and examined the cabin, and found a few household goods and farming utensils stowed in it. The articles had been brought there by emigrants in what were called dug-outs. I believe the boat bringing my goods was the first boat that ever ascended the river, other than Indian-trading boats. . . .

From the cabin I found a trail leading out towards Springfield, and I started on the trail afoot and alone. I had to wade a slough in the bottom knee-deep in water, and before I got to the first house on my road, fifteen miles out . . ., I met two teams going to the river; and as neither of them would have full loads, I turned back and made up their loads. As no one lived near, I had no fear of thieves. The whisky was in the most danger if found by the Indians, and was among the first articles hauled away. Besides, the wheat was about ready to cut, and at that day it was an uphill business and a drag to cut wheat without the aid of whisky. Upon my arrival at Springfield I employed teams to haul the goods. As there were about twenty-five tons of them, it took more than a month to do this, but it was finally accomplished without having the first thing disturbed or missing. . . .

Upon my arrival I found my store house was not quite ready, for the want of nails, and you may believe it was a rough concern; but it answered my purpose. This was the first store house erected in Springfield or in the county, and I was the first one to sell goods in Springfield. For some time my sales were about as much to Indians as to the whites. For the first two years I had no competition, and my customers were widely and thinly scattered. . . .

Soon after opening my store, my father sent to me from Kentucky a youth, aged sixteen, a son of one of his valued neighbors, to act as store boy and clerk. This youth was John Williams, now better known as Col. Williams. He proved to be a valuable assistant, and lived with me as one of the family until 1831, when I sold my goods to him and established him in business. He was very successful, and soon improved and cultivated a large farm in connection with his store. In after years he established the First National Bank in Springfield, of which he was president and the principal stockholder. He also built and owned the Northwestern Railroad, from Springfield to Havana, fifty miles. A short time since he sold his store, his bank stock, and his railroad, and has now partly retired from business, though he still cultivates his large farm and attends to the leasing and care of his valuable property in Springfield. . . .

After moving to my farm, I soon found myself much in need of an additional plowman. A boy came to me and said he wanted to work. He had the chills every other day, and could only plow on his well days and do some light work on his chill days. His name was Robert North. He was about the most scrawny looking chap I ever saw, and could neither read nor write. But as I was much in need of a plow boy I took him on trial, uncouth and sickly as he was. He was so slow in his movements that he kept me on nettles. But his first day's plowing convinced me he would do. He had plowed as much and had done as good work as any of the other hands. He soon got well of the chills, and made me a most valuable hand. I taught him to read and write. He lived with me ten years, got married and went to farming on his own hook, in which he was successful. He died two years ago, at the age of seventy, after accumulating in land and cash more than $150,000.

After North married and left me, I hired a young man by the name of Charles Fairchild, about twenty-one years old. He was all go-ahead, a brisk worker, and was my leader. The only fault I found in him was that he would tire out too quick and would break down my other hands. He resided with me several years; is still living and a thrifty farmer.

These were faithful men, who worked for and looked after my interest as though it had been their own; and when it was necessary for anything to be done, day or night, rain or shine, nothing would stop them. I think I did a good part by them, and was proud to see them successful.

8. *1829—*"OLD HICKORY" TAKES OVER

❲ *Thousands of Westerners—the term was applied, for many years, to all who lived west of Pittsburgh—became a new force in politics. Their hero was Andrew Jackson, the hard-bitten frontiersman from Tennessee who knew the country beyond the Alleghenies as no President from Virginia or Massachusetts—and all before him had come from those two states—could possibly know it. In 1828, after a narrow miss four years earlier, Jackson was elected. His inauguration, on March 4th of the following year, marked the beginning of a new era. Anne Royall, a popular writer of the time, described it.*

At length the *Fourth of March* arrived. It being a fair day, to gratify the people who had been literally pouring into the City for several days, to witness the Inauguration, the Committee of Arrangements had resolved the ceremony should take place in the East Portico of the Capitol, so that the crowd, which no building could hold, might be gratified. This was the calculation. But, doubtless, no arrangement was more completely defeated. Excepting a parcel of boys, black people, and those who had the good fortune to mix with them, and stand up on the square in front of the Capitol, the Inauguration was a perfect blank.

When I arrived at the Capitol, which was long before the hour, I stepped out on the platform to see the preparations, and found my friend, Senator Smith, of Maryland, giving directions to the men who were spreading carpets, and placing chairs and settees for the Judges of the Supreme Court, Foreign Ministers, and other high and mighty characters. Looking up, I beheld Colonel Towson at the other end, directing the men also in placing the seats, he, also, being one of the Committee of Arrangements. The Colonel saluted me with great gallantry, and took me under his protection, but a hundred Colonels would have found it impossible to protect my toes that day against hostile feet, which in the end was verified.

President Adams had called a session of the new Senate, upon retiring from office, to enable his successor to appoint his cabinet, and perform other Executive business. The new Senate met about 11 o'clock, in the Senate Chamber, to be sworn in. I had selected a seat convenient

Anne Royall, *Letters from Alabama* (Washington, 1830), 170–71.

to the door, behind the bar of the Senate, so that I could step at once into the portico.

The lobby round the bar, was exclusively reserved for the ladies and such Members of Congress as might choose to attend. The gallery, which has been made entirely new, during the summer, was also filled with ladies. All this being understood, I amused myself in conversing with my friends, awaiting the arrival of General Jackson, the Judges, and the Foreign Ministers. At length, the Foreign Ministers were announced, and General Smith met them at the door and conducted them to their seats, to the left of the chair, and very near my Royal self. Next came the Judges, and took their seats on the right of the chair; and, lastly, the President elect. The Ministers were covered with gold lace; the Judges were dressed in black silk gowns—and General Jackson was the plainest dressed man in the Chamber. He was dressed in a suit of black, and with a cane in his hand he entered the Chamber. After taking off his hat, he bowed respectfully, and was conducted by General Smith to a seat in front of the chair, at the foot of the Foreign Ministers. He was thin and pale, and his hair, which was black when I first saw him, was now, almost white, and his countenance was melancholy. He showed no embarrassment, however, but surveyed the company with a mild and friendly aspect; sometimes resting upon his cane, while every eye was bent upon him. Shortly after he entered, the new Senators, two or three at a time, stepped up to the chair, where the usual oath was administered, and they then resumed their seats. It yet wanted several minutes of twelve, and every one watched the clock, which always is kept in the Senate Chamber, with deep attention. Within a minute or two of the time, I arose and walked out to select an eligible place to witness the Inauguration. I did reach the door by hard squeezing; but such another sight baffles description. Not only every seat, but every inch of the platform was crowded, by men, women, and children. These had forced the guards, and taken possession. I was shoved and pushed from one place to another, squeezed, and betrampled; and at length wedged up, about an inch from the door: but as for moving backwards or forwards, it was out of the question. How the President, the Judges, Foreign Ministers, and Senators, &c. got out of the Senate Chamber, I am at a loss to divine; for I saw nothing of the President, but the top of his head. The chairs, intended for the Honorables, were filled with women, standing on them, and the whole appeared one mass of solid people. One half of those in the Senate Chamber were unable to get out.

I had been watching an opportunity, and one offering, I squeezed my way back; nor did I hear one word of the President's address; much less did I hear him take the oath.

My only chance now, was to witness the procession on its return, and Senator Rowan advised me to go to the Library; but that, and all the rooms were fast locked. After wandering about, I found a messenger who unlocked a lower room, and I sat in the window, but was under promise to let no one else in, and to keep the door locked. The firing of the cannon, and the shouting of the multitude, soon proclaimed the new President; and shortly after this the crowd came thundering down the steps, and President Jackson appeared bare headed, leaning upon two gentlemen, one on each side, while he was followed by a dense crowd, who rent the air with shouts. The earth was literally, covered with people, who maintained neither order nor regularity. Some ran, some walked, and some jumped the walls. The square, the Avenue, all was now all motion; and to have a better view, I ran up stairs to look out of some of the upper windows; and after viewing the crowd some minutes, I stepped into the Senate Chamber, where Judge Story was reading the Inauguration Speech, which I having listened to, I sought my way home, which was but a few steps distant; and if ever I am caught in such another crowd, while I live, it will be an accident.

9. *1830*—WEBSTER PLEADS FOR A STRONG NATION

❮ *Even though Jackson, a strong nationalist, sat in the White House, signs of the conflict that would eventually lead to civil war appeared. In 1830 Robert Y. Hayne, Senator from South Carolina, took the floor to expound an extreme doctrine of states' rights. Hayne's speech gave Daniel Webster, Senator from Massachusetts, a chance for which he had been waiting. In one of the greatest speeches ever delivered in Congress, Webster demolished his opponent.*

Peter Harvey, Webster's friend and biographer, drew the scene from the recollections of Edward Everett and Webster himself.

I heard Mr. Everett, in Mr. Webster's presence, relate an incident connected with the reply to Hayne, which is worth repeating.

Mr. Everett did not hear the Hayne speech, to which Mr. Webster was to reply. "There was," he said, "a very great excitement in Washington, growing out of the controversies of the day, and the action of the South; and party spirit ran uncommonly high. There seemed to be a preconcerted action of the part of the Southern members to break down the Northern men, and to destroy their force and influence by a premeditated onslaught.

"Mr. Hayne's speech was an eloquent one, as all know who ever read it. He was considered the foremost Southerner in debate, except

Peter Harvey, *Reminiscences and Anecdotes of Daniel Webster* (Boston, 1877), 149-53.

Calhoun, who was Vice-president and could not enter the arena. Mr. Hayne was the champion of the Southern side. Those who heard his speech felt much alarm, for two reasons; first, on account of its eloquence and power, and second, because of its many personalities. It was thought by many who heard it, and by some of Mr. Webster's personal friends, that it was impossible for him to answer the speech.

"I shared a little myself in that fear and apprehension," said Mr. Everett. "I knew from what I heard concerning General Hayne's speech, that it was a very masterly effort, and delivered with a great deal of power and with an air of triumph. I was engaged on that day in a committee of which I was chairman, and could not be present in the Senate. But, immediately after the adjournment, I hastened to Mr. Webster's house, with, I admit, some little trepidation, not knowing how I should find him. But I was quite reassured in a moment after seeing Mr. Webster, and observing his entire calmness. He seemed to be as much at his ease and as unmoved as I ever saw him. Indeed, at first, I was a little afraid from this that he was not quite aware of the magnitude of the contest. I said at once :—

" 'Mr. Hayne has made a speech?'

" 'Yes, he has made a speech.'

" 'You reply in the morning?'

" 'Yes,' said Mr. Webster; 'I do not propose to let the case go by default, and without saying a word.'

" 'Did you take notes, Mr. Webster, of Mr. Hayne's speech?'

"Mr. Webster took from his vest pocket a piece of paper about as big as the palm of his hand, and replied, 'I have it all: that is his speech.'

"I immediately rose," said Mr. Everett, "and remarked to him that I would not disturb him longer; Mr. Webster desired me not to hasten, as he had no wish to be alone; but I left.

"The next morning when I entered the Senate Chamber and listened to his reply, of course that was an end of apprehension. The speech was such a triumphant answer, such a complete refutation, not only in the judgment of friends but of foes, that it left nothing to be wished for."

. . . There are many anecdotes about what took place between Mr. Hayne and Mr. Webster, and among them a great many absurdities. I had read a large number of these stories; and I asked Mr. Webster about the truth of them. Mr. Webster replied:

"Not one of them is true."

He said, however, that it was true that, when he had finished his speech, some Southern member, whose name he did not mention, approached him cordially and said :—

"Mr. Webster, I think you had better die now, and rest your fame on that speech."

Mr. Hayne was standing near and heard the remark, and said:—

"You ought not to die: a man who can make such speeches as that ought never to die."

Mr. Webster met General Hayne at the President's reception on the evening of that day, and, as he came up to him, Mr. Webster remarked pleasantly:—

"How are you tonight?"

"None the better for you, sir," was the General's humorous reply.

10.   *1842*—A FOURTEEN-YEAR-OLD BOY GOES OFF TO SEA

⟦ *Webster's nationalism fitted the facts of American life. It was the nation—Young America—that was peopling a wilderness, not the sovereign states. It was the nation that was extending its commerce around the world. The ships that sailed from New Bedford or Salem to California, or the China Sea, or the coast of Chile, flew the American flag rather than the emblem of Massachusetts.*

And ships sailed almost in fleets from American ports in the years when pioneers swarmed to the Mississippi, then leaped to the farther shore. The United States had the hardwoods for stout hulls, tall trees for masts, pitch for caulking, hemp for ropes, and most important of all, thousands of boys who wanted to make the sea their career. One of these, Charles P. Low, described the manner in which, at the age of fourteen, he became a sailor.

My brother Abbot came home from China with quite a good-sized fortune. . . . After his marriage with Miss Ellen Dow, in March, 1841, he built a topsail schooner called the *Mazeppa,* one of the handsomest vessels of the kind I ever saw, destined for the East India and China trade. My brothers went down to Sandy Hook when she sailed and took me with them. Just before the steam tug cast off, I got into one of the bread lockers in hopes they would not miss me, and thus I could get away to sea; but they were on the watch for me and my brother Josiah set the captain and mate after me, who soon found me half-suffocated, and sent me on board the tug. But this attempt, and the story my brothers told my parents about my plan of going on a farm and about my running away, had its effect upon them, and they realized that I must go to sea and try it. But it was some time yet before my wishes were gratified.

In the mean time I was making myself ready. By daily visits to ships

Some Recollections by Captain Charles P. Low, 1847–1873 (Boston: Geo. H. Ellis Co., 1906), 13–30.

and talking to the sailors in the boarding-house opposite I learned a great deal, and later on I went to a navigation school and studied navigation under an old sea captain.

In May, 1842, my brother William married Miss Bedell of Brooklyn, and it was understood that in the fall they were to go to China. So about the middle of October they engaged passage in the *Horatio*, Captain Howland, master, and, what was better than that, my brother Abbot secured a berth for me as boy on board the same ship. After he had secured it, he wanted to know how I was going to make a living, as boys had no wages. I immediately replied, "As soon as the voyage is over, I will ship again." My brother William told me I need not be afraid of starving, he would see me all right. My father gave me fifty dollars and a sailor's outfit, which cost about thirty dollars more, and my freedom; that is, I was not to depend upon him any further, but make my own way in the world.

The fifth day of November, 1842, was the day set for sailing and I could hardly wait, I was so anxious to be off. At ten o'clock a.m. the tug came alongside, and my brothers and sisters and some six or eight of the Bedell girls, sisters of my brother William's wife, went down to Sandy Hook to see us off. The day was pleasant, and we had a good start. After leaving the pilot and guests we were kept hard at work stowing the anchors and getting sail on the ship. It being a fair wind we did not stop work till all the studding-sails were set and we were nearly out of sight of land. After the decks were cleared up all hands were called aft and the watches chosen. We had for officers: Captain Howland; first mate, Mr. Wood; second mate, Mr. Howard; third mate, Mr. Jennings. The first mate was a short, well-built man and a good sailor and officer. The second mate was a taller and larger man, and a very smart man in every way, but he was the most profane man I ever met. Mr. Jennings, the third mate, was an active, good-natured fellow and understood his work. In fact they were all about as well fitted for their positions as I have ever known men to be. The watches were chosen by the first and second mates. One chooses a man, and then the other chooses, till the crew are equally divided. The captain then addresses the men, telling them he expects them to be quick at a call and to do their duty at all times, and that if they do, they will be well fed and have a pleasant voyage, but if they do not, they will have a rough time of it. At six p.m. the captain's watch went below, ready to turn out at eight p.m. and stay on deck till midnight. The rule on board ship is for the captain to take the ship out, and the mate to bring her home; that is, the captain's watch, which is looked out for by the second mate, has the first eight hours on deck,—that is, from eight to twelve p.m. and from four to eight a.m. And, coming home, the mate's watch has the same time the first night out.

The sailmaker and carpenter and we four boys had bunks in the between-decks, just forward of the cabin. The men all slept forward in the forecastle. The ship not being full of cargo, there was plenty of room. The sailmaker and carpenter both worked down in the between-decks. Our cargo consisted of two or three hundred tons of pig lead, lumber, and cotton goods, which filled up the lower hold. Water, ship stores, and spare sails were all that were in between-decks.

The first two days out we had fine weather, but the ship rolled enough to make all the boys seasick. I escaped, however, not feeling the least uncomfortable, but enjoying it all. The third day came on with fresh winds, which soon amounted to a gale, and orders were given to send down the royal yards, and I jumped for the main rigging, when the mate sung out to me, "Where in h——l are you going to?"

I said I was going to send down the royal yard. He wanted to know what I knew about it. I merely replied that I could send it down.

"Then go ahead, and be quick about it!" he said, at the same time calling an ordinary seaman to go up with me; and I thought he told him to help me only if I got stuck. But I was confident I could do it, and I did it. Having got the heaviest of all three down first, after securing the lifts and braces to the masts, I came down, and the mate said, "Well done, Charlie!" Afterwards when everything was snug, he called me and wanted to know if I had been to sea before, and, if not, where I had learned to send down a royal yard. I told him, and he wanted to know if I could box the compass. I told him I could and that I should like to steer the ship. He said he would give me a chance as soon as the weather was better. . . .

The living I stood very well, for I had a ravenous appetite. Mondays we had salt beef and bread for breakfast, dinner, and supper, with a mixture at breakfast called coffee, a quart to each one, boiled with molasses. It did very well to soak biscuit in, and after a while I could drink it and think it good. Tuesday we had salt pork for breakfast, bean soup and salt pork for dinner, and a quart of vinegar was allowed us on bean day. Friday we had the same bill of fare. Wednesday we had scouse, or beef hash mixed with potatoes, or if no potatoes, ship's biscuits soaked and mixed with the beef. I was very fond of scouse.[1] This was a good breakfast. For dinner we had, in addition to salt beef, boiled rice. Each man and boy had six large spoonfuls of molasses to eat with the rice. The sailmaker used to measure our allowance of molasses, and he would stint us boys if he could, so as to have more for himself. Thursday we had scouse for breakfast and flour pudding, or duff, for dinner. Friday the same as Tuesday, bean soup. Saturday codfish and potatoes or rice. Sunday's bill of fare was the same, except that our

---

[1] Short for lobscouse: meat stewed with vegetables and ship's biscuit.

flour pudding or duff had a few raisins which made it plum pudding. Every night we had a quart of a mixture called tea, boiled the same as the coffee, with molasses for sweetening. Such was the bill of fare through the outward bound voyage, and I shall refer no more to that. I got used to it and enjoyed all my meals. . . .

As the weeks flew by I became more in love with my sea life, and I got along well with officers and men. I was perfectly fearless. I could hold my weight with one hand, and I was as much at home on the royal yard as on deck.

One afternoon the watch on deck to which I belonged were sent aloft to bend a new main-topgallant sail. It was blowing fresh. The sail was hoisted up to the masthead by the bunt, or middle. The third mate was out on the topgallant yard, and I took the earing—a piece of ratline stuff that fastens the sail to the yard arm—and ran out on top of the yard with it to the third mate. He turned pale to see me, and told me to get down on the foot rope as quickly as possible. While there bending the sail, the other watch were called from below to reef the topsail. It was blowing a gale and it was as much as we could do to get the sail bent and furled. I thought nothing of what I had done and after the sails were reefed and everything made snug, it was my watch below and I went down in the forecastle to talk with the men. I had hardly got there when the second mate called for me, and gave me an awful scolding and told me if I attempted to run out on a topgallant yard again, he would take my hide off. At the same time I could see he thought well of me for doing it; and my brother afterward told me that Mr. Howard said I was the smartest boy he ever saw on board a ship.

11. *1850*—"THERE SHE BLOWS!"

❨ *Before the first great oil field was opened in 1859, the world de-pended on the whale for light. His huge carcass provided oil for lamps; spermaceti, a soft white inflammable substance, for candles; and flexible bones for the tight corsets worn by every woman who made any pretense to style.*

The sea-faring American took to whaling. Even before the Revo-lution, Nantucket, near the landing place of the Pilgrims, had be-come the greatest whaling port in the world. Wars crippled the industry, but not for long. Early in the nineteenth century Yankee captains ventured farther and farther, and in greater numbers than ever, in search of whales. When the industry reached its peak, about 1845, the United States had more than 700 whaling ships at sea.

Henry T. Cheever, *The Whale and His Captors* (Glasgow, 1850), 37–39, 42–43.

Voyages as far as New Zealand or the Bering Sea, lasting three or four years, were commonplace.

Few occupations offered more hard work and danger than whaling. Both features of the life are brought out in the narrative of the Reverend Henry T. Cheever, a missionary who took passage on the COMMODORE PREBLE *when the ship touched at the Hawaiian Islands in 1850.*

For the first time in our now ten weeks' passage from the Hawaiian Islands, on this New Zealand Cruising Ground we heard, day before yesterday, that life-kindling sound to a weary whaleman, THERE SHE BLOWS! The usual questions and orders from the deck quickly followed. "Where away?" "Two points on the weather bow!" "How far off?" "A mile and a half!" "Keep your eye on her!" "Sing out when we head right!" It turned out that three whales were descried from aloft in different parts, and in a short time, when we were deemed near enough, the captain gave orders to "Stand by and lower" for one a little more than half a mile to windward.

Three boats' crews pulled merrily away, glad of something to stir their blood, and with eager hope to obtain the oily material wherewith to fill their ship and make good their "lay." The whale was going leisurely to windward, blowing every now and again two or three times, then "turning tail," "up flukes," and sinking. The boats "headed" after him, keeping a distance of nearly one quarter of a mile from each other, to scatter (as it is called) their chances.

Fortunately, as the oarsmen were "hove up," that is, had their oars a-peak, about the place where they expected the whale would next appear, the huge creature rose hard by the captain's boat, and all the harpooner in the bow had to do was to plunge his two keen cold irons, which are always secured to one tow-line, into the monster's blubber-sides. This he did so well as to hit the "fish's life," at once, and make him spout blood forthwith. It was the first notice the poor fellow had of the proximity of his powerful captors, and the sudden piercing of the barbed harpoons to his very vitals made him caper and run most furiously.

The boat spun after him with almost the swiftness of a top, now diving through the seas and tossing the spray, and then lying still while the whale sounded; anon in swift motion again when the game rose, for the space of an hour. During this time another boat "got fast" to him with its harpoons, and the captain's cruel lance had several times struck his vitals. He was killed, as whalemen call it, that is, mortally wounded, an hour before he went into "his flurry," and was really dead or turned up on his back.

The loose boat then came to the ship for a hawser to fasten round his flukes; which being done, the captain left his irons in the carcass and pulled for the ship, in order to beat to windward, and, after getting alongside, to "cut him in." This done, and the mammoth carcass secured to the ship by a chain round the bitts, they proceeded to reeve the huge blocks that are always made fast for the purpose to the fore and main mast head, and to fasten the cutting-in tackle. The captain and two mates then went over the sides on steps well secured, and having each a breast-rope to steady them and lean upon. The cooper then passed them the long-handled spades, which he was all the time grinding and whetting, and they fell lustily to work, chopping off the blubber. . . .

Soon after we had finished cutting in, about eight o'clock in the evening, the wind increased almost to a gale, making it impossible to try out that night. But today, while the ship is lying to, the business has begun in good earnest; the blubber-men cutting up in the blubber room: others pitching it on deck: others forking it over to the side of the "try-works"; two men standing by a "horse" with a mincing knife to cleave the pieces into many parts for the more easy trying out, as the rind of a joint of pork is cut by the cook for roasting: the boat-steerers and one of the mates are pitching it into the kettles, feeding the fires with the scraps, and bailing the boiling fluid into copper tanks, from which it is the duty of another to dip into casks. The decks present that lively though dirty spectacle which whalemen love, their faces all begrimed and sooty, and smeared with oil, so that you cannot tell if they be black or white. A farmer's golden harvest in autumn is not a pleasanter sight to him, than it is to a whaler to have his decks and blubberroom "blubber-log," the try-works a-blazing, cooper a-pounding, oil a-flowing, everybody busy and dirty night and day. Donkey-loads of Chilian or Peruvian gold, filling into the custom-house at Valparaiso and Lima, or a stream of Benton's yellow-boys flowing up the Mississippi, or bags of the Californian dust riding into San Francisco, have no such charms for him as cutting in a hundred-barrel whale and turning out oil by the hogshead.

The whale now taken proves to be a cow whale, forty-five feet long and twenty-five round, and it will yield between seventy and eighty barrels of right whale oil. This is about the ordinary size of the New Zealand whale, a mere dwarf in comparison with that of the northwest, which sometimes yields, it is said, three hundred barrels, ordinarily one hundred and fifty, or one hundred and eighty.

CHAPTER XI

BEYOND THE MISSISSIPPI

1831 – 1852

1.   *1833*—TO THE ROCKIES FOR FURS

❲ *The first colonists in North America had hoped to find gold. Instead, they found furs, but furs could be sold for gold. The wealthy classes in Europe wanted fur garments both for warmth and as a sign of their social standing; the same motives led to a demand in America as the cities of the East grew and prospered.*

When Lewis and Clark reported that the Rocky Mountains swarmed with fur-bearing animals, venturesome men lost no time in going after their pelts. Manuel Lisa, a Spanish merchant living in St. Louis, sent the first big expedition up the Missouri in 1807. Almost every year thereafter companies left St. Louis to spend a year or more in the mountains, trapping and trading goods with the Indians for peltries. When an expedition was successful it yielded a small fortune, but if the season was bad, or a sudden

Charles Larpenteur, *Forty Years a Fur Trader on the Upper Mississippi* (Chicago: R. R. Donnelley & Sons Co., 1933), 17–26.

*squall overturned a loaded keelboat on the return trip, months of
hardship went for nothing.*

*In 1833, when Charles Larpenteur joined a party organized by
Robert Campbell, a noted trapper, the western fur trade was at its
height. Leaving St. Louis in several groups, the men assembled at
Lexington in western Missouri and started from there for the fur
country. Larpenteur, who had been born in France but had lived
most of his twenty-six years in Baltimore, saw his companions and
their way of life with the fresh vision of one who was making his
first trip.*

On the 12th of May we took our departure for the mountains, and
at the same time the keel boat left Lexington Landing, manned by thirty
men with the cordell on their shoulders, some of them for the distance
of about 1800 miles. Our party consisted of 40 enlisted men; Robert
Campbell, boss in charge; Louis Vasquez, an old mountain man; Mr.
Johnesse, a clerk in charge of the men, whose place it was to remain
in the rear to aid in readjusting the loads, which would get out of order,
and to have an eye to the whole cavalcade. . . .

Now hard times commenced. At first the mules kicking off packs and
running away was amusing, for those who were all right, but mighty
disagreeable for the poor fellows who were out of luck. I had my share
of this, but it was not to be compared with the troubles of some of my
comrades. This kind of kicking up lasted three or four days in full
blast; it finally subsided, yet there would be a runaway almost every
day. Our fare consisted of bacon and hard-tack—no sugar nor coffee—
for three or four days, after which we each received a small piece of
sheep meat, as we had a drove to last us until we got into the buffalo.
While the sheep lasted we had but that alone. . . . About a week after
we had been under march the guard was established, and I was appointed an officer. It became the duty of the officer every third day to
post his men around the camp, as soon as all the animals were brought
in and picketed in the circle of the camp; those men were to remain
quite still at their stations; the officer was to cry out "All's well" every
20 minutes, and the men to cry out the same, so as to find out whether
they were asleep or awake. Should any one fail to reply, it was then
the duty of the officer to go the rounds to find out the individual, and
if caught asleep to take his gun to the boss' tent; then in the morning
he would be informed of what he had to undergo, which was a $5 fine
and three walks. The men on guard were not permitted to move from
their stations, as it was considered dangerous on account of Indians
being known to creep up to camp and watch to shoot someone whom
they could discover strolling about; so the officer was in more danger
than his men. The usual time of guard was 2½ hours. Having traveled

all day, being obliged to remain quiet at one's post was very trying on the sleeping organs, and consequently there would be some poor fellow trudging along on foot almost every day.

Our route, as well as I can remember, crossed the Little and Big Blue rivers and continued along the south side of the Platte. I complained, as my messmates did, of the sheep meat, but they consoled me as well as themselves by speaking of the fine feast we soon would have on the buffalo, which they said they would prefer to all the good messes that could be gotten up in the States. Three days after we had reached the Platte the hunters brought in one evening a load of meat; but the cry of "buffalo meat!" was heard long before they came in, and there was great rejoicement in camp. Sheep meat could be had very cheap that evening, and it was amusing to see the cooks hunting their kettles—some cursing them for being too small, as though it was the poor kettle's fault for its size; but it was not long before they found the kettles were large enough. Then came trouble—there was no wood to be found about camp, and all the fuel we could obtain was the stalks of some large dried weeds, the wild sunflower. Now and then some hungry fellow would bring in a small armful of that kind of fuel, and his first words would be, "Is the kettle boiling?" Upon being answered in the negative a long string of bad expressions would be heard, the mildest being, "Waugh! I believe that damned kettle won't never boil!" Thanks to the virtue of sunflower stalks, however, it boiled at last, and every countenance became pleasant at the thought of tasting that much-talked-of buffalo meat. When it was thought cooked by the old voyageurs, preparations were made to dish it out; but, as we had no pans, a clean place was looked for on the grass, and the contents of the kettle were poured out. All hands seated around the pile hauled out their long butcher knives, opened their little sacks of salt, and then began operations. But it was not long before bad expressions were used again in regard to the highly praised quality of buffalo meat. "I can't chew it"—"Tougher'n whalebone"—"If that's the stuff we've got to live on for eighteen months, God have mercy on us!" For my part I thought about the same, but said nothing; and after I had chewed as long as I could without being able to get it in swallowing condition, I would seize an opportunity to spit it into my hand, and throw it out unseen behind me. My comrades asked me how I liked buffalo meat; I replied I thought it might be some better than it was, and they said, "Never mind, Larpenteur; wait until we get among the fat cows—then you will see the difference." At this time of the year, in the early part of June, the cows are not fit to kill; for they have their young calves, and are very poor. For several days after this sheep meat would have kept up its price, and perhaps would have risen in value; but none was allowed to come into market, what little there was being reserved for the boss' mess. So we had to go it on buffalo alone; but, thank Providence! we soon got into fine fat cows, and fared well. . . .

We soon reached the [Laramie] river, where we were ordered to dismount and go to work making a boat out of the hides of the buffalo—quite a new kind of boat to me. But the boat was made, and the party with all the goods were crossed over by sunset. The next day, or the day after, according to custom Mr. Campbell sent Mr. Vasquez with two men to hunt up some trappers, in order to find out where the rendezvous would be, and we awaited their return at this place. They were gone eight days, which time we enjoyed in hunting and feasting on the best of buffalo meat. On the arrival of the trappers and hunters a big drunken spree took place. Our boss, who was a good one, and did not like to be backward in such things, I saw flat on his belly on the green grass, pouring out what he could not hold in. Early next morning everything was right again, and orders were given to catch up and start. Everything moved quite smoothly until we reached the Divide,[1] where my faithful old Simon[2]—I may say the whole trinity—played out on me. About two hours before camping time the pack of one of my mules got so much out of order that I was obliged to stop to lash it. Mr. Simon, who was in the habit of waiting for me on occasions of that kind, changed his notion and took it into his head to follow the party without me; the well-packed one followed suit, and it was all I could do to prevent the third one from leaving before getting his pack on; but as soon as that was done the gentleman took to his heels, and all three got into camp about an hour before me. The want of Simon was the cause of my being obliged to wade a small creek—tributary to the Sweetwater—which was very cold, although it was the 2d of July. I was wet up to my waist, and it was my guard late that night. When I was awakened to go on guard my clothes were still wet, and on that morning, the 3d of July, water froze in our kettles nearly a quarter of an inch thick. I felt quite chilly and was sick for about eight days.

2. *1839*—THE RENDEZVOUS

❮ *As the western fur trade developed, the men who managed it devised what they called the "rendezvous system." Instead of sending out their own trappers, they set a time and place, a year in advance, where their pack train would meet the Indians and the independent trappers, or "mountain men," and exchange trade goods for the year's catch of furs. The rendezvous described here was held on the Green River, in the southwestern part of the present state*

F. A. Wislizenus, *A Journey to the Rocky Mountains in the Year 1839* (St. Louis, 1912), 84–90.
[1] At South Pass, which Jedediah Smith had discovered in 1823.
[2] Larpenteur's mule.

of Wyoming. The account was written by Adolph Wislizenus, a German political refugee who, after practicing medicine for three years in Illinois, joined a party of the Fur Company of St. Louis in order to see the West.

This year's meeting place had been fixed on the right bank of the Green River at the angle formed by its junction with Horse Creek. We were now about a day's journey from the place. Starting off in company in the afternoon, we covered, at a more rapid pace than usual, about twelve miles. . . . It was the Fourth of July, the great holiday of the United States. Our camp, however, presented its humdrum daily appearance. We stretched out around the fires, smoked and, in expectation of what the morrow would bring, went quietly asleep. The next morning we started early, and reached toward noon the Green River, so long desired. . . . The journey which we had made from the border of Missouri, according to our rough calculation, was near 1,200 miles.

We reached the camping place. What first struck our eye was several long rows of Indian tents (lodges), extending along the Green River for at least a mile. Indians and whites were mingled here in varied groups. Of the Indians there had come chiefly Snakes, Flatheads and Nezperces, peaceful tribes, living beyond the Rocky Mountains. Of whites the agents of the different trading companies and a quantity of trappers had found their way here, visiting this fair of the wilderness to buy and to sell, to renew old contracts and to make new ones, to make arrangements for future meetings, to meet old friends, to tell of adventures they had been through, and to spend for once a jolly day. These trappers, the "Knights without fear and without reproach," are such a peculiar set of people that it is necessary to say a little about them. The name in itself indicates their occupation. They either receive their outfit, consisting of horses, beaver traps, a gun, powder and lead, from trading companies, and trap for small wages, or else they act on their own account, and are then called freemen. The latter is more often the case. In small parties they roam through all the mountain passes. No rock is too steep for them; no stream too swift. Withal, they are in constant danger from hostile Indians, whose delight it is to ambush such small parties, and plunder them, and scalp them. Such victims fall every year. One of our fellow travelers, who had gone to the mountains for the first time nine years ago with about one hundred men, estimated that by this time half the number had fallen victims to the tomahawks of the Indians. But this daily danger seems to exercise a magic attraction over most of them. Only with reluctance does a trapper abandon his dangerous craft; and a sort of serious home-sickness seizes him when he retires from his mountain life to civilization. In manners and customs, the trappers have borrowed much from the Indians. Many of them, too, have taken Indian women as wives. Their dress is generally of leather. The hair of the head is usually allowed to grow long. In place of money, they use beaver skins, for which they can satisfy all their needs at the forts by way of trade. A pound of beaver skins is usually paid for with four dollars worth of goods; but the goods themselves are sold at enormous prices, so-called mountain prices. A pint of meal, for instance, costs from half a dollar to a dollar; a pint of coffee-beans, cocoa beans or sugar, two dollars each; a pint of diluted alcohol (the only spirituous liquor to be had), four dollars; a piece of chewing tobacco of the commonest sort, which is usually smoked, Indian fashion, mixed with herbs, one to two dollars. Guns and ammunition, bear traps, blankets, kerchiefs, and gaudy finery for the squaws, are also sold at enormous profit. At the yearly rendezvous the trappers seek to indemnify themselves for the sufferings and privations of a year spent in the wilderness. With their hairy bank notes, the beaver skins, they can obtain all the luxuries of the mountains, and live for a few days like lords. Coffee and chocolate is cooked; the pipe is kept aglow day and night; the spirits circulate; and whatever is not spent in such ways the squaws coax out of them, or else it is squandered at cards. Formerly single trappers on such occasions have often wasted a thousand dollars. But the days of their glory seem to be past, for constant hunting has very much reduced the number of beavers. This diminution in the beaver catch made itself noticeable at this year's rendezvous in the quieter behavior of the trappers. There was little drinking of spirits, and almost no gambling. Another decade perhaps and the original trapper will have disappeared from the mountains.

The Indians who had come to the meeting were no less interesting than the trappers. There must have been some thousands of them. Their tents are made of buffalo hides, tanned on both sides and sewed together, stretched in cone shape over a dozen poles, that are leaned against each other, their tops crossing. In front and on top this leather can be thrown back, to form door and chimney. The tents are about twelve feet high and twenty feet in circumference at the ground, and give sufficient protection in any kind of weather. I visited many tents, partly out of curiosity, partly to barter for trifles, and sought to make myself intelligible in the language of signs as far as possible. An army of Indian dogs very much resembling the wolf, usually beset the entrance. From some tents comes the sound of music. A virtuoso beats a sort of kettle drum with bells around with all his might, and the chorus accompanies him with strange monotone untrained sounds that showed strong tendency to the minor chords. A similar heart-rending song drew me to a troop of squaws that were engrossed in the game of "the hand," so popular with the Indians. Some small object, a bit of wood, for instance, is passed from hand to hand among the players seated in a circle; and it is someone's part to guess in whose hands the object is. During the game the chorus steadily sings some song as monotonous as those to which bears dance. But the real object is to gamble in this way for some designated prize. It is a game of hazard. In this case, for example, a pile of beads and corals, which lay in the midst of the circle, was the object in question. Men and women are so carried away by the game, that they often spend a whole day and night at it. Other groups of whites and Indians were engaged in barter. The Indians had for the trade chiefly tanned skins, moccasins, thongs of buffalo leather or braided buffalo hair, and fresh or dried buffalo meat. They have no beaver skins. The articles that attracted them most in exchange were powder and lead, knives, tobacco, cinnabar, gaily colored kerchiefs, pocket mirrors and all sorts of ornaments. Before an Indian begins to trade he demands sight of everything that may be offered by the other party to the trade. If there is something there that attracts him, he, too, will produce his wares, but discovers very quickly how much or how little they are coveted. If he himself is not willed to dispose of some particular thing, he obstinately adheres to his refusal, though ten times the value be offered him. . . .

The rendezvous usually lasts a week. Then the different parties move off to their destinations and the plain that today resounded with barbarous music, that was thronged with people of both races, with horses and dogs, returns to its old quiet, interrupted only now and then by the muffled roar of the buffalo and the howl of the wolf.

3.   *1835*—ON THE OREGON TRAIL

❨ *Not all the parties leaving St. Louis had the fur country as their destination: many sought farms in the fertile valley of the Willamette River. Missionaries, intent on saving the souls of the Indians, led the van of the movement. First among them were the Methodists, who established a mission near the present city of Salem, Oregon, in 1834. Their success spurred the Presbyterians to action. In 1835 the Reverend Samuel Parker and the Reverend Marcus Whitman, who was also a physician, headed for Oregon with the caravan of the American Fur Company. Parker described their experiences on the Oregon Trail.*

Wednesday, July 1st. I rested last night as quietly as I should have done upon a good bed, in a civilized country; and was cheerful in committing myself to God, to awake in this, or in the eternal world, as he should direct. . . .

Samuel Parker, *Journal of an Exploring Tour Beyond the Rocky Mountains* (Ithaca, New York, 1844), 52–53, 79–81, 84–85.

We proceeded to-day a few miles up the Loup fork, and unexpectedly found a good fording place, where we crossed the river, which in this place is nearly a mile wide. After going a few miles up the river, we halted for the night. The manner of our encamping, is to form a large hollow square, encompassing an area of about an acre, having the river on one side; three wagons forming a part of another side, coming down to the river; and three more in the same manner on the opposite side; and the packages so arranged in parcels, about three rods apart, as to fill up the rear, and the sides not occupied by the wagons. The horses and mules, near the middle of the day, are turned out under guard, to feed for two hours; and the same again towards night, until after sunset, when they are taken up and brought into the hollow square, and fastened with ropes twelve feet long, to pickets driven firmly into the ground. The men are divided into small companies, stationed at the several parcels of goods and wagons, where they wrap themselves in their blankets and rest for the night; the whole, however, are formed into six divisions to keep guard, relieving each other every two hours. This is to prevent hostile Indians from falling upon us by surprise, or coming into the camp by stealth and taking away either horses or packages of goods. . . .

[August 12th.] After stopping for the night upon the New Fork, a branch of Green river, we arose on the 12th, at the first breaking of the day, and continued our forced marches. Although we were emerging from the mountains, yet peaks covered with perpetual snow were seen in almost every direction, and the temperature of the air was uncomfortably cold. . . . In the afternoon we came to the Green river, a branch of the Colorado, in latitude 42°, where the caravan hold their rendezvous. This is a widely extended valley, which is pleasant, with a soil sufficiently fertile for cultivation, if the climate was not so cold. Like the country we have passed through, it is almost entirely prairie, with some woods skirting the streams of water.

The American Fur Company have between two and three hundred men constantly in and about the mountains, engaged in trading, hunting and trapping. These all assemble at rendezvous upon the arrival of the caravan, bring in their furs, and take new supplies for the coming year, of clothing, ammunition, and goods for trade with the Indians. But few of these men ever return to their country and friends. Most of them are constantly in debt to the company, and are unwilling to return without a fortune; and year after year passes away, while they are hoping in vain for better success. . . .

While we continued in this place, Doct. Whitman was called upon to perform some very important surgical operations. He extracted an iron arrow, three inches long, from the back of Capt. Bridger, which was received in a skirmish, three years before, with the Blackfeet In-

227

dians. It was a difficult operation, because the arrow was hooked at the point by striking a large bone, and a cartilaginous substance had grown around it. The Doctor pursued the operation with great self-possession and perseverance; and his patient manifested equal firmness. The Indians looked on meanwhile, with countenances indicating wonder, and in their own peculiar manner expressed great astonishment when it was extracted. . . .

A few days after our arrival at the place of rendezvous, and when all the mountain men had assembled, another day of indulgence was granted to them, in which all restraint was laid aside. These days are the climax of the hunter's happiness. I will relate an occurrence which took place near evening, as a specimen of mountain life. A hunter, who goes technically by the name of the great bully of the mountains, mounted his horse with a loaded rifle, and challenged any Frenchman, American, Spaniard, or Dutchman, to fight him in single combat. Kit Carson, an American, told him if he wished to die, he would accept the challenge. Shunar defied him. C. mounted his horse, and with a loaded pistol, rushed into close contact, and both almost at the same instant fired. C's ball entered S's hand, came out at the wrist, and passed through the arm above the elbow. Shunar's ball passed over the head of Carson; and while he went for another pistol, Shunar begged that his life might be spared. Such scenes, sometimes from passion, and sometimes for amusement, make the pastime of their wild and wandering life. They appear to have sought for a place where, as they would say, human nature is not oppressed by the tyranny of religion, and pleasure is not awed by the frown of virtue. . . . Their toils and privations are so great, that they more readily compensate themselves by plunging into such excesses, as in their mistaken judgment of things, seem most adapted to give them pleasure. They disdain the commonplace phrases of profanity which prevail among the impious vulgar in civilized countries, and have many set phrases, which they appear to have manufactured among themselves, and which, in their imprecations, they bring into almost every sentence and on all occasions. By varying the tones of their voices, they make them expressive of joy, hope, grief, and anger. In their broils among themselves, which do not happen every day, they would not be ungenerous. They would see "fair play," and "spare the last eye;" and would not tolerate murder, unless drunkenness or great provocation could be pleaded in extenuation.

Their demoralizing influence with the Indians has been lamentable, and they have practiced impositions upon them, in all the ways that sinful propensities dictate. It is said they have sold them packs of cards at high prices, calling them the Bible; and have told them, if they should refuse to give white men wives, that God would be angry with them and punish them eternally; and on almost any occasion when their wishes have been resisted, they have threatened them with the wrath of God. If these things are true in many instances, yet from personal observation, I should believe, their more common mode of accomplishing their wishes has been by flattery and presents; for the most of them squander away their wages in ornaments for their women and children. . . .

4. *1846*—THE DONNERS STARVE IN THE SIERRAS

❦ *The trip to Oregon never lacked hardship. Many who undertook it found lonely graves along the way. But no tragedy of the trail ever approached that of the Donner party. After leaving Springfield, Illinois, in the summer of 1846, this group of well-to-do emigrants followed the Oregon Trail to what is now Utah, and then headed for the Sacramento Valley by an unfamiliar route. Caught at Truckee Lake in the Sierras by early snows, they were marooned for the winter. Half of the party survived, but only by eating the flesh of those who died. Patrick Breen was one of several who kept diaries.*

TRUCKEY'S LAKE, November 20, 1846

Came to this place on the thirty-first of last month; went into the pass; the snow so deep we were unable to find the road, and when within three miles from the summit, turned back to this shanty on Truckey's Lake; Stanton came up one day after we arrived here; we again took our teams and wagons, and made another unsuccessful attempt to cross in company with Stanton; we returned to this shanty; it continued to snow all the time. We now have killed most part of our cattle, having to remain here until next spring, and live on lean beef, without bread or salt. It snowed during the space of eight days, with little intermission, after our arrival, though now clear and pleasant, freezing at night; the snow nearly gone from the valleys.

November 21. Fine morning; wind northwest; twenty-two of our company about starting to cross the mountains this day, including Stanton and his Indians. . . .

Nov. 23. Same weather; wind west; the expedition across the mountains returned after an unsuccessful attempt. . . .

Nov. 30. Snowing fast . . .; no living thing without wings can get about.

Dec. 1. Still snowing; wind west; snow about six or seven and a half feet deep; very difficult to get wood, and we are completely housed up; our cattle are killed but two or three, and these, with the horses

---

C. F. McGlashan, *History of the Donner Party* (San Francisco, 1880), 93–159. In this excerpt scattered diary entries have been brought together.

and Stanton's mules, all supposed to be lost in the snow; no hopes of finding them alive. . . .

Dec. 6. The morning fine and clear; Stanton and Graves manufacturing snow-shoes for another mountain scrabble; no account of mules. . . .

Dec. 9. Commenced snowing about eleven o'clock; wind northwest; took in Spitzer yesterday, so weak that he can not rise without help; caused by starvation. Some have a scanty supply of beef; Stanton trying to get some for himself and Indians; not likely to get much. . . .

Dec. 16. Fair and pleasant; froze hard last night; the company started on snow-shoes to cross the mountains; wind southeast.

Dec. 17. Pleasant; William Murphy returned from the mountain party last evening; Baylis Williams died night before last; Milton and Noah started for Donner's eight days ago; not returned yet; think they are lost in the snow. . . .

Dec. 21. Milton got back last night from Donner's camp. Sad news; Jacob Donner, Samuel Shoemaker, Rhinehart, and Smith are dead; the rest of them in a low situation; snowed all night with a strong southwest wind. . . .

Dec. 25. Began to snow yesterday, snowed all night, and snows yet rapidly; extremely difficult to find wood; uttered our prayers to God this Christmas morning; the prospect is appalling, but we trust in Him. . . .

Dec. 30. Fine clear morning; froze hard last night. Charles Burger died last evening about 10 o'clock. . . .

Jan. 4. Fine morning; looks like spring. Mrs. Reed and Virginia, Milton Elliott, and Eliza Williams started a short time ago with the hope of crossing the mountains; left the children here. It was difficult for Mrs. Reed to part with them.

Jan. 6. Eliza came back yesterday evening from the mountains, unable to proceed; the others kept ahead.

Jan. 8. Mrs. Reed and the others came back; could not find their way on the other side of the mountains. They have nothing but hides to live on. . . .

Jan. 15. Clear today again. Mrs. Murphy blind; Landrum not able to get wood; has but one ax between him and Keseberg. It looks like another storm; expecting some account from Sutter's soon.

Jan. 17. Eliza Williams came here this morning; Landrum crazy last night; provisions scarce; hides our main subsistence. May the Almighty send us help.

Jan. 21. Fine morning; John Baptiste and Mr. Denton came this morning with Eliza; she will not eat hides. Mrs.———sent her back to live or die on them. . . .

Jan. 27. Commenced snowing yesterday; still continues today.

Lewis Keseberg, Jr., died three days ago; food growing scarce; don't have enough fire to cook our hides. . . .

Jan. 31. The sun does not shine out brilliant this morning; froze hard last night; wind northwest. Landrum Murphy died last night about ten o'clock. . . .

Feb. 4. Snowed hard until twelve o'clock last night; many uneasy for fear we shall all perish with hunger; we have but little meat left, and only three hides; Mrs. Reed has nothing but one hide, and that is on Graves' house; Milton lives there, and likely will keep that. Eddy's child died last night. . . .

Feb. 8. Fine, clear morning. Spitzer died last night, and we will bury him in the snow; Mrs. Eddy died on the night of the seventh. . . .

Feb. 10. Beautiful morning; thawing in the sun; Milton Elliott died last night at Murphy's cabin, and Mrs. Reed went there this morning to see about his effects. John Denton trying to borrow meat for Graves; had none to give; they had nothing but hides; all are nearly out of meat, but a little we have; our hides are nearly all eat up, but with God's help spring will soon smile upon us. . . .

Feb. 19. Froze hard last night. Seven men arrived from California yesterday with provisions, but left the greater part on the way. Today it is clear and warm for this region; some of the men have gone to Donner's camp; they will start back on Monday. . . .

Feb. 25. Today Mrs. Murphy says the wolves are about to dig up the dead bodies around her shanty, and the nights are too cold to watch them, but we hear them howl.

Feb. 26. Hungry times in camp; plenty of hides, but the folks will not eat them; we eat them with tolerably good appetite, thanks to the Almighty God. Mrs. Murphy said here yesterday that she thought she would commence on Milton and eat him. I do not think she has done so yet; it is distressing. The Donners told the California folks four days ago that they would commence on the dead people if they did not succeed that day or the next in finding their cattle, then ten or twelve feet under the snow, and they did not know the spot or near it; they have done it ere this. . . .

March 1. Ten men arrived this morning from Bear Valley, with provisions. We are to start in two or three days, and cache our goods here. They say the snow will remain until June.

5. *1831*—THE TRADERS START FOR SANTA FE

❡ *Furs drew men to the mountains; farms enticed them to Oregon. Trade called them to the Southwest and opened the great trail to Santa Fe.*

Josiah Gregg, *The Commerce of the Prairies* (Chicago: R. R. Donnelley & Sons Co., 1926), 30, 36–40.

*The sleepy little capital of New Mexico contained no more than
3,000 inhabitants, but it was the trading center of some 40,000 New
Mexicans, all eager to barter their gold and silver and furs for the
knives and calico and "Yankee notions" that their own country
could not provide. But the Spanish authorities rigidly excluded
American traders, and smugglers were either imprisoned or made
to pay heavy fines. Then, in 1821, Mexico won her independence.
Thereafter traders from the North were welcome. Almost at once
the heavy wagons rolled across the plains—westward from Independence, Missouri, to the eastern slopes of the Sangre de Cristo
Mountains, then south and west to the end of the range and around
it to Santa Fe. A few weeks later they would return by the same
route. If the members of a caravan escaped disaster by accident and
succeeded in fighting off the Comanche and Pawnee Indians they
would find themselves well paid for five or six months of work, no
matter how hard and dangerous.*

*By 1831, when Josiah Gregg made the first of his many trips to
Santa Fe, the trade had grown to such an extent that the caravan
he accompanied consisted of nearly 100 wagons, loaded with merchandise valued at $200,000. Here Gregg describes the start of the
trading party from Council Grove, 150 miles west of Independence.*

Early on the 26th of May we reached the long looked-for rendezvous
of Council Grove, where we joined the main body of the caravan. . . .
The heterogeneous appearance of our company, consisting of men from
every class and grade of society, with a little sprinkling of the softer
sex, would have formed an excellent subject for an artist's pencil. It
may appear, perhaps, a little extraordinary that females should have
ventured across the prairies under such forlorn auspices. Those who accompanied us, however, were members of a Spanish family who had
been banished in 1829 in pursuance of a decree of the Mexican congress
and were now returning to their homes in consequence of a suspension
of the decree. Other females, however, have crossed the prairies to
Santa Fe at different times, among whom I have known two respectable French ladies, who now reside in Chihuahua.

The wild and motley aspect of the caravan can be but imperfectly
conceived without an idea of the costumes of its various members. The
most fashionable prairie dress is the fustian frock of the city-bred merchant furnished with a multitude of pockets capable of accommodating
a variety of extra tackling. Then there is the backwoodsman with his
linsey or leather hunting-shirt—the farmer with his blue jean coat—the
wagoner with his flannel-sleeve vest—besides an assortment of other
costumes which go to fill up the picture.

In the article of firearms there is also an equally interesting medley.
The frontier hunter sticks to his rifle, as nothing could induce him to

carry what he terms in derision "the scatter-gun." The sportsman from the interior flourishes his double-barreled fowling-piece with equal confidence in its superiority. The latter is certainly the most convenient description of gun that can be carried on this journey; as a charge of buck-shot in night attacks (which are the most common) will of course be more likely to do execution than a single rifle-ball fired at random. The repeating arms have lately been brought into use upon the prairies and they are certainly very formidable weapons, particularly when used against an ignorant savage foe. A great many were furnished beside with a bountiful supply of pistols and knives of every description, so that the party made altogether a very brigand-like appearance. . . .

Although the usual hour of starting with the prairie caravans is after an early breakfast, yet on this occasion we were hindered till in the afternoon. The familiar note of preparation, "Catch up! Catch up!" was now sounded from the captain's camp, and re-echoed from every division and scattered group along the valley. On such occasion a scene of confusion ensues which must be seen to be appreciated. The woods and dales resound with the gleeful yells of the light-hearted wagoners, who, weary of inaction and filled with joy at the prospect of getting under way, become clamorous in the extreme. Scarcely does the jockey on the race-course ply his whip more promptly at that magic word "Go" than do these emulous wagoners fly to harnessing their mules at the spirit-stirring sound of "Catch up." Each teamster vies with his fellows who shall be soonest ready; and it is a matter of boastful pride to the first to cry out "All's set!"

The uproarious bustle which follows—the hallooing of those in pursuit of animals—the exclamation which the unruly brutes call forth from their wrathful drivers; together with the clatter of bells—the rattle of yokes and harness—the jingle of chains—all conspire to produce a clamorous confusion which would be altogether incomprehensible without the assistance of the eyes; while those alone would hardly suffice to unravel the labyrinthian maneuvers and hurly-burly of this precipitate breaking up. It is sometimes amusing to observe the athletic wagoner hurrying an animal to its post—to see him heave upon the halter of a stubborn mule, while the brute as obstinately sets back, determined not to move a peg till his own good pleasure thinks it proper to do so—his whole manner seeming to say, "Wait till your hurry's over!" I have more than once seen a driver hitch a harnessed animal to the halter and by that process haul his mulishness forward, while each of his four projected feet would leave a furrow behind; until at last the perplexed master would wrathfully exclaim, "A mule will be a mule any way you can fix it!"

"All's set!" is finally heard from some teamster—"All's set" is directly responded from every quarter. "Stretch out!" immediately vociferates the captain. Then the "Heps!" of drivers—the cracking of whips

233

—the trampling of feet—the occasional creak of wheels—the rumbling of wagons—form a new scene of exquisite confusion, which I shall not attempt further to describe. "Fall in!" is heard from headquarters, and the wagons are forthwith strung out along the long, inclined plain which stretches to the heights beyond Council Grove.

6.   *1831*—SANTA FE AT LAST

⟦ *Ten weeks after leaving Council Grove, Gregg's Santa Fe caravan reached its destination. The drowsy old city suddenly came to life.*

Some distance beyond the Colorado a party of about a dozen (which I joined) left the wagons to go ahead to Santa Fe. . . .

A few miles before reaching the city the road . . . emerges into an open plain. Ascending a table-ridge, we spied in an extended valley to the northwest occasional groups of trees skirted with verdant corn and wheat fields, with here and there a square block-like protuberance reared in the midst. A little farther and just ahead of us to the north irregular clusters of the same opened to our view. "Oh, we are approaching the suburbs!" thought I, on perceiving the cornfields and what I supposed to be brick-kilns scattered in every direction. These and other observations of the same nature becoming audible, a friend at my elbow said, "It is true those are heaps of unburnt bricks, nevertheless they are *houses*—this is the city of Santa Fe."

Five or six days after our arrival the caravan at last hove in sight, and wagon after wagon was seen pouring down the last declivity at about a mile distance from the city. To judge from the clamorous rejoicings of the men and the state of agreeable excitement which the muleteers seemed to be laboring under, the spectacle must have been as new to them as it had been to me. It was truly a scene for the artist's pencil to revel in. Even the animals seemed to participate in the humor of their riders, who grew more and more merry and obstreperous as they descended towards the city. I doubt, in short, whether the first sight of the walls of Jerusalem was beheld by the crusaders with much more tumultuous and soul-enrapturing joy.

The arrival produced a great deal of bustle and excitement among the natives. *"Los Americanos!"*—*"Los carros!"*—*"La entrada de caravana!"* were to be heard in every direction; and crowds of women and boys flocked around to see the new-comers; while crowds of *leperos* hung about, as usual, to see what they could pilfer. The wagoners were by no means free from excitement on this occasion. Informed of the ordeal they had to pass, they had spent the previous morning in rubbing up; and now they were prepared, with clean faces, sleek-combed

---

Gregg, *Commerce of the Prairies*, 99, 101–05.

hair, and their choicest Sunday suit to meet the fair eyes of glistening black that were sure to stare at them as they passed. There was yet another preparation to be made in order to show off to advantage. Each wagoner must tie a brand new cracker to the lash of his whip; for on driving through the streets and the *plaza publica* every one strives to outvie his comrades in the dexterity with which he flourishes this favorite badge of his authority.

Our wagons were soon discharged in the ware-rooms of the custom house; and a few days' leisure being now at our disposal, we had time to take that recreation which a fatiguing journey of ten weeks had rendered so necessary. The wagoners and many of the traders, particularly the novices, flocked to the numerous fandangoes which are regularly kept up after the arrival of a caravan. But the merchants generally were anxiously and actively engaged in their affairs—striving who should first get his goods out of the custom house and obtain a chance at the hard chink of the numerous country dealers, who annually resort to the capital on these occasions.

7. *1836*—THE ALAMO

❮ *Texas, though a dependency of Mexico, attracted many settlers from the United States. By the mid-1830's some 25,000 had taken up their residence there. The newcomers, different in nationality, language, and religion from the country to which they were subject, soon showed that they would not be satisfied with less than a large measure of self-government. But Santa Anna, who proclaimed himself dictator of Mexico in 1834, made it clear that he would grant the Texans no more freedom than the residents of Chihuahua or Vera Cruz. Both sides prepared to settle their differences by arms. Fighting broke out in the fall of 1835, with the Americans victorious in the first engagements. In March, 1836, the Texans declared their independence. Santa Anna moved to crush the rebellion. With an overwhelming force he surrounded San Antonio, where a body of Texans, commanded by Lt. Col. William Barret Travis, a twenty-seven-year-old lawyer, occupied the stout-walled Alamo Mission. Two dispatches from Colonel Travis describe the first weeks of the siege. No defender could tell the whole story, for none survived.*

To THE PEOPLE IN TEXAS, AND ALL AMERICANS IN THE WORLD:
COMMANDANCY OF THE ALAMO, BEJAR, Feb. 24, 1836.
FELLOW-CITIZENS AND COMPATRIOTS:

I am besieged by a thousand or more of the Mexicans, under Santa Anna. I have sustained a continual bombardment and cannonade for

---

Henry Stuart Foote, *Texas and the Texans* (Philadelphia, 1841), II, 218–22.

twenty-four hours, and have not lost a man. The enemy have demanded a surrender at discretion, otherwise the garrison is to be put to the sword, if the fort is taken. I have answered the summons with a cannon-shot, and our flag still waves proudly from the walls. *I shall never surrender or retreat:* then I call on you, in the name of Liberty, of Patriotism, and of every thing dear to the American character, to come to our aid with all despatch. The enemy are receiving reinforcements daily, and will no doubt increase to three or four thousand in four or five days. Though this call may be neglected, I am determined to sustain myself as long as possible, and die like a soldier, who never forgets what is due to his own honour and that of his country. *Victory or Death!*

W. BARRET TRAVIS,
Lieutenant-Colonel, Commanding.

P.S. The Lord is on our side. When the enemy appeared in sight, we had not three bushels of corn. We have since found, in deserted houses, eighty or ninety bushels, and got into the walls twenty or thirty head of beeves.   T.

TO THE PRESIDENT OF THE CONVENTION
COMMANDANCY OF THE ALAMO, BEJAR, March 3, 1836.
SIR:

. . . . From the 25th to the present date, the enemy have kept up a bombardment from two howitzers (one a five and a half inch, and the other an eight inch), and a heavy canonade from two long nine-pounders, mounted on a battery on the opposite side of the river, at the distance of four hundred yards from our walls. During this period, the enemy have been busily employed in encircling us with intrenched encampments on all sides. . . . Notwithstanding all this, a company of thirty-two men from Gonzales, made their way into us on the morning of the 1st inst. at three o'clock, and Col. J. B. Bonham (a courier from Gonzales) got in this morning at eleven o'clock, without molestation. I have so fortified this place, that the walls are generally proof against cannon-balls; and I still continue to intrench on the inside, and strengthen the walls by throwing up the dirt. At least two hundred shells have fallen inside of our works without having injured a single man; indeed, we have been so fortunate as not to lose a man from any cause, and we have killed many of the enemy. The spirits of my men are still high, although they have had much to depress them. We have contended for ten days against an enemy whose numbers are variously estimated at from fifteen hundred to six thousand men, with Gen. Ramirez Sezma and Col. Bartres, the aid-de-camp of Santa Anna, at their head. A report was circulated that Santa Anna himself was with the enemy, but I think it was false. A reinforcement of about one thousand men is now entering Bexar from the west, and I think it more than probable that Santa Anna is now in town, from the rejoicing we hear. . . .

I look to the *colonies alone* for aid; unless it arrives soon, I shall have to fight the enemy on his own terms. I will, however, do the best I can under the circumstances, and I feel confident that the determined valour and desperate courage, heretofore evinced by my men, will not fail them in the last struggle. . . .

The power of Santa Anna is to be met here or in the colonies; we had better meet them here, than to suffer a war of desolation to rage in our settlements. A blood-red banner waves from the church of Bexar, and in the camp above us, in token that the war is one of vengeance against rebels; they have declared us as such, and demanded that we should surrender at discretion, or that this garrison should be put to the sword. Their threats have had no influence on me or my men, but to make all fight with desperation, and that high-souled courage which characterizes the patriot, who is willing to die in defence of his country's liberty and his own honour. . . .

The bearer of this will give your honourable body, a statement more in detail, should he escape through the enemy's lines. *God and Texas! —Victory or Death!!*

> Your obedient ser't.
> W. BARRET TRAVIS
> *Lieut. Col. Comm.*

At day-break of the 6th inst. the enemy surrounded the fort with their infantry, with the cavalry forming a circle outside to prevent escape on the part of the garrison; the number consisted of at least 4000 against 140! General Santa Anna commanded in person, assisted by four Generals and a formidable train of artillery. Our men had been previously much fatigued and harassed by night-watching and incessant toils, having experienced for some days past, a heavy bombardment and several real and feigned attacks. But, American valour and American love of Liberty displayed themselves to the last; they were never more conspicuous: twice did the enemy apply to the walls their scaling ladders, and twice did they receive a check; for our men were determined to verify the words of the immortal Travis, "to make the victory worse to the enemy than a defeat." A pause ensued after the second attack, which was renewed the third time, owing to the exertions of Santa Anna and his officers; they then poured in over the walls "like sheep"; the struggle, however, did not even there cease— unable from the crowd and for want of time to load their guns and rifles, our men made use of the butt-ends of the latter, and continued to fight and to resist, until life ebbed out through their numberless wounds, and the enemy had conquered the fort, but not its brave, its matchless defenders: they perished, but they yielded not: only one (Warner) remained to ask for quarter, which was denied by the unrelenting enemy—total extermination succeeded, and the darkness of death occupied the memorable Alamo, but recently so teeming with gallant spirits and filled with deeds of never-failing remembrance. We envy not the feelings of the victors, for they must have been bitter and galling; not proud ones. Who would not be rather one of the Alamo heroes, than of the living of its merciless victors?. . . .

From the commencement to its close, the storming lasted less than an hour. Major Evans, master of ordnance, was killed when in the act of setting fire to the powder magazine, agreeably to the previous orders from Travis. The end of David Crockett of Tennessee, the great hunter of the West, was as glorious as his career through life had been useful. He and his companions were found surrounded by piles of assailants, whom they had immolated on the altar of Texas liberties. The countenance of Crockett was unchanged: he had in death that freshness of hue, which his exercise of pursuing the beasts of the forest and the prairie had imparted to him. Texas places him, exultingly, amongst the martyrs in her cause. Col. Travis stood on the walls cheering his men, exclaiming "Hurra, my boys!" till he received a second shot, and fell; it is stated that a Mexican general (Mora) then rushed upon him, and lifted his sword to destroy his victim, who, collecting all his last expiring energies, directed a thrust at the former, which changed their relative positions; for the victim became the victor, and the remains of both descended to eternal sleep; but not alike to everlasting fame. . . .

It is stated that about fifteen hundred of the enemy were killed and wounded in the last and previous attacks.

8.   *1846*—ZACHARY TAYLOR WINS THE BATTLE OF MONTEREY

⟦ *Despite the loss of the Alamo, the Texans won their independence, and at once let it be known that they would welcome annexation by the United States. The North, fearful of the admission of new slave states, objected so strongly that nine years passed before Texas was allowed to come into the Union. Mexico regarded the annexation as an act of war and broke off diplomatic relations. When attempts to re-establish them failed, President Polk ordered General Zachary Taylor, commanding an American army in Texas, to advance to the Rio Grande. There he clashed with Mexican forces and defeated them in the battles of Palo Alto and Resaca de la Palma. Congress declared war.*

John R. Kenly, *Memoirs of a Maryland Volunteer* (Philadelphia, 1873), 105–28.

American military plans called for an advance into northern Mexico. Late September found Taylor's army in front of the strongly fortified city of Monterey. He attacked on September 21. The battle, vividly described by John R. Kenly, a volunteer from Maryland, lasted three days. During the night of the 23rd the Mexicans withdrew, leaving the city in American hands.

September 21, 1846. . . . The reveille soon sounded throughout our camp, the slumbering fires of the past night were replenished with wood, coffee was cooked, and by sunrise our men had breakfasted. . . . We moved out of the woods . . . and after thirty minutes' hard marching, emerged from a cornfield at the distance of five hundred yards from and directly in front of a fort (Teneria), which opened upon us immediately. . . .

We advanced toward the fort with steadiness and rapidity, receiving its fire of round and grape shot, and the musketry of its infantry supports, when there came across our line of advance, and apparently in close proximity, the sound of an eighteen-pound ball sent from the citadel. *We were being enfiladed.* Still we advanced; another shot from the citadel, and the leg of Lieutenant Dilworth, of the First Infantry, was taken off as he stepped. If the gun which had fired that shot had been aimed the eighth of an inch more to the left, there is no telling how many would have been crippled. Still we advanced, notwithstanding this additional fire on our exposed flank, until we were within a little less than one hundred yards of the citadel. . . . Just at the moment the fruits of our gallant charge were within our grasp, our brigade commander committed the unpardonable blunder of changing the point of attack. . . . If there had been any faltering in his troops, if there were any impassable obstacle in our front, then there might have been some excuse for changing the direction of the brigade; but, going with the speed that we were, the hesitation caused by all not comprehending the movement was of itself sufficient to break the *élan* of the charge. . . .

The Third and First Infantry were on our right, and necessarily by the flank movement preceded us into the street leading into the heart of the town, and they caught the severity of the fire of the Mexicans lying in wait for our advance. It was a terrific fire from all sides, and as we hurried up the street we passed the dead, the dying, and those who were seeking shelter of the two leading battalions. I was well up with the head of our battalion, and did not look behind, but I have no doubt that men of ours sought shelter as had those who preceded them. I say, however, that the mass of our men followed as far as the mass of the brigade, and that was as far as brave men could go. There was no going any farther; the brigade was gone as an organization, and the last order given in that town by Colonel Garland, prior to the order to retreat, was obeyed by some twenty or thirty officers and men; the rest were unable to fight or do more than they had done, and were lying in the streets by which we had reached the shambles in which we were now cooped. . . .

The Fourth Brigade was gone, but its commanding officer was at his post. As angry as I was, I could not but admire the courage of Colonel Garland, for even in that storm of missiles he seemed unwilling to withdraw. Finally he said to the few about him, "We must withdraw." Watson, turning to me, asked which way I was going. I replied, "With the men." He said, "I am going this way," and crossed to an open gateway on the north side of the street, and this was the last I saw of him. . . .

September 22. A heavy cannonading was kept up all last night, and the rockets from the town illuminated the mountains in the rear to such an extent that the scenery was grand, almost sublime. At reveille we were ordered to be ready to leave at a moment's warning, and the stiffened limbs of the men yielded unwilling obedience to orders to fall in. During the morning it was reported that the Mexicans were assembling on the plain, and the division was formed, when my company was detailed to move to the front to support Bragg's Battery, near the city. I left the camp with my men, and once more took the road to the town. We soon perceived that there was heavy fighting on the hill next the Loma Independencia, upon which was the bishop's palace, and we saw the soldiers fighting; it was the most exciting scene I had ever beheld, for now they were advancing to the assault on the palace. How my heart beat! for I felt that if they could carry the palace the town was ours. On rushed the Americans, in full view as we marched, met with the fire from the Mexicans; but still they pressed on, and now they were getting in the works. Almost simultaneously with the entry of the Americans, we saw the Mexicans leaping from the windows, and running from the rear of the palace down the hill toward the city. We saw the Mexican flag lowered, and such a cheer as was sent up was never heard before on that plain. . . .

The bishop's palace carried, it was clear that the town was gone, for this hill entirely commanded Monterey and its environs, and it was only a question of time as to when it would surrender. . . .

At reveille on the morning of Wednesday, September 23d, we were again ordered to hold ourselves in readiness to leave, as a final attack was to be made on the town by the whole of the two divisions. At 8:30 the long roll sounded and the troops sprang to their arms; at 9 o'clock a.m. we marched from our camp, still in the wood of San Domingo, but called by us Walnut Springs, and followed our well-known road to the city; we halted within half a mile from the town, when the First

Division moved forward into line of battle, and the command was given, *"In place, rest."* . . . . We were comparatively safe from fire, and our interest and excitement increased every hour; bombs were flying continually from every side; volleys of musketry, lighting up the smoke with a lurid glare, were mingled with the dull heavy roar of cannon flashing their jets of flame through the dark cloud enveloping friend and foe, and rolling down upon us, reeking with the smell of battle. I would have given an arm to have been ordered to the attack, and all were alike excited. As the fighting continued, I never beheld men in such a condition as ours; it was impossible to keep them in the ranks. They would jump up and sit down, fix and unfix bayonets, open their cartridge-boxes, unbutton their coats, stamp with their feet, swear the most horrid oaths, and it needed but one single cry of "Forward!" to have thrown that division like a torrent into the city, to aid their hard-pressed comrades. . . .

As night approached, the firing gradually dropped off, save that now and then a whizzing, which seemed more spiteful because less in quantity, might be heard cutting the air as the missile sped on its flight; now and then the explosion of a single bomb lit up the darkness of cloud and smoke with a thousand pictures of light and shadow; but as the cold shades of evening fell upon us, a silence, heavy and profound, was over camp and field, town and mountains, the living and the dead.

9. *1847*—THE BATTLE OF THE BEAUTIFUL VIEW

❮ *After the Battle of Monterey, Santa Anna raised a new army and moved north to drive the American invaders from Mexican soil. He found Taylor at a mountain pass near the hacienda of Buena Vista. On February 22, 1847, Santa Anna attacked. A hard and bloody battle followed. At the end of the second day Major W. H. L. Wallace of the First Illinois Volunteers feared defeat. But that night the Mexicans retreated, leaving the Americans victorious.*

"Our bugles sang truce and the night cloud had lowered." I went down with Colonel Weatherford to our camp to get something to eat and some blankets to lie upon, for I did not expect to sleep much. We found the camp, and especially my tent, crowded with wounded. I was surprised at the coolness of my feelings as I looked upon the ghastly wounds and shattered limbs and heard the deep stifled groans of my suffering countrymen. But the fight was not yet over. I felt then an absolute certainty that we should have to re-enact the scenes of today as soon as light came.

Isabel Wallace, Ed., *Life and Letters of W. H. L. Wallace* (Chicago, 1909), 50–52.

I got a blanket from a friend and again went on to the hill. There was no moon, a slight breeze rustled the flag close to me, around lay the forms of our wearied men reposing in their blankets on their arms —across the hills to the front the fires of the enemy's camp burned brightly; and occasionally as the breeze rose and lulled, I could hear the creaking of wheels and the noise of some movement. This confirmed me in the belief that we should have another and harder fight in the morning. I imagined that I could see a column moving down the road, and I was certain they were planting heavy ordnance on the hill in front of us to command our position. I believe that every man of our command had determined to die on that hill. I felt there was nothing for us but victory or death. We had seen enough through the day to convince us we had no quarter to expect. Our wounded friends butchered in cold blood—the savage ferocity of the lancers cut off all hope in that quarter. Retreat was equally impossible. A body of two thousand lancers had entered through the Palomas pass and were hovering about town, and had been slightly engaged during the day with a detachment from town. We had reason to believe that larger bodies had been sent toward Monterey, and what I have since ascertained to be the case, the mountains and valleys on either side of us were filled and covered with rancheros from all the neighboring towns and settlements—even as far as Parras and Monclova, watching the result of the fight and ready to participate in the pillage and slaughter of our defeat.

Under all these circumstances courage was no virtue, or at least a *virtue* of necessity. With these thoughts and feelings I lay down with Colonel Weatherford. Neither of us spoke. But my fatigue soon overcame me and I went to sleep and slept till near daylight. I got up, the Mexican fires burned dim, and most of them were entirely out. I could hear no noise, but I thought I could discover a cloud of dust far up the road. I could not then hope they were gone. I stood upon the breastwork, looking out keenly—day broke—it grew gradually light. I looked to the foot of the mountain at Battery No. 3 and thought I could see the dim outlines of the column that rested there at dark the night before. The light increased and I saw what I had taken for a column to be a row of palmetto. I looked up the road and saw distinctly the dust of their retreating column. Oh, what a feeling of relief came over me. I set up a shout of *victory*—it was a mockery, however, I had the day before felt very much as I should suppose a *whipped* man would feel— and I've no doubt—*inter nos*—had it been just as convenient for us, as for Santa Anna to *vamos* we would have been off for Monterey.

But no matter for that, we were in possession of the field—the enemy was retiring, leaving his dead and wounded, or a large portion of them, on the ground. . . .

We collected the wounded, who were suffering awfully from hunger and thirst as well as their wounds, and sent them to hospitals in town. During the day we collected and buried our dead, amounting to two hundred and seventy. The remains of Colonels Hardin, McKee and Clay were taken to Saltillo and there interred. The wounded, both American and Mexican, were collected and cared for in the hospitals there.

It was amusing to see our volunteers when the poor famished Mexicans were brought in—for we took a large number of prisoners through the day. "Damn them," they would say, "they ought to have their throats cut, but let's give the poor devils something to eat," and it was a treat to see them eat. They had been in a half starving condition during their forced march from San Luis Potosi. When coffee and biscuit were placed before them they showed even in their famished state some signs of surprise and gratitude. This was the greatest victory of all, a victory unstained by blood and the feelings for its success unchecked by any mournful thoughts.

10. *1847*—THE CAPTURE OF VERÁ CRUZ

❲ *While Taylor held northern Mexico, another army under General Winfield Scott prepared to invade the country from the east and strike at Mexico City, as Cortes had done three centuries earlier. On March 9, under the immediate direction of General William J. Worth, the troops hit the beaches at Vera Cruz in the first amphibious operation in American military history. After a siege lasting a little less than three weeks, the city surrendered. Landing and surrender are described by Raphael Semmes, flag-lieutenant to the naval commander, Commodore David Conner.*

As the ships approached their allotted anchoring ground, they came to . . . in the most harmonious and exact order, each one dropping her anchor and swinging into her appropriate place, without the least confusion, and with the most admirable precision. Indeed, so thoroughly and admirably had Commodore Conner organized the whole movement; from the transfer of the troops from the vessels in which they had arrived, to the ships of war; to the placing them with haversack and musket on the enemy's beach, that it was next to impossible that anything could go wrong. The surf-boats, 67 in number, and each one manned by experienced seamen of the navy, were hauled alongside of the ships; the soldiers, with their arms and accoutrements, were passed into them; and as each boat received her complement, she shoved off, and laid on her oars, at a little distance, until the others should be

Raphael Semmes, *Service Afloat and Ashore during the Mexican War* (Cincinnati, 1851), 126–28, 145–47.

ready. The post of honor on this memorable occasion, was given to Brevet Brigadier-General Worth, who had so recently distinguished himself before Monterey—it being decided by the general-in-chief, that his division—the 1st division of regulars, which afterward became so celebrated in the valley of Mexico—should be the first to flout our flag in the enemy's face. Accordingly, when all was ready, the general, whose fine military person and bearing, had already won the hearts of such of the officers of the navy as had come in contact with him, descended into one of the man-of-war's boats prepared for him, and placing himself at the head of his troops, moved, in a semi-circle, toward the shore. Commodore Conner had previously directed the two steamers, *Spitfire,* Commander Tatnall, and *Vixen,* Commander Sands, with five-gun schooners, to anchor in line, abreast of the beach, to cover the landing, in case any opposition should be made. This part of the movement had already been handsomely executed. Nothing could exceed the beauty of this spectacle, as viewed from the poop of the flagship. It was just before sunset, an hour at which all the beauties of the Mexican coast are wont to stand out in bold and beautiful relief. The day had continued as clear as it had begun, and the sea-breeze, as it died gradually away, had left behind it a glazed and unruffled sea. The magnificent mountain of Orizaba, with its snow-clad summit, which had been hid from view most of the day, suddenly revealed itself, with startling distinctness and grandeur; the distant Cofre of Perote loomed up, also, in blue and mystic beauty, and the bold and rugged outline of the coast, seemed more bold and rugged still, from the refracting power of the atmosphere.

The walls of the town and castle, the domes of the churches, and the rigging and mast-heads of the foreign men-of-war, anchored at Sacrificios, all filled with curious and eager spectators, completed a scene which made a lively impression upon the minds of all beholders. The boats reaching the shore, in fine style, the troops debarked in good order; and in a few minutes afterward a detachment, which had wound its way up one of the sand-hills, unfurled the American flag, and waving it proudly over their heads, planted it in the land of Cortez. As if by common consent a shout, such as seamen only can give, arose at this moment from the decks of all the ships-of-war present, which was joined in, and prolonged, by such portions of the army as had not yet landed. The debarkation now went briskly forward, and before ten o'clock, p.m., the whole force present, consisting of about twelve thousand men, was safely landed, without the occurence of a single mistake or accident; an event unparalleled in the history of similar operations, and of which any naval commander might well be proud. . . .

The 29th of March, the day of the surrender, was a *gala* day, with the navy and army before Vera Cruz. The sun rose brilliantly in an unclouded sky, and the sea-breeze came in gently and delightfully from the S. E. A green meadow of considerable extent, immediately south of the city, had been chosen as a place where the enemy was to lay down his arms; and thither, at an early hour, repaired a host of spectators from the camp, the city, and the shipping—including the foreign men-of-war—to witness the ceremony. General Worth was chosen as the marshal of the day, and the officer to receive the surrender. A limited number was picked out from each corps of the army, to represent their brethren; and Commodore Perry had detailed for the occasion, a number of officers and seamen to be present, on the part of the squadron. At ten o'clock, the hour appointed in the articles of capitulation, the Mexican flags, which had been hoisted, as usual, at sunrise, on the castle of San Juan de Ulloa, and the forts of Santiago and Conception, were struck in these several places, saluted by the Mexican batteries; and in a few moments afterward, our glorious stripes and stars were unfolded to the breeze, under salutes from our own batteries and the squadron, and looked proudly forth over those arid sand-hills, and that wide gulf which had witnessed so many revolutions of empire during the last three hundred years. At this moment the enemy's troops were defiling out of the city gate; and, although the temptation seemed to be almost irresistible with the American multitude there assembled, to salute our proud banners with one long and loud hurra! good taste and a sense of propriety, which, I venture to say, have not often been equaled, restrained them. The Mexicans were about five thousand strong. They were arrayed in their best uniforms—many of those of the officers being covered with the stars and embroidery of which this people is so fond—and marched, with music playing, beneath the standards of their respective corps. Accompanying the soldiery, were many women and children—the women loaded down with their simple household effects, and the children trudging on by their sides, looking with amazement and wonder upon the spectacle before them.

Our men, on whose bronzed features were visible the joint emotions of pride of conquest, and sympathy for the fallen, were drawn up, under arms, in two lines, between which their late enemies passed. As each corps of the Mexican army reached a designated spot, the soldiers, in succession, divested themselves of their accoutrements, laid down these and their muskets, and passed on to the open fields, under parole, which they had previously given, "of not serving again in the present war, unless duly exchanged." All persons retained their private effects; and the officers were permitted, beside, to retain their horses with their caparisons, and their side-arms. This solemn and novel spectacle lasted several hours, and presented one of those striking pictures which linger in the imagination, long after the reality has passed away. The two gallant armies, arrayed in the pomp and panoply of war; the officers of the squadron, clad in their more modest blue and gold; the seamen, with their rolling gait and holiday attire; the meadow, the hills, the sea, and the glorious sunshine, all presented one of those *coups d' oeil* which the pencil alone can portray. General Worth was the "observed of all observers"; sitting his horse as proudly as a marshal of France in the best days of the republic, and receiving the submission of the enemy, with a mingled dignity and grace, which he knew so well how to assume, and which became him so well. Thus ended the surrender of Vera Cruz.

11.   *1847*—ACTION AT THE MILL OF THE KING

❴ *After a brilliant campaign Scott's army stood outside Mexico City. Several strong points had to be taken before the capital could be occupied. One of these was Molino del Rey. The fighting there was described by Lieutenant Robert Anderson, who would be in command of Fort Sumter at the outbreak of the Civil War.*

The fall of Mexico City, on September 14, brought the war to an end.

Tuesday, September 7th, three p.m.

We have been ready for the last three hours to move at a moment's warning. The truce was broken yesterday, by the Mexicans, and this morning, Genl. Santa Anna, I hear, wrote and sent a very impertinent "buncombe" letter to the Genl. Their troops, at all events, commenced moving out of the City early this morning, and are now drawn up in line of battle with their left resting on Ft. Chapultepec. Genl. Scott and Staff are engaged in reconnoitring his position, so that not many hours can elapse before we have another battle. . . .

Should God spare my life, I will resume this letter the earliest moment after victory. . . .

MEXICO, September 22nd.

This day two weeks ago since I was wounded. Oh, how devotedly I should offer thanks to our Heavenly Father for His preservation of my life on that dreadful day. . . .

Leaving our quarters about half-past two a.m., 8th Sept., we, after being kept a long time in the streets of Tacubaya, reached our position in front of the building called the Foundry, and better known as "El Molino de Rey"; our men were ordered to lie down on the road, so as to conceal themselves from the observation of the troops in Ft. Chapultepec. We remained there until a few discharges had been made by our Arty. when, just before sunrise, we were ordered to advance.

Robert Anderson, *An Artillery Officer in the Mexican War* (New York, 1911), 310–13.

The firing of musketry and cannon was at this time very severe on our left. We approached and when within about two hundred yards of the Foundry, we were received with an awful shower of grape and musketry, the column was ordered to halt, and the men ordered to shelter themselves against the wall on our right, the angle here making a shoulder which partially protected our troops. . . .

When we had remained a short time there, two of Capt. Drum's guns were unlimbered and, seeing that there were few men at the first, which they were bringing up by hand, I, more for example's sake than anything else, assisted at it. This gun was placed in position, and commenced firing. I then stepped a few paces back, and observing that the men were slow in bringing the other gun forward, I took hold of the trail, which I left as soon as it was in position, and when I saw men enough at it to manage it.

I then hurried towards the Regt., which was then some paces in the rear, when I felt a severe blow against my right shoulder; it was like the blow from the ball in a leaded cane;—I supposed that it was a *spent ball* which had hit me, and fallen to the ground—another step and I felt a tingling pricking sensation in my left arm. I, without raising my hand or giving any intimation of being wounded, regained my Command, and on my remarking to some Officer that I believed I had been touched by a spent ball, was told that there was blood on my cloak. In a few minutes, I heard some one call out, "Come on, they are abandoning their battery." I stepped out and saw Lt. Prince, 4th Infy., in the road, waving his hand (the 4th and 6th Regts. Infy. were in front or advance of us). I immediately called out "Forward 3rd Arty.," and rushed forward. Lt. Prince was shot down while he was calling out. I found myself under the enclosure of the Foundry, the enemy still lining its walls.

My wound giving me much pain, had now rendered me a little less vigorous than I was, and I was joined by Lt. Andrews and Capt. Ayres and went forward. Mr. Andrews begged me to send for more men, as the Mexicans were in too great force for us to enter the passageway . . . , the enemy being in considerable numbers in the enclosure and on the walls around it. Getting a half dozen men more, I went forward and entered the enclosure under a pretty galling fire. As I passed through the passageway, a ball grazed my right leg, grazing the bone outside about three inches below the knee.

We had tolerably warm work in retaining possession of this place, and in killing and driving the enemy from it. He made repeated attempts to dislodge us, but, thanks to God, did not succeed. In about two hours officers came in with re-inforcements, who ranked me, and then all the fighting, responsibility, and excitement being over, and my wound becoming stiff, I realized that I felt discomfort from my wound. A drink of spirits from a soldier's canteen revived me, but in a few minutes I fell. . . .

12.   *1848*—GOLD!

❲ *For more than 300 years California was a province first of Spain, then of Mexico. By 1846, when the Mexican War broke out, a scattering of Americans had settled there. The United States sent in troops quickly, and acquired the region by treaty after the end of the war.*

In its first two years under the Stars and Stripes California changed little. The inhabitants herded their cattle and cultivated their orchards and vineyards in the unhurried manner they had followed for centuries. But on January 24, 1848, an event occurred on the baronial estate of John Augustus Sutter, on the American River near its junction with the Sacramento, that soon transformed a pastoral paradise into the scene of a mad scramble for wealth. Sutter, a one-time citizen of Switzerland, tells the story.

I was sitting one afternoon just after my siesta, engaged, by-the-bye, in writing a letter to a relation of mine at Lucern, when I was interrupted by Mr. Marshall, a gentleman with whom I had frequent business transactions—bursting into the room. From the unusual agitation in his manner I imagined that something serious had occurred, and, as we involuntarily do in this part of the world, I at once glanced to see if my rifle was in its proper place. You should know that the mere appearance of Mr. Marshall at that moment in the Fort, was quite enough to surprise me, as he had but two days before left the place to make some alterations in a mill for sawing pine planks, which he had just run up for me some miles higher up the Americanos. When he had recovered himself a little, he told me that, however great my surprise might be at his unexpected reappearance, it would be much greater when I heard the intelligence he had come to bring me. "Intelligence," he added, "which if properly profited by, would put both of us in possession of unheard-of wealth—millions and millions of dollars, in fact." I frankly own, when I heard this that I thought something had touched Marshall's brain, when suddenly all my misgivings were put at an end by his flinging on the table a handful of scales of pure virgin gold. I was fairly thunderstruck and asked him to explain what all this meant, when he went on to say, that according to my instructions, he had thrown the mill-wheel out of gear, to let the whole body of the water in the dam find a passage through the tail race, which was previously too narrow to allow the water to run off in sufficient quantity,

From an 1854 print reproduced in Harry T. Peters, *California on Stone* (Garden City, 1935), 28, 67–69.

whereby the wheel was prevented from efficiently performing its work. By this alteration the narrow channel was considerably enlarged, and a mass of sand & gravel carried off by the force of the torrent. Early in the morning after this took place, Mr. Marshall was walking along the left bank of the stream when he perceived something which he at first took for a piece of opal—a clear transparent stone, very common here—glittering on one of the spots laid bare by the sudden crumbling away of the bank. He paid no attention to this, but while he was giving directions to the workmen, having observed several similar glittering fragments, his curiosity was so far excited, that he stooped down & picked one of them up. "Do you know," said Mr. Marshall to me, "I positively debated within myself two or three times whether I should take the trouble to bend my back to pick up one of the pieces and had decided on not doing so when further on, another glittering morsel caught my eye—the largest of the pieces now before you. I condescended to pick it up, and to my astonishment found that it was a thin scale of what appears to be pure gold." He then gathered some twenty or thirty pieces which on examination convinced him that his suppositions were right. His first impression was, that this gold had been lost or buried there, by some early Indian tribe—perhaps some of those mysterious inhabitants of the West, of whom we have no account, but who dwelt on this continent centuries ago, and built those cities and temples, the ruins of which are scattered about these solitary wilds. On proceeding, however, to examine the neighbouring soil, he discovered that it was more or less auriferous. This at once decided him. He mounted his horse, and rode down to me as fast as it could carry him with the news.

At the conclusion of Mr. Marshall's account, and when I had convinced myself, from the specimens he had brought with him, that it was not exaggerated, I felt as much excited as himself. I eagerly inquired if he had shown the gold to the work people at the mill and was glad to hear that he had not spoken to a single person about it. We agreed not to mention the circumstance to any one and arranged to set off early the next day for the mill. On our arrival, just before sundown, we poked the sand around in various places, and before long succeeded in collecting between us more than an ounce of gold, mixed up with a good deal of sand. I stayed at Mr. Marshall's that night, and the next day we proceeded some little distance up the South Fork, and found that gold existed along the whole course, not only in the bed of the main stream, where the [water] had subsided but in every little dried-up creek and ravine. Indeed I think it is more plentiful in these latter places, for I myself, with nothing more than a small knife, picked out from a dry gorge, a little way up the mountain, a solid lump of gold which weighed nearly an ounce and a half.

Notwithstanding our precautions not to be observed, as soon as we came back to the mill, we noticed by the excitement of the working people that we had been dogged about, and to complete our disappointment, one of the Indians who had worked at the gold mine in the neighbourhood of La Paz cried out in showing us some specimens picked up by himself,—"Oro!—Oro—Oro!!!"

13. *1849*—TO CALIFORNIA BY THE ISTHMUS OF PANAMA

❡ *The fact that gold had been discovered in California could not be kept secret. By May, 1848, the word had reached San Francisco. Workmen dropped their tools, merchants closed their stores, teachers shut their classrooms and rushed for the gold fields. News of the discovery was published in mid-August, but the skeptical East paid little attention until President Polk made an official announcement in a message to Congress in early December. With that, goldfever swept the country, and thousands fought for some means of transportation to the west coast.*

While most California emigrants followed the overland trails, those who could afford the passage money took ship. Assuming that they could find accommodations, they had their choice of two routes: around Cape Horn, or to Panama, where they crossed the Isthmus and reshipped on the Pacific side.

One of those who took the Panama route in 1849 was Bayard Taylor, a popular lecturer and writer who went west to report the gold rush for the New York TRIBUNE. *Taylor sailed from New York in June, then crossed the Isthmus from Chagres to the ancient city of Panama. His own narrative describes the remainder of the voyage.*

There were about seven hundred emigrants waiting for passage, when I reached Panama. All the tickets the steamer could possibly receive had been issued and so great was the anxiety to get on, that double price, $600, was frequently paid for a ticket to San Francisco. A few days before we came, there was a most violent excitement on the subject, and as the only way to terminate the dispute, it was finally agreed to dispose by lot of all the tickets for sale. The emigrants were all numbered, and those with tickets for sailing vessels or other steamers excluded. The remainder then drew, there being fifty-two tickets to near three hundred passengers. This quieted the excitement for the time, though there was still a continual under-current of speculation and intrigue which was curious to observe. The disappointed candidates, for the most part, took passage in sailing vessels, with a prospect of seventy

Bayard Taylor, *Eldorado, or Adventures in the Path of Empire* (New York, 1850), 29–33, 36, 51–53.

days' voyage before them. A few months previous, when three thousand persons were waiting on the Isthmus, several small companies started in the log canoes of the natives, thinking to reach San Francisco in them! After a voyage of forty days, during which they went no further than the Island of Quibo, at the mouth of the Gulf, nearly all of them returned; the rest have not since been heard of.

The passengers were engaged in embarking all the afternoon of the second day after my arrival. The steamer came up to within a mile and a half of the town, and numbers of canoes plied between her and the sea-gateway. Native porters crowded about the hotels, clamoring for luggage, which they carried down to the shore under so fervent a heat that I was obliged to hoist my umbrella. One of the boatmen lifted me over the swells for the sake of a *medio,* and I was soon gliding out along the edge of the breakers, startling the pelicans that flew in long lines over the water. I was well satisfied to leave Panama at the time; the cholera, which had already carried off one-fourth of the native population, was making havoc among the Americans, and several of the *Falcon's* passengers lay at the point of death. . . .

A voyage from Panama to San Francisco in the year 1849, can hardly be compared to sea-life in any other part of the world or at any previous period. Our vessel was crowded fore and aft: exercise was rendered quite impossible and sleep was each night a new experiment, for the success of which we were truly grateful. We were roused at daylight by the movements on deck, if not earlier, by the breaking of a hammock-rope and the thump and yell of the unlucky sleeper. Coffee was served in the cabin; but, as many of the passengers imagined that, because they had paid a high price for their tickets, they were conscientiously obligated to drink three cups, the late-comers got a very scanty allowance. The breakfast hour was nine, and the table was obliged to be fully set twice. At the first tingle of the bell, all hands started as if a shot had exploded among them; conversation was broken off in the middle of a word; the deck was instantly cleared, and the passengers, tumbling pell-mell down the cabin-stairs, found every seat taken by others who had probably been sitting in them for half an hour. The bell, however, had an equally convulsive effect upon these. There was a confused grabbing motion for a few seconds, and lo! the plates were cleared. A chicken parted in twain as if by magic, each half leaping into an opposite plate; a dish of sweet potatoes vanished before a single hand; beef-steak flew in all directions; and while about half the passengers had all their breakfast piled at once upon their plates, the other half were regaled by a "plentiful lack." The second table was but a repetition of these scenes, which dinner—our only additional meal—renewed in the afternoon. To prevent being driven, in self-defence, into the degrading habit, eight of us secured one end of the second table, shut off by the mizen-mast from the long arms that might otherwise have grabbed our share. Among our company of two hundred and fifty, there were, of course, many gentlemen of marked refinement and intelligence from various parts of the Union—enough, probably, to leaven the large lump of selfishness and blackguardism into which we were thrown. I believe the controlling portion of the California emigration is intelligent, orderly, and peaceable; yet I never witnessed so many disgusting exhibitions of the lowest passions of humanity, as during the voyage. At sea or among the mountains, men completely lose the little arts of dissimulation they practise in society. They show in their true light, and very often, alas! in a light little calculated to encourage the enthusiastic believer in the speedy perfection of our race. . . .

We had on board a choice gang of blacklegs, among whom were several characters of notoriety in the United States, going out to extend the area of their infernal profession. About a dozen came on from New Orleans by the *Falcon* and as many from New York by the *Crescent City*. They established a branch at Panama, immediately on their arrival, and two or three remained to take charge of it. They did not commence very fortunately; their first capital of $500 having been won in one night by a lucky padre. Most of them, with the devil's luck, drew prizes in the ticket lottery, while worthy men were left behind. After leaving Acapulco, they commenced playing *monte* on the quarter-deck, and would no doubt have entrapped some unwary passengers, had not the Captain put a stop to their operations. These characters have done much, by their conduct on the Isthmus and elsewhere, to earn for us the title of "Northern barbarians," and especially, by wantonly offending the religious sentiment of the natives. I was told of four who entered one of the churches with their hats pulled fast over their brows, and, marching deliberately up the aisle, severally lighted their cigars at the four tapers of the altar. The class was known to all on board and generally shunned. . . .

At last the voyage is drawing to a close. Fifty-one days have elapsed since leaving New York, in which time we have, in a manner, coasted both sides of the North-American continent, from the parallel of 40° N. to its termination, within a few degrees of the Equator, over seas once plowed by the keels of Columbus and Balboa, of Grijalva and Sebastián Viscaíno. All is excitement on board; the Captain has just taken his noon observation. We are running along the shore, within six or eight miles' distance; the hills are bare and sandy, but loom up finely through the deep blue haze. A brig bound to San Francisco, but fallen off to the leeward of the harbor, is making a new tack on our left, to come up again. The coast trends somewhat more to the westward, and a notch or gap is at last visible in its lofty outline.

An hour later; we are in front of the entrance to San Francisco Bay. The mountains on the northern side are 3,000 feet in height, and come boldly down to the sea. As the view opens through the splendid strait, three or four miles in width, the island rock of Alcatraz appears, gleaming white in the distance. An inward-bound ship follows close on our wake, urged on by wind and tide. There is a small fort perched among the trees on our right, where the strait is narrowest, and a glance at the formation of the hills shows that this pass might be made impregnable as Gibraltar. The town is still concealed behind the promontory around which the Bay turns to the southward, but between Alcatraz and the island of Yerba Buena, now coming into sight, I can see vessels at anchor. High through the vapor in front, and thirty miles distant, rises the peak of Monte Diablo, which overlooks everything between the Sierra Nevada and the Ocean. On our left opens the bight of Sousolito, where the U.S. propeller *Massachusetts* and several other vessels are at anchor.

At last we are through the Golden Gate—fit name for such a magnificent portal to the commerce of the Pacific! Yerba Buena Island is in front; southward and westward opens the renowned harbor, crowded with the shipping of the world, mast behind mast and vessel behind vessel, the flags of all nations fluttering in the breeze! Around the curving shore of the Bay and upon the sides of three hills which rise steeply from the water, the middle one receding so as to form a bold amphitheatre, the town is planted and seems scarcely yet to have taken root, for tents, canvas, plank, mud and adobe houses are mingled together with the least apparent attempt at order and durability. But I am not yet on shore. The gun of the *Panama* has just announced our arrival to the people on land. We glide on with the tide, past the U.S. ship *Ohio* and opposite the main landing, outside of the forest of masts. A dozen boats are creeping out to us over the water; the signal is given—the anchor drops—our voyage is over.

14.   *1849*—ALONZO DELANO REACHES SACRAMENTO

❲ *Some 80,000 people poured into California in 1849. Of these, perhaps 25,000 traveled by sea, 55,000 by land. Alonzo Delano, one of the 55,000, described his emotions when he saw Sacramento City, the end of the long journey.*

September 17. . . . I was stiff and sore from the exertion of the previous day, but hope impelled me on with ardent fervor, and suffering from thirst, I was desirous of gaining the point where it could be as-

---

A. Delano, *Life on the Plains and Among the Diggings* (Auburn and Buffalo, 1853), 230–33, 248–50.

suaged. This was half a mile distant, at the foot of a steep hill—a part of the way over perpendicular ledges of rock, from which I let myself down with difficulty. On reaching the brink of a fine mountain creek, now called Cow Creek, I kindled a fire, and prepared a refreshing draught of coffee. Anxious as I was, I could not prevail upon myself to leave the delicious stream for two hours. After filling my flask, I again climbed the hill to the road. Ascending to the top of an inclined plain, the long-sought, the long-wished-for and welcome valley of the Sacramento, lay before me, five or six miles distant.

How my heart bounded at the view! how every nerve thrilled at the sight! It looked like a grateful haven to the tempest-tossed mariner, and with long strides, regardless of the weariness of my limbs, I plodded on, anxious to set foot upon level ground beyond the barren, mountain desert. I could discern green trees, which marked the course of the great river, and a broad, level valley, but the day was too smoky for a very extended view. There was the resting place, at least for a few days, where the dangerous and weary night-watch was no longer needed; where the habitations of civilized men existed, a security from the stealthy tread of the treacherous savage; where our debilitated frames could be renewed, and where our wandering would cease. Perspiring and fainting from exertion, I reached the foot of the last hill, and stood upon the plain. Yet here I was disappointed, for instead of the high grass and rich soil that I expected to find, for four or five miles after reaching the valley the earth was dry and baked by the sun; the scanty vegetation was dried and crisp, and the ground was strewn with round stones, which seemed to have been thrown there by volcanic force, or washed by the floods from the hills. But onward I pressed, till I reached the first trees which I had seen from the mountains, and found that they grew along the margin of Deer Creek, which I followed a mile, when the sight of a chimney attracted my attention. It was the house of Colonel Davis, eight miles from the foot hills. My sensations were singular on approaching the house. Although it was a simple abode, standing within a rough paling, it was the first peaceful dwelling of civilized man which I had seen for months. While I hurried to it, I felt an almost irresistible repugnance to approach, and when at length I sat down on the porch, I felt lost and bewildered with a degree of astonishment at seeing men and women moving about at their usual avocations. I could only give short replies to interrogatories which were made, and after sitting nearly an hour in a kind of half stupidity, I found resolution enough to inquire where the trains were encamped.

"About a mile below," was the reply, and I got up and walked off, leaving, probably, no very favorable impression as to my conversational powers.

On reaching the encampments below, and seeing the hundreds of white tents and wagons, with multitudes of cattle cropping the grass, I felt once more at home: all uneasy sensations vanished, and I wondered how I had been so perfectly stupid at the house. I met many traveling acquaintances, and was soon invited to share the hospitality of friends for the night.

Lawson's was on the opposite side of the creek, and a little before evening I went over, and found two or three small adobe buildings, one of which was called by courtesy a store, having a little flour, whisky, and a few groceries for sale. Around the trading post were lounging gangs of naked Indians of both sexes, drunken Mexicans, and weary emigrants, enjoying respite from excessive fatigue in the flowing bowl; and take it all in all, it did not give me a very flattering impression of the morals of the citizens of the first settlement. My first act was to provide for the creature comfort; and purchasing a little beef, bread, sugar and cheese, I returned to the camp, to enjoy a feast to which I had long been a stranger. . . .

On the fifth day after leaving Lawson's, we encamped on the bank of the American River, where there was a broad, grassy bottom, and where there were thousands of emigrants encamped, and it seemed as if we were again transported to the plains, amid the universal emigrant army.

We had driven half of the previous night to reach our resting place; and we now learned that we were within three miles of Sacramento City and Sutter's Fort. After a frugal dinner of hard bread and water, Doctor Hall, Mr. Rood and myself doffed our soiled garments, and after assuming habiliments more in accordance with civilized life, we set out for town, leaving our cattle and wagon in the care of Mr. Pope. Taking off our clothes on reaching the ford, we waded across the American, a clear and beautiful stream, about four hundred feet wide, and reached the city of tents about four o'clock in the afternoon. And here I found myself more than two thousand miles from home, in a city which had risen as if by enchantment since I had crossed the Missouri, a stranger, wayworn and jaded by a long journey, half famished for want of even the necessaries of life, practicing domestic economy to the fullest extent, with every prospect before me of continuing in the practice of that useful science; for, on examining the state of my treasury, I found myself the wealthy owner of the full sum of four dollars!

15. *1852*—"NATURE'S GREAT LOTTERY"

❡ *Once in California, how did the miners take out the gold? "Dame Shirley," pen name of Louise Amelia Knapp Smith Clappe, de-*

Louise Amelia Knapp Smith Clappe, *The Shirley Letters*, Thomas C. Russell, Ed. (San Francisco, 1922, 213–19. Originally printed in *Pioneer Magazine*, 1854–55.

scribed the process. Mrs. Clappe was the wife of a physician at a mining camp in the Sierras.

FROM OUR LOG CABIN,
INDIAN BAR, April 10, 1852.

Having got our gold mines discovered, and claimed, I will try to give you a faint idea of how they work them. Here, in the mountains, the labor of excavation is extremely difficult, on account of the immense rocks which form a large portion of the soil. Of course no man can work out a claim alone. For that reason, and also for the same that makes partnerships desirable, they congregate in companies of four or six, generally designating themselves by the name of the place from whence the majority of the members have emigrated; as, for example, the Illinois, Bunker Hill, Bay State, etc., companies. In many places the surface soil, or in mining phrase, the top dirt, pays when worked in a Long-Tom. This machine (I have never been able to discover the derivation of its name) is a trough, generally about twenty feet in length and eight inches in depth, formed of wood, with the exception of six feet at one end, called the "riddle" (query, why "riddle?"), which is made of sheet-iron perforated with holes about the size of a large marble. Underneath this colander-like portion of the long-tom, is placed another trough, about ten feet long, the sides six inches, perhaps, in height, which, divided through the middle by a slender slat, is called the riffle-box. It takes several persons to manage properly a long-tom. Three or four men station themselves with spades at the head of the machine, while at the foot of it stands an individual armed "wid de shovel an' de hoe." The spadesmen throw in large quantities of the precious dirt, which is washed down to the riddle by a stream of water leading into the long-tom through wooden gutters or sluices. When the soil reaches the riddle, it is kept constantly in motion by the man with the hoe. Of course, by this means, all the dirt and gold escapes through the perforations into the riffle-box below, one compartment of which is placed just beyond the riddle. Most of the dirt washes over the sides of the riffle-box, but the gold, being so astonishingly heavy, remains safely at the bottom of it. When the machine gets too full of stones to be worked easily, the man whose business it is to attend to them throws them out with his shovel, looking carefully among them as he does so for any pieces of gold which may have been too large to pass through the holes of the riddle. I am sorry to say that he generally loses his labor. At night they pan out the gold, which has been collected in the riffle-box during the day. Many of the miners decline washing the top dirt at all, but try to reach as quickly as possible the bed-rock, where are found the richest deposits of gold. The river is supposed to have formerly flowed over this bed-rock, in the crevices of which it left, as it passed away, the largest portions of the so eagerly sought for ore. The group of mountains amidst which we are living is a spur of the Sierra Nevada, and the bed-rock, which in this vicinity is of slate, is said to run through the entire range, lying, in distance varying from a few feet to eighty or ninety, beneath the surface of the soil. On Indian Bar the bed-rock falls in almost perpendicular benches, while at Rich Bar the friction of the river has formed it into large, deep basins, in which the gold, instead of being found, as you would naturally suppose, in the bottom of it, lies, for the most part, just below the rim. A good-natured individual bored *me,* and tired *himself,* in a hopeless attempt to make me comprehend that this was only a necessary consequence of the under-current of the water, but with my usual stupidity upon such matters I got but a vague idea from his scientific explanation, and certainly shall not mystify *you* with my confused notions thereupon.

When a company wish to reach the bed-rock as quickly as possible, they sink a shaft (which is nothing more nor less than digging a well) until they "strike it." They then commence drifting coyote holes, as they call them, in search of crevices, which, as I told you before, often pay immensely. These coyote holes sometimes extend hundreds of feet into the side of the hill. Of course they are obliged to use lights in working them. They generally proceed until the air is so impure as to extinguish the lights, when they return to the entrance of the excavation and commence another, perhaps close to it. When they think that a coyote hole has been faithfully worked, they clean it up, which is done by scraping the surface of the bed-rock with a knife, lest by chance they have overlooked a crevice, and they are often richly rewarded for this precaution.

Now I must tell you how those having claims on the hills procure the water for washing them. The expense of raising it in any way from the river is too enormous to be thought of for a moment. In most cases it is brought from ravines in the mountains. A company, to which a friend of ours belongs, has dug a ditch about a foot in width and depth, and more than three miles in length, which is fed in this way. I wish that you could see this ditch. I never beheld a *natural* streamlet more exquisitely beautiful. It undulates over the mossy roots and the gray old rocks like a capricious snake, singing all the time a low song with the "liquidest murmur," and one might almost fancy it the airy and coquettish Undine herself. When it reaches the top of the hill, the sparkling thing is divided into five or six branches, each one of which supplies one, two, or three long-toms. There is an extra one, called the waste-ditch, leading to the river, into which the water is shut off at night and on Sundays. This race (another and peculiar name for it) has already cost the company more than five thousand dollars. They sell the water to others at the following rates: Those that have the first use

257

of it pay ten per cent upon all the gold that they take out. As the water runs off from their machine, (it now goes by the elegant name of "tailings"), it is taken by a company lower down, and as it is not worth so much as when it was clear, the latter pay but seven per cent. If any others wish the tailings, now still less valuable than at first, they pay four per cent on all the gold which they take out, be it much or little. The water companies are constantly in trouble, and the arbitrations on that subject are very frequent.

I think I gave you a vague idea of fluming in a former letter; I will not, therefore, repeat it here, but will merely mention that the numerous fluming companies have already commenced their extensive operations upon the river.

As to the rockers, so often mentioned in story and song, I have not spoken of them since I commenced this letter. The truth is, that I have seldom seen them used, though hundreds are lying ownerless along the banks of the river. I suppose that other machines are better adapted to mining operations in the mountains.

Gold mining is Nature's great lottery scheme. A man may work in a claim for many months, and be poorer at the end of the time than when he commenced, or he may take out thousands in a few hours. It is a mere matter of chance. A friend of ours, a young Spanish surgeon from Guatemala, a person of intelligence and education, told us that after working a claim for six months he had taken out but six ounces.

CHAPTER XII

THE FABRIC OF SOCIETY

1832 – 1855

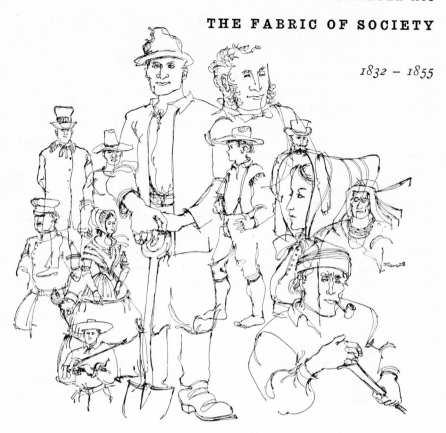

1.   *1834*—DAVY CROCKETT DESCRIBES LOWELL'S "MILE OF GALS"

❨ *At the same time that the nation was spilling its people across the Mississippi and thence to Santa Fe, Oregon, and California, its older regions were developing a complex society. Where formerly nearly everyone had made a living on the farms, or as a shopkeeper or craftsman in the towns and cities, now a class of factory workers was springing into existence. In 1812 a young Bostonian, Francis Cabot Lowell, had returned from a trip to England determined to set up in the United States a textile factory of the kind he had seen in Lancashire. With the aid of an expert machinist he perfected a loom to be run by water power rather than by hand. Lowell raised capital, bought a site on the Charles River, and launched a factory that succeeded in the mass production of coarse sheetings. Lowell died in 1817, but by that time the industry he had founded was*

David Crockett, *An Account of Col. Crockett's Tour to the North and Down East* (Philadelphia, 1835), 91–99.

*firmly established. Before many years its center—and showpiece—
was the city of Lowell, named in his honor. There hundreds of
young women, living in dormitories under strict supervision, tended
the spindles and looms, and attracted all sorts of curious visitors.
One of these was the celebrated frontiersman, Davy Crockett.
Whether or not Davy wrote the account of the tour that bears his
name is a question, but the narrative has the same qualities of
naiveté, keenness of observation, and humor that characterized the
man himself.*

Next morning I rose early, and started for Lowell in a fine carriage,
with three gentlemen who had agreed to accompany me. I had heard
so much of this place that I longed to see it; not because I had heard
of the "mile of gals"; no, I left that for the gallantry of the President,
who is admitted, on that score, to be abler than myself: but I wanted
to see the power of machinery, wielded by the keenest calculations of
human skill; I wanted to see how it was that these northerners could
buy our cotton, and carry it home, manufacture it, bring it back, and
sell it for half nothing; and in the mean time, be well to live, and make
money besides.

We stopped at the large stone house at the head of the falls of the
Merrimac river, and having taken a little refreshment, went down
among the factories. The dinner bells were ringing, and the folks pouring out of the houses like bees out of a gum. I looked at them as they
passed, all well dressed, lively, and genteel in their appearance; indeed,
the girls looked as if they were coming from a quilting frolic. We
took a turn round, and after dining on a fine salmon, again returned,
and entered the factories.

The out-door appearance was fully sustained by the whole of the
persons employed in the different rooms. I went in among the young
girls, and talked with many of them. No one expressed herself as tired
of her employment, or oppressed with work: all talked well, and looked
healthy. Some of them were very handsome; and I could not help observing that they kept the prettiest inside, and put the homely ones on
the outside rows. . . .

There are more than five thousand females employed in Lowell; and
when you come to see the amount of labour performed by them, in
superintending the different machinery, you will be astonished.

Twelve years ago, the place where Lowell now rises in all its pride
was a sheep-pasture. It took its name from Francis C. Lowell, the pro-
jector of its manufactories, and was incorporated in 1826—then a mere
village. The fall, obtained by a canal from the Merrimac river, is thirty-
two feet, affording two levels for mills, of thirteen and seventeen feet;
and the whole water of the river can be used.

There are about fourteen thousand inhabitants. It contains nine meeting-houses; appropriates seven thousand five hundred dollars for free schools; provides instruction for twelve hundred scholars, daily; and about three thousand annually partake of its benefits. It communicates with Boston by the Middlesex canal (the first ever made in the United States); and in a short time the rail-road to Boston will be completed, affording every facility of intercourse to the seaboard.

This place has grown by, and must depend on, its manufactures. Its location renders it important, not only to the owners, but to the nation. Its consumption not only employs the thousands of its own population, but many thousands far away from them. It is calculated not only to give individual happiness and prosperity, but to add to our national wealth and independence; and instead of depending on foreign countries, to have our own material worked up in our own country.

Some of the girls attended three looms; and they make from one dollar seventy-five cents to three dollars per week, after paying their board. These looms weave fifty-five yards per day; so that one person makes one hundred and sixty-five yards per day. Every thing moves on like clock-work, in all the variety of employments; and the whole manufacture appears to be of the very best.

The owner of one of the mills, Mr. Lawrence, presented me with a suit of broadcloth, made out of wool bought from Mark Cockral, of Mississippi, who sold them about four thousand pounds; and it was as good cloth as the best I ever bought for best imported.

The calico made here is beautiful, and of every variety of figure and colour. To attempt to give a description of the manner in which it is stamped and coloured is far beyond my abilities. One thing I must state, that after the web is wove, and before they go further, it is actually passed over *a red-hot cylinder,* to scorch off the furze. The number of different operations is truly astonishing; and if one of my country-women had the whole of the persons in her train that helped to make her gown, she would be like a captain on a field-muster: and yet, when you come to look at the cost, it would take a trunk full of them to find these same people in living for one day.

I never witnessed such a combination of industry, and perhaps never will again. I saw the whole process, from the time they put in the raw material, until it came out completely finished. In fact, it almost came up to the old story of a fellow walking into a patent machine with a bundle of wool under his arm, and coming out at the other end with a new coat on.

Nothing can be more agreeable than the attention that is paid by every one connected with these establishments. Nothing appears to be kept secret; every process is shown, and with great cheerfulness. I regret that more of our southern and western men do not go there,

261

as it would help much to do away with their prejudices against these manufactories. . . .

I met the young gentlemen of Lowell, by their particular request, at supper. About one hundred sat down. Every thing was in grand order, and went off well. They toasted *me*, and I enlightened *them* by a speech as good as I could make: and, indeed, I considered them a good sett of fellows, and as well worth speaking to as any ones I had met with. The old saying, "them that don't work should not eat," don't apply to them, for they are the rale workies, and know how to act genteel, too; for, I assure you, I was not more kindly, and hospitably, and liberally treated any where than just by these same people.

After supper I went to my lodgings for the night. Next morning I took another range round the town, and returned to Boston.

2. *1832*—"OULD" IRELAND ON NEW SOIL

⟨ *Almost from the beginning, people from countries other than England found homes in the North American colonies. The Dutch were the original settlers of New York; the Swedes, with the Dutch, established the first European footholds in what is now Delaware. In the eighteenth century large numbers of Germans took up land in Pennsylvania; that province, as well as Virginia and the Carolinas, attracted many thousands of Scotch-Irish.*

The Revolution and the War of 1812 slowed down the tide of immigration, but after 1815 it swelled again. Ireland—the "ould sod" rather than Protestant Ulster—furnished the first horde of newcomers. In the home country the average Irishman could hope for nothing better than a half-starved existence; in the New World he could find a job at good pay on the construction gangs that were building canals and railroads.

Though the Irishman was welcome as a laborer, his uncouth manners made him a social outcast. But Charles J. Latrobe, the English traveler, was acute enough to see that these raw immigrants would eventually outgrow the characteristics that disturbed staid citizens and become a valued part of the fabric of American society.

Of all emigrants, the Englishman experiences the most difficulty in settling down in a new country. . . . He has not the buoyant elasticity and gaiety of the Frenchman. He has not been subjected to kicks and cuffs like the German; he has not the careless hilarity of the Irishman, and wants the patient endurance and pliancy of the Scotchman.

These latter classes of settlers, even if they should have formed false

---

Latrobe, *The Rambler in North America*, II, 222–23.

views of the country, are still able to bend to circumstances, and make the most of what is frequently a bad bargain.

Here comes a ship load of Irish. They land upon the wharfs of New York in rags and open-knee'd breeches, with their raw looks and bare necks; they flourish their cudgels, throw up their torn hats and cry,— "Hurrah for Gineral Jackson!" They get drunk and kick up a row;— lend their forces to any passing disturbance, and make early acquaintance with the interior of the lock-ups. From New York they go in swarms to the canals, railroads, and public works, where they perform the labour which the Americans are not inclined to do: now and then they get up a fight among themselves in the style of ould Ireland, and perhaps kill one another, expressing great indignation and surprise when they find that they must answer for it, though they are in a free country. By degrees, the more thrifty get and keep money, and diving deeper into the continent, purchase lands; while the intemperate and irreclaimable vanish from the surface. The Americans complain, and justly, of the disorderly population which Ireland throws into the bosom of the Union, but there are many reasons why they should be borne with. They, with the poor Germans, do the work which without them could hardly be done. Though the fathers may be irreclaimable, the children become good citizens,—and there is no finer race in the world both for powers of mind and body than the Irish, when favoured by education and under proper control. In one thing the emigrant Irish of every class distinguish themselves above the people of other nations, and that is in the love and kindly feeling which they cherish towards their native land, and towards those whom they have left behind; a fact proved by the large sums which are yearly transmitted from them to the mother country, in aid of their poverty-stricken relatives.

3.   *1833*—A GERMAN FAMILY SETTLES IN ILLINOIS

❲ *In the 1830's and 1840's German immigrants to the United States rivalled the Irish in numbers. Many of the Germans, however, were driven from home by political repression rather than by the difficulty of making a living. Yet the educated German had almost as hard a time adjusting himself to American life as the unschooled Irishman. Gustave Koerner, university graduate, describes the clash of old-world habits with the customs that prevailed in the young state of Illinois.*

On the third of August . . . Mr. Engelmann, Sophie, Ruppelius, myself, and Doctor Engelmann, started for the upper farm. A farm-

Thomas J. McCormack, Ed., *Memoirs of Gustave Koerner, 1809–1896* (Cedar Rapids, 1909), I, 296–300.

wagon drawn by two yoke of oxen had been hired to move our goods from St. Louis. Early in the morning it came to our door. It was a large wagon, with a long and high box, and held nearly all our things. Doctor Engelmann was on horseback. We others walked to the ferry-boat, but once over the river, we seated ourselves comfortably on some of the mattresses. It was terribly hot and the dust at many places was six inches deep. . . .

About two o'clock in the afternoon we reached Belleville. On Main Street, our caravan, which had excited the curiosity of the few people there, halted at a tavern, the Virginia House. No wonder that we excited astonishment. The doctor was on a very fine horse. Mr. Engelmann, of imposing stature and wearing a mustache and chin beard a la Henri Quatre, looked like a military officer of high rank; Sophie appeared as a young lady, while Ruppelius and I carried double-barreled shot-guns. Beards at that time were not worn by Americans,—save English side-whiskers, by the select few. The fashion of wearing beards did not arise till after the Mexican War in 1848, when our citizen soldiers mostly returned bearded. And this decidedly reputable, but very foreign-looking party, came in an ox wagon! A year or two afterwards, when emigration was pouring into this region of the country, our appearance would not have been particularly noticed.

When we alighted a tall, lean, white-haired man, as straight as a pole, in a shabby blue swallow-tailed dress-coat with brass buttons and nankeen, rather shortlegged trousers, a brownish, worn-out high hat on his head, very self-possessed, and with a very red nose and closed lips, showed us into a small room, serving as a general hall and parlor at the same time. It was Major Doyle, a Virginian, who had evidently seen better days, but who now condescended to keep an inn at Belleville. We went in, and as I expressed a desire to wash, we were shown through the kitchen into a small yard, where there was a shaky sort of a long pine bench, on which stood two tin wash pans. A little black boy drew a bucket of water from the well, and with the help of a pint tin cup poured the water into the wash pans, one of which had several holes in it stopped up with strings of tow.

After we had washed, we bethought ourselves of having something to eat. I asked the Major very innocently for some lunch. He seemed very much surprised. "Sir," said he to me, "supper will be ready at six o'clock. We have nothing in the house to eat between meals." Mr. Engelmann grew somewhat angry. "What—is this a tavern and we can get no kind of refreshment? You ought to take down the sign from your house." While we were discussing the matter, Mrs. Doyle, a small, round, but very kindly looking lady, entered the room. Finding out what was going on, she remarked, looking up at the Major in a sort of beseeching way, that she could make us a cup of coffee. She had no bread: they made their bread for each meal; but she would send down to the baker's shop and get us some. Butter she had.

Of course, we accepted her offer. In the meantime, however, Mr. Engelmann thought it right to order a bottle of wine. The Major looked still more astonished. "We keep no liquors in this house." Mr. Engelmann now grew quite excited; for that in a tavern a man could get nothing to drink appeared to him the height of absurdity, the more so as the landlord bore the evident marks of being a hard drinker. However, things were arranged. There was, right across the way, the Major said, a liquor store kept by a man by the name of Carr, nicknamed Brandy Carr, where we could get wine; so I went over and for seventy-five cents I bought a bottle of very good St. Julien. We refreshed ourselves, and after awhile the coffee came in, which was, as Southern people know how to make it, pretty good.

About four o'clock we resumed our journey. It was a beautiful road; nearly all the way fine, tall, beautiful timber, whiteoak, walnut, hickory, wild cherry, maple and sycamore; now and then there were openings, where wild roses, blackberry and hawthorne bushes grew. We passed also some fine farms. At last, about six miles from Belleville, at the Shiloh meeting-house, we turned from the main road to the south, and through a fine woodland we saw before us the old farmhouse. . . .

Our life on the upper farm was really a romantic one. American and German neighbors called frequently. As Doctor George and I spoke English "pretty plain," as the Americans said, we soon got acquainted with our American neighbors. They were all very kind and accommodating. Some were great hunters and good for nothing else, but clever fellows after all.

4. *1835*—THE OLD TIME RELIGION

❨ *In new communities, whether in the Old West, the New South, or the vast lands beyond the Mississippi, the settler found himself free from many restraints of law and custom. The agencies of government—legislatures and courts—tended to become less formal; so did the churches. Religious rituals—Congregational, Presbyterian, Church of England—which men and women had followed for generations gave way to highly emotional services consisting only of preaching, singing, and conversion.*

To many thousands the camp meeting became the highest form of religious experience, as well as a welcome escape from grubbing

Thomas Low Nichols, *Forty Years of American Life, 1821–1861* (London, 1864), I, 77–81.

for a living. Thomas Low Nichols, a physician with a keen eye for the eccentricities of his countrymen, described the typical backwoods revival.

In the European Churches, Greek, Lutheran, Roman, or English, children, baptized in infancy, are afterwards confirmed, considered members of the church, and receive its sacraments. In America, among what are called the Evangelical denominations, there must be, at some period, what is called conversion, getting religion, a change of heart, followed by a public relation of religious experience, a profession of faith, and formal reception into the church. The non-professor becomes a professor, and a church member. But this change is commonly the result of periodical and epidemic religious excitements, termed revivals. These sometimes appear to come spontaneously, or, as supposed, by the special outpouring of the Divine Spirit, but they are more often induced by peculiarly earnest and excited preaching, camp meetings, protracted meetings, and systematic efforts to excite the community to religious feeling. Certain energetic and magnetic preachers are called revival preachers, and are hired to preach day and night in one place until there is a revival, and then go to another. Some of these receive considerable sums for their services, and cause revivals wherever they appear.

The camp meetings are mostly held by the Methodists. They gather from a wide district, with tents, provisions, and cooking utensils; form a regular camp in some picturesque forest, by some lake or running stream; a preacher's stand is erected, seats are made of plank, straw laid in a space railed off in front of the preachers for those who are struck with conviction or who wish to be prayed for to kneel upon, and then operations commence.

Ten or twelve preachers have collected, under the leadership of some old presiding elder or bishop, who directs the proceedings. Early in the morning, the blowing of a horn wakes the camp to prayers, singing, and a bountiful breakfast: then the day's work begins. People flock in from the surrounding country. Sonorous hymns, often set to popular song-tunes, are sung by the whole congregation, pealing through the forest aisles. Sermon follows sermon, preached with the lungs of Stentors and the fervour of an earnest zeal. Prayer follows prayer. The people shout, "Amen!" "Bless the Lord!" "Glory to God!" "Glory! Hallelujah!" They clap their hands, and shout with the excitement. Nervous and hysterical women are struck down senseless, and roll upon the ground. "Mourners" crowd to the anxious seats, to be prayed for. There is groaning, weeping, shouting, praying, singing. Some are suddenly converted, and make the woods ring with joyful shouts of "Glory!" and these exhort others to come and get religion. After three or four hours of this exciting and exhausting work, a benediction is given, and all hands go to work to get dinner. Fires are burning behind each tent, great pots are smoking with savoury food, and, while spiritual affairs are the main business, the physical interests are not neglected. After dinner comes a brief session of gossip and repose. Then there are prayer meetings in the different tents, and the scenes of the morning are repeated at the same time in a dozen or twenty places, and the visitor who takes a place in the centre of the camp may hear exhortations, prayers, and singing going on all together and on every side, while at times half a dozen will be praying and exhorting at once in a single group, making "confusion worse confounded."

. . . Then the horn blows again, and all gather before the preacher's stand, where the scenes of the morning are repeated with increased fervour and effect. A dozen persons may be taken with "the power"—of the Holy Ghost as believed—falling into a state resembling catalepsy. More and more are brought into the sphere of the excitement. It is very difficult for the calmest and most reasonable person to avoid its influence.

At night, after an interval for supper, the camp is lighted up by lanterns upon the trees and blazing fires of pine-knots. The scene is now wild and beautiful. The lights shine in the tents and gleam in the forest; the rude but melodious Methodist hymns ring through the woods; the ground is glittering with the phosphoric gleam of certain roots which trampling feet have denuded of their bark; the moon shines in the blue vault above the tree tops, and the melancholy scream of the loon, a large waterfowl, comes across the lake on the sighing breeze of night. In this wild and solemn night-scene, the voice of the preacher has a double power, and the harvest of converts is increased. A procession is formed of men and women, who march round the camp singing an invitation to the unconverted. They march and sing—

> "Sinners, will you scorn the Saviour?
>   Will you drive Him from your arms?
> Once He died for your behaviour,
>   Now He calls you to His charms."

Or they fill the dim primeval forest with that tumultuous chorus—

> "I am bound for the Kingdom!
> Will you go to Glory with me?
>   O Hallelujah! O Halle hallelujah!
> I am bound for the Kingdom!
> Will you go to Glory with me?
>   O Hallelujah! O praise ye the Lord!"

The recruits fall in—the procession increases. When all are gathered up who can be induced to come, they bring them to the anxious-seats, where they are exhorted and prayed for, with tears, groans, and shouting, and cries of "Glory!"

Then there are prayer meetings in the tents again, with the accumulated excitement of the whole day and evening. At ten o'clock the long, wild note of the horn is heard from the preacher's stand: the night watch is set. Each tent is divided into two compartments, one for men, the other for women; straw is littered down, and all lie down in close rows upon the ground to sleep, and silence reigns in the camp, broken only by the mournful note of the waterfowl and the neighing of horses, fastened, with their forage, under the trees. These meetings last a week or longer.

5. *1844–1847*—THREE YEARS AT BROOK FARM

(*At the opposite end of the scale from the emotional religion of the frontier stood Transcendentalism, the doctrine that held that God pervaded all nature and could be discovered by anyone who would devote himself to plain living and high thinking. Ordinary society offered too many distractions for the Transcendentalists. The ideal life, as they defined it, could best be found in communities where like-minded members would divide the work among them and devote themselves to cultural and intellectual activities.*

The most famous of the Transcendental communities was Brook Farm, founded by George Ripley at West Roxbury, Massachusetts, in 1841. For several years the experiment promised success, but in the end human selfishness, the lack of business capacity, and a disastrous fire forced the members to disband. We see the community decline through the eyes of a young woman who joined it in the spring of 1844.

BROOK FARM, Sunday, April 14, '44.

DEAR BROTHER FRANK,

. . . Now my business is as follows (but perhaps liable to frequent change): I wait on the breakfast table (½ hour), help M. A. Ripley clear away breakfast things, etc. (1½ hours), go into the dormitory group till eleven o'clock,—dress for dinner—then over to the Eyrie and sew till dinner time,—half past twelve. Then from half past one or two o'clock until ½ past five, I teach drawing in Pilgrim Hall and sew in the Eyrie. At ½ past five go down to the Hive, to help set the tea table, and afterwards I wash tea cups, etc., till about ½ past seven. Thus I make out a long day of it, but alternation of work and pleasant company and chats make it pleasant. I am about entering a flower garden group and assisting Miss Russell in doing up muslins. I have one very

Amy L. Reed, Ed., *Letters from Brook Farm* (Poughkeepsie, 1928), 7–9, 51–52, 136–38, 177–78.

pleasant drawing class, consisting of the young ladies and the young men, José, Martin Cushing, etc. The other class is composed of the children in the regular school. We enjoy ourselves here very well, and I can't but think that after some weeks I shall become perfectly attached to the place—I have felt perfectly at home from the first. We need more leisure, or rather, we should like it. There are so many, and so few women to do the work, that we have to be nearly all the time about it. I can't find time to write till it comes evening, and then we generally assemble in little bands somewhere for a little talk or amusement. . . .

BROOK FARM, Dec. 14, '44.

DEAREST ANNA,

. . . Have I told you about our retrenchment?. . . . You know it is one of our rules not to incur any debt, but to pay as we go along—well, we found that we could not be sure of commanding ready money this winter sufficient to pay our expenses, so we agreed to retrench in our table fare, in order to make a saving and come within the means we can command. It was really cheering to see how readily this measure was adopted. We now set one of the long tables in our old style for boarders, scholars and visitors,—and a *few associates* who feel that their *health* requires (!) the use of meat, tea, etc. At the other tables we have no meat, no tea, nor butter, nor sugar. This "retrenchment" has afforded us no little amusement. We are not at a loss for something to eat,— have good potatoes, turnips, squashes, etc., etc., and puddings. At our breakfast table I counted nine different articles this morning; so we can't complain of want of variety. Our New York friends are pitying us very much and wonder what we can have left to eat. For my own part, I think much good will come out of it. I trust our people will find by and by that meat and tea have lost their relish, and that there is something better. Perhaps we shall have fewer head-aches, etc. Charlie N. sat at the *no* retrenchment table at *one* meal, but has come home to us again, and is excepted from the general rule and allowed to have tea and butter brought to him. Our breakfast these short days is ready precisely at seven and, in order to make people punctual, Mr. Capen carries the dishes off at exactly half-past. Here again, friend N. is excepted, as he ought to be. We hear that many small associations are stopped, or will stop soon.—Some good will come of this. *We* only have to *retrench*. Friends of Association in New York and elsewhere are beginning to see the need of concentrating their efforts in some one undertaking, and it is to Brook Farm that they look. Mr. Kay regards our condition as much more prosperous and hopeful than when he was here in the summer. No matter if we are to have a hard winter in some respects, we know how to make sunshine around us and to wear smiling faces. What a hindrance to us is our climate! . . .

BROOK FARM, Sunday, Dec. 7, 1845.

MY DEAR ANNA,

. . . You speak of a crisis,—this is one of the things I can't write fully about, and whatever I may say will be confidential. We have reached, I believe, our severest crisis. If we survive it, we shall probably go on safely and not be obliged to struggle thro' another. I think here lies the difficulty,—we have not had business men to conduct our affairs—we have had *no* strictly business transactions from the beginning, and those among us who have some business talents, see this error, and feel that we cannot go on as we have done. They are ready to give up if matters cannot be otherwise managed, for they have no hope of success here under the past and present government. All important matters have been done up in council of one or two or three individuals, and everybody else kept in the dark (perhaps I exaggerate somewhat) and now it must be so no longer;—our young men have started "enquiry meetings," and it must be a sad state of things that calls for such measures. We are perplexed by debts, by want of capital to carry on any business to advantage,—by want of our Phalanstery or the means to finish it. From want of wisdom we have failed to profit by some advantages we have had. And then Brisbane is vague and unsteady; the help he promised us from his efforts comes not—but on the contrary, he and other friends to the cause in New York, instead of trying to concentrate all efforts upon Brook Farm as they promised, have wandered off,—have taken up a vast plan of getting $100,000 and starting anew, so they are for disposing of us in the shortest manner,— would set their foot upon us, as it were, and divert what capital might come to us. . . .

My hopes are here; our council seems to be awake and ready for action; if we get the money, we will finish the building,—then we will enlarge our school, which should bring us in a handsome income. Our sash and blind business is very profitable, and may be greatly enlarged in the spring, the tailor's business is good, the tin block, and why do I forget the printing, and the Farm? Also we shall have together a better set of people than ever before. Heaven help us, and make us wise, for the failure of Brook Farm must defer the cause a long time. This place as it is (take it all in all) is the best place under the sky; why can't people see this, and look upon it hopefully and encouragingly?. . . .

BROOK FARM, Sat. eve., Mar. 29, [1847].

DEAREST ANNA,

. . . It is sad to see Brook Farm dwindling away, when it need not have been so. How it has struggled against all sorts of diseases and accidents, and defects of organization! With what vitality it has been endowed! How reluctantly it will give up the ghost! But is it not doomed to die by and by of consumption? Oh! I love every tree and wood haunt —every nook and path, and hill and meadow. I fear the birds can never sing so sweetly to me elsewhere,—the flowers can never greet me so smilingly. I can hardly imagine that the same sky will look down upon me in any other spot,—and where, where in the wide world shall I ever find warm hearts all around me again? Oh! you must feel with me that none but a Brook Farmer can know how chilling is the cordiality of the world.

But I am ready for anything that must be. I can give all up, knowing well that a more blessed home than we can imagine will yet be prepared for humanity. No words can tell my thankfulness for having lived here, and for every experience here, whether joyful or painful. It certainly is very unusual for me, and I think it may be quite wrong, to look for less in the future than we have derived from the past, but it does seem as tho' in this wide waste of the world, life could not possibly be so rich as it has been here. . . .

6. *1847*—EMILY DICKINSON ATTENDS MOUNT HOLYOKE SEMINARY

⟨ By the nineteenth century colleges had become a well-established feature of American life. The example of John Harvard and the Massachusetts General Court, which brought Harvard College into existence in 1636, had been followed in scores of other instances in the East, and the new states of the West would soon be dotted with institutions of higher learning. Progressive Americans, moreover, were conceding that even females were endowed with minds. In 1837 Oberlin College admitted women on an equality with men, and the same general period saw the founding of "female seminaries" that would eventually become outstanding colleges. One of the best known of these was Mount Holyoke, at South Hadley, Massachusetts. Emily Dickinson, later to be recognized as one of the country's finest poets, attended for one year.

MT. HOLYOKE SEMINARY. Nov. 6, 1847

MY DEAR ABIAH,

I am really at Mt. Holyoke Seminary and this is to be my home for a long year. Your affectionate letter was joyfully received and I wish that this might make you as happy as your's did me. It has been nearly six weeks since I left home and that is a longer time, than I was ever away from home before now. I was very homesick for a few days and it seemed to me I could not live here. But I am now contented and quite

Arthur C. Cole, *A Hundred Years of Mount Holyoke College* (New Haven: Yale University Press, 1940), 391–93. Reprinted by permission.

happy, if I can be happy when absent from my dear home and friends. You may laugh at the idea, that I cannot be happy when away from home, but you must remember that I have a very dear home and that this is my first trial in the way of absence for any length of time in my life.

As you desire it, I will give you a full account of myself since I first left the paternal roof. I came to S. Hadley six weeks ago next Thursday. I was much fatigued with the ride and had a severe cold besides, which prevented me from commencing my examinations until the next day, when I began. I finished them in three days and found them about what I had anticipated, though the old scholars say, they are more strict than they have ever been before. As you can easily imagine, I was much delighted to finish without failures and I came to the conclusion then, that I should not be at all homesick, but the reaction left me as homesick a girl as it is not usual to see. I am now quite contented and am very much occupied now in reviewing the Junior studies, as I wish to enter the middle class. The school is very large, and though quite a number have left, on account of finding the examinations more difficult than they anticipated, yet there are nearly 300 now. Perhaps you know that Miss Lyon is raising her standard of scholarship a good deal, on account of the number of applicants this year and on account of that she makes the examinations more severe than usual. You cannot imagine how trying they are, because if we cannot go through them all in a specified time, we are sent home. I cannot be too thankful that I got through as soon as I did and I am sure that I never would endure the suspense which I endured during those three days again for all the treasures of the world.

I room with my Cousin Emily, who is a Senior. She is an excellent room-mate and does all in her power to make me happy. You can imagine how pleasant a good room-mate is for you have been away to school so much. Everything is pleasant and happy here and I think I could be no happier at any other school away from home. Things seem much more like home than I anticipated and the teachers are all very kind and affectionate to us. They call on us frequently and urge us to return their calls and when we do, we always receive a cordial welcome from them.

I will tell you my order of time for the day, as you were so kind as to give me your's. At 6 o'clock, we all rise. We breakfast at 7. Our study hours begin at 8. At 9 we all meet in Seminary Hall for devotions. At 10¼ I recite a review of Ancient History in connection with which we read Goldsmith and Grimshaw. At 11 I recite a lesson in "Pope's Essay on Man" which is merely transposition. At 12 I practise Calisthenics and at 12¼ read until dinner which is at 12½. After dinner from 1½ until 2 I sing in Seminary Hall. From 2¾ until 3¾ I practise upon the Piano. At 3¾ I go to Section, where we give in all our accounts for the day, including Absence—Tardiness—Communications—Breaking Silent

Study hours—Receiving Company in our rooms and ten thousand other things which I will not take time or place to mention. At 4½ we go into Seminary Hall and receive advice from Miss Lyon in the form of a lecture. We have supper at 6 and silent study hours from then until the retiring bell, which rings at 8¾ but the tardy bell does not ring until 9¾, so that we don't often obey the first warning to retire.

Unless we have a good and reasonable excuse for failure upon any of the items that I mentioned above, they are recorded and a *black mark* stands against our names. As you can easily imagine, we do not like very well to get "exceptions" as they are called scientifically here. My domestic work is not difficult and consists in carrying the knives from the 1st tier of tables at morning and noon, and at night washing and wiping the same quantity of knives. I am quite well and hope to be able to spend the year here free from sickness. You have probably heard many reports of the food here and if so I can tell you, that I have yet seen nothing corresponding to my ideas on that point, from what I have heard. Everything is wholesome and abundant and much nicer than I should imagine could be provided for almost 300 girls. We have also a great variety upon our tables and frequent changes. One thing is certain and that is, that Miss Lyon and all the teachers, seem to consult our comfort and happiness in everything they do and you know that is pleasant. When I left home I did not think I should find a companion or a dear friend in all the multitude. I expected to find rough and un-cultivated manners, and to be sure I have found some of that stamp, but on the whole, there is an ease and grace and a desire to make one an-other happy, which delights and at the same time surprises me very much. I find no Abby or Abiah or Mary but I love many of the girls. Austin came to see me when I had been here about two weeks and brought Viny and Abby. I need not tell you how delighted I was to see them all nor how happy it made me to hear them say that "they were *so lonely.*" It is a sweet feeling to know that you are missed and that your memory is precious at home. . . .

Abiah, you must write me often and I shall write you as often as I have time. But you know I have many letters to write now I am away from home. Cousin Emily says "give my love to Abiah."

From your aff. EMILY, E. D.

7. *1849*—"THE SCARLET LETTER" FINDS A PUBLISHER

❨ *As the United States matured it offered an audience and a living —of sorts—to men of letters. Yet the way was hard. Nathaniel Haw-thorne was so discouraged by the small sales of his* TWICE-TOLD TALES *that he refused to admit that he had finished a novel called*

James T. Fields, *Yesterdays with Authors* (Boston, 1901), 47–51.

THE SCARLET LETTER. *James T. Fields, Boston publisher, describes how he discovered the existence of the manuscript and arranged for its publication.*

I first saw Hawthorne when he was about thirty-five years old. He had then published a collection of his sketches, the now famous "Twice-Told Tales." Longfellow, ever alert for what is excellent and eager to do a brother author a substantial service, at once came before the public with a generous estimate of the work in the North American Review; but the choice little volume, the most promising addition to American literature that had appeared for many years, made little impression on the public mind. Discerning readers, however, recognized the supreme beauty in this new writer, and they never afterwards lost sight of him. . . .

When Mr. George Bancroft, then Collector of the Port of Boston, appointed Hawthorne weigher and gauger of the custom-house, he did a wise thing, for no public officer ever performed his disagreeable duties better than our romancer. Here is a tattered little official document signed by Hawthorne when he was watching over the interests of the country: it certifies his attendance at the unloading of a brig, then lying at Long Wharf in Boston. I keep this precious relic side by side with one of a similar custom-house character, signed *Robert Burns.*

I came to know Hawthorne very intimately after the Whigs displaced the Democratic romancer from office. In my ardent desire to have him retained in the public service, his salary at that time being his sole dependence,—not foreseeing that his withdrawal from that sort of employment would be the best thing for American letters that could possibly happen,—I called, in his behalf, on several influential politicians of the day, and well remember the rebuffs I received in my enthusiasm for the author of the "Twice-Told Tales." One pompous little gentleman in authority, after hearing my appeal, quite astounded me by his ignorance of the claims of a literary man on his country. "Yes, yes," he sarcastically croaked down his public turtle-fed throat, "I see through it all, I see through it; this Hawthorne is one of them 'ere visionists, and we don't want no such a man as him round." So the "visionist" was not allowed to remain in office, and the country was better served by him in another way.

In the winter of 1849, after he had been ejected from the custom-house, I went down to Salem to see him and inquire after his health, for we had heard that he had been suffering from illness. He was then living in a modest wooden house in Mall Street, if I remember rightly the location. I found him alone in a chamber over the sitting-room of the dwelling; and as the day was cold, he was hovering near a stove. We fell into talk about his future prospects, and he was, as I feared I should find him, in a very desponding mood. "Now," said I, "is the time for you to publish, for I know during these years in Salem you must have got something ready for the press." "Nonsense," said he; "what heart had I to write anything, when my publishers (M. and Company) have been so many years trying to sell a small edition of the 'Twice-Told Tales'?" I still pressed upon him the good chances he would have now with something new. "Who would risk publishing a book for *me*, the most unpopular writer in America?" "I would," said I, "and would start with an edition of two thousand copies of anything you write." "What madness!" he exclaimed. "Your friendship for me gets the better of your judgment. No, no," he continued; "I have no money to indemnify a publisher's losses on my account." I looked at my watch and found that the train would soon be starting for Boston, and I knew there was not much time to lose in trying to discover what had been his literary work during these last few years in Salem. I remember that I pressed him to reveal to me what he had been writing. He shook his head and gave me to understand he had produced nothing. At that moment I caught sight of a bureau or set of drawers near where we were sitting; and immediately it occurred to me that hidden away somewhere in that article of furniture was a story or stories by the author of the "Twice-Told Tales," and I became so positive of it that I charged him vehemently with the fact. He seemed surprised, I thought, but shook his head again; and I rose to take my leave, begging him not to come into the cold entry, saying I would come back and see him again in a few days.

I was hurrying down the stairs when he called after me from the chamber, asking me to stop a moment. Then quickly stepping into the entry with a roll of manuscript in his hands, he said: "How in Heaven's name did you know this thing was there? As you have found me out, take what I have written, and tell me, after you get home and have time to read it, if it is good for anything. It is either very good or very bad,—I don't know which." On my way up to Boston I read the germ of "The Scarlet Letter"; before I slept that night I wrote him a note all aglow with admiration of the marvellous story he had put into my hands, and told him that I would come again to Salem the next day and arrange for its publication. I went on in such an amazing state of excitement when we met again in the little house, that he would not believe I was really in earnest. He seemed to think I was beside myself, and laughed sadly at my enthusiasm.

8. *1855*—AN INTERVIEW WITH WASHINGTON IRVING

《 *Unlike Hawthorne, Washington Irving, the country's first profes-sional author, found success at the outset of his career. The* SALMA-

James Grant Wilson, *Bryant and His Friends: Some Reminiscences of the Knickerbocker Writers* (New York, 1886), 160–72.

GUNDI *papers, whimsical essays and sketches published in 1807 and 1808, when Irving was only twenty-five, gave him a reputation as a writer and wit. "Diedrich Knickerbocker's"* HISTORY OF NEW YORK *made its author famous. Later works—*THE SKETCH BOOK, THE ALHAMBRA, *biographies of Columbus and Washington—upheld Irving's reputation and yielded him a modest fortune. While these and other books were appearing he achieved distinction in diplomatic posts at Madrid and London.*

In 1846 Irving retired to "Sunnyside," his home on the Hudson River. There, four years before his death, he received James Grant Wilson, then a young man about to begin a literary career of his own.

It was a sunny September morning that the writer set out from New York in an early train, on a visit to Sunnyside and its . . . honoured proprietor—almost the last of the great literary lights that witnessed the dawn of the nineteenth century. . . .

Arrived at Irvington we procured the only attainable vehicle the place could boast of,—an old, shaky, two-seated box waggon, drawn by a steed bearing a striking resemblance to Geoffrey Crayon's descriptions of the charger bestrode by the enraptured pedagogue on the occasion of the famous gathering at Mynheer Van Tassel's—and were in due time set down at the porch of Sunnyside, pleasantly situated on the banks of the river where its owner thanked God he was born. The quaint-looking mansion is a graceful combination of the English cottage and Dutch farm-house, covered with ivy brought from Melrose Abbey, and embowered amid trees and shrubbery. . . .

The simplicity of the interior arrangement struck me as characteristic of the simple and unperverted tastes of its owner, and its cottage ornaments were suggestive of his delightful pictures of English country life. Entering by a rustic doorway, covered with climbing roses, and passing through a tiled hall, you enter the drawing-room, a low-roofed apartment, on the walls of which hung the Jarvis portrait, painted when Mr. Irving was twenty-seven years of age; an engraving of Faed's picture of Scott and his friends at Abbotsford, presented to him by a son of Sir Walter Scott's eminent publisher, Archibald Constable; together with several other paintings and engravings, and well filled with parlour furniture, a piano, and tables covered with books and magazines of the day.

The family at that time consisted of the bachelor author, who had "no termagant wife to dispute the sovereignty of the Roost" with him; his eldest brother, Ebenezer, ten years his senior; a nephew, Pierre M. Irving, and his wife; and two nieces, daughters of the brother above mentioned, who were ever ministering to the slightest wish of their honoured uncle. . . .

As I sat at his board in the dining-room, from which is seen the majestic Hudson with its myriad of sailing-vessels and steamers, and heard him dilate upon the bygone days and the giants that were on the earth then—of his friends Scott and Byron, of Moore and Lockhart . . .; and as the old man pledged the health of his kinsfolk and guest, it seemed as if a veritable realm of romance were suddenly opened. . . .

In reply to our inquiry as to his opinion of the poets of the present day, Irving said, "I ignore them all. I read no poetry written since Byron's, Moore's, and Scott's." "What!" I exclaimed, "not Paulding's 'Backwoodsman'?" Whereupon he laughed, most heartily, and answered, "Well, if I did, I should take it in homoeopathic doses." This was followed by some friendly praise of Paulding's prose writings. . . . After some friendly words about his former literary partner and some of the younger members of the literary guild, the elderly author said, "He and I were very fortunate in being born so early. We should have no chance now against the battalions of better writers." He alluded in terms of the highest admiration to Motley's "History of the Dutch Republic," and in the same connection complained, "There are a great deal too many books written nowadays about countries, and places, and people, that when I was young no one knew, or wanted to have any knowledge of whatever; and it is morally impossible for any mortal to read or digest one half of them.". . . .

Returning to the drawing-room, Mr. Irving sat down in his favourite seat, a large, well-cushioned and capacious arm-chair. . . . His sanctum sanctorum was a small room, well filled with books, neatly arranged on the shelves, that extended completely around the room. In the centre stood a table, with a neat writing-desk, on which, seated in the well-lined easy elbow-chair, Geoffrey Crayon had written many of his modern works, including his "Life of Washington." His hours for literary labour were in the morning, "but," said he, "unlike Scott, I can do no work until I get breakfast, and it is between breakfast and dinner that I do all my writing." He appeared gratified at our allusion to the fact that Niagara and Irving were the two topics connected with this country in which we found intelligent Englishmen, or rather Britons, most interested during our sojourn there the previous season. . . .

In strolling over his charming grounds, we came upon those of his opulent neighbour, Mr. Moses H. Grinnell, who married a niece of Mr. Irving, which were kept in the most perfect order, when he remarked, "My place in its rough and uncultivated condition sets off finely my neighbour Grinnell's"; and on my replying that I thought it was precisely the reverse, he indulged in a quiet laugh, and looked very much as if he quite agreed with me. . . .

On our return we found a party of five ladies and gentlemen, under the escort of a relative, who had come up from New York to see "Diedrich Knickerbocker" and his loved domain. Upon returning from a ramble over the grounds and those of Mr. Grinnell with the Southern party and the Misses Irving, we found the amiable author upon the front porch gazing over the river and the distant hills at the setting sun, the *tout ensemble* presenting a fine scene for a painter. I shall never forget it; the mild, dreamy, and happy expression of that old man's countenance as he sat with his shawl around him looking over the broad Tappaan Zee at the sun's departing rays. I never saw him again.

9. *1842*—NOAH LUDLOW FINDS THAT ACTORS CAN BE GENTLEMEN

❮ *Long before American writers could find a sufficient number of readers to give them encouragement, actors played to eager audiences. Even in colonial times theatrical troupes performed regularly in all the larger cities. But while the people welcomed the farces and melodramas, they kept their fingers crossed as far as the actors and actresses were concerned. Could these traveling showmen really be respectable citizens? They doubted it. Noah Ludlow, a famous actor and manager, knew the popular attitude well enough, but even he was surprised at the aggravated form in which he met public distrust at Vicksburg, Mississippi. Fortunately, all residents of the southern city did not hold the "profession" in contempt.*

About the middle of November, our audiences [at St. Louis], which had not been very extensive for some weeks, began to show evident signs of shrinkage, and a sensitiveness to the touch of Jack Frost; and the wild geese—sensible birds!—were flying southward, and I determined to follow their example. Mr. James Thorne, then with us, informed me there was a small temporary theatre in Vicksburg, that he had been the manager of not long before, and that he had no doubt that I could get it on my own terms. I wrote as he directed me, and without any difficulty made an arrangement for occupancy of it for one month or more, at my discretion. I . . . closed the St. Louis Theatre about the last of November, taking our departure on a steamer for Vicksburg, where we arrived safely in four or five days, and commenced climbing the hills of that highly aristocratic city.

After landing at Vicksburg and getting my baggage to a hotel, I started out to look for the theatre; and after climbing hills until I had scarcely any breath left, I found it, as Smith would have said, a-w-a-a-a-y out of town. It appeared to have been a warehouse originally, fitted up very roughly, and would hold three or four hundred people.

Noah M. Ludlow, *Dramatic Life As I Found It* (St. Louis, 1880), 555–56.

THE FABRIC OF SOCIETY

Knowing that I had to pass at least a month in that city, and having a dislike to hotels as boarding-houses, I started out to hunt up private boarding, and succeeded, without any difficulty, in finding a nice, clean-looking house, and bargained with the lady for a room and my meals. Before leaving her, I asked her if she could accommodate me with a night-key, for, being a member of a theatrical company that had just arrived in town, I should be out late at nights, and did not wish to keep anyone up for the purpose of letting me in. The moment I said the word "theatrical," I observed that she changed color. With a half-smothered voice she said, "Theatre"; and then, with mock civility, "I am very sorry, sir, but I cannot accommodate you;" and would have closed the door in my face, but that I suddenly stepped back and retreated down the steps, muttering to myself, "Betsy, take in the shirts, the players have come!" the old story told of a woman in a country town of England. I was then directed to a private house where I was told they occasionally took one or two boarders. To this house I went. It was a building that had been erected for the use of a Railroad Bank. It was large, had a number of fine rooms, and was occupied by Dr. M——n and family. I rang the door-bell, asked for Dr. M., and was shown into a very well furnished, small reception-room. The doctor soon presented himself, and was a fine specimen of the Virginia gentleman. I told him what I wished, and concluded with saying that, if agreeable, I would like to stop a month or more with him. "Certainly, sir," he replied, "you appear to be a gentleman." "I will first make you assured of that," I replied. "I have a letter here to Mr. H——t, of your city; you can read it, and form your opinion accordingly." "Not at all, sir," said he; "it is not necessary." Hesitating a moment, I then said, "But, sir, I am an *actor*, and perhaps that may be objectionable." "By no means," he rejoined; "I like you the better with that knowledge." "And you are absolutely willing to take me as a boarder after being informed that I am an *actor!*" "Sir," said he, in a good-natured, jolly manner, "I would not take you if you were anything else!" and the dialogue ended in a hearty laugh by both. The doctor had me located in a very pleasant room, and I was never more comfortable in my life than while under his roof.

10.   *1850*—THE SWEDISH NIGHTINGALE CONQUERS
NEW YORK

⟨ *The United States was late in developing musicians of concert rank. Good music, in fact, did not become popular in America until the population had received a large influx of Europeans, particularly Germans. But the people could always be lured by showmanship. When the greatest of all promoters, P. T. Barnum, brought Jenny*

Allen Nevins, Ed., *The Diary of Philip Hone* (New York, 1927), II, 901–04.

Lind, the "Swedish Nightingale," to this country in 1850, her tour was a sensation. Philip Hone, wealthy patron of the arts, recorded the excitement that greeted her appearance in New York.

Tuesday, September 3.—*Jenny Lind.* "Sing a song of six-pence," at the rate of a thousand dollars a night. Our good city is in a new excitement. So much has been said, and the trumpet of fame has sounded so loud, in honor of this new importation from the shores of Europe, that nothing else is heard in our streets, nothing seen in the papers, but the advent of the "Swedish Nightingale." Jenny Lind arrived on Sunday, in the *Atlantic.* This noble steamer was a most fitting fiddle-case, a suitable cage for such a bird. The wharf was thronged with anxious expectants of her landing, and thousands of silly bird-fanciers following the "nightingale" to the Irving House impeded her flight. Five hundred ladies assembled to be introduced to her. Presents are showered, choice flowers exhale their fragrance, and luscious fruits court the embrace of her lips. Milliners, dressmakers and costumers contend for the honor of furnishing gratuitously her wardrobe. A serenade of two hundred and forty performers "blew a blast so loud and dread" as soon as the clock of the City Hall announced the departure of the Sabbath.

Thursday, September 5.—The committee appointed by Mr. Barnum to award the prize of $200 for the best song to be sung by Jenny Lind, at her first concert here, have adjudged it to Bayard Taylor, for his song entitled, "Welcome to America." The Committee state, in their report, that the number of competitors for this prize amounted to seven hundred; a large proportion of the productions were "not fit to feed the pigs."

Thursday, September 12.—The Jenny Lind excitement in New York seems to have increased to fever heat. Her second rehearsal was given with renewed spirit and effect, and received with new enthusiasm. Tickets have been sold to the amount of $55,000. The good people of New York are anxious to part with their money *for a song,* and the "nightingale" will make a profitable exchange of her *notes* for specie.

The Nightingale. Jenny Lind's second concert took place on Tuesday, and was attended as numerously and enthusiastically as the first; crowds follow her wherever she goes. She has been compelled to leave the Irving House, in my neighborhood, to escape from the persecution. This Siren, the tenth Muse; the *Angel,* as Barnum calls her; the *nightingale,* by which she is designated by the would-be *dilettanti,*—has secured the affection as well as the admiration of the mass of the people by an act of munificence, as well as good policy. Her contract with Mr. Barnum has been changed. Instead of $1,000 a night, she gets one-half of the net profits; her share of which for the first night, after deducting the large expenses of a first performance, amounting to the enormous sum of $12,600, all of which, with unprecedented liberality, she distributed among the charitable and benevolent institutions of the city. The list is headed by the fire department fund, to which she gives $3,000, to the musical fund $2,000, and the balance is divided in sums of $500 each to all the other charities. The noble gratuity to the firemen is a great stroke of policy. It binds to her the support and affection of the red-shirt gentlemen, who will go to hear her sing as long as they can raise the money for a ticket, and will worship the *nightingale* and fight for her to the death, if occasion should require. New York is conquered; a hostile army or fleet could not effect a conquest so complete.

11. *1853*—AN AMERICAN PIANIST HAS HIS TROUBLES

❰ *Louis Gottschalk was born in New Orleans in 1829. Sent to Paris at the age of thirteen to study the piano, he became the pupil and friend of the composer Berlioz. Chopin predicted a great future for the young American. When Gottschalk toured Europe at the age of twenty, ovations greeted his playing. In 1853 he returned to the United States. There, on his father's advice, he made the mistake of refusing an offer from Barnum. Gottschalk soon discovered that his countrymen could stay away from concert halls in droves. (A few years later they flocked to hear him.)*

When, in 1853, I returned to the United States, which I had left eleven years before (at eleven years of age), my reputation, wholly Parisian, had not, thus to speak, crossed the Atlantic. Two or three hundred concerts, given in Belgium, in Italy, in France, Spain, Switzerland, etc., had given me a name; but this name, so young, was not yet acclaimed in America. My first concert at New York was a success, but the receipts did not amount to one-half of the expenses. The second, given at Niblo's theatre, was a fiasco; in the two concerts I lost twenty-four hundred dollars. The excellent Wallace had offered me, with that good-natured kindness which was so natural to him, to conduct the orchestra, and Hoffman, the admirable and conscientious pianist, whom at all times I have ever found ready to oblige me, played with me two pieces on two pianos. In these two concerts I then lost twenty-four hundred dollars. It was a decided failure. Barnum then made me the offer of an engagement for a year, offering me twenty thousand dollars and my expenses paid; but my father had his prejudices (unjust) against Barnum, in whom he obstinately insisted in seeing only a showman of learned beasts. I refused. We left, my father and I, for New Orleans, my native city. My fellow-citizens received me in triumph. I was at that

Louis Moreau Gottschalk, *Notes of a Pianist* (1881), 124–26.

time the only American artist who had received the sanction of the European public, and, the national self-love assisting, I was received with an indescribable enthusiasm by the Louisianians, less, without doubt, because I deserved it—I already have said so—but because I was first celebrated in Paris under the name of the "Pianiste compositeur Louisianais." From my birth I had always lived in affluence—thanks to the successful speculations entered into by my father. Certain of being able to rely upon him, I quietly permitted myself to follow those pursuits in which I anticipated only pleasure and enjoyment. Poorly prepared for the realities of American life by my long sojourn in the factitious and enervating atmosphere of Parisian salons, where I easily discounted the success which my youth, my independent position, the education which I had received, and a certain originality in the compositions which I had already published, partly justified, I found myself taken unawares, when one day, constrained by necessity and the death of my father, hastened by a series of financial disasters, I found myself without other resources than my talents to enable me to perform the sacred duties bequeathed to me by him. I was obliged to pay his debts, which my concerts at New Orleans had already in part lightened the weight of, and to sustain in Paris a numerous family, my mother and six brothers and sisters. Of all misery, the saddest is not that which betrays itself by its rags. Poverty in a black coat, that poverty which, to save appearances, smiles, with death at the heart, is certainly the most poignant; then I understood it.

Nevertheless, my brilliant success in Europe was too recent for me not to perceive a near and easy escape from my sad troubles. I believed success still possible. I then undertook a tour in New England. At Boston my first receipts exceeded one hundred dollars; at the second concert I made forty-nine dollars. . . . Throughout all New England (where, I am anxious to say, some years later I found the most sympathetic reception), there was but a succession of losses. A. S., in a newspaper, devoted a whole column to my "kid gloves"; another to my handsome appearance, and my French manners. At P., after my first concert, at which there were seventeen persons, one editor gave a facetious account, in which he asserted that he hated music, but that mine was less insupportable to him, because, in the noise that I drew from my piano, there was no music. Be that as it may, I lost sixteen hundred dollars in a few months.

CHAPTER XIII

A NATION DIVIDING

1834 – 1860

1. *1834*—AN ENGLISHWOMAN FINDS SLAVERY WANTING

⟨ *In one of his debates with Douglas, Abraham Lincoln made a fundamental observation on American life. "We have in this nation," he said, "this element of domestic slavery. It is a matter of absolute certainty that it is a disturbing element. . . . I suggest that the difference of opinion, reduced to its lowest terms, is no other than the difference between the men who think slavery wrong and those who do not think it wrong."*

Many Americans condemned slavery on moral grounds. It was wrong, they believed, for one human being to hold another in bondage. Most of the objectors, however, recognized the difficulty of abolishing the institution quickly, although the Abolitionists held that all men ought to be free regardless of the Constitution or practical considerations. In any event, men's views were likely to be colored by what they considered to be the merits or demerits of the

Harriet Martineau, *Retrospect of Western Travel* (New York, 1838), I, 214–20.

283

slave system. Did it, in actual practice, elevate the Negro, or did it degrade him and his white masters as well? Harriet Martineau, an English traveler and journalist, had one answer after a prolonged tour of the United States.

Our stationary rural life in the South was various and pleasant enough; all shaded with the presence of slavery, but without any other drawback. There is something in the make-shift, irregular mode of life which exists where there are slaves, that is amusing when the cause is forgotten.

The waking in the morning is accomplished by two or three black women staring at you from the bedposts. Then it is five minutes' work to get them out of the room. Perhaps, before you are half dressed, you are summoned to breakfast. You look at your watch, and listen whether it has stopped, for it seems not to be seven o'clock yet. You hasten, however, and find your hostess making the coffee. The young people drop in when the meal is half done, and then it is discovered that breakfast has been served an hour too early, because the clock has stopped, and the cook has ordered affairs according to her own conjectures. Everybody laughs, and nothing ensues. After breakfast a farmer in homespun—blue trousers and an orange-brown coat, or all-over gray—comes to speak with your host. A drunken white has shot one of his negroes, and he fears no punishment can be obtained, because there were no witnesses of the deed but blacks. A consultation is held whether the affair shall go into court; and, before the farmer departs, he is offered cakes and liqueur.

Your hostess, meantime, has given her orders, and is now engaged in a back room, or out in the piazza behind the house, cutting out clothes for her slaves; a very laborious work in warm weather. There may be a pretence of lessons among the young people, and sometimes more than pretence if they happen to have a tutor or governess; but the probability is that their occupations are as various as their tempers. Rosa cannot be found; she is lying on the bed in her own room reading a novel; Clara is weeping for her canary, which has flown away while she was playing with it; Alfred is trying to ascertain how soon we may all go out to ride; and the little ones are lounging about the court, with their arms round the necks of blacks of their own size. You sit down to the piano or to read, and one slave or another enters every half hour to ask what is o'clock. Your hostess comes in at length, and you sit down to work with her; she gratifies your curiosity about her "people," telling you how soon they burn out their shoes at the toes, and wear out their winter woollens, and tear up their summer cottons; and how impossible it is to get black women to learn to cut out clothes without waste; and how she never inquires when and where the whipping is done, as it is the overseer's business, and not hers. She has not been seated many minutes when she is called away, and returns saying how babyish these people are, and that they will not take medicine unless she gives it to them; and how careless of each other, so that she has been obliged to stand by and see Diana put clean linen upon her infant, and to compel Bet to get her sick husband some breakfast. . . .

The carriage and saddle-horses are scrambling on the gravel before the door, and the children run in to know if they may ride with you. . . . The carriage goes at good speed, and yet the fast pace of the saddle-horses enables the party to keep together. . . .

Your host paces up to the carriage window to tell you that you are now on A.'s plantation. You are overtaking a long train of negroes going to their work from dinner. They look all over the colour of the soil they are walking on: dusky in clothing, dusky in complexion. An old man, blacker than the rest, is indicated to you as a native African; and you point out a child so light as to make you doubt whether he be a slave. A glance at the long heel settles the matter. You feel that it would be a relief to be assured that this was a troop of monkeys dressed up for sport, rather than that these dull, shuffling animals should be human.

There is something inexpressibly disgusting in the sight of a slave woman in the field. I do not share in the horror of the Americans at the idea of women being employed in outdoor labour. It did not particularly gratify me to see the cows always milked by men (where there were no slaves); and the hay and harvest fields would have looked brighter in my eyes if women had been there to share the wholesome and cheerful toil. But a negro woman behind the plow presents a very different object from the English mother with her children in the turnip-field, or the Scotch lassie among the reapers. In her pre-eminently ugly costume, the long, scanty, dirty woollen garment, with the shabby large bonnet at the back of her head, the perspiration streaming down her dull face, the heavy tread of the splay foot, the slovenly air with which she guides her plow, a more hideous object cannot well be conceived, unless it be the same woman at home, in the negro quarter, as the cluster of slave dwellings is called.

You are now taken to the cotton-gin, the building to your left, where you are shown how the cotton, as picked from the pods, is drawn between cylinders so as to leave the seeds behind; and how it is afterward packed, by hard pressure, into bales. The neighbouring creek is dammed up to supply the water-wheel by which this gin is worked. You afterward see the cotton-seed laid in handfuls round the stalks of the young springing corn, and used in the cotton field as manure.

Meantime you attempt to talk with the slaves. You ask how old that very aged man is, or that boy; they will give you no intelligible answer. Slaves never know, or never will tell their ages, and this is the reason why the census presents such extraordinary reports on this point, declaring a great number to be above a hundred years old. If they have a kind master, they will boast to you of how much he gave for each of them, and what sums he has refused for them. If they have a hard master, they will tell you that they would have more to eat and be less flogged, but that massa is busy, and has no time to come down and see that they have enough to eat. Your hostess is well known on this plantation, and her kind face has been recognized from a distance; and already a negro woman has come to her with seven or eight eggs, for which she knows she shall receive a quarter dollar. You follow her to the negro quarter, where you see a tidy woman knitting, while the little children who are left in her charge are basking in the sun, or playing all kinds of antics in the road; little shining, plump, clear-eyed children, whose mirth makes you sad when you look round upon their parents, and see what these bright creatures are to come to. You enter one of the dwellings, where everything seems to be of the same dusky hue: the crib against the wall, the walls themselves, and the floor, all look one yellow. More children are crouched round the wood fire, lying almost in the embers. You see a woman pressing up against the wall like an idiot, with her shoulder turned towards you, and her apron held up to her face. You ask what is the matter with her, and are told that she is shy. You see a woman rolling herself about in a crib, with her head tied up. You ask if she is ill, and are told that she has not a good temper; that she struck at a girl she was jealous of with an axe, and the weapon being taken from her, she threw herself into the well, and was nearly drowned before she was taken out, with her head much hurt.

The overseer has, meantime, been telling your host about the fever having been more or less severe last season, and how well off he shall think himself if he has no more than so many days' illness this summer: how the vegetation has suffered from the late frosts, pointing out how many of the oranges have been cut off, but that the great magnolia in the centre of the court is safe. You are then invited to see the house, learning by the way the extent and value of the estate you are visiting, and of the "force" upon it. You admire the lofty, cool rooms, with their green blinds, and the width of the piazzas on both sides [of] the house, built to compensate for the want of shade from trees, which cannot be allowed near the dwelling for fear of moschetoes. You visit the icehouse, and find it pretty full, the last winter having been a severe one. You learn that, for three or four seasons after this icehouse was built, there was not a spike of ice in the state, and a cargo had to be imported from Massachusetts.

When you have walked in the field as long as the heat will allow, you step into the overseer's bare dwelling, within its bare enclosure, where fowls are strutting about, and refresh yourself with a small tumbler of milk; a great luxury, which has been ordered for the party. The overseer's fishing-tackle and rifle are on the wall, and there is a medicine chest and a shelf of books. He is tall, sallow, and *nonchalant*, dropping nothing more about himself and his situation than that he does not know that he has had more than his share of sickness and trouble in his vocation, and so he is pretty well satisfied.

2. *1846*—SIR CHARLES LYELL SEES THE "PECULIAR INSTITUTION" IN A DIFFERENT LIGHT

⟨ *Sir Charles Lyell, England's foremost geologist of the nineteenth century, came to a different conclusion.*

There are 500 negroes on the Hopeton estate, a great many of whom are children, and some old and superannuated. The latter class, who would be supported in a poor-house in England, enjoy here, to the end of their days, the society of their neighbours and kinsfolk, and live at large in separate houses assigned to them. The children have no regular work to do till they are ten or twelve years old. We see that some of them, at this season, are set to pick up dead leaves from the paths, others to attend the babies. When the mothers are at work, the young children are looked after by an old negress, called Mom Diana. . . .

The out-door laborers have separate houses provided for them; even the domestic servants, except a few who are nurses to the white children, live apart from the great house—an arrangement not always convenient for the masters, as there is no one to answer a bell after a certain hour. But if we place ourselves in the condition of the majority of the population, that of servants, we see at once how many advantages we should enjoy over the white race in the same rank of life in Europe. In the first place, all can marry; and if a mistress should lay on any young woman here the injunction so common in English newspaper advertisements for a maid of all work "no followers allowed," it would be considered an extraordinary act of tyranny. The laborers begin work at six o'clock in the morning, have an hour's rest at nine for breakfast, and many have finished their assigned task by two o'clock, all of them by three o'clock. In summer they divide their work differently, going to bed in the middle of the day, then rising to finish their task, and afterward spending a great part of the night in chatting, merry-making, preaching, and psalm-singing. At Christmas they claim a week's holidays, when they hold a kind of Saturnalia, and the owners can get no work done. Although there is scarcely any drinking, the master rejoices when this season is well over without mischief. The

Sir Charles Lyell, *A Second Visit to the United States of North America* (New York, 1849), I, 262–66.

287

negro houses are as neat as the greater part of the cottages in Scotland (no flattering compliment it must be confessed), are provided always with a back door, and a hall, as they call it, in which is a chest, a table, two or three chairs, and a few shelves for crockery. On the door of the sleeping apartment they keep a large wooden padlock, to guard their valuables from their neighbors when they are at work in the field, for there is much pilfering among them. A little yard is often attached, in which are seen their chickens, and usually a yelping cur, kept for their amusement.

The winter, when the whites enjoy the best health, is the trying season for the negroes, who are rarely ill in the rice-grounds in summer, which are so fatal to the whites, that when the planters who have retreated to the sea-islands revisit their estates once a fortnight, they dare not sleep at home. Such is the indifference of the negroes to heat, that they are often found sleeping with their faces upward in a broiling sun, instead of lying under the shade of a tree hard by. We visited the hospital at Hopeton, which consists of three separate wards, all perfectly clean and well-ventilated. One is for men, another for women, and a third for lying-in women. The latter are always allowed a month's rest after their confinement, an advantage rarely enjoyed by hard-working English peasants. Although they are better looked after and kept more quiet, on these occasions, in the hospital, the planters are usually baffled; for the women prefer their own houses, where they can gossip with their friends without restraint, and they usually contrive to be taken by surprise at home.

The negro mothers are often so ignorant or indolent, that they can not be trusted to keep awake and administer medicine to their own children; so that the mistress has often to sit up all night with a sick negro child. In submitting to this, they are actuated by mixed motives—a feeling of kindness, and a fear of losing the services of the slave; but these attentions greatly attach the negroes to their owners. In general, they refuse to take medicine from any other hands but those of their master or mistress. The laborers are allowed Indian meal, rice, and milk; and occasionally pork and soup. As their rations are more than they can eat, they either return part of it to the overseer, who makes them an allowance of money for it at the end of the week, or they keep it to feed their fowls, which they usually sell, as well as their eggs, for cash, to buy molasses, tobacco, and other luxuries. When disposed to exert themselves, they get through the day's task in five hours, and then amuse themselves in fishing, and sell the fish they take; or some of them employ their spare time in making canoes out of large cypress trees, leave being readily granted them to remove such timber, as it aids the landowner to clear the swamps. They sell the canoes for about four dollars, for their own profit. . . .

One day, when walking alone, I came upon a "gang" of negroes, who were digging a trench. They were superintended by a black "driver," who held a whip in his hand. Some of the laborers were using spades, others cutting away the roots and stumps of trees which they had encountered in the line of the ditch. Their mode of proceeding in their task was somewhat leisurely, and eight hours a day of this work are exacted, though they can accomplish the same in five hours, if they undertake it by the task. The digging of a given number of feet in length, breadth, and depth is, in this case, assigned to each ditcher, and a deduction made when they fall in with a stump or root. The names of gangs and drivers are odious, and the sight of the whip was painful to me as a mark of degradation, reminding me that the lower orders of slaves are kept to their work by mere bodily fear, and that their treatment must depend on the individual character of the owner or overseer. That the whip is rarely used, and often held for weeks over them, merely *in terrorem*, is, I have no doubt, true on all well-governed estates; and it is not that formidable weapon which I have seen exhibited as formerly in use in the West Indies. It is a thong of leather, half an inch wide and a quarter of an inch thick. No ordinary driver is allowed to give more than six lashes for any offense, the head driver twelve, and the overseer twenty-four. When an estate is under superior management, the system is remarkably effective in preventing crime. The most severe punishment required in the last forty years, for a body of 500 negroes at Hopeton, was for the theft of one negro from another. In that period there has been no criminal act of the highest grade, for which a delinquent could be committed to the penitentiary in Georgia, and there have been only six cases of assault and battery. As a race, the negroes are mild and forgiving, and by no means so prone to indulge in drinking as the white man or the Indian. There were more serious quarrels, and more broken heads, among the Irish in a few years, when they came to dig the Brunswick Canal, than had been known among the negroes in all the surrounding plantations for half a century. The murder of a husband by a black woman, whom he had beat violently, is the greatest crime remembered in this part of Georgia for a great length of time.

3. *1854*—THE FEDERAL GOVERNMENT RETURNS A FUGITIVE SLAVE

❮ *No matter how enlightened some slaveholders might be, many slaves each year tried to escape to the North—and freedom. In 1850, as a part of the famous Compromise of that year, Congress passed a stringent Fugitive Slave Law. Under that law a slave named*

Charles E. Stevens, *Anthony Burns, A History* (Boston, 1856), 143–50.

Anthony Burns, who had escaped from a Virginia plantation in the spring of 1854, was arrested in Boston, and ordered to be returned to his master. The decision brought the anti-slavery citizens of Massachusetts to the verge of open conflict with the armed forces of the United States. This account by an eye-witness conveys the tension that marked the removal of Burns to the ship that would return him to bondage.

At eleven o'clock, Court Square presented a spectacle that became indelibly engraved upon the memories of men. The people had been swept out of the Square, and stood crowded together in Court street, presenting to the eye a solid rampart of living beings. At the eastern door of the Court House, stood the cannon, loaded, with its mouth pointed full upon the compact mass. By its side stood the officer commanding the detachment of United States troops, gazing with steady composure in the same direction. It was the first time that the armed power of the United States had ever been arrayed against the people of Massachusetts. Men who witnessed the sight, and reflected upon its cause, were made painfully to recognize the fact, before unfelt, that they were the subjects of two governments. . . .

At length, about two o'clock, the column was formed in the Square. First came a detachment of United States Artillery, followed by a platoon of United States Marines. After these followed the armed civil posse of the Marshal, to which succeeded two platoons of Marines. The cannon, guarded by another platoon of Marines, brought up the rear. When this arrangement was completed, Burns, accompanied by an officer on each side with arms interlocked, was conducted from his prison through a passage lined with soldiers, and placed in the centre of the armed posse. Immediately after the decision, Mr. Dana and Mr. Grimes had asked permission to walk with Burns arm in arm, from the Court House to the vessel at the wharf; and the Marshal had given them his consent. At the last moment, he sought them out and requested that they would not insist upon the performance of his promise, because, in the opinion of some of the military officers, such a spectacle would add to the excitement. Mr. Dana declined to release the Marshal from his promise. The latter persisted in urging the abandonment of the purpose.

"Do I understand you," asked Mr. Dana, "to say distinctly that we *shall not* accompany Burns, after having given your promise that we might?"

The Marshal winced under the pressure of this pointed question, but after a momentary reluctance answered firmly, "Yes." Accordingly, without a single friend at his side, and hemmed in by a thick-set hedge of gleaming blades, Burns took his departure.

The route from the Court House to the wharf had by this time become thronged with a countless multitude. It seemed as if the whole population of the city had been concentrated upon this narrow space. In vain the military and police had attempted to clear the streets; the carriage-way alone was kept vacant. On the sidewalks in Court and State streets, every available spot was occupied; all the passages, windows, and balconies, from basement to attic, overflowed with gazers, while the roofs of the buildings were black with human beings. It was computed that not less than fifty thousand people had gathered to witness the spectacle.

At different points along the route, were displayed symbols significant of the prevailing sentiment. A distinguished member of the Suffolk Bar, whose office was directly opposite the courtroom, and who was, at the time, commander of the Ancient and Honorable Artillery, draped his windows in mourning. The example was quickly followed by others. From a window opposite the Old State House, was suspended a black coffin, upon which was the legend, *The Funeral of Liberty*. At a point farther on toward the wharf, a venerable merchant had caused a rope to be stretched from his own warehouse across State street to an opposite point, and the American flag, draped in mourning, to be suspended therefrom with the union down. . . .

Along this Via Dolorosa, with its cloud of witnesses, the column now began to move. No music enlivened its march; the dull tramp of the soldiers on the rocky pavements, and the groans and hisses of the bystanders, were the only sounds. As it proceeded, its numbers were swelled by unexpected additions. Unauthorized, the zealous commander of the mounted Dragoons joined it with his corps. The Lancers, jealous of their rivals, hastened to follow the example: thus vanguard and rearguard consisted of Massachusetts troops. In its progress, it went past the Old State House. . . . Just below, it passed over the ground where, in the Massacre of 1770, fell Attucks, the first negro martyr in the cause of American liberty.

Opposite the Custom House, the column turned at a right angle into another street. This cross movement suddenly checked the long line of spectators which had been pressing down State street, parallel with the other body; but the rear portion, not understanding the nature of the obstruction, continued to press forward, and forced the front from the sidewalk into the middle of the street. To the chafed and watchful military, this movement wore the aspect of an assault on the *cortege;* instantly some Lancers, stationed near, rode their horses furiously at the surging crowd, and hacked with their sabres upon the defenceless heads within their reach. Immediately after, a detachment of infantry charged upon the dense mass, at a run, with fixed bayonets. Some were pitched headlong down the cellar-ways, some were forced into the passages, and up flights of stairs, and others were overthrown upon the pavement, bruised and wounded.

While this was passing, the procession moved on and reached the wharf. A breach of trust had secured to the Federal authorities the use of this wharf for their present purpose. It was the property of a company, by whom it had been committed in charge to an agent. Without their knowledge and against their wishes, he had granted to the Marshal its use on this occasion. When arraigned afterward by his employers for such betrayal of trust, he replied that he had since been rewarded by an appointment to a place in the Custom House.

At the end of the wharf lay a small steamer which had been chartered by the United States Government. On board this vessel Burns was conducted by the Marshal, and immediately withdrawn from the sight of the gazing thousands into the cabin below. The United States troops followed, and, after an hour's delay, the cannon was also shipped. At twenty minutes past three o'clock the steamer left the wharf, and went down the harbor.

4. *1854*—STEPHEN A. DOUGLAS DEFIES AN ANTI-SLAVERY
AUDIENCE

❨ *Anti-slavery feeling was not confined to Boston. After Stephen A. Douglas, United States Senator from Illinois, forced the Kansas-Nebraska Bill through Congress in the spring of 1854, he found himself denounced by the very people who had elected him two years earlier. For Douglas had included in the bill a provision to repeal the Missouri Compromise, which had prohibited slavery in new territories this far north. Douglas's bill provided that when Kansas and Nebraska were ready for statehood, they could decide for themselves whether to come into the Union as slave states or free states. Large numbers of Northerners saw in this measure an opportunity for slavery to move into a part of the country that had been considered to be permanently free.*

When Douglas arrived in Chicago after the adjournment of Congress he met a bitterly hostile reception. His ardent supporter, James W. Sheahan, editor of the CHICAGO TIMES, *claimed that the crowd was a "mob" of Know-Nothings who hated Douglas's Irish supporters as much as they hated him. After two hours, Douglas gave up the attempt to speak. "It is now Sunday morning," he shouted at his hecklers; "I'll go to church and you may go to hell!"*

Congress adjourned about the first of August. Mr. Douglas left Washington soon after, and reached his home in Chicago about the

James W. Sheahan, *The Life of Stephen A. Douglas* (New York, 1860), 271–73.

25th. In the mean time there had been extensive preparations by the Know-nothings and their allies to prevent any appeal by him to the people, such as he had made in Philadelphia. Some of the reverend gentlemen with whom he had had a controversy about their remonstrance took an active part in the matter. There was a thorough and complete organization established not only in Chicago, but throughout all the northern part of Illinois, to meet him every where with personal insult, and, if possible, to prevent his being heard. After he had been in the city some days, public notice was given that, on the night of the 1st of September, he would address his constituents at North Market Hall. The mayor of the city, the Hon. I. L. Milikin, was invited and consented to preside. The announcement of his intention to speak was received with great excitement. The newspapers warned the public to be there, and not to allow him to deceive the people by his sophistries. One paper, appealing directly to the prejudices of the Know-nothings, announced that Mr. Douglas had selected a body-guard of five hundred Irishmen, who, with arms in their hands, were to be present, and compel the people to silence while he spoke, and thus he would claim that they had, by not objecting, admitted his arguments and defense to be complete. Strange as it may seem that such a statement should obtain credence in an intelligent community, yet the fact is unquestionable. In a day or two after, another paper, hostile to Mr. Douglas, declared that there was a feverish sentiment prevailing in the community indicating a season of violence, and proved its assertion by citing the fact that every revolver and pistol in the stores of the city had been sold, and that there were orders for a large number yet unfilled. . . .

Under such circumstances as these assembled the meeting on that September evening. During the afternoon the flags of such shipping as was owned by the most bitter of the Fusionists were hung at half-mast; at dusk the bells of numerous churches tolled with all the doleful solemnity that might be supposed appropriate for some impending calamity. As the evening closed in, crowds flocked to the place of meeting. At a quarter before eight o'clock Mr. Douglas commenced to address the multitude. The whole area in front of the building, and the street running east to Dearborn and west to Clark Street, were soon densely packed. The roofs of houses opposite, and windows, balconies, and every available standing-spot, were occupied. He had hardly commenced before he was hailed with a storm of hisses; he paused until silence was comparatively restored, when he told the meeting that he came there to address his constituents, and intended to be heard. He was instantly assailed by all manner of epithets and abuse. He stood his ground firmly, contesting with that maddened and excited crowd. His friends—and he had friends there, warm, devoted, and unyielding Democrats—were indignant, and were disposed to resent some of the most indecent outrages. Mr. Douglas appealed to them to be calm; to leave him to deal with the mob before him. He denounced the violence exhibited as a preconcerted thing, and in defiance of yells, groans, cat-calls, and every insulting menace and threat, he read aloud, so that it was heard above the infernal din, a letter informing him that, if he dared to speak, he would be maltreated.

We never saw such a scene before, and hope never to see the like again. What we have described is a pretty fair description of what took place during that protracted struggle. Until ten o'clock he stood firm and unyielding, bidding the mob defiance, and occasionally getting in a word or two upon the general subject. . . . We have conversed since then with men who were present at that mob; with men who went there as members of the order, pledged to stand by and protect each other; with men who were armed to the teeth in anticipation of a scene of bloody violence, and they have assured us that nothing prevented blood-shed that night but the bold and defiant manner in which Douglas main-tained his ground. Had he exhibited fear, he would not have com-manded respect; had he been suppliant, he would have been spurned; had he been craven, and retreated, his party would in all probability have been assaulted with missiles, leading to violence in return. But, standing there before that vast mob, presenting a determined front and unyielding purpose, he extorted an involuntary admiration from those of his enemies who had the courage to engage in a personal en-counter; and that admiration, while it could not overcome the purpose of preventing his being heard, protected him from personal violence.

5. *1858*—THE LINCOLN-DOUGLAS DEBATES

❴ *In operation the Kansas-Nebraska Bill soon led to turmoil. Pro-slavery groups, largely from the neighboring state of Missouri, invaded Kansas in an effort to fix slavery there, only to find them-selves facing Northern immigrants determined that the future state should be free. By casting thousands of illegal votes the proslavery forces elected a legislature and adopted a constitution which the free-soilers refused to recognize. Both sides resorted to violence. At times the territory verged on civil war.*

Conditions in Kansas led large numbers of moderate antislavery Whigs and Democrats to join the Republican party, organized in 1854 in opposition to the Kansas-Nebraska policy. After two years of hesitation Abraham Lincoln, leader of the anti-Nebraska forces in Illinois, became a member. When Stephen A. Douglas, whom the Republicans blamed for the Kansas mess, came up for re-election to the Senate in 1858, he found Lincoln opposing him.

Memoirs of Gustave Koerner, II, 58–69 *passim.*

Gustave Koerner, German-American political leader, sketches one of the most memorable campaigns in the country's history.

On June 15th, the Republican Convention met in Springfield. Twelve hundred delegates attended. Richard Yates was made temporary, and I permanent, chairman. It adopted in the main the Republican State platform of 1856. It disapproved of the Dred Scott decision, maintained the right of Congress to prohibit slavery in the Territories and its duty to exercise it, approved the recent decision of the Supreme Court of Illinois, which declared that property in persons was repugnant to the constitution of Illinois, and that slavery was the creature of local and municipal law. A resolution that Abraham Lincoln was the first and only choice of the Republicans of Illinois was adopted with the most deafening applause. James Miller, the old Republican incumbent, was nominated for State Treasurer and Newton Bateman for Superintendent of Public Instruction.

The Convention met again in the evening. Mr. Lincoln, having been requested to address the Convention, took his stand on the right hand of the President, and delivered the ever-memorable speech containing the passage: "A house divided against itself cannot stand. I believe this government cannot endure permanently half slave and half free. I do not expect the Union to be dissolved. I do not expect the house to fall, but I do expect it to cease to be divided. It will become all one thing or all the other. Either the opponents of slavery will arrest the further spread of it, and place it where the public mind shall rest in the belief that it is in the course of ultimate extinction,—or its advocates will push it forward until it shall become alike lawful in all the States, old as well as new, North as well as South. Have we no tendency to the latter condition?"

Other speakers followed him and the Convention adjourned amid the wildest enthusiasm. . . .

The first speech Judge Douglas made was at Chicago. His friends had made the most ample preparations for an ovation. Notice had been given for weeks, half-price excursion trains carried large numbers from the country into town. Bands of music and torch-light processions brought large masses to the front of the Tremont House, from the balcony of which he addressed the crowd. Bengal fires illuminated the scene, and when he appeared he was greeted with tumultuous cheers. He was fighting for his political life. His massive form supported his ample head, covered with a thick growth of black hair. His deep-set, dark blue eyes shed their lustre under his heavy brows. The features of his firm, round face were wonderfully expressive of the working of his feelings. Calm in stating facts, passionate when he attacked, disdainful when he was forced to defend, his gestures were sometimes violent, and often exceptionally so. His voice was strong, but not modulated. Bold in his assertions, maledictory in his attacks, impressive in language, not caring to persuade, but intent to force the assent of his hearers, he was the Danton, not the Mirabeau, of oratory. . . .

Lincoln, who happened to be in the city, sat quietly on the same balcony. After Douglas got through, he was loudly called for. He rose, and stated that this ovation was gotten up for his friend Judge Douglas, but that if the good people of Chicago would listen to him, he would speak to them to-morrow evening at the same time and place. Without time for parade or showy demonstration the throng that listened to Lincoln next evening, as might have been expected from the political complexion of the city, was larger and really more enthusiastic than the one of the night before.

No greater contrast could be imagined than the one between Lincoln and Douglas. The latter was really a very little giant physically, measuring five feet and nothing, while Lincoln, when standing erect, towered to six feet three inches.[1] Lincoln, awkward in his posture and leaning a little forward, stood calm and collected, addressing his hearers in a somewhat familiar, yet very earnest, way, with a clear, distinct, and far-reaching voice, generally well modulated, but sometimes rather shrill. When unmoved, his features seemed overshadowed by an expression of sadness, though at times he could assume a most humorous, and even comical, look; but, when aroused, he appeared like a prophet of old. Neither he nor Douglas indulged in rhetoric; both were mainly argumentative. But while Douglas, powerful as was his speech, never showed anything like genius, there came from Lincoln occasionally flashes of genius and burning words, revelations as it were from the unknown, that will live as long as the English language lives. Lincoln was deeply read in the Bible and Shakespeare. He did not quote from them, but his style showed plainly his close intimacy with the Scriptures and the great bard. Douglas was eminently talented; Lincoln was original. But what made Lincoln vastly more effective in this contest was that even the most obtuse hearer could see at once that Douglas spoke for himself, and Lincoln for his cause.

The day after Lincoln's speech, July 15th, both went down on the train to Springfield,—Lincoln as a quiet passenger, Douglas as a sort of triumphator. He had a special car, had a secretary and a reporter, and a number of devoted friends with him. A band of music accompanied him, and on an attached platform car a gun was planted, which was fired off to announce his arrival at every station. His car was decorated with flags and emblems. Preparations had been made at every

---

[1] In fact, Douglas was five feet four inches tall, Lincoln six feet four.

station to receive him with music and the booming of cannon. The station platforms were crowded with men, women and children.

At Bloomington, where an appointment had been made for Douglas to speak, processions, salutes of cannon, fireworks, an immense crowd, —everything, in fact,—had been made ready to glorify the idol of the Illinois Democracy. Lincoln listened quietly. At Springfield Douglas met with a similar reception, and he spoke in the afternoon at Edwards' Grove for three hours. His friends pronounced it the best speech of his campaign. But now came Lincoln's turn. He spoke in Springfield at night. His speech was not only a masterpiece of argument, but so full of splendid humor that it kept the audience in roars of laughter. . . .

Lincoln now had measured swords, and in spite of his innate modesty was sagacious enough to see that he was Douglas's match in every respect. He proposed to canvass the State jointly, dividing the time between them. Douglas alleging that his friends had already made appointments for him, which he could not recall and which occupied nearly all his time, consented, however, to seven joint debates at Ottawa, Freeport, Quincy, Galesburg, Jonesborough, Charleston and Alton. Those joint meetings drew immense crowds. Douglas, impetuous, denunciatory, frequently lost his temper, made unguarded statements of facts which he had to take back, but magnetized the big crowd by his audacity and supreme self-confidence. Lincoln impressed his audiences by his almost too extreme fairness, his always pure and elevated language, and his appeals to their higher nature. Douglas, on the contrary, roused the existing strong prejudices against the negro race to the highest pitch, and not unfrequently resorted to demagogism unworthy of his own great reputation as a statesman. . . .

Douglas continued his canvass over the State in the same royal style in which he had commenced it in his appointments at Springfield and Bloomington. Large sums were sent into Illinois by his outside friends, and he himself raised, it was said, fifty thousand dollars, by mortgaging his real estate. Lincoln, now and then with a few friends, traveled as an ordinary passenger, though of course he met with enthusiastic demonstrations wherever he spoke. At the end of the canvass, when a friend asked him how much the campaign had cost him, he answered: "He was afraid that he had not spent less than five hundred dollars." Both candidates spoke almost every day from the 10th of July to the day of election. The highly excited elections in 1840 and 1856 bore no comparison with the political tempest which raged this year all over the Prairie State. . . .

I attended only the last joint meeting, shortly before the election, at Alton. I arrived there in the morning, and found Lincoln in the hotel sitting-room. He at once said: "Let us go up and see Mary." I had not seen Mrs. Lincoln, that I recollected, since meeting her at the Lexington parties, when she was Miss Todd. "Now, tell Mary what you think of our chances! She is rather dispirited." I was certain, I said, of our carrying the State and tolerably certain of our carrying the Legislature. St. Clair was perfectly safe. The outlook in Madison was good. We had just then been reading the St. Louis morning papers, where it was announced that more than a thousand Douglas men had chartered a boat to attend the Alton meeting, and that they represented the Free Soil party in Missouri and were enthusiastic for Douglas's election. We discussed fully the singular position that party had taken under the lead of Frank Blair, who had been the great champion of the cause of our party in Missouri, ever since the repeal of the Missouri Compromise. I found Lincoln a little despondent. He had come quietly down from Springfield with his wife that morning, unobserved, and it was not until an hour or so that his friends were made aware of his arrival.[2] He was soon surrounded by a crowd of Republicans; but there was no parade or fuss, while Douglas, about noon, made his pompous entry, and soon afterwards the boat from St. Louis landed at the wharf, heralded by the firing of guns and the strains of martial music.

The speaking commenced at two o'clock. The stand was on the public square. It was occupied by the speakers and by the Lincoln and Douglas Reception Committees of Alton. Mr. Lincoln took me with him on the platform. Here I met, for the first time since 1856, Judge Douglas, who in his genial manner shook hands with me, apparently quite cordially. But I was really shocked at the condition he was in. His face was bronzed, which was natural enough, but it was also bloated, and his looks were haggard, and his voice almost extinct. In conversation he merely whispered. In addressing his audience he made himself understood only by an immense strain, and then only to a very small circle immediately near him. He had the opening and conclusion. His speech, however, was as good as any he had delivered. Lincoln, although sunburnt, was as fresh as if he had just entered the campaign, and as cool and collected as ever. Without any apparent effort he stated his propositions clearly and tersely, and his whole speech was weighted with noble and deep thoughts. There were no appeals to passion and prejudice.

The Alton speech contained, by general admission, some of the finest passages of all the speeches he ever made. When Douglas's opening speech had been made, he was vociferously cheered. When, after Lincoln's speech, which made a powerful impression, Douglas made his reply, there was hardly any applause when he closed.

---

[2] Both Lincoln and Douglas traveled to Alton on a river steamer from Quincy, where they had debated on October 13.

6. *1859—JOHN BROWN'S BODY DANGLES FROM A ROPE*

❬ *Most Americans were willing, so far, to settle the slavery question by constitutional means. Not John Brown. This fanatical Abolitionist believed that only the flow of blood would bring slavery to an end. In Kansas he and several of his sons had murdered pro-slavery settlers in cold blood. In 1858 he had raided plantations in Missouri and carried off slaves to Canada. In 1859 he plotted the boldest stroke of all. With a small band of devoted followers he would seize the United States armory and arsenal at Harpers Ferry, Virginia. The slaves of the countryside would rise, and, armed with government weapons, overthrow their white masters. Brown and his men made their attack on the evening of October 16, 1859. They captured the armory and arsenal, then waited for slaves to join them. Instead of slaves, troops came. The following morning the soldiers, commanded by Col. Robert E. Lee, carried the buildings by assault, taking Brown and four others prisoners. Two men had escaped, ten lay dead or dying.*

In a trial marked by scrupulous fairness John Brown was convicted of murder, conspiracy, and treason to the state of Virginia, and sentenced to death by hanging. David Hunter Strother, representing HARPER'S WEEKLY, *described the execution.*

On Friday, December 2nd the notorious John Brown was executed at Charlestown, Virginia,[1] according to the sentence of the law. . . .

As early as nine o'clock . . . the field (adjoining the town of Charlestown), which had been selected for the place of execution, was occupied by a considerable body of soldiers, horse, foot, & artillery. A line of sentinels encircled the enclosure preventing access by the fences and a guard of infantry and artillery was posted at the gate by which spectators were required to enter.

I repaired to the field some time before the appointed hour that I might choose a convenient position to witness the final ceremony. The gibbet was erected on a gentle swell that commanded a view of the country for many miles around. From the scaffold which I ascended the view was of surpassing beauty. On every side stretching away into the blue distance were broad & fertile fields dotted with corn shocks and white farm houses glimmering through the leafless trees—emblems of prosperity and peace. Hard by was the pleasant village with its elegant suburban residences and bordering the picture east & west were

Boyd B. Stutler, "The Hanging of John Brown," *American Heritage, The Magazine of History,* No. 2, February, 1955, 6–9.
[1] Now West Virginia.

the blue mountains thirty miles apart. In the Blue Ridge which lay to the eastward appeared the deep gap through which the Potomac and Shenandoah pour their united streams at Harpers Ferry, eight miles distant.

Near at hand stood long lines of soldiers resting on their arms while all the neighboring hills in sight were crowded with squadrons of cavalry. The balmy south wind was blowing which covered the landscape with a warm & dreamy haze reminding one rather of May than December. From hence thought I, the old man may see the spot where his enormous crime first took the form of action—he may see the beautiful land his dark plots had devoted to bloody ruin, he may see in the gleaming of a thousand swords and these serried lines of bayonets— what might be well calculated to make wiser men than he, thoughtful.

At eleven o'clock, escorted by a strong column of soldiers, the prisoner entered the field. He was seated in a furniture waggon on his coffin with his arms tied down above the elbows, leaving the forearms free. The driver with two others occupied the front seat while the jailer sat in the after part of the waggon. I stood with a group of half a dozen gentlemen near the steps of the scaffold when the prisoner was driven up. He wore the same seedy and dilapidated dress that he had at Harpers Ferry and during his trial, but his rough boots had given place to a pair of particoloured slippers and he wore a low crowned broad brimmed hat (the first time I had ever seen him with a hat). He had entirely recovered from his wounds and looked decidedly better & stronger than when I last saw him. As he neared the gibbet his face wore a grim & grisly smirk which, but for the solemnity of the occasion, might have suggested ideas of the ludicrous. He stepped from the waggon with surprising agility and walked hastily toward the scaffold pausing a moment as he passed our group to wave his pinioned arm & bid us good morning. I thought I could observe in this a trace of bravado—but perhaps I was mistaken, as his natural manner was short, ungainly and hurried. He mounted the steps of the scaffold with the same alacrity and there as if by previous arrangement, he immediately took off his hat and offered his neck for the halter which was as promptly adjusted by Mr. Avis the jailer. A white muslin cap or hood was then drawn over his face and the Sheriff not remembering that his eyes were covered requested him to advance to the platform. The prisoner replied in his usual tone, "You will have to guide me there."

The breeze disturbing the arrangement of the hood the Sheriff asked his assistant for a pin. Brown raised his hand and directed him to the collar of his coat where several old pins were quilted in. The Sheriff took the pin and completed his work.

He was accordingly led forward to the drop, the halter hooked to the

beam, and the officers supposing that the execution was to follow immediately took leave of him. In doing so, the Sheriff enquired if he did
not want a handkerchief to throw as a signal to cut the drop. Brown
replied, "No, I don't care; I don't want you to keep me waiting un-
necessarily."

These were his last words, spoken with that sharp nasal twang peculiar to him, but spoken quietly & civilly, without impatience or the
slightest apparent emotion. In this position he stood for five minutes
or more, while the troops that composed the escort were wheeling into
the positions assigned them. I stood within a few paces of him and
watched narrowly during these trying moments to see if there was any
indication of his giving way. I detected nothing of the sort. He had
stiffened himself for the drop and waited motionless 'till it came.

During all these movements no sound was heard but the quick stern
words of military command, & when these ceased a dead silence reigned.
Col. Smith said to the Sheriff in a low voice, "We are ready." The civil
officers descended from the scaffold. One who stood near me whispered
earnestly, "He trembles, his knees are shaking." "You are mistaken,"
I replied, "it is the scaffold that shakes under the footsteps of the
officers." The Sheriff struck the rope a sharp blow with a hatchet, the
platform fell with a crash—a few convulsive struggles & a human soul
had gone to judgment.

7. *1860—OLD ABE LINCOLN FOR PRESIDENT!*

❲ *Lincoln had failed, in 1858, to defeat Douglas for the United
States Senate, but the campaign had made the Illinois Republican
a national figure. Even so, when the Republican National Convention met at Chicago on May 16, 1860, Lincoln seemed to be only
one of several minor candidates for the presidential nomination.
Most political observers believed that the choice would fall on either
William H. Seward, Senator from New York, or Salmon P. Chase,
Governor of Ohio. But in the first two days of the convention the
Chase boom failed to develop, while Lincoln's strength grew amazingly. When the balloting began it was apparent that the contest
would be between him and Seward.*

Murat Halstead reported the convention for the CINCINNATI
COMMERCIAL.

The Seward men generally abounded in confidence Friday morning
[May 18]. The air was full of rumors of the caucusing the night before, but the opposition of the doubtful States to Seward was an old

---

Murat Halstead, *Caucuses of 1860: A History of the National Political Conventions* (Columbus,
1860), 143–54.

story; and after the distress of Pennsylvania, Indiana & Co., on the subject of Seward's availability, had been so freely and ineffectually expressed from the start, it was not imagined their protests would suddenly become effective. The Sewardites marched as usual from their head-quarters at the Richmond House after their magnificent band, which was brilliantly uniformed—epaulets shining on their shoulders, and white and scarlet feathers waving from their caps—marched under the orders of recognized leaders, in a style that would have done credit to many volunteer military companies. They were about a thousand strong, and protracting their march a little too far, were not all able to get into the wigwam. This was their first misfortune. They were not where they could scream with the best effect in responding to the mention of the name of William H. Seward.

When the Convention was called to order, breathless attention was given the proceedings. There was not a space a foot square in the wigwam unoccupied. There were tens of thousands still outside, and torrents of men had rushed in at the three broad doors until not another one could squeeze in. . . .

Every body was now impatient to begin the work. Mr. Evarts of New York nominated Mr. Seward. Mr. Judd of Illinois nominated Mr. Lincoln. Mr. Dudley of New Jersey nominated Mr. Dayton. Mr. Reeder of Pennsylvania nominated Simon Cameron. Mr. Cartter of Ohio nominated Salmon P. Chase. Mr. Caleb Smith of Indiana seconded the nomination of Lincoln. Mr. Blair of Missouri nominated Edward Bates. Mr. Blair of Michigan seconded the nomination of William H. Seward. Mr. Corwin of Ohio nominated John McLean. Mr. Schurz of Wisconsin seconded the nomination of Seward. Mr. Delano of Ohio seconded the nomination of Lincoln. The only names that produced "tremendous applause," were those of Seward and Lincoln.

Every body felt that the fight was between them, and yelled accordingly.

The applause, when Mr. Evarts named Seward, was enthusiastic. When Mr. Judd named Lincoln, the response was prodigious, rising and raging far beyond the Seward shriek. Presently, upon Caleb B. Smith seconding the nomination of Lincoln, the response was absolutely terrific. It now became the Seward men to make another effort, and when Blair of Michigan seconded his nomination,

> "At once there rose so wild a yell,
> Within that dark and narrow dell;
> As all the fiends from heaven that fell
> Had pealed the banner cry of hell."

The effect was startling. Hundreds of persons stopped their ears in pain. The shouting was absolutely frantic, shrill and wild. No Camanches, no panthers ever struck a higher note, or gave screams with more infernal intensity. Looking from the stage over the vast amphi-theatre, nothing was to be seen below but thousands of hats—a black, mighty swarm of hats—flying with the velocity of hornets over a mass of human heads, most of the mouths of which were open. Above, all around the galleries, hats and handkerchiefs were flying in the tempest together. The wonder of the thing was, that the Seward outside pressure should, so far from New York, be so powerful.

Now the Lincoln men had to try it again, and as Mr. Delano of Ohio, on behalf "of a portion of the delegation of that State," seconded the nomination of Lincoln, the uproar was beyond description. Imagine all the hogs ever slaughtered in Cincinnati giving their death squeals together, a score of big steam whistles going (steam at 160 lbs. per inch), and you conceive something of the same nature. I thought the Seward yell could not be surpassed; but the Lincoln boys were clearly ahead, and feeling their victory, as there was a lull in the storm, took deep breaths all round, and gave a concentrated shriek that was posi-tively awful, and accompanied it with stamping that made every plank and pillar in the building quiver.

Henry S. Lane of Indiana leaped upon a table, and swinging hat and cane, performed like an acrobat. The presumption is, he shrieked with the rest, as his mouth was desperately wide open; but no one will ever be able to testify that he has positive knowledge of the fact that he made a particle of noise. His individual voice was lost in the aggregate hurricane.

The New York, Michigan and Wisconsin delegations sat together, and were in this tempest very quiet. Many of their faces whitened as the Lincoln *yawp* swelled into a wild hozanna of victory.

The Convention now proceeded to business. The New England States were called first, and it was manifest that Seward had not the strength that had been claimed for him there. Maine gave nearly half her vote for Lincoln. New Hampshire gave seven out of her ten votes for Lin-coln. Vermont gave her vote to her Senator Collamer, which was under-stood to be merely complimentary. It appeared, however, that her dele-gation was hostile or indifferent to Seward, otherwise there would have been no complimentary vote to another. Massachusetts was divided. Rhode Island and Connecticut did not give Seward a vote. So much for the caucusing the night before. Mr. Evarts of New York rose and gave the vote of that State, calmly, but with a swelling tone of pride in his voice—"The State of *New York* casts her *seventy votes* for *William H. Seward!*" The seventy votes was a plumper, and there was slight ap-plause, and that rustle and vibration in the audience indicating a sensa-tion. The most significant vote was that of Virginia, which had been expected solid for Seward, and which now gave him but eight and gave Lincoln fourteen. The New Yorkers looked significantly at each other as this was announced. Then Indiana gave her twenty-six votes for Lincoln. . . . It was seen that Lincoln, Cameron and Bates had the strength to defeat Seward, and it was known that the greater part of the Chase vote would go for Lincoln.

The Secretary announced the vote:

William H. Seward, of New York............................173½
Abraham Lincoln, of Illinois....................................102
Edward Bates, of Missouri.. 48
Simon Cameron, of Pennsylvania............................... 50½
John McLean, of Ohio... 12
Salmon P. Chase, of Ohio.. 49
Benjamin F. Wade, of Ohio....................................... 3
William L. Dayton, of New Jersey............................... 14
John M. Reed, of Pennsylvania................................... 1
Jacob Collamer, of Vermont...................................... 10
Charles Sumner, of Massachusetts............................... 1
John C. Fremont, of California................................... 1
Whole number of votes cast, 465; necessary to a choice, 233.

The Convention proceeded to a second ballot. Every man was fiercely enlisted in the struggle. The partisans of the various candidates were strung up to such a pitch of excitement as to render them incapable of patience, and the cries of "Call the roll" were fairly hissed through their teeth. The first gain for Lincoln was in New Hampshire. The Chase and the Fremont vote from that State were given him. His next gain was the whole vote of Vermont. This was a blighting blow upon the Seward interest. The New Yorkers started as if an Orsini bomb had exploded. And presently the Cameron vote of Pennsylvania was thrown for Lincoln, increasing his strength forty-four votes. The fate of the day was now determined. New York saw "checkmate" next move, and sullenly proceeded with the game, assuming unconsciousness of her inevitable doom. On this ballot Lincoln gained seventy-nine votes! Seward had 184½ votes; Lincoln 181. . . .

While this ballot [the third] was taken amid excitement that tested the nerves, the fatal defection from Seward in New England still further appeared—four votes going over from Seward to Lincoln in Massachusetts. The latter received four additional votes from Pennsylvania and fifteen additional votes from Ohio. It was whispered about— "Lincoln's the coming man—will be nominated this ballot." When the roll of States and Territories had been called, I had ceased to give attention to any votes but those for Lincoln, and had his vote added up as it was given. The number of votes necessary to a choice were two hundred and thirty-three, and I saw under my pencil as the Lincoln column was completed, the figures 231½—one vote and a half to give him the nomination. In a moment the fact was whispered about. A hundred pencils had told the same story. The news went over the house wonderfully, and there was a pause. There are always men anxious to distinguish themselves on such occasions. There is nothing that politicians like better than a crisis. I looked up to see who would be the man to give the decisive vote. . . . In about ten ticks of a watch, Cartter of Ohio was up. I had imagined Ohio would be slippery enough for the crisis. And sure enough! Every eye was on Cartter, and every body who understood the matter at all, knew what he was about to do. He is a large man with rather striking features, a shock of bristling black hair, large and shining eyes, and is terribly marked with the small-pox. He has also an impediment in his speech, which amounts to a stutter; and his selection as chairman of the Ohio delegation was, considering its condition, altogether appropriate. He had been quite noisy during the sessions of the Convention, but had never commanded, when mounting his chair, such attention as now. He said, "I rise (eh), Mr. Chairman (eh), to announce the change of four votes of Ohio from Mr. Chase to Mr. Lincoln." The deed was done. There was a moment's silence. The nerves of the thousands, which through the hours of suspense had been subjected to terrible tension, relaxed, and as deep breaths of relief were taken, there was a noise in the wigwam like the rush of a great wind, in the van of a storm—and in another breath, the storm was there. There were thousands cheering with the energy of insanity.

A man who had been on the roof, and was engaged in communicating the results of the ballotings to the mighty mass of outsiders, now demanded by gestures at the sky-light over the stage, to know what had happened. One of the Secretaries, with a tally sheet in his hands, shouted—"Fire the Salute! Abe Lincoln is nominated!" As the cheering inside the wigwam subsided, we could hear that outside, where the news of the nomination had just been announced. And the roar, like the breaking up of the fountains of the great deep that was heard, gave a new impulse to the enthusiasm inside. Then the thunder of the salute rose above the din, and the shouting was repeated with such tremendous fury that some discharges of the cannon were absolutely not heard by those on the stage. Puffs of smoke, drifting by the open doors, and the smell of gunpowder, told what was going on.

The moment that half a dozen men who were on their chairs making motions at the President could be heard, they changed the votes of their States to Mr. Lincoln. . . .

After a rather dull speech from Mr. Browning of Illinois, responding in behalf of Lincoln, the nomination was made unanimous, and the Convention adjourned for dinner. The town was full of the news of Lincoln's nomination, and could hardly contain itself. There were bands of music playing, and processions marching, and joyous cries heard on every hand, from the army of trumpeters for Lincoln of Illinois, and the thousands who are always enthusiastic on the winning side. But hundreds of men who had been in the wigwam were so prostrated by the excitement they had endured, and their exertions in shrieking for Seward or Lincoln, that they were hardly able to walk to their hotels. There were men who had not tasted liquor, who staggered about like drunkards, unable to manage themselves. The Seward men were terribly stricken down. They were mortified beyond all expression, and walked thoughtfully and silently away from the slaughterhouse, more ashamed than embittered. They acquiesced in the nomination, but did not pretend to be pleased with it; and the tone of their conversations, as to the prospect of electing the candidate, was not hopeful. It was their funeral, and they would not make merry.

A Lincoln man who could hardly believe that the "Old Abe" of his adoration was really the Republican nominee for the Presidency, took a chair at the dinner-table at the Tremont House, and began talking to those around him, with none of whom he was acquainted, of the greatness of the events of the day. One of his expressions was, "Talk of your money and bring on your bullies with you!—the immortal principles of the everlasting people are with Abe Lincoln, of the people, by—." "Abe Lincoln has no money and no bullies, but he has the people by—." A servant approached the eloquent patriot and asked what he would have to eat. Being thus recalled to temporal things he glared scornfully at the servant and roared out, "Go to the devil—what do I want to eat for? Abe Lincoln is nominated, G— d—— it; and I'm going to live on air—the air of Liberty by —." But in a moment he inquired for the bill of fare, and then ordered "a great deal of everything"— saying if he must eat he might as well eat "the whole bill." He swore he felt as if he could "devour and digest an Illinois prairie." And this was one of thousands. . . .

The city was wild with delight. The "Old Abe" men formed processions, and bore rails through the streets. Torrents of liquor were poured down the hoarse throats of the multitude. A hundred guns were fired from the top of the Tremont House. The Chicago Press and Tribune office was illuminated. That paper says:

"On each side of the counting-room door stood a *rail*—out of the three thousand split by 'honest Old Abe' thirty years ago on the Sangamon River bottoms. On the inside were two more, brilliantly hung with tapers."

I left the city on the night train on the Fort Wayne and Chicago road. The train consisted of eleven cars, every seat full and people standing in the aisles and corners. I never before saw a company of persons so prostrated by continued excitement. The Lincoln men were not able to respond to the cheers which went up along the road for "old Abe." They had not only done their duty in that respect, but exhausted their capacity. At every station where there was a village, until after two o'clock, there were tar barrels burning, drums beating, boys carrying rails; and guns, great and small, banging away. The weary passengers were allowed no rest, but plagued by the thundering jar of cannon, the clamor of drums, the glare of bonfires, and the whooping of the boys, who were delighted with the idea of a candidate for the Presidency, who thirty years ago split rails on the Sangamon River—classic stream now and for evermore—and whose neighbors named him "honest."

CHAPTER XIV

CIVIL WAR

1861 – 1865

1. *1861*—SOUTH CAROLINA SECEDES FROM THE UNION

❡ *On the 6th of November, 1860, Abraham Lincoln was elected President. Many Southern leaders had warned that if the Republicans won the election the slave-holding states would secede from the Union. The North refused to take the warnings seriously. But the South meant its threats. South Carolina, whose former Senator John C. Calhoun had devoted much of his life to expounding the doctrine of secession, took the lead. Soon after Lincoln's election the governor summoned a convention to meet at Columbia.*

Samuel Wylie Crawford, an army surgeon stationed at Charleston, witnessed the passage of the Ordinance of Secession.

Hardly had the Convention assembled at Columbia when a resolution was introduced by Chancellor J. A. Inglis to the effect that "it is the opinion of the Convention that the State should forthwith secede from

---

Samuel Wylie Crawford, *The Genesis of the Civil War* (New York, 1887), 47-55.

the Federal Union known as the United States of America, and that a committee be appointed to draft an ordinance to be adopted at the Convention in order to accomplish this purpose of secession." . . . It passed without a dissenting voice.

Meantime, a contagious disease having broken out in the city, the Convention resolved to change its session to Charleston, and it reassembled in that city on the eighteenth. . . .

In the large room of Institute Hall, the Convention reassembled at 4 o'clock on the afternoon of the 18th of December. Crowds of excited people thronged the streets and open squares of the city, and filled the passage and stairways of the hall. Congratulations were exchanged on every side, while earnest dissatisfaction was freely expressed that the passage of the Secession Ordinance had been delayed.

Blue cockades and cockades of palmetto appeared in almost every hat; flags of all descriptions, except the National colors, were everywhere displayed. Upon the gavel that lay upon the Speaker's table, the word "Secession" had been cut in deep black characters. The enthusiasm spread to the more practical walks of trade, and the business streets were gay with bunting and flags, as the tradespeople, many of whom were Northern men, commended themselves to the popular clamor by a display of coarse representations on canvas of the public men, and of the incidents daily presenting themselves, and of the brilliant future in store for them. . . .

Early on the morning of the 20th knots of men were seen gathered here and there through the main streets and squares of Charleston. The Convention was not to meet until 12 o'clock, but it was understood that the Committee were ready to report the Ordinance of Secession, and that it would certainly pass the Convention that day. The report soon spread. Although this action had been fully anticipated, there was a feverish anxiety to know that the secession of the State was really accomplished, and as the hour of noon approached, crowds of people streamed along the avenues towards St. Andrew's Hall and filled the approaches. A stranger passing from the excited throng outside into the hall of the Convention would be struck with the contrast. Ordinary business was quietly disposed of; the Mayor and Governor and the officials of the Legislature were invited to seats upon the floor; committees authorized by previous resolutions were announced by the President, the more noticeable being that of the late United States Judge Magrath, to head the Committee on so much of the President's message as related to the property in the harbor, and W. P. Miles on Foreign Relations looking to the ordeal in Washington. Quietly the Convention had met, and had been opened with prayer to God. There was no excitement. There was no visible sign that the Commonwealth of South Carolina was about to take a step more momentous for weal or woe than had yet been known in her history.

Then followed the introduction of a resolution by Mr. R. B. Rhett, that a committee of thirteen be appointed to report an ordinance providing for a convention to form a Southern Confederacy, as important a step as the secession of the State itself. It was referred to the appropriate committee, when Chancellor Inglis of Chesterfield, the Chairman of the Committee to report an ordinance proper of secession, arose and called the attention of the President.

An immediate silence pervaded the whole assemblage as every eye turned upon the speaker. Addressing the chair, he said that the Committee appointed to prepare a draft of an ordinance proper, to be adopted by the Convention in order to effect the secession of South Carolina from the Federal Union, respectfully report that they have had the matter under consideration, and believe that they would best meet the exigencies of the occasion by expressing in the fewest and simplest words all that was necessary to effect the end proposed, and so to exclude everything which was not a necessary part of the "solemn act of secession." They therefore submitted the following:

"AN ORDINANCE

to dissolve the Union between the State of South Carolina and other States united with her under the compact entitled 'The Constitution of the United States of America.'

"We, the people of the State of South Carolina, in convention assembled, do declare and ordain, and it is hereby declared and ordained, that the Ordinance adopted by us in convention, on the 23d day of May, in the year of our Lord, one thousand seven hundred and eighty-eight, whereby the Constitution of the United States was ratified, and also all the acts and parts of acts of the General Assembly of this State ratifying amendments of the said Constitution, are hereby repealed, and that the union now subsisting between South Carolina and other States under the name of 'The United States of America' is hereby dissolved."

A proposition that business be suspended for fifteen minutes was not agreed to, and the question was at once put, with the result of a unanimous vote, at 1:30 p.m., of 169 yeas, nays none. An immediate struggle for the floor ensued. Mr. W. Porcher Miles moved that an immediate telegram be sent to the Members of Congress, at Washington, announcing the result of the vote and the Ordinance of Secession. It was then resolved to invite the Governor and both branches of the Legislature to Institute Hall, at seven o'clock in the evening, and that the Convention should move in procession to that hall, and there, in the presence of the constituted authorities of the State and the people, sign the Ordinance of Secession. That a clergyman of the city should be invited to attend, and upon the completion of the signing of the Ordinance, he should "return thanks to Almighty God in behalf of the people of this State and to invoke His blessings upon our proceedings." The Ordinance was then turned over to the Attorney-General and the solicitors to be engrossed.

The invitations to the Senate and House of Representatives having been accepted, the Convention moved in procession at the hour indicated to Institute Hall, amid the crowds of citizens that thronged the streets, cheering loudly as it passed. The galleries of the hall were crowded with ladies, who waved their handkerchiefs to the Convention as it entered, with marked demonstration. On either side of the President's chair were two large palmetto trees. The Hall was densely crowded. The Ordinance, having been returned engrossed and with the great seal of the State, attached by the Attorney-General, was presented and was signed by every member of the Convention, special favorites being received with loud applause. Two hours were thus occupied. The President then announced that "the Ordinance of Secession has been signed and ratified, and I proclaim the State of South Carolina," said he, "an independent Commonwealth."

At once the whole audience broke out into a storm of cheers; the ladies again joined in the demonstration; a rush was made for the palmetto trees, which were torn to pieces in the effort to secure mementos of the occasion. As soon as the passage of the Secession Ordinance at St. Andrew's Hall was accomplished, a messenger left the house and rode with the greatest speed to the camp of the First Regiment of Rifles, South Carolina Militia, Colonel Pettigrew, one mile distant, where in front of the paraded regiment the Ordinance was read amid the loud acclamations of the men.

The adjournment of the Convention was characterized by the same dignity that had marked its sessions. Outside, the whole city was wild with excitement as the news spread like wild-fire through its streets. Business was suspended everywhere; the peals of the church bells mingling with salvos of artillery from the citadel. Old men ran shouting down the street. Every one entitled to it, appeared at once in uniform. In less than fifteen minutes after its passage, the principal newspaper of Charleston had placed in the hands of the eager multitude a copy of the Ordinance of Secession. Private residences were illuminated, while military organizations marched in every direction, the music of their bands lost amid the shouts of the people. The whole heart of the people had spoken. . . .

2.   *1861*—THE CONFEDERATES TAKE FORT SUMTER

⟨ *By March 4, 1861, when Lincoln was inaugurated, seven states had declared themselves out of the Union and had formed the Con-*

"The Diary of Emma E. Holmes," in Katharine M. Jones, *Heroines of Dixie* (Indianapolis: Bobbs-Merrill Co., 1955), 18–22.

federate States of America. Whenever they could, the states had taken over Federal forts and arsenals within their borders. But in Charleston harbor a Union garrison under Major Robert Anderson held Fort Sumter. With provisions at the fort running low, Lincoln had to decide whether to send a relief expedition or order Anderson to give up the fort. The President decided on an expedition, but notified the Confederate authorities that he was dispatching provisions only, not reinforcements. The Confederates determined to take the fort before relief arrived.

Emma E. Holmes, a young woman lamed by a recent illness, recorded the events of four stirring days in her diary.

Charleston, South Carolina

Thursday 11th [April 1861] is a day never to be forgotten in the annals of Charleston. A despatch was received from Jeff. Davis with orders to demand the surrender of Fort Sumter immediately. At 2 P.M. two aide-de-camps went to Anderson with the summons, giving him until six to decide. The whole afternoon and night the Battery was thronged with spectators of every age and sex, anxiously watching and waiting with the momentary expectation of hearing the roar of cannon, opening on the fort, or on the fleet which was reported off the bar. Everybody was restless and all who could go, were out.

Friday April 12, 1861. . . . Beauregard went a second time last night at ten to urge the surrender but Anderson refused. The first time Anderson said if the fort was not battered he would have to surrender in three days for want of food. All last night the troops were under arms and at half past four this morning the heavy booming of cannon woke the city from its slumbers. The Battery was soon thronged with anxious hearts, and all day long they have continued—a dense, quiet, orderly mass—but not a sign of fear or anguish is seen. Everybody seems relieved that what has been so long dreaded has come at last, and so confident of victory that they seem not to think of the danger of their friends. Everybody seems calm and grave.

I am writing about half past four in the afternoon—just about twelve hours since the first shot was fired—and during the whole time shot and shell have been steadily pouring into Fort Sumter from Fort Stevens where our "Palmetto boys" have won the highest praise from Beauregard, from Fort Moultrie and the floating battery, placed at the cove. These are the principal batteries and just before dinner we received despatches saying *no one* has yet been hurt on either Morris or Sullivan's island and though the floating battery and Fort Stevens have both been hit several times, *no damage* has been done, while two or three breaches have been made in Fort Sumter. For more than two hours our batteries opened on Anderson, before he returned a single shot, as if husbanding his resources. At times the firing has been very rapid, then slow and irregular and at times altogether upon Fort Moultrie.

Though every shot is distinctly heard and shakes our house, I feel calm and composed. . . .

There are some few ladies who have been made perfectly miserable and nearly frantic by their fear of the safety of their loved ones, but the great body of the citizens seem to be so impressed with the justice of our Cause that they place entire confidence on the God of Battles.

Every day brings hundreds of men from the up-country and the city is besides filled with their anxious wives and sisters and mothers who have followed them.

Saturday April 13, 1861.

All yesterday evening and during the night our batteries continued to fire at regular intervals. About six in the afternoon the rain commenced and poured for some hours. The wind rose and it became quite stormy. But this morning was clear and brilliantly beautiful. Yesterday was so misty it was difficult to see what was going on at the forts. The wind was from the west today, which prevented us from hearing any firing and we were becoming anxious to know the meaning of stillness, when Uncle James sent to tell us Fort Sumter was on fire. . . .

The scene at Fort Sumter must have been awful beyond description. They had soon been compelled to leave their barbette guns, from their exposed situation, many being disabled by our balls. Anderson fired his guns until he was compelled to retire to the case mates from the fury of the fire, on three sides at one time. . . . Both on Friday and Saturday, Anderson put his flag at half-mast as a signal of distress—the barracks being on fire three times on Friday—but "his friends" took no notice of it, and was not understood by our men though all sympathized deeply with him, and shouted applause every time he fired.

In the meantime the scene to the spectators in the city was intensely exciting. The Battery and every house, house top and spire was crowded. On White Point Garden were encamped about fifty cadets, having in charge, five, six, & twelve pounders placed on the eastern promenade. It was thought the vessels might attempt to come in and bombard the city, and workmen were busy all day in mounting four twenty-fours directly in front of Cousin S.'s.

With the telescope I saw the shots as they struck the fort, and the masonry crumbling, while on Morris Island we saw the men moving about on the sand hills. All were anxious to see, and most had opera-glasses which they coolly used till they heard a report from Sumter, when they dodged behind the sand hills. . . .

During the morning a demand for cartridge bags for the Dahlgreen guns was made. The elder ladies cut and about twenty girls immediately went to work, all seated on the floor, while we set one to watch and report.

Soon the welcome cry was heard "the flag is down" but scarcely had the shout died away, when it was reported to be up again, but only visible with the glass. The staff being shot off, it was hastily fastened just above the parapets and very soon after at one o'clock the stars and stripes were struck and the white flag floated alone. We could scarcely believe it at first but the total cessation of hostilities soon proved it true.

After the staff was shot off Mr. Wigfall, who was on Morris Island, not being able to see the flag when it was replaced, determined to demand the surrender in Beauregard's name. He sprang into a boat rowed by three Negroes, asked H. Gourdin Young of the P.G. to accompany him and went to the fort while shot and shell were falling all around from the batteries on Sullivan's Island. He crept into a port hole, asked to see Anderson and demanded the surrender. He was asked why the batteries continued firing as the White flag was up beside the U.S. flag. Wigfall answered that as long as the latter floated the firing would continue. It was immediately hauled down.

In the meantime a steamer had started from the City with several other aides, but they found Wigfall had anticipated them. The terms granted are worthy of South Carolina to a brave antagonist. Major Anderson and his garrison are to be allowed to march out with military honors—saluting their flag before taking it down. All facilities will be afforded for his removal together with company arms and property and all private property. He is allowed to determine the precise time of yielding up the Fort and may go by sea or land as he chooses. He requested that he might be sent on in the "Isabel" to New York. . . .

As soon as the surrender was announced, the bells commenced to ring, and in the afternoon, salutes of the "magic seven" were fired from the cutter, "Lady Davis," school ship, and "Cadet's Battery" in honor of one of the most brilliant and bloodless victories in the records of the world. After thirty three hours consecutive cannonading not one man hurt on either side—no damages of any consequence done to any of our fortifications, though the officers' quarters at Fort Moultrie and many of the houses on Sullivan's Island were riddled, and though the outer walls of Fort Sumter were much battered and many of the guns disabled, besides the quarters burnt, still as a military post it is uninjured. . . .

Sunday 14th. Major Anderson appointed 12 o'clock today to give up the fort. The Governor, his wife & suite, General Beauregard—suite— and many other military men besides Mrs. Isaac Hayne and Hattie

Barnwell who went down with Lieut. Davis' sister, went down on board
a steamer, whence they witnessed the ceremony of raising the Confederate and Palmetto flags. . . . Anderson and his men embarked on
board the "Isabel" but as the tide prevented them from leaving immediately, they were obliged to be witnesses of the universal rejoicing. . . .

3. *1861*—LINCOLN LEARNS OF BULL RUN

❨ *Lincoln answered the attack on Fort Sumter with a proclamation
calling for troops. Both North and South sprang to arms. By the
middle of May thousands of Union soldiers had reached Washington. The North called for action, and "On to Richmond!" became the slogan of editorial writers and patriotic speakers.*

*Yielding to the clamor, the Union authorities decided to strike
the Confederate forces grouped around Manassas Junction twenty-
five miles southwest of Washington. On Sunday, July 21, a Federal
army under General Irvin McDowell attacked the Confederate lines
along Bull Run Creek. Washington residents, including many Congressmen, expected an easy victory and drove out to see the sport.
At first it seemed that they would not be disappointed, but by mid-
afternoon the tide of battle turned and the Federal forces began a
retreat that became a rout.*

*John G. Nicolay, Lincoln's private secretary, made a diary record
of the way news of the battle and its outcome came to the White
House.*

[Noon, 21st] I think General McDowell's object is to get to the rear
of the enemy's position before he will offer a general battle. Actions are,
however, almost always controlled more or less by accidents which cannot be foreseen. . . . Even while I write this, dispatches come which
indicate that a considerable part of the force is engaged, so that we may
know by tonight whether we are to be successful in this fight. . . . Of
course everybody is in great suspense. General Scott talked confidently
this morning of success, and very calmly and quietly went to church at
eleven o'clock.

3½ P.M. . . . During say two hours the President has been receiving
dispatches at intervals of fifteen minutes from Fairfax Station, in
which the operator reports the fluctuations of the firing as he hears it, at
the distance of three or four miles from the scene of action. For half
an hour the President has been somewhat uneasy as these reports
seemed to indicate that our forces were retiring.

After getting his dinner he went over to see General Scott whom he

Helen Nicolay, *Lincoln's Secretary, A Biography of John G. Nicolay* (New York: Longmans,
Green & Co., 1949), 108–10. Reprinted by permission.

found asleep. He woke the General and presented his view of the case to him. But the General told him these reports were worth nothing as indications either way—that the changes in the currents of wind, the echoes, &c &c., made it impossible for a distant listener to determine the course of a battle. The General still expressed his confidence in a successful result, and composed himself for another nap when the President left.

From about four to six dispatches continued to come in saying the battle had extended along nearly the whole line—that there had been considerable loss on both sides, but that the secession lines had been driven back two or three miles (some of the dispatches said to the Junction). One of General Scott's aides came in and reported substantially that General McDowell would immediately attack and capture the Junction, perhaps yet tonight, but certainly by tomorrow morning.

At six o'clock, the President having in the meanwhile gone out to ride, Mr. Seward came into the President's room with a terribly frightened and excited look, and said to John and me, who were sitting there:

"Where is the President?"

"Gone to ride," we replied.

"Have you any late news?" said he.

I began reading Hansen's dispatch to him.

Said he, "Tell no one. That is not so. The battle is lost. The telegraph says that McDowell is in full retreat, and calls on General Scott to save the capital," &c. "Find the President, and tell him to come immediately to General Scott's."

In about an hour the President came in. We told him, and he started off immediately. John and I continued to sit at the windows and could now distinctly hear heavy cannonading on the other side of the river. It is now eight o'clock, but the President has not yet returned, and we have heard nothing further.

Monday morning, July 23d. Thus go the fortunes of war. Our worst fears are confirmed. The victory which seemed in our grasp at four o'clock yesterday afternoon is changed to an overwhelming defeat—a total and disgraceful rout of our men. The whole army is in retreat, and will come back as far as the lines of fortifications on the other side of the river. These have all the time been kept properly garrisoned and are strong enough to make the city perfectly secure.

4. 1862—THE "MONITOR" AND THE "MERRIMACK" FIGHT TO A DRAW

❲ *At the outbreak of the war Confederate forces captured the United States steam frigate* MERRIMACK, *scuttled in shallow water*

Chicago History (Chicago Historical Society), Vol. III, No. 11, 340–45.

and partly burned. The Southern authorities decided to cover the ship's upper works with heavy iron plates and convert her into a ram or floating battery. Nine months later, renamed the VIRGINIA, *she was ready for action, the first ironclad in naval history. On March 8, 1862, she found the Federal blockading squadron, all wooden ships, off Newport News. In a few hours she sank the* CUMBERLAND *and put the* CONGRESS *and the* MINNESOTA *out of action.*

All Washington, except Gideon Welles, the Secretary of the Navy, went into panic. The MERRIMACK, *officials predicted, could sink every Union ship, bombard every coastal city, come up the Potomac to Washington and destroy the government buildings. Welles had confidence in a new little ship of his own. The* MONITOR, *invented by a Swedish-American engineer named John Erickson, was simply a revolving turret on a low deck above an iron hull. She was no match in size for the* MERRIMACK, *but she mounted two heavy guns, and would be hard to sink.*

The two ships met on March 9th. Neither could sink the other, but their drawn battle made junk of the world's navies. A seaman on the MONITOR *tells the story of the engagement.*

Battle was fought Sunday, March 9, '62
at Hampton Roads, Va. 8 to 12 a.m.

MY DEAR FATHER:

We had a very unpleasant passage out. The first night went off well. The next day it blew hard from nw. From the Capes of Delaware to Smith Island we had heavy seas. They rolled over her [the *Monitor*] several feet deep. The water ran down around the tower bottom and wheel house. The sea broke into the blower pipes and caused a great deal of trouble and into the smoke funnels and caused the gas to escape into the fire room. The engineers and firemen on duty were brought out almost lifeless and we had for some time no control of the ship. All that night no one slept much. . . . About 2 a.m. the wheel ropes got off the wheel and we were broadside to seas rolling over & over in all kinds of ways.

In the morning we got in with the land; we were very glad. Off Cape Henry we got a pilot. He told us that at 2 p.m. the *Merrimac*[1] came down from Norfolk and steamed to Newport News. She sunk the *Cumberland* frigate by running her ram into her and then taking raking positions and killed 120 men at the guns. They fought till she went over on her port side lying with her mastheads out of water. The rest of the crew and officers saved themselves the best way they could or were taken prisoners.

---

[1] Though officially named the *Merrimack,* the word is almost invariably spelled without the "k."

The *Congress* frigate fought for some time until she [was] struck through the deck [which] set her on fire. We saw her burning when we came in. By and by she blew up. We got to Hampton about 8 p.m. of the 8th of March, Saturday. After anchoring the Captain [Lt. John L. Worden] went on board the flagship and got orders to proceed to the scene of demolition and if he could to save the *Minnesota,* then aground at Newport News. So up we went and anchored close to her (the *Merrimac*) intending to attack her in the morning, having already exchanged some broadsides before dark. In the morning we saw the *Merrimac* and two wooden steamers under Sewell's Point. We got under way immediately and soon after, went to quarters on a slim breakfast and but little rest.

I was down on the berth deck with the powder division and all I know is from others. The shot, shell, and grape flew by with a whizz and struck all over. We were struck 21 times by the *Merrimac,* [and by] 2 shots from the *Minnesota.* Seven shots struck the tower, 7 or 8 tore up the edge of the deck & side, one shell burst right in the portholes but hurt no one ; another stuck fast in a dent it made in the tower 2½ inches deep, right on a rivet. Those that struck the sides dented & bent the iron plates but not so much as to hinder us from immediate action. One shot took a corner of the pilot house like you would rough a piece of bread in spreading it. Another, fired about 20 yards from the fore part of the house, cracked the iron bar and the dust from the projectile flew into the eyes of the Captain. He had to go out of the house and his face was covered with blood and smoke. After the action closed we sent him on shore and he went up to Washington to get the best medical aid and see the President.

The Quarter Master, Peter Williams, the Asst. Secy. of the Navy says he will give a Master Mate's rate for his reward. Pete saw more of her [the *Merrimac*] than any one else. He saw right into the bore of the gun and the loader was a nigger. Pete says, "Captain, that is for us," and rip! she came. After that we fired but few shots. After an action of about 4 hours we made her run with the after ports down in the water as though she was badly injured, the men running out of the ports into the boats and two wooden [ships] towing her. We gave the wooden boats a shot and made the timber fly. They went off to Norfolk.

We put two shots one after the other into one place on her [the *Merrimac's*] water line, another just above ; 2 shots passed through her roof, several glanced off, and one went through her quarter. We struck her prow or ram and sent the splinters about. The iron flew lively from her very often. She flew a Black Flag with a white cross. Her flag staff we blew a piece off ; the flag with one shot was cut half away. We made a hole in her roof that a man stood straight up in when she passed by the point after action.

318

Thousands of soldiers, men of war people, and shore folks were looking at us, and some of the best glasses in the country were in use. We fought over 4 miles of ground and steamed around and around her, keeping at close quarters. We could steam faster than she. We can make about 6 knots, she not so much. We fired away at the *Merrimac* for some time before she took notice of us. Our Captain says, "Hold your fire; I will put you alongside directly," so after our first fire rip she came right into us and our 175 lbs. of shot went right through her. Just think of them at but a few feet and theirs not going through our tower. We were very close all the action. Twice we touched and the shot and shell did everlastingly fly around the decks. They tried to put rifle bullets into the holes in the ports and sights but did not.

Our Captain was as cool as a man playing a game of chess. He passed the word to keep cool and not lose a shot. One man was knocked down by the head of a bolt but was all right in a few hours. The other Master was in the tower and had his knee against the side of the tower and a shell struck the tower on the outside at the same time. He was knocked down by it but was soon about again. The concussions caused a little uneasiness in the ears of the men in the tower, but not much. I was in charge down below with the powder division attending to shot, &c. The time passed very quick away and everyone was in the best humor until our Captain was wounded, and then our pilot house was thought to be unsafe so we did not follow up the *Merrimac*. If it had not been for that we might have sunk her outright.

We returned to save the *Minnesota*. In the night she got off and returned to Hampton Roads. In the morning we steamed to Hampton Roads and as we passed the ships we were cheered by everyone, the men of our ship returning it. The soldiers and people of the forts also, and every one of the guard and passing boats. The feeling everywhere was of the most excitable enthusiasm & gratitude. We have been up & down the harbor and to Newport News and hundreds of officers, soldiers, & seamen have been aboard and gave us their account of what they saw and how they feel about it.

Our orders are to keep on the defensive for awhile and to look out for the *Merrimac*. The batteries around Sewell's Point we can see and today the Sawyer Jim on the Rip Raps were firing shell right onto the point, the shells bursting about but I don't know with what effect yet.

We have had changes in officers. Another Captain has come. His name is Jeffers, a man they say is a good fighter. He says he will carry us as well as our other Captain.

I am well and hope you all are. I don't know how long it will be before we have another fight. We are anxious for it. We cleared away for action yesterday noon and steamed over to the point but no vessel was there. The fort has ceased firing on our passing vessels. Today they are removing the troops away from some of the batteries. We hear that we have injured her [the fort] very much and the Captain and 2 Lieutenants are also much hurt, 17 men killed, &c. We have papers from the North, of March 11, giving us great praise for our fight. The Captain of a French steamer has been on board and was highly pleased. He witnessed the fight. The *Rinaldo*, Capt. Montague of H.B.M. that took Mason & Slidell from Boston to Bermuda was on board and said his wooden ship was good for nothing alongside of us, that 3 or 4 such as this could whip the world.

I will now close. If any one of my friends want to know what was done, just pass the letter around, for it is the longest I ever wrote or will do again.

I remain your son,

I will write again.   JOHN

5. *1862*—LINCOLN DECIDES TO ISSUE THE PROCLAMATION OF EMANCIPATION

❮[*The North went to war to preserve the Union, not to abolish slavery. But as the fighting dragged on without a decisive Federal victory, Lincoln became convinced that he could not afford to forego the advantages which a blow at slavery would give the Union. If Federal victory promised to end slavery, France and Great Britain would not dare intervene on the side of the South, as they had indicated they might. Emancipation, moreover, would encourage slaves to leave their masters, and if they could be enlisted in the Union armies, they would be an important addition to the manpower of the North.*

Lincoln brought the subject of emancipation before his Cabinet in July, 1862, but laid it aside when William H. Seward, Secretary of State, objected that the time was not opportune. The Northern military situation was so bad, Seward believed, that a proclamation would be considered a sign of weakness—in his own words, "the last shriek on the retreat." But the Battle of Antietam, fought on September 17, 1862, removed this objection. Five days later Lincoln summoned his Cabinet. Salmon P. Chase, Secretary of the Treasury, recorded the memorable meeting in his diary.

Sept. 22, Monday. To Department about nine. State Department messenger came, with notice to Heads of Departments to meet at 12.— Received sundry callers.—Went to White House.

All the members of the Cabinet were in attendance. There was some

David Donald, Ed., *Inside Lincoln's Cabinet: The Civil War Diaries of Salmon P. Chase* (New York: Longmans, Green & Co., 1954), 148–52.

general talk; and the President mentioned that Artemus Ward had sent him his book. Proposed to read a chapter which he thought very funny. Read it, and seemed to enjoy it very much—the Heads also (except Stanton) of course. The Chapter was 'Highhanded Outrage at Utica.'

The President then took a graver tone and said:—

"Gentlemen: I have, as you are aware, thought a great deal about the relation of this war to Slavery; and you all remember that, several weeks ago, I read to you an Order I had prepared on this subject, which, on account of objections made by some of you, was not issued. Ever since then, my mind has been much occupied with this subject, and I have thought all along that the time for acting on it might very probably come. I think the time has come now. I wish it were a better time. I wish that we were in a better condition. The action of the army against the rebels has not been quite what I should have best liked. But they have been driven out of Maryland, and Pennsylvania is no longer in danger of invasion. When the rebel army was at Frederick, I determined, as soon as it should be driven out of Maryland, to issue a Proclamation of Emancipation such as I thought most likely to be useful. I said nothing to any one; but I made the promise to myself, and (hesitating a little)—to my Maker. The rebel army is now driven out, and I am going to fulfil that promise. I have got you together to hear what I have written down. I do not wish your advice about the main matter—for that I have determined for myself. This I say without intending any thing but respect for any one of you. But I already know the views of each on this question. They have been heretofore expressed, and I have considered them as thoroughly and carefully as I can. What I have written is that which my reflections have determined me to say. If there is anything in the expressions I use, or in any other minor matter, which anyone of you thinks had best be changed, I shall be glad to receive the suggestions. One other observation I will make. I know very well that many others might, in this matter, as in others, do better than I can; and if I were satisfied that the public confidence was more fully possessed by any one of them than by me, and knew of any Constitutional way in which he could be put in my place, he should have it. I would gladly yield it to him. But though I believe that I have not so much of the confidence of the people as I had some time since, I do not know that, all things considered, any other person has more; and, however this may be, there is no way in which I can have any other man put where I am. I am here. I must do the best I can, and bear the responsibility of taking the course which I feel I ought to take."

The President then proceeded to read his Emancipation Proclamation, making remarks on the several parts as he went on, and showing that he had fully considered the whole subject, in all the lights under which it had been presented to him.

After he had closed, Gov. Seward said: "The general question having been decided, nothing can be said further about that. Would it not, however, make the Proclamation more clear and decided, to leave out all reference to the act being sustained during the incumbency of the present President; and not merely say that the Government 'recognizes,' but that it will maintain, the freedom it proclaims?"

I followed, saying: "What you have said, Mr. President, fully satisfies me that you have given to every proposition which has been made, a kind and candid consideration. And you have now expressed the conclusion to which you have arrived, clearly and distinctly. This it was your right, and under your oath of office your duty, to do. The Proclamation does not, indeed, mark out exactly the course I should myself prefer. But I am ready to take it just as it is written, and to stand by it with all my heart. I think, however, the suggestions of Gov. Seward very judicious, and shall be glad to have them adopted."

The President then asked us severally our opinions as to the modifications proposed, saying that he did not care much about the phrases he had used. Everyone favored the modification and it was adopted. Gov. Seward then proposed that in the passage relating to colonization, some language should be introduced to show that the colonization proposed was to be only with the consent of the colonists, and the consent of the States in which colonies might be attempted. This, too, was agreed to; and no other modification was proposed.

6.   *1863*—THE BLUE LINE BREAKS PICKETT'S CHARGE AT GETTYSBURG

(*Although the Union armies won some important victories in the West, the first two years of the war in the East brought a succession of defeats: Bull Run in 1861, the Peninsula, Second Bull Run, and Fredericksburg in 1862, Chancellorsville in the spring of 1863. The Confederacy had proved that it could defend its own territory.*

To Robert E. Lee, commanding the Army of Northern Virginia, the time seemed ripe for an invasion of the North. Late in June, 1863, he threw his 80,000 battle-hardened veterans across the Potomac into Maryland, then marched into southern Pennsylvania. The Army of the Potomac retreated along a parallel route, thus shielding Washington and Baltimore. On July 1, at Gettysburg, Pennsylvania, the two armies stumbled into each other. In two days of bitter fighting the Union forces, commanded by General George G. Meade, held their positions. On the third day Lee decided on a desperate gamble: he would strike the Federal center with the pick

---

Frank Aretas Haskell, *The Battle of Gettysburg* (Madison, Wisconsin, 1910), 110-30.

of his army, the divisions of Pickett and Pettigrew. After a tre-
mendous artillery duel, the Confederate troops started across the
mile of level land that lay before the Federal line, protected by a
stone wall on the crest of a low ridge. Frank A. Haskell, a staff
officer of the 2nd Division, Second Army Corps, describes the cli-
mactic hour that followed.

At three o'clock almost precisely the last shot hummed, and bounded and fell, and the cannonade was over. . . . Men began to breathe more freely, and to ask, What next, I wonder? The battery men were among their guns, some leaning to rest and wipe the sweat from their sooty faces, some were handling ammunition boxes and replenishing those that were empty. Some batteries from the artillery reserve were moving up to take the places of the disabled ones; the smoke was clearing from the crests. There was a pause between acts, with the curtain down, soon to rise upon the great final act, and catastrophe of Gettysburg. . . .

We were near our horses when we noticed Brigadier General Hunt, Chief of Artillery of the Army, near Woodruff's Battery, swiftly moving about on horseback, and apparently in a rapid manner giving some orders about the guns. Thought we, what could this mean? In a moment afterwards we met Captain Wessels and the orderlies who had our horses; they were on foot leading the horses. Captain Wessels was pale, and he said, excited: "General, they say the enemy's infantry is advancing." We sprang into our saddles, a score of bounds brought us upon the all-seeing crest. To say that men grew pale and held their breath at what we and they there saw, would not be true. Might not six thousand men be brave and without shade of fear, and yet, before a hostile eighteen thousand, armed, and not five minutes' march away, turn ashy white? None on that crest now need be told that *the enemy is advancing.* Every eye could see his legions, an overwhelming resistless tide of an ocean of armed men sweeping upon us! Regiment after regiment and brigade after brigade move from the woods and rapidly take their places in the lines forming the assault. Pickett's proud division, with some additional troops, hold their right; Pettigrew's (Worth's) their left. The first line at short interval is followed by a second, and that a third succeeds; and columns between support the lines. More than half a mile their front extends; more than a thousand yards the dull gray masses deploy, man touching man, rank pressing rank, and line supporting line. The red flags wave, their horsemen gallop up and down; the arms of eighteen thousand men, barrel and bayonet, gleam in the sun, a sloping forest of flashing steel. Right on they move, as with one soul, in perfect order, without impediment of ditch, or wall or stream, over ridge and slope, through orchard and meadow, and cornfield, magnificent, grim, irresistible. All was orderly and still upon our crest; no noise and no confusion. The men had little need of commands, for the survivors of a dozen battles knew well enough what this array in front portended, and, already in their places, they would be prepared to act when the right time should come. The click of the locks as each man raised the hammer to feel with his fingers that the cap was on the nipple; the sharp jar as a musket touched a stone upon the wall when thrust in aiming over it, and the clicking of the iron axles as the guns were rolled up by hand a little further to the front, were quite all the sound that could be heard. Cap-boxes were slid around to the front of the body; cartridge boxes opened, officers opened their pistol-holsters. Such preparations, little more was needed. . . .

General Gibbon rode down the lines, cool and calm, and in an unimpassioned voice he said to the men, "Do not hurry, men, and fire too fast, let them come up close before you fire, and then aim low and steadily." . . . .

Our skirmishers open a spattering fire along the front, and, fighting, retire upon the main line. . . . Then the thunders of our guns, first Arnold's then Cushing's and Woodruff's and the rest, shake and reverberate again through the air, and their sounding shells smite the enemy. . . . All our available guns are now active, and from the fire of shells, as the range grows shorter and shorter, they change to shrapnel, and from shrapnel to canister; but in spite of shells, and shrapnel and canister, without wavering or halt, the hardy lines of the enemy continue to move on. The Rebel guns make no reply to ours, and no charging shout rings out today, as is the Rebel wont; but the courage of these silent men amid our shots seems not to need the stimulus of other noise. The enemy's right flank sweeps near Stannard's bushy crest, and his concealed Vermonters rake it with a well-delivered fire of musketry. The gray lines do not halt or reply, but withdrawing a little from that extreme, they still move on. And so across all that broad open ground they have come, nearer and nearer, nearly half the way, with our guns bellowing in their faces, until now a hundred yards, no more, divide our ready left from their advancing right. The eager men there are impatient to begin. Let them. First, Harrow's breastworks flame; then Hall's; then Webb's. As if our bullets were the fire coals that touched off their muskets, the enemy in front halts, and his countless level barrels blaze back upon us. The Second Division is struggling in battle. The rattling storm soon spreads to the right, and the blue trefoils are vieing with the white. All along each hostile front, a thousand yards, with narrowest space between, the volleys blaze and roll; as thick the sound as when a summer hail-storm pelts the city roofs; as thick the fire as when the incessant lightning fringes a summer cloud. . . .

The jostling, swaying lines on either side boil, and roar, and dash their flamy spray, two hostile billows of a fiery ocean. Thick flashes stream from the wall, thick volleys answer from the crest. No threats or expostulation now, only example and encouragement. All depths of passion are stirred, and all combatives fire, down to their deep foundations. Individuality is drowned in a sea of clamor, and timid men, breathing the breath of the multitude, are brave. The frequent dead and wounded lie where they stagger and fall—there is no humanity for them now, and none can be spared to care for them. The men do not cheer or shout; they growl, and over that uneasy sea, heard with the roar of musketry, sweeps the muttered thunder of a storm of growls. Webb, Hall, Devereux, Mallon, Abbott among the men where all are heroes, are doing deeds of note. Now the loyal wave rolls up as if it would overlap its barrier, the crest. Pistols flash with the muskets. My "Forward to the wall" is answered by the Rebel counter-command, "Steady, men!" and the wave swings back. Again it surges, and again it sinks. These men of Pennsylvania, on the soil of their own homesteads, the first and only to flee the wall, must be the first to storm it. "Major———, *lead* your men over the crest, they will follow." "By the tactics I understand my place is in rear of the men." "Your pardon, sir; I see *your* place is in rear of the men. I thought you were fit to lead." "Capt. Sapler, come on with your men." "Let me first stop this fire in the rear, or we shall be hit by our own men." "Never mind the fire in the rear; let us take care of this in front first." "Sergeant, forward with your color. Let the Rebels see it close to their eyes once before they die." The color sergeant of the 72d Pa., grasping the stump of the severed lance in both his hands, waved the flag above his head and rushed towards the wall. "Will you see your color storm the wall alone?" One man only starts to follow. Almost half way to the wall, down go color bearer and color to the ground—the gallant sergeant is dead. The line springs the crest of the solid ground with a great roar, heaves forward its maddened load, men, arms, smoke, fire, a fighting mass. It rolls to the wall—flash meets flash, the wall is crossed—a moment ensues of thrusts, yells, blows, shots, and undistinguishable conflict, followed by a shout universal that makes the welkin ring again, and the last and bloodiest fight of the great battle of Gettysburg is ended and won.

7. *1863*—VICKSBURG FALLS

❨ *At the very hour when Pickett's charge was breaking against the low stone wall at Gettysburg, General U. S. Grant and General John C. Pemberton were arranging terms for the surrender of the Con-*

Mary Ann Loughborough, *My Cave Life in Vicksburg* (New York, 1864), 40–42, 47–50, 55–62, 136–39.

federate stronghold of Vicksburg, which Pemberton commanded. Since the middle of May, 1863, Grant had held this Southern city on a high bluff above the Mississippi in a grip that could not be broken. Mrs. J. M. Loughborough tells the story of the siege, which ended on July 4, as it appeared to Vicksburg residents.

Sunday, the 17th . . . of May, as we were dressing for church, and had nearly completed the arrangement of shawls and gloves, we heard the loud booming of cannon. Frightened, for at this time we knew not *what* "an hour would bring forth," seeing no one who might account for the sudden alarm, we walked down the street, hoping to find some friend who could tell us if it were dangerous to remain away from home at church. . . . After walking a square or two, we met an officer, who told us the report we heard proceeded from our own guns, which were firing upon a party of soldiers, who were burning some houses on the peninsula on the Louisiana shore; he told us, also, it had been rumored that General Pemberton had been repulsed. . . . Still, as the bell of the Methodist church rang out clear and loud, my friend and I decided to enter, and were glad that we did so, for we heard words of cheer and comfort in this time of trouble. . . .

As we returned home, we passed groups of anxious men at the corners, with troubled faces; very few soldiers were seen; some battery men and officers, needed for the river defences, were passing hastily up the street. . . . Now and then a worn and dusty soldier would be seen passing with his blanket and canteen; soon, straggler after straggler came by, then groups of soldiers worn and dusty with the long march. "What can be the matter?" we all cried, as the streets and pavements became full of these worn and tired-looking men. We sent down to ask, and the reply was: "We are whipped; and the Federals are after us." We hastily seized veils and bonnets, and walked down the avenue to the iron railing that separates the yard from the street. . . .

We almost feared to retire that night; no one seemed to know whether the Federal army was advancing or not; some told us that they were many miles away, and others that they were quite near. How did we know but in the night we might be awakened by the tumult of their arrival! . . .

The next morning all was quiet; we heard no startling rumors; the soldiers were being gathered together and taken out into the rifle pits; Vicksburg was regularly besieged, and we were to stay at our homes and watch the progress of the battle. The rifle pits and intrenchments were almost two miles from the city. We would be out of danger, so we thought; but we did not know what was in preparation for us around the bend of the river. The day wore on; still all was quiet. At night our hopes revived: the Federal troops had not yet come up—another calm night and morning. At three o'clock that evening, the artillery boomed from the intrenchments, roar after roar, followed by the rattle of musketry: the Federal forces were making their first attack. Looking out from the back veranda, we could plainly see the smoke before the report of the guns reached us. . . .

The discharges of musketry were irregular. . . . At every report our hearts beat quicker. The excitement was intense in the city. Groups of people stood on every available position where a view could be obtained of the distant hills, where the jets of white smoke constantly passed out from among the trees. . . .

Next day, two or three shells were thrown from the battle field, exploding near the house. This was our first shock, and a severe one. We did not dare to go in the back part of the house all day. . . .

In the evening we were terrified and much excited by the loud rush and scream of mortar shells; we ran to the small cave near the house, and were in it during the night, by this time wearied and almost stupefied by the loss of sleep.

The caves were plainly becoming a necessity, as some persons had been killed on the street by fragments of shells. The room that I had so lately slept in had been struck by a fragment of a shell during the first night, and a large hole made in the ceiling. I shall never forget my extreme fear during the night, and my utter hopelessness of ever seeing the morning light. Terror stricken, we remained crouched in the cave, while shell after shell followed each other in quick succession. I endeavored by constant prayer to prepare myself for the sudden death I was almost certain awaited me. My heart stood still as we would hear the reports from the guns, and the rushing and fearful sound of the shell as it came toward us. As it neared, the noise became more deafening; the air was full of the rushing sound; pains darted through my temples; my ears were full of the confusing noise; and, as it exploded, the report flashed through my head like an electric shock, leaving me in a quiet state of terror the most painful that I can imagine—cowering in a corner, holding my child to my heart—the only feeling of my life being the choking throbs of my heart, that rendered me almost breathless. As singly they fell short, or beyond the cave, I was aroused by a feeling of thankfulness that was of short duration. Again and again the terrible fright came over us in that night. . . .

So constantly dropped the shells around the city, that the inhabitants all made preparations to live under the ground during the siege. M——sent over and had a cave made in a hill near by. We seized the opportunity one evening, when the gunners were probably at their supper, for we had a few moments of quiet, to go over and take possession. We were under the care of a friend of M——, who was paymaster on the staff of the same General with whom M—— was Adjutant. We had neighbors on both sides of us; and it would have been an amusing sight to a spectator to witness the domestic scenes presented without by the number of servants preparing the meals under the high bank containing the caves.

Our dining, breakfasting, and supper hours were quite irregular. When the shells were falling fast, the servants came in for safety, and our meals waited for completion some little time; again they would fall slowly, with the lapse of many minutes between, and out would start the cooks to their work.

Some families had light bread made in large quantities, and subsisted on it with milk (provided their cows were not killed from one milking time to another), without any more cooking, until called on to replenish. Though most of us lived on corn bread and bacon, served three times a day, the only luxury of the meal consisting in its warmth, I had some flour, and frequently had some hard, tough biscuit made from it, there being no soda or yeast to be procured. At this time we could, also, procure beef. A gentleman friend was kind enough to offer me his camp bed, a narrow spring mattress, which fitted within the contracted cave very comfortably; another had his tent fly stretched over the mouth of our residence to shield us from the sun. . . . Our quarters were close, indeed; yet I was more comfortable than I expected I could have been made under the earth in that fashion. . . .

We were now swiftly nearing the end of our siege life: the rations had nearly all been given out. For the last few days I had been sick; still I tried to overcome the languid feeling of utter prostration. My little one had swung in her hammock, reduced in strength, with a low fever flushing in her face. M—— was all anxiety, I could plainly see. A soldier brought up, one morning, a little jaybird, as a plaything for the child. After playing with it for a short time, she turned wearily away. "Miss Mary," said the servant, "she's hungry; let me make her some soup from the bird." At first I refused: the poor little plaything should not die; then, as I thought of the child, I half consented. With the utmost haste, Cinth disappeared; and the next time she appeared, it was with a cup of soup, and a little plate, on which lay the white meat of the poor little bird.

On Saturday a painful calm prevailed: there had been a truce proclaimed; and so long had the constant firing been kept up, that the stillness was now absolutely oppressive. . . .

The next morning, M—— came up, with a pale face, saying: "It's all over! The white flag floats from our forts! Vicksburg has surrendered!"

8.   *1864*—LINCOLN CONFERS THE SUPREME COMMAND
   ON GRANT

❮ *For nearly three years Lincoln hunted for a general who could lead the Union armies to victory. Vicksburg pointed to Grant. Later in 1863, when Federal forces won a succession of battles at Chatta-nooga, where Grant commanded, Lincoln made his choice. Congress revived the grade of Lieutenant General with the understanding that it would be conferred on Grant, and the War Department called the Western commander to Washington. John G. Nicolay describes the first meeting of the President and the "man of the hour."*

Executive Mansion, March 8, 1864—In obedience to an invitation from the Sec. of War Gen. Grant reached the city about 5 P.M. By some sort of negligence there was no one at the depot to receive him, but he found his way to Willard's with the two members of his staff who accompanied him.

Reception tonight. The weather was bad; but the *Republican* having announced that Grant would attend the reception, it brought out a considerable crowd. At about 9½ P.M. the General came in—alone again excepting his staff—and he and the President met for the first time. The President, expecting him, knew from the buzz and movement in the crowd that it must be the General; and when a man of modest mien and unimposing exterior presented himself, the President said:

"This is General Grant, is it not?"

The General replied, "Yes."

and the two greeted each other more cordially, but still with that modest deference, felt rather than expressed in word or action, so appropriate to both—the one the honored ruler, the other the honored victor of the nation and the time.

The crowd too partook of the feeling of the occasion. There was no rude jostling, or pushing, or pulling, but unrestrained the circle kept its respectful distance, until after a brief conversation the President gave the General in charge of Seward to present to Mrs Lincoln, at the same time instructing me to send for the Secretary of War. After paying his respects to Mrs Lincoln the General was taken by Seward to the East Room, where he was greeted with cheer after cheer by the assembled crowd, and where he was forced to mount a sofa from whence he could shake hands with those who pressed from all sides to see him. It was at least an hour before he returned, flushed, heated and perspiring with the unwonted exertion.

The President went upstairs, and returning in a little while, sat down

Helen Nicolay, *Lincoln's Secretary, A Biography of John G. Nicolay* (New York: Longmans, Green & Co., 1949), 194–97.

near where the General, the Secretary of War and I were sitting.

"Tomorrow," said the President to the General, "at such time as you may arrange with the Sec. War, I desire to make to you a formal presentation of your commission as Lieut. Genl. I shall then make a very short speech to you, to which I desire you to reply for an object; and that you may be properly prepared to do so I have written what I shall say—only four sentences in all—which I will read from my MS. as an example which you may follow and also read your reply, as you are perhaps not as much accustomed to speaking as I, myself—and I therefore give you what I shall say that you may consider it and form your reply. There are two points that I would like to have you make in your answer, 1st, to say something which shall prevent or obviate any jealousy of you from any of the other generals in the service, and 2d, something which shall put you on as good terms as possible with this Army of the Potomac. Now, consider whether this may not be said to make it of some advantage; and if you see any objection whatever to doing it, be under no restraint whatever in expressing that objection to the Secretary of War who will talk further with you about it."

The General asked at what time this presentation would take place.

"The Secretary of War and yourself may arrange the time to suit your convenience. I will be ready, whenever you shall have prepared your reply."

"I can be ready in thirty minutes," said the General.

One o'clock tomorrow was finally fixed as the hour, after which the General took his leave, accompanied by the Sec. of War.

The President, as I learned in reply to a question to him, is contemplating bringing the General East to see whether he can not do something with the unfortunate Army of the Potomac.

During the reception a dispatch was brought to me announcing that the Union ticket had been today carried in N.H. by 3000.

March 9, 1864—The presentation ceremony of General Grant's commission as Lieut.-General took place today at 1 P.M. in the Cabinet Chamber. The newspapers give the proceedings and addresses in full. Both the President and the General read their remarks from MSS. The General had hurriedly and almost illegibly written his speech on the half of a sheet of note paper, in lead pencil, and being quite embarrassed by the occasion, and finding his own writing so very difficult to read, made rather sorry and disjointed work of enunciating his reply. I noticed too that in what he said, while it was brief and to the point, he had either forgotten or disregarded entirely the President's hints to him of the night previous.

During this afternoon Gov. Chase sent the President a copy of his letter to Judge Hall of Ohio withdrawing his name from the presidential canvass.

9. *1864*—LEE SHATTERS GRANT'S ASSAULT ON COLD HARBOR

⟦ *Grant's war plan called for two massive movements, both at the same time. Sherman, with the Army of the West, would strike at Atlanta; the Army of the Potomac would advance on Richmond. The campaign against Richmond began on May 5, 1864. After a month of fighting so costly that Northern newspapers were calling the Union commander a butcher, the Army of the Potomac was within sight of its goal. There Grant made the mistake of ordering an assault on the strongly entrenched Confederate position of Cold Harbor. The action is described by Theodore Lyman, a colonel on the staff of General Meade, who still commanded the Army of the Potomac under Grant's supervision.*

June 2, 1864

. . . We set out in the morning by half-past seven and, partly by roads, partly by cross-cuts, arrived at Kelly's via Woody's house. Of all the wastes I have ever seen, this first sight of Cool Arbor[1] was the most dreary! Fancy a baking sun to begin with; then a foreground of breast-works; on the left, Kelly's wretched house; in front, an open plain, trampled fetlock deep into fine, white dust and dotted with caissons, regiments of many soldiers, and dead horses killed in the previous cavalry fight. On the sides and in the distance were pine woods, some red with fires which had passed through them, some grey with the clouds of dust that rose high in the air. It was a Sahara intensified, and was called Cool Arbor! Wright's Headquarters were here, and here, too, I first beheld "Baldy" Smith, a short, quite portly man, with a light-brown imperial and shaggy moustache, a round, military head, and the look of a German officer, altogether. After getting all information, General Meade ordered a general assault at four p.m. but afterwards countermanded it, by reason of the exhausted state of the 2d Corps.
. . . . Towards evening Warren was to close in to his left and join with the rest of the line, his right resting near Bethesda Church, while Burnside was to mass and cover his movement; but they made a bad fist of it between them. The enemy, the moment the march began, rushed in on the skirmishers. A division, 5th Corps, got so placed that it bore the whole brunt (and a fine division too). Between the two corps— both very willing—the proper support was not put in. The enemy in force swung round by Via's house and gobbled up several miles of our telegraph wire, besides several hundred prisoners. We *ought* to have just eaten them up; but as it was, we only drove them back into some rifle-pits we had formerly abandoned, and then the line was formed as

George R. Agassiz, Ed., *Meade's Headquarters, 1863–1865: Letters of Colonel Theodore Lyman* (Boston, 1912), 140–48.
[1] Lyman's rendering of Cold Harbor.

331

originally ordered, with Burnside swung round to cover our right flank from Bethesda Church towards Linney's house, while the enemy held Via's house and a line parallel to our own. . . .

June 3, 1864

We had very severe fighting this morning, all along the lines. . . . The Rebel lines were about parallel with ours and they were throwing up dirt as hard as they could. No country could be more favorable for such work. The soldiers easily throw up the dirt so dry and sandy with their tin plates, their hands, bits of board, or canteens split in two, when shovels are scarce; while a few axes, in experienced hands, soon serve to fell plenty of straight pines, that are all ready to be set up, as the inner face of the breastwork. I can't say I heard with any great hope the order, given last night, for a general assault at 4:30 the next morning! You see Wright and Smith took their front line and drove them back Wednesday afternoon [June 1]. Thursday afternoon was twenty-four, and Friday morning would be thirty-six hours, for them to bring up and entrench their whole army. If we *could* smash them up, the Chickahominy lay behind them; but I had no more hope of it, after Spotsylvania, than I had of taking Richmond in two days. Half-past four found us at Kelly's, the Headquarters of General Wright; the brave General himself, however, had gone to the front. At that moment the cannon opened, in various directions, and the Rebels replied vigorously. There has been no fight of which I have seen so little as this. The woods were so placed that the sound, even, of the musketry was much kept away, and the fighting, though near us, was completely shut from view. All the warfare for us was an occasional roundshot, or shell, that would come about us from the Rebel batteries. In the direction of the 18th Corps the crash of the musketry was very loud, but elsewhere, scarcely to be noticed. . . . About five we had a gleam of hope for our success. News came that Barlow had carried their works and taken seventeen guns; and so he did; but it is one thing to get in, another to stay in. His men advanced heroically and went over the breastworks with a rush; but the enemy had reserves massed behind, well knowing that his extreme right was seriously threatened. Before our supports could get up, their forces were down on our men, while a hearty enfilade of cannister was kept up from flanking batteries. Barlow was driven out with heavy loss, and succeeded in getting off only about 300 of the prisoners he took. Like good soldiers, however, his men stopped and turned about, close to the works, and there entrenched themselves. At six we got notice that Russell's division could not carry the line in their front. Ricketts, however, on the right of the 6th Corps, got their first line, and so did the 18th Corps on his right; but the 18th people were forced back, and this left Ricketts a good deal exposed to enfilade; but he held on. A singular thing about the whole attack, and one that demonstrated the staunchness of the troops, was, that our men, when the fire was too hot for them to advance and the works too strong, did not retreat as soldiers often do, but lay down where some small ridge offered a little cover, and there staid, at a distance from the enemy varying from forty to perhaps 250 yards. When it was found that the lines could not be carried, General Meade issued orders to hold the advanced position, all along, and to trench. The main fight lasted, I suppose, some three hours, but there was sharp skirmishing and artillery firing the whole day. The Rebels threw cannister in large quantities, doing much damage. . . .

At nine at night the enemy made a fierce attack on a part of Gibbon's division, and, for a time, the volleys of musketry and the booming of the cannon were louder, in the still night, than the battle had been by day. But that sort of thing has not done with the Rebels, since the brilliant attack of Johnson, the second night of the Wilderness. This time they were repulsed completely. It was then that our men called out: "Come on! Come on! Bring up some more Johnnies! You haven't got enough!"

. . . To-night all the trenching tools were ordered up and the lines were strengthened, and saps run out, so as to bring them still closer to the opposing ones. And there the two armies slept, almost within an easy stone-throw of each other; and the separating space ploughed by cannon-shot and clotted with the dead bodies that neither side dared to bury! I think nothing can give a greater idea of deathless tenacity of purpose, than the picture of these two hosts, after a bloody and nearly continuous struggle of thirty days, thus lying down to sleep, with their heads almost on each other's throats! Possibly it has no parallel in history. So ended the great attack at Cool Arbor. The losses were far greater for us than for the Rebels. From what I can gather I doubt not we lost four or five to one. We gained nothing save a knowledge of their position and proof of the unflinching bravery of our soldiers. . . .

10. *1865*—A CONFEDERATE SOLDIER HEADS FOR HOME

❨ *Sherman took Atlanta in September, 1864, then marched eastward to Savannah, which he captured on December 22. Five weeks later he started northward to join Grant before Richmond. Confederate forces under General Joseph E. Johnston could offer little opposition. Many Southern soldiers, aware of the hopelessness of their cause, struck out for home. One of these was Lizzie's brother Jim, whose letter was picked up in Raleigh, North Carolina, two weeks before Johnston surrendered.*

Spencer Glasgow Welch, *A Confederate Surgeon's Letters to His Wife* (New York and Washington, 1911), 121.

DEER SISTER LIZZY: i hev conkludid that the dam fulishness uv tryin to lick shurmin Had better be stoped. we hav bin gettin nuthin but hell & lots uv it ever sinse we saw the dam yankys & i am tirde uv it. shurmin has a lots of pimps that dont care a dam what they doo. and its no use tryin to whip em. if we dont git hell when shirmin starts again i miss my gess. if i cood git home ide tri dam hard to git thare. my old horse is plaid out or ide trie to go now. maibee ile start to nite fur ime dam tired uv this war fur nuthin. if the dam yankees Havent got thair yit its a dam wunder. Thair thicker an lise on a hen and a dam site ornraier. YOUR BROTHER JIM.

11. *1865*—THE CONFEDERATES EVACUATE RICHMOND

❪ *After the bloody repulse at Cold Harbor, Grant slipped around Lee's flank and moved against Petersburg south of Richmond, hoping by this approach to force the Confederates from their capital. But Petersburg was stoutly defended, and Grant had to start siege operations. Richmond held out for nearly nine months, but by April, 1865, its situation was desperate. Mrs. John P. McGuire, a clerk in the Confederate Commissary Department, describes the evacuation.*

Richmond, Virginia

April 3.—Agitated and nervous, I turn to my diary to-night as the means of soothing my feelings. We have passed through a fatal thirty-six hours. Yesterday morning we went, as usual, to St. James's Church, hoping for a day of peace and quietness, as well as of religious improvement and enjoyment. The sermon being over, as it was the first Sunday in the month, the sacrament of the Lord's Supper was administered. While the sacred elements were being administered, the sexton came in with a note to General Cooper, which was handed him as he walked from the chancel, and he immediately left the church. It made me anxious; but such things are not uncommon, and caused no excitement in the congregation. The services being over, we left the church, and our children joined us, on their way to the usual family gathering in our room on Sunday. . . .

John remarked to his father, that he had just returned from the War Department, and that there was sad news—General Lee's lines had been broken, and the city would probably be evacuated within twenty-four hours. . . .

In an hour J. received orders to accompany Captain Parker to the South with the Corps of Midshipmen. Then we began to understand

Mrs. John P. McGuire, *Diary of a Southern Refugee, During the War* (New York, 1867), 342–49.

that the Government was moving, and that the evacuation was indeed going on. The office-holders were now making arrangements to get off. Every car was ordered to be ready to take them south. Baggage-wagons, carts, drays, and ambulances were driving about the streets; every one going off that could go. The people were rushing up and down the streets, vehicles of all kinds were flying along, bearing goods of all sorts and people of all ages and classes who could go beyond the cor- poration lines. We tried to keep ourselves quiet. We could not go south, nor could we leave the city at all in this hurried way. . . .

Last night, when we went out to hire a servant to go to Camp Jack- son for our sister, we for the first time realized that our money was worthless here, and that we are in fact penniless. About midnight she walked in, escorted by two of the convalescent soldiers. We collected in one room, and tried to comfort one another. . . .

Oh, who shall tell the horror of the past night! Union men began to show themselves; treason walked abroad. About two o'clock in the morning we were startled by a loud sound like thunder; the house shook and the windows rattled; it seemed like an earthquake in our midst. It was soon understood to be the blowing up of a magazine below the city. In a few hours another exploded on the outskirts of the city, much louder than the first, and shivering innumerable plate-glass windows all over Shockoe Hill. It was then daylight, and we were standing out upon the pavement. The lower part of the city was burning.

About seven o'clock I set off to go to the central depot to see if the cars would go out. As I went from Franklin to Broad Street, and on Broad, the pavements were covered with broken glass; women, both white and coloured, were walking in multitudes from the Commissary offices and burning stores with bags of flour, meal, coffee, sugar, rolls of cotton cloth, etc., coloured men were rolling wheel-barrows filled in the same way. I went on and on towards the depot, and as I proceeded shouts and screams became louder. The rabble rushed by me in one stream. "Who are those shouting? What is the matter?" I seemed to be answered by a hundred voices, "The Yankees have come." I turned to come home, but what was my horror when I reached Ninth Street, to see a regiment of Yankee cavalry come dashing up, yelling, shouting, hallooing, screaming! All Bedlam let loose could not have vied with them in diabolical roarings. I stood riveted to the spot; I could not move nor speak. Then I saw the iron gate of our time-honoured and beautiful Capitol Square, on the walks and greensward of which no hoof had been allowed to tread, thrown open and the cavalry dash in. I could see no more. . . . I came home. . . .

The Federal soldiers were roaming about the streets; either whis- key or the excess of joy had given some of them the appearance of being beside themselves. We had hoped that very little whiskey would be found in the city, as, by the order of the Mayor, casks were emptied yesterday evening in the streets, and it flowed like water through the gutters; but the rabble had managed to find it secreted in the burning shops, and bore it away in pitchers and buckets. . . .

The fire was progressing rapidly, and the crashing sound of falling timbers was distinctly heard. Dr. Read's church was blazing. The War Department was falling in; burning papers were being wafted about the streets. The Commissary Department, with our desks and papers, was consumed already. Warwick & Barksdale's mill was sending its flames to the sky. Cary and Main Streets seemed doomed throughout; Bank Street was beginning to burn, and now it had reached Franklin. . . . Almost every house is guarded; and the streets are now (ten o'clock) perfectly quiet. The moon is shining brightly on our captivity. God guide and watch over us!

12.   *1865*—LEE SURRENDERS

❨ *After evacuating Richmond Lee hoped to make a dash to the west, escape his besiegers, and unite his forces with Johnston's in North Carolina. But the Union army was alert, powerful, and fast. A week after leaving Richmond, Lee found himself at Appomattox Court House, boxed in by overwhelming numbers. Further resistance would have been sheer murder. The Confederate leader sent a flag of truce. Armistead L. Long, Lee's military secretary, describes the surrender.*

Colonel C. S. Venable of General Lee's staff graphically tells what took place at headquarters on that eventful morning [April 9]. . . .

"At three o'clock on the morning of that fatal day General Lee rode forward, still hoping that we might break through the countless hordes of the enemy who hemmed us in. Halting a short distance in rear of our van-guard, he sent me on to General Gordon to ask him if he could break through the enemy. I found General Gordon and General Fitz Lee on their front line in the dim light of the morning arranging an attack. Gordon's reply to the message (I give the expressive phrase of the gallant Georgian) was this: 'Tell General Lee I have fought my corps to a frazzle, and I fear I can do nothing unless I am heavily supported by Longstreet's corps.'

"When I bore this message back to General Lee he said, 'Then there is nothing left me but to go and see General Grant, and I would rather die a thousand deaths.'

"Convulsed with passionate grief, many were the wild words which

Armistead L. Long, *Memoirs of Robert E. Lee* (New York, 1887), 420–24.

336

we spoke as we stood around him. Said one, 'Oh, general, what will history say of the surrender of the army in the field?'

"He replied, 'Yes, I know they will say hard things of us: they will not understand how we were overwhelmed by numbers. But that is not the question, colonel: the question is, Is it right to surrender this army? If it is right, then *I* will take *all* the responsibility.' "

The artillery had been withdrawn from the heights, as above stated, and parked in the small valley east of the village, while the infantry, who were formed on the left, stacked arms and silently waited the result of the interview between the opposing commanders.

The flag of truce was sent out from General Gordon's lines. Grant had not yet come up, and while waiting for his arrival General Lee seated himself upon some rails which Colonel Talcott of the Engineers had fixed at the foot of an apple tree for his convenience. This tree was half a mile distant from the point where the meeting of Lee and Grant took place, yet widespread currency has been given to the story that the surrender took place under its shade, and "apple-tree" jewelry has been profusely distributed from the orchard in which it grew.

About 11 o'clock General Lee, accompanied only by Colonel Marshall of his staff, proceeded to the village to meet General Grant, who had now arrived. The meeting between the two renowned generals took place at the house of a Mr. McLean at Appomattox Court-house, to which mansion, after exchanging courteous salutations, they repaired to settle the terms on which the surrender of the Army of Northern Virginia should be concluded.

A conversation here took place which General Grant, as he himself tells us, led to various subjects divergent from the immediate purpose of the meeting, talking of old army matters and comparing recollections with General Lee. As he says, the conversation grew so pleasant that he almost forgot the object of the meeting.

General Lee was obliged more than once to remind him of this object, and it was some time before the terms of the surrender were written out. The written instrument of surrender covered the following points: Duplicate rolls of all the officers and men were to be made, and the officers to sign paroles for themselves and their men, all agreeing not to bear arms against the United States unless regularly exchanged. The arms, artillery, and public property were to be turned over to an officer appointed to receive them, the officers retaining their side-arms and private horses and baggage. In addition to this, General Grant permitted every man of the Confederate army who claimed to own a horse or mule to retain it for farming purposes, General Lee remarking that this would have a happy effect. As for the surrender by General Lee of his sword, a report of which has been widely circulated, General Grant disposes of it in the following words: "The much-talked of surrendering of Lee's sword and my handing it back, this and much more that has been said about it is the purest romance."

After completion of these measures General Lee remarked that his men were badly in need of food, that they had been living for several days on parched corn exclusively, and requested rations and forage for 25,000 men. These rations were granted out of the car-loads of Confederate provisions which had been stopped by the Federal cavalry. As for forage, Grant remarked that he was himself depending upon the country for that. The negotiations completed, General Lee left the house, mounted his horse, and rode back to headquarters.

It is impossible to describe the anguish of the troops when it was known that the surrender of the army was inevitable. Of all their trials, this was the greatest and hardest to endure. There was no consciousness of shame; each heart could boast with honest pride that its duty had been done to the end, and that still unsullied remained its honor. When, after his interview with Grant, General Lee again appeared, a shout of welcome instinctively ran through the army. But instantly recollecting the sad occasion that brought him before them, their shouts sank into silence, every hat was raised, and the bronzed faces of the thousands of grim warriors were bathed with tears.

As he rode slowly along the lines hundreds of his devoted veterans pressed around the noble chief, trying to take his hand, touch his person, or even lay a hand upon his horse, thus exhibiting for him their great affection. The general then, with head bare and tears flowing freely down his manly cheeks, bade adieu to the army. In a few words he told the brave men who had been so true in arms to return to their homes and become worthy citizens.

Thus closed the career of the noble Army of Northern Virginia.

13.   *1865*—THE DEATH OF LINCOLN

❧ *In Washington a half-mad actor brooded over the South's defeat. At ten o'clock on the evening of April 14th John Wilkes Booth entered Ford's Theatre, slipped into the President's box from the rear, and fired a derringer at point-blank range. Gideon Welles, Secretary of the Navy, committed the events of the tragic night to his diary.*

I had retired to bed about half past-ten on the evening of the 14th of April, and was just getting asleep when Mrs. Welles, my wife, said some one was at our door. Sitting up in bed, I heard a voice twice call to John, my son, whose sleeping-room was on the second floor directly over the front entrance. I arose at once and raised a window, when my

John T. Morse, Jr., Ed., *Diary of Gideon Welles* (Boston, 1911), II, 282–89.

messenger, James Smith, called to me that Mr. Lincoln, the President, had been shot, and said Secretary Seward and his son, Assistant Secretary Frederick Seward, were assassinated. James was much alarmed and excited. I told him his story was very incoherent and improbable, that he was associating men who were not together and liable to attack at the same time. "Where," I inquired, "was the President when shot?" James said he was at Ford's Theatre on 10th Street. "Well," said I, "Secretary Seward is an invalid in bed in his house yonder on 15th Street." James said he had been there, stopped in at the house to make inquiry before alarming me.

I immediately dressed myself, and, against the earnest remonstrance and appeals of my wife, went directly to Mr. Seward's, whose residence was on the east side of the square, mine being on the north. James accompanied me. As we were crossing 15th Street, I saw four or five men in earnest consultation, standing under the lamp on the corner by St. John's Church. Before I had got half across the street, the lamp was suddenly extinguished and the knot of persons rapidly dispersed. For a moment and but a moment I was disconcerted to find myself in darkness, but, recollecting that it was late and about time for the moon to rise, I proceeded on, not having lost five steps, merely making a pause without stopping. Hurrying forward into 15th Street, I found it pretty full of people, especially so near the residence of Secretary Seward, where there were many soldiers as well as citizens already gathered.

Entering the house, I found the lower hall and office full of persons, and among them most of the foreign legations, all anxiously inquiring what truth there was in the horrible rumors afloat. I replied that my object was to ascertain the facts. Proceeding through the hall to the stairs, I found one, and I think two, of the servants there holding the crowd in check. The servants were frightened and appeared relieved to see me. I hastily asked what truth there was in the story that an assassin or assassins had entered the house and assaulted the Secretary. They said it was true, and that Mr. Frederick was also badly injured. They wished me to go up, but no others. At the head of the first stairs I met the elder Mrs. Seward, who was scarcely able to speak but desired me to proceed up to Mr. Seward's room. I met Mrs. Frederick Seward on the third story, who, although in extreme distress, was, under the circumstances, exceedingly composed. I asked for the Secretary's room, which she pointed out,—the southwest room. As I entered, I met Miss Fanny Seward, with whom I exchanged a single word, and proceeded to the foot of the bed. Dr. Verdi and, I think, two others were there. The bed was saturated with blood. The Secretary was lying on his back, the upper part of his head covered by a cloth, which extended down over his eyes. His mouth was open, the lower jaw dropping down. I exchanged a few whispered words with Dr. V. Secretary Stanton, who came after but almost simultaneously with me, made inquiries in a louder tone till admonished by a word from one of the physicians. We almost immediately withdrew and went into the adjoining front room, where lay Frederick Seward. His eyes were open but he did not move them, nor a limb, nor did he speak. Doctor White, who was in attendance, told me he was unconscious and more dangerously injured than his father.

As we descended the stairs, I asked Stanton what he had heard in regard to the President that was reliable. He said the President was shot at Ford's Theatre, that he had seen a man who was present and witnessed the occurrence. I said I would go immediately to the White House. Stanton told me the President was not there but was at the theatre. "Then," said I, "let us go immediately there." He said that was his intention, and asked me, if I had not a carriage, to go with him. In the lower hall we met General Meigs, whom he requested to take charge of the house, and to clear out all who did not belong there. General Meigs begged Stanton not to go down to 10th Street; others also remonstrated against our going. Stanton, I thought, hesitated. Hurrying forward, I remarked that I should go immediately, and I thought it his duty also. He said he should certainly go, but the remonstrants increased and gathered round him. I said we were wasting time, and, pressing through the crowd, entered the carriage and urged Stanton, who was detained by others after he had placed his foot on the step. I was impatient. Stanton, as soon as he had seated himself, turned round, rose partly, and said the carriage was not his. I said that was no objection. He invited Meigs to go with us, and Judge Cartter of the Supreme Court mounted with the driver. At this moment Major Eckert rode up on horseback beside the carriage and protested vehemently against Stanton's going to 10th Street; said he had just come from there, that there were thousands of people of all sorts there, and he considered it very unsafe for the Secretary of War to expose himself. I replied that I knew not where he would be more safe, and that the duty of both of us was to attend the President immediately. Stanton concurred. Meigs called to some soldiers to go with us, and there was one on each side of the carriage. The streets were full of people. Not only the sidewalk but the carriage-way was to some extent occupied, all or nearly all hurrying towards 10th Street. When we entered that street we found it pretty closely packed.

The President had been carried across the street from the theatre, to the house of a Mr. Peterson. We entered by ascending a flight of steps above the basement and passing through a long hall to the rear, where the President lay extended on a bed, breathing heavily. Several surgeons were present, at least six, I should think more. Among them I was glad to observe Dr. Hall, who, however, soon left. I inquired of Dr. H., as I entered, the true condition of the President. He replied the President was dead to all intents, although he might live three hours or perhaps longer.

The giant sufferer lay extended diagonally across the bed, which was not long enough for him. He had been stripped of his clothes. His large arms, which were occasionally exposed, were of a size which one would scarce have expected from his spare appearance. His slow, full respiration lifted the clothes with each breath that he took. His features were calm and striking. I had never seen them appear to better advantage than for the first hour, perhaps, that I was there. After that, his right eye began to swell and that part of his face became discolored.

Senator Sumner was there, I think, when I entered. If not he came in soon after, as did Speaker Colfax, Mr. Secretary McCulloch, and the other members of the Cabinet, with the exception of Mr. Seward. A double guard was stationed at the door and on the sidewalk, to repress the crowd, which was of course highly excited and anxious. The room was small and overcrowded. The surgeons and members of the Cabinet were as many as should have been in the room, but there were many more, and the hall and other rooms in the front or main house were full. One of these rooms was occupied by Mrs. Lincoln and her attendants, with Miss Harris. Mrs. Dixon and Mrs. Kinney came to her about twelve o'clock. About once an hour Mrs. Lincoln would repair to the bedside of her dying husband and with lamentation and tears remain until overcome by emotion.

[April 15.] A door which opened upon a porch or gallery, and also the windows, were kept open for fresh air. The night was dark, cloudy, and damp, and about six it began to rain. I remained in the room until then without sitting or leaving it, when, there being a vacant chair which some one left at the foot of the bed, I occupied it for nearly two hours, listening to the heavy groans, and witnessing the wasting life of the good and great man who was expiring before me.

About 6 A.M. I experienced a feeling of faintness and for the first time after entering the room, a little past eleven, I left it and the house, and took a short walk in the open air. It was a dark and gloomy morning, and rain set in before I returned to the house, some fifteen minutes [later]. Large groups of people were gathered every few rods, all anxious and solicitous. Some one or more from each group stepped forward as I passed, to inquire into the condition of the President, and to ask if there was no hope. Intense grief was on every countenance when I replied that the President could survive but a short time. The colored people especially—and there were at this time more of them, perhaps, than of whites—were overwhelmed with grief.

Returning to the house, I seated myself in the back parlor, where the Attorney-General and others had been engaged in taking evidence concerning the assassination. Stanton, and Speed, and Usher were there, the latter asleep on the bed. There were three or four others also in the room. While I did not feel inclined to sleep, as many did, I was somewhat indisposed. I had been so for several days. The excitement and bad atmosphere from the crowded rooms oppressed me physically.

A little before seven, I went into the room where the dying President was rapidly drawing near the closing moments. His wife soon after made her last visit to him. The death-struggle had begun. Robert, his son, stood with several others at the head of the bed. He bore himself well, but on two occasions gave way to overpowering grief and sobbed aloud, turning his head and leaning on the shoulder of Senator Sumner. The respiration of the President became suspended at intervals, and at last entirely ceased at twenty-two minutes past seven.

CHAPTER XV

POST-WAR YEARS

1865 – 1893

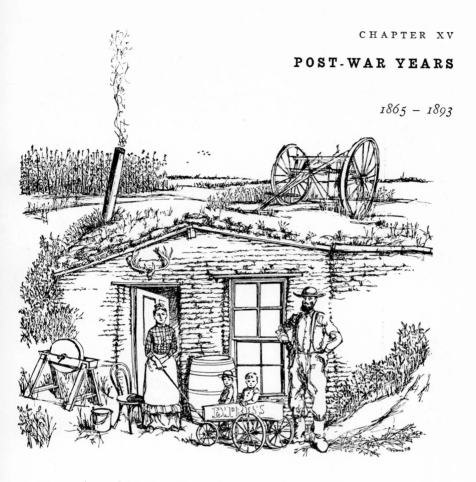

1. *1865*—THE SOUTH'S SOCIAL REVOLUTION

❮ *The biggest problem the South faced at the end of the war was that of adjusting its social and economic life to the presence of four million suddenly-free Negroes. In the diary of Henry W. Ravenal, a planter and botanist of Aiken, South Carolina, we see how a man of conscience and good will approached a social revolution. The entries cover the last three weeks of May, 1865.*

T. 9   Rode into Aiken this morning. Bought 23 lbs soft soap at 10 cts per lb to be paid in specie or provisions. Confederate notes are now universally refused except on the Railroad to Augusta. This morning I had not a cent but we sent out a few vegetables which sold for 85 cts, & this is the whole fortune I own in money. We are beginning life again in our financial affairs. Many negroes in Aiken hearing they were free in Augusta have gone over to hear from the Yankees the truth. Some

Arney Robinson Childs, Ed., *The Private Journal of Henry William Ravenal, 1859–1887* (Columbia, S. C.: University of South Carolina Press, 1947), 231–32, 238–40.

343

are returning disappointed. . . . Most that we hear is mere rumor. The press is now muzzled—& all news comes to us through the sieve of Yankee eyes. We are bound hand & foot . . . we can now see the naked truth that our great struggle for independance & the right of self government is lost. I need not enumerate here the reasons by which we justified our efforts at independance. The right of secession was denied & upon that we went to war. We struggled under great disadvantages for four years. We commenced without a govt. & had to organize one— we had fewer men—scarcely any of the materials of war, workshops or artizans—Our ports were blockaded & we were thus cut off from foreign supplies—The nations of Europe gave us no sympathy & closed their ports against our privateers, thus denying us a belligerent right which had never previously been denied to any people. From sheer exhaustion of our means, we have at length been compelled to yield. God in His good providence has not seen fit to grant us our prayer & hearts desires. If it is his will that we are not to be a nation, but only a part of the United States again, so be it. I acquiesce in this decision & accept it as His act. I know that if it had been in the order of His providence to establish our independance, we should have gained it. I accept the final issue & submit myself with cheerfulness to His will. . . . .

F. 12 Yesterday I went over to Augusta to purchase a few supplies. Specie & green backs (U. S. currency) is the only money now available. I bought sugar at 20 per lb, Coffee at 75 cts—tea at $3. per lb. The stock of goods has not yet been replenished but in a few days, trade will be opened with Savannah. There is a Yankee force stationed in the town & I saw a number of the soldiers strolling about the streets, chatting & laughing with our men. They seem to feel quite at home. . . . A large number of idle negroes are about the streets coming in from the country & leaving their masters. The Military authorities decline to interfere in any way. They do not tell the negroes they are free, but refuse to return them to their owners. They say they have receivd no instructions upon the subject. If this state of things continue it is virtually emancipating them, as there is no power or authority in the civil powers to act, whilst the city is under military rule. . . . .

Th. 25 We still remain in doubt as to the emancipation policy. No official announcement except Presdt. Lincolns amnesty proclamation, has been published. Military officers however in Charleston & Mobile are prescribing in their orders the mode in which the "freedmen" are to work & the terms on which they must be engaged. I think there is no doubt emancipation will be the settled policy, but whether immediate or gradual will be decided by Congress. The party in power now are radical abolitionists & will do all in their power to urge it forward. Both policy & humanity would dictate that it should be gradual, so that both parties at the South may accommodate themselves to so radical a change in social & political economy—And for the interest of the nation at large, this change should be gradual, & thus avoid the shock to the industrial resources of the country. Fanaticism & Reason have nothing in common.

My negroes have made no change in their behaviour, & are going on as they have always hitherto done. Until I know that they are legally free, I shall let them continue. If they become free by law then the whole system must be changed. If the means which I now possess of supporting the old & the young are taken away, they must then necessarily look for their support to their own exertions. How they can support themselves at present, I cannot see. Labour is more abundant (from the return of so many soldiers) & food still scarce & money yet more scarce & difficult to be got. I have three or four of my negroes who are only working out their food. If Emancipation prevails, the negro must become a labourer in the field, as the whites will soon occupy all the domestic & mechanic employments. . . .

M. 29 I went in to Aiken this morning & called at the hotel to inquire if any officer in Aiken was authorized to administer the Oath of Allegiance. They expected in a day or two to have it done here. It is necessary now in order to save property, have personal protection, or exercise the rights of citizenship, or any business calling. Every one who is allowed, is now taking the oath, as the Confederate govt. is annulled, the state govt. destroyed, & the return into the Union absolutely necessary to our condition as an organized community. As Gen. Gillmore's order based upon Chief Justice Chase's opinion announces the freedom of the negroes there is no further room to doubt that it is the settled policy of the country. I have today formally announced to my negroes the fact, & made such arrangements with each as the new relation rendered necessary. Those whose whole time we need, get at present clothes & food, house rent & medical attendance. The others work for themselves giving me a portion of their time on the farm in lieu of house rent. Old Amelia & her two grandchildren, I will spare the mockery of offering freedom to. I must support them as long as I have any thing to give.

T. 30 My negroes all express a desire to remain with me. I am gratified at the proof of their attachment. I believe it to be real & unfeigned. For the present they will remain, but in course of time we must part, as I cannot afford to keep so many, & they cannot afford to hire for what I could give them. As they have always been faithful & attached to us, & have been raised as family servants, & have all of them been in our family for several generations, there is a feeling towards them somewhat like that of a father who is about to send out his children on the world to make their way through life. Those who have brought the present change of relation upon us are ignorant of these

345

ties. They have charged us with cruelty. They call us, man stealers, robbers, tyrants. The indignant denial of these charges & the ill feelings engendered during 30 years of angry controversy, have culminated at length in the four years war which has now ended. It has pleased God that we should fail in our efforts for independance—& with the loss of independance, we return to the Union under the dominion of the abolition sentiment. The experiment is now to be tried. The negro is not only to be emancipated, but is to become a citizen with all the right & priviledges! It produces a financial, political & social revolution at the South, fearful to contemplate in its ultimate effects. Whatever the result may be, let it be known & remembered that neither the negro slave nor his master is responsible. It has been done by those who having political power, are determined to carry into practice the sentimental philanthropy they have so long & angrily advocated. Now that is fixed. I pray God for the great issues at stake, that he may bless the effort & make it successful—make it a blessing & not a curse to the poor negro.

2. *1873*—"BLACK PARLIAMENT"

❨ *The Southern Negro was totally unprepared for freedom. Yet the Radical Republicans of the North, now in control of the Federal government, gave the freed slave the vote, disfranchised most native Southerners, and so controlled the local election machinery that large numbers of Negroes won seats in state legislatures. There they were readily manipulated by "carpetbaggers" (unscrupulous Northerners intent on making fortunes), and "scalawags" (Southerners who accepted the new regime for ends of their own). The result was a burlesque on self-government.*

South Carolina offered one of the worst examples of farce, extravagance, and corruption. James S. Pike, who described the "Black Parliament" of 1873, was a Northern newspaperman of strong anti-slavery principles and a stanch Republican. What he saw in South Carolina, which he called "The Prostrate State," was an indictment of policies which he had long supported.

Yesterday, about 4 P.M., the assembled wisdom of the State . . . issued forth from the State-House. About three-quarters of the crowd belonged to the African race. They were of every hue, from the light octoroon to the deep black. They were such a looking body of men as might pour out of a market-house or a court-house at random in any Southern State. Every negro type and physiognomy was here to be seen, from the genteel serving-man to the rough-hewn customer from

James S. Pike, *The Prostrate State: South Carolina Under Negro Government* (New York, 1874), 10–15, 19–21.

the rice or cotton field. Their dress was as varied as their countenances. There was the second-hand black frock-coat of infirm gentility, glossy and threadbare. There was the stove-pipe hat of many ironings and departed styles. There was also to be seen a total disregard of the proprieties of costume in the coarse and dirty garments of the field; the stub-jackets and slouch hats of soiling labor. In some instances, rough woolen comforters embraced the neck and hid the absence of linen. Heavy brogans, and short, torn trousers, it was impossible to hide. The dusky tide flowed out into the littered and barren grounds, and, issuing through the coarse wooden fence of the inclosure, melted away into the street beyond. These were the legislators of South Carolina. . . .

We will enter the House of Representatives. Here sit one hundred and twenty-four members. Of these, twenty-three are white men, representing the remains of the old civilization. These are good-looking, substantial citizens. They are men of weight and standing in the communities they represent. They are all from the hill country. The frosts of sixty and seventy winters whiten the heads of some among them. There they sit, grim and silent. They feel themselves to be but loose stones, thrown in to partially obstruct a current they are powerless to resist. They say little and do little as the days go by. They simply watch the rising tide, and mark the progressive steps of the inundation. . . .

This dense negro crowd they confront do the debating, the squabbling, the law-making, and create all the clamor and disorder of the body. These twenty-three white men are but the observers, the enforced auditors of the dull and clumsy imitation of a deliberative body, whose appearance in their present capacity is at once a wonder and a shame to modern civilization. . . .

Deducting the twenty-three members referred to, who comprise the entire strength of the opposition, we find one hundred and one remaining. Of this one hundred and one, ninety-four are colored, and seven are their white allies. Thus the blacks outnumber the whole body of whites in the House more than three to one. . . . As things stand, the body is almost literally a Black Parliament. . . . The Speaker is black, the Clerk is black, the door-keepers are black, the little pages are black, the chairman of the Ways and Means is black, and the chaplain is coal-black. . . .

But the old stagers admit that the colored brethren have a wonderful aptness at legislative proceedings. They are "quick as lightning" at detecting points of order, and they certainly make incessant and extraordinary use of their knowledge. No one is allowed to talk five minutes without interruption, and one interruption is the signal for another and another, until the original speaker is smothered under an avalanche of them. Forty questions of privilege will be raised in a day. At times, nothing goes on but alternating questions of order and of

347

privilege. The inefficient colored friend who sits in the Speaker's chair cannot suppress this extraordinary element of the debate. Some of the blackest members exhibit a pertinacity of intrusion in raising these points of order and questions of privilege that few white men can equal. Their struggles to get the floor, their bellowings and physical contortions, baffle description. The Speaker's hammer plays a perpetual tattoo all to no purpose. The talking and the interruptions from all quarters go on with the utmost license. Every one esteems himself as good as his neighbor, and puts in his oar, apparently as often for love of riot and confusion as for any thing else. It is easy to imagine what are his ideas of propriety and dignity among a crowd of his own color, and these are illustrated without reserve. The Speaker orders a member whom he has discovered to be particularly unruly to take his seat. The member obeys, and with the same motion that he sits down, throws his feet on to his desk, hiding himself from the Speaker by the soles of his boots. In an instant he appears again on the floor. After a few experiences of this sort, the Speaker threatens, in a laugh, to call "the gemman" to order. This is considered a capital joke, and a guffaw follows. The laugh goes round, and then the peanuts are cracked and munched faster than ever; one hand being employed in fortifying the inner man with this nutriment of universal use, while the other enforces the views of the orator. This laughing propensity of the sable crowd is a great cause of disorder. They laugh as hens cackle—one begins and all follow.

But underneath all this shocking burlesque upon legislative proceedings, we must not forget that there is something very real to this uncouth and untutored multitude. It is not all sham, nor all burlesque. They have a genuine interest and a genuine earnestness in the business of the assembly which we are bound to recognize and respect, unless we would be accounted shallow critics. They have an earnest purpose, born of a conviction that their position and condition are not fully assured, which lends a sort of dignity to their proceedings. The barbarous, animated jargon in which they so often indulge is on occasion seen to be so transparently sincere and weighty in their own minds that sympathy supplants disgust. The whole thing is a wonderful novelty to them as well as to observers. Seven years ago these men were raising corn and cotton under the whip of the overseer. Today they are raising points of order and questions of privilege. They find they can raise one as well as the other. They prefer the latter. It is easier, and better paid. Then, it is the evidence of an accomplished result. It means escape and defense from old oppressors. It means liberty. It means the destruction of prison-walls only too real to them. It is the sunshine of their lives. It is their day of jubilee. It is their long-promised vision of the Lord God Almighty. Shall we, then, be too critical over the spectacle? Perhaps we might more wisely wonder that they can do so well in so short a time. . . .

3. *1871*—THE KU KLUX KLAN DISCIPLINES A NEGRO

❨ *Many Southerners reacted violently to the Negro as voter and officeholder. To put him in his place some elements banded together in a secret organization called the "Invisible Empire of the South," better known as the Ku Klux Klan. Its members wore white robes and masks and always carried out their missions at night. Their methods come out in the testimony of Gadsden Steel, a Negro witness at a trial for the murder of Jim Williams, also a Negro.*

Testimony of Gadsden Steel

Gadsden Steel, a witness for the prosecution, being duly sworn, testified as follows:

Direct Examination by Mr. Corbin.

Q. Where do you live?

A. In North Carolina.

Q. Where did you live last spring—in March?

A. Near Yorkville and McConnellsville, York County.

Q. How long had you lived in York County, prior to that time?

A. Until about the middle of April. I moved to North Carolina about the middle of April.

Q. How long had you lived in York County before you moved to North Carolina?

A. Until that time, all my life.

Q. Were you a voter in York County?

A. Yes, sir.

Q. Vote at the last election?

A. Yes, sir.

Q. Are you twenty-one years of age?

A. Twenty-six.

Q. What ticket did you vote?

A. Voted the Radical ticket.

Q. Vote for Mr. Wallace?

A. Yes, sir.

Q. Now, tell the jury about the Ku Klux coming to your house last March, on the night that Jim Williams was killed; what they said and did, and what you said, and all about it.

Proceedings in the Ku Klux Trials, at Columbia, S. C., in the United States Circuit Court, November Term, 1871 (Columbia, 1872), 232–35.

A. They came to my house on a Monday night.

Q. What Monday night was that?

A. I don't exactly know what day of the month it was.

Q. Well, sales day, in March?

A. No, sir; I don't exactly know.

Q. Which Monday?

A. It was on a Monday night; I don't know what day of the month it was.

Q. The first or third?

A. I don't know exactly whether it was the first or third; I cannot exactly tell.

Q. Very well, tell what occurred.

A. They came to my house about ten o'clock, and I was in bed at that time; and I was asleep; and my wife she heard them before I did, and she shook me and woke me up, and told me she heard a mighty riding and walking, and said I had better get up, she thought it was Ku Klux. I jumped up, and put on my pantaloons, and stepped to the door, and looked out, and very close to the door I seen the men, and I stepped right back into the house; so when they knocked the door open they couldn't see me; and they came in and called for me to give up my gun, and I says I has no gun; and when I spoke they all grabbed me, and taken me out into the yard.

Q. What sort of looking people were they?

A. They was all disguised; as far as I could see—they was all disguised, and struck me three licks over the head, and jobbed the blood out of me, right forninst my eye, with a pistol, and down by my mouth here, [indicating;] and four of them walked around to Mr. Moore's; and, when they started off, one touched the other, and said let's go around, and see this man, and then the crowd that had me taken me to Mr. Moore's, and asked Mr. Moore if I had a gun; and he said no, not that he knew of; and they asked if I had a pistol, and he said no; they asked if I belonged to that company; he said no.

Q. What company?

A. Jim Williams' company; asked him was I a bad boy, and run about into any devilment; he said no; I was a very fine boy, as far as he knew; they asked how I voted; he said I voted the Radical ticket; they says, "There, G—d d—n you, I'll kill you for that;" they took me on out in the lane, and says, "come out and talk to No. 6;" they locked arms with me, and one took me by the collar, and put a gun agin me, and marched me out to No. 6; when I went out there, he was sitting on his horse; I walked up to him; he bowed his head down to me, (illustrating with a very low bow), and says, "How do you do," and horned me in the breast with his horns; had horns on the head about so long, (indicating about two feet;) I jumped back from him, and they punched me, and said "Stand up to him, G—d d—n you, and talk to him;" I told them I would do so; he told me that he wanted me to tell him who had guns.

Q. Who said that?

A. No. 6; I told him I knew a heap that had guns, but hadn't them now; they had done give them up; well, says he, ain't Jim Williams got the guns? I says I heard folks say that he has them, but I do not know whether he has them or not. Then he says to me: "We want you to go and show us the way to Jim Williams' house." Says I, "I have never been there since he built on that road." Says they, "We want you to go and show us to where his house is; if you don't show us to where his house is we will kill you;" and then one looked up to the moon and says: "Don't tarry here too long with this d—n nigger; we have to get back to hell before daybreak. It won't do to tarry here too long." Says he, "get on." There was a man standing to the right of me with his beast; his head was turned from me; I stepped around and got on behind him, and rode on around until they turned towards the school house, about sixty yards down the road, and he asked me did I want to go, and I told him no. Says I, the fix that I am in, if you don't do anything to me, may kill me. I hadn't nothing on but a shirt, pantaloons and drawers. They started in a lope then, and he hollowed to No. 6 that he could not keep up, that I was too heavy. Says he, "this God damned nigger is too heavy." No. 6 hollows back to him, "let him down," and he rode close enough to the fence so that I could get down, and I stepped off; says he, "you go home and go to bed, and if you are not there when we come along, we will kill you the next time we call on you; we are going on to kill Williams, and are going to kill all these damned niggers that votes the Radical ticket; run, God damn you, run." I ran into the yard, and I heard somebody talking near the store, and I slipped up beside the palings, and it was Dr. Love and Andy Lindsey talking, and Love seen me, and says, "Gadsden, did they hurt you;" "no," says I, "not much; they punched the blood out in two places, and knocked me two or three times about the head, but they did not hurt me very much." Says he, "you go to bed and I don't think they will trouble you very much." I went home and put on my clothes, and goes up to the mill to get the other boys out of the way, for fear they might go on them, but they were out, and the others were lying in bed, and I waked the others up, and we all went out into the old field and laid there until the chickens crowed for day, and went back to Mr. Moore's, near the house, and lay there till clear day-light, and I goes into the yard there, and Mr. Moore came to me and looked over my face and seen where they had punched the blood out of me, and says then for me to go on to my work and make myself easy, that they should not come and bother me any more; I never seen any more of them after that.

Q. Now, what time the next day did you learn that Jim Williams was dead?

A. It was about 8 o'clock when I heard of it.

Q. Did you go down near him?

A. No, sir; I didn't go. I was busy employed, and didn't go. I didn't quit my work to go. I was working at the mill, and some come there to the mill very early that morning and told it.

Q. Told you what?

A. Well, they didn't tell me, but they told Mr. Dover and Mr. Guthrie that he was killed.

Q. Who?

A. I don't know who it was that said it was Jim Williams. They said he was killed, but the man that said it I didn't know. They was white men.

Q. Jim Williams was killed that night, was he?

A. Yes, sir; he was killed that night.

Q. Repeat, if you please, what that man told you when he let you go off from the horse; what they said to you?

A. When they let me off the horse, they said: "You go home and go to bed, and if you are not there in the morning when we come along, the next time we call, we will kill you. We are going to kill all you d—n niggers that vote these Radical tickets. We are going to kill Jim, and are going to kill all these d—n niggers that vote the Radical ticket." The man that I was riding behind, he was the one that talked to me.

4. *1868*—THE IMPEACHMENT TRIAL OF ANDREW JOHNSON

《 *Andrew Johnson, Lincoln's successor, came to the Presidency as a Radical Republican, committed to the policy of giving equality to the Negro and making the South suffer for having brought on the Civil War. But after a few weeks in office Johnson's attitude changed, and he began to follow Lincoln's plan of restoring the old Union with as little modification as possible except for emancipation. Conflict with the Radicals was inevitable. The President vetoed Radical measures; Congress passed them over his vetoes. Johnson's hasty temper and lack of tact made bad feeling worse. Finally, when he ignored the Tenure of Office Act, which forbade the President to remove, without the consent of the Senate, an office-holder who had been appointed with the consent of the Senate, Radicals in the House of Representatives decided to force Johnson from office by the impeachment method.*

Under the Constitution, an impeachment is voted by the House,

Margarita Spalding Gerry, Ed., *Through Five Administrations: Reminiscences of Colonel William H. Crook* (New York, 1910), 124–34.

*and then the charges are tried by the Senate, with the Chief Justice
of the United States presiding. William H. Crook, one of Johnson's
bodyguards, describes the historic event—the only time that a President of the United States has been brought to trial.*

The formal opening of the trial was on the 13th of March. The
President's counsel asked for forty days in which to prepare the arguments. They were rather ungraciously refused, and were allowed ten
days instead. The court then adjourned until the 23d. . . .

On the 23d of March, when the actual trial began, the President
took leave of three of his counsel—Mr. Evarts, Mr. Curtis, and Mr.
Nelson—who had come to the White House for a final discussion. I
was near them as they stood together in the portico. Mr. Johnson's
manner was entirely calm and unconcerned. He shook hands with each
of them in turn, and said:

"Gentlemen, my case is in your hands; I feel sure that you will protect my interests." Then he returned to his office. I went off with the
gentlemen. By the desire of the President, I accompanied them to the
Capitol every day.

When, from my seat in the gallery, I looked down on the Senate
chamber, I had a moment of almost terror. It was not because of the
great assemblage; it was rather in the thought that one could feel in
the mind of every man and woman there that for the first time in the
history of the United States a President was on trial for more than his
life—his place in the judgment of his countrymen and of history.

There was a painful silence when the counsel for the President filed
in and took their places. They were seated under the desk of the presiding officer—in this case, Chief-Justice Chase—on the right-hand side
of the Senate chamber. The managers for the prosecution were already
in their seats. Every seat in the gallery was occupied.

The dignity with which the proceedings opened served to heighten
the sense of awe. It persevered during the routine business of reading
the journal and while the President's reply was being read; but when
Manager Butler arose to make the opening address for the prosecution,
there was a change.

His speech was a violent attack upon the President. It was clever.
Actually blameless incidents were made to seem traitorous. The address
was so bitter, and yet so almost theatrical, that it seemed unreal. I
wondered at the time why it so impressed me. In Butler's later action—
to which I shall hereafter refer—came a possible explanation of this
impression.

The trial lasted three weeks. The President, of course, never appeared. In that particular the proceedings lacked a spectacular interest
they might have had. Every day the President had a consultation with

his lawyers. For the rest, he attended to the routine work of his position. He was absolutely calm through it all. The very night of the 23d he gave a reception to as many of the members of Congress as would come. I was fully prepared to have the White House deserted, but, instead of that, it was crowded. I wondered why men who hated the President so bitterly could accept his hospitality until I came to a group of about fifteen Radicals gathered together in the East Room, where they had proceeded after paying their respects to the President. They were laughing together, and teasing one another like boys.

"What are you here for?" I heard.

"And you—what are you doing here yourself?"

"Why, I wanted to see how Andy takes it," was the answer. I thought to myself as I passed them that they were getting small satisfaction out of that, for no one could have seen the slightest difference in Mr. Johnson's manner. He greeted every one as pleasantly as though it were a surprise party come to congratulate him on his statesmanship. . . .

As the trial proceeded, the conviction grew with me—I think it did with every one—that the weight of evidence and of constitutional principle lay with the defence. There were several clever lawyers on the prosecution, and Butler had his legal precedents skilfully marshalled, but the greater part of the proceedings showed personal feeling and prejudice rather than proof. Every appeal that could be made to the passions of the time was utilized. "Warren Hastings," "Charles I," "Irresponsible tyranny," were always on the lips of the prosecution.

In comparison, the calm, ordered, masterly reasoning of the defence must have inspired every one with a conviction of the truth of their cause. Their efforts were of varying ability and character, of course. The minds of these men were as diverse as their faces. Mr. Nelson was a short, stout man with a ruddy face. Mr. Evarts, who was then laying the foundation for his future unquestioned eminence, was an active, thin man. Mr. Groesbeck, who was ill during the trial, and was forced to have his clerk read his argument, had, with appropriateness, considering his name, a prominent, curved nose. Mr. Nelson's address was the most emotional of them all. His appeal was largely for sympathy, for admiration of the man Andrew Johnson; it was personal. Mr. Groesbeck was the surprise of the trial. He had been able to take very little part in the proceedings, but his argument was remarkably fine. Mr. Evarts's address was clearly reasoned. Mr. Curtis's argument, in my opinion, was the finest of them all.

But the legal struggle, after all, with that assemblage of violent passions was hardly the contest that counted. The debate was for the benefit of the country at large; while the legal lights argued, the enemies of the President were working in other ways. The Senate was thoroughly canvassed, personal argument and influence were in constant use. Every personal motive, good or bad, was played upon. Long before the final ballot, it became known how most of the men would probably vote. Toward the end the doubtful ones had narrowed down to one man—Senator Ross, of Kansas. Kansas, which had been the fighting-ground of rebel guerilla and Northern abolitionist, was to have, in all probability, the determining vote in this contest.

Kansas was, from inception and history, abolitionist, radical. It would have been supposed that Senator Ross would vote with the Radicals. He had taken the place of James H. Lane, who had shot himself. Lane was a friend of the President, and, had he lived, in all probability would have supported him. But Ross had no such motive. It became known that he was doubtful; it was charged that he had been subject to personal influence—feminine influence.

Then the cohorts of the Senate and the House bore down upon the Senator from Kansas. Party discipline was brought to bear, and then ridicule. Either from uncertainty, or policy, or a desire to keep his associates in uncertainty, Ross refused to make an announcement of his policy. In all probability he was honestly trying to convince himself. . . .

On May 15th, a rainy, dismal day, the Lincoln Monument in front of the city hall was dedicated. Either the anxiety of Congress to have the impeachment over, or, more probably, a desire to show contempt for Andrew Johnson, who was to preside, caused both Houses to refuse to adjourn to honor the memory of the dead President. I accompanied Mr. Johnson and saw the exercises, which were finished without the recognition of our legislators.

On May 16th the vote was taken.

Every one who by any possible means could get a ticket of admission to the Senate chamber produced it early that morning at the Capitol. The floor and galleries were crowded.

The journal was read; the House of Representatives was notified that the Senate, "sitting for the trial of the President upon the articles of impeachment," was ready to receive the other House in the Senate chamber. The question of voting first upon the eleventh article was decided.

While the clerk was reading the legal statement of those crimes of which, in the opinion of the House of Representatives, the President was guilty, some people fidgeted and some sat with their hands tensely clasped together. At the end, the Chief-Justice directed that the roll be called. The clerk called out:

"Mr. Anthony." Mr. Anthony rose.

"Mr. Anthony"—the Chief-Justice fastened his eyes upon the Senator—"how say you? Is the respondent, Andrew Johnson, President of the United States, guilty or not guilty of a high misdemeanor as charged in this article?"

"Guilty," answered Mr. Anthony.

A sigh went round the assemblage. Yet Mr. Anthony's vote was not in doubt. A two-thirds vote of thirty-six to eighteen was necessary to convict. Thirty-four of the Senators were pledged to vote against the President. Mr. Fowler, of Tennessee, it was known, would probably vote for acquittal, although there was some doubt. Senator Ross was the sphinx; no one knew his position.

The same form was maintained with each Senator in turn. When Fowler's name was reached, every one leaned forward to catch the word.

"Not guilty," said Senator Fowler.

The tension grew. There was a weary number of names before that of Ross was reached. When the clerk called it, and Ross stood forth, the crowd held its breath.

"Not guilty," called the Senator from Kansas.

It was like the bubbling over of a caldron. The Radical Senators, who had been laboring with Ross only a short time before, turned to him in rage; all over the house people began to stir. The rest of the roll-call was listened to with lessened interest, although there was still the chance for a surprise. When it was over, and the result—thirty-five to nineteen—was announced, there was a wild outburst, chiefly groans of anger and disappointment, for the friends of the President were in the minority.

I did not wait to hear it, for, barely waiting for the verdict to be read—it was no surprise to me, as I had been keeping tally on a slip of paper—I ran down-stairs at the top of my speed. In the corridor of the Senate I came across a curious group. In it was Thad Stevens, who was a helpless cripple, with his two attendants carrying him high on their shoulders. All about the crowd, unable to get into the court-room, was calling out: "What was the verdict?" Thad Stevens's face was black with rage and disappointment. He brandished his arms in the air, and shouted in answer:

"The country is going to the devil!"

I ran all the way from the Capitol to the White House. I was young and strong in those days, and I made good time. When I burst into the library, where the President sat with Secretary Welles and two other men whom I cannot remember, they were quietly talking. Mr. Johnson was seated at a little table on which luncheon had been spread in the rounding southern end of the room. There were no signs of excitement.

"Mr. President," I shouted, too crazy with delight to restrain myself, "you are acquitted!"

All rose. I made my way to the President and got hold of his hand. The other men surrounded him, and began to shake his hand. The President responded to their congratulations calmly enough for a moment, and then I saw that tears were rolling down his face.

5. *1869*—FINISHING THE UNION PACIFIC

❡ *In the midst of the Civil War Congress faced the necessity of building a railroad to link the far West with the rest of the nation. To this end it incorporated the Union Pacific Railroad Company and authorized it to build westward from Iowa, and at the same time empowered the Central Pacific to push eastward from California to join the Union Pacific. Both roads were aided by grants of government land. Construction went slowly until 1865, when thousands of discharged soldiers exchanged their muskets for picks and shovels and joined the other thousands of Chinese and Mexicans already at work. The two roads came together at Promontory, Utah, on May 10, 1869. Officials staged a celebration which at least one of those who was present, Alexander Toponce, never forgot.*

I saw the Golden Spike driven at Promontory, Utah, on May 10, 1869. . . .

On the last day, only about 100 feet were laid, and everybody tried to have a hand in the work. I took a shovel from an Irishman, and threw a shovel full of dirt on the ties just to tell about it afterward.

A special train from the west brought Sidney Dillon, General Dodge, T. C. Durant, John R. Duff, S. A. Seymour, a lot of newspaper men, and plenty of the best brands of champagne.

Another train made up at Ogden carried the band from Fort Douglas, the leading men of Utah Territory, and a small but efficient supply of Valley Tan.

It was a very hilarious occasion; everybody had all they wanted to drink all the time. Some of the participants got "sloppy," and these were not all Irish and Chinese by any means.

California furnished the Golden Spike. Governor Tuttle of Nevada furnished one of silver. General Stanford [Governor Safford?] presented one of gold, silver, and iron from Arizona. The last tie was of California laurel.

When they came to drive the last spike, Governor Stanford, president of the Central Pacific, took the sledge, and the first time he struck he missed the spike and hit the rail.

What a howl went up! Irish, Chinese, Mexicans, and everybody

"Reminiscences of Alexander Toponce, Pioneer," in B. A. Botkin and Alvin F. Harlow, Eds., *A Treasury of Railroad Folklore* (New York, 1953), 124–25.

yelled with delight. "He missed it. Yee." The engineers blew the whistles and rang their bells. Then Stanford tried it again and tapped the spike and the telegraph operators had fixed their instruments so that the tap was reported in all the offices east and west, and set bells to tapping in hundreds of towns and cities. . . . Then Vice President T. C. Durant of the Union Pacific took up the sledge and he missed the spike the first time. Then everybody slapped everybody else again and yelled, "He missed it too, yow!"

It was a great occasion, every one carried off souvenirs and there are enough splinters of the last tie in museums to make a good bonfire.

When the connection was finally made the Union Pacific and the Central Pacific engineers ran their engines up until their pilots touched. Then the engineers shook hands and had their pictures taken and each broke a bottle of champagne on the pilot of the other's engine and had their picture taken again.

The Union Pacific engine, the "Jupiter," was driven by my good friend, George Lashus, who still lives in Ogden.

Both before and after the spike driving ceremony there were speeches, which were cheered heartily. I do not remember what any of the speakers said now, but I do remember that there was a great abundance of champagne.

6. *1870*—A COWBOY ON THE LONG TRAIL

❲ *The twenty-five years that followed the Civil War were the years of the cowboy's glory. This rugged workman of the western plains lived a life of loneliness, hardship, and danger, yet he was proud of his vocation and rarely traded it for another except of necessity. His work reached its climax in the long drive from the range to the shipping points in Kansas. For weeks he would be under constant strain, ever watchful for a stampede, on guard always against marauding Indians. James H. Cook, an old time "waddy" (cowboy), describes his first trip northward from central Texas.*

When Mr. Roberts informed me that I was to be one of his trail waddies, I immediately moved all my personal belongings over to his camp. I was allowed to take five of the best saddle horses which I had been riding, to be used on the trail. Roberts's trail crew consisted of twelve riders and the cook, besides himself. We were now to be favored by having one man whose duty would be to drive two yoke of oxen on our canvas-covered supply wagon and to cook for the outfit. We were most fortunate in having with us on that trip a man who was one of

James H. Cook, *Fifty Years on the Old Frontier* (New Haven, 1923), 39–49.

358

the best ox drivers or bull-whackers, as well as cooks, that ever popped a bull-whip over a cattle trail. The men who usually did this work were veterans on the frontier, who had seen long service with wagon trains drawn by oxen. Too much praise or credit cannot be given to those old-time trail cooks who were numbered among the *good* ones. A camp cook could do more toward making life pleasant for those about him than any other man in an outfit, especially on those trail trips. A good-natured, hustling cook meant a lot to a trail boss. A cheery voice ringing out about daybreak, shouting, "Roll out there, fellers, and hear the little birdies sing their praises to God!" or "Arise and shine and give God the glory!" would make the most crusty waddie grin as he crawled out to partake of his morning meal—even when he was extremely short of sleep.

On the morning when we were to start up the trail, all was in readiness. Those selected to go with this herd were for the most part white men. The others were well known to be good hands with cattle. About a dozen extra men were to help us for a few days while we were breaking in the herd to accustom them to being held by riders both night and day (for we should have no more corrals). They were also to help us out of the brush country to the open plains. After reaching this open country the extra men would turn back and help bring up any herd or herds that were to follow.

On the trail we were each allowed to take a pair of bed blankets and a sack containing a little extra clothing. No more load than was considered actually necessary was to be allowed on the wagon, for there would be no wagon road over most of the country which we were to traverse, and there was plenty of rough country, with creeks and steep-banked rivers to be crossed. We had no tents or shelter of any sort other than our blankets. Our food and cooking utensils were the same as those used in cow camps of the brush country. No provision was made for the care of men in case of accident. Should anyone become injured, wounded, or sick, he would be strictly "out of luck." A quick recovery and a sudden death were the only desirable alternatives in such cases, for much of the time the outfit would be far from the settlements and from medical or surgical aid.

On the first day I was told to help drive the saddle horses and to keep them with the wagon. The wagon started, and we followed with the horses, the cattle herd following us in the trail made by the oxen and wagon. Roberts pointed out the course which he desired the outfit to follow, and then rode on ahead to select our first camp ground. After going a few miles he found a place with water and some fairly open ground upon which to bed the cattle down for the night. Returning to us, he told us where to go and where the wagon was to be located, so that it would not be too close to the herd.

When we reached the designated spot, the work oxen were hobbled and turned loose and a meal prepared of corn bread, broiled meat, and coffee. Along toward night about half the men who had been driving the cattle came in and had supper. They then caught our fresh horses and returned to the herd, allowing their companions to come in. After these men had eaten and caught fresh horses, they helped to hobble the entire horse herd, after which they all returned to the cattle. . . .

After the first night we divided the night-herding into two watches, half of the entire outfit being on guard at a time. When we were out of the brush country the extra help turned back, and as the cattle were now pretty well broken to being night-herded, we divided the watch into three tricks, three men going on guard with the cattle at a time and one man on each watch over the horses. Every night all the horses were hobbled, but they had to be herded just the same, for everything depended upon our holding to our horse herd. Horses stampede at night just the same as cattle, and are a great deal harder to hold if not hobbled. In those days there were plenty of Indians who would have been only too happy to relieve us of the care of them. . . .

One night we were camped on a little creek that ran into the Llano River at its head. Throughout that day we had seen a lot of fresh Indian signs. I was on the first watch with the horses. Roberts had arranged for me to be on guard with the horse herd during the early part of each evening and also just at the break of day, those hours being the Indian's favorite times for deviltry. I was known to be the best shot in that outfit, and I was expected to score straight bull's-eyes and not get "buck fever," no matter how plentiful, hideous, or dangerously close the human targets.

The country was rough and broken, and here and there were large cedar thickets or brakes. I was holding the horses pretty close to the wagon immediately after supper, and everyone noticed that the animals were very restless. In those days, for some unknown reason, a white man's horse was generally afraid of the sight or scent of an Indian, just as Indian ponies were afraid of a white man. When our animals scented Indians they sniffed the air, snorted, ran together, and showed terror by their looks and actions.

At last Roberts came out where I was holding the horses and told me I had better put them into a little opening in the center of a big cedar brake near the wagon. I replied that I was afraid to go in there to herd: the Indians could then slip up close and kill me with an arrow, for I could not see them. However, Roberts said there would be a great deal less danger in the brakes, as the Indians were likely to run in between the horses and the wagon, if these were on the open prairie, and run the entire herd off as well as kill me. Roberts continued: "They cannot run their horses in that brake." So in we went, he assisting me to drive in the animals. Roberts then returned to camp, cautioning me to keep a sharp lookout.

It required all the nerve I possessed to remain there with those horses. I had to ride hard to keep them in the space: they kept snorting and trying to scatter. I circled around them as fast as I could and kept them herded in as small a space as possible. When riding on the side of the herd nearest camp, I was only about seventy-five yards from the wagon. After what seemed an age, I heard one of the boys from the cattle herd come into camp and arouse the men who were to relieve us. Frank Dennis was the man who relieved me. He was one of the old school cowboys, and as brave a man as ever lived.

The night was very dark and a little chilly. One of the boys had put a lot of dry wood on the campfire, so that I could see the men there very plainly. It did not take them long to get out after being called, for all hands slept with their clothes on, and every rider kept his night horse close by, all saddled, every hour of the night. I started toward camp when I saw Frank advancing. He had thrown his bed blanket over his head and shoulders, Indian fashion, in place of an overcoat. As I passed him I said: "Frank, you will have to ride hard to hold the horses." He was blinded, he said, from having been so long in the light of the campfire; so I rode back with him and around the horses once or twice. At last he replied, "All right, Jim, I can see them now, and I'll set 'em for a while." I started for camp again and, riding up to the campfire, swung down off my horse, with my rifle in my hand—for I had been carrying it, ready to shoot at a moment's notice, all the evening.

Just as my foot touched the ground I heard a couple of dozen shots in quick succession. I turned my head and could see the flash from the guns. I fired one shot in the direction of the flashes. My horse had also turned his head when the shots were fired. A bullet struck him in the forehead, and he went down at my feet. I jumped away from that campfire as quickly as possible and crawled under a big cedar tree, the branches of which came very close to the ground. The next moment most of the horse herd came tearing right through camp. We had ropes stretched from the wagon wheels to some trees to make a corral in which to catch horses, and the horses ran against the ropes, upsetting the wagon.

Every man in camp ran for his life into the thicket. The horses which were tied about near camp, all saddled, ran on their ropes and broke them and decamped with the other animals—all save one horse. Some Indian had slipped into camp before the firing started, cut the picket-rope of this horse, and led him away.

The horses ran into the cattle herd, and away went the cattle into a big cedar brake containing many old dead trees. There was a smashing and crashing and about as great an uproar as any cowboy ever heard.

The men with the cattle did not dare yell at the animals or sing to them, lest Indians locate and slip an arrow into somebody.

I lay quite still under the tree. After a time I heard Roberts's voice calling out: "Don't let 'em get away with the horses, boys! Stay with 'em! Come on, boys, where are you?" I do not know where Roberts disappeared to when the horses stampeded through camp, but he certainly went somewhere—for a few minutes. I don't see, either, how he expected us to hold that horse herd. One by one I could hear the boys answer him. I did not like to get out from beneath that tree, but I did not care to be called a coward, so I joined him, although I thought it the most foolish thing we could possibly do. It was so dark that an Indian could slip up within three feet of a man and not be seen.

Frank Dennis not appearing, I made up my mind that he had been killed. I said to Roberts, "Let's go and see if we can find Frank. I know where he was riding, and I saw the shooting." We went and searched, but could find no trace of the missing cowboy. We then wandered about until daylight.

The men who had been with the cattle then came in, bringing some of the horses, and said that they had held the cattle and that the herd was then about half a mile from camp. I had my saddle, but several of our saddles, of course, were gone. So bareback riding was the order of the day for some of the men. I gave my saddle to Roberts.

About sunrise Frank Dennis came into camp. He was a little pale, but quite cheerful. He said, "Well, fellers, good morning; we had a very pleasant night of it, didn't we?" When he swung down from his horse I saw that there was blood on his clothes, and that his hand was tied up in his handkerchief, which was soaked with blood. He then told us his story.

After I had left him he rode around the herd a time or two. It seems that a large bunch of Indians had crawled up to within about fifteen feet of the line where he was riding, and as he passed they blazed away at him. He was so close to them, and looked so big, with a blanket wrapped about him, that I suppose they thought they could not help getting him, and that the firing would stampede the horses to boot. The redskins would then have run to their own horses, tied close at hand, mounted, and followed and secured our stampeded animals.

But their plans did not work very well. They succeeded in shooting a hole through the center of Frank's left hand, as well as in giving him two or three little flesh wounds and shooting about a dozen holes through his blanket and saddle. One shot tore the saddle-horn off, and an arrow lodged between his saddle and saddle-blanket. The horse herd had scattered in every direction after passing camp. Some ran into the cattle herd, where they were held by the boys with the herd, and one bunch of horses was chased up a cañon by the Indians for some distance. The horses were unable to get out of it because of the perpendicular bluffs, and the Indians were afraid to try to drive them back down the cañon, so they had to let the animals go. As it was, the savages got away with about a fourth of our horses.

7. *1867*—CUSTER REPELS AN INDIAN FORAY

⟦ *After Appomattox the United States expected to be at peace. Years passed before the hope was realized. For a quarter of a century the Plains Indians kept up an intermittent warfare that engaged a large part of the small regular army. Many officers who had achieved fame in the Civil War participated in the fighting. One of these was George A. Custer, a cavalryman who had won the two stars of a major general at the age of twenty-five. In the peacetime army, Custer was glad to accept a lieutenant colonel's commission. In 1867, at the head of the Seventh Cavalry, he took part in his first Indian campaign, an expedition against the Sioux. His account of a minor engagement reveals why the Indian was such a hard foe to conquer. Boldness, bravery, skill in horsemanship often led to Indian victory—and would bring a smashing one nine years later, when Custer and his entire command would die in the Battle of the Little Big Horn.*

Soon after arriving at camp a small party of Indians was reported in sight in a different direction. Captain Louis Hamilton, a lineal descendant of Alexander Hamilton, was immediately ordered to take his troop and learn something of their intentions. The Indians resorted to their usual tactics. There were not more than half a dozen to be seen—not enough to appear formidable. These were there as a decoy. Captain Hamilton marched his troop toward the hill on which the Indians had made their appearance, but on arriving at its crest found that they had retired to the next ridge beyond. This manœuver was repeated several times, until the cavalry found itself several miles from camp. The Indians then appeared to separate into two parties, each going in different directions. Captain Hamilton divided his troop into two detachments, sending one detachment, under command of my brother, after one of the parties, while he with twenty-five men continued to follow the other.

When the two detachments had become so far separated as to be of no assistance to each other, the Indians developed their scheme. Suddenly dashing from a ravine, as if springing from the earth, forty-three Indian warriors burst out upon the cavalry, letting fly their arrows and filling the air with their wild war-whoops. Fortunately Captain Hamil-

George A. Custer, *My Life on the Plains,* Milo M. Quaife, Ed. (Chicago: R. R. Donnelley & Sons Co., 1952), 144–50.

ton was an officer of great presence of mind as well as undaunted courage. The Indians began circling about the troops, throwing themselves upon the sides of their ponies and aiming their carbines and arrows over the necks of their well-trained war-steeds. Captain Hamilton formed his men in order to defend themselves against the assaults of their active enemies. The Indians displayed unusual boldness, sometimes dashing close up to the cavalry and sending in a perfect shower of bullets and arrows. Fortunately their aim, riding as they did at full speed, was necessarily inaccurate.

All this time we who had remained in camp were in ignorance of what was transpiring. Dr. Coates, whose acquaintance has been made before, had accompanied Captain Hamilton's command, but when the latter was divided the doctor joined the detachment of my brother. In some unexplained manner the doctor became separated from both parties, and remained so until the sound of the firing attracted him toward Captain Hamilton's party. When within half a mile of the latter, he saw what was transpiring; saw our men in the center and the Indians charging and firing from the outside. His first impulse was to push on and endeavor to break through the line of savages, casting his lot with his struggling comrades. This impulse was suddenly nipped in the bud. The Indians, with their quick, watchful eyes, had discovered his presence, and half a dozen of their best mounted warriors at once galloped toward him.

Happily the doctor was in the direction of camp from Captain Hamilton's party, and comprehending the peril of his situation at a glance, turned his horse's head toward camp, and applying the spur freely set out on a ride for life. The Indians saw this move, but were not disposed to be deprived of their victim in this way. They were better mounted than the doctor, his only advantage being in the start and the greater object to be attained. When the race began he was fully four miles from camp, the day was hot and sultry, the country rough and broken, and his horse somewhat jaded from the effects of the ride of the morning. These must have seemed immense obstacles in the eyes of a man who was riding for dear life. A false step, a broken girth, or almost any trifle might decide his fate.

How often, if ever, the doctor looked back, I know not; his eyes more probably were strained to catch a glimpse of camp or of assistance accidentally coming to his relief. Neither the one nor the other appeared. His pursuers, knowing that their success must be gained soon, if at all, pressed their fleet ponies forward until they seemed to skim over the surface of the green plain, and their shouts of exultation falling clearer and louder upon his ear told the doctor that they were surely gaining upon him. Fortunately our domestic horses, until accustomed to their presence, are as terrified by Indians as by a huge wild beast, and will fly from them if not restrained. The yells of the approaching Indians served, no doubt, to quicken the energies of the doctor's horse and impelled him to greater efforts to escape.

So close had the Indians succeeded in approaching that they were almost within arrow range and would soon have sent one flying through the doctor's body, when to the great joy of the pursued and the corresponding grief of his pursuers camp suddenly appeared in full view scarcely a mile distant. The ponies of the Indians had been ridden too hard to justify their riders in venturing near enough to provoke pursuit upon fresh animals. Sending a parting volley of bullets after the flying doctor, they turned about and disappeared. The doctor did not slacken his pace on this account, however; he knew that Captain Hamilton's party was in peril, and that assistance should reach him as soon as possible. Without tightening rein or sparing spur he came dashing into camp, and the first we knew of his presence he had thrown himself from his almost breathless horse and was lying on the ground, unable, from sheer exhaustion and excitement, to utter a word.

The officers and men gathered about him in astonishment, eager and anxious to hear his story, for all knew that something far from any ordinary event had transpired to place the doctor in such a condition of mind and body. As soon as he had recovered sufficiently to speak, he told us that he had left Captain Hamilton surrounded by a superior force of Indians, and that he himself had been pursued almost to the borders of camp.

This was enough. The next moment the bugle rang out the signal "To horse," and in less time than would be required to describe it, horses were saddled and arms ready. Then "there was mounting in hot haste." A moment later the command set off at a brisk trot to attempt the rescue of their beleaguered comrades.

Persons unfamiliar with the cavalry service may mentally inquire why, in such an emergency as this, the intended reinforcements were not pushed forward at a rapid gallop? But in answer to this it need only be said that we had a ride of at least five miles before us in order to arrive at the point where Captain Hamilton and his command had last been seen, and it was absolutely necessary to so husband the powers of our horses as to save them for the real work of conflict.

We had advanced in this manner probably two miles, when we discerned in the distance the approach of Captain Hamilton's party. They were returning leisurely to camp, after having succeeded in driving off their assailants and inflicting upon them a loss of two warriors killed and several wounded. The Indians could only boast of having wounded a horse belonging to Captain Hamilton's party.

8. *1863–1865*—A NORWEGIAN FAMILY MAKES A HOME IN IOWA

❴ *While the cowboys rode herd and the miners panned gold and the cavalry chased the Indians, settlers pushed ever westward. The low hills of Iowa, the plains of Kansas, Nebraska, and the Dakotas drew many Europeans who sought not quick wealth but modest farms that they could call their own. They found life hard in the new country, and different from what they had known in the old, but while their letters are often tinged with homesickness they rarely express regret. Those which follow were written by Gro Svendsen, who had settled, with her husband, in northwestern Iowa.*

1863

DEAR PARENTS, SISTERS, AND BROTHERS (always in my thoughts):

I have often thought that I ought to tell you about life here in the New World. Everything is so totally different from what it was in our beloved Norway. You never will really know what it's like, although you no doubt try to imagine what it might be. Your pictures would be all wrong, just as mine were.

I only wish that I could be with you to tell you all about it. Even if I were to write you countless pages, I still could not tell you everything.

I remember I used to wonder when I heard that it would be impossible to keep the milk here as we did at home. Now I have learned that it is indeed impossible because of the heat here in the summertime. One can't make cheese out of the milk because of flies, bugs, and other insects. I don't know the names of all these insects, but this I do know: If one were to make cheese here in the summertime, the cheese itself would be alive with bugs. Toward late autumn it should be possible to keep the milk. The people who have more milk than they need simply feed it to the hogs.

It's difficult, too, to preserve the butter. One must pour brine over it or salt it; otherwise it gets full of maggots. Therefore it is best, if one is not too far from town, to sell the butter at once. This summer we have been getting from eight to ten cents a pound. Not a great profit. For this reason people around here do not have many cows—just enough to supply the milk needed for the household. It's not wise to have more than enough milk, because the flies are everywhere. Even the bacon must be preserved in brine, and so there are different ways of doing everything.

I have so much to tell you. We have no twilight here in the summertime. Even in June, on the longest day of the year, the sun doesn't rise

Pauline Farseth and Theodore C. Blegen, Eds., *Frontier Mother: The Letters of Gro Svendsen* (Northfield, Minn.: Norwegian-American Historical Association, 1950), 39–41, 70–73.

before 4:23 and sets at 7:40. The nights are as dark as they are at home in autumn. We never have rain without thunder and lightning. The thunderstorms are so violent that one might think it was the end of the world. The whole sky is aflame with lightning, and the thunder rolls and crashes as though it were right above our heads. Quite often the lightning strikes down both cattle and people, damages property, and splinters sturdy oak trees into many pieces. Even though one did not fear the thunder in Norway, one can easily become frightened here.

Then there is the prairie fire or, as they call it here, "Faieren." This is terrifying, and the fire rages in both the spring and the fall. Whatever it leaves behind in the fall, it consumes in the spring, so there is nothing left of the long grass on the prairies, sloughs, and marshes. It is a strange and terrible sight to see all the fields a sea of fire. Quite often the scorching flames sweep everything along in their path—people, cattle, hay, fences. In dry weather with a strong wind the fire will race faster than the speediest horse. No one dares to travel without carrying matches, so that if there is a fire he can fight it by building another and in this way save his life and prevent burns, which sometimes prove fatal.

Snakes are found here in the summertime and are also a worry to us. I am horribly afraid of them, particularly the rattlesnake. The rattlesnake is the same as the *klapperslange*. I have seen many of them and thousands of ordinary snakes.

I could tell you even more, but possibly many who read this letter may think I am exaggerating. I assure you that all that I have told you I have experienced myself. If they do not believe me, they should come over and find out for themselves. Then they would tell you the same things I tell you.

By the way, no one leaving Norway should sell all his possessions as most people do. Everything that is useful in Norway is also useful here. The women can make use of all their clothes, with the exception of their headdress, bodice, jackets, and kerchiefs. All these they could sell, but all the other clothes they could make over and wear here. Everything Norwegian is of better quality than what can be bought here. So I am very grateful to you, my parents, every time I touch anything I have received from you. Bedding, too, should be brought along, as it's colder here in the winter than in Norway. Even those who criticize Norway and praise America must admit this. I could tell you much more but haven't time. . . .

ESTHERVILLE, EMMETT CO., IOWA

December 3, 1865

PRECIOUS PARENTS, SISTERS, AND BROTHERS:

. . . We have had a good year, a rich harvest both from the grain that we sowed as well as from the wild fruit and grain. We have plowed and fenced in three acres of new land. On this plot we raised ninety bushels of corn, twenty-four bushels of potatoes, and a plant called sugar cane or sorghum. This sugar cane is pressed and cooked into syrup or molasses. From our patch of sugar cane we got nine gallons of syrup (a gallon is equal to four *potter*). The man whose pressing and cooking machine we used also got nine gallons so we actually got eighteen gallons all told. We also got some fruit from our garden. It would take too long to list all of it, but I must tell you something about a fruit called "watermelon." We have an enormous quantity of them; I can't compare them to anything I ever saw in Norway. They are as big as a child's head; some are larger. They are round, and the inside is red or yellow. The melons are sweet and juicy. They are eaten just as they are taken from the field, provided they are ripe. I have cooked molasses from them, and I have also brewed juice several times. (Hops grow wild here. They are very plentiful, and we use them throughout the year.) We sometimes sell melons to wayfarers passing by. We usually get ten cents apiece for them. However, most of the melons we shared with our friends and neighbors, many of whom had walked several miles in order to get a chance to taste our watermelons and muskmelons. The latter fruit is not quite so good as the first.

Our harvest was not abundant, but since it was enough to supply our needs for the year and since it was raised on land that we call our own, I want to tell you about it.

This summer we plowed up three acres of land that we plan to sow with wheat next year. Had we known that Ole would come back, we would have plowed up more land this summer. Not knowing when he would return, we let it go with just three acres. By the time he did come home, it was too late to plow any more, so we're letting it go till next summer. So you see we haven't so many acres "under the plow" as they say, but it's not so easy to get ahead if one attempts too much.

This winter we are feeding twenty-one head of cattle, two pigs (a sow and a boar), two horses (a mare and a colt), and three sheep belonging to brother Ole. We also have two bulls belonging to brother Sevat Svendsen. We are paid cash for feeding these cattle. All told we have sixteen farm animals of our own, not counting the young cattle.

We have only four cows. The heifer will bear her first calf this winter, and then we shall have five cows if all goes well. We have only one sheep. (The lamb died this spring when it was gelded.) I have sheared the sheep twice this year. The wool, which was of excellent quality, weighed all of seven pounds.

We butchered two pigs this week, one fully grown, the other eight or nine months old. We had fattened them since last September so they were quite large.

I also want to tell you that this fall we have sold butter for thirty-five dollars—not so much, but I am satisfied for the time being.

Last fall we built a stable for twelve head of cattle. We built it of timber, and right now we are building another like it, but this one is a little larger. They are built a short distance from each other so that we can have a shed between for the bulls (about like the Sansat stable). I can't compare them to the stables in Norway, but around here they are supposed to be among the best. There are many varieties of stable to be seen here. Some are built of branches and hay; others of sod or turf. I have even seen a barn where the walls were built of layers of manure piled up one above the other.

Our house is very small and humble, but it's a shelter from the cold winter. I shall say no more about it. However, next spring, if we are all here and all is well, we hope to build a large and comfortable house. We shall build even though it costs a great deal of money to build houses in this country.

The spring of 1864 we bought twelve and a half acres of woodland for one hundred dollars, or eight dollars an acre. We borrowed the money from old Svend at seven percent interest with five years to pay. The trees are exceptionally fine, so if we should want to sell the land again, it would not be difficult to get twice the amount that we paid for it. There is not a great deal of woodland here, and therefore that type of land is much in demand and the prices are steadily rising.

Our woodland is six miles from home, a long way to haul the wood; but the road is good. The main road is just outside our door, and it runs past the very edge of the woods. The woodland is two miles from the sawmill in the village of Estherville.

We have had very little pastoral service so far, but we soon hope to get more. A certain Pastor Torgersen has taken it upon himself to visit this congregation two or three times a year. I think we have been very fortunate this fall to have had two services. Two years ago we had thirteen Norwegian families in this congregation, and now we have thirty families and more are constantly moving in. Maybe in time we may be so many that we can have our own pastor.

I have told you in part just how we live. It's so incomplete, but as I did want to tell you everything, even the merest trifle, I have included many things that I should have omitted. I hope you will not disapprove.

Now I have used up all the paper, and I still have so much more to tell you. You no doubt will have to pay extra postage for this letter. . . .

9. *1877*—MAKING A SOD HOUSE

❪ *As settlers took up land on the plains they found wood so scarce that they were forced to build their houses of sod. Howard Ruede,*

Howard Ruede, *Sod-House Days: Letters from a Kansas Homesteader, 1877–78,* John Ise, Ed. (New York: Columbia University Press, 1937), 27–29, 43.

a Kansas homesteader, describes the making of the kind of habitation that served many thousands until they could save enough money for permanent homes.

AT SNYDER'S, KILL CREEK, KANSAS
March 27, 1877

. . . This is a sod house, plastered inside. The sod wall is about 2 feet thick at the ground, and slopes off on the outside to about 14 inches at the top. The roof is composed of a ridge pole and rafters of rough split logs, on which is laid corn stalks, and on top of those are two layers of sod. The roof has a very slight pitch, for if it had more, the sod would wash off when there is a heavy rain.

Perhaps you will be interested in the way a sod house is built. Sod is the most available material, in fact, the only material the homesteader has at hand, unless he happens to be one of the fortunates who secured a creek claim with timber suitable for house logs.

Occasionally a new comer has a "bee," and the neighbors for miles around gather at his claim and put up his house in a day. Of course there is no charge for labor in such cases. The women come too, and while the men lay up the sod walls, they prepare dinner for the crowd, and have a very sociable hour at noon. A house put up in this way is very likely to settle and get out of shape, but it is seldom deserted for that reason.

The builder usually "cords up" the sods, though sometimes he crosses the layers, making the walls about two feet thick, but a little experience shows that the extra thick walls are of no real advantage. When the prairie is thoroughly soaked by rain or snow is the best time for breaking sod for building. The regulation thickness is 2½ inches, buffalo sod preferred on account of its superior toughness. The furrow slices are laid flat and as straight as a steady-walking team can be driven. These furrow slices, 12 inches wide, are cut with a sharp spade into 18-inch lengths, and carefully handled as they are laid in the wall, one length reaching across the wall, which rises rapidly even when the builders are green hands. Care must be taken to break joints and bind the corners of the house. "Seven feet to the square" is the rule, as the wall is likely to settle a good deal, especially if the sod is very wet when laid. The door and window frames are set in place first and the wall built around them. Building such a house is hard work.

When the square is reached, the crotches (forks of a tree) are set at the ends and in the middle of the house and the ridge pole—usually a single tree trunk the length of the building, but sometimes spliced—is raised to its place by sheer strength of arm, it being impossible to use any other power. Then rails are laid from the ridge log to the walls and covered with any available material—straight sorghum stalks, willow switches and straw, or anything that will prevent the sod on the roof from falling between the rafters. From the comb of the roof to the earthen floor is usually about nine feet.

The gables are finished before the roof is put on, as in roofing the layer of sod is started at the outer edge of the wall. If the builder is able, he has sawed cottonwood rafters and a pine or cottonwood board roof covered with sod. Occasionally a sod house with a shingle roof is seen, but of course this costs more money.

At first these sod houses are unplastered, and this is thought perfectly all right, but such a house is somewhat cold in the winter, as the crevices between the sods admit some cold air; so some of the houses are plastered with a kind of "native lime," made of sand and a very sticky native clay. This plaster is very good unless it happens to get wet. In a few of the houses this plaster is whitewashed, and this helps the looks very much. Some sod houses are mighty comfortable places to go into in cold weather, and it don't take much fire to keep them warm. I will have to be contented with a very modest affair for a while, but perhaps I can improve it later. . . .

April 10, 1877

. . . I made out an estimate of the cost of our house. This does not include what was paid for in work: Ridgepole and hauling (including two loads of firewood) $1.50; rafters and straw, 50¢; 2 lb. nails, 15¢; hinges 20¢; window 75¢; total cash paid, $4.05. Then there was $4 worth of lumber, which was paid for in work, and $1.50 for hauling it over, which, together with hauling the firewood, 50¢, makes $10.05 for a place to live in and firewood enough to last all summer. . . .

10.   *1893*—THE RUSH FOR THE CHEROKEE STRIP

❪ *The last part of the West to be opened for settlement was the Cherokee Strip, owned by the Cherokee Indians until 1891, when the United States government purchased it. Seth K. Humphrey describes the mad rush that took place when the Strip was opened to homesteaders on September 16, 1893.*

The Cherokee Strip—more correctly, the Cherokee Outlet—was a stretch of prairie country about sixty miles wide extending for two hundred miles along the north line of the Indian Territory. North of it was Kansas; on the south, the four-year-old Territory of Oklahoma. Its great extent and its location next to settled country drew the biggest crowd of adventurers ever gathered for the single purpose of col-

Seth K. Humphrey, *Following the Prairie Frontier* (copyright 1931, University of Minnesota), 229–57.

lecting a farm from the government. There were also a few farmers present. . . .

The rush was to be made from a line-up on both the Kansas and Oklahoma boundaries. I chose the Kansas state line, since two of my brothers, land men like myself, were living within twenty miles of the Cherokee border. At this point a railroad crossed the strip, running southward to Oklahoma and Texas. My older brother and I, being landowners and therefore ineligible as homesteaders, were making the run solely for the fun of it; and to get an extra kick out of the experience we were going in on bicycles. . . .

Days before the run matters began to look ominous. Already there were twice as many waiting boomers as waiting farms, and heaven knew what the proportion would be on the day of the rush. The idea was penetrating the deluded crowd that this was to be a race, not a prairie schooner parade to a happy new home. . . .

At last the eventful morning broke, a day exactly like all the rest, hot and dry, a south wind rising with the sun—dead ahead, and a hard proposition for bicyclists. We had stayed overnight in the little hotel of a town within a mile of the border, several of us in one room; but at least we two of the bicycle corps did not have to mix up with the jam of horses about the place. And we had another decided advantage in not having horses to look after in a hot prairie wilderness where there was not a well, scarcely a stream not gone to a dry bed, and only an occasional water tank on the one railroad running south to Texas. This water would be of service only to the comparative few who could locate near by.

Naturally there was wild eagerness to make the run next to the railroad, not only because of its water tanks in a dry country, but because farm land near it was desirable, as well as the town lots in the several sites that had been laid out near the tank stations. A boomer could take a farm or a town lot, but not both.

So at this point in the waiting line an immense number of "town siters" were added to the crowd of land-seekers. For their special accommodation a train of ten cattle cars was to be run, which was to stop for a moment at each town site. Its engine toed the starting line, along with all the rest of us, waiting, with steam up and loaded to the cow catcher with a human swarm, for the crack of the gun at twelve o'clock noon. The train was to run no faster than eight miles an hour, so as to have no advantage over the horsemen; but a flock of dollar bills fluttering around the engine warped the trainmen's judgment and they ran it at fifteen. Another fight-provoker, this, in the already hectic scrap for land. My brother and I, out for excitement, found ourselves in the right spot to get it. . . .

A quarter to twelve. The line stiffened and became more quiet with the tension of waiting. Out in front a hundred yards and twice as far apart were soldiers, resting easily on their rifles, contemplating the line. I casually wondered how they would manage to dodge the onrush; perhaps they were wondering that too. The engine, a few hundred feet away, coughed gently at the starting line; its tender and the tops of its ten cattle cars trailing back into the state of Kansas, were alive with men. Inside the cars the boomers were packed standing, their arms sticking out where horns ought to be. . . .

Five minutes. Three minutes. The soldiers now stood with rifles pointing upward, waiting for the first sound of firing to come along their line from the east. A cannon at its eastern end was to give the first signal; this the rifles were to take up and carry on as fast as sound could travel the length of the Cherokee Strip.

All set!

At one minute before twelve o'clock my brother and I, noticing that the soldier out in front was squinting upward along his rifle barrel and intent on the coming signal, slipped out fifty feet in front of the line, along the railroad embankment. It was the best possible place from which to view the start. It has been estimated that there were somewhere around one hundred thousand men in line on the Kansas border. Within the two-mile range of vision that we had from our point of vantage there were at least five thousand and probably nearly eight.

Viewed from out in front the waiting line was a breath-taking sight. We had seen it only from within the crowd or from the rear. The back of the line was ragged, incoherent; the front was even, smooth, solid. It *looked* like the line-up that it was. I thought I had sensed the immensity of the spectacle, but that one moment out in front gave me the unmatched thrill of an impending race with six thousand starters in sight.

First in the line was a solid bank of horses; some had riders, some were hitched to gigs, buckboards, carts, and wagons, but to the eye there were only the two miles of tossing heads, shiny chests, and restless front legs of horses. The medley of grotesque speed outfits, the stupendous gamble, the uniqueness of the farce and the tragedy of it— these were submerged in the acute expectancy of a horse race beyond words, incomparable.

While we stood, numb with looking, the rifles snapped and the line broke with a huge, crackling roar. That one thundering moment of horseflesh by the mile quivering in its first leap forward was a gift of the gods, and its like will never come again. The next instant we were in a crash of vehicles whizzing past us like a calamity. . . .

The funniest of all the starters was the engine with its ten carloads of men. From our stand fifty feet directly in front of it I was contemplating it as the chief absurdity of the race when the rush began. The engine tooted incessantly and labored hard, but of course she could not get under way with anything like the quickness of the horses. They left her as good as tied to her cattle train. The incongruity of starting a contrivance like that with a lot of horses and calling it a race made us laugh—not only because she waddled behind so ridiculously at the start but because we knew that the crowd aboard intended to be far ahead of the horsemen long before the finish of the race, if moral suasion or cash inducement could make the old girl cough a little faster than the rules allowed.

Of course everybody on the train was mad with excitement, particularly since they were packed in without a chance to vent their emotions in any but some noise-making way. With the first toots of the engine came revolver shots from the crowds all along the tops of the cars, and at least a few from those penned up inside. The fusillade, which kept up all the while the train was pulling out past us, had a most exhilarating effect; my old gun, I suddenly noticed, was barking with the rest of them. . . .

At six o'clock we were only twenty miles in; but that twenty miles loomed up like a day's work. Inflating and mending tires had taken a good deal of time, for we had been riding on the sharp stubble left by the fires; this hard ride over burned ground we could not have foreseen. The deflation of our own energy by the rough prairie and a head wind, too, had slowed us down to little better than a walk. Six miles ahead was Pond Creek, the first town site of any importance. We could make that in the morning, after taking in the hectic first-night events on the prairie. . . .

Very soon after sunset came darkness and with it a multitude of stars such as the heavens display only in a dry atmosphere. There was a blaze of light above, but it was pitch dark below; the brilliant starlight of an exceedingly clear air seems to have little power to illuminate the earth. But these sights did not even interest us. Dog-tired, we rolled up in our blankets, rested our heads on our bicycle wheels, and dropped off to sleep.

A little before midnight, we woke to a distant clatter of hoofs, shouting, and shooting. "Number—section—township—range—. Keep off and get off!" Then crack! crack! went the rifles, after each call, from the pretty country we had been admiring at sundown. . . .

After a hearty breakfast we pumped up our sorry tires and packed up to start south for the town sites. Ever since daybreak boomers had been straggling northward, bound for Kansas and all points east. One young fellow who stopped for a moment while we were eating breakfast was a fair sample of this crowd. He asked for water, and we gave him a biscuit, for we hadn't a drop of water left. He had staked a claim in our nice little valley, along with a half dozen others on the same tract; and of course, as in such cases all over the Strip, nobody under heaven could know who had arrived first. But for him the delicate question had been settled by the gay horsemen in the pitch darkness of the night before. By the time they were through with him he felt assured that he must have arrived about a week late.

"I wouldn't live here next to such neighbors, anyway," he told us with considerable heat. At this safe distance and in the daylight his feelings had turned to indignation, but he was still trembling a little.

We did our best to soothe him by pointing out that he had escaped several years of doubtful litigation by accepting the hint of the clean-up crowd to vacate; but there was no need to tell him, since he had lost his claim, that even if he had stayed he never would have had those men for neighbors. Farming in the Cherokee Strip was the last thing any of these gun-toters, to say nothing of the speed sports and most of the others, intended to do. True, somebody would have to live on these claims for five years as homesteaders, but not they; their plan was to get possession, file on it, then sell their relinquishments to farmers.

In the Cherokee Strip was to be repeated the history of every move into the prairie frontier: a first crop of settlers, mostly fly-by-nights, followed by a second contingent, composed largely of true farmers.

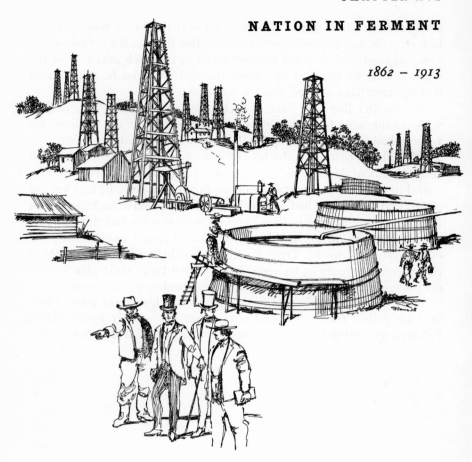

1. *1862*—ANDREW CARNEGIE DESCRIBES THE FIRST OIL BOOM

❲ *Between 1865 and 1900 the United States transformed itself from an agricultural to an industrial nation. The change had started before the Civil War with the beginnings of the factory system in New England and the construction of railroads, but it did not attain real momentum until after Appomattox.*

Peace released thousands of men for productive work on the farms and in the factories. It also stimulated demand—to replace what war had destroyed and to meet the needs of a suddenly enlarged civilian population. Factories expanded in size and number and multiplied their output by producing with machines instead of by hand. By using farm machinery and bringing new land under cultivation farmers created the surplus with which they could buy

Autobiography of Andrew Carnegie (Boston: Houghton Mifflin Co., 1924), 136–39. Published by permission of Houghton Mifflin Company.

the products of the factories. Fast-growing railroads made the ex-
change of goods and commodities quick and cheap.

The industrialization of the country depended upon three basic
factors: (1) a growing, prosperous population; (2) ingenuity and
inventiveness; and (3) natural resources. Of natural resources, none
would be more important than oil. This fundamental source of
power was discovered in western Pennsylvania in 1859. When
Andrew Carnegie, then a twenty-six-year-old railroad telegrapher,
visited the field three years later, the boom was at its height.

It was in 1862 that the great oil wells of Pennsylvania attracted attention. My friend Mr. William Coleman, whose daughter became, at a
later date, my sister-in-law, was deeply interested in the discovery, and
nothing would do but that I should take a trip with him to the oil regions. It was a most interesting excursion. There had been a rush to the
oil fields and the influx was so great that it was impossible for all to
obtain shelter. This, however, to the class of men who flocked thither,
was but a slight drawback. A few hours sufficed to knock up a shanty,
and it was surprising in how short a time they were able to surround
themselves with many of the comforts of life. They were men above
the average, men who had saved considerable sums and were able to
venture something in the search for fortune.

What surprised me was the good humor which prevailed everywhere. It was a vast picnic, full of amusing incidents. Everybody was
in high glee; fortunes were supposedly within reach; everything was
booming. On the tops of the derricks floated flags on which strange
mottoes were displayed. I remember looking down toward the river and
seeing two men working their treadles boring for oil upon the banks of
the stream, and inscribed upon their flag was "Hell or China." They
were going down, no matter how far.

The adaptability of the American was never better displayed than in
this region. Order was soon evolved out of chaos. When we visited the
place not long after we were serenaded by a brass band the players of
which were made up of the new inhabitants along the creek. It would
be safe to wager that a thousand Americans in a new land would organize themselves, establish schools, churches, newspapers, and brass
bands—in short, provide themselves with all the appliances of civilization—and go ahead developing their country before an equal number
of British would have discovered who among them was the highest in
hereditary rank and had the best claims to leadership owing to his
grandfather. There is but one rule among Americans—the tools to
those who can use them.

Today Oil Creek is a town of many thousand inhabitants, as is also
Titusville at the other end of the creek. The district which began by

furnishing a few barrels of oil every season, gathered with blankets from the surface of the creek by the Seneca Indians, has now several towns and refineries, with millions of dollars of capital. In those early days all the arrangements were of the crudest character. When the oil was obtained it was run into flat-bottomed boats which leaked badly. Water ran into the boats and the oil overflowed into the river. The creek was dammed at various places, and upon a stipulated day and hour the dams were opened and upon the flood the oil boats floated to the Allegheny River, and thence to Pittsburgh.

In this way not only the creek, but the Allegheny River, became literally covered with oil. The loss involved in transportation to Pittsburgh was estimated at fully a third of the total quantity, and before the oil boats started it is safe to say that another third was lost by leakage. The oil gathered by the Indians in the early days was bottled in Pittsburgh and sold at high prices as medicine—a dollar for a small vial. It had general reputation as a sure cure for rheumatic tendencies. As it became plentiful and cheap its virtues vanished. What fools we mortals be!

The most celebrated wells were upon the Storey farm. Upon these we obtained an option of purchase for forty thousand dollars. We bought them. Mr. Coleman, ever ready at suggestion, proposed to make a lake of oil by excavating a pool sufficient to hold a hundred thousand barrels (the waste to be made good every day by running streams of oil into it), and to hold it for the not far distant day when, as we then expected, the oil supply would cease. This was promptly acted upon, but after losing many thousands of barrels waiting for the expected day (which has not yet arrived) we abandoned the reserve. Coleman predicted that when the supply stopped, oil would bring ten dollars a barrel and therefore we would have a million dollars worth in the lake. We did not think then of Nature's storehouse below which still keeps on yielding many thousands of barrels per day without apparent exhaustion.

2. *1899*—JOHN D. ROCKEFELLER JUSTIFIES THE STANDARD
OIL COMPANY

⟪ *One of the features of the industrial transformation of the nation was the development of great corporations. Many Americans viewed huge companies with distrust. By their wealth and power such companies could and often did ruin small competitors and establish monopolies. No corporation came in for more public criticism on this ground than the Standard Oil Company, which the business*

Testimony before the Industrial Commission, in Thomas G. Manning and David M. Potter, *Government and the American Economy, 1870–Present* (New York: Henry Holt & Co., 1950), II, 91–92. .

genius of John D. Rockefeller and a few associates built from a local Cleveland refinery to an industrial giant with world-wide operations.

But there was much to be said in favor of the large corporation. Rockefeller, testifying before the Industrial Commission, a government investigating body, made a case not only for Standard Oil, but also for big business generally.

I ascribe the success of the Standard to its consistent policy to make the volume of its business large through the merits and cheapness of its products. It has spared no expense in finding, securing, and utilizing the best and cheapest methods of manufacture. It has sought for the best superintendents and workmen and paid the best wages. It has not hesitated to sacrifice old machinery and old plants for new and better ones. It has placed its manufactories at the points where they could supply markets at the least expense. It has not only sought markets for its principal products, but for all possible by-products, sparing no expense in introducing them to the public. It has not hesitated to invest millions of dollars in methods of cheapening the gathering and distribution of oils by pipe lines, special cars, tank steamers, and tank wagons. It has erected tank stations at every important railroad station to cheapen the storage and delivery of its products. It has spared no expense in forcing its products into the markets of the world among people civilized and uncivilized. It has had faith in American oil, and has brought together millions of money for the purpose of making it what it is, and holding its markets against the competition of Russia and all the many countries which are producers of oil and competitors against American oil. . . .

Much that one man can not do alone two can do together, and once admit the fact that cooperation, or, what is the same thing, combination, is necessary on a small scale, the limit depends solely upon the necessities of business. Two persons in partnership may be a sufficiently large combination for a small business, but if the business grows or can be made to grow, more persons and more capital must be taken in. The business may grow so large that a partnership ceases to be a proper instrumentality for its purposes, and then a corporation becomes a necessity. . . .

I speak from my experience in the business with which I have been intimately connected for about 40 years. Our first combination was a partnership and afterwards a corporation in Ohio. That was sufficient for a local refining business. But dependent solely upon local business we should have failed years ago. We were forced to extend our markets and to seek for export trade. This latter made the seaboard cities a necessary place of business, and we soon discovered that manufacturing for export could be more economically carried on at the seaboard, hence refineries at Brooklyn, at Bayonne, at Philadelphia, and necessary corporations in New York, New Jersey, and Pennsylvania.

We soon discovered as the business grew that the primary method of transporting oil in barrels could not last. The package often cost more than the contents, and the forests of the country were not sufficient to supply the necessary material for an extended length of time. Hence we devoted attention to other methods of transportation, adopted the pipe-line system, and found capital for pipe-line construction equal to the necessities of the business.

To operate pipe lines required franchises from the States in which they were located, and consequently corporations in those States, just as railroads running through different States, are forced to operate under separate State charters. To perfect the pipe-line system of transportation required in the neighborhood of fifty millions of capital. This could not be obtained or maintained without industrial combination. The entire oil business is dependent upon this pipe-line system. Without it every well would shut down and every foreign market would be closed to us.

The pipe-line system required other improvements, such as tank cars upon railways, and finally the tank steamer. Capital had to be furnished for them and corporations created to own and operate them.

Every step taken was necessary in the business if it was to be properly developed, and only through such successive steps and by such an industrial combination is America today enabled to utilize the bounty which its land pours forth, and to furnish the world with the best and cheapest light ever known, receiving in return therefor from foreign lands nearly $50,000,000 per year, most of which is distributed in payment of American labor.

3. *1870–1890*—THE RAILROADS OPEN THE WEST

❲ *Like other great corporations, the big railroad systems were often pictured as economic villains. Sometimes they deserved the characterization. Promoters frequently ignored the rights of stockholders, favored shippers received secret rebates, freight rates were boosted to what the traffic would bear, and legislatures were bribed more or less openly. But the coin had another side. Regardless of the misdeeds of those who controlled them, the railroads were one of the greatest constructive forces in the nation. Their influence in developing the West was effectively described by Edwin A. Pratt, an English author.*

Edwin A. Pratt, *American Railways* (London, 1903), 128–36, 165–67.

My first experience of western travel—regarding Chicago as the dividing line—was a journey from Chicago to Denver, a trip of 1083 miles, by the Rock Island system. . . . That line is, in the main, a single-track one as a matter of course. In very few parts of the west is the traffic heavy enough to warrant the laying of a second pair of rails, except at passing points and in the neighbourhood of railway stations where sidings are necessary. There is one western railway system at least which has 6000 miles of track, but only about eighty miles of double track altogether. Then the wayside railway stations in the west are still more primitive than those in the east, and in many instances their interior cubic space cannot be very much greater than that of one of the expanded freight cars that pass them by on wheels. Still one cannot say that they are not big enough for the amount of business done, such business being, as a rule, mainly the transportation of live stock. . . .

From Chicago to Omaha, on the Missouri River, and for a good stretch beyond, the line passed mainly through the corn-belt district, as it is called, and the expanse of land devoted to maize crops was a sample only, of the immense amount of territory over which the industry is carried on in this section of the United States. Here at least there seemed to be the opportunity for a good freight traffic for the railways.

But the appearance of things was very different when we reached the prairies. My acquaintance with them was made at Kanorado, . . . so called after the two States of Kansas and Colorado, the dividing line of which runs down the main street. Kanorado was the first prairie town I had visited, and I made an inventory of it. On the one side— that is, in the State of Colorado—there was an "hotel" (the most important building of all, at that moment, from my point of view), a combined post-office and store, and a store that was a store only. These were reached along some boards which represented the "side-walk." On the other side of the street—that is, in the State of Kansas—there was still another store, a dwelling-house, and some sheds. All the structures were of wood. Such was the constitution of the town, but there were some scattered houses as well visible in the "suburbs," the total population of Kanorado being at least 50. . . .

It was worth remembering, however, that many well-populated towns in the America of to-day have developed from just such primitive conditions as these. That is to say, they began with a handful of wooden dwellings and soon attracted still more people, who, as a matter of convenience, erected their houses on each side of the line. After a time a regularly laid-out town would spring up, the paths by which the inhabitants had crossed the metals would become streets, and in due course those streets would have tramways, which would themselves cross and recross the railway on the same level. . . .

The general character of a prairie railway may be judged from the fact that for a distance of some hundreds of miles the train passed through no place that was inhabited by more than a few score of people. Every ten or fifteen miles there was a cluster of houses and farms dignified with a name on the railway map, and with a diminutive building alongside the line that served the purposes of a railway station. Otherwise there was nothing but boundless prairie, stretching out as far as the eye could reach, the monotonous level of the perfectly flat plains, with their covering of snow, mingling with the misty horizon. . . . I must confess that I could not but admire the enterprise of railway pioneers who had stretched their line of rail across these immense tracts of territory mainly in the hope of tapping whatever sources of traffic might lie beyond them. A certain amount of business is, it is true, got from the prairies, for a good deal of cattle-feeding goes on, especially in the background of the district through which we passed; but it is the through traffic that is aimed at, and American railways will be built across 400, 500, or 600 miles or more of unsettled territory, from which little or no revenue can be derived, in the expectation of finding a promised land beyond. . . .

We reached Denver at last, nearly ten hours late on the journey of 1083 miles. Still, we got there. And, getting there, I understood more clearly why it is that American railways are built for stretches of many hundreds of miles across the comparatively uninhabited prairie lands. Without counting what might be further west, here was as handsome, as populous, and as prosperous a city as one could hope to find in America, outside of such really great collections of humanity as are represented by places like New York, Philadelphia, and Chicago. . . .

Denver itself was only organized as a town in 1858, and as a city it represents the growth of little more than about three decades; yet today it has a population of 150,000. . . . The railways that were built in hope years ago, anticipating the growth of the country later on, are thus at last getting their reward. . . .

Little by little the railways crossed the plains where the Navajoes, the Apaches, and the Utes had carried on their warfare against civilization, and where, as one trader, indulging in reminiscences, put it to me, "you could sometimes see nothing but one vast mass of buffaloes, without a single break." Even as late as 1870 the Indians were a source of considerable trouble on the Santa Fe Trail.

At last, in February 1879, the Atchison, Topeka, and Santa Fe crossed the Raton Pass. . . . The first train entered Las Vegas in the following July, and Albuquerque was reached in 1880. For engineering reasons the main line was made to diverge to the south of Santa Fe, to which a short branch line was constructed from Lamy. But this was a matter of detail. The fact remained that the railway had absorbed the trail, and had opened up for New Mexico an era of progress and prosperity far in excess of anything that had been achieved for her in the whole period of 275 years that had elapsed since the Spanish flag was first raised in the now United States city of Santa Fe. A land that had slumbered and slept, or had done no more than just supply her daily requirements throughout the centuries, awoke to new life. Now that a journey which once took a fortnight even by stage-coach, or seventy days by ox-team, could be made comfortably by train in a day and a night, there was a substantial migration to a district where the mineral wealth was great, where irrigation alone was needed to cause the desert to become abundantly fertile, and where the dry and clear atmosphere promised a fresh lease of life to sufferers from pulmonary complaints who could not endure the moist temperature of the eastern States. So the existing cities began to expand; brick buildings supplemented the low adobe structures,—made with sun-dried mud-blocks,—which were previously alone to be found there (at Santa Fe itself there was not a single two-storey house until the advent of the railway); mines which the Indians had filled up or closed down when, in 1680, they revolted against their Spanish taskmasters, were reopened; new industries were introduced, and valleys where hitherto silence had reigned supreme became populated and helped to enrich a country which had seemed to be lagging behind in the general progress of the United States. . . .

The Spanish conqueror may have done heroic deeds with his sword, but it was left for the humbler railway navvy,[1] working with pick and shovel, to convert New Mexico into a land of abundant promise and of practical utility to the world at large.

4.   *1885*—EDISON: A SKETCH BY HIS SECRETARY

❲ *Few men left as deep a mark on industry and society as Thomas A. Edison, who invented the phonograph, made vital improvements in the incandescent lamp, and discovered the so-called "Edison effect" which became the basis of the vacuum tube. Edison's long-time secretary, Alfred O. Tate, pictures a very human man whose real character, like his achievements, has long been clouded by myth.*

One of Edison's friends in eulogizing him after his death said that he was the last great empirical experimenter. The dictionary defines

---

From the book *Edison's Open Door: The Life Story of Thomas A. Edison,* by Alfred O. Tate. Copyright, 1938, by E. P. Dutton & Co., Inc. Reprinted by permission of the publishers.
[1] The English term for a railroad construction worker.

empirical as "depending on experience alone without due regard to science or theory," and an empirical experimenter as "one who relies on practical experience." Edison certainly at times employed methods that might be regarded as unorthodox, but it would be wrong to assume that he was not abreast of science. He not only subscribed to but read all the scientific journals. He had a thoroughly modern scientific library which constantly was augmented and which did not remain unread.

No one but himself could know to what extent he drew upon science and theory. He must have employed theory, because no forward step can be taken in experimentation unless the mind is projected ahead of it. Science may be described as "systemized knowledge." It has many branches, but in those which Edison pursued he unquestionably was familiar with all "systemized knowledge" associated with them, and demonstrated at times his ability to project it.

In the year 1875 he discovered the waves that now enter every household "through the air" to provide entertainment. They were called the "Edison Effect" or "Etheric Force," and a number of patents were issued to him covering devices designed to utilize them.

Edison was not a mathematician. He had a method of his own of solving mathematical problems. His lack of knowledge of this science never seemed to be a handicap. His mind seemed to alight on the answer in one swift flight which perhaps he himself could not explain. It has been said that Newton never could demonstrate a problem in Euclid. The answers were to him so obvious that he could not restrain his mental processes long enough to follow the steps of a demonstration. That is the way Edison's mind seemed to work. His esteem for mathematicians could not be described as extravagant. He had been subjected to the ridicule of these scientists in his earlier days when he was conducting his "empirical" experiments on the incandescent lamp. They lived to regret it.

One day I walked into a room where Edison was working at a bench. Arthur Kennelley, his mathematician, was just leaving the room and he was laughing. I went over to Edison and asked him what was the joke.

"Tate," he exclaimed impatiently, "these mathematicians make me tired. When you ask them to work out a sum they take a piece of paper, cover it with rows of A's and B's and X's and Y's, decorate them with a lot of little numbers, scatter a mess of flyspecks over them [his disrespectful synonym for decimals was much more Rabelaisian than this] and then give you an answer that's all wrong!"

. . . I recall one of Edison's empirical experiments. He wanted to find a solvent of hard rubber. Science had not discovered it. Theory was helpless. So he resorted to empiricism. He had a storeroom of scientific chemicals that was complete. He immersed in vials containing one of each of these chemicals a small section of hard rubber. I do not recall how many there were, but it was an impressive collection. Later on I asked him how the experiment had turned out. "I got it," he said, and mentioned the name of the solvent which, not being a chemist, I have forgotten, except that it was an acetate.

But I have Edison's word for it that he was not a scientist. He subscribed to a newspaper clipping bureau and when the basket containing letters to be submitted to him was put before him each morning these clippings were placed on top, as he always wanted to read them first. It was not vanity. It was curiosity.

On one of these occasions when I was sitting beside him, he passed a clipping over to me in which he was referred to as a scientist. Then he said, "That's wrong! I'm not a scientist. I'm an inventor. Faraday was a scientist. He didn't work for money. Said he hadn't time. But I do. I measure everything I do by the size of a silver dollar [silver dollars were current coin then]. If it don't come up to that standard then I know it's no good."

His meaning was clear. If his work would sell, if the public would buy and pay their silver dollars for it, then he would know that it was useful. And that was his vocation—the production of new and useful inventions. He was a utilitarian inventor, and money was the only barometer that could be employed to indicate success. But I do not concur in his disclaimer. He also was a Scientist most highly esteemed and admired by his contemporaries throughout the world.

Edison had beautiful hands, more sensitive than those of a woman. Often I have watched them hovering over an instrument to make delicate adjustments, with the rest of his body as rigid as a statue. At these times they seemed to assume an individuality of their own. Always I associated them with the strings of a harp. They seemed to belong there. But there was one thing those hands were unable to accomplish. They could not count money.

One evening we were dining together at Delmonico's to go later to the apartment of Ed Rice of the famous theatrical firm of Rice and Dixey. At that time Henry Dixey was appearing in *Adonis,* which ran for a period that broke all previous records and made Dixey the most popular stage artist in New York. Rice played some of his delightful piano compositions for us and Dixey entertained us with some of his wonderful card tricks. After dinner, when the bill was presented, Edison took a roll of notes out of his pocket, flattened it on the table, and began to pick at it. He disarranged it. Then he patted it around the edges, smoothed it out, and began to pick at it again. Then in disgust he pushed the pile across the table to me and said: "Here, Tate! You take the damn thing. Stick it in your pocket and pay our bills tonight."

The reason for this was that he never, or very seldom, carried money, and while he made large sums, little of it passed through his hands in the form of currency. At his laboratory in Orange, if he had occasion to go to New York, I had carefully to see that he was provided with money. Otherwise he would have started without any. He derived no pleasure from the expenditure of money for personal gratification. He was indifferent concerning food with the exception of pie. When intensively preoccupied with work in his laboratory his meals were sent there from his home, but invariably he would let them stand until cold and frequently I have seen him eat the pie which always formed a part of his fare and leave everything else untouched. This irregularity was the habit of a lifetime and undoubtedly was the cause of the stomach acidity which assailed him at not infrequent intervals.

But in the expenditure of money for experimentation he never stopped to count the cost. It made no difference to him what the cost might be when he had an objective in view. This factor never entered his mind. He evaluated money not as something to be conserved or accumulated but as a vehicle essential to the progress of his work. If beyond this a surplus was accumulated, he was gratified, not because it represented wealth, but because it constituted tangible evidence of the utility of his inventions.

In those early days when the Edison Electric Light Company shares were quoted at an enormous premium, and when he had relatively little money, he never sold a share. He was bitterly opposed to speculation. There was no title of reproach and contempt that he could confer on anyone more withering than that of speculator. I can hear him now annihilating someone of whose pursuits in this hazardous field he disapproved with the blasting denunciation, "Oh! he's a speculator!" And yet he staked, lost and won millions in his own field of adventure. It is the objective that reveals and establishes character in the great gamble of industrial development. Edison played a square game.

5.   *1898*—THE INFANT DAYS OF ADVERTISING

❨ *Nothing illustrates the difference between the business world of the nineteenth century and that of today more strikingly than advertising. Albert D. Lasker, generally credited with being the father of modern advertising, describes the field as he found it in 1898, when, at the age of eighteen, he went to work for the Chicago firm of Lord & Thomas.*

I presume that at the time I went to work for Lord & Thomas there were from ten to fourteen [advertising] agencies in the United States. I do not believe there were more than that, and I do not believe that the total of general advertising in the United States *through agencies*

"The Personal Reminiscences of Albert Lasker," *American Heritage, The Magazine of History,* No. 1, December, 1954, 76–77. Reprinted by permission of the Oral History Research Office, Columbia University.

was more than $15,000,000. Today [1949] any one advertising firm which does $15,000,000 is merely a moderate size firm—doing well, but nothing special.

While advertising was used somewhat, it was not known what the force was that made it effective. The general conception was that advertising was "keeping the name before the people." Advertising would pay in some cases, and it wouldn't pay in others. When I came to Lord & Thomas, their total copywriting staff consisted of one man on half time. He worked mornings for Lord & Thomas and worked afternoons for Montgomery Ward and Company. If I remember, he got $40 or $50 a week all told.

Lord & Thomas did the advertising of Armour & Company, but the total of that account wasn't very much. They did Anheuser-Busch. I presume Anheuser-Busch spent $120,000 a year, and was one of the largest advertisers in America. They handled Cascarets, which was in those days one of the four or five largest advertisers in the country. They spent $300,000, and Lord & Thomas owned a third of the Cascaret business. It was a cathartic.

They had several railroads, but the railroad accounts didn't amount to anything in cash, for it was all done on an exchange basis. They exchanged transportation to the papers for space, and they paid Lord & Thomas the commission in transportation. The papers and we in turn would *sell* the transportation to cut-rate agencies. In Chicago on Clark Street I imagine there were fifteen or twenty of these cut-rate agencies. They had signs in front giving perhaps half rate for the same tickets you would buy at the station—and for the same trains! Subsequently a law was passed forbidding any transportation being sold, save at the full rate.

I found that Lord & Thomas did a business of $800,000 the year I came with them. From that, they made $28,000. They were one of the three largest firms in the business. During all the time I was with the business, the same three firms which were the largest firms when I came, remained the largest practically all of the time—J. Walter Thompson, N. W. Ayer, Lord & Thomas. N. W. Ayer was the largest firm, and shortly after I came to Lord & Thomas, they became by *far* the largest. Ayer & Son got the first million dollar account, and here is how.

The Moore Brothers in Chicago were, I believe, the lawyers who had thought up the modern trust. They had brought several hundred local cracker factories together under the name of the National Biscuit Company. They paid these several hundred local cracker factories with stock. I *think* this was the first trust.[2]

They wanted a common trade-mark, and the idea in putting that

---

[2] Mr. Lasker was wrong. The first trust was the Standard Oil Company, formed secretly in 1879, announced publicly in 1882. And in the National Biscuit combine, the Moore brothers were the promoters rather than the lawyers.

trust together was that they could do national promotion. It was really the birth of the national promotion idea. Ayer & Son thought of the title—U-Needa-Biscuit—and had as a trade-mark (I don't know why) a boy in storm slickers. The new corporation, by combining the local appropriations for advertising of the scores of absorbed companies, could muster a national appropriation of $1,000,000. Nothing like that had ever been heard of. Before that, no advertiser had an account larger than Cascarets—which was around $300,000. The U-Needa-Biscuit appropriation gave wings to the idea of advertising.

Most of the advertising then was patent medicine advertising. It was all largely a gamble. The first few years that I was in advertising (and it had been that way for years) most bankers were very opposed to advertising as being a gambling device. Many times when a firm began advertising, their bankers sent for them and said, "Unless you quit this, we'll withdraw your credit." They could not see any *tangible* addition to their security in advertising. They looked upon it as a gamble that might take away from their security. They would loan the same people large sums of money to build plants of brick and mortar—the product of which they might not be able to sell—but there was a violent prejudice generally among bankers against firms which advertised.

In Battle Creek, Michigan, a Doctor Kellogg had worked out a diet treatment with various taboos—for instance, coffee was taboo. Out of grain, he made substitute foods. He ran a sanitarium there where people came for this diet.

One of his patients was a man named C. W. Post, who came to Battle Creek from Texas. Post partook of these substitute foods and became cured of his ailment. He therefore became convinced that this type of substitute food should be generally made known to the public—that there was a service to be rendered and a profit to be made.

Post stayed in Battle Creek after he was cured and started a small plant to make his own brands. These he called Postum and Grape Nuts. Postum was a substitute for coffee; Grape Nuts was a cereal breakfast food to be served ready cooked. Post advertised these with simulated news copy, the same as the patent medicine people used, and he was successful from the beginning.

Dr. Kellogg never forgave Post. Kellogg felt that Post was a plagiarist, but from a small beginning Post built the great institution from which later grew the General Foods Corporation. Kellogg subsequently relented as to offering his goods to the public through advertising and proceeded to manufacture for general consumption. Some years later he originated Corn Flakes.

Kellogg was successful—and Post was successful. All of a sudden, in 1902 or '03, a boom in cereal foods was born—a boom comparable to a real estate boom. People came from all over the country and started cereal food factories in Battle Creek. At one time I believe there were

24 of them. Brokerage firms sold stock in these companies all over the country.

When I went to Battle Creek for Lord & Thomas, the atmosphere was the same as in the oil towns. Food company stocks soared in price with each passing hour and of course in the end most of the money invested was lost. When it was all over, only Post and Kellogg remained. The rest disappeared.

All that I have already described about Battle Creek, the format of copy and U-Needa-Biscuit was really concurrent with my starting to work. It was on this background that I entered the advertising world.

6. *1906–1908*—HENRY FORD BUILDS THE MODEL T

❮ *Henry Ford revolutionized the automobile business—and American life—when he produced the Model T, a durable car priced so low that any workingman could hope to own one and operate it within his means. Charles E. Sorensen, Danish-born pattern-maker who joined Ford in 1904 (and rose in the ranks to the position of general superintendent), describes the birth of the best-known automobile ever produced.*

Early one morning in the winter of 1906–7, Henry Ford dropped in at the pattern department of the Piquette Avenue plant to see me. "Come with me, Charlie," he said, "I want to show you something."

I followed him to the third floor and its north end, which was not fully occupied for assembly work. He looked about and said, "Charlie, I'd like to have a room finished off right here in this space. Put up a wall with a door in big enough to run a car in and out. Get a good lock for the door, and when you're ready, we'll have Joe Galamb come up in here. We're going to start a completely new job."

The room he had in mind became the maternity ward for Model T.

It took only a few days to block off the little room . . . and to set up a few simple power tools and Joe Galamb's two blackboards. The blackboards were a good idea. They gave a king-sized drawing which, when all initial refinements had been made, could be photographed for two purposes: as a protection against patent suits attempting to prove prior claim to originality and as a substitute for blueprints. A little more than a year later Model T, the product of that cluttered little room, was announced to the world. . . .

The first steel that we were to use on experimental Model T transmission was the carbonizing type. When the gears were cut and finished they were packed into heavy cast boxes and surrounded with a carbon material, then put in furnaces and brought up to heat and held for some

Reprinted from *My Forty Years with Ford*, by Charles E. Sorensen, by permission of W. W. Norton & Company, Inc. Copyright 1956 by Charles E. Sorensen. Pages 96–97, 101–02, 109–10.

time at that temperature. We wanted to find out how deep this carbon should go into the steel. . . .

It was primarily these new types of steel that would determine what Model T would look like. Every day it became more evident that soon Mr. Ford would come up with something revolutionary.

Of course, with his mind working the way it was at that time, there was no reason why he should be involved in administration or production. The current Models N, R, and S were to be stepping stones for the future car. The funds had to be found and the sales program had to be enlarged to the point where there was large enough volume to accommodate the change. I could see a big difference in Mr. Ford after he got into Galamb's room and began development work for Model T.

He kept saying to me, "Charlie, we are on the right track here now. We're going to get a car now that we can make in great volume and get the prices way down . . . ."

Actually it took four years and more to develop Model T. Previous models were the guinea pigs, one might say, for experimentation and development of a car which anyone could afford to buy, which anyone could drive anywhere, and which almost anyone could keep in repair. . . .

I could add a great deal about problems that had to be worked out before Model T was evolved, but detailed recital of them is not important. The real importance is what came out of them.

We worked through the whole year of 1907 on these problems. By early 1908 we had built several test cars which we tried out on the roads. I did a lot of driving myself. Mr. Ford invariably went with me, and we made trips as far away as Indianapolis and northern Michigan. Most of the roads were terrible, which was one reason why we took them; a car which survived them met the acid test. There is no better comparison of highways then and now than today's elaborate proving grounds which cost the big auto companies millions of dollars to produce synthetic hazards that, back in 1908, we got for free.

By March, 1908, we were ready to announce Model T, but not to produce it. On October 1 of that year the first car was introduced to the public. From Joe Galamb's little room on the third floor had come a revolutionary vehicle. In the next eighteen years, out of Piquette Avenue, Highland Park, River Rouge, and from assembly plants all over the United States came 15,000,000 more.

7. *1913*—SORENSEN DEVISES THE MODERN ASSEMBLY LINE

❮[*Although less well known than the Model T, the complete assembly line was an equally important contribution of the Ford organiza-*

Reprinted from *My Forty Years with Ford,* by Charles E. Sorensen, by permission of W. W. Norton & Company, Inc. Copyright 1956 by Charles E. Sorensen. Pages 115–18.

tion. Here Sorensen describes his part in devising the method of production that made American industry the envy of the world.

We have seen how Model T slowly evolved. An equally slow evolution was the final assembly line, the last and most spectacular link in mass production. Both "just grew," like Topsy. But, whereas the car evolved from an idea, mass production evolved from a necessity; and it was long after it appeared that the idea and its principles were reduced to words.

Today, we do not hear so much about "mass production" as we do about "automation." Both evolve from the same principle: machine-produced interchangeable parts and orderly flow of those parts first to subassembly, then to final assembly. The chief difference is that mechanized assembly is more complete in automation; where men once tended machine tools, the job is now done electronically, with men, fewer of them, keeping watch over the electronics.

Interchangeable parts were not new in 1913. Johann Gutenberg, the first printer in the Western world to use movable type, employed that principle five hundred years ago. Eli Whitney used interchangeable parts when making rifles in the early days of the Republic; and in early days of this century Henry Leland, who later sold out to Ford, applied the same principle in the first Cadillac cars. Overhead conveyors were used in many industries, including our own. So was substitution of machine work for hand labor. Nor was orderly progress of the work anything particularly new; but it was new to us at Ford until . . . Walter Flanders showed us how to arrange our machine tools at the Mack Avenue and Piquette plants.

What was worked out at Ford was the practice of moving the work from one worker to another until it became a complete unit, then arranging the flow of these units at the right time and the right place to a moving final assembly line from which came a finished product. Regardless of earlier uses of some of these principles, the direct line of succession of mass production and its intensification into automation stems directly from what we worked out at Ford Motor Company between 1908 and 1913.

Henry Ford is generally regarded as the father of mass production. He was not. He was the sponsor of it. . . . Another misconception is that the final assembly line originated in our Highland Park plant in the summer of 1913. It was born then, but it was conceived in July of 1908 at the Piquette Avenue plant and not with Model T but during the last months of Model N production.

The middle of April, 1908, six weeks after public announcement of plans for Model T, Walter Flanders resigned. . . . Mr. Ford told Ed Martin and me to "go out and run the plant, and don't worry about titles." Ed, as plant superintendent, ran the production end. I was assistant plant superintendent and handled production development. This was a natural evolution from my patternmaking, which turned out wooden models of experimental new parts designs.

My daily routine was to arrive at the plant at 7:30 and look over the shipping department's record of the previous day's output. Any bugs in production would show up in those records. Next, I made a round of the second floor where Model N bodies were being readied for bolting to the chassis. At that time all our cars were being put together on the third floor on the east side of the building. . . . On the west side of the third floor was an elevator; all the parts were brought up and stored until needed for assembly.

As may be imagined, the job of putting the car together was a simpler one than handling the materials that had to be brought to it. Charlie Lewis, the youngest and most aggressive of our assembly foremen, and I tackled this problem. We gradually worked it out by bringing up only what we termed the fast-moving materials. The main bulky parts, like engines and axles, needed a lot of room. To give them that space, we left the smaller, more compact, light-handling material in a storage building on the northwest corner of the grounds. Then we arranged with the stock department to bring up at regular hours such divisions of material as we had marked out and packaged.

This simplification of handling cleaned things up materially. But at best, I did not like it. *It was then that the idea occurred to me that assembly would be easier, simpler, and faster if we moved the chassis along, beginning at one end of the plant with a frame and adding the axles and the wheels; then moving it past the stockroom, instead of moving the stockroom to the chassis.* I had Lewis arrange the materials on the floor so that what was needed at the start of assembly would be at that end of the building and the other parts would be along the line as we moved the chassis along. We spent every Sunday during July planning this. Then one Sunday morning, after the stock was laid out in this fashion, Lewis and I and a couple of helpers put together the first car, I'm sure, that was ever built on a moving line.

8. *1886*—GOMPERS HEADS THE AMERICAN FEDERATION OF LABOR

❲ *Well before the Civil War workingmen had seen the advantages of organizing unions to further their own interests in such fundamental matters as wages and working hours. For the most part, the early unions were local associations of men of the same craft. Efforts to organize on a national scale and to combine different*

From the book *Seventy Years of Life and Labor* by Samuel Gompers. Copyright, 1925, by E. P. Dutton & Co., Inc. Renewal, 1952, by Gertrude Cleaves Gompers. Reprinted by permission of the publishers. Pp. 268–74.

*unions in one inclusive federation met with indifferent success until
1886, when the American Federation of Labor was formed. That
the Federation lasted and prospered was due largely to Samuel
Gompers, a London-born cigarmaker who had made his own craft
union a model organization. The first years, however, taxed even
Gompers' devotion and energy.*

The Columbus meetings [in 1886] unanimously decided that a Federation should be formed and that all trade union organizations should
be eligible. . . . The convention provided for a president with a salary
of $1,000 per year and added as part of its constitution "that the president shall devote his entire time to the interests of the Federation." I
was nominated for president but I was greatly disinclined to accept any
salaried labor office and therefore declined. John McBride of the Miners
was nominated and he frankly stated that he could not afford to accept
a position to which he would have to devote his entire time upon such a
meager salary. The office fairly went begging and finally I was again
nominated and persuaded in the interest of the movement to accept the
nomination and election. . . . We authorized a Federation seal; the
payment of one hundred dollars as annual salary to the treasurer; the
publication of an official monthly journal to be sold for fifty cents per
year; the issuance of charters by the president when no protest was
involved. . . . Finally we authorized the president to hire an office boy
—and the Federation took on the form of permanence.

This was in November and the constitution was to go into effect on
March 1 of the following year, and so there was no salary paid me for
the intervening months. It was a difficult economic struggle for me to
devote my entire time for those months without receiving salary or
compensation for I had a wife and six children in addition to myself to
support. Somehow I managed through it all. My family and I just put
ourselves in the psychological position of a strike or lockout and somehow the period was tided over. . . .

The first little office, which was about ten by eight, had a door, a
small window, and a brick floor. It was cold in winter and hot in summer. The furniture was make-shift, consisting of a kitchen table brought
down from our scanty house furnishings and a box for my chair. My
second boy, Henry, who helped me when not in school, and who now
takes great pride in the fact that he was the first office boy of the Federation, helped to contrive office furnishings. My daughter, Rose, had a
child's writing desk that someone had given her. Henry took this down
to the "office," put legs under it, and nailed it to the wall under the
window. Thus equipped, with a box for a seat, Henry was busy during
the summer all day long writing wrappers for the paper and doing
many errands. He devised files for the office. Just across the street was
a grocery store, the friendly proprietor of which contributed empty

tomato boxes which Henry transformed into files. Our filing system was very simple. I personally marked each letter, circular, or pamphlet and Henry filed according to the designated subjects. As I was eager for information and had a reverence for the printed word, we soon collected a quantity of valuable information. One essential I had to buy during the first fall was a stove and pipe which cost $8.50. So I managed for a few months.

However, as soon as we had a few pennies we tried to make improvements. We invested one dollar in pine wood and cuttings out of which to construct real files. . . . We were very happy getting conveniences in the office, and when it was all done we felt very rich. It may be hard to understand how genuinely satisfied I was in feeling that I was building something constructive, something that would be helpful, although, of course, I could not foresee the results that were to come. . . . It is pathetic and tragic to look back over those struggles of the early labor movement, to remember the hardships we endured and the makeshifts that we utilized to develop the labor movement of today. . . .

Money was scarce. There was not always enough for paper and ink. Henry remembers as one of his duties as office boy, going to the school around the corner to borrow a little ink until we could get money to buy a new bottle. Sometimes there was money to pay Henry his three dollars for his week's work, sometimes there was money to pay my week's salary. But whether there was money or not, in the morning we started to work from our home on Sixty-ninth Street and Second Avenue and usually walked to work with our lunch under our arms. If we had ten cents we might ride back—if not we walked. But we did the day's work, ate our sandwich apiece at noon, and got back home when we could. More often than not, it was midnight before I got home—there were meetings, speeches to make, conferences to attend, for the cause of labor is no easy mistress to serve.

In June we had sufficient money to begin publishing the *Trade Union Advocate*. It was a busy period of the month when the paper went to press. I wrote all the copy in long hand and read all the proof. Henry wrote all the wrappers. When the issue was sent round from the printer, Henry and I worked hard at folding and getting the papers ready for the mail. Usually, a few cigarmakers volunteered to help with this work as they were in the same office and could see our difficulties. When all were ready, we loaded them into mail sacks, hired a truck, rode on the end of the truck over to the post-office, where the mail was weighed and paid for. If I had ten cents left we rode home, if I had more we had a sandwich apiece, but if I didn't have money we walked and got home in the early hours of the morning.

I often spent my own money for Federation work rather than stop work because none other was available. There was little enough for all purposes, with a family of eight to be cared for. We had no luxuries —not always the necessaries. Many a time the children had to stay home while shoes or clothes were repaired—there were no changes. When my shoes needed repairing, I wore old slippers in the office while Henry took the shoes over to the shoe shop to be mended before evening. My brother Alexander takes delight in recounting the time when I was going away to a convention, but had no clothes to wear. Finally, after arduous excitement, I succeeded in getting enough to buy a suit.

But those days of privation were not unhappy. My wife never interposed an objection to any decision I thought best. Many a night the children went to bed hungry, but I always tried to make it up to them the next morning at breakfast.

9. *1894—THE PULLMAN STRIKE: THE COMPANY'S CASE*

《 *In 1894 one of the bitterest strikes in the history of American industry closed down the works of the Pullman Palace Car Company at Pullman, on the southern outskirts of Chicago. George M. Pullman, president of the company, had made the town a model community and was sincerely interested in the welfare of his employees. He could not understand why they should be so ungrateful as to strike, even though their wages had been reduced below the subsistence level. Honest mystification runs through the statement he made to a committee of workmen two days before the men walked out.*

At the commencement of the very serious depression last year, we were employing at Pullman 5,816 men, and paying out in wages there $305,000 a month. Negotiations with intending purchasers of railway equipment that were then pending for new work were stopped by them, orders already given by others were cancelled, and we were obliged to lay off, as you are aware, a large number of men in every department, so that by November 1, 1893, there were only about 2,000 men in all departments, or about one-third of the normal number. I realized the necessity for the most strenuous exertions to procure work immediately, without which there would be great embarrassment, not only to the employees and their families at Pullman, but also to those living in the immediate vicinity, including between 700 and 800 employees who had purchased homes and to whom employment was actually necessary to enable them to complete their payments.

I canvassed the matter thoroughly with the manager of the works

Chicago *Herald*, June 26, 1894.

and instructed him to cause the men to be assured that the company would do everything in its power to meet the competition which was sure to occur because of the great number of large car manufacturers that were in the same condition, and that were exceedingly anxious to keep their men employed. I knew that if there was any work to be let, bids for it would be made upon a much lower basis than ever before.

The result of this discussion was a revision in piecework prices, which, in the absence of any information to the contrary, I supposed to be acceptable to the men under the circumstances. Under these conditions, and with lower prices upon all materials, I personally undertook the work of the lettings of cars, and by making lower bids than other manufacturers, I secured work enough to gradually increase our force from 2,000 up to about 4,200, the number employed, according to the April pay rolls, in all capacities at Pullman.

This result has not been accomplished merely by reduction in wages, but the company has borne its full share by eliminating from its estimates the use of capital and machinery, and in many cases going even below that and taking work at considerable loss, notably the 55 Long Island cars, which was the first large order of passenger cars let since the great depression and which was sought for by practically all the leading car builders in the country. My anxiety to secure that order, so as to put as many men at work as possible, was such that I put in a bid at more than $300 per car less than the actual cost to the company. The 300 stock cars built for the Northwestern road and the 250 refrigerator cars now under construction for the same company will result in a loss of at least $12 per car, and the 25 cars just built for the Lake Street elevated road show a loss of $79 per car. I mention these particulars so that you may understand what the company has done for the mutual interests and to secure for the people at Pullman and vicinity the benefit of the disbursement of the large sums of money in these and similar contracts, which can be kept up only by the procurement of new orders for cars, for, as you know, about three-fourths of the men must depend upon contract work for employment.

I can only assure you that if this company now restores the wages of the first half of 1893, as you have asked, it would be a most unfortunate thing for the men, because there is less than sixty days of contract work in sight in the shops under all orders and there is absolutely no possibility, in the present condition of affairs throughout the country, of getting any more orders for work at prices measured by the wages of May, 1893. Under such a scale the works would necessarily close down and the great majority of the employees be put in idleness, a contingency I am using my best efforts to avoid.

To further benefit the people of Pullman and vicinity we concentrated all the work that we could command at that point, by closing our

Detroit shops entirely and laying off a large number of men at our other repair shops, and gave to Pullman the repair of all cars that could be taken care of there.

Also, for the further benefit of our people at Pullman we have carried on a large system of internal improvements, having expended nearly $160,000 in internal improvements since August last in work which, under normal conditions, would have been spread over one or two years. The policy would be to continue this class of work to as great an extent as possible, provided, of course, the Pullman men show a proper appreciation of the situation by doing whatever they can to help themselves to tide over the hard times which are so seriously felt in every part of the country.

There has been some complaint made about rents. As to this I would say that the return to this company on the capital invested in the Pullman tenements for the last year and the year before was 3.82 per cent. There are hundreds of tenements in Pullman renting for from $6 to $9 per month, and the tenants are relieved from the usual expenses of exterior cleaning and the removal of garbage. . . .

10.   1894—THE PULLMAN STRIKE: THE WORKMEN'S CASE

⟦ *A statement by Pullman workmen a month after the beginning of the strike reveals differences between labor and management too deep to be settled except by a test of strength. The workmen's statement was a plea for intervention by the American Railway Union, which came to the aid of the strikers ten days later. By refusing to handle Pullman cars the railroad workers brought about a general transportation stoppage. After much rioting and property damage the strike was broken by the use of federal troops.*

MR. PRESIDENT AND BROTHERS OF THE AMERICAN RAILWAY UNION:
We struck at Pullman because we were without hope. We joined the American Railway Union because it gave us a glimmer of hope. Twenty thousand souls, men, women, and little ones, have their eyes turned toward this convention to-day, straining eagerly through dark despondency for a glimmer of the heaven-sent message you alone can give us on this earth.

In stating to this body our grievances it is hard to tell where to begin. You all must know that the proximate cause of our strike was the discharge of two members of our grievance committee the day after George M. Pullman, himself, and Thomas H. Wickes, his second vice-president, had guaranteed them absolute immunity. The more remote

United States Strike Commission, *Report and Testimony on the Chicago Strike of 1894* (Washington, 1895), 87–88.

causes are still imminent. Five reductions in wages, in work, and in conditions of employment swept through the shops at Pullman between May and December, 1893. The last was the most severe, amounting to nearly 30 per cent, and our rents had not fallen. We owed Pullman $70,000 when we struck May 11. We owe him twice as much to-day. He does not evict us for two reasons: One, the force of popular sentiment and public opinion; the other because he hopes to starve us out, to break through in the back of the American Railway Union, and to deduct from our miserable wages when we are forced to return to him the last dollar we owe him for the occupancy of his houses.

Rents all over the city in every quarter of its vast extent have fallen, in some cases to one-half. Residences, compared with which ours are hovels, can be had a few miles away at the prices we have been contributing to make a millionaire a billionaire. What we pay $15 for in Pullman is leased for $8 in Roseland; and remember that just as no man or woman of our 4,000 toilers has ever felt the friendly pressure of George M. Pullman's hand, so no man or woman of us all can ever hope to own one inch of George M. Pullman's land. Why, even the very streets are his. His ground has never been platted of record, and to-day he may debar any man who has acquired rights as his tenant from walking in his highways. . . .

Pullman, both the man and the town, is an ulcer on the body politic. He owns the houses, the schoolhouses, and churches of God in the town he gave his once humble name. The revenue he derives from these, the wages he pays out with one hand—the Pullman Palace Car Company, he takes back with the other—the Pullman Land Association. He is able by this to bid under any contract car shop in this country. His competitors in business, to meet this, must reduce the wages of their men. This gives him the excuse to reduce ours to conform to the market. His business rivals must in turn scale down; so must he. And thus the merry war—the dance of skeletons bathed in human tears— goes on. . . .

Our town is beautiful. In all these thirteen years no word of scandal has arisen against one of our women, young or old. What city of 20,000 persons can show the like? Since our strike, the arrests, which used to average four or five a day, has dwindled down to less than one a week. We are peaceable; we are orderly, and but for the kindly beneficence of kindly-hearted people in and about Chicago we would be starving. . . .

George M. Pullman, you know, has cut our wages from 30 to 70 per cent. George M. Pullman has caused to be paid in the last year the regular quarterly dividend of 2 per cent on his stock and an extra slice of 1½ per cent, making 9½ per cent on $30,000,000 of capital. George M. Pullman, you know, took three contracts on which he lost less than

$5,000. Because he loved us? No. Because it was cheaper to lose a little money in his freight car and his coach shops than to let his workingmen go, but that petty loss, more than made up by us from money we needed to clothe our little ones, was his excuse for effecting a gigantic reduction of wages in every department of his great works, of cutting men and boys and girls with equal zeal, including everyone in the repair shops of the Pullman Palace cars on which such preposterous profits have been made. . . .

11.   *1891*—SWEATSHOPS IN CHICAGO

❨ *Before the passage of laws regulating working hours and conditions industry was not always mindful of human values. One of the worst offenders was the clothing industry, where much of the work was done in sweatshops. Those of Chicago, described by the novelist and newspaperman Joseph Kirkland, had their counterparts in New York, Rochester, and all other centers of the garment trade.*

The *sweat-shop* is a place where, separate from the tailor-shop or clothing-warehouse, a "sweater" (middleman) assembles journeyman tailors and needle-women, to work under his supervision. He takes a cheap room outside the dear and crowded business centre, and within the neighborhood where the work-people live. Thus is rent saved to the employer, and time and travel to the employed. The men can and do work more hours than was possible under the centralized system, and their wives and children can help, especially when, as is often done, the garments are taken home to "finish." (Even the very young can pull out basting-threads.) This "finishing" is what remains undone after the machine has done its work, and consists in "felling" the waists and leg-ends of trousers (paid at one and one-half cents a pair), and, in short, all the "felling" necessary on any garment of any kind. For this service, at the prices paid, they cannot earn more than from twenty-five to forty cents a day, and the work is largely done by Italian, Polish, and Bohemian women and girls.

The entire number of persons employed in these vocations may be stated at 5,000 men (of whom 800 are Jews), and from 20,000 to 23,000 women and children. The wages are reckoned by piece-work and (outside the "finishing") run about as follows:

Girls, hand-sewers, earn nothing for the first month, then as unskilled workers they get $1 to $1.50 a week, $3 a week, and (as skilled workers) $6 a week. The first-named class constitutes fifty per cent

Joseph Kirkland, "Among the Poor of Chicago," *The Poor in Great Cities* (New York, 1895), 227–30.

of all, the second thirty per cent, and the last twenty per cent. In the general work, men are only employed to do button-holing and pressing, and their earnings are as follows: "Pressers," $8 to $12 a week; "under-pressers," $4 to $7. Cloak operators earn $8 to $12 a week. Four-fifths of the sewing-machines are furnished by the "sweaters" (middlemen); also needles, thread, and wax.

The "sweat-shop" day is ten hours; but many take work home to get in overtime; and occasionally the shops themselves are kept open for extra work, from which the hardest and ablest workers sometimes make from $14 to $16 a week. On the other hand, the regular work-season for cloakmaking is but seven months, and for other branches nine months, in the year. The average weekly living expenses of a man and wife, with two children, as estimated by a self-educated workman named Bisno, are as follows: Rent (three or four small rooms), $2; food, fuel, and light, $4; clothing, $2, and beer and spirits, $1. . . .

A city ordinance enacts that rooms provided for workmen shall con-tain space equal to five hundred feet of air for each person employed; but in the average "sweat-shop" only about a tenth of that quantity is to be found. In one such place there were fifteen men and women in one room, which contained also a pile of mattresses on which some of the men sleep at night. The closets were disgraceful. In an adjoining room were piles of clothing, made and unmade, on the same table with the food of the family. Two dirty little children were playing about the floor. . . .

The "sweating system" has been in operation about twelve years, during which time some firms have failed, while others have increased their production tenfold. Meantime certain "sweaters" have grown rich; two having built from their gains tenement-houses for rent to the poor workers. The wholesale clothing business of Chicago is about $20,-000,000 a year.

12.　*1900*—A SLOVAK WEDDING

❨ *Much of the heavy, hard work of the country was done by recent immigrants from Europe. After the Civil War, what had previously been a steady stream of newcomers swelled into a flood. Between 1860 and 1870 their number exceeded 5,000,000, most of whom came over in the last five years of the decade. The flood would con-tinue and even increase until the first World War.*

After 1885 the character of immigration changed radically. Where formerly the immigrants had come principally from Great Britain, Ireland, Germany, and the Scandinavian countries, now they came in the main from Italy, Russia, and the various states of

Edward A. Steiner, *On the Trail of the Immigrant* (Chicago, 1906), 207–10.

Austria-Hungary. Many Americans found the customs of the new-comers strange indeed. Edward Steiner, an Iowa college professor, describes some of the proclivities of Slovak miners whom he visited in Pennsylvania.

Although the Slovak is a quiet and peaceful citizen, on feast day he does not consider his religious nature sufficiently stirred without a fight, which is usually a crude, bungling affair, devoid of the science which accompanies such an episode among the Irish, and also without the deadly results of an Italian fracas.

On the wedding day of Yanko and Katshka, the silence of the camp is broken by the sound of a screeching violin, followed by the wailing of a clarinet and the grunting of a bass viol. Above the discord of noise made by these instruments is heard the voice of the bridegroom, who leads the dances with the song: "I am so glad I have you, I have you, and I wouldn't sell you to any one."

Usually the Slav dancers provide the notes and the bank notes also; for at the end of the piece half a dozen stalwart men will throw themselves in front of the musicians, each one of them demanding in exchange for the money tossed upon the table, his favorite tune to which he sings his native song. The result is half a dozen men, each singing or trying to sing, a different song, all of them pushing, crowding, and at last fighting, until in the middle of the room you will find an entanglement of human beings which beats itself into an unrecognizable mass. The wedding lasts three days, the ceremony often taking place after the first day's festivities. The order of proceedings and the length of the feast vary, according to imported traditions which among the Slavs are different in every district.

Of course the whole mining camp is an interested spectator and guests usually do not wait for a formal invitation. The ceremony over, the wedding dinner is served, and never in all the Carpathian Mountains was there such feasting as there is in the Alleghenies. "Polak" steak, cabbage with raisins, beets, slices of bacon, links of sausages, sweet potatoes, and, "last but not least," the great American dish, conqueror of all foreign tastes—pie; huge, luscious and full of unheard-of delicacies. Beer flows as freely as milk and honey flowed in the promised land; again the musicians play and if the bridegroom has voice enough left he will sing the song of "The sweetheart he is so glad to have and wouldn't sell to any one, no, not to any one." Barrel after barrel is emptied until the pyramids of Egypt have small rivals in those built entirely of beer barrels in the little mining town in Pennsylvania. Many of the drinkers fall asleep as soundly as Rameses ever did before he was embalmed, while others are making ready for the end of the feast—the fight, for "no fight, no feast" is the proverb. Somebody calls a Slovak a Polak, or vice versa; some young man casts glances at some young maiden otherwise engaged—and the fight is on. I have never discovered just the reason for the fight, and one might as well search for the cause of a cyclone, but the results are nearly the same: furniture, heads, and glasses all in the same condition—broken; everybody on the ground like twisted forest trees, while one hears between long black curses the peaceful snores of the unconscious drunk. The next day and the next the programme is repeated, and this is the Slovak's only diversion, unless it be a saint's day, when history repeats itself and he once more practices his two vices, drinking and fighting.

13. *1889—BIG CITY CRIME*

❡ Heavy immigration, the rapid development of industry, and the amazing growth of the cities between 1865 and 1900 produced a ferment that had many different phases. One was crime. There have always been lawbreakers, but when most people lived on the farms or in small towns there were few habitual criminals. Big cities offer criminal opportunities so numerous and so tempting that they breed a criminal class.

Jacob Riis, journalist and reformer who had come to the United States in 1870 at the age of twenty-one, writes of the gangs of New York as he knew them in the 1880's. His report shows that the juvenile gangs of today are not a new phenomenon.

The gang is an institution in New York. The police deny its existence while nursing the bruises received in nightly battles with it that tax their utmost resources. The newspapers chronicle its doings daily, with a sensational minuteness of detail that does its share toward keeping up its evil traditions and inflaming the ambition of its members to be as bad as the worst. The gang is the ripe fruit of tenement-house growth. It was born there, endowed with a heritage of instinctive hostility to restraint by a generation that sacrificed home to freedom, or left its country for its country's good. . . . New York's tough represents the essence of reaction against the old and the new oppression, nursed in the rank soil of its slums. Its gangs are made up of the American-born sons of English, Irish, and German parents. They reflect exactly the conditions of the tenements from which they sprang. Murder is as congenial to Cherry Street or to Battle Row, as quiet and order to Murray Hill. The "assimilation" of Europe's oppressed hordes, upon which our Fourth of July orators are fond of dwelling, is perfect. The product is our own.

Such is the genesis of New York's gangs. Their history is not so easily written. It would embrace the largest share of our city's criminal history for two generations back, every page of it dyed red with blood.

Jacob A. Riis, *How the Other Half Lives* (New York, 1890), 218–21, 227–29.

. . . Bravado and robbery are the real purposes of the gangs; the former prompts the attack upon the policeman, the latter that upon the citizen. Within a single week last spring, the newspapers recorded six murderous assaults on unoffending people, committed by young highwaymen in the public streets. How many more were suppressed by the police, who always do their utmost to hush up such outrages "in the interests of justice," I shall not say. There has been no lack of such occurrences since, as the records of the criminal courts show. In fact, the past summer has seen, after a period of comparative quiescence of the gangs, a reawakening to renewed turbulence of the East Side tribes, and over and over again the reserve forces of a precinct have been called out to club them into submission. It is a peculiarity of the gangs that they usually break out in spots, as it were. When the West Side is in a state of eruption, the East Side gangs "lie low," and when the toughs along the North River are nursing broken heads at home, or their revenge in Sing Sing, fresh trouble breaks out in the tenements east of Third Avenue. This result is brought about by the very efforts made by the police to put down the gangs. In spite of local feuds, there is between them a species of ruffianly Freemasonry that readily admits to full fellowship a hunted rival in the face of the common enemy. The gangs belt the city like a huge chain from the Battery to Harlem—the collective name of the "chain gang" has been given to their scattered groups in the belief that a much closer connection exists between them than commonly supposed—and the ruffian for whom the East Side has become too hot, has only to step across town and change his name, a matter usually much easier for him than to change his shirt, to find a sanctuary in which to plot fresh outrages. The more notorious he is, the warmer the welcome, and if he has "done" his man he is by common consent accorded the leadership in his new field.

From all this it might be inferred that the New York tough is a very fierce individual, of indomitable courage and naturally as blood-thirsty as a tiger. On the contrary he is an arrant coward. His instincts of ferocity are those of the wolf rather than the tiger. It is only when he hunts with the pack that he is dangerous. Then his inordinate vanity makes him forget all fear or caution in the desire to distinguish himself before his fellows, a result of his swallowing all the flash literature and penny-dreadfuls he can beg, borrow, or steal—and there is never any lack of them—and of the strongly dramatic element in his nature that is nursed by such a diet into rank and morbid growth. He is a queer bundle of contradictions at all times. Drunk and foul-mouthed, ready to cut the throat of a defenceless stranger at the toss of a cent, fresh from beating his decent mother black and blue to get money for rum, he will resent as an intolerable insult the imputation that he is "no gentleman." Fighting his battles with the coward's weapons, the brass-knuckles and the deadly sand-bag, or with brick-bats from the housetops, he is still in all seriousness a lover of fair play, and as likely as not, when his gang has downed a policeman in a battle that has cost a dozen broken heads, to be found next saving a drowning child or woman at the peril of his own life. . . . Ready wit he has at all times, and there is less meanness in his makeup than in that of the bully of the London slums; but an intense love of show and applause, that carries him to any length of bravado, which his twin-brother across the sea entirely lacks. I have a very vivid recollection of seeing one of his tribe, a robber and murderer before he was nineteen, go to the gallows unmoved, all fear of the rope overcome, as it seemed, by the secret, exultant pride of being the centre of a first-class show, shortly to be followed by that acme of tenement-life bliss, a big funeral. . . .

Inspector Byrnes is authority for the statement that throughout the city the young tough has more "ability" and "nerve" than the thief whose example he successfully emulates. He begins earlier, too. Speaking of the increase of the native element among criminal prisoners exhibited in the census returns of the last thirty years, the Rev. Fred. H. Wines says, "their youth is a very striking fact." Had he confined his observations to the police courts of New York, he might have emphasized that remark and found an explanation of the discovery that "the ratio of prisoners in cities is two and one-quarter times as great as in the country at large," a computation that takes no account of the reformatories for juvenile delinquents, or the exhibit would have been still more striking. Of the 82,200 persons arrested by the police in 1889, 10,505 were under twenty years old. The last report of the Society for the Prevention of Cruelty to Children enumerates, as "a few typical cases," eighteen "professional cracksmen," between nine and fifteen years old, who had been caught with burglars' tools, or in the act of robbery. Four of them, hardly yet in long trousers, had "held up" a wayfarer in the public street and robbed him of $73. One, aged sixteen, "was the leader of a noted gang of young robbers in Forty-ninth Street. He committed murder, for which he is now serving a term of nineteen years in State's Prison." Four of the eighteen were girls and quite as bad as the worst. In a few years they would have been living with the toughs of their choice without the ceremony of a marriage, egging them on by their pride in their lawless achievements, and fighting side by side with them in their encounters with the "cops."

14. *1902—A "BOSS" EXPLAINS THE SYSTEM*

⟨ *The kind of crime with which the police were concerned was of little consequence in comparison with corrupt politics. The great*

From *The Autobiography of Lincoln Steffens,* copyright, 1931, by Harcourt, Brace and Company, Inc. and reprinted with their permission. Vol. I, 411–14.

cities, with their thousands of immigrants unused to the ways of democracy, gave unscrupulous politicians their opportunity. Enough votes could be manipulated so that city councils could be controlled, and then the granting of franchises for public utilities and contracts for paving and other services could be made a highly profitable business. By the end of the nineteenth century city after city—New York, Philadelphia, Chicago, Cincinnati, St. Louis—had become notoriously graft-ridden.

The situation was attacked by a group of young journalists whose exposures, in books and magazines, won them the title of "muckrakers." Of these, none was better known than Lincoln Steffens, whose articles in McClure's Magazine *spurred many reform movements. In his* Autobiography *Steffens describes a frank interview with the boss of Philadelphia.*

In desperation . . . I called at the office of the boss, Israel W. Durham. His secretary shook his head. "Don't think Mr. Durham will see you; too busy." He would ask. He came out with his eyes and mouth open in surprise. "Go in," he said, and I went in, and saw a man well worth knowing. He was sitting, a slight figure, relaxed at his desk. "Not well," I thought. Only his eyes were quick; they were kind, inquiring. He did not rise. As I halted on his threshold, he nodded a smiling welcome.

"Close the door," he said quietly. "I want to ask you a couple of questions."

"Oh, no, you don't," I protested. "I came to this town for information, and everybody is asking me questions, like you. I draw the line. You've got to answer me first."

He smiled. "All right," he said. "Your turn first, then mine. What do you want to know?"

There had been a burst, a volcanic eruption, of "steals" and "jobs," all in the administration of Mayor Ashbridge. I asked Durham how they dared do such a wild, wholesale business in such a short time. He did not mind the assumption, in my question, that the franchise grants were steals and that he knew it. He waited a moment; then asked me quietly if I meant to quote him.

No, I said. I was really puzzled and wanted only to understand the politics of the Ashbridge administration; technically it looked like bad politics, "bad bad politics," I remember saying. He shook his head slowly, thoughtfully, no.

"In the first place," he said, "Ashbridge wished it so. He wanted but one term in office, and having no further ambition, he wanted to crowd as much business as we would let him into that one term. And we—we talked it all over. With the mayor known to be for one term only we would have to stay here and take the permanent blame. The responsibility fell upon me. But we reasoned—"

"Well," I urged, when he halted there, "you could put over one of those steals in New York or anywhere else, but one would be enough to strain any machine I know of. And five or—more!" He smiled.

"We reasoned," he resumed, "we agreed among ourselves that it was exactly the five or—more that would save us."

He let me express my bewilderment; then he cleared it as by a lightning flash.

"If we did any of these things alone the papers and the public would concentrate on it, get the facts, and fight. But we reasoned that if we poured them all out fast and furious, one, two, three—one after the other—the papers couldn't handle them all and the public would be stunned and—give up. Too much."

We sat there, he amused, I as stunned as his public.

"Well, you Pennsylvania politicians know something even Tammany doesn't know."

He nodded. "Yes," he said. "We know a lot they don't know. We know that public despair is possible and that that is good politics."

So that was why my hotel host, and the reformers, and the professors at the university, and the good citizens generally, said there was nothing to be done.

"Yes," Iz Durham answered. "The Bullitt Charter was a great thing for us. It was the best, last throw of the reformers, and when we took that charter and went right on with our business, we took the heart out of our reform forever."

"Then," I summed it up, "then Philadelphia is a city where reform is over."

He nodded, watching me humorously, while I went on theorizing out loud. . . .

"If this process goes on," I said, "then this American republic of ours will be a government that represents the organized evils of a privileged class."

. . . He protested. "But I had some questions to ask you," he said, "and you promised to answer mine if I answered yours."

"Sure, I did. What's your question?"

"In your articles on St. Louis," he began, "you said that the boss there, Ed Butler, governed the city with a minority of both parties. Here we have to have a majority of both parties. How does Butler do it his way?"

I explained in general that by controlling the shifting, the purchasable, and the organized voters, he could influence the nominations of both parties and then, at the polls, either all of one party or the best crooks from both tickets. That did not satisfy Durham. He saw that, but he wanted to know how it was worked out in detail, in the wards, for example, and then in the conventions and Legislature. I became enthusiastic. I had been interested in those details myself and had inquired into them; I had not written the results, and no one else had ever asked for them. To Durham, a politician, they were fascinating, and forgetting his use for them, I talked on like an enthusiast to a willing listener, as one artist to another. And I satisfied him on two points.

"Yes," he said thoughtfully when I had finished my exposition of the technique of grafting politics with a minority of each party. "Yes," he reflected again. "That's all right. That would work, I can see. And" —slapping his knee, he exclaimed—"it's cheap, too, cheaper than our way."

And, then, as he moved with me to the door, he said quite seriously, "I think that I get you now."

The sudden personal turn stalled me. "What do you mean, get me?"

"Well," he said, "we've been looking you over since you came to town, reading your other stuff and wondering how you, a reformer, get on to the game the way you do; you know the way it's done."

"Yes?" I said. "And what is the explanation you say you've got?"

"Oh, I can see that you are a born crook that's gone straight."

CHAPTER XVII

ENJOYING LIFE—AND LEARNING

1865 – 1906

1.   *1890–1900*—NEW YORK IN THE GOLDEN NINETIES

❰ *The industrial development of the nation between 1865 and 1900 brought wealth and a certain amount of leisure to many Americans. In increasing numbers they began to spend at least some time in enjoying themselves. Sport in one form or another became popular. Even in cramped cities thousands could zip along on the "safety" bicycle, perfected in 1888, and enjoy the sights and the summer breezes in open trolley cars. A New Yorker, Henry Collins Brown, describes these and other pleasures of his youth.*

It was the advent of the Bicycle that created the present enormous

Henry Collins Brown, *In the Golden Nineties* (Hastings-on-Hudson, N. Y., 1928), 52–53, 57–58, 65–66.

vogue for athletics amongst women. Of course, there had previously been some ladylike tennis and croquet playing, skating and archery on the distaff side, but it was only by a small minority, in a spirit of high adventure, or as an excuse to wear some jaunty, if tight fitting, sporting costumes. The real beginning of swimming the Channel for mommer, popper, the babies on our block, and the Star Spangled Banner; of tennis quarrels, and similar amenities of feminine sport, is found in the great bicycle craze of the Nineties, which put the world awheel. "Daisy Bell" and her bicycle built for two, was the lyric expression of this furore. Bicycles were at first constructed for skirted females. Then some intrepid women revived the bloomer, which had caused so much laughter and indignation way back in the Fifties, and rode men's bikes in them. Society took up the fad, and organized the Michaux Club on Broadway near 53rd Street, then still an equine neighborhood. Pictures of society belles in fetching bicycle costumes, including the popular Tyrolean hat, appeared in the Sunday papers, and of course, what Society favored, who could resist? It took only a few months for the fad to make a conquest of the entire population. . . .

Another mode of transit, supplementing the pioneer work of the bicycle in carrying people afield, was the trolley. This newly-invented vehicle had by this time about wholly superseded the old, slow-moving horse car. The greater speed of this new transportation system made it a popular vehicle, especially in those remote sections of Greater (?) New York where lamps were still lighted only in the dark of the moon.

The power that furnished the transit also furnished the light. The small incandescent lamp was perfected by this time and the cheerful brightness of the trolley car at night soon suggested its use for a novel purpose—neighborhood outings. For a trifling expense a car could be illuminated from one end to the other in a perfect blaze of multi-colored lights, producing at once a carnival spirit that was quite irresistible. Many of the companies bedecked these cars at their own expense and found the added patronage adequately justified the cost. In these outlying districts, especially in Brooklyn and the small towns around the city, these trolley parties became quite the fad and all through the summer this delightful pastime was vastly popular and entertained whole communities.

In the city itself this same attraction made itself felt, and encouraged a new class of passengers known as "pleasure riders," who paid their nickels merely for the sake of the ride and the cooling breezes incidental thereto. This had hitherto been the monopoly of the poorer East Side classes. Particularly on Broadway did it flourish, the cars then running without change from Harlem to the Battery. The noisy family parties of the Third Avenue line found an antithesis in the more sedate, and also more varied types, of the Broadway line. Down Columbus

409

Avenue, curving into the "White Light" district, then into the semi-gloom below Madison Square, and the deserted wholesale and financial quarters the car sped. After a pleasant hour or less it finally disgorged its cooled and gratified passengers into the still delightful precincts of Battery Park, with its view of the bay and the twinkling lights of the moving craft on its dark and romantic waters. . . .

It was not until the early nineties that the hansom appeared on our streets in any numbers. Its four-wheeled predecessor in the cab ranks was generally termed a "coupe." The New Yorker of that day was not a cab-riding biped. Except on those rare occasions when for some particular reason he desired to create an impression, the street cars served his purpose quite adequately and cheaply. . . .

The coming of the hansom gave a considerable impetus to cab riding here. There was an old maxim among cab patrons—"Never ride in a cab with two men on the box." This harmless observation carried a world of meaning to the initiated; numerous robberies occurred when the warning was disregarded. The lure of driving has always held an irresistible appeal to ex-convicts, ticket of leave men, robbers, etc. Perhaps it is the temporary contact with genteel life that fascinates them. At all events not only in the Nineties but even in our own day this same attraction persists, and the taxi cab bandit is only the legitimate successor of the two men on the box of which we speak.

The hansom had only room for two passengers, and its open front made it very pleasant for sightseeing. It was also much handier to navigate than the old four-wheeler. Ladies, in particular, liked the hansom to see and be seen, and it soon became the most popular form of *de luxe* transit. In fact, the first taxicabs on our streets were built on the hansom pattern.

New York's first "rubber-neck" wagon was the old Fifth Avenue stage which rumbled over the granite stones of that renowned thoroughfare drawn by a pair of dejected steeds that often excited the commiseration of the S.P.C.A. and were the occasion of their official interference. The original stages had not outside accommodation for passengers. In fact, business on the line was not very brisk as it ran parallel with the Madison Avenue cars and public preference for the smooth rails instead of the jolting stones was pronounced. But the strangers and the sightseers all wanted to see the outside of the millionaires' mansions along the 'bus line. The company issued little booklets containing a directory of these fabled domiciles which were faithfully consulted by the passengers interested. The tendency to this form of "rubber necking" became so pronounced that the company installed seats on the roofs of its vehicles and, to the great relief of the general public, also improved their horse power. Business picked up wonderfully, and thus began the present admirable system in vogue.

2. *1875–1900*—ALBERT G. SPALDING RECOUNTS BASEBALL HISTORY

❨ *Baseball, in the general form that we know it, was played as early as 1845, but the game did not achieve real popularity until after the Civil War. One of the first great players was Albert G. Spalding. As a pitcher (for the Forest City team of Rockford, Illinois, and for the National League clubs of Boston and Chicago), as a manager, and as the founder of a great sporting goods house, Spalding devoted his life to the game. In his time he saw many changes.*

The first glove I ever saw on the hand of a ball player in a game was worn by Charles C. Waite, in Boston, in 1875. He had come from New Haven and was playing at first base. The glove worn by him was of flesh color, with a large, round opening in the back. Now, I had for a good while felt the need of some sort of hand protection for myself. In those days clubs did not carry an extra carload of pitchers, as now. For several years I had pitched in every game played by the Boston team, and had developed severe bruises on the inside of my left hand. When it is recalled that every ball pitched had to be returned, and that every swift one coming my way, from infielders, outfielders or hot from the bat, must be caught or stopped, some idea may be gained of the punishment received.

Therefore, I asked Waite about his glove. He confessed that he was a bit ashamed to wear it, but had it on to save his hand. He also admitted that he had chosen a color as inconspicuous as possible, because he didn't care to attract attention. He added that the opening on the back was for purpose of ventilation.

Meanwhile my own hand continued to take its medicine with utmost regularity, occasionally being bored with a warm twister that hurt excruciatingly. Still, it was not until 1877 that I overcame my scruples against joining the "kid-glove aristocracy" by donning a glove. When I did at last decide to do so, I did not select a flesh-colored glove, but got a black one, and cut out as much of the back as possible to let the air in.

Happily, in my case, the presence of a glove did not call out the ridicule that had greeted Waite. I had been playing so long and had become so well known that the innovation seemed rather to evoke sympathy than hilarity. I found that the glove, thin as it was, helped considerably, and inserted one pad after another until a good deal of relief was afforded. If anyone wore a padded glove before this date I do not know it. The "pillow mitt" was a later innovation.

Albert G. Spalding, *America's National Game* (1911), 475–81.

About this time, 1875–76, James Tyng, catcher for the Harvard Base Ball Club, appeared on the Boston grounds one day, and, stepping to his position, donned the first wire mask I had ever seen. This mask had been invented and patented by Mr. Fred W. Thayer, a Harvard player. . . . Like other protective innovations at that stage of the game, it was not at first well received by professionals. Our catcher, James White, was urged to try it, and after some coaxing consented. I pitched him a few balls, some of which he missed, and finally, becoming disgusted at being unable to see the ball readily, he tore off the mask and, hurling it toward the bench, went on without it.

This wire mask, with certain modifications, is the same that has been used by catchers ever since. . . .

To Roger Bresnahan, manager of the St. Louis Nationals, belongs the credit of the recent introduction of shinguards for the catcher.

When sliding, as an aid to the base runner, began, I am not prepared to state with authority. I do know, however, that its introduction was not by "King" Kelly, as has sometimes been claimed. As early as 1866 (Kelly began to play as a lad in 1873), at a game at Rochelle, Illinois, Robert Addy startled the players of the Forest Citys by a diving slide for second base. None of us had ever witnessed the play before, though it may have been in vogue. Certainly we were quite nonplussed, and just as surely the slogan, "Slide, Kelly, slide," had not been heard at that time.

All the varied modifications of the slide have been well known for many years, and, but for the fact that different players adopt different methods of "getting there," not many changes have been introduced, some reaching the bases "head-on," others feet foremost, still others sliding sideways, and a few by a low dodge and grab of the sack with one hand.

The bunt sacrifice hit is a comparatively recent introduction to the game. Years before it was thought of much attention had been given to placing hits in exposed portions of the field, and some batsmen had gained considerable proficiency in the science. Others made a specialty of the long, high drive, in the hope of a muff or of aiding base runners to advance after the ball had been caught, with only one man out. But to stop the ball at close infield, with the expectation of giving advantage to base runners, and with the forlorn chance of beating the ball to first, was not adopted systematically as a feature of the game until much later. I regret that I am not able to give the name of the player who introduced this very important innovation or the time of its first presentation.

As a matter of fact, from the time of the adoption of regular playing rules by the old Knickerbockers, changes in the technique of Base Ball have been remarkably few in number as compared with the great advances in skill and science of play. The ball has been recently improved, but is still of practically the same size and weight. Bats are substantially of the same form and material as at the beginning of professional Base Ball. The masks and gloves and mitts have been somewhat bettered in material and workmanship, and uniforms and shoes are better; but the same general quality of fabric and fashion are yet employed in their making.

3. *1884*—FOOTBALL IN THE DARK AGES

⟪ *Football, like baseball, has a long history, though it was not played under rules like those now in effect until 1869, when Rutgers defeated Princeton in the first intercollegiate game. After that contest the sport was taken up by many colleges, particularly in the East. For many years, however, it remained an informal kind of athletic activity, without the professional coaches, expensive equipment, and strenuous promotion it enjoys today. Amos Alonzo Stagg, whose coaching career covered more than fifty years, describes the game as it was played when he was an undergraduate at Yale.*

I arrived at Yale in September, 1884, and turned out for the squad. The college bought its first athletic field that year, the one hundred and eighty-third of its history. Being situated in the heart of New Haven, it had to go far out to the farther bank of the West River to find sufficient cheap vacant land. Paying good money for a playground caused talk and revived faculty criticism of the attention being given to athletics. Prof. E. L. Richards, who promoted the present Yale gym, dug into the records on his own initiative, proved that disciplinary cases had decreased sharply and progressively since 1875, and silenced the conservatives.

The old gym was a primitive thing where freshmen were marshaled in street dress and forced to swing Indian clubs and dumbbells. No bath followed and the drill probably did as much harm as good. One of the joys of growing to sophomore stature was escaping the gym. Informal football and baseball practice customarily was held on the gym lot, where Harkness Dormitory now stands. Conditions at Yale were representative of the larger colleges.

There were no coaches, trainers, rubbers, or even a water boy. Occasional graduated players were drifting back to advise the football team, but the captain still was a captain, not a coach's foreman. He chose the team, ran it, and was not always above playing favorites. Once elected, he was answerable to no one. . . . Once under Camp's captaincy the Yale squad came near dissolving in mid-season over a

Amos Alonzo Stagg and Wesley Winans Stout, *Touchdown!* (New York, 1927), 73-75.

quarrel between the forwards and the backs. Camp and his fellow backs favored the newer running mass style of play. The rush line was unanimous naturally for the old open, kicking, passing, individual running game in which they could be as spectacular as the backs.

Camp was particularly fearful of a muddy field for the Thanksgiving Day game with Princeton, with Eaton and Fred Remington, heavy ends, and insisted on drilling the line in mass formations. The line revolted. That night Camp summoned the squad to his room in Durfee Hall, told them that the responsibility was his, that he either would run the team or get off, resigned and left the room. Ten minutes of heated debate followed. The rush line was as little convinced as ever, but so disturbed at the threatened loss of Camp's leadership that they coaxed him back. Camp led the eleven against Princeton and won, but Yale played the old open game.

Camp resigned another time. There were no training rules or training table, but the squad had pledged themselves not to leave the campus for ten days before the Princeton game, and to be in bed by eleven each night. Catching Johnny Moorehead sneaking back from the theater one night late, Camp called every man out of bed and quit on the spot. Moorehead offered his own resignation instead, and Camp reconsidered. As Moorehead played in the Princeton game, he seems to have been restored to grace.

At Princeton as early as 1879 the students had so criticized the football squad for smoking that the players gradually gave up tobacco during the season. In those years at Princeton the team customarily practiced at noon and jogtrotted half a mile to a mile at sundown. A full three-quarters-of-an-hour period of continuous playing against the scrubs was Yale's daily practice, and injuries were disregarded. There was no freshman rule, but no particular attempt was made to interest the incoming class. Two or three dependable substitutes were all that a team thought of needing. The freshman who made the varsity was either a natural player or had played in prep school. The bulk of the newcomers never had seen the game. If they turned out, they were expected to teach themselves.

4. *1892*—CORBETT KNOCKS OUT SULLIVAN

⟦ *One of the most colorful figures in the history of American sport was John L. Sullivan, heavyweight boxer who defeated all challengers from 1877, when he first entered the ring, until 1892, when he was knocked out by James J. Corbett in a match at New Orleans. Corbett, a highly literate man, tells his own story of the fight.*

James J. Corbett, *The Roar of the Crowd* (Garden City, N.Y., 1926), 197–201. Reprinted by permission of Mrs. James J. Corbett, Flushing, N.Y.

"Time" was called, and the first round was on.

Now, I knew that the most dangerous thing I could do was to let Sullivan work me into a corner when I was a little tired or dazed, so I made up my mind that I would let him do this while I was still fresh. Then I could find out what he intended doing when he got me there. In a fight, you know, when a man has you where he wants you, he is going to deliver the best goods he has.

From the beginning of the round Sullivan was aggressive—wanted to eat me up right away. He came straight for me and I backed and backed, finally into a corner. While I was there I observed him setting himself for a right-hand swing, first slapping himself on the thigh with his left hand—sort of a trick to balance himself for a terrific swing with his right. But before he let the blow go, just at the right instant, I sidestepped out of the corner and was back in the middle of the ring again, Sullivan hot after me.

I allowed him to back me into all four corners, and he thought he was engineering all this, that it was his own work that was cornering me. But I had learned what I wanted to know—just where to put my head to escape his blow if he should get me cornered and perhaps dazed. He had shown his hand to me.

In the second round he was still backing me around the ring. I hadn't even struck at him yet, and the audience on my right hissed me for running away and began to call me "Sprinter." Now I could see at a glance that Sullivan was not quite near enough to hit me, so suddenly I turned my side to him, waved both hands to the audience and called out, "Wait a while! You'll see a fight."

. . . At the end of the round I went to my corner and said to Brady and Delaney, "Why I can whip this fellow slugging!"

At this there was a panic in my corner, all of them starting to whine and pleading with me.

"You said you were going to take your time," they said. "What are you going to take any chances for?"

"All right," I replied, to comfort them, "But I'll take one good punch at him this round, anyway."

So far Sullivan hadn't reached me with anything but glancing blows, and it was my intention, when the third round started, to hit him my first punch, and I felt that it *must* be a good one! If my first punch didn't hurt him, he was going to lose all respect for my hitting ability.

So, with mind thoroughly made up, I allowed him to back me once more into a corner. But although this time I didn't intend to slip out, by my actions I indicated that I was going to, just as I had before. As we stood there, fiddling, he crowding almost on top of me, I glanced, as I had always done before, first to the left, then to the right, as if looking for some way to get out of this corner. He, following my eye

415

and thinking I wanted to make a getaway, determined that he wouldn't let me out this time!

For once he failed to slap himself on the thigh with his left hand, but he had his right hand all ready for the swing as he was gradually crawling up on me. Then, just as he finally set himself to let go a vicious right I beat him to it and loosed a left-hand for his face with all the power I had behind it. His head went back and I followed it up with a couple of other punches and slugged him back over the ring and into his corner. When the round was over his nose was broken.

At once there was pandemonium in the audience! All over the house, men stood on their chairs, coats off, swinging them in the air. You could have heard the yells clear to the Mississippi River!

But the uproar only made Sullivan the more determined. He came out of his corner in the fourth like a roaring lion, with an uglier scowl than ever, and bleeding considerably at the nose. I felt sure now that I would beat him, so made up my mind that, though it would take a little longer, I would play safe.

From that time on I started doing things the audience were seeing for the first time, judging from the way they talked about the fight afterwards. I would work a left-hand on the nose, then a hook into the stomach, a hook up on the jaw again, a great variety of blows, in fact; using all the time such quick side-stepping and footwork that the audience seemed to be delighted and a little bewildered, as was also Mr. Sullivan. That is, bewildered, for I don't think he was delighted.

In the twelfth round we clinched, and, with the referee's order, "Break away," I dropped my arms, when Sullivan let go a terrific right-hand swing from which I just barely got away; as it was it just grazed the top of my head. Some in the audience began to shout "foul!" but I smiled and shook my head, to tell them, "I don't want it that way."

So the next eight rounds continued much in the fashion of toreador and the bull, Sullivan making his mad rushes and flailing away with his arms; rarely landing on me, but as determined as ever. Meanwhile I was using all the tricks in my boxing repertoire, which was an entirely new one for that day and an assortment that impressed the audience. Then I noticed that he was beginning to puff and was slowing down a little.

When we came up for the twenty-first round it looked as if the fight would last ten or fifteen rounds longer. Right away I went up to him, feinted with my left and hit him with a left-hand hook alongside the jaw pretty hard, and I saw his eyes roll. . . . Summoning all the reserve force I had left I let my guns go, right and left, with all the dynamite Nature had given me, and Sullivan stood dazed and rocking. So I set myself for an instant, put just a little more in a right and hit him alongside the jaw. And he fell helpless on the ground, on his stomach, and rolled over on his back! The referee, his seconds, and mine picked him up and put him in his corner; and the audience went wild.

5. 1895—FRANK DURYEA WINS THE FIRST AMERICAN AUTOMOBILE RACE

⟨ *Automobile racing in the United States began at Chicago on Thanksgiving Day, 1895, only three years after Frank and Charles Duryea had produced the first American-made car. It was appropriate that Frank Duryea, who tells his own story, should have been the first of the two drivers to cover the fifty-mile course. His time: ten hours and twenty-three minutes.*

I now started with draughtsmen on plans for a new car, of which I had, from time to time, been making rough sketches during the past summer. But my work was interrupted by the necessity of preparing the old car for the race promoted by H. H. Kohlsaat of the *Chicago Times-Herald*. This race was set for November 2, and as driver, the Company sent me out to Chicago with the car on that date. Only the Mueller Benz and the Duryea cars were ready to start, so the race was postponed to Thanksgiving Day, November 28, 1895. . . .

Thanksgiving Day, when it arrived, found me again in Chicago with the car. . . .

A heavy snow had fallen during the night and we experienced hard going as we drove out to Jackson Park from our quarters on Sixteenth Street.

Of nearly a hundred entries, only six cars lined up for the start. Of these six, two were electric vehicles entered by Morris and Salom of Philadelphia, and Sturgis of Chicago. Of the four gasoline-engined vehicles, H. Mueller & Co. of Decatur, Illinois, R. H. Macy & Co. of New York, and The De la Vergne Refrigerating Machine Co. of New York, each came to the start with an imported German Benz. The Duryea Motor Wagon Company's entry was the only American-made gasoline car to start.

The word "go" was given at 8:55, and the Duryea was the first car away.

With me as umpire was Mr. Arthur W. White. The machine made good going of the soft unpacked snow in Jackson Park, but when we came to the busier part of the city, the street surface consisted of ruts and ice hummocks, in which the car slewed badly from side to side.

While still in the lead, the left front wheel struck a bad rut at such

---

J. Frank Duryea, *America's First Automobile* (Springfield, Mass.: Donald M. Macaulay, 1942), 20–23.

an angle that the steering arm was broken off. This arm had been threaded and screwed firmly to a shoulder, and it was a problem to extract the broken-off threaded part of the arm. When this was finally accomplished, we, fortunately, located a blacksmith shop where we forged down, threaded and replaced the arm.

While thus delayed, the Macy Benz passed us and held the lead as far as Evanston, where we regained it.

Having made the turn at Evanston, elated at being in the lead again, we started on the home trip.

We had not yet come to Humboldt Park when one of the two cylinders ceased firing. . . .

This repair was completed in fifty-five minutes and we got going, feeling that the Macy Benz must surely be ahead of us, but learned later that the Macy did not get that far. Breaking the way through the snow in Humboldt and Garfield Parks furnished heavy work for the motor, but also indicated that all competitors were behind us.

After a stop for gasoline, and a four-minute wait for a passing train at a railroad crossing, we continued on to the finish in Jackson Park, arriving at 7:18 P.M.

The motor had at all times shown ample power, and at no time were we compelled to get out and push.

After receiving congratulations from the small group still remaining at the finish line, among whom were the Duryea Motor Wagon Company party, I turned the car and drove back to its quarters on Sixteenth Street.

The Mueller Benz, the only other machine to finish, was driven across the line at 8:53 by the umpire, Mr. Charles B. King, Mr. Mueller having collapsed from fatigue.

6. *1875–1900*—WALTER DAMROSCH REVEALS THE RIVALRY
OF MUSICIANS

⟨ *Money and leisure led to the enjoyment of the arts as well as sports. The American audience was swelled, moreover, by immigrants from European countries with long musical traditions. From Europe, too, came nearly all the musicians heard in American concert halls. For those who became permanent residents, the way to a successful career was not always smooth. Walter Damrosch, himself a conductor of note, describes some of the difficulties which his father, Leopold Damrosch, encountered.*

In 1873 Anton Rubinstein, greatest of Russian pianists, accompanied

Walter Damrosch, *My Musical Life* (New York: Charles Scribner's Sons, 1923), 22–26. Reprinted by permission.

by the violinist, Wieniawski, came to America by invitation of Steinway and Sons. He dined at our house and expressed wonder that my father had not yet been able to achieve a position in New York commensurate with his reputation and capacity. My father explained to him how difficult the situation was and that the entire orchestral field was monopolized by Theodore Thomas. He told Rubinstein that when he had first arrived in New York he had met Thomas at the music store of Edward Schubert in Union Square and that after the introduction Thomas had said to him:

"I hear, Doctor Damrosch, that you are a very fine musician, but I want to tell you one thing: whoever crosses my path I crush."

Thomas at that time really believed that America was not large enough to contain more than one orchestra, but he lived long enough to see my father surpass him at the head of a symphony orchestra, as founder of the first great musical festival in New York and, above all, of opera in German at the Metropolitan.

In 1881 the first symphony orchestra on a permanent basis had been founded in Boston by Colonel Higginson, and before Thomas's death there were half a dozen great subsidized orchestras actively operating in the United States, a number which has since then increased to twelve.

Rubinstein said to my father: "Why don't you begin by founding an oratorio society, and that will lead to other things?"

My father consulted a few devoted friends, and the Oratorio Society of New York was accordingly founded in 1873 and began rehearsals in the Trinity Chapel with a chorus of about eighteen singers, my mother's glorious voice leading the sopranos and my very humble and little self among the altos. The first performance took place in the warerooms of the Knabe Piano Company the following winter, at which time the chorus had increased to sixty singers. The programme was a remarkable one for that period, containing a capella chorus and accompanied choruses by Bach, Mozart, Handel, Palestrina, and Mendelssohn.

From this small beginning the society developed until it became the foremost representative of choral music in New York. . . .

Indirectly, but logically, the founding of the Oratorio Society led to the founding of the Symphony Society of New York in 1877, which at last gave my father an orchestra with which he could demonstrate his abilities as a symphonic conductor.

The differences between him and Thomas were very marked. Thomas, who had educated himself entirely in America, had always striven for great cleanliness of execution, a metronomical accuracy and rigidity of tempo, and a strict and literal (and therefore rather mechanical) observance of the signs put down by the composers. America owed him a great debt of gratitude for the high quality of his programmes. My father had been educated in a more modern school of interpretation, and his readings were emotionally more intense. . . .

Both conductors had their violent partisans, and, as they were at that time literally the only orchestral conductors in America, feeling ran very high. My father was the last comer, and Thomas was well fortified in the field, with a group of wealthy men to support him. The first years for my father were very hard and a portion of the New York papers assailed him bitterly, continuously, and with vindictive enmity. Again and again dreams of murder would fill my boyish heart when I would read one of these attacks in the morning paper.

It was hard work to keep the two societies going and to enable them to meet the bills for hall rent, soloists, and orchestra. There was as yet but a small public for the higher forms of music, and again and again it looked as if further efforts would have to be abandoned. But my father persevered and struggled on, making a living for his family by teaching violin, composition, and singing, and occasionally getting a fee of "a hundred dollars in gold" as violin soloist or in a chamber-music concert, officiating as musical director in a church and as conductor of the German male choral society, the Arion. . . .

Orchestral conditions were bad compared with to-day. There was no such thing as a "permanent orchestra." The musicians of the Symphony Society, for instance, played in six symphony concerts during the winter, each preceded by a public rehearsal. They also officiated at four concerts of the Oratorio Society, and this was almost the extent of their efforts in that direction. The rest of the time they made their living by teaching, playing in theatres, at dances, and some of them even at political or military processions and mass meetings. If a better "job" came along than the symphony concert they would simply send my father a substitute. Small wonder that occasionally their lips gave out and the first horn or trumpet would break on an important note during a symphony concert. And yet, in spite of this disheartening condition, my father succeeded in infusing the orchestral players with such emotional intensity, and in imparting so lofty an interpretation to them, that the audiences of that day were often roused to the greatest enthusiasm; and I would tuck my arm very proudly into his as we marched home from a concert, even though we knew that the subscription to the concert was not more than eight hundred dollars and the single sale at the box office had not reached the hundred dollar mark.

7.   *1895–1896*—OTIS SKINNER RECALLS A TROUPER'S TRIALS

❨ *No art flourished like the theater. Every large city had its dozen or more playhouses, while traveling troupes offered theatrical en-*

Otis Skinner, *Footlights and Spotlights* (Indianapolis, 1924), 241–42, 244–47. Reprinted by permission of Cornelia Otis Skinner.

tertainment ranging from minstrel shows to Shakespeare in the "opera houses" of the small towns. But the actor's profession was a hazardous one, yielding, often as not, more experience than money. Otis Skinner, a familiar figure of the American stage for more than fifty years, describes a trouper's trials.

The tour took us to Boston where our engagement was played at the Park Theatre managed by the male *Mrs. Malaprop* of the theatrical world—John Stetson. This big, bass, blustering individual had sprung from street life in Boston to the position of prosperous manager. His usual manner was that of a war tank—he went through things if they stood in his way. One look at his aggressive face, square jaw and aggressive *dead* eye was enough to cause timid ones to step aside. Perhaps many of the stories of his "malapropisms" were apocryphal, but he unquestionably had a penchant for big-sounding words. Once upon his return from Europe he expressed his satisfaction in being again on *terra cotta.*

A Biblical play was being presented at the Boston Globe Theatre under Stetson's management. Observing a tableau of "The Last Supper," seen through a gauze drop, Stetson was disturbed because the scene looked scant, and demanded that more people be shown.

"But, Mr. Stetson," said the stage director, "there were only twelve apostles."

"I know what I want," said Stetson, "gimme twenty-four!"

For all his idiosyncrasies he was immensely popular, and he had a sympathetic side not difficult to approach. I discovered this in the dilemma which confronted us at the close of the engagement. Business had been quite terrible, and on the last Saturday night it was disclosed that not only were we indebted to the theatre for house charges but we hadn't the wherewithal to move to the next stand. My manager put the matter frankly before John Stetson. He accepted our I. O. U. for the indebtedness and advanced funds to enable us to move on. . . .

The pendulum of my travels swung east, then west—finally toward the Pacific Coast. We stopped at Lincoln, Nebraska, the early habitat of William F. Cody—"Buffalo Bill." It chanced that Bill's Wild West Show was in town that day. Under any condition I probably should not have had a full house, but what chance had *Hamlet* against Buffalo Bill?

The meager audience was listening to the early sorrows of the Prince of Denmark with apparent sympathy when the colonel came into the theatre a little the worse for wear. All day long his friends and neighbors had been celebrating his advent with great conviviality. He looked at the little collection of people in the orchestra seats with a glazed eye that straightway kindled into indignation.

"Do you know what I'm going to do?" he exclaimed. "Look at that house! I'm going down that aisle and tell them that Otis Skinner is the best damned actor in America." Being thwarted in his threat, he came behind the scenes, deciding he preferred to issue his proclamation from the stage. Again he was dissuaded and I invited him to my dressing-room where he sat on a trunk swaying a bit unsteadily. The door flew open and my wife came in quite unaware that I had a visitor. The colonel rose, every inch a gentleman and a soldier, and stood erect, unswerving. He was in the presence of a lady: Off came the well-known sombrero. The colonel was a very prince. The introduction was formal. Scenting an air of restraint, if indeed no other atmospheric condition, my wife quickly withdrew and Buffalo Bill relaxed immediately to the trunk again.

Late one afternoon I stood on the platform of the Union Pacific Railway Station at Omaha with my face toward the setting sun. My company was aboard, our tickets—good for three months—from Omaha to California and back to the Missouri River were paid for. I felt I was on the threshold of adventure. Only a few days before I had received a letter from an acquaintance saying: "Dear Skinner: I hear you are about to go West. Don't! The plains are white with the bones of actors who have tried to get back."

My manager, reading a suggestion of doubt in my face, asked if I felt like weakening on the proposition.

"The first stop is Denver, and there's an awful lot of country west of that," he said.

"Well, that's where we're going," I answered, and we stepped aboard the train.

Denver, Salt Lake City and finally California!

We played from San Francisco to San Diego and back. The land of gold brought me nothing but the fairy-gold of legend. When I turned my face eastward at the end of June I was confronted by three thousand miles of railway and scant means of getting a company of twenty people, a carload of scenery, my wife and myself to our destination—Chicago.

I owed everybody—printers, transfer companies, scenic artists, property makers, my working force, and, above all, my actors. These last were patient and forebearing with me and took our reverses like true soldiers of fortune.

We had our railroad tickets back to the Missouri River—nothing more.

My manager camped in the office of the superintendent of the Southern Pacific Railroad at Sacramento for an entire day waiting a chance to plead with that potent person for authority to allow our scenery and baggage to go through as far as Omaha. Finally he got an audience with the hard-boiled official, and his pent-up eloquence as he pictured the desperation of our situation, won the day. We were off to pick up a few pence at Ogden and Salt Lake City. We traveled by day in the coach, and at night our women were given berths in the Pullman while we men took to the tourist sleeper. What cash there was in the treasury was held by Buckley against the necessities of meal stations where we breakfasted, lunched and dined *en famille* as frugally as possible. A frightful thing occurred on the way. At a cashier's desk of a meal station while the bell was ringing for the departure of the train, Buckley laid down a twenty-dollar gold piece among his silver, under the impression that it was a dollar, and didn't discover his mistake until we were fifty miles away. Then in our melancholy, befell the miracle— manna dropped from Heaven! At the supper station, nineteen dollars which we thought gone forever, returned to us by telegraph from the scene of the awful blunder.

Ogden and Salt Lake City helped us out a little—then a few Nebraska towns, and finally Omaha! There we played to enough cash to purchase our transportation to Chicago.

Our crusade was over.

8. *1865–1880*—THE NEW ENGLAND WRITERS

❡ *Long before the end of the nineteenth century the United States had a flourishing national literature. Most revered among its authors were those of the New England school, all elderly men when William Dean Howells, editor of the* ATLANTIC MONTHLY, *came to know them.*

Now and then I met Doctor Holmes at Longfellow's table, but not oftener than now and then, and I never saw Emerson in Cambridge at all except at Longfellow's funeral. In my first years on the *Atlantic* I sometimes saw him, when he would address me some grave . . . civilities, after I had been newly introduced to him, as I always had to be on these occasions. . . .

Some years before he died I sat between him and Mrs. Rose Terry Cooke, at an *Atlantic* Breakfast where it was part of my editorial function to preside. When he was not asking me who she was, I could hear him asking her who I was. . . . His remembrance absolutely ceased with an event, and yet his character, his personality, his identity fully persisted. . . .

In manner, he was very gentle, like all those great New England men, but he was cold, like many of them, to the new-comer, or to the old-comer who came newly. . . . I once heard him speak critically of

---

William Dean Howells, *Literary Friends and Acquaintances* (New York, 1900), 132–35, 140–42, 163–64, 167–68, 196–97, 227–30, 250.

Hawthorne, and once he expressed his surprise at the late flowering brilliancy of Holmes's gift in the *Autocrat* papers after all his friends supposed it had borne its best fruit. But I recall no mention of Longfellow, or Lowell, or Whittier from him. At a dinner where the talk glanced upon Walt Whitman he turned to me as perhaps representing the interest posterity might take in the matter, and referred to Whitman's public use of his privately written praise as something altogether unexpected. . . .

The first time I saw Whittier was in Fields's room at the publishing office, where I had come upon some editorial errand to my chief. He introduced me to the poet: a tall, spare figure of black in Quaker cut, with a keen, clean-shaven face, black hair, and vivid black eyes. It was just after his poem, *Snow Bound,* had made its great success, in the modest fashion of those days, and had sold not two hundred thousand but twenty thousand, and I tried to make him my compliment. I contrived to say that I could not tell him how much I liked it; and he received the inadequate expression of my feeling with doubtless as much effusion as he would have met something more explicit and abundant. . . . In him . . . the Quaker calm was bound by the frosty Puritanic air, and he was doubly cold to the touch of the stranger, though he would thaw out to old friends, and sparkle in laugh and joke. I myself never got so far with him as to experience this geniality, though afterwards we became such friends as an old man and a young man could be who rarely met. . . .

Francis Parkman . . . like so many other Boston men of letters, was of patrician family, and of those easy fortunes which Clio prefers her sons to be of; but he paid for these advantages by the suffering in which he wrought at what is, I suppose, our greatest history. He wrought at it piecemeal, and sometimes only by moments, when the terrible headaches which tormented him, and the disorder of the heart which threatened his life, allowed him a brief respite for the task which was dear to him. He must have been more than a quarter of a century in completing it, and in this time, as he once told me, it had given him a day-laborer's wages; but of course money was the least return he wished from it. I read the irregularly successive volumes of *The Jesuits in North America, The Old Regime in Canada,* the *Wolfe and Montcalm,* and the others that went to make up the whole history with a sufficiently noisy enthusiasm, and our acquaintance began by his expressing his gratification with the praises of them that I had put in print. We entered into relations as contributor and editor, and I know that he was pleased with my eagerness to get as many detachable chapters from the book in hand as he could give me for the magazine, but he was of too fine a politeness to make this the occasion of his first coming to see me. He had walked out to Cambridge, where I then lived, in pursuance of a regimen which, I believe, finally built up his health; that it was unsparing, I can testify from my own share in one of his constitutionals in Boston, many years later. . . .

He came to me during my final year in Boston for nothing apparently but to tell me of his liking for a book of mine describing boy-life in Southern Ohio a half-century ago. He wished to talk about many points of this, which he found the same as his own boy-life in the neighborhood of Boston; and we could agree that the life of the Anglo-Saxon boy was pretty much the same everywhere. He had helped himself into my apartment with a crutch, but I do not remember how he had fallen lame. It was the end of his long walks, I believe, and not long afterwards I had the grief to read of his death. I noticed that perhaps through his enforced quiet, he had put on weight; his fine face was full; whereas when I first knew him, he was almost delicately thin of figure and feature. He was always of a distinguished presence, and his face had a great distinction. . . .

For three privileged years I lived all but next-door neighbor of Doctor Holmes in that part of Beacon Street whither he removed after he left his old home in Charles Street, and during these years I saw him rather often. We were both on the water side, which means so much more than the words say, and our library windows commanded the same general view of the Charles rippling out into the Cambridge marshes and the sunsets, and curving eastward under Long Bridge, through shipping that increased onward to the sea. He said that you could count fourteen towns and villages in the compass of that view, with the three conspicuous monuments accenting the different attractions of it: the tower of Memorial Hall at Harvard; the obelisk on Bunker Hill; and in the centre of the picture that bulk of Tufts College which he said he expected to greet his eyes the first thing when he opened them in the other world. . . .

In this pleasant study he lived among the books, which seemed to multiply from case to case and shelf to shelf, and climb from floor to ceiling. Everything was in exquisite order, and the desk where he wrote was as scrupulously neat as if the slovenly disarray of most authors' desks were impossible to him. He had a number of ingenious little contrivances for helping his work, which he liked to show you; for a time a revolving book-case at the corner of his desk seemed to be his pet; and after that came his fountain-pen, which he used with due observance of its fountain principle, though he was tolerant of me when I said I always dipped mine in the inkstand; it was a merit in his eyes to use a fountain-pen in anywise. After you had gone over these objects with him, and perhaps taken a peep at something he was examining through his microscope, he sat down at one corner of his hearth, and invited you to an easy-chair at the other. His talk was always considerate of your wish to be heard, but the person who wished to talk when he could listen to Doctor Holmes was his own victim, and always the loser. If you were well advised you kept yourself to the question and response which manifested your interest in what he was saying, and let him talk on, with his sweet smile, and that husky laugh he broke into at times. Perhaps he was not very well when you came in upon him; then he would name his trouble, with a scientific zest and accuracy, and pass quickly to other matters. . . .

He had, indeed, few or none of the infirmities of age that make themselves painfully or inconveniently evident. He carried his slight figure erect, and until his latest years his step was quick and sure. . . . If you met him on the street, you encountered a spare, carefully dressed old gentleman, with a clean-shaven face and a friendly smile, qualified by the involuntary frown of his thick, senile brows; well coated, lustrously shod, well gloved, in a silk hat, latterly wound with a mourning-weed. Sometimes he did not know you when he knew you quite well, and at such times I think it was kind to spare his years the fatigue of recalling your identity; at any rate, I am glad of the times when I did so. In society he had the same vagueness, the same dimness; but after the moment he needed to make sure of you, he was as vivid as ever in his life. He made me think of a bed of embers on which the ashes have thinly gathered, and which, when these are breathed away, sparkles and tinkles keenly up with all the freshness of a newly kindled fire. . . .

Longfellow . . . was the most perfectly modest man I ever saw, ever imagined, but he had a gentle dignity which I do not believe any one, the coarsest, the obtusest, could trespass upon. In the years when I began to know him, his long hair and the beautiful beard which mixed with it were of one iron-gray, which I saw blanch to a perfect silver, while that pearly tone of his complexion, which Appleton so admired, lost itself in the wanness of age and pain. When he walked, he had a kind of spring in his gait, as if now and again a buoyant thought lifted him from the ground. It was fine to meet him coming down a Cambridge street; you felt that the encounter made you a part of literary history, and set you apart with him for the moment from the poor and mean. When he appeared in Harvard Square, he beatified if not beautified the ugliest and vulgarest looking spot on the planet outside of New York. You could meet him sometimes at the market, if you were of the same provision-man as he; and Longfellow remained as constant to his tradespeople as to any other friends. He rather liked to bring his proofs back to the printer's himself, and we often found ourselves together at the University Press, where the *Atlantic Monthly* used to be printed. But outside of his own house Longfellow seemed to want a fit atmosphere, and I love best to think of him in his study, where he wrought at his lovely art with a serenity expressed in his smooth, regular, and scrupulously perfect handwriting. It was quite vertical, and rounded, with a slope neither to the right or left, and at the time I knew him first, he was fond of using a soft pencil on printing paper, though commonly he wrote with a quill. Each letter was distinct in shape, and between the verses was always the exact space of half an inch. I have a good many of his poems written in this fashion, but whether they were the first drafts or not I cannot say; very likely not. Towards the last he no longer sent his poems to the magazines in his own hand, but they were always signed in autograph. . . .

For four years I did not take any summer outing from Cambridge myself, and my associations with Elmwood and with Lowell are more of summer than of winter weather meetings. But often we went our walks through the snows, trudging along between the horse-car tracks which enclosed the only well-broken-out paths in that simple old Cambridge. . . .

At the time I speak of there was certainly nothing in Lowell's dress or bearing that would have kept the common life aloof from him, if that life were not always too proud to make advances to any one. In this retrospect, I see him in the sack coat and rough suit which he wore upon all out-door occasions, with heavy shoes, and a round hat. I never saw him with a high hat on until he came home after his diplomatic stay in London; then he had become rather rigorously correct in his costume, and as conventional as he had formerly been indifferent. In both epochs he was apt to be gloved, and the strong, broad hands, which left the sensation of their vigor for some time after they had clasped yours, were notably white. At the earlier period, he still wore his auburn hair somewhat long; it was darker than his beard, which was branching and full, and more straw-colored than auburn, as were his thick eyebrows; neither hair nor beard was then touched with gray, as I now remember. When he uncovered, his straight, wide, white forehead showed itself one of the most beautiful that could be; his eyes were gay with humor, and alert with all intelligence. He had an enchanting smile, a laugh that was full of friendly joyousness, and a voice that was exquisite music. Everything about him expressed his strenuous physical condition: he would not wear an overcoat in the coldest Cambridge weather; at all times he moved vigorously, and walked with a quick step, lifting his feet well from the ground. . . .

I believe neither in heroes nor in saints; but I believe in great and good men, for I have known them, and among such men Lowell was of the richest nature I have known. His nature was not always serene or pellucid; it was sometimes roiled by the currents that counter and cross in all of us; but it was without the least alloy of insincerity, and it was never darkened by the shadow of a selfish fear.

9. *1863–1871—WALT WHITMAN: POET AND PERSON*

❲ *Of all nineteenth-century authors, the two who owed least to the English literary tradition were Mark Twain and Walt Whitman. In* LEAVES OF GRASS, *first published in 1855, Whitman departed completely from the accepted forms of poetry, and sang of himself and his country with a lustiness that shocked many readers. Yet he never lost the admiration of John Burroughs, the author and naturalist, who met the poet in 1863. Whitman became the subject of the first of Burroughs' many books.*

Those who entertain great expectations Walt Whitman will probably disappoint at first sight. I have known and seen him for years, under various surroundings, in company, on rambles, by the sick cots in the army hospitals, and elsewhere; and I should describe him, offhand, as a cheerful, rather quiet man, easily pleased with others, letting them do most of the talking, seeking not the least conquest or display, never exhibiting any depression of spirits, asking very few questions, and at first view making the impression on any unsuspecting stranger of a good-willed, healthy character, without the least ostensible mark of the philosopher or the poet; but all the while, though thus passive and receptive, yet evidently the most masculine of beings.

Observed more closely, he suggests ideas as of the Beginners, the Adamic men. One notes the great strength of his face, of the fullest Greek pattern, and combining the quality of weight with that which soars and ascends; head high-domed and perfectly symmetrical, with no bulging of the forehead; brows remarkably arching; nose straight and broad, with a strong square bridge; gray beard, in bushy fleeces or locks; florid countenance, well seamed; blue eyes, with very heavy projecting lids; and in physiognomy, as in his whole form withal, a certain cast of chivalry:

"Douglas! Douglas! tender and true."

While not incapable, also, on due occasions, of measureless obstinacy and hauteur.

The "eccentricity" of Walt Whitman, though it has been part of the material of many a paragraphist and magazine writer for the last ten years, has not a particle of real foundation. The truth simply is, that as to "fashion" and all the mere fopperies and conventional trimmings, which American society is perhaps more the slave of than any European people, he quietly ignores them in his dress and demeanor, as will always any man of full physique and noble and independent nature. No essential, however, no universal law, nothing belonging to the gentleman in the true sense, does he ever ignore. Far above oddity or queer-

---

John Burroughs, *Notes on Walt Whitman as Poet and Person* (New York, 1871), 85–87.

ness, I think the verdict of every good observer, noticing him with attention, will finally be that, if anything makes him eccentric, it is because he, above all the rest, is so free from eccentricity. . . .

It may be because everything in his personal appearance is so relentlessly averaged to the idea of a complete man, that strangers involuntarily ascribe to him all sorts of characters, according to their first impressions. I knew a lady who persisted in calling him "Doctor," and even consulting him professionally, without ever stopping to inquire about, and even after she had been told, the truth. During his services in the army hospitals . . . various myths were floating about concerning him. Now he was a benevolent Catholic priest—then some unknown army general, or retired sea captain; and at one time he was the owner of the whole Cunard line of steamers. To be taken for a Californian has been common. . . .

There probably lives not another man so genuinely and utterly indifferent to literary abuse, or to "public opinion," either when favorable or unfavorable. He has never used the usual means to defend his reputation. It has been his fate to have his book and his personal character atrociously intercepted from their due audience with the public, whose minds have been plied and preoccupied by detractions, and the meanest misreports and falsehoods.

10. *1906*—MARK TWAIN MEETS HIS BIOGRAPHER

❲ *In such books as* LIFE ON THE MISSISSIPPI, HUCKLEBERRY FINN, *and* TOM SAWYER, *Mark Twain (Samuel L. Clemens) had made enduring literature out of material which writers in the genteel tradition would have considered beneath their dignity. Long before the winter night in 1906 when Mark Twain attended a dinner at the Players' Club in New York both his reputation and his place in the affections of the American people were assured. Yet that dinner was a memorable one, for there the aging author met Albert Bigelow Paine, then one of the editors of* ST. NICHOLAS MAGAZINE. *From that meeting, which Paine describes, would come a truly great book:* MARK TWAIN, A BIOGRAPHY.

The night of January 5, 1906, remains a memory apart from other dinners. Brander Matthews presided, and Gilder was there, and Frank Millet and Willard Metcalf and Robert Reid, and a score of others; some of them are dead now, David Munro among them. It so happened that my seat was nearly facing the guest of the evening, who, by custom of The Players, is placed at the side and not at the end of the long

Albert Bigelow Paine, *Mark Twain, A Biography* (New York, 1912), IV, 1260–65. Reprinted by permission of Louise Paine Moore, table. He was no longer frail and thin, as when I had first met him. He had a robust, rested look; his complexion had the tints of a miniature painting. Lit by the glow of the shaded candles, relieved against the dusk richness of the walls, he made a picture of striking beauty. One could not take his eyes from it, and to one guest at least it stirred the farthest memories. I suddenly saw the interior of a farm-house sitting-room in the Middle West, where I had first heard uttered the name of Mark Twain, and where night after night a group gathered around the evening lamp to hear the tale of the first pilgrimage, which, to a boy of eight, had seemed only a wonderful poem and fairy tale. To Charles Harvey Genung, who sat next to me, I whispered something of this, and how, during the thirty-six years since then, no other human being to me had meant quite what Mark Twain had meant—in literature, in life, in the ineffable thing which means more than either, and which we call "inspiration," for lack of a truer word. Now here he was, just across the table. It was the fairy tale come true.

Genung said:

"You should write his life."

His remark seemed a pleasant courtesy, and was put aside as such. . . . By and by the speaking began—delightful, intimate speaking in that restricted circle—and the matter went out of my mind.

When the dinner had ended, and we were drifting about the table in general talk, I found an opportunity to say a word to the guest of the evening about his *Joan of Arc,* which I had recently re-read. To my happiness, he detained me while he told me of the long-ago incident which had led to his interest, not only in the martyred girl, but in all literature. I think we broke up soon after, and descended to the lower rooms. At any rate, I presently found the faithful Charles Genung privately reasserting to me the proposition that I should undertake the biography of Mark Twain. Perhaps it was the brief sympathy established by the name of Joan of Arc, perhaps it was only Genung's insistent purpose—his faith, if I may be permitted the word. Whatever it was, there came an impulse, in the instant of bidding good-by to our guest of honor, which prompted me to say:

"May I call to see you, Mr. Clemens, some day?"

And something, dating from the primal atom, I suppose—prompted him to answer:

"Yes, come soon."

This was on Wednesday night, or rather on Thursday morning, for it was past midnight, and a day later I made an appointment with his secretary to call on Saturday.

I can say truly that I set out with no more than the barest hope of success, and wondering if I should have the courage, when I saw him, even to suggest the thought in my mind. . . . I arrived at 21 Fifth

Avenue and was shown into that long library and drawing-room combined, and found a curious and deep interest in the books and ornaments along the shelves as I waited. Then I was summoned, wondering why I had come on so futile an errand, and trying to think of an excuse to offer for having come at all.

He was propped up in bed—in that stately bed—sitting, as was his habit, with his pillows placed at the foot, so that he might have always before him the rich, carved beauty of its headboard. He was delving through a copy of *Huckleberry Finn*, in search of a paragraph concerning which some random correspondent had asked explanation. He was commenting unfavorably on this correspondent and on miscellaneous letter-writing in general. He pushed the cigars toward me, and the talk of these matters ran along and blended into others more or less personal. By and by I told him what so many thousands had told him before: what he had meant to me, recalling the childhood impressions of that large, black-and-gilt-covered book with its wonderful pictures and adventures—the Mediterranean pilgrimage. Very likely it bored him—he had heard it so often—and he was willing enough, I dare say, to let me change the subject and thank him for the kindly word which David Munro had brought. I do not remember what he said then, but I suddenly found myself suggesting that out of his encouragement had grown a hope—though certainly it was something less—that I might someday undertake a book about himself. I expected the chapter to end at this point, and his silence which followed seemed long and ominous.

He said, at last, that at various times through his life he had been preparing some autobiographical matter, but that he had tired of the undertaking, and had put it aside. He added that he had hoped his daughters would one day collect his letters; but that a biography—a detailed story of personality and performance, of success and failure—was of course another matter, and that for such a work no arrangement had been made. He may have added one or two other general remarks; then, turning those piercing agate-blue eyes directly upon me, he said:

"When would you like to begin?"

. . . . "Whenever you like. I can begin now."

. . . . "Very good," he said. "The sooner, then, the better. Let's begin while we are in the humor. The longer you postpone a thing of this kind the less likely you are ever to get at it."

. . . That was always his way. He did nothing by halves; nothing without unquestioning confidence and prodigality. He got up and showed me the lovely luxury of the study, with its treasures of material. I did not believe it true yet. It had all the atmosphere of a dream, and I have no distinct recollection of how I came away.

11. *1898*—WHY THEY WENT TO COLLEGE

⟪ *The same forces which led to increasing interest in music, the theater, and literature fostered higher education. Colleges and universities grew in number and size faster than the population. Yet not all students had a passion for knowledge. Many, perhaps most, were impelled by a vague conviction that they would find a college "education" worth its cost in time and money. Henry Seidel Canby, author and editor, draws on his experience at Yale to argue, somewhat cynically, that the conviction was well founded.*

I went to college at a time when an old curriculum was still tottering like a rotted house about to fall and in parts already fallen. Before my day college education had been disciplinary. The curriculum was a beautiful unity; neat, harmonious, and inspiring confidence because so many generations had worked out the rules for extracting the maximum of mental discipline from the age-tested subjects of which it was composed. It consisted of the classics, long since emptied of the noble excitements of the Renaissance, but efficiently organized into exercises in grammar and bilinguality; of mathematics; of rhetoric; and of some philosophy, literature, and history—all taught by men who believed in hard work upon hard subjects as the first of the intellectual virtues. It was a training rather than an education, yet it had the merits of all systems carried through to a logical conclusion. The professors of that day were taskmasters and looked their part. Some of them still survived in our expansive period, bearded men, a little dusty, whose clothes and faces were as emphatically different from the world's as were the old-time clergymen's. Men sure of themselves, severe, arid, uncompromising, uninventive, uninterested in the constantly new thing which we call life, yet often unexpectedly wise and serene. Or so they seemed in the decay of the age of discipline.

For of course it had to decay, since its discipline was based upon a superstitious belief in the exclusive validity of an inherited learning. By our time not even the professors really believed in the efficacy of the old curriculum. They had faith in their own subjects still, but were patently aware that few agreed with them. How many classrooms do I remember where instruction consisted in a calling-up of one man after another to translate from a heavily cribbed text of Latin, Greek, or French! How many an English recitation where in sleepy routine the questions went round: "What does our author say about Lucifer's ambitions? Who was Ben Jonson and what were his relations to Shakespeare?" Never in business, in law, even in religion, has there been

Henry Seidel Canby, *American Memoir* (Boston: Houghton Mifflin Co., 1947), 162–69. Reprinted by permission.

more sham, bunk, and perfunctoriness than in the common education of
the American college in that easy-going time. It seemed to me incredible
that a mature and civilized person, who in private life had an impeccable character and often geniality and charm, should be willing to earn
a living (and usually a meager living) by asking trivial questions day
after day of young men who had either memorized the answers as the
easiest way of getting on with college life and their real education or
constructed a system of bluff so transparent that only a defeatist who
did not believe in education would have stood for it. I understand more
now how hard it was for a scholar to get enough to live on in those
days. Even so I wonder when I think of men I knew who persisted in
this rigmarole for forty years. . . .

If this had been all to college education in those days, there would
have been no alumni turning back to *alma mater,* and certainly no book,
but only a dirge, to write about the American college. It was, of course,
not the real college education at all. That was a life, a powerful, condi-
tioning life, from which only the "grinds" and rare sophisticates escaped
without a molding of character and intellect, and a complete reshaping
of behavior.

Why did they go to college, those thousands upon mounting thousands that crowded into the campuses in those decades? Entrance
examinations were stiffened to hold them back (a boon to tutoring
schools), subjects which, like Greek, the public schools refused to teach,
were kept in the requirements in the hope of barring the gate. Yet
still they came until in many an institution all obstacles were swept
away and the prosperous multitude was greeted with a triumphant
despair.

They came for the best of reasons. They swarmed from the drab
experience of small town or commercial city, direct or via the boarding
schools, because they had heard of college life, where, instead of the
monotony of school discipline or the bourgeois experience which had
succeeded their confident childhood, there was singing, cheering, drinking, and the keenest competition for honor and prestige, a life rich in
the motives which were being stifled in the struggle for power in the
adult world outside. They desired romance, they sought distinction, and
were not unwilling to spend some bookish labor in order to win the
opportunities of a class that called itself educated.

These were the naïves, and perhaps by far the largest number of as-
pirants. The shrewder and less romantic shared some of these antici-
pations, but mingled with them ambitions much more realistic. They
had learned in the preparatory schools that the college world was a
career as well as a Utopia; and furthermore, a career where the sharp
and energetic might overcome handicaps of birth, poverty, or even of
character. They knew that this college boasted of its democracy, which

433

actually was no social democracy at all, since class lines (once drawn) were tighter than in the outside world. They knew well that it was a democracy of opportunity. In the home town you were either born into the right group, and, if your family kept its money, stayed there; or, with greater or less difficulty, depending upon where you lived, forced yourself into society and its privileges by the sheer power of money. Self-made riches came hard. But in college life there were other stairways that led to security. Money counted, social standing outside counted, yet the son of a shopkeeper could get as far on athletic prowess as the gilded child of privilege on his family momentum. Good looks counted also, more, I should say, in the men's than in the women's colleges; and so did good clothes if worn in the collegiate manner which required the slovenly use of expensive and well-cut garments. Wit, and the gift of being amusing, especially when tight, were very helpful; and so was political sagacity. And, as I have said, there were routes upward for boys who could write what the college magazine wanted, or make the kind of music that undergraduates liked; and a broad path, much trodden in my day, for the energetically pious who could organize religion, and sell God to the right kind of undergraduate. . . .

These shrewd and realistic students who went to college as careerists were well aware that this college climbing led to much more than a college success. From a commonplace family in a commonplace town, with no prospect ahead but a grind of money-making and association with other stuffy nobodies, the youngster whose parents had invested in a college education, might hope to pass by his own native abilities into the brave, trans-lunary world of great cities and the gilded corridors of their privileged sets. For if he could once place himself in the right college group, his own would take care of him, provided that he did not too egregiously disappoint them in his later career. From henceforth he would not be Jones of Columbus, but Jones of "Bones" or some other tight-ringed fraternity. Thanks to his ability to catch a ball, or to organize, or to be friendly, or to drink like a gentleman, or even to capitalize his charm, he was tapped as of the elect at age twenty or twenty-one, and had precisely that advantage (and no more) which rank and privilege still gave in the Old World. If there was a good job in a brokerage firm, he would get it, because of his connections. If there was a right club where he was going, he could join it. And all this he himself could win, unaided by the power of money or the accident of social position, and find himself, after a few brief years of struggle, companioned with the sons of plutocrats and the aristocracy. . . .

In short, college life, which was so often criticized or laughed at, did educate for adult life afterward, and especially for American life in what was its most typical if not its most admirable aspect. It inculcated ideals that were viable in America as it was then, and these ideals were adaptations of general idealism (even of Christianity) to the needs of an industrialized, get-rich-quick country. It educated specifically for the harsh competitions of capitalism, for the successful and often unscrupulous pursuit by the individual of power for himself, for class superiority, and for a success measured by the secure possession of the fruits of prosperity. I do not see how a better education could have been contrived for a youth that wanted the wealth, the position, the individual power that was being worshiped just then in America—and wanted to get them quickly, easily, and with no public dishonesty.

CHAPTER XVIII

THE UNITED STATES
BECOMES A WORLD POWER

1898 – 1910

1. *1898*—WE GO TO WAR WITH SPAIN

❨ *In the last decade of the nineteenth century a wave of imperialism swept the United States. We had become a great industrial nation, we had confidence in our democracy, we were proud of our educational and scientific progress. Our "manifest destiny"—a phrase popular fifty years earlier—beckoned us beyond our borders. Voice after voice stirred the country to face the challenge offered by backward peoples. Senators, missionaries, professors, editors proclaimed that the United States had "the mission of conducting the political civilization of the modern world," that it was the duty of the American people, "by virtue of the call of God," to "give the world the life more abundant both for here and hereafter." "We are face to face with a strange destiny," the Washington* POST *declared in an editorial typical of many that appeared all over the country. "The taste of Empire is in the mouth of the people even as the taste of blood*

H. H. Kohlsaat, *From McKinley to Harding: Personal Recollections of Our Presidents* (New York, 1923), 66–68.

in the jungle. It means an Imperial policy, the Republic, renascent, taking her place with the armed nations."

With public opinion—never of course unanimous—in such a temper, revolution broke out in the Spanish dependency of Cuba. For many years American expansionists had coveted the fertile island; now both self-interest and humanitarian motives made its affairs a matter of pressing concern. American capital was deeply involved in Cuban sugar raising and refining, in mining, and in shipping, and suffered heavily after the beginning of the insurrection. The cruelty of the Spanish authorities, exploited by sensational newspapers, shocked millions of readers. The belief spread that the United States must intervene if it were not to be false to its destiny.

Grover Cleveland, President when the Cuban revolt broke out in 1895, resisted the pressure. So did his successor, William McKinley, until the sinking of the battleship MAINE *aroused an irresistible demand for action. Even so, McKinley was reluctant. H. H. Kohlsaat, publisher of the Chicago* TIMES-HERALD, *found the President troubled on the eve of war.*

February 15, 1898, the *Maine* was blown up in Havana harbor. The event stirred the country against Spain. In April, I received a wire from Secretary Cortelyou, as follows: "The President wants to see you."

At Harper's Ferry a telegram invited me to dine with the President and Mrs. McKinley. My train was two hours behind time, making it too late for dinner. So I wired that I would come as soon as possible.

There was a piano recital in the Blue Room of the White House. Mrs. McKinley was seated near the pianist, looking very frail and ill. The President was in the centre of the room on an S-shaped settee. There were eighteen or twenty guests present. As I stood in the doorway some one said: "The President is trying to catch your eye." He motioned me to sit by him and whispered: "As soon as she is through this piece go and speak to Mrs. McKinley and then go to the Red Room door. I will join you." I did as requested, and when he had shaken hands with some of the late arrivals we went into the Red Room. We sat on a large crimson-brocade lounge. McKinley rested his head on his hands, with elbows on knees. He was in much distress, and said: "I have been through a trying period. Mrs. McKinley has been in poorer health than usual. It seems to me I have not slept over three hours a night for over two weeks. Congress is trying to drive us into war with Spain. The Spanish fleet is in Cuban waters, and we haven't enough ammunition on the Atlantic seacoast to fire a salute."

He broke down and cried like a boy of thirteen. I put my hand on his shoulder and remained silent, as I thought the tension would be relieved by his tears. As he became calm, I tried to assure him that the country would back him in any course he should pursue. He finally said:

"Are my eyes very red? Do they look as if I had been crying?"

"Yes."

"But I must return to Mrs. McKinley at once. She is among strangers."

"When you open the door to enter the room, blow your nose very hard and loud. It will force tears into your eyes and they will think that is what makes your eyes red." He acted on this suggestion and it was no small blast.

After the musicale the President and I went into the old cabinet room and talked until very late.

A few days afterward Congress put $50,000,000 in McKinley's hands —with no string on it. War was declared April 21, 1898.

Ten days later, May 1, 1898, the battle of Manila Bay was fought. I visited the President a few days after the victory. McKinley said: "When we received the cable from Admiral Dewey telling of the taking of the Philippines I looked up their location on the globe. I could not have told where those darned islands were within 2,000 miles!"

2.   *1898—*DEWEY WINS THE BATTLE OF MANILA BAY

❨ *When war was declared Commodore George Dewey, commanding the Asiatic squadron, had just finished fitting out his four cruisers and two gunboats at Hong Kong. Orders came by cable to attack the Spanish fleet at Manila in the Philippines, with the stern warning, "You must capture vessels or destroy." Dewey slipped into Manila Bay at midnight on April 30. The following morning he sighted the Spanish fleet under the guns of Cavite dockyard. The action that followed is described by Joseph L. Stickney, a newspaper correspondent who served as Dewey's aide during the battle.*

As Commodore Dewey had planned, the fleet arrived within five miles of Manila at daybreak. What must have been the astonishment in the Spanish lines when the sun rose, and they looked out on the American ships that had come in during the night!

While, as yet, the fleet retained the appearance of calm that had characterized its approach, now many eyes on board lighted with the fire of war, as they sighted the Spanish fleet, under command of Rear Admiral Montojo, lying off Cavite. . . .

With the American flag flying from all mastheads, the ships moved on. . . . As the ships passed in front of Manila, action was begun by

---

Joseph L. Stickney, *War in the Philippines* (Haverhill, Mass., 1899), 38–48.

the Spaniards. Three batteries, mounting guns powerful enough to send shells to the distance of five miles, opened fire. The *Concord* replied, but Commodore Dewey, after two shots, made signal to stop firing, since there was danger of the shells carrying destruction and death into the crowded city beyond.

At six minutes past five o'clock, when nearing Cavite, there was a splash and roar, and two great jets of water were thrown high in air ahead of the flagship. The fleet had come upon the first of the submarine mines. Of course it was possible and probable that the whole harbor was filled with torpedoes. At any moment they were liable to explode beneath the ships; but Commodore Dewey had foreseen this when he entered the bay, and it did not now cause him to change his plans. . . .

Steaming at the comparatively slow speed of eight knots, our ships approached Cavite. From the peak of each vessel and from every masthead floated the "stars and stripes"—the largest regulation ensign being displayed. In the lead was, of course, the *Olympia,* followed by the *Baltimore,* the *Raleigh,* the *Petrel,* the *Concord* and the *Boston,* in the order named. The revenue cutter *McCulloch* and the merchant steamers attached to the squadron as coal carriers were ordered to keep well out of range in the bay, and they naturally did not try to come nearer. . . .

Presently, we came near enough to distinguish the Spanish ships in the Bay of Cavite. Most prominently in view at first was a sort of cream-colored vessel, apparently at anchor. This we recognized as the *Castilla.* She was moored, head and stern, with her port battery to seaward, just outside the point of low land that makes out like a lobster's claw and protects the inner anchorage. Behind the *Castilla,* with all steam up and moving to and fro in the back bay, were the *Reina Cristina,* flagship, the *Isla de Luzon,* the *Isla de Cuba,* the *Don Juan de Austria,* the *Don Antonio de Ulloa,* the *Marques del Duero,* the *General Lezo,* the *Argos,* several torpedo boats and the transport *Isla de Mindanao.* The latter steamed away as fast as she could and was beached some distance up the coast, where she was burned by the *Concord* later in the day.

When we were at a distance of about 6,000 yards a puff of very white cloud arose from a clump of bushes on shore. It was a pretty sight, for the smoke floated away in fantastic shapes above the red clay shore and the bright green foliage. . . . Within four seconds we heard the scream of the shot, as it passed far over us, and we knew that the first gun in the battle of Manila Bay had failed to do us any damage. Then the Spanish flagship, taking a lesson probably from the excessive elevation given to the shore gun, fired several times in quick succession, with an aim as much too short as the battery's had been too high. Yet one or two of her projectiles passed between our masts on the rebound from the water. More puffs of flame from the shore in different places showed that the Spaniard's were better protected than we had supposed. Soon all the Spanish vessels were aflame with rapid gun fire. Shell after shell flew close over our superstructure or skimmed past the head of our Commodore and his staff on our forward bridge.

Still our courtly chief made no sign. In the usual service white uniform, wearing, however, a gray traveling cap on his head, having been unable to find his uniform cap after the guns in his cabin had been cleared for action, the Commodore paced the bridge, watching the enemy's hot fire as if he were a disinterested spectator of an unusual display of fireworks. . . .

Suddenly a shell burst directly over the center of the ship. As the projectile flashed over the head of the man who held the destiny of the fleet in his grasp, it became evident that the moment of activity had come. Even the powerful will of their leader could no longer restrain the surging war fever of the crew. A boatswain's-mate, who had been bending over, looking eagerly ahead with his hand on the lock string of the after 5-inch gun, sprung up and cried out: "Boys, remember the *Maine!*" Instantly the watchword was repeated by the two hundred men at the guns. The hoarse shout was caught up in the turrets and fire rooms. It echoed successively through all the decks of the silent ship, till finally, in a sullen whisper, "Remember the *Maine*" stole up through the ventilators from the lowest parts of the hold to the officers on the bridge. . . .

"You may fire when you are ready, Captain Gridley," said the Commodore. This order sufficed, and at 5:41 in the morning, at a distance of three miles, America roared forth her first battle cry to Spain from the starboard 8-inch gun in the forward turret of the *Olympia*.

The *Baltimore* and the *Boston* were not slow in following the example of the flagship, and almost immediately their 8-inch guns were sending 250-pound shells toward the *Castilla* and the *Reina Cristina*. The battle now began to rage fierce and fast. Encouraged by the fact that the range was too great for accuracy, and that the American gunners were obliged to guess the distance, the Spaniards fired more rapidly. Shots from their ship and shore guns came through the air in a screaming shower; time-fuse shells were constantly bursting about the American fleet, and their fragments, scattering in all directions, would strike the water like shrapnel or cut the hull and rigging of the ships.

The *Olympia* was the target for most of the Spanish guns, because she was the flagship and because she steered directly for the center of the Spanish line. One shell struck close by a gun in the ward room. The signal halyards were cut from Lieutenant Brumby's hand, as he stood on the after bridge. One great projectile, with almost human intuition, came straight toward the forward bridge, but burst less than a hundred feet away. A fragment cut the rigging directly over the heads of Commander Lamberton and myself. Another struck the bridge railings in line with us, and still another, about as large as a flat iron, gouged a hole in the deck a few feet below the Commodore.

The *Baltimore's* crew had several narrow escapes. One shot struck her and passed through her, but fortunately hit no one. Another ripped up her main deck, disabled one 6-inch gun, and exploded a couple of 3-pounder shells, wounding eight men. . . .

The *Boston* received a shell in her port quarter. It burst in Ensign Doddridge's stateroom and caused a hot fire, as did also one that burst in the port hammock netting; but both these fires were quickly extinguished. One shell passed through the *Boston's* foremast, just in front of Captain Wildes on the bridge. The entire battle was a series of incidents of this sort and the wonder is that they were no more than incidents.

Even now, when the Spaniards had brought all their guns into action, the Americans had not yet responded with all their strength. Commodore Dewey was reserving his force. The men naturally chafed at this continued restraint, but they laughed good naturedly among themselves. Sometimes, when a shell would burst close aboard or would strike the water and pass overhead, with the peculiar sputtering noise characteristic of the tumbling of a rifled projectile, some of the more nervous would dodge mechanically.

At a distance of 4,000 yards, owing to her deep draught, the Commodore was obliged to change his course and run the *Olympia* parallel to the Spanish column. At last, as she brought her port broadside toward the foe, Commodore Dewey said:

"Open with all the guns," and the roar that went forth shook the vessel from end to end. The battle was indeed on. Above the snarling of the *Olympia's* 5-inch rapid-firers was heard the prolonged growl of her turret 8-inchers. The other ships joined in, and Cavite Harbour was no longer comfortable for the Spaniards. . . .

The fight had now lasted about two hours and a half, when for about four hours hostilities were suspended and the fleet lay inactive in the center of the bay. During this time it was found that there remained in the magazines of the *Olympia* only 85 rounds of 5-inch ammunition, and that the stock of 8-inch charges was sufficiently depleted to make another two hours' fighting impossible. The *Baltimore* was discovered to have the best supply, so when, at 10:50 o'clock, the signal for close action went up again, she was given the place of honor in the lead, the *Olympia* following and the other ships as before. As the *Baltimore* began firing at the Spaniards at 11:16 o'clock she made a series of hits as if at target practice.

In this second attack the Spaniards replied very slowly, chiefly from their shore guns. The Americans now recognized the results of their morning's work, for the Spanish flagship and the *Castilla* were burning fiercely, and we had heard the explosion of the magazines on board the *Reina Cristina*. For some reason the *Castilla* did not blow up, although she burned fiercely as late as Monday night. This was undoubtedly due to the fact that her magazines had been flooded before she was abandoned by her crew. Commodore Dewey now signalled the *Raleigh*, the *Boston*, the *Concord* and the *Petrel* to go into the inner harbour and destroy all the enemy's ships.

The work of the little *Petrel*, Commander E. P. Wood, commanding, is worthy of special mention. Her draught was so light that she was able to approach within 1,000 yards. From this close range she commanded everything flying the Spanish flag and fired with the greatest accuracy. Lieutenant E. M. Hughes, with an armed boat's crew, set fire to the *Don Juan de Austria*, the *Marques del Duero* and the *Isla de Cuba*. The large transport *Manila* and many tug boats and small craft were also captured. The other ships did their duty as well, and soon not a red and yellow ensign remained aloft, except one fluttering from a battery far up the coast. The *Don Antonio de Ulloa* was the last vessel to be abandoned. She at last lurched over and sank. The Spanish flag on the arsenal was hauled down at 12:30, the white flag was hoisted in its place, and the power of the Spanish Dons in the Philippines was at an end.

3.   *1898*—THE ROUGH RIDERS CHARGE SAN JUAN HILL

❲ *In the middle of May Spain's Atlantic fleet, under Admiral Cervera, took refuge in the harbor of Santiago, Cuba, where it was immediately bottled up by an American naval force commanded by Admiral W. T. Sampson. A few weeks later 18,000 troops, both regulars and volunteers, landed on the near-by coast. On the first of July they attacked San Juan Hill and El Caney, the principal defenses of the city. One division under Henry W. Lawton took El Caney; J. L. Kent's division and Theodore Roosevelt's Rough Riders bogged down in a jam before San Juan Hill, and finally advanced from sheer desperation. Richard Harding Davis, picturesque newspaper correspondent and author, describes the charge that made Roosevelt a national hero.*

General Kent's division, which was to have been held in reserve, according to the plan, had been rushed up in the rear of the First and Tenth, and the Tenth had deployed in skirmish order to the right. The

---

Richard Harding Davis, *The Cuban and Porto Rican Campaigns* (New York, 1898), 213–23.

trail was now completely blocked by Kent's division. Lawton's division, which was to have reinforced on the right, had not appeared, but incessant firing from the direction of El Caney showed that he and Chaffee were fighting mightily. The situation was desperate. Our troops could not retreat, as the trail for two miles behind them was wedged with men. They could not remain where they were for they were being shot to pieces. There was only one thing they could do—go forward and take the San Juan hills by assault. It was as desperate as the situation itself. To charge earthworks held by men with modern rifles, and using modern artillery, until after the earthworks have been shaken by artillery, and to attack them in advance and not in the flanks, are both impossible military propositions. But this campaign had not been conducted according to military rules, and a series of military blunders had brought seven thousand American soldiers into a chute of death, from which there was no escape except by taking the enemy who held it by the throat, and driving him out and beating him down. So the generals of divisions and brigades stepped back and relinquished their command to the regimental officers and the enlisted men.

"We can do nothing more," they virtually said. "There is the enemy."

Colonel Roosevelt, on horseback, broke from the woods behind the line of the Ninth, and finding its men lying in his way, shouted: "If you don't wish to go forward, let my men pass, please." The junior officers of the Ninth, with their Negroes, instantly sprang into line with the Rough Riders, and charged at the blue block-house on the right.

I speak of Roosevelt first because, with General Hawkins, who led Kent's division, notably the Sixth and Sixteenth Regulars, he was, without doubt, the most conspicuous figure in the charge. General Hawkins, with hair as white as snow, and yet far in advance of men thirty years his junior, was so noble a sight that you felt inclined to pray for his safety; on the other hand, Roosevelt, mounted high on horseback, and charging the rifle-pits at a gallop and quite alone, made you feel that you would like to cheer. He wore on his sombrero a blue polka-dot handkerchief, à la Havelock, which, as he advanced, floated out straight behind his head, like a guidon. Afterward, the men of his regiment who followed this flag, adopted a polka-dot handerchief as the badge of the Rough Riders. These two officers were notably conspicuous in the charge, but no one can claim that any two men, or any one man, was more brave or more daring, or showed greater courage in that slow, stubborn advance than did any of the others. . . .

I think the thing which impressed one the most, when our men started from cover, was that they were so few. It seemed as if someone had made an awful and terrible mistake. One's instinct was to call them to come back. You felt that someone had blundered and that these few men were blindly following out some madman's mad order. It was not heroic then, it seemed merely terribly pathetic. The pity of it, the folly of such a sacrifice was what held you.

They had no glittering bayonets, they were not massed in regular array. There were a few men in advance, bunched together, and creeping up a steep, sunny hill, the top of which roared and flashed with flame. The men held their guns pressed across their breasts and stepped heavily as they climbed. Behind these first few, spreading out like a fan, were single lines of men, slipping and scrambling in the smooth grass, moving forward with difficulty, as though they were wading waist high through water, moving slowly, carefully, with strenuous effort. It was much more wonderful than any swinging charge could have been. They walked to greet death at every step, many of them, as they advanced, sinking suddenly or pitching forward and disappearing in the high grass, but the others waded on, stubbornly, forming a thin blue line that kept creeping higher and higher up the hill. It was as inevitable as the rising tide. It was a miracle of self-sacrifice, a triumph of bulldog courage, which one watched breathless with wonder. The fire of the Spanish riflemen, who still stuck bravely to their posts, doubled and trebled in fierceness, the crests of the hills crackled and burst in amazed roars, and rippled with waves of tiny flame. But the blue line crept steadily up and on, and then, near the top, the broken fragments gathered together with a sudden burst of speed, the Spaniards appeared for a moment outlined against the sky and poised for instant flight, fired a last volley and fled before the swift-moving wave that leaped and sprang up after them.

The men of the Ninth and the Rough Riders rushed to the block-house together, the men of the Sixth, of the Third, of the Tenth Cavalry, of the Sixth and Sixteenth Infantry, fell on their faces along the crest of the hills beyond, and opened upon the vanishing enemy. They drove the yellow silk flags of the cavalry and the Stars and Stripes of their country into the soft earth of the trenches, and then sank down and looked back at the road they had climbed and swung their hats in the air. And from far overhead, from these few figures perched on the Spanish rifle-pits, with their flags planted among the empty cartridges of the enemy, and overlooking the walls of Santiago, came, faintly, the sound of a tired, broken cheer.

4. *1898*—THE "OREGON" AT GUANTANAMO BAY

⟦ *The spring of 1898 found the* OREGON, *a first-class battleship of 10,288 tons, at San Francisco. With war imminent, she was ordered*

The Voyage of the Oregon from San Francisco to Santiago (Boston: Merrymount Press, 1898), as quoted in William Matthews and Dixon Wecter, *Our Soldiers Speak, 1775–1918* (Boston, 1943), 244–48.

*to the Caribbean. On March 19 she pulled up her anchor and began
a race with time that thrilled the nation—down the Pacific Coast,
through the Straits of Magellan, and up the Atlantic Coast to Key
West, which she reached on May 26. From there she joined Sampson's blockading squadron outside Santiago. After June 1 until
Cervera brought on the Battle of Santiago by coming out of the
harbor the* OREGON's *story is told by one of her seamen, R. Cross,
who kept a diary for his sisters.*

June 1. I herd the first shot in this war to day, Santiago de Cuba
and with the flying squadron.

June 2. we had a wild goose chase.

June 10. we went down to Guantanamo Bay to put some coal on
and landed 40 Marines in the Morning. we wer the first to put foot on
Cuban soil in this war. The 9th the Marblehead and Dolphin Bombarded
the place and made them look like Munkys; they ran away and left
every thing behind them.

June 11. came back to Santiago on the 10th. and laying off hear
as befor.

June 14. the New Orleans was ordered to run in close to the shore
and do som Bombarding By her self Just to break the Monotony and to
let us believe we wer at war. we don a good Job all right, she silenced
the east Battry and the west one too, and made them show up a water
Battry which we did not know any thing about. havent herd how many
got kild or wounded on the other side. But I know they never hert any
one on this side. Got some news from Guantanamo to day. Col. Hunt-
ington and his Marines of 800 Had a Brush with the Spanish, it is
reported that 6 marines wer kild and Doctor Gibbs was shot through
the head by accident. There is at Guantanamo Bay the Texas, Marblehead and Porter and 800 Marines; they expect to have the cable work
soon and the Harbor well under Hand. I forgot to say the Vesuvius
landed 3 shots of dinomite in the Harbor on the night of the 13th at
Santiago and did great damage to the Shore Batterys; the latest report
is that the Cubans are flocking in to Huntingtons camp.

June 16. At 3.30 A.M. this morning all hands was called and the
coffie was passed around with som hardtack and cand Beef at 4 A.M.
Turn to, some 15 or 20 Minutes later Gen Quarters sounded. Then we
went at it to try and see if we could not knock thoes Batterys off the
earth. Bombarded untill 7:15 A.M. Nobody knows how much damage
was don, except we silenced all the Batterys they had and made them
show up a nother one inside of the harbor of which there seems to be
lots of them. I will say right hear that if we take this place its going
to be a hot old Job, and som of us will think we run up against a
Hornets nest when we get in side. they have been talking of forsing

the Chanell and Capt Clark signaled over to the flag ship and asked permishion to take the leed, and I am sure we will stay with him as long as the ship floats for we love him. The Vesuvius fired three more shots last night at about 12. dont know what damage was don But I know we are all tired of this fooling. if they would only send some soldiers down here from the regular army, say 6 Regiments of Infantry and 3 of Cavalry, I think, with what we could put up, that forse would more than be a match for them and take the place with all ease. The latest Bulitin of the day is that the Forses at Guantanamo have bin Joined by some Cubans and had a Brush with the Spanish, and the report is that 40 wer kild on the Spanish side and 17 taken prisoners of war, one Spanish Lut. 2 Corp and 14 Privates. On our side 3 Cubans Kild and 2 wounded, 3 Marines wounded and 17 overcome by the heat. But all recovered. Routed the Spanish and distroyed the water suply and Block House. The Dolphin held there posision from the water frount and the Texas sunk 2 small Gun boats.

June 20. Bully for the Soldiers, they are hear at last, "I thought they would com tomorrow," some of the papers say there is 20,000 of them, that is enough to eat the plase up for lunch. Well I hope we will soon crack this nut that is so hard to crack. I hear there is 15000 Spanish soldiers over hear.

June 22. the soldiers are landing all O.K. and doing well, and only a few horses and 2 men lost so far, so the Flag Ship says.

June 26. Started in this morning to see if we coulden knock down that Spanish old Morro or else knock somthing cruckit around it. Well we pelted away for an hour or more and the flag ship signaled over to the Iowa to close in and pump at the Smith Key Battry. The Iowa signaled Back that her forward Turet was out of order, so it fel to us, we went in to 700 yards of the shore Battry and did knock down the Spanish flag with an 8 inch shell and knocked over one of there Big Guns. I belive if the flag ship had not called us off Capt Clark would have went in along side of old Morro and give him a tutching up.

June 28. I am geting tired of trying to keep cases on this thing. there is nothing doing but laying around hear like a lot of sharks watching for a fish.

July 4. The fish has come out to see us. On the 3rd the Spanish fleet came out of the Harbor to fight and get a way if possible. (I would have put this down on the 3rd But I dident have time and was too tired that night so I put it off for today.) Well the Fleet came out and went to Davy Joneses locker. it was Just 9.25 A.M. first call had sounded on our ship for Quarters and we all had our best dudds on; we wer going to listen to the Articles of War this morning and to have chirch right affter, But we never did. all of a sudden the Ordly on watch made a dive for the Cabin head first, and told the old man the Fleet was coming out of the Harbor. the old man jumpt up a standing. as soon as some of the men seen the ships there, they went to there Quarters with out any further delay. I was standing on the Quarter Deck waiting for the last call to go. I heard the news and looking around the affter Terets seen the first one. I thought she looked Biger than a Mountain. But then I thought afterwards we could cut her down to her natchral size. of corse it takes longer to tell about it than it taken us to get ready, for we wer allways ready, and all we had to do was to sound the Bells and stand By our Guns, they wer allways loaded so all we had to do was to turn on the fors draught and pull the triger.

By 9:27 the Oregon fired the first shot of the Battle of July 3rd. 1898 at the first ship that come out of the Harbor. I dont remember the ships as they come out, But we went in to meet them and passed them som good shots as they cep coming. about 7 or 9 minuts after they got started good, one of our 6 inch guns blew up one of the Torpedo Boats, struck her squar amidships, she sunk like a rock with all on board. and right hear is where I had to stop for a moment to admire one of there Guners. I do think he was one of the bravest men I ever had the pleasure to look upon. That man must have known he was going to a shure Deth, he stud on Deck and cep firing at us all the time, and the last time I seen him he was Just going up in the air. As the ships came out of the harbor they sircled to the right, or Westward, and Capt Clark knew they were trying to escape. they did not think the old Oregon was such a runer as she was a fighter, so we Just tailed on with them and giving them shot for shot. In about 20 minuts the first ship went on the Beach, plumb knocked out, and 15 minuts later the secon one went on the Beach, a short ways from the first. Then came the tug of war for we had to run to catch the Vizcaya and the Colon, but we catched them both. the Vizcaya was about 4000 yards ahead and the Colon was about 3 miles ahead, and the poor men in the fireroom was working like horses, and to cheer them up we passed the word down the ventlators how things was going on, and they passed the word back if we would cut them down they would get us to where we could do it. So we got in rainge of the Vizcaya and we sent her ashore with the secondary Battry and 6 inch guns, and then we settled down for a good chase for the Colon. I thought she was going to run a way from us. But she had to make a curv and we headed for a point that she had to come out at. We all think there is no man in the Navy like Capt Clark, he is a Brave man, he stud on the Forward 13 inch turet through the thickest of this fight and directed his ship to the final results.

Coming back to Santiago we waited untill we got to where the first ship went on the Beach and there fired the national salut. We have 3 Spanish prisoners on board and they thought we wer at it a gain, and it was all the sick Bay man could do as to quiet them. I hear there is over 1800 Prisoners and 650 kild and 800 wounded on the third. the three men on board tells the sickbayman that we run through there fleet coming around hear, for the next day they found a Pork barrel ful of holes and had on the head U.S.S. Oregon. We all seem to think we could take care of our selves Just the same. it is Just 6.50 P.M. now and the men all say there is no flag flying on the Morro. But I can see Just as good as any and I can not see any either, But then I think we are too far out.

July 5. At about 11.45 the danger Signal was flashed by the lookout from the Massachusetts, she being the one to show her serchlight at the entrance of the Harbor for the night, the Spanish was trying to sink one of there old ships in the Chanel so as not to let us in. But Just 3 or 4 shots from the Massachusetts Big 13 inch Guns help them to do the Job, for she sunk befor they got to the Chanal. there is Spanish menowar and Torpedo boats strung all along the Beach for 60 miles.

July 10. We are laying off now in Guantanamo Bay filing out to go to Porto Rico or on the Coast of Spain.

This is all in regards to the trip of the Oregon.

5.   *1898*—A SOLDIER'S LIFE

⟦ *The Spanish-American War proved that a new generation could fight as well as the men of Antietam, Gettysburg, and the Wilderness. It also demonstrated that both the high command and the War Department had learned little since 1865. Supply was inexcusably inefficient, sanitary provisions criminally lacking. Of the 5,000 men who died in the hostilities, disease accounted for all but 400. More than half a century later an Illinois militia captain could write angrily of the sufferings to which the men were needlessly subjected.*

We of the Spanish War who are still living can look back on our war experience, and can thank our Heavenly Father for being alive today. It's remarkable what our bodies can stand, when I think back on our Picnic Island days in Tampa, Florida—raw men in a heavy rain, a fierce storm blowing our pup tents out into the sea, no protection, our clothing soaked to the skin. Then came the issue of canned corned beef at sea that stunk so that we had to throw it into the sea—our landing at Sebony in Cuba, camping at the foot of a hill, large land crabs crawling over us at night, our long march toward San Juan Hill through jungles and swamps, joining up with the Rough Riders on Kettle Hill, heavy rains pouring down, no tents for cover, every man for himself, standing in trenches in a foot of water and mud, day and night. When

Letter of Jacob Judson, Captain, Company E, First Regiment, Illinois National Guard, April 15, 1956. Manuscript Collection, Chicago Historical Society. Printed by permission of the author.

off duty we kneaded our feet to get them back in shape. When the sun came out our boys would help each other by wringing out our wet clothes and blankets, quickly cutting down limbs of trees, and constructing an overhead protection by laying on palm leaves. Abel Davis and I found a spot under a tree about 30 feet from Teddy Roosevelt's tent.

For lack of proper nourishment men were becoming weak, ration issue consisting of a slice of sow belly, hardtack, and some grains of coffee that we had to crack between stones or rocks. Then came the issue of fleece-lined underwear in a 132 climate, and orders to burn the underwear we brought from home—result, you would see the boys in the river streams, backs covered with boils. Fleece-lined underwear and sow belly do not go in a 132 climate. Then came on malaria. It was my duty on mornings to take our sick boys to the Division hospital. There were no doctors in attendance, just a hospital corps sergeant who issued pills out of one bottle for all ailments. Sick men laying on cots, their mouths, ears and noses full of flies. I would go over to these poor boys and with my finger clear their mouths of flies—not so much as a piece of paper to cover their faces. Then our boys laying day and night on the edge of the sinks; because of their malaria they had no control of their bowels, weakened by malaria, kidneys diseased, guts rotted by foul food and water. Morning sick detail would come along and take away any that died, their bodies buried on a hillside, heavy rains washing away the soil, making necessary a second burial.

I was one of the fortunate boys. It had been my privilege to train Abel Davis when he joined up with the First. We were very close pals. Abel Davis had a brother who was a doctor in Chicago; this doctor gave Abel a box containing medicines for malaria and other tropical ailments, so when I came down with malaria Abel took care of me. Doctors were scarce; most of them were down with malaria themselves. Abel pulled me through; he then came down with the malaria himself, and I used his medicines until he got on his feet. If it was not for that box of medicines I think both Abel's bones and mine would lay in Cuban hills today.

Colonel Teddy Roosevelt said to his daughter-in-law, Mrs. Teddy Roosevelt, Jr.: "The Spanish War was but a drop in the bucket as compared with the war following." This statement was no doubt true; the war following had troops spread all over Europe, but the soldier had full modern equipment, was properly clothed, had healthy, nourishing food and the very best medical care, none of which was given the Spanish War soldier.

So when the war ended and we landed at Montauk, Long Island, our boys were thin, underweight, yellow as lemons, and it took us years to recover. So I say: Let us thank God for taking care of us all these years. . . .

6. *1910*—BUILDING THE PANAMA CANAL: THE
ENGINEERING GENIUS

❨ *The long dash of the* Oregon *around South America demonstrated the need for a canal connecting the Atlantic and Pacific. If the United States were to defend the island possessions, principally Puerto Rico and the Philippines, which it had won in the Spanish-American War, it had to have a quick means of access to the two oceans. The task was a gigantic one, at which a French company had already failed. As soon as the war was over, the United States government acquired the French rights, obtained permission from the new Republic of Panama, and, in 1904, began construction. For the success of the undertaking Colonel George Washington Goethals, appointed chief engineer in 1907, was primarily responsible. Arthur Bullard, a contemporary journalist who wrote under the name of Albert Edwards, offers a picture of Goethals at work.*

"Tell me something about Colonel Goethals."

My friend was a keen observer who had already given me much information about the life and work on the Canal Zone. "You want a line on the old man?" he said after a moment's consideration. "Well, the most distinctive picture of him I have is this. I used to live at Culebra. One night I was sitting out on the porch of my quarters, smoking. There were only a few lights here and there in the Administration Building. One by one they went out, all except that in the old man's office. It was getting on toward ten when his window went dark. It was the dry season. A full moon, as big as a dining-room table, was hanging down about a foot and a half above the flagstaff—a gorgeous night. The old man came out and walked across the grass to his house. He didn't stop to look up at the moon; he just pegged along, his head a little forward, still thinking. And he hadn't been in his own house ten minutes before all the lights were out there. He'd turned in, getting ready to catch that early train. The only time the Colonel isn't working is from 10 P.M. to 6 A.M., when he's asleep."

That seems to be the thing which impresses our men down here most of all about the Boss. He is always on the Job. . . .

The Administration Building is a barnlike, corrugated-iron-roofed structure on the top of Culebra Hill. Before entering it you get the impression of a noteworthy lack of fuss and feathers. Through a broad corridor, hung with maps and blue prints of the work, you reach the office, where the Chairman's private secretary and chief clerk reign over a vast filing system. You will travel far before you see a more smoothly

---

Albert Edwards, *Panama: The Canal, the Country and the People* (New York, 1912), 497–505.

running office. Does the Colonel want a copy of the letter to the Spanish Government about contract laborers? Does he want to look over the specifications in the contract for the new unloading cranes for the Balboa dock, or By-law 37 of the International Brotherhood of Railroad Engineers, or the excavation record of steam-shovel 333? Or is it the personal file of employee No. 33,333—the date of his birth, the color of his hair, how many times he has been docked for sleeping overtime, or the cause of his last quarrel with his wife? A push-button starts an electric buzz, and inside of two minutes the desired document is on his desk.

There are few men at the head of as large an undertaking who are so easy of access. If you have to wait a few minutes, you can find plenty to hold your interest. The walls are covered with maps and blue prints. This is true of every wall in the Canal Zone. There may be private homes along the line where the rooms are decorated with familiar photographs of the Venus de Milo and the Coliseum; but every official wall is plastered with blue prints.

But you will not have to wait long before you are ushered into the Throne Room—more maps and blue prints—and you are face to face with the most absolute autocrat in the world.

Many people have described Colonel Goethals as having a boyish face; but they must have seen him with his hat on, for his hair is white. If, as they say, his face looks twenty and his hair sixty, I could not see it, for his eyes—which dominate—look forty. He is broad-shouldered and erect. He carries his head the way they did at West Point before it became fashionable for the cadets to wear stays. Above everything, he looks alert and "fit." Although he does not spare himself, he has not lost a day from malaria.

Of course the first thing you do will be to hand him your perfectly useless "letter from my Congressman." Useless, because even if you have no letter he will show you every courtesy he can without interfering with the Job; and he will not interfere with the Job even if you bring letters from all the Congressmen.

Like every man who accomplishes an immense amount of work, he is a great believer in routine.

Six mornings a week he is "out on the line," and he takes the early train. He took me along on one of these inspection trips. It was before seven when we reached Pedro Miguel, and we walked back through the Cut to Empire. It was four hours of bitter hard tramping, for the Colonel kept to no beaten track. Whatever interested him he wished to see at close range. So it was something of a luxury to have a few minutes of "good walking" on railway ties. And dodging the incessant rush of dirt-trains and running for shelter when the whistle warns that the dynamite squad is on the point of shooting a "dobe" charge require no

451

small expenditure of energy. I have often walked through the Cut, but never before nor since at the clip the Colonel sets. They say that a feeling of fatigue is one of the first symptoms of the Chagres fever. As we climbed out of the Cut at Empire—it is an interminably long flight of stairs, and the sun gets hot in the tropics by eleven—I was sure I was in for a severe attack. The Colonel said blithely, "The only way to keep your health in this climate is to take a little exercise every morning." Doubtless it is true, but I had rather die quickly than keep alive at that rate.

His afternoons go in routine desk work, signing papers, approving reports, and so forth. It is part of his system that he discourages oral reports. Everything comes to him on paper. If he wants to talk with any of his subordinates, he generally does it during his morning trips—on the spot. Perhaps the phrase he uses most frequently is, "Write it down."

The afternoon office work is much interrupted by callers. The stream of tourists grows steadily, and the Colonel realizes that it is we, the people of the United States, who are doing this Canal Job. Any one of us who is sufficiently interested to come down and look it over is welcome.

"Whenever I have anything to study out, work which requires uninterrupted attention," he said, "I go back to the office at night." This happens generally three or four, and often seven, nights a week.

The most remarkable part of Colonel Goethal's routine is his Sunday Court of Low, Middle, and High Justice. Even as the Caliphs of Bagdad sat in the city gate to hear the plaints of their people, so, in his very modern setting—principally maps and blue prints—the Colonel holds session every Sunday morning. . . .

I had the good fortune to be admitted one Sunday morning to the audience chamber.

The first callers were a negro couple from Jamaica. They had a difference of opinion as to the ownership of thirty-five dollars which the wife had earned by washing. Colonel Goethals listened gravely until the fact was established that she had earned it, then ordered the man to return it. He started to protest something about a husband's property rights under the English law. "All right," the Colonel said, decisively. "Say the word, and I'll deport you. You can get all the English law you want in Jamaica." The husband decided to pay and stay.

Then came a Spanish laborer who had been maimed in an accident. The Colonel called in his chief clerk and told him to help the unfortunate man prepare his claim. "See that the papers are drawn correctly and have them pushed through."

A man came in who had just been thrown out of the service for brutality to the men under him. This action was the result of an investigation before a special committee. The man sought reinstatement. The Colonel read over the papers in the case, and when he spoke his language was vigorous: "If you have any new evidence, I will instruct the committee to reopen your case. But as long as this report stands against you, you will get no mercy from this office. If the men had broken your head with a crowbar, I would have stood for them. We don't need slave-drivers on this job."

Then a committee from the Machinists' Union wanted an interpretation on some new shop rules. A nurse wanted a longer vacation than the regulations allow. A man and his wife were dissatisfied with their quarters. A supervisor of steam-shovels who had two or three "high records for monthly excavations" to his credit came in to ask advice about applying for another job under the Panama Government. The end of the Canal work is approaching, and the far-sighted men are beginning to look into the future. "Of course I can't advise you," the Colonel said. "You know I would hate to see you go. But, if you decide that it is wise, come in and see me. I may be able to give you some introductions which will help you." (And, as every one knows that a letter of introduction from the Chairman of the Commission would look like an order to the Panama Government, there is another man who will want to vote for Goethals for President in 1916!) Then a man came in to see if he could get some informal inside information on a contract which is soon to be let. His exit was hurried. . . .

The procession kept up till noon—pathos, patience-trying foolishness, occasional humor. "Once in a while," the Colonel said, "something turns up which is really important for me to know. And, anyway, they feel better after they have seen me, even if I cannot help them. They feel that they got a fair chance to state their troubles. They are less likely to be breeding discontent in the quarters. But it is a strain."

One sees the Colonel at his best in these Sunday morning hours. You see the immensely varied nature of the things and issues which are his concern. Engineering in the technical sense seems almost the least of them. There is the great human problem of keeping this working force in good order, of caring for the welfare and contentment of this community of exiles—exiled to what was once the most unhealthy jungle in the world. And he sits there, week after week, the paternal authority to which all may come with their unofficial troubles. English, French, American negroes, Spanish and Italian peasants, coolies from India, with all the complications which come from their varied languages and customs—Mrs. Blank, whose husband drinks too much; diamond-drill operator No. 10, who has an abscess of the liver and wants a word of encouragement before he goes to Ancon Hospital for the operation. It is as remarkable a sight as I have ever seen to watch him at it. He is a good listener until he is quite sure he has got to the nubbin of the matter, and then, like a flash, the decision is made and given. And I think there are very few indeed who go away thinking that they have been denied justice. But, as he said, it must be a strain.

This routine of Colonel Goethals is followed week by week, year after year. It is broken only by occasional trips to Washington. And every one knows that the political end of the Job is more wearing than the regular grind. He has not had a real vacation since he took up this Job of ours.

7. *1910*—BUILDING THE PANAMA CANAL: VANQUISHING THE MOSQUITO

⟨ Perhaps not even the engineering genius of Colonel Goethals could have made the Panama Canal a reality had it not been for the work of William C. Gorgas, chief sanitary engineer. In the failure of the French, epidemics of yellow fever had been as important as the stubborn jungle and the rugged mountains. Gorgas had proved that yellow fever could be stamped out by eliminating the particular mosquito that carried it, but at Panama, skepticism and opposition hindered his work. Finally given large powers by President Roosevelt, Gorgas not only wiped out the disease in the Canal Zone, but also made the cities of Panama and Colon as healthy as any in the United States.

Albert Edwards describes the man and his methods.

Of all the sights on the Canal Zone there is none more worthy of note than a dilapidated galvanized iron ash-can in the hills back of Paraiso.

Half an hour's stiff climb from the village will bring you to where it stands in a little hollow in the side of the mountain. If you look up hill, you see a dense wall of tropical jungle. It is a tangle of unbelievable vegetation—a felt-like fabric of green; palms, mahogany, cocobolo, and lignum-vitæ for the woof, and countless varieties of vines and creepers, great ferns, and many-branched grasses for the web. It is embroidered with bizarre patterns in scarlet and yellow blossoms and ghostly orchids. It takes a sharp *machete* and a strong arm to penetrate it. It stands there untouched by civilization—primeval—just as it stood when Balboa tore his way through it to fame four centuries ago. The life which spawns within its dense shade is not only vegetable. Strange beasts are there—tapirs, sloths, iguana, the giant lizard, and snakes. It is the home of the boa, and many lesser but more venomous breeds. More innumerable even than the varieties of plants are the species of

Edwards, *Panama*, 511–13, 521–23.

insects. With acute ears you will hear the faint murmur of their life, the never-ceasing rustle of myriad microscopic feet on the rotting leaves; of myriad minute and filmy wings beating the dead, sodden air. The tropical jungle has a sinister aspect, an evident menace, which is unknown in the North.

Turn about, and you will look down into and across the valley of the Rio Grande. In the bottom is a haze of murky smoke, shot through with flashes of white steam. Through rifts in those man-made clouds you get glimpses of rushing dirt trains, of straining monsters of steam and steel, of an army of active, hurrying men. The clang of iron on iron, the shriek of steam-whistles, perhaps the roar of a dynamite blast, beat up against your ears. On the sides of the hills you see villages—clusters of homes, well-kept lawns where all that is beautiful in the jungle has been separated from what is noxious and brought under cultivation: noble groups of palms, red and yellow and green shrubbery, flaming bushes of hibiscus; you see mothers in crisp white dresses playing with their babies; and if it chances to be the right hour, you will see a rout of children, as husky youngsters as you could find in East Orange, tumble out of the school-house.

Now look down at your feet. Two or three little threads of water trickle down the sides of the hollow in the hill where you are standing and join forces in a little brook. The hand of man is as evident here as in the bottom of the valley. All the vegetation is close cropped on either side the rivulet—the jungle has been pushed back several yards. The banks of the little stream are no longer covered with dense moss and fern, as they were when the Spaniards came—as they were thirty years ago when the French started a colony in Paraiso. They are black and barren—smeared with unsightly grime. Just at the spot where the three threads of water join there is a rough plank across, and on it the ash-can. Just such an unattractive affair as the men of the Street Cleaning Department empty into their carts every morning in New York City. Only this one is uglier still, as it, like the banks of the stream, is smeared with the black oil. A piece of lampwick hangs out near the bottom, and from it there falls every few seconds a drop of the blackness. Splashing into the water, it spreads out—wider and wider, till it touches each bank—into an iridescent film. It looks like the stuff they use for oiling automobile roads. It is a compound of crude carbolic acid, resin, and caustic soda, called larvacide. These disreputable-looking ash-cans—there are many of them all through the hills at the head-waters of each stream—have a very intimate connection with the mighty work down in the valley and with the healthy bloom on the cheeks of those village children. They are outposts—frontier stations—in the war against the mosquito. . . .

And if you talk with these men who are fighting disease—the engineer, who with transit and chain is laying out drainage ditches; the man who has the responsibility of guarding the purity of the drinking-water; the rat-catcher, who strolls about with a Flobert rifle and a pocket full of poison; the red-headed young doctor who vaccinates you at Colon; or even the bacteriologist who finds his interesting researches "disturbed"—they will speak of themselves as "ditch-diggers." And no dynamite operator nor steam-shovel man will deny their right to say, "We've got sixty per cent. of the dirt out of Culebra Cut," or "We beat the record laying concrete at Gatun this week."

One of the Larvacide Brigade pointed out to me a rusty mass of French machinery going to pieces in the jungle. "They didn't know the difference between a mosquito and a bumblebee," he said by way of explanation. And he had hit the nail on the head. Like as not, our mighty modern engines would be going to scrap alongside of the old French ones except for the devoted, intelligent work of these sanitary men.

The responsible head of the men who have done this marvelous work —and no words at my command can express the wonder of it—is W. C. Gorgas, Chief Sanitary Officer. As Colonel Goethals is, in a way, pater-familias of the community, so Colonel Gorgas is the family physician. Goethals is farther aloof and authoritative. Gorgas is genial and sympathetic. They say "he can give you liquid quinine and jolly you into thinking you like it." That is just what he did to the people of Panama City and Colon during the early yellow-fever epidemic. Nobody likes to have his home fumigated. The Panamanians are immune to the fever. Most of them are too ignorant to understand the reason why they must be turned out of their homes for twenty-four hours. The more intelligent are easy-going, used to avoiding such inconveniences by bribing petty officials. All of them are, from a sanitary point of view, slipshod and careless. Gorgas succeeded in fumigating every house in Panama City within two weeks. He did it by jollying them—slapping the men on the shoulders, smiling at the women, and playing "one little pig went to market, one little pig stayed at home," on the toes of the babies. Even the Panamanians who are most unfriendly to Americans admit that Gorgas is a good fellow, and every child that knows him wants to sit in his lap.

Before coming here he had had charge of cleaning up Havana, and he knew how it should be done. Doubtless there were other American army doctors who had had similar experience and understood the work as well. But beyond the technique of his profession Gorgas knew the Latin American people, their manner of life and their prejudices. He knew how to make them swallow quinine and at least half believe they liked it. It was necessary to fumigate those houses, and we would have done it even if it had been necessary to call in the marines and proclaim martial law. But Gorgas, with his wonderful tact, did it without using force or in any way increasing the enmity to the Gringo. It was not only a remarkably effective sanitary accomplishment, but an exceedingly clever bit of diplomacy.

They tell a story about Gorgas in Cuba, and people who know him say that it sounds true.

In the early days there were many who made light of the mosquito work. Gorgas went to one of his superiors for some money to carry on his campaign.

"Is it worth while to spend all this money just to save the lives of a few niggers?" the Commandant protested.

"That's not the point, General," Gorgas shot back at him. "We're spending it to save *your* life. And that's worth while."

He got the money.

CHAPTER XIX

THE PROGRESSIVE ERA

1896 – 1916

1. *1896*—THE GREAT COMMONER

❦ *The second half of the nineteenth century saw the growth of great corporations and huge fortunes; it also witnessed a sharp reaction against these concentrations of wealth and power. The farmer at the mercy of the weather and the railroad, the small dealer squeezed by trusts, the borrower who despaired of paying his debts —to these the era was one of oppression rather than opportunity. When facile doctors of the economy argued for "cheaper money"— unlimited silver coinage at the inflationary rate of sixteen silver dollars to one of gold—the distressed classes of the country embraced the remedy eagerly and tossed their hats in the air for William Jennings Bryan, who had won the Democratic nomination for the Presidency by an impassioned speech in which he had denounced the gold standard and proclaimed: "You shall not press down upon*

G. W. Steevens, *The Land of the Dollar* (Edinburgh and London, 1897), 80–87.

the brow of labor this crown of thorns, you shall not crucify mankind upon a cross of gold!"

G. W. Steevens, an English journalist, sized up Bryan as he saw him campaigning in Washington in September, 1896.

When I walked down to the station five minutes before his train was due, I found it dense with men and women, white, whitey-brown, and black, who overflowed into the streets. In a torrid wind that fanned them lazily off the baked bricks and pavements, they waited with a crowd's usual mixture of expectancy and listlessness. . . .

There was a trembling in the crowd by the door. An open carriage with four horses and two colossal negroes in livery swung up to the pavement. Next moment William J. Bryan was standing bareheaded inside it. A compact, black-coated figure, a clean-shaven, clear-cut face, a large, sharp nose, and a square mouth and jaw. With the faint blue stubble on his face, and his long grizzly hair, he suggests an actor to the English mind. But you could not mistake him for a bad actor. Cheers rang out down the street, and hats flew in the air; and so he drove off serene and upright, pleased but not surprised, with a smile on his lips and a light in his eye—the very type of a great demagogue. . . .

I wandered up to the park, where the great meeting was to be held, and drifted into the crowd. The platform was built in front of a large stage, whereon sat perhaps a thousand people. It was draped with bunting, flags flew from every corner, and it was festooned with hundreds of incandescent lights. Along to the speaker's left was another stand. At one end of this a brazen-lunged band punctuated the speeches with "Shouting out the battle-cry of freedom," and similar appropriate airs. In front of the platform was massed the dense company, about ten thousand strong: this was not an extraordinarily large meeting for America. Out of the sea of soft felt hats rose an occasional club banner, and parts of the crowd were as thick with American ensigns as a wheatfield with poppies. A speaker was declaiming with vigour and eloquence from the platform, but the crowd took not the least notice. In the pauses of their conversation they occasionally caught a phrase, and whooped commendingly. But they were not there to hear arguments; they were there to hear Bryan, and Bryan at the moment was dining. Now and again an enthusiast threw into the air a sheaf of bills, bearing the opinions of Abraham Lincoln on the money-power, and the ominous hot wind, which was plainly bringing up a thunder-storm, distributed them over the crowd. The crowd was only languidly interested in free silver, but it was down on the money-power. That is the kernel of this election. . . .

Suddenly, above the periods of the orator and the whistling of the wind, the band crashes out "See the conquering hero comes." Instantly

the whole park awoke. A forest of little American flags sprang up on
the stand and waved furiously. A deafening scream went up from the
whole ground. "Unfurl," said a voice at my elbow; I looked up, and
behold I was standing under the flaunting standard of the North Carolina Bryan Club. I felt the position was a false one—the more so when
the staff snapped in the wind and the banner extinguished me; but
nobody had leisure to think of such things. The mass of heads and flags
in the stand was still heaving tumultuously; it took the candidate a
matter of minutes to swim through to the platform, yet the piercing
quality of the shrieking never varied. Then he appeared, calm but
radiant. Ten thousand hats flew in the air—ten thousand and one, counting mine, which with the stolidity of my race I merely waved—and the
screams rose yet more shrilly. A little girl in silver tripped along the
platform rail, and presented a bunch of silver roses. The shrieks became delirium. For a moment the square, black figure stood absolutely
still. Then slowly he reached forth the hand, like St. Paul in the Bible.
The din went on unabated. Still very slowly, he raised an arm above
his head and made passes—one, two, three—in each direction of the
crowd. Gradually silence crept over the mass of heads, and then the
orator opened his lips. In a voice low but plain, hoarse but very rich, he
began. He was glad to see once more those among whom he had spent
four years of official life. "We'll give you four years more," shrieked my
friend from the station. A broad and winning smile broke over the
candidate's mouth, and again the mob screamed. A most admirable
demagogue! "That's smart," said a little man behind me; "did ye see
how it made him laugh?" Everybody saw; everybody was meant to
see. Then again, when rain began to fall, somebody held up an umbrella
over the orator's head. The wind blew it inside out. But the orator
crammed a broad felt hat on to his head, turned up his coat collar with
a sturdy gesture, and then spread out his arms to his hearers. Once
more they cracked their throats with applause. "They won't get him
down from there so easy," cried a delighted elector. Nature herself,
turned gold-bug, was powerless to deter the people's hero from his
mission.

As for the speech, why trouble to inquire about it? It reads well in
this morning's newspaper, though I thought it smacked of platitude and
tautology. Certainly it was most effectively delivered, and telling gestures drove every point hard home. But the matter—'twas no matter
what he said. They had come to see and hear, but not to reason. Each
man was more concerned to set his own little radius laughing with a
smart bit of comment than to hear what the man they cheered had to
say. "Did ye see him?" was the question one put to another—not "What
did he say?" Both for good and evil, the free American citizen is no
disciple of anybody; it would take a smart man to teach him. So the

whole meeting was just a spectacular effect. And nobody knew and acted on that truth better than William J. Bryan.

Then came the storm. First a clap of thunder, then a cloud of dust, then flag-staves cracking, and finally such a fusilade of heavy raindrops as England never sees. Three-quarters of the audience took to their heels like a routed army. The rest squatted down close to the ground in bunches of two or three under an umbrella, till the park might have been dotted with toads under toadstools. Minute by minute the pitiless downpour went on. Then the remaining quarter split asunder from the centre. "He's gone!" and in fifteen seconds the park was as bare as if Bryan never had been. But as I plashed home I saw the four-horsed carriage, with the nodding helmets of mounted police, driving rapidly off, with a further running, yelling escort of devotees. And I saw the black, square figure turn from side to side, buoyant and elastic, glad and exultant over the popular applause. A born demagogue, if I ever saw one!

2. *1896*—MC KINLEY: THE FRONT PORCH CANDIDATE

❲ *To Steevens we are also indebted for a picture of William Mc-Kinley, of Canton, Ohio, candidate of the Republican Party. McKinley, who stood for the gold standard and a high protective tariff and saw nothing to be concerned about in big business, refused to make an active campaign. Instead, he stayed in Canton and addressed visiting delegations from the front porch of his home.*

When all is said and done, Canton has no more than 40,000 inhabitants at the outside. This is not so big but that a good proportion of its citizens know Mr. M'Kinley to speak to, and nearly all by sight. His mother still lives here in a tiny cottage by the roadside. And here he sits among his fellow-citizens, and waits to be made the governor of the largest civilised population in the world. There is a democracy among towns as among men, and it has been well said that if the United States have no capital they have also no provinces. The good side of this is that otherwise such democracy must quickly crush out individuality. The dubious side of it is the frequent opinion that, "If Bill M'Kinley gets in, he ought to do something for Canton." But, whether for one reason or the other, there is no doubt about Canton's enthusiasm for its citizen. I walked to his house under banner after banner; no shop window and few private houses lacked at least one of his portraits. So I came to the two-storeyed wooden house with green window-frames and red shutters, one of a row. Before it was a broken fence, part iron,

Steevens, *Land of the Dollar*, 128–32.

part wood. Also the place where a lawn should have been, but not a blade had the feet of pious pilgrims left there.

If you want to see a presidential candidate you ring the bell and walk in and see him. That is what he is there for. I rang and walked in; Mr. M'Kinley was sitting on a rocking-chair in a little office not ten feet from the door. His strong, clean-shaven face has a suggestion of Charles Bradlaugh; there is the same lofty and massive forehead, the same mastiff power of chin and jaw. Clear eyes, wide nose, full lips— all his features suggest dominant will and energy rather than subtlety of mind or emotion. He had on the frockcoat in which he was presently to address deputations, and loosely tied brown slippers in which he was not. He also was not unmindful of the spittoon. Yet with that he is gifted with a kindly courtesy that is plainly genuine and completely winning. . . . His personality presents a rare combination of strength and charm. But when it came to the question of being interviewed, though the charm remained, the strength got the better of it. No. He had made it a rule from the first moment of his candidature, and in no single instance had he departed from it. He was quite ready to admit that the contest was peculiarly well worth coming to see; indeed, he was inclined to believe that the whole country was an interesting one. He went so far as to presume that the election was of some importance to many people even outside the United States. But to be interviewed—the indomitable chin began to tighten up on the masterful jaw, and I left off asking him.

Well, if I could not interview, at least I could be interviewed. So Mr. M'Kinley turned me over with a gracious farewell to some of his political and journalistic friends. . . . I am leaving by this evening's fast train. In the meantime Mr. M'Kinley's staff provided me with refreshment, and took me to see a delegation. Three special trains, swathed in golden-yellow bunting, came clanking in, and a whooping, screaming multitude surged out on to the platform. Every man, woman, and child wore a brilliant yellow badge, and most added yellow flowers, yellow caps, a portrait of M'Kinley, a tinsel emblem of devotion to the gold standard, a fancy button, and a miniature edition of the Stars and Stripes. You could not move on the platform, and you could not hear yourself speak. What a hopeless mob! But suddenly "Fall in!" cried a voice. And before I quite knew what was happening the multitude had left the station and was formed up four abreast in the street beyond. Then the word was given to march. First came the leader on a grey horse, clear ahead. Then a rank of mounted marshals, every man with his badge and decorations, the horses with ribbons on the bridles and Stars and Stripes for saddle-cloths. Behind them came two carriages abreast, tricked out in every colour in which bunting is made. Then three huge ensigns, and almost as huge a mastiff, neck and tail tied up in golden yellow, led solemnly on a yellow leash. Then a gold-laced brass band. After them a long procession of ladies, all the black jackets splashed yellow; and after them a company of men with red, white, and blue umbrellas displayed. Next a great yellow banner with the name and style of the deputation—Portage County, Ohio. Then a battalion of men, all in blazing yellow caps, and then a band of boys; then another battalion of men; then another band; more men with a banner; another band; more ensigns; more banners—white this time, with coloured devices; then another battalion with yellow slouch hats to bring up the rear. Every man kept step. The whole array was so long that each band could hardly carry far enough to mark the time for its own particular division. Yet it never lost step or broke its formation. Horse and foot, men and women, a kaleidoscope of yellow and red and blue, music crashing, and colours flaunting, the long column wound itself in and out and about the streets of Canton.

When Mr. M'Kinley came forward in the tabernacle to speak—it was too dripping wet to receive them at his porch—the place was like a field of buttercups, but buttercups leaping into the air and yelling themselves hoarse. His speech was not long, and, to tell the truth, it was not interesting. He is no orator as Bryan is. Indeed he is almost the least effective speaker I have heard here. He read his address from a paper held before him, not without a stumble or two: he was distinct and dignified, but after the pageantry and shouting it was something of a fall to the commonplace. He pointed out with great force that Portage County was the finest in the States. But there was neither argument nor eloquence, and though for the peroration he imported a thrill into his voice it did not pass to his hearers. I suppose he and they could not help remembering that he had said much the same to the last county, and would repeat it in a few hours to the next. The next has come in and marched up by now, has been addressed, and has shed itself over the town.

3.   *1901*—THEODORE ROOSEVELT AND THE SQUARE DEAL

⟨ *When McKinley was re-elected in 1900 his Vice President was Theodore Roosevelt, the Rough Rider who had been elected Governor of New York in 1898. In that office Roosevelt's liberalism and his aggressive pursuit of good government upset the conservatives who controlled the New York Republican Party, and after two years they were happy to shunt him into the second place on the national ticket. Six months after the inauguration Czolgosz's pistol gave McKinley a mortal wound. On September 14, 1901, Roosevelt succeeded to the Presidency.*

Liberals the country over were jubilant. So, as Lincoln Steffens found, was Roosevelt. The "muckraking" journalist describes the origin of a slogan as famous in its time as the "New Deal" would be thirty years later.

The gift of the gods to Theodore Roosevelt was joy, joy in life. He took joy in everything he did, in hunting, camping, and ranching, in politics, in reforming the police or the civil service, in organizing and commanding the Rough Riders. . . .

But the greatest joy in T. R.'s life was at his succession to the Presidency. I went to Washington to see him; many reformers were there to see the first reformer president take charge. We were like the bankers T. R. described to me later, much later, when his administration suddenly announced a bond issue.

"It was just as if we had shot some big animal and the carcass lay there exposed for a feast. The bankers all over the country rose like buzzards, took their bearings, and then flew in a flock straight here to—the carrion."

So we reformers went up in the air when President McKinley was shot, took our bearings, and flew straight to our first president, T. R. And he understood, he shared, our joy. He was not yet living in the White House. He used the offices, which were then in the main building, upstairs on the second floor; he worked there by day, but he had to go home at night to his own residence till the McKinleys were moved out and the White House was made ready for Mrs. Roosevelt. His offices were crowded with people, mostly reformers, all day long, and the president did his work among them with little privacy and much rejoicing. He strode triumphant around among us, talking and shaking hands, dictating and signing letters, and laughing. Washington, the whole country, was in mourning, and no doubt the president felt that he should hold himself down; he didn't; he tried to, but his joy showed in every word and movement. I think that he thought he was suppressing his feelings and yearned for release, which he seized when he could. One evening after dusk, when it was time for him to go home, he grabbed William Allen White with one hand, me with the other, and saying, "Let's get out of this," he propelled us out of the White House into the streets, where, for an hour or more, he allowed his gladness to explode. With his feet, his fists, his face and with free words he laughed at his luck. He laughed at the rage of Boss Platt and at the tragic disappointment of Mark Hanna; these two had not only lost their President McKinley but had been given as a substitute the man they had thought to bury in the vice-presidency. T. R. yelped at their downfall. And he laughed with glee at the power and place that had come to him. The assassination of McKinley had affected him, true, but in a romantic way. He described what he would do if an assassin attacked him. He looked about him in the shadows of the trees we were passing under—he looked for the dastardly coward that might pounce upon him, and, it seemed to me, he hoped the would-be murderer would appear then and there—say at the next dark corner—as he described, as he enacted, what he, the president, would do to him, with his fists, with his feet, with those big, clean teeth. It would have frightened the assassin to see and hear what it was T. R. would have done to him; it may have filled Bill White with terror; what I sensed was the passionate thrill the president was actually finding in the assassination of his assassin.

I had come to Washington to find out whether the fighting reformer president, who used to see things as I saw them, saw them now as I saw them now, and what he meant to do with them. I spent my afternoons in the press gallery of the Senate and the House, watching the senators and representatives I knew about in the States at work representing—what? . . . The Senate was the chamber of the bosses. Two senators from each State, one represented the political machine that betrayed the people of his State, the other represented the leading business men of his State whom the boss worked for there. The U. S. Senate represented corruption, business, as I saw it in those days; it was a chamber of traitors, and we used to talk about the treason of the Senate. . . .

"The representatives and the senators," I said, "those that I know, those who come from States that I have investigated are picked men, chosen for their tried service to the system in their States. They stand for all you are against; they are against all you are for. They have the departments filled with men they have had sent here to be rewarded for anti-social service, and as vacancies occur, they will want you to appoint rascals of similar records."

He nodded. He knew that. T. R. saw the machine; he did not see the system. He saw the party organizations of the politicians; he saw some of the "bad" trusts back of the bad politics, but he did not see the good trusts back of the bad trusts that were back of the bad machines. He did not see that the corruption he resisted was a process to make the government represent business rather than politics and the people.

"I am on to the crooked machines," he said, "and the machinists, too. Yes, even in the Congress."

"What are you going to do about them and their demands for jobs for their heelers?"

"Deal with them," he snapped. "If they'll vote for my measures I'll appoint their nominees to Federal jobs. And I'm going to tell them so. They think I won't, you know. I'm going to call in a couple of machine senators and a few key congressmen and tell them I'll trade". . . .

That was his policy with the bosses, the political and the business agents in and out of the Senate and the House. He played the game with them; he did business with them; and he told them he would, from the very start. He did not fight, he helped build up, the political machine—and he made it partly his. I think that that was one of his purposes: to build up the party organization with enough of his appointees and to lead it with such an expectation of reward and punishment that it would nominate and help elect him to the presidency. T. R. was a politician much more than he was a reformer; in the phraseology of the radicals, he was a careerist, an opportunist with no deep insight into issues, but he was interesting, picturesque.

I accused him of this superficiality once during his first term, when he was keeping his promise to carry out McKinley's policies. That was his excuse for doing "nothing much." He was "being good" so as to be available for a second term.

"You don't stand for anything fundamental," I said, and he laughed. He was sitting behind his desk; I was standing before it. He loved to quarrel amiably with his friends, and it was hard to hit him. So now, to get in under his guard and land on his equanimity, I said with all the scorn I could put into it, "All you represent is the square deal."

"That's it," he shouted, and rising to his feet, he banged the desk with his hands. "That's my slogan: the square deal. I'll throw that out in my next statement. The square deal." And he did.

4.   *1908*—ROOSEVELT AND THE STRENUOUS LIFE

❡ *Theodore Roosevelt had been a sickly boy, afflicted with asthma, handicapped by poor eyesight. As he grew older he found health through vigorous exercise, and thereafter made a fetish of it. Captain Archie Butt, whom Roosevelt made his military aide in 1908, describes a typical afternoon with the President.*

I went walking with the President this afternoon: rather I should say climbing and swimming, for there was far more of that than walking. . . .

We drove from the White House at 4:15 and reached the boulder bridge near the centre of the park in less than a half hour. I had on heavy marching shoes, leggings, and a flannel shirt. He was dressed in what appeared to me to be a handsome cutaway coat, but wore a campaign hat. I thought, therefore, that we would have a mild walk, especially as he had been laid up with his leg and Doctor Rixey had advised him to take it quietly for a while. I think this very advice inspired him to test his strength and see what his leg could endure.

Archie Butt to his mother, October 10, 1908. From: *The Letters of Archie Butt* edited by Lawrence F. Abbott. Copyright 1924 by Doubleday & Co. Inc. Reprinted by permission of the publishers. Pages 119–23.

As we got out of the carriage he dismissed it and told the two detectives who had followed us on wheels not to attempt to follow us, and so we started. We made a circuitous route through the underbrush and at length came out farther up the creek, where there were no paths and few openings to the water and many overhanging cliffs and rocks. He pushed through the brush like an Indian scout and when he got to the water's edge he began to clamber out on the ridges and overhanging rocks. Sometimes we had to pass ourselves along the outer faces of rocks with hardly enough room in the crevices for fingers or feet. Each time I made it after him he would express his delight and surprise that I had done it so nimbly. I did not tell him how each time I thought it would be my last, nor did I show the real fear I had of falling.

My chief anxiety was for him. I felt that he had no right to jeopardize his health and life as he was doing. Finally we reached one cliff that went straight up from the water, made a turn, and the ledge he would have to make hung over some very nasty and jagged projections, so that if he should fall it might prove most serious to him.

I watched his ascent, therefore, with alarm. The rocks were slippery, and just as he was on the point of making the highest point, imagine my horror when I saw him lose hold, slip, and go tumbling down. He went feet foremost fortunately, and he showed great presence of mind by shoving himself away from the rocks as he fell. Had he swerved his head would have been certain to strike some projection.

I stood paralyzed with fear. I could see what it would mean to have him meet with any accident of this kind. However, he missed all sharp projections and fell straight in the water. It was deep, but he did not go over his head, the water only reaching to his shoulders. With a laugh he clambered to the bank again and started once more. I knew that there would be no use trying to dissuade him from the effort, so I watched him with more anxiety the second time than I had felt the first time. He made it on the second trial and then came my effort. I felt so relieved about him (and I knew he felt chagrined at having fallen) that it was really a matter of indifference to me whether I went into the water or not. On the contrary, however, I went over the ridge like a cat. It was the best climb I made during the afternoon.

But his innings were coming later. We trudged on for about an hour more, sometimes crawling, sometimes climbing. Just about dark we reached a point on the creek where we had to swim it.

"Are you willing to try it?" he laughed, and plunged in.

I followed. He called back to swim hard and straight, which I did, and soon we were on the other side, shivering but laughing, and then he told me how near Fitz Lee came to drowning at that point one afternoon; that after three efforts he had refused to permit him to make another effort and made him take the detour. We then skirted the Zoo and finally came to a ledge of rocks that rose, I should say, forty feet in the air and was much higher when taken in conjunction with the sloping and rocky surface below it. He said it was dangerous and he doubted if it could be made on account of the rain and darkness. All these rocks and climbs were familiar to him, and he knew what could be done. He started up, and to my surprise he made it. I began the ascent and got midway and could not budge another inch. I could not see anything and when I glanced below it appeared about as dangerous to go back as to try to go over. I could hear him calling from above not to attempt to follow, that it was too slippery and that it would be fatal to fall. I made one or two more efforts and then decided that I was beaten and started back. But I had better gone on. I simply had to slide down and when I reached the bottom I was pretty nearly used up. He made the detour and joined me about fifty yards further on, coming out of the precipitous jungle like a bear, but laughing and evidently buoyed up over his prowess. Indeed I felt proud of him, too. I told him how chagrined I was not to have been able to follow him.

"Never mind," he said, "you did not fall into the water. So we are quits."

That was the only reference that had been made to the mishap.

This all sounds like hard work, doesn't it? and yet it was one of the most enjoyable afternoons of my life.

5. *1909—TAFT AND ROOSEVELT: A CONTRAST*

❬ *When William Howard Taft succeeded Theodore Roosevelt on March 4, 1909, the new President asked Captain Butt to remain as military aide. Butt had difficulty in adjusting himself to a personality altogether different from that of his former chief.*

. . . I had looked forward this week to a good rest when the President and Mrs. Taft would be away much as a schoolboy looks forward to the absence of a teacher; but on Wednesday, after riding with the President, he asked me what Mr. Roosevelt usually did regarding aides on trips of an official character. I told him that sometimes he took them and oftentimes did not, but that Mr. Roosevelt was afraid always of the cry of militarism, and while he liked to have his military aides near him, he often requested them to go in citizen's clothes in order to avoid criticism. President Taft said he thought his well known theory, that the military should always be secondary to the civilian, would free him from criticism of this nature, and whenever I accompanied him to wear

Archie Butt to his sister, March 21, 1909. From: *Taft and Roosevelt, The Intimate Letters of Archie Butt* by Archie Butt. Copyright 1930 by Doubleday & Co. Inc. Reprinted by permission of the publishers. Vol. I, 17-21.

my uniform, and to so inform his newly appointed senior aide, Colonel Crosby. He then said he wanted me to accompany him to New York on the following morning, and as the train was to leave at eight o'clock there was little time for me to break a score of engagements.

You may have kept track of him, and incidentally of me, through the press, but no newspaper accounts could convey to you the fatigue of those two days. He has marvelous powers of physical endurance, and he keeps one engagement after another with wonderful promptitude and with little evidence of wear on the nervous tissue.

He has the faculty of sleeping sitting up, and while this may indicate some trouble somewhere in his great bulk, I am inclined to think it indicative rather of a phlegmatic temperament. It certainly comes to his assistance just now, when he has little opportunity to rest save as he can catch these little cat naps on trains and between interviews. He went fast asleep sitting at the White House last night while Speaker Cannon was talking to him, and this, too, when the Speaker was leaning over his chair and talking most earnestly on behalf of Jim Watson.

From the minute we left Washington I began to miss excitement, which always attended President Roosevelt on these trips. Even before we left Washington, President Taft took no notice of the crowd—it was not a large one—which had assembled at the depot. He entered his car and never came out to wave a good-bye, and I think even the depot employees missed the "Good-bye, good-luck" of the ex-President. There was a large crowd at Baltimore, and the President never went even to the platform to wave his hand—and so it was all the way to New York. Of course, I am committed to the Roosevelt school of policy and think that the people have a right to expect some return attention from the President when it assembles anywhere to see him pass. But I do not think Mr. Taft will ever care a hang about this form of popularity, although I wish he would, for it reads well all over the country that the President was met by a crowd here and a throng there, who demanded a speech. Mr. Roosevelt always said he was a poor campaigner and that he could only be made to speak when some vital issue was at stake.

At the depot in Jersey City and on the New York side there was a great lot of people gathered, but we were so surrounded by police and secret service men that we had little trouble in reaching our motor. We took the closed motor in Jersey City and never got out of it until we reached Mr. Henry Taft's house in New York. The President did not even look out of the window to respond to the *banzai* of the people of the street. Jimmie Sloan, the secret service man, whispered to me:

"What an opportunity he is missing! For God's sake, captain, get him to lift his hat when the people yell, for if he don't they will stop yelling when he will want them most."

469

"It's all right, Jimmie," I said. "He will get shaken down after a while, and things will all come right."

"Never," he said. "The other man has educated the public to know what to expect, and this one will be a dead card if he don't change."

It was no use to argue with Jimmie. He, too, had been too long under the magic wand of Roosevelt to see things in any other way.

As we approached New York I still wore my dress uniform, which is merely a modest, neat blue blouse. I said that I should change it for my full-dress uniform, but hesitated to do so, as the other was conspicuous for a New York audience such as we would see at the Grover Cleveland memorial exercises in Carnegie Hall.

"It makes no difference to me," said the President, "but you can't put on too much to please Mrs. Taft."

"It seems to me," she said, "that you are the one who likes the gold lace about. I find that you miss it when it is not there."

"I believe I do," laughed the President, "but I find that things go smoother when I have an officer with me. Somehow they seem to know how to do things without asking me to decide every time."

I think that it is so, for I have noticed that when I ask him, for instance, if he wants to see the newspaper men, he will say "No," but if I bring them to him he receives them and I think is glad to do so.

He wrote his speech on Cleveland, going to New York. He had not thought of it until he got on the train, and soon after leaving Baltimore he sent for his stenographer and dictated it in less than an hour. I know it was finished by the time he reached Philadelphia. In speaking of his habit to delay this class of work he said that it came from laziness chiefly; that he always put off writing a speech as long as possible, while Mr. Roosevelt always had to give expression to what he thought as soon as he thought it.

"If Roosevelt accepted an invitation to make a speech he would begin to think what he would say after the first hour, and the second he would have outlined his speech, and before the twenty-four were over he would have written it in full. Then he would read it to those whose judgment he valued and often would make changes here and there, but this method resulted in splendid productions."

President Roosevelt once told me that he nearly always outlined his speeches on horseback and would dictate them that same night.

Sometimes the method of President Taft works to his detriment. For instance, he had accepted an invitation of the Yale graduates for a dinner at the Waldorf on Friday evening, and he expected to write his speech on the way to New Haven, where he went Friday morning and where he was to attend a meeting of the Corporation Board at noon. After the meeting we went to a luncheon at President Hadley's, and coming back in the train the President went to one room to dictate his speech, but was tired and slept most of the way back, sitting upright, and in consequence his speech at the dinner was a failure; in fact, it was no speech at all, and he felt himself that it was not up to the occasion. There were over sixteen hundred men at this dinner, and the scene beggars description. It was one of the most wonderful personal tributes ever paid a man, I imagine, and the speeches of Sheffield and Hadley were masterpieces of their kind. The only thing lacking was one from the President corresponding in dignity or humor or eloquence to those which had preceded his, but again to quote Jimmie Sloan:

"He fell down."

But it made no difference to those splendid enthusiastic graduates, for they are so loyal to this son of Yale that, had he said nothing at all, it would have pleased them as well. The spirit of the Yale men is splendid. They seem to have accepted the unwritten resolution among themselves to ask for nothing but to give support and loyalty and to feel love and pride in him, the first Yale man to reach the Presidency. . . .

As we reached the Taft house there was a line of photographers ready to snap us as we entered, and they remained about the place the entire time we were there. When we got in the house the President took Miss Boardman and went dancing about the room like a schoolboy. He dances well and is as nimble on his feet as a cat. I have found out three things he does well. He dances well, he curses well, and he laughs well.

6. *1912*—ROOSEVELT BOLTS THE PARTY

❨ *Although Roosevelt had picked Taft as his successor, the originator of the Square Deal soon came to the conclusion that the huge, easy-going Ohioan had betrayed the faith. But when Roosevelt tried to prevent Taft's renomination at the 1912 Republican National Convention, held in Chicago, he found the Taft forces in complete control of the party machinery. In the end Roosevelt bolted the convention, led his followers from the Coliseum to Orchestra Hall, and then and there founded the Progressive Party.*

William Allen White, attending the convention in the dual role of delegate and editor of the Emporia, Kansas, GAZETTE, *describes the dramatic development, though not, to his everlasting regret, as an eyewitness.*

The Republican national convention was meeting that week under a guard of nearly a thousand policemen. They crowded the aisles. They ranged through the galleries to maintain order. Not that disorder had broken out, but the marchers in the streets, the great throngs in the gal-

This selection from William Allen White, *The Autobiography of William Allen White,* copyright 1946 by The Macmillan Company, is used with the publisher's permission. Pp. 469–73.

lery were so overwhelmingly bent upon the nomination of Roosevelt that his inevitable defeat seemed to be a good reason for the cordon of police that ran through the hall like a blue smear around the buff upturned faces of the delegates. I had been elected Republican national committeeman before the convention met, so I sat for the most part with the reporters where I could look down into the human caldron that was boiling all around me. The committee on credentials had done its work. It had seated enough contested delegates to nominate Taft. The parliamentary question which was before the house in the first day or two of the convention came in a motion to require the contestants on both sides to stand aside and let the uncontested delegates vote on the temporary organization of the convention. That motion, if passed, would, of course, have given Roosevelt control by about the same small majority that Taft had when the committee had seated practically all his contested delegates. There was parliamentary precedent to justify the prevalence of either the yeas or the nays; but with the contested delegates voting for themselves the Taft forces easily controlled the temporary organization which would also set up the permanent organization.

The Roosevelt delegates presented, as their candidate for permanent chairman, the name of Wisconsin's governor, McGovern, whom the Wisconsin delegates heroically deserted. The other La Follette delegates followed the La Follette suit. McGovern was defeated for election as permanent chairman by Elihu Root, who took the chair. He became the symbol of the Taft machine. He was a man then in his sixties, probably the most learned, even erudite, distinguished, and impeccable conservative Republican in the United States. He had served as United States Senator, as Secretary of State, as Secretary of War. He was the idol of the American bar. He had authority. When he clicked the gavel on the marble block that topped the speaker's table, order ensued almost hypnotically. The gaunt thin-lined features of this man so conspicuously the intellectual leader of a convention which had been melted by rage into a rabble, stood there calm, serene, and sure in his domination of the scene. He looked down upon the sweating wrathful faces in the pit where the delegates sat, swept his eyes around the vast horseshoe of spectators who jammed the gallery until they sometimes crowded the police guards off their feet. But Root's hands did not tremble, his face did not flicker. He was master. He knew probably what we afterwards found out, that the railing approaches to his rostrum were wound with barbed wire, that he was commander of the police, and could have checked a riot by raising his hand. He knew also that hundreds of his outraged fellow Republicans, men who had once been his friends, were glaring at him with eyes distraught with hate. I have never seen mass passion sway men before or since as that great multitude was moved those first hours after Root took command. . . .

Root in his morning coat and gray trousers, a lean, almost hatchet-faced man in his late sixties, repressed, almost reticent in his stingy use of words exactly chiseled out of the moment's need, was the greatest corporation lawyer in the United States, a man born on an endowed college campus, representing the impeccable respectability of invested capital. All his life he had been on the money side of lawsuits representing the invested economic surplus of a thrifty and not too scrupulous plutocracy. As befitted such a character in such a miracle play as we were staging in those days, Root was probably the most erudite and polished statesman of his day. Foreign travel had made him a cosmopolitan. Service in the United States Senate and in the Capital had given him that gentle, almost wistful cynicism that garbs the American aristocrat who stems back to Concord or to the James River. He was from every angle the perfect symbol of a propertied class struggling for its privileges which it honestly deems to be its rights. It was deeply symbolic that invested capital should be encased in dark-striped trousers and morning coat, wielding the gavel as a king would wave his scepter, with a dignity that made a show of indignation superfluous.

Beside him many times the convention saw the young Rooseveltian leader, Herbert Hadley. He wore a long gun-barrel double-breasted knee-length coat, and often in controversy smilingly pushed back a flap, shoved his hand into a trouser pocket, using the other for gesticulation, and smiled the guileless smile of lingering youth—boyish, disarming, as he spoke for the lost cause. He came to that rostrum because he had been fighting for ten years all that Root had defended for forty years. Hadley was a reformer. As prosecuting attorney in Kansas City he had been the foe of crooks, big and little; and as prosecuting attorney he had flashed on the national screen sharply, effectively, rather mercilessly cross-examining John D. Rockefeller the elder, who was the lion totem of the clan of predatory respectability in American industry. Hadley was the David to Rockefeller's Goliath. As governor of Missouri he had led the state in adopting the current reforms popular in that hour. There they stood in that vast charade that was picturing, *ad lib.*, the conflict inherent in Christian civilization, the conflict between aggrandized enterprise and its various ramifications of commercial and industrial rapacity, on the one hand, and the protest against that pious pillage, man's sense of pity for the exploited, his uneasy sense of wrong that was disturbing the middle class, and the inner urge for justice which has been the motor of human progress as man has struggled for the thing called liberty through the ages. They were old, old forces in an ancient miracle play of human history that were clashing there that sultry June day in the Chicago Coliseum—Root and Hadley, not villain and hero, not the dragon and St. George, but Samson blind in Gaza and Laocoön and his struggle with his snakes.

Slowly, motion by motion, phase by phase, the steamroller crushed its way toward the nomination of Taft. And here is a funny American expression: In the midst of all the rancor and wormwood pumping in the hearts of the delegates, every time a motion was offered by the Taft people, a thousand toots and imitation whistles of the steamroller engine pierced the air sharply, to be greeted with laughter that swept the galleries. An American crowd will have a terrible time behind barricades, or surging up Pennsylvania Avenue to overwhelm the White House. It will probably laugh itself to death on the way. Kipling said it of the American: "His sense of humor saves him whole."

Looking back, I don't remember how I wrote my stories for the newspapers. . . . I can remember wiggling in and out of the crowded Florentine Room of the Roosevelt headquarters like an overfed ferret, nosing out little inside notes of news for my daily articles. I can remember quiet talks with Roosevelt in his room alone. He was becoming deadly as his defeat approached. We discussed the possible bolt. We discussed the formation of a new party. There again I rejected it; but there again I was determined to follow my leader after I had advised him against a course which seemed inevitable. He knew I would follow. Then a curtain falls, and I do not remember when the decision was made that Roosevelt should bolt the nomination of Taft and run, either with a rump nomination or with the backing of a new party. Personally I favored the new party rather than a rump nomination; but I do not know when the decision was made to take the latter course. I was not present when the Roosevelt forces decided to do so. . . .

For some reason I did my own filing that night, which meant that I prepared three carbon copies and the original. I could file to about half of the newspapers with one copy through the Western Union, but maybe a fourth of them required filing through the Postal Telegraph Company on a carbon, and ten or a dozen of them required separate filings. Two of them near by, in cities like Milwaukee or Detroit, received their copies by mail. After I had written my story that night, a two-hour job, I used another hour or such a matter filing what I had written. By that time it was well along into the middle of the evening. I came back to the hotel and sat down alone to have the first good meal I had had since breakfast. All day I had been subsisting on sandwiches and hot dogs at the restaurants under the rostrum at the Coliseum. It must have been nine o'clock, perhaps later, and I was still feeding rather luxuriously and abundantly, when I noticed the dining room filling up. Ed Mullaney, one of the Kansas bolting delegates, came in, sat down beside me, and asked:

"Why weren't you over to Orchestra Hall?"

I told him why, and he began to laugh. "Well," he said, "you missed the big show."

I said, "What show?"

"Oh," he said, grinning and knowing how funny it was, "we have organized the Progressive Party. Roosevelt made a ripsnorting speech, and the crowd tore the roof off and we are on our way!"

7. *1912*—THE DEMOCRATS NOMINATE WOODROW WILSON

⟨ *In the Democratic Party, no less than the Republican, progressive elements pushed against the tough crust of conservatism. The leader of the progressives was William Jennings Bryan, too shopworn to be a real contender for the nomination, but still the most powerful figure in the convention that met at Baltimore in late June, 1912. Before the balloting began Bryan pushed through a resolution renouncing "any candidate who is the representative of or under obligation to J. Pierpont Morgan, Thomas F. Ryan, August Belmont, or any other member of the privilege-hunting or favor-seeking class." If the resolution could not be specifically applied to Champ Clark, the candidate of the conservatives, it could at least be interpreted as condemning the interests for which Clark stood.*

The favorite of the progressives was Woodrow Wilson, who had stepped from the presidency of Princeton University to the state house of New Jersey in 1910. Chosen by cynical bosses as a respectable front, Wilson had quickly repudiated his original backers and given the state a more enlightened administration than it had enjoyed in fifty years. William Allen White describes the "Governor's" arrival on the national scene.

The convention had hardly opened before Bryan attacked his foes by name in a rather absurd resolution. It made a sensation, and the Clark forces finally decided to laugh it off by letting it pass unanimously without opposition. They made it ridiculous in the convention, but Bryan made it dramatic in the country.

Bryan was a curious figure in that convention. The sixteen years that had elapsed since the boy orator of the Platte stampeded the convention at Chicago had broadened his girth, thinned his hair, taken youth out of him. He was slightly stooped, and had not the cast of countenance of maturity, but a little too much weight in jowl and belly. He was beginning to dress, of summers, in an alpaca coat with a white vest and wrinkled trousers. He had never paid much attention to clothes, and he had a frowzy look. It was evident from the parliamentary dowdiness of his resolution attacking Ryan and Belmont that his thinking was slightly askew. But his speech supporting his motion certainly had

This selection from William Allen White, *The Autobiography of William Allen White,* copyright 1946 by The Macmillan Company, is used with the publisher's permission. Pp. 478–81.

enough fire in it to draw howling approval from the galleries, and also of what was evidently a majority of the convention. It was a sinister exhibition, that response to the Bryan resolution. It was different from the clamor that greeted Roosevelt's leadership at Chicago, more emotional, more unrestrained, more savage. The academic group which was designed to control the Democratic party under the leaders like Wilson certainly had not made over the party. It was still Irish, and the rebel yell still ripped through the applause like a scythe down the swath.

On the first ballot, Clark took the lead. He registered a majority in the early balloting. As Clark was gathering his majority, it became evident that Wilson would be his opponent. Other Democratic candidates lost strength, which generally went to Wilson. After Clark had assembled his majority, he held it for several sessions.

To say that, does not carry the sense of drama. To understand the drama we must realize that, ballot by ballot, the country was standing around the billboards of newspapers in great crowds, watching the Baltimore struggle. The cleavage between progressives and conservatives which had been opened by the Chicago convention was deepened and widened in the hearts of the American people by the spectacle at Baltimore. Clark, who was a better politician than Taft, had not revealed his conservatism. That showed forth in the character of his supporting delegates, and after he held his majority for a day the nation realized, as the convention had realized from the first click of the temporary chairman's gavel, that Clark and Bryan were fighting the battle that Roosevelt had lost to Taft.

I was almost as deeply moved, watching Wilson's strength develop, as I had been at Chicago, where I had a personal stake in the ballot. I had met Wilson at Madison, Wisconsin, two years before. I had watched his career as governor of New Jersey, when he had, by sheer intellectual strength, given his state the primary, the direct election of United States Senators, by the contemporary subterfuge of allowing candidates for the State Senate and legislature to pledge themselves to a candidate for United States Senator. Wilson was for the workmen's compensation law, for child-labor enactments, and for the whole progressive program. He had dramatized himself skillfully, and stood as a progressive Democrat just as La Follette, Roosevelt and other state satellites in the Republican party had become branded with the liberal sign. So I found myself cheering whenever Wilson gained a state in the balloting. I know now from looking back over my newspaper reports that I filed at the convention that I reasoned that the conservative vote outside of the deep South was negligible and that if we had Roosevelt running against Wilson, the country was sure of a progressive President. And in my heart, loyal as I was to Roosevelt, it made no great difference to me whether Roosevelt or Wilson won. Although I was capable of emotional strain and surface prejudice, my ingrained habit of seeing both sides helped me to size up the realities of the political situation, and I gave my loyalty to the progressive cause rather than to the Progressive party.

I had no great personal liking for Wilson. When I met him, he seemed to be a cold fish. I remember I came home from the meeting at Madison, Wisconsin, and told Mrs. White that the hand he gave me to shake felt like a ten-cent pickled mackerel in brown paper—irresponsive and lifeless. He had a highty-tighty way that repulsed me. When he tried to be pleasant he creaked. But he had done a fine liberal job in New Jersey. I liked the way he gathered the Irish politicians about him and let them teach him the game in his gubernatorial fights. In every contest he rang true. So, as the convention dragged on, far past the four or five days that it ordinarily took to hold a national convention, my respect for Wilson grew and my admiration waxed warm. And when the Nebraska delegation, after days and days of balloting for Clark, broke to Wilson, I stood on the reporters' table top and cheered, until I was hoarse, with the galleries; while Tammany and the irreconcilable reactionaries in some of the southern states, and Tom Taggart, the Indiana boss, clung to the spars and lifeboats of the wrecked Clark liner, and all the country knew that Clark's day was done—that the progressives were about to win a victory in Baltimore to offset the defeat in Chicago.

Once at the last, as the convention was balloting until long past midnight, we were routed out of our beds almost at dawn and hurried into the convention to watch the break-up of the wreck that had been the Clark majority. It was then, I think, that I danced on my table and yelled to my heart's content. Wilson's strength in the convention slowly mounted until it tipped over the two-thirds majority needed for the nomination. But I did not exult much after that first demonstration of Wilson's power. It was tragic to see Clark's strength crumbling. I say tragic because it was indeed that disintegration of failure which one sees in well-built drama. Human nature is not always lovely in failure, and I sat watching the rise of Wilson and the fall of Clark—seeing men scurry from the Clark camp to the other to save their political hides, watching them sneak into the Wilson camp or go with banners. . . .

In reporting the convention I did not conceal my frank bias for the Wilson cause. I was a liberal before I was a Republican or a progressive, and was proud then of my heart's loyalty to the cause. Certainly I did not try to write a colorless story. I wrote frankly as a partisan of the liberals in both conventions, and while I told the truth as I saw it, my story was the story of the progressive split in each. There was no nonsense about concealing the cause of the rift, or smoothing it over as a personal triumph for either Taft or Wilson. I painted the conservatives black, and probably made the liberals white-winged angels—which they were not. They were only men, two-legged and frail, walking in strange new roads drawn by something they did not quite understand, following a pattern of political conduct that they could not quite resist, in a drama whose lines they improvised out of the promptings of their hearts.

8. *1913*—WILSON'S DAY OF DEDICATION

❨ *With the opposition divided between the regular Republicans and Roosevelt's Progressives, Wilson won handily. On March 4, 1913, he took the oath of office with the avowed purpose of inaugurating an era of government for the common people rather than for the privileged few. Joseph P. Tumulty, who had been Wilson's private secretary at Trenton and would serve his chief in the same capacity at Washington, describes the new President's approach to his responsibilities.*

A presidential inauguration is a picturesque affair even when the weather is stormy, as it frequently is on the fourth of March in Washington. It is a brilliant affair when the sun shines bright and the air is balmy, as happened on March 4, 1913, when Woodrow Wilson took the oath of office at noon, delivered his inaugural address a few minutes later, reviewed the parade immediately after luncheon, and before nightfall was at his desk in the White House transacting the business of the Government. To the popular imagination Inauguration Day represents crowds and hurrahs, brass bands and processions. The hotels, restaurants, and boarding houses of Washington overflow with people from all parts of the country who have come to "see the show." The pavements, windows, and housetops along Pennsylvania Avenue from the east front of the Capitol to the western gate of the White House are crowded with folk eager to see the procession with its military column and marching clubs. From an improvised stand in front of the White House, surrounded by his friends, the new President reviews the parade. . . .

So it was when the Democrats came into office on March 4, 1913, after sixteen years of uninterrupted Republican control and for only the third time in the fifty-two years since Buchanan had walked out of the White House and Lincoln had walked in. Hungry Democrats flocked to Washington, dismayed Republicans looked on in silence or with sardonic comment. Democratic old-timers who had been waiting, like Mr. Micawber, for "something to turn up" through long lean years, mingled

---

Joseph P. Tumulty, *Woodrow Wilson As I Know Him* (Garden City, 1921), 139–43.

in the hotel lobbies with youths flushed with the excitement of a first experience in the political game and discussed the "prospects," each confident that he was indispensable to the new administration. Minor office-holders who had, so they said, been political neutrals during the past administration, anxiously scanned the horizon for signs that they would be retained. "Original Wilson men" from various parts of the country were introducing themselves or being introduced by their friends. And there were the thousands, with no axes to grind, who had come simply to look on, or to participate in a long-postponed Democratic rejoicing, or to wish the new President Godspeed for his and the country's sake. . . .

To the new President the day was, as he himself said, not one of "triumph" but of "dedication." For him the occasion had a significance beyond the fortunes of individuals and parties. Something more had happened than a replacement of Republicans by Democrats. He believed that he had been elected as a result of a stirring of the American conscience against thinly masked "privilege" and a reawakening of American aspiration for government which should more nearly meet the needs of the plain people of the country. He knew that he would have to disappoint many a hungry office-seeker, whose chief claim to preferment lay in his boast that he "had always voted the Democratic ticket." Among the new President's first duties would be the selection of men to fill offices and, of course, in loyalty to his party, he would give preference to Democrats, but it did not please him to think of this in terms of "patronage" and "spoils." With the concentration of a purposeful man he was anxious chiefly to find the best people for the various offices, those capable of doing a day's work and those who could sense the opportunities for service in whole-hearted devotion to the country's common cause. His inaugural address met the expectations of thoughtful hearers. It was on a high plane of statesmanship, uncoloured by partisanship. It was the announcement of a programme in the interest of the country at large, with the idea of trusteeship strongly stressed. There was nothing very radical in the address: nothing to terrify those who were apprehensive lest property rights should be violated. The President gave specific assurance that there would be due attention to "the old-fashioned, never-to-be-neglected, safeguarding of property," but he also immediately added "and of individual right." Legitimate property claims would be scrupulously respected, but it was clear that they who conceived that the chief business of government is the promotion of their private or corporate interests would get little aid and comfort from this administration. The underlying meaning of the President's progressivism was clear: the recovery of old things which through long neglect or misuse had been lost, a return to the starting point of our Government, government in the interest of the many, not

of the few: "Our work is a work of restoration;" "We have been refreshed by a new insight into our life." . . .

After Chief Justice White administered the oath of office, the President read the brief address, of which the following are the concluding
words:

"This is not a day of triumph; it is a day of dedication. Here muster,
not the forces of party, but the forces of humanity. Men's hearts wait
upon us; men's lives hang in the balance; men's hopes call upon us to
say what we will do. Who shall live up to the great trust? Who dares
fail to try? I summon all honest men, all patriotic, all forward-looking
men, to my side. God helping me, I will not fail them, if they will but
counsel and sustain me!"

9.   *1916*—WILSON WINS IN A PHOTO FINISH

❮ *Midway in Wilson's presidency the First World War erupted.
The President pleaded for neutrality in thought as well as deed, and
concentrated on his domestic program. In 1916 he was nominated
without opposition, but he faced a reunited Republican Party headed
by a strong candidate, Charles Evans Hughes, who had resigned
from the United States Supreme Court to make the race. Wilson
campaigned on his domestic record and on a foreign policy which
had kept the country out of war, but the war could not be excluded
as a political issue. Millions of Americans took sides with the bel-
ligerents to such an extent that party loyalties were affected and the
outcome made unpredictable. Tumulty, always loyal, describes the
calmness with which the President accepted what appeared, erro-
neously, to be defeat.*

The happenings of Election Day, 1916, will long linger in my memory. I was in charge of the Executive offices located at Asbury Park,
while the President remained at Shadow Lawn, awaiting the news of
the first returns from the country. The first scattered returns that filtered in to the Executive offices came from a little fishing town in
Massachusetts early in the afternoon of Election Day, which showed a
slight gain for the President over the election returns of 1912. Then
followed early drifts from Colorado and Kansas, which showed great
Wilson gains. Those of us who were interested in the President's cause
were made jubilant by these early returns. Every indication, though im-
perfect, up to seven o'clock on the night of the election, forecasted the
President's reëlection.

In the early afternoon the President telephoned the Executive of-

Tumulty, *Woodrow Wilson As I Know Him*, 216–19, 222–23.

fices to inquire what news we had received from the country and he was apprised of the results that had come in up to that time. Then, quickly, the tide turned against us in the most unusual way. Between seven and nine o'clock the returns slowly came in from the East and Middle West that undeniably showed a drift away from us.

About nine-thirty o'clock in the evening I was seated in my office, when a noise outside in the hallway attracted my attention and gave me the impression that something unusual was afoot. The door of my office opened and there entered a galaxy of newspaper men connected with the White House offices, led by a representative of the New York *World,* who held in his hands a bulletin from his office, carrying the news of Hughes' election. The expression in the men's faces told me that a crisis was at hand. The *World* man delivered his fateful message of defeat for our forces, without explanation of any kind. To me the blow was stunning, for the New York *World* had been one of our staunchest supporters throughout the whole campaign, and yet, I had faith to believe that the news carried in the bulletin would be upset by subsequent returns. Steadying myself behind my desk, I quickly made up my mind as to what my reply should be to the *World* bulletin and to the query of the newspaper men whether we were ready to "throw up the sponge" and concede Hughes' election. Concealing the emotion I felt, I dictated the following statement, which was flashed through the country:

When Secretary Tumulty was shown the *World* bulletin, conceding Hughes' election, he authorized the following statement: "Wilson will win. The West has not yet been heard from. Sufficient gains will be made in the West and along the Pacific slope to offset the losses in the East."

Shortly after the flash from the *World* bulletin was delivered to me, conceding Hughes' election, the President again telephoned me from Long Branch to find out the latest news of the election. From what he said he had already been apprised by Admiral Grayson of the bulletin of the New York *World.* Every happening of that memorable night is still fresh in my memory and I recall distinctly just what the President said and how philosophically he received the news of his apparent defeat. Laughingly he said: "Well, Tumulty, it begins to look as if we have been badly licked." As he discussed the matter with me I could detect no note of sadness in his voice. In fact, I could hear him chuckle over the 'phone. He seemed to take an impersonal view of the whole thing and talked like a man from whose shoulders a great load had been lifted and now he was happy and rejoicing that he was a free man again. When I informed him of the drifts in our favour from other parts of the country and said that it was too early to concede anything, he said: "Tumulty, you are an optimist. It begins to look as if the defeat might be overwhelming. The only thing I am sorry for, and that cuts me to the quick, is that the people apparently misunderstood us. But I have no regrets. We have tried to do our duty." So far as he was concerned, the issue of the election was disposed of, out of the way and a settled thing. That was the last telephone message between the President and myself until twenty-four hours later, when the tide turned again in our favour. . . .

Just about the break of day on Wednesday morning, as David Lawrences, Ames Brown, and my son Joe were seated in my office, a room which overlooked a wide expanse of the Atlantic Ocean, we were notified by Democratic headquarters of the first big drift toward Wilson. Ohio, which in the early evening had been claimed by the Republicans, had turned to Wilson by an approximate majority of sixty thousand; Kansas followed; Utah was leaning toward him; North Dakota and South Dakota inclining the same way. The Wilson tide began to rise appreciably from that time on, until state after state from the West came into the Wilson column. At five o'clock in the morning the New York *Times* and the New York *World* recanted and were now saying that the election of Mr. Hughes was doubtful. . . .

Mr. Wilson arose the morning after the election, confident that he had been defeated. He went about his tasks in the usual way. The first news that he received that there had been a turn in the tide came from his daughter, Margaret, who knocked on the door of the bathroom while the President was shaving and told him of the "Extra" of the New York *Times,* saying that the election was in doubt, with indications of a Wilson victory. The President thought that his daughter was playing a practical joke on him and told her to "tell that to the Marines," and went on about his shaving.

When the President and I discussed the visit of his daughter, Margaret, to notify him of his reëlection, he informed me that he was just beginning to enjoy the reaction of defeat when he was notified that the tide had turned in his favour. This will seem unusual, but those of us who were close to the man and who understood the trials and tribulations of the Presidency, knew that he was in fact for the first time in four years enjoying the freedom of private life.

CHAPTER XX

THE FIRST WORLD WAR

1914 – 1921

1.   *1914*—EUROPE GOES TO WAR

⟨ *On June 28, 1914, in Sarajevo—a city in Austria-Hungary which most Americans had never heard of—a young Serbian assassinated the Archduke Francis Ferdinand, heir to the Austrian throne. The incident was the spark that touched off explosive forces that had been gathering for years—the national aspirations of minorities within the Austro-Hungarian empire, the growing feeling of solidarity between the Slavic peoples, Germany's ambition to dominate Europe, French and British fears of German conquest. Ten days after the assassination Austria-Hungary declared war on Serbia. Russia countered with a general mobilization. The following day, August 1, Germany declared war on Russia. In England, Walter Hines Page, American Ambassador to Great Britain, knowing that England and France were bound to Russia by alliances, saw that a general European war was inevitable. On a quiet Sunday evening Page wrote down his thoughts.*

Burton J. Hendrick, Ed., *The Life and Letters of Walter H. Page* (Garden City, 1922), I, 301–03. Reprinted by permission of the estate of Burton J. Hendrick.

BACHELOR'S FARM, OCKHAM, SURREY.
Sunday, August 2, 1914

The Grand Smash is come. Last night the German Ambassador at St. Petersburg handed the Russian Government a declaration of war. To-day the German Government asked the United States to take its diplomatic and consular business in Russia in hand. Herrick, our Ambassador in Paris, has already taken the German interests there.

It is reported in London to-day that the Germans have invaded Luxemburg and France.

Troops were marching through London at one o'clock this morning. Colonel Squier came out to luncheon. He sees no way for England to keep out of it. There is no way. If she keeps out, Germany will take Belgium and Holland, France would be betrayed, and England would be accused of forsaking her friends.

People came to the Embassy all day to-day (Sunday), to learn how they can get to the United States—a rather hard question to answer. I thought several times of going in, but Greene and Squier said there was no need of it. People merely hoped we might tell them what we can't tell them.

Returned travellers from Paris report indescribable confusion—people unable to obtain beds and fighting for seats in railway carriages.

It's been a hard day here. I have a lot (not a big lot either) of routine work on my desk which I meant to do. But it has been impossible to get my mind off this Great Smash. It holds one in spite of one's self. I revolve it and revolve it—of course getting nowhere.

It will revive our shipping. In a jiffy, under stress of a general European war, the United States Senate passed a bill permitting American registry to ships built abroad. Thus a real emergency knocked the old Protectionists out, who had held on for fifty years! Correspondingly the political parties here have agreed to suspend their Home Rule quarrel till this war is ended. Artificial structures fall when a real wind blows.

The United States is the only great Power wholly out of it. The United States, most likely, therefore, will be able to play a helpful and historic part at its end. It will give President Wilson, no doubt, a great opportunity. It will probably help us politically and it will surely help us economically.

The possible consequences stagger the imagination. Germany has staked everything on her ability to win primacy. England and France (to say nothing of Russia) really ought to give her a drubbing. If they do not, this side of the world will henceforth be German. If they do flog Germany, Germany will for a long time be in discredit.

I walked out in the night a while ago. The stars are bright, the night is silent, the country quiet—as quiet as peace itself. Millions of men are in camp and on warships. Will they all have to fight and many of them die—to untangle this network of treaties and alliances and to blow off huge debts with gunpowder so that the world may start again?

2. *1917*—WILSON ASKS FOR A DECLARATION OF WAR AGAINST GERMANY

〖 *For nearly three years the United States remained neutral. The old American aversion to European entanglements dictated a hands-off policy. Moreover, public opinion was divided. Millions, of German and Austrian ancestry, sympathized with the Central Powers. Other millions, shocked by Germany's invasion of Belgium and by her ruthless submarine warfare, openly hoped for French and British victory. Gradually the feeling grew that German success would be a world-wide calamity. When Germany announced that on February 1, 1917, she would resume unrestricted submarine warfare, which she had given up some months earlier, only an incident was needed to bring the United States into the conflict. The next month saw the sinking of two unarmed merchant ships. Wilson summoned Congress to meet on April 2. Robert Lansing, Secretary of State, tells the story of that momentous day.*

The issuance of the call for Congress to meet on Monday, April 2, 1917, was interpreted by the press and people of the United States to mean that President Wilson would ask the two Houses of Congress to declare war against Germany. Doubt no longer remained in the public mind that that decision had been reached. If there had been such doubt, it would have been dispelled by the activities of the War and Navy Departments, which were working feverishly to put the army and navy on a war footing preparatory to the United States' entry into the conflict.

The President spent Sunday, April first, preparing the address which he was to deliver the next day. At ten o'clock that night he telephoned me about certain matters pertaining to armed neutrality which he desired to incorporate in his address. He also suggested the preparation of a joint resolution which could be introduced in Congress. I told him that I thought the resolution could be better prepared after the address had been completed, and he agreed that it would be the wiser course. The following morning (Monday) the President sent me an extract from his speech, which was to be the basis of a joint resolution, and I immediately prepared such a document. This I read to the Presi-

From *War Memories of Robert Lansing,* copyright © 1935, used by special permission of the publishers, The Bobbs-Merrill Company, Inc. Pp. 238–43.

dent over our private telephone and he approved it. Copies were then taken by Mr. Woolsey to the Capitol and placed in the hands of Senator Swanson and Mr. Flood, who would have charge of the resolution in the Senate and House of Representatives, respectively. Later in the day these managers telephoned me suggesting certain minor changes in the phraseology of the resolution, which seemed to me entirely acceptable.

Shortly after the final form of the resolution was agreed upon with the managers, Attorney-General Gregory came to my office to discuss the proclamation which should be issued. While we were in conference Mr. Wilson unexpectedly arrived, an incident which excited the press correspondents tremendously. He gave us the benefit of his views on the matter under discussion, but no decision was reached at that time as to whether there should be one or two proclamations. I took the opportunity to urge upon the President that in going to the Capitol that evening (it had been decided that he would address the two Houses in joint session at eighty-thirty o'clock) he should have an ample military escort. Mr. Gregory strongly supported this precautionary measure. We both felt that with public feeling so greatly aroused there might be some fanatical pro-German, anarchist or pacifist who would be mad enough to attack the President either in going to or coming from the Capitol. The President was very unwilling to accept a guard, scoffing at and making light of the danger of bodily violence. However, after he departed, it was arranged with the Secretary of War that a cavalry squadron should protect his automobile and keep back the crowds from coming too near to the entrance to the Hall of the House of Representatives, where the joint session was to meet.

At eight o'clock, Monday evening, April second, the great auditorium of the House was crammed to overflowing. To the left of the Speaker sat the members of the Cabinet and immediately behind them the ambassadors of foreign powers; in front of the Speaker's desk were the members of the Supreme Court; the benches immediately behind the Court were left vacant for the senators; the diplomatic gallery was filled with foreign ministers and others entitled to diplomatic privileges; the seats in the executive gallery were occupied by members of the President's family and the wives of Cabinet officers; the galleries reserved for the use of members and the public galleries were crowded to suffocation, while people sat on the steps and stood in the doorways which led into the corridors. Every possible space was occupied by those who had been fortunate enough to obtain tickets of admission to the building.

Shortly before eight-thirty it was announced that the Senate had arrived. Those having seats on the floor of the House and the people in the galleries arose and stood as this distinguished body advanced slowly down the center aisle of the Hall and took the seats which had been reserved for them, Vice-President Marshall, who led them, proceeding to the raised dais and taking a chair beside the Speaker. A moment later the Clerk of the House announced "The President of the United States." Mr. Wilson came through the doorway to the left of the Speaker, followed by his bodyguard of Secret Service men, and with deliberation mounted to the reading desk in front of and a little below the high platform on which sat the Vice-President and the Speaker. The solemnity of the occasion was evinced by the unbroken silence which prevailed. Not a whisper was to be heard in all the vast throng. Not a smile showed on the hundreds of faces turned toward the President as he stood with determination showing in the lines of his face, which seemed unusually pale and stern as he gazed over the white sea of faces awaiting to hear the message that he, as the spokesman of one hundred million people, was about to deliver.

In low measured tones and with that fine command of his emotions which Mr. Wilson always possessed, he began to speak:

"Gentlemen of the Congress:
"I have called the Congress into extraordinary session because there are serious, very serious, choices of policy to be made, and made immediately, which it was neither right nor constitutionally permissible that I should assume the responsibility of making."

He then proceeded to review the record of submarine warfare since the German promises were given in the *Sussex* case, pointing out that the new policy announced by the Imperial German Government on January thirty-first had "swept every restriction aside." He asserted that he was for a while unable to believe that the policy would be carried out, but that he had been compelled to believe that it would be by the conduct of the Germans. He then went on to show the illegality and inhumanity of the German practices, during which he declared:

"Property can be paid for; the lives of peaceful and innocent people cannot be. The present German submarine warfare against commerce is a warfare against mankind.
"It is a war against all nations. American ships have been sunk, American lives taken, in a way which it has stirred us very deeply to learn of, but the ships and people of other neutral and friendly nations have been sunk and overwhelmed in the waters in the same way. There has been no discrimination. The challenge is to all mankind."

Mr. Wilson then reviewed the attempted efforts to protect American shipping by armed neutrality, which, he asserted, were ineffectual at best and, in the circumstances, "worse than ineffectual" and that, as we must now choose our next step, there was one choice we could not make and that was submission.

He paused a moment and then continued with an earnestness and firmness which thrilled his listeners:

"With a profound sense of the solemn and even tragical character of the step I am taking and of the grave responsibilities which it involves, but in unhesitating obedience to what I deem my constitutional duty, I advise that the Congress declare the recent course of the Imperial German Government to be in fact nothing less than war against the government and people of the United States; that it formally accept the status of belligerent which has thus been thrust upon it; and that it take immediate steps not only to put the country in a more thorough state of defense but also to exert all its power and employ all its resources to bring the Government of the German Empire to terms and end the war."

This was the pinnacle of his speech. A sigh could be heard breaking the complete silence with which the audience had awaited in breathless anticipation of this fateful utterance. I can see now the light of enthusiastic approval illumine the face of Chief Justice White as he listened to the distinct and measured words of the speaker. Many eyes were suffused with tears, but they were not tears of sorrow, but the tears of emotions which had been stirred to their depths by the occasion and by the momentous declaration which had been uttered. In all my experience there was no incident so thrilling, so intense, so profoundly moving as this point in Mr. Wilson's great address when he asked for war against the German Government.

The President described the attitude of the United States toward the war and toward the peace to follow it in this language:

". . . We are now about to accept gauge of battle with this natural foe to liberty and shall, if necessary, spend the whole force of the nation to check and nullify its pretensions and its power. We are glad, now that we see the facts with no veil of false pretense about them, to fight thus for the ultimate peace of the world and for the liberation of its peoples, the German peoples included; for the rights of nations great and small and the privilege of men everywhere to choose their way of life and of obedience. The world must be made safe for democracy. Its peace must be planted upon the tested foundations of political liberty. We have no selfish ends to serve. We desire no conquest, no dominion. We seek no indemnities for ourselves, no material compensation for the sacrifices we shall freely make. We are but one of the champions of the rights of mankind. We shall be satisfied when those rights have been made as secure as the faith and the freedom of nations can make them."

The closing sentences of this remarkable address are well worth reading, not only because of their excellence of language, but because they contain the very essence of President Wilson's foreign policy after the United States entered the war, a policy which he consistently pursued not only during the progress of hostilities but afterward as he sat at the peace table in Paris. Whether his ideas were right or wrong, whether they were visionary or practical, makes no difference. Mr. Wilson's consistency of purpose stands unassailable.

"It is a distressing and oppressive duty, Gentlemen of the Congress, which I have performed in thus addressing you. There are, it may be, many months of fiery trial and sacrifice ahead of us. It is a fearful thing to lead this great peaceful people into war, into the most terrible and disastrous of all wars, civilization itself seems to be hanging in the balance. But the right is more precious than peace, and we shall fight for the things which we have always carried nearest our hearts,—for democracy, for the right of those who submit to authority to have a voice in their own governments, for the rights and liberties of small nations, for a universal dominion of right by such a concert of free peoples as shall bring peace and safety to all nations, and make the world itself at last free. To such a task we can dedicate our lives and our fortunes, everything that we are and everything that we have, with the pride of those who know that the day has come when America is privileged to spend her blood and her might for the principles that gave her birth and happiness and the peace which she has treasured. God help her, she can do no other."

As the sound of Mr. Wilson's voice ceased and he seated himself, there was for several seconds, which seemed like long minutes, a dead silence. It was the finest tribute ever paid to eloquence. Then spontaneously and as if with one voice the vast audience broke into a tumult of applause that was deafening. They clapped, they stamped, they cheered, they fairly yelled their approval and support.

No one who witnessed that scene in the Hall of Representatives, where the whole Government of the United States was assembled, will ever forget the soul-stirring moment when the patriotism of the nation spoke in no uncertain tones and shouted approval of the President's demand that the German challenge be accepted and that the Republic wage war to the uttermost against the Prussian-ruled Empire. The scene is indelibly impressed on the memory, a vivid picture which can never fade or grow dim. It was a great event in American history, an event big with possibilities which touched the very destiny of the United States if not of the whole world. The tremendous forces set in motion on that April evening were to continue without check or abatement until achievement and victory were attained, until Autocracy was crushed by the irresistible might of Democracy.

3.   *1917—*"LAFAYETTE, WE ARE HERE"

⟦ *In June Major General John J. Pershing, whom Wilson selected to command the troops that the country would send overseas, proceeded to France with his staff. Floyd Gibbons, war correspondent of the* CHICAGO TRIBUNE, *describes the reception which the war-worn French accorded to the vanguard of the American Expeditionary Force.*

Floyd Gibbons, *"And They Thought We Wouldn't Fight"* (New York, 1918), 52–60.

We landed that day at Boulogne, June 13th, 1917. Military bands massed on the quay, blared out the American National Anthem as the ship was warped alongside the dock. Other ships in the busy harbour began blowing whistles and ringing bells, loaded troop and hospital ships lying near by burst forth into cheering. The news spread like contagion along the harbour front.

As the gangplank was lowered, French military dignitaries in dress uniforms resplendent with gold braid, buttons and medals, advanced to that part of the deck amidships where the General stood. They saluted respectfully and pronounced elaborate addresses in their native tongue. They were followed by numerous French Government officials in civilian dress attire. The city, the department and the nation were represented in the populous delegations who presented their compliments, and conveyed to the American commander the unstinted and heartfelt welcome of the entire people of France.

Under the train sheds on the dock, long stiff-standing ranks of French poilus wearing helmets and their light blue overcoats pinned back at the knees, presented arms as the General walked down the lines inspecting them. At one end of the line, rank upon rank of French marines, and sailors with their flat hats with red tassels, stood at attention awaiting inspection.

The docks and train sheds were decorated with French and American flags and yards and yards of the mutually-owned red, white and blue. Thousands of spectators began to gather in the streets near the station, and their continuous cheers sufficed to rapidly augment their own numbers.

Accompanied by a veteran French colonel, one of whose uniform sleeves was empty, General Pershing, as a guest of the city of Boulogne, took a motor ride through the streets of this busy port city. He was quickly returned to the station, where he and his staff boarded a special train for Paris. I went with them. . . .

The sooty girders of the Gare du Nord shook with cheers when the special train pulled in. The aisles of the great terminal were carpeted with red plush. A battalion of bearded poilus of the Two Hundred and Thirty-seventh Colonial Regiment was lined up on the platform like a wall of silent grey, bristling with bayonets and shiny trench helmets.

General Pershing stepped from his private car. Flashlights boomed and batteries of camera men manœuvred into positions for the lens barrage. The band of the Garde Républicaine blared forth the strains of the "Star Spangled Banner," bringing all the military to a halt and a long standing salute. It was followed by the "Marseillaise."

At the conclusion of the train-side greetings and introductions, Marshal Joffre and General Pershing walked down the platform together.

The tops of the cars of every train in the station were crowded with workmen. As the tall, slender American commander stepped into view, the privileged observers on the car-tops began to cheer.

A minute later, there was a terrific roar from beyond the walls of the station. The crowds outside had heard the cheering within. They took it up with thousands of throats. They made their welcome a ringing one. Paris took Pershing by storm. . . .

General Pershing and M. Painlevé, Minister of War, took seats in a large automobile. They were preceded by a motor containing United States Ambassador Sharp and former Premier Viviani. The procession started to the accompaniment of martial music by massed military bands in the courtyard of the station. . . .

The crowds overflowed the sidewalks. They extended from the building walls out beyond the curbs and into the streets, leaving but a narrow lane through which the motors pressed their way slowly and with the exercise of much care. From the crowded balconies and windows overlooking the route, women and children tossed down showers of flowers and bits of coloured paper.

The crowds were so dense that other street traffic became marooned in the dense sea of joyously excited and gesticulating French people. Vehicles thus marooned immediately became islands of vantage. They were soon covered with men and women and children, who climbed on top of them and clung to the sides to get a better look at the khaki-clad occupants of the autos.

Old grey-haired fathers of French fighting men bared their heads and with tears streaming down their cheeks shouted greetings to the tall, thin, grey-moustached American commander who was leading new armies to the support of their sons. Women heaped armfuls of roses into the General's car and into the cars of other American officers that followed him. Paris street gamins climbed the lamp-posts and waved their caps and wooden shoes and shouted shrilly.

American flags and red, white and blue bunting waved wherever the eye rested. English-speaking Frenchmen proudly explained to the uninformed that "Pershing" was pronounced "Peur-chigne" and not "Pair-shang."

Paris was not backward in displaying its knowledge of English. Gay Parisiennes were eager to make use of all the English at their command, that they might welcome the new arrivals in their native tongue.

Some of these women shouted "Hello," "Heep, heep, hourrah," "Good morning," "How are you, keed?" and "Cock-tails for two." Some of the expressions were not so inappropriate as they sounded.

Occasionally there came from the crowds a good old genuine American whoop-em-up yell. This happened when the procession passed groups of American ambulance workers and other sons of Uncle Sam,

491

wearing the uniforms of the French, Canadian and English Corps.

They joined with Australians and South African soldiers on leave to cheer on the new-coming Americans with such spontaneous expressions as "Come on, you Yanks," "Now let's get 'em," and "Eat 'em up, Uncle Sam."

The frequent stopping of the procession by the crowds made it happen quite frequently that the automobiles were completely surrounded by enthusiasts, who reached up and tried to shake hands with the occupants. Pretty girls kissed their hands and blew the invisible confection toward the men in khaki. . . .

Through such scenes as these, the procession reached the great Place de la Concorde. In this wide, paved, open space an enormous crowd had assembled. As the autos appeared the cheering, the flower throwing, the tumultuous kiss-blowing began. It increased in intensity as the motors stopped in front of the Hôtel Crillon into which General Pershing disappeared, followed by his staff.

Immediately the cheering changed to a tremendous clamorous demand for the General's appearance on the balcony in front of his apartments.

"Au balcon, au balcon," were the cries that filled the Place. The crowd would not be denied.

General Pershing stepped forth on the balcony. . . . A soft breeze from the Champs Elysées touched the cluster of flags on the General's right and from all the Allied emblems fastened there it selected one flag.

The breeze tenderly caught the folds of this flag and wafted them across the balcony on which the General bowed. He saw and recognised that flag. He extended his hand, caught the flag in his fingers and pressed it to his lips. All France and all America represented in that vast throng that day cheered to the mighty echo when Pershing kissed the tri-colour of France.

It was a tremendous, unforgettable incident. It was exceeded by no other incident during those days of receptions and ceremonies, except one. That was an incident which occurred not in the presence of thousands, but in a lonely old burial ground on the outskirts of Paris. This happened several days after the demonstration in the Place de la Concorde.

On that day of bright sunshine, General Pershing and a small party of officers, French and American, walked through the gravel paths of Picpus Cemetery in the suburbs of Paris, where the bodies of hundreds of those who made the history of France are buried.

Several French women in deep mourning curtsied as General Pershing passed. His party stopped in front of two marble slabs that lay side by side at the foot of a granite monument. From the General's party a Frenchman stepped forward and, removing his high silk hat, he addressed the small group in quiet, simple tones and well-chosen English words. He was the Marquis de Chambrun. He said:

"On this spot one can say that the historic ties between our nations are not the result of the able schemes of skilful diplomacy. No, the principles of liberty, justice and independence are the glorious links between our nations.

"These principles have enlisted the hearts of our democracies. They have made the strength of their union and have brought about the triumph of their efforts.

"To-day, when, after nearly a century and a half, America and France are engaged in a conflict for the same cause upon which their early friendship was based, we are filled with hope and confidence.

"We know that our great nations are together with our Allies invincible, and we rejoice to think that the United States and France are reunited in the fight for liberty, and will reconsecrate, in a new victory, their everlasting friendship of which your presence to-day at this grave is an exquisite and touching token."

General Pershing advanced to the tomb and placed upon the marble slab an enormous wreath of pink and white roses. Then he stepped back. He removed his cap and held it in both hands in front of him. The bright sunlight shone down on his silvery grey hair. Looking down at the grave, he spoke in a quiet, impressive tone four simple, all-meaning words:

"Lafayette, we are here."

4. *1917*—THE RAINBOW DIVISION GOES OVER

❨ *The menace of German submarines and mines made every American convoy a hazardous venture. The experience of the Forty-second, or Rainbow, Division, composed of National Guard units from all the states, was typical. The division embarked at Hoboken, New Jersey, in mid-October on three big liners—the* PRESIDENT GRANT, *the* PRESIDENT LINCOLN, *and the* COVINGTON—*and several smaller ships. The story of the crossing is told by Captain Yates Sterling, Jr., who commanded the convoy from the quarter-deck of the* PRESIDENT LINCOLN.

The embarking of the troops at Hoboken was a very drab business. The ships were ready but neither the material nor the personnel had been given a trial in feeding and housing such an enormous number of men. In fact, in all of the ships many dock-yard workmen were on board until the last gangway was put ashore. The commissary depart-

Journal of the Naval Institute Proceedings, September, 1925.

ment, led by the most experienced naval paymasters, but padded out with many raw recruits, could only imagine how it was to be done. Many of the soldiers were to catch sight of the ocean for the first time. German propaganda had insinuated the subconscious belief, not at all borne out by conscious reasoning, that the ocean was as thickly strewn with submarines and mines as Fifth Avenue with automobiles, or Broadway with chorus girls. One could hear the troops talking in low tones at night, fearing to raise their voices above a whisper.

The convoy sailed at night. No white lights of any kind were lighted except in the engine and fire rooms, and below decks where it was sure lights could not be seen from outside. In other localities where it was necessary for some illumination, in order to regulate troop traffic, pale blue lights were used which gave a gruesome and none too cheerful aspect to the moist and hot berthing spaces below decks, crowded to the ceiling with men.

The ships were untried. The personnel were in great part composed of men who knew but little of life at sea. Even the old timers were unfamiliar with the present conditions made necessary by war. It was imperative immediately upon leaving port to form the convoy. Big ships maneuvered at close distance to each other and at almost full speed. The captains and the principal officers were familiar with cruising in formation, but many of the watch officers engaged in this difficult maneuver for the first time. Captains remained on or near the navigating bridge at all times. The safety of their ships lay heavy on their minds.

Once on the ocean and in the broad white light of day much of the unreasoned fears passed. It was a long way to longitude 20 W, where the submarines began their piratical work and the convoy would require eight days at least to arrive within the danger zone.

There were many things to be done. The organization so carefully worked over by the executive officers for taking care of the troops had to be frequently tested, amended, and again tried until everything was as good as could be made. One important change was made in the abandon ship method. An attempt had been made in the organization to assign specified men to definitely located rafts or boats. This was all thrown out and the troops under their officers were formed instead on the upper open decks in groups of seventy-five or one hundred and merely told when the order to abandon ship was given to use the nearest jacob ladders and life lines plentifully provided and just "step into the water," where life rafts would be plentifully provided. The temperature of the water at that time was about 45° Fahrenheit; however, later, off the coast of France, it was only about 50°.

The navy crews were made as large as berthing facilities allowed, but there was so much work to be done that many additional details were given to the Army; guards at boat drills, magazine guards, and so forth. Of course, all troop spaces were policed and guarded by the Army.

Brigadier General Chas. P. Summerall, commanding the 67th Field Artillery Brigade, was the commanding officer of troops on the *Lincoln*. His one idea seemed to be to help the Navy in their new work. He appreciated the shortage of skilled men and said to the commanding officer, "Captain, in our outfit, we have every known trade; we've even got sailors if you need them." That ship used soldiers freely.

The convoy sailed in line-abreast formation and, at night, with no lights showing. When the moon was obscured the next ship abreast could be seen as a deeper shadow in the gloom unless by chance she edged in too close and then to the captain and officer of the deck she loomed like a mountain too near for comfort. On the other hand, if the end ships were kept too wide they were liable to lose touch entirely during darkness and at daylight be miles ahead or miles astern of the formation. In the beginning careful routing of convoys was difficult, especially as the ocean was fairly full of neutral shipping. Often a tramp steamer would find itself heading through a convoy at night. Its actions would at once reflect the coolness of the man on the tramp's bridge. It might be expected to charge down one way, then change its mind and come charging back another way. It went without saying that troopships took no chances; they discounted brains on the bridge of the tramp and gave him a wide berth. Then there was the danger of running pell-mell into a big merchant convoy on a converging course, especially nearing the coast of France. Then quick action by the convoy commander of the fast troopships was required to avoid a mishap.

Every man of the artillery brigade carried by the *President Lincoln* will doubtlessly not soon forget, even after his hazardous service at the front in France, the two hours that vessel was stopped in the war zone, east of longitude 20°, to repair a disabled air pump. The troops were all at their abandon ship stations with life preservers adjusted. The gun crews were alert, and all lookouts on their toes to discover a periscope. The rest of the convoy swept on and quickly disappeared beyond the horizon. A lone destroyer remained, circling about the huge vessel at high speed. The two hours seemed an eternity to those in authority. Possibly there was not a submarine within a hundred miles, yet one might have been near enough to make an attack and, if so, 6,000-odd men would have been set adrift five hundred miles from land, mostly on life rafts to which they could only cling, and with the water temperature 50°. There were six destroyers altogether guarding the convoy. If all six performed rescue work they could not accommodate with standing room all of the shipwrecked men on this one big ship, and to perform this act of mercy, they must desert the remainder of the convoy they were guarding and seek port at full speed.

Just before this convoy arrived at St. Nazaire, the entrance to the River Loire was mined by an enemy submarine, so the convoy was conducted by a circuitous route, through tortuous channels and between menacing rocks to a point inside of the mined area.

The little French pilot boarded the ship and received a cordial welcome from the happy troops. The atmosphere of constraint suddenly disappeared as the big convoy entered the sheltered waters of Quiberon Bay and they were anxious to let off steam that had been bottled up for two weeks. The regimental bands played with a renewed vigor. Everybody was happy. The submarines had been fooled.

At the entrance to the river a thick blanket of fog was encountered. To the westward was the open sea and only a short distance away the mine field. The pilot said, shrugging expressive shoulders, "I cannot see the buoy, therefore we must stop and anchor." Six loaded transports awaited the finding of that buoy. Meanwhile, worse luck, the guarding destroyers considering their duty completed had all turned northward and had disappeared in the fog. They had other convoys to protect.

It is not a pleasant feeling to poke the big blunt bow of a 20,000-ton liner into a fog to find a tiny buoy surrounded on all sides by treacherous rocks, shoals, and enemy mines, and amidst the strongest known currents; but, on the other hand, there was the necessity to anchor in that dangerous locality six ships carrying 20,000 men. One submarine might, by some evil streak of devil's luck, sink all of them and on the threshold of France.

"There's the buoy!" Everyone seemed to understand the importance of keeping that buoy in sight. Night was fast falling but once within the headlands of the river, the fog melted. Up the river the convoy steamed and the biggest turned in toward the locks in order to enter at the top of the tide. "How long are you?" asked the pilot of the captain of the biggest ship, while that ship was entering the lock. When told, the pilot looked serious for a few minutes, apparently calculating. "It's all right," he finally announced; "there's ten feet to spare." It was the largest ship that had ever entered that locked harbor. The captain was confident all the time that the all-knowing ones at home had made sure of the fit—yet it was none too much to spare.

Sunny France was in tears on the arrival of the convoy but the populace were out in full force to welcome the troops. There was no more soul-stirring sight than those six huge ships loaded down with khaki-clad men, their white faces gleaming in the flood of great cargo and illuminating lights on the docks, passing each other close aboard as one after another was docked into the small harbor and berthed alongside the piers. Bands were playing "Over There," "It's a Long Long Trail," "Keep the Home Fires Burning," and so forth. Each ship, as it entered the harbor, cheered those it passed, until there was a continuous roar of young American voices mingled with stirring music and song. The rain, an insidious French drizzle, could not dampen the soldiers' spirits.

They were "over there"!

5. *1918*—THE HOME FRONT

❴ *The war involved civilian populations to an extent undreamed of before 1914. In a letter to the American Ambassador to Great Britain, Franklin K. Lane, Secretary of the Interior, described life in Washington in the spring of 1918—and made a shrewd prediction as to the effect the war would have on the American economy.*

. . . Let me give you a glimpse of my day, just to compare it with your own and by way of contrasting life in two different spheres and on different sides of the ocean. I get to my office at nine in the morning and my day is broken up into fifteen-minute periods, during which I see either my own people or others. I really write none of my own letters, simply telling my secretaries whether the answer should be "yes" or "no." I lunch at my own desk and generally with my wife, who has charge of our war work in the Department. We have over thirteen hundred men who have gone out of this Department into the Army. . . . My day is broken into by Cabinet meeting twice a week, meeting of the Council of National Defense twice a week, and latterly with long sessions every afternoon over the question of what railroad wages should be.

My office is a sort of place of last resort for those who are discouraged elsewhere, for Washington is no longer a city of set routine and fixed habit. It is at last the center of the nation. New York is no longer even the financial center. The newspapers are edited from here. Society centers here. All the industrial chiefs of the nation spend most of their time here. It is easier to find a great cattle king or automobile manufacturer or a railroad president or a banker at the Shoreham or the Willard Hotel than it is to find him in his own town. The surprising thing is that these great men who have made our country do not loom so large when brought to Washington and put to work. . . . Every day I find some man of many millions who has been here for months and whose movements used to be a matter of newspaper notoriety, but I did not know, even, that he was here. I leave my office at seven o'clock, not having been out of it during the day except for a Cabinet or Council meeting, take a wink of sleep, change my clothes and go to a dinner, for this, as you will remember, is the one form of entertainment that

Anne Wintermute Lane and Louise Herrick Wall, Eds., *The Letters of Franklin K. Lane* (Boston, 1922), 274–78.

Washington has permitted itself in the war. The dinners are Hooverized,
—three courses, little or no wheat, little or no meat, little or no sugar,
a few serve wine. And round the table will always be found men in
foreign uniforms, or some missionary from some great power who
comes begging for boats or food. These dinners used to be places of
great gossip, and chiefly anti-administration gossip, but the spirit of the
people is one of unequaled loyalty. The Republicans are as glad to have
Wilson as their President as are the Democrats, I think sometimes a
little more glad, because many of the Democrats are disgruntled over
patronage or something else. The women are ferocious in their hunt for
spies, and their criticism is against what they think is indifference to
this danger. Boys appear at these dinners in the great houses, because
of their uniforms, who would never have been permitted even to come
to the front door in other days, for all are potential heroes. Every
woman carries her knitting, and it is seldom that you hear a croaker
even among the most luxurious class. Well, the dinner is over by half
past ten, and I go home to an hour and a half's work, which has been
sent from the office, and fall at last into a more or less troubled sleep.
This is the daily round.

I have not been to New York since the war began. I made one trip
across the continent speaking for the Liberty Loan, day and night.
And this life is pretty much the life of all of us here. The President
keeps up his spirits by going to the theatre three or four times a week.
There are no official functions at the White House, and everybody's
teeth are set. The Allies need not doubt our resolution. England and
France will break before we will, and I do not doubt their steadfast
purpose. It is, as you said long ago, their fault that this war has come,
for they did not realize the kind of an enemy they had, either in spirit,
purpose, or strength. But we will increasingly strengthen that western
gate so that the Huns will not break through.

We do things fast here, but I never realized before how slow we are
in getting started. It takes a long time for us to get a new stride. I did
not think that this was true industrially. I have known that it was true
politically for a long time, because this was the most backward and
most conservative of all the democracies. We take up new machinery of
government so slowly. But industrially it is also true. When told to
change step we shift and stumble and halt and hesitate and go through
all kinds of awkward misses. This has been true as to ships and aëro-
planes and guns, big and little, and uniforms. Whatever the government
has done itself has been tied by endless red tape. It is hard for an army
officer to get out of the desk habit, and caution, conservatism, sureness,
seem even in time of crisis to be more important than a bit of daring.
In my Department, I figure that it takes about seven years for the
nerve of initiative and the nerve of imagination to atrophy, and so, per-

haps, it is in other departments. It took five months for one of our war bureaus to get out a contract for a building that we were to build for them. Fifteen men had to sign the contract. And of course we have been impatient. But things are bettering every day. The men in the camps are very impatient to get away. But where are the ships to do all the work? The Republicans cannot chide us with all of the unpreparedness, for they stood in the way of our getting ships three years ago. The gods have been against us in the way of weather so we have not brought down our supplies to the seaboard, but we have not had the ships to take away that which was there; or coal, sometimes, for the ships.

From now, however, you will see a steadier, surer movement of men, munitions, food, and ships. The whole country is solidly, strongly with the President. There are men in Congress bitterly against him but they do not dare to raise their voices, because he has the people so resolutely with him. The Russian overthrow has been a good thing for us in one way. It will cost us perhaps a million lives, but it will prove to us the value of law and order. We are to have our troubles, and must change our system of life in the next few years.

A great oil man was in the office the other day and told me in a plain, matter-of-fact way, what must be done to win—the sacrifices that must be made—and he ended by saying, "After all, what is property?" This is a very pregnant question. It is not being asked in Russia alone. Who has the right to anything? My answer is, not the man, necessarily, who has it, but the man who can use it to good purpose. The way to find the latter man is the difficulty.

We will have national woman suffrage, national prohibition, continuing inheritance tax, continuing income tax, national life insurance, an increasing grip upon the railroads, their finances and their operation as well as their rates. Each primary resource, such as land and coal and iron and copper and oil, we will more carefully conserve. There will be no longer the opportunity for the individual along these lines that there has been. Industry must find some way of profit-sharing or it will be nationalized. These things, however, must be regarded as incidents now; and the labor people, those with vision and in authority, are very willing to postpone the day of accounting until we know what the new order is to be like. . . .

6.   *1918*—THE UNITED STATES MARINES AT BELLEAU WOOD

❨ *In early June the German Seventh Army, driving toward Paris, attempted to cross the River Marne at Château-Thierry. When the*

Kemper F. Cowing and Courtney Ryley Cooper, *Dear Folks at Home* (Boston, 1919), 236–43.

499

French retreated American troops were thrown in to stem the advance. In Belleau Wood the Fourth Marine Brigade stopped the enemy cold, but of the 8,000 Marines who went into battle, only 2,000 escaped death or wounds. One of the survivors was Sergeant Karl P. Spencer, who related his experiences in a letter to his mother.

My Dear Mother: I am taking this opportunity to write. The Lord only knows when I will be able to get the letter off. Yesterday and today I received beaucoup first-class mail and a package of eats from Paris, plum pudding and chocolate bars. Believe me, Mother, one appreciates such luxuries after existing for six days on Argentine bully beef, French bread, salmon and water. Twice the Red Cross and Y.M.C.A. (God bless them!) have sent us jam and cakes and chocolates and cigarettes. I smoke cigarettes (when I have them) like a trooper, and especially when I am lying in my hole in the ground and the shells are breaking all around; they quiet one's nerves, I believe.

In my last letter I spoke of our moving to the rear; instead, that very day word came for us to go into the front line that night. Were we disgusted? Gee, but you should have heard us rave and swear! We have been in the trenches since March 14th, and in this sector nearly four weeks; no leaves; no liberty; no rest; they must think the Marines are supermen or maybe mechanical devices for fighting. But then we have it straight from General Pershing that what's left of the Marine Corps will parade in Paris July 4th. Glory be, if this is only true. According to the fighting we've done we rate something out of the ordinary, and, of course, you know the Marines are credited with saving Paris. You have read exaggerated accounts of our exploits, perhaps you would be pleased to hear the truth. It is a long, long story so don't weaken.

Get you a map, locate Château-Thierry, back up ten kilometres toward Paris by way of Meaux (Meaux was being evacuated when we arrived), and there you find the location of our battle-ground. The Germans were advancing ten kilometres a day when in swept the Marines, relieving the retreating boys and with the Eighty-second and Eighty-third Companies in skirmish formation, attacking, the Huns were stopped and in three hours lines were pushed back four kilometres. Our losses were slight, for the Germans were not prepared to meet a stone wall resistance such as they bumped up against and certainly they had no idea of an offensive movement being launched.

The German infantry had been moving at so rapid a pace that their artillery could not keep up with them. As a result it was easy sailing for us. You should have seen those Huns running; they dropped everything and started toward Berlin. Twenty German planes were counted overhead that evening; they wanted to find out what the devil had interfered with their well-laid plans; what they saw was a wheat-field full of Marines and for miles behind the lines hundreds of trucks going forward at full speed, loaded with men, provisions and munitions. The Kaiser certainly had a set-back.

To continue with the battle, our objective was a railway station, but between us and our objective was a machine-gun Hill 142, and here the Germans made a last stand. The hill is a sort of plateau rising out of Belleau Woods, but between it and the woods are patches of wheat and beyond the hill the ground slopes gently down to the railway station. The hilltop is covered with immense rock and behind these the Germans placed their machine guns and made their stand, and held out for three weeks. The Eighty-second and Eighty-third made one attack against this position. We formed in the wheat-field in wave formation, and with our captain and major leading we rushed up that hill in the face of twenty machine guns. The woods were also full of German snipers.

The attack failed; we lost all our officers and half our company. We were just starting when out from behind a rock comes an unarmed German with arms up in the air shouting "Kamerad!" A dozen Marines rushed forward with fixed bayonets and stuck that man full of holes— orders were to take no prisoners. Many a brave Marine fell that day. That was our last attack. Since then six separate attacks were made on that hill and not until the other night did the Marines take it. Between the time of our attack and the successful one, the German artillery was moved up and we suffered much from shell fire.

The attack the 25th was wonderfully successful. We, the Eighty-second Company, were in support, but were not called upon. At 3 P.M. the American artillery opened up on the hill. The Germans suspected something and immediately began gassing our rear and shelling the support—us. After two hours of fearful bombarding, at 5.05 P.M. two companies of Marines marched up that hill in wave formation and never halted until they had taken the position. Their losses were heavy, for the whizz-bangs, 77's, and other German guns were playing a tune all over that hill and about one hundred Maxims were spitting fire into the ranks of our brave men, but at heart those Germans are cowards, and when they saw the jig was up they surrendered. Six hundred prisoners, old men, and boys of eighteen and nineteen years, and fifty machine guns were taken. One Marine private took sixty prisoners, and by himself marched them away.

The inevitable followed. A counter-attack. Four hundred Huns attempted to retake the hill; a great many were taken prisoners, and several hundred gassed by our battery. To-day we hold the hill and the prospect of an early relief is bright. Not a great deal is to be feared from these defeated divisions, for the Marines have their "Nanny."

Finish to-morrow, Mother, for it's getting too dark to write.

June 28, 1918. I saw a wonderfully thrilling sight several days ago—an air battle. For several hours a Hun plane had been flying low, up and down our lines, observing our activities and probably signaling his artillery our range. He was loafing over our position, when out from the clouds above darts a frog plane straight for the Hun, when within range the frog opened up with his machine gun and the next minute the German plane was nothing but a ball of fire. The aviator tried his best to get back to the German lines, but the wind was blowing our way, so Heinie darn near burned himself to death: but he turned and volplaned toward our line, and when within a few feet of the ground he sprang out of his machine, killing himself. Three Boche planes were down that day in this one sector. Some of our men went out this morning to salvage the dead Germans. They returned with watches, razors, iron crosses, pictures, knives, German money, *gats,* and all sorts of souvenirs. I don't like salvaging, for the odor of a dead German is stifling. Nix on that stuff. The only souvenir I care to bring back to U.S.A. is yours truly.

This has been a banner day for us. Our ration detail returned this A.M. with Y.M.C.A. donations—chocolate, cookies, raisins, sugar and syrup, and cigarettes. This P.M. more mail arrived, K.C. papers and two pair of white lisle sox from Jones Store, Paris. I put one pair on immediately, although my feet were dirty and darn near black, due to the absence of water and abundance of sand. Two weeks ago I had a bath. That was a memorable day. The major decided that his boys needed washing, so he marched the whole battalion about twelve kilometres to the rear to a small village on the Marne River. The town had been evacuated, so we made ourselves at home. New potatoes, green peas, onions, and honey. I had honey that day, but I certainly paid for it. Several of us put on respirators, wrapped up well and invaded the beehives. I finished with eleven bee stings and a great quantity of excellent honey. After that escapade I filled my tummy and then went for a plunge in the river Marne. We were a happy crew that evening.

Water up here is scarce. We send after drinking-water at night. One dares not wander very far from his hole during the day, except on duty, of course, for those deadly whizz-bangs are very muchly in evidence. A whizz-bang (so-called because of the sound it makes when hitting near by—you hear the whizz and immediately the bang) is a trench-mortar affair, calibre 88 cm., shot from a small gun about one and one half to two feet long, and smooth-bore. The shell has very little trajectory (in fact, the Germans use them for sniping), is filled with shrapnel, and its concussion is terrific. Damn it, I certainly hate these things! You can hear other shells coming and quite often can dodge them, but these whizz-bangs come fast and low.

The only writing I shall ever do when I return home will be a theme or so for some English Prof. There will be so much war bunk after this affair is over that the people will become sick of the word "war." I used to be ambitious. I desired a war cross and honor, but my ideas have changed. I have seen too many men with those ambitions go down riddled with bullets. (One of our lieutenants was shot twenty times while trying to rush a machine-gun position.) So I've come to the conclusion that I am of more value and credit to my country, to you and myself, as a live soldier, obedient and ready for duty, than as a dead hero. No grand-standing—just good honest team work and common sense. Don't be disillusioned—if I live long enough I may rate a sir. . . .

Sunday afternoon, June 30, 1918. Oh, what a relief! Last night we were relieved on the front line. . . . We were many miles behind the lines. We struck camp in a large woods. At 3 A.M. we had a hot meal; turned in later and slept until 11 A.M. when we ate again. Since then I have been swimming and feel like a different man. Received your June 10th letter a short while ago. More Y.M.C.A. supplies blew in, so with a full stomach and a feeling of security from those "Dutch" shells I am fairly happy. From a reliable source we are told that our battalion will parade in Paris July 4th and will be decorated for the fighting we have done this month. Will write you later whether or not this comes to pass.

7. *1918*—THE WAR ENDS

❲ *In the spring of 1918 the Germans launched the first of four great drives that continued until mid-summer. Their armies gained ground, but they failed to break the defending lines. Late in September Marshal Foch, now the supreme Allied commander, ordered an offensive along the entire line. Everywhere the drive succeeded. The German government, recognizing that defeat was inevitable, made overtures for peace. Weeks of diplomatic fencing followed, but when revolutions broke out in Munich, Berlin, and other cities, and the Kaiser abdicated, Germany was helpless. She could only sign an armistice and await whatever terms the victors might propose.*

Among the civilian populations the armistice brought wild rejoicing; the war-weary troops found it hard to comprehend. Colonel Thomas R. Gowenlock, a combat intelligence officer of the First Division, describes their numbed reception of the end.

On the morning of November 11 I sat in my dugout in Le Gros Faux, which was again our division headquarters, talking to our Chief

From: *Soldiers of Darkness* by Thomas R. Gowenlock. Copyright 1936, 1937 by Doubleday & Co., Inc. Reprinted by permission of the publishers. Pp. 264–66.

of Staff, Colonel John Greely, and Lieutenant Colonel Paul Peabody, our G-1. A signal corps officer entered and handed us the following message:

Official Radio from Paris—6:01 A.M., Nov. 11, 1918.
Marshal Foch to the Commander-in-Chief.
1. Hostilities will be stopped on the entire front beginning at 11 o'clock, November 11th (French hour).
2. The Allied troops will not go beyond the line reached at that hour on that date until further orders.

[signed]   MARSHAL FOCH
5:45 A.M.

"Well—*fini la guerre!*" said Colonel Greely.

"It sure looks like it," I agreed.

"Do you know what I want to do now?" he said. "I'd like to get on one of those little horse-drawn canal boats in southern France and lie in the sun the rest of my life."

My watch said nine o'clock. With only two hours to go, I drove over to the bank of the Meuse River to see the finish. The shelling was heavy and, as I walked down the road, it grew steadily worse. It seemed to me that every battery in the world was trying to burn up its guns. At last eleven o'clock came—but the firing continued. The men on both sides had decided to give each other all they had—their farewell to arms. It was a very natural impulse after their years of war, but unfortunately many fell after eleven o'clock that day.

All over the world on November 11, 1918, people were celebrating, dancing in the streets, drinking champagne, hailing the armistice that meant the end of the war. But at the front there was no celebration. Many soldiers believed the Armistice only a temporary measure and that the war would soon go on. As night came, the quietness, unearthly in its penetration, began to eat into their souls. The men sat around log fires, the first they had ever had at the front. They were trying to reassure themselves that there were no enemy batteries spying on them from the next hill and no German bombing planes approaching to blast them out of existence. They talked in low tones. They were nervous. After the long months of intense strain, of keying themselves up to the daily mortal danger, of thinking always in terms of war and the enemy, the abrupt release from it all was physical and psychological agony. Some suffered a total nervous collapse. Some, of a steadier temperament, began to hope they would someday return to home and the embrace of loved ones. Some could think only of the crude little crosses that marked the graves of their comrades. Some fell into an exhausted sleep. All were bewildered by the sudden meaninglessness of their existence as soldiers—and through their teeming memories paraded that swiftly moving cavalcade of Cantigny, Soissons, St. Mihiel, the Meuse-Argonne and Sedan.

What was to come next? They did not know—and hardly cared. Their minds were numbed by the shock of peace. The past consumed their whole consciousness. The present did not exist—and the future was inconceivable.

8. *1919*—WILSON COLLAPSES

⟨ *To Woodrow Wilson, the World War was a war to end war. The instrument by which that purpose would be achieved was the League of Nations, which the President succeeded in incorporating in the peace treaty framed at Versailles in 1919. Returning to the United States in July, Wilson found strong though not insurmountable opposition to the League covenant. But he was a stubborn man, and he had made his last compromise. Rather than accept amendments which might have resulted in approval by the Senate, he determined to appeal to the people. Months of overwork had brought him to the verge of collapse; the long hard speaking tour taxed him beyond endurance. The devoted Tumulty records the tragic story.*

When it became evident that the tide of public opinion was setting against the League, the President finally decided upon the Western trip as the only means of bringing home to the people the unparalleled world situation.

At the Executive offices we at once set in motion preparations for the Western trip. One itinerary after another was prepared, but upon examining it the President would find that it was not extensive enough and would suspect that it was made by those of us—like Grayson and myself—who were solicitous for his health, and he would cast them aside. All the itineraries provided for a week of rest in the Grand Canyon of the Colorado, but when a brief vacation was intimated to him, he was obdurate in his refusal to include even a day of relaxation, saying to me, that "the people would never forgive me if I took a rest on a trip such as the one I contemplate making. This is a business trip, pure and simple, and the itinerary must not include rest of any kind." . . .

Uncomplainingly the President applied himself to the difficult tasks of the Western trip. While the first meeting at Columbus was a disappointment as to attendance, as we approached the West the crowds grew in numbers and the enthusiasm became boundless. The idea of the League spread and spread as we neared the coast. Contrary to the impression in the East, the President's trip West was a veritable triumph for him and was so successful that we had planned, upon the comple-

Tumulty, *Woodrow Wilson As I Know Him*, 438, 446–48.

tion of the Western trip, to invade the enemy's country, Senator Lodge's own territory, the New England States, and particularly Massachusetts. This was our plan, fully developed and arranged, when about four o'clock in the morning of September 26, 1919, Doctor Grayson knocked at the door of my sleeping compartment and told me to dress quickly, that the President was seriously ill. As we walked toward the President's car, the Doctor told me in a few words of the President's trouble and said that he greatly feared it might end fatally if we should attempt to continue the trip and that it was his duty to inform the President that by all means the trip must be cancelled; but that he did not feel free to suggest it to the President without having my cooperation and support. When we arrived at the President's drawing room I found him fully dressed and seated in his chair. With great difficulty he was able to articulate. His face was pale and wan. One side of it had fallen, and his condition was indeed pitiful to behold. Quickly I reached the same conclusion as that of Doctor Grayson, as to the necessity for the immediate cancellation of the trip, for to continue it, in my opinion, meant death to the President. Looking at me, with great tears running down his face, he said: "My dear boy, this has never happened to me before. I felt it coming on yesterday. I do not know what to do." He then pleaded with us not to cut short the trip. Turning to both of us, he said: "Don't you see that if you cancel this trip, Senator Lodge and his friends will say that I am a quitter and that the Western trip was a failure, and the Treaty will be lost." Reaching over to him, I took both of his hands and said: "What difference, my dear Governor, does it make what they say? Nobody in the world believes you are a quitter, but it is your life that we must now consider. We must cancel the trip, and I am sure that when the people learn of your condition there will be no misunderstanding." He then tried to move over nearer to me to continue his argument against the cancellation of the trip; but he found he was unable to do so. His left arm and leg refused to function. I then realized that the President's whole left side was paralyzed. Looking at me he said: "I want to show them that I can still fight and that I am not afraid. Just postpone the trip for twenty-four hours and I will be all right."

But Doctor Grayson and I resolved not to take any risk, and an immediate statement was made to the inquiring newspaper men that the Western trip was off.

Never was the President more gentle or tender than on that morning. Suffering the greatest pain, paralyzed on his left side, he was still fighting desperately for the thing that was so close to his heart—a vindication of the things for which he had so gallantly fought on the other side. Grim old warrior that he was, he was ready to fight to the death for the League of Nations.

9.   *1921*—WILSON'S LAST DAY IN OFFICE

〖 *Wilson was completely incapacitated for months. He finally re-covered sufficiently to administer the government, but by that time the Senate had rejected the League of Nations, his hope for a peaceful world. Tumulty describes the President on his last day in office, his health gone but his courage unbroken.*

I was greatly concerned lest the President should be unable by reason of his physical condition to stand the strain of Inauguration Day. Indeed, members of his Cabinet and intimate friends like Grayson and myself had tried to persuade him not to take part, but he could not by any argument be drawn away from what he believed to be his duty—to join in the inauguration of his successor, President-elect Harding. The thought that the people of the country might misconstrue his attitude if he should remain away and his firm resolve to show every courtesy to his successor in office were the only considerations that led him to play his part to the end. . . .

On this morning, March 4, 1921, he acted like a man who was happy now that his dearest wish was to be realized. As I looked at Woodrow Wilson, seated in his study that morning, in his cutaway coat, awaiting word of the arrival of President-elect Harding at the White House, to me he was every inch the President, quiet, dignified; ready to meet the duties of the trying day upon which he was now to enter, in his countenance a calm nobility. It was hard for me to realize as I beheld him, seated behind his desk in his study, that here was the head of the greatest nation in the world who in a few hours was to step back into the uneventful life of a private citizen.

A few minutes and he was notified that the President-elect was in the Blue Room awaiting his arrival. Alone, unaided, grasping his old blackthorn stick, the faithful companion of many months, his "third leg," as he playfully called it, slowly he made his way to the elevator and in a few seconds he was standing in the Blue Room meeting the President-elect and greeting him in the most gracious way. No evidence of the trial of pain he was undergoing in striving to play a modest part in the ceremonies was apparent either in his bearing or attitude, as he greeted the President-elect and the members of the Congressional Inaugural Committee. He was an ill man but a sportsman, determined to see the thing through to the end. President-elect Harding met him in the most kindly fashion, showing him the keenest consideration and courtesy.

And now the final trip to the Capitol from the White House. The ride to the Capitol was uneventful. From the physical appearance of

Tumulty, *Woodrow Wilson As I Know Him,* 506-11.

the two men seated beside each other in the automobile, it was plain to the casual observer who was the out-going and who the in-coming President. In the right sat President Wilson, gray, haggard, broken. He interpreted the cheering from the crowds that lined the Avenue as belonging to the President-elect and looked straight ahead. It was Mr. Harding's day, not his. On the left, Warren Gamaliel Harding, the rising star of the Republic, healthy, vigorous, great-chested, showing every evidence in his tanned face of that fine, sturdy health so necessary a possession in order to grapple with the problems of his country. One, the man on the right, a battle-scarred veteran, a casualty of the war, now weary and anxious to lay down the reins of office; the other, agile, vigorous, hopeful, and full of enthusiasm for the tasks that confronted him. Upon the face of the one were written in indelible lines the scars and tragedies of war; on that of the other, the lines of confidence, hope, and readiness for the fray.

The Presidential party arrived at the Capitol. Woodrow Wilson took possession of the President's room. Modestly the President-elect took a seat in the rear of the room while President Wilson conferred with senators and representatives who came to talk with him about bills in which they were interested, bills upon which he must act before the old clock standing in a corner of the room should strike the hour of twelve, noon, marking the end of the official relationship of Woodrow Wilson with the affairs of the Government of the United States. It was about eleven-thirty. Senators and congressmen of both parties poured into the office to say good-bye to the man seated at the table, and then made their way over to congratulate the President-elect. . . .

Presently there appeared at the door a gray-haired man of imperious manner. Addressing the President in a sharp, dry tone of voice, he said: "Mr. President, we have come as a committee of the Senate to notify you that the Senate and House are about to adjourn and await your pleasure." The spokesman for the committee was Henry Cabot Lodge, the distinguished senator from Massachusetts, the implacable political foe of the man he was addressing.

It was an interesting study to watch the face and manner of Woodrow Wilson as he met the gaze of Senator Lodge who by his attacks had destroyed the great thing of which the President had dreamed, the thing for which he had fought and for which he was ready to lay down his life. It appeared for a second as if Woodrow Wilson was about to give full sway to the passionate resentment he felt toward the man who, he believed, had unfairly treated him throughout the famous Treaty fight. But quickly the shadow of resentment passed. A ghost of a smile flitted across his firm mouth, and steadying himself in his chair, he said in a low voice: "Senator Lodge, I have no further communication to make. I thank you. Good morning."

Senator Lodge and the committee withdrew from the room. I looked at the clock in the corner. A few minutes more and all the power which the weary man at the table possessed would fall from his shoulders. All left the room except the President, Mrs. Wilson, Admiral Grayson, and myself.

The old clock in the corner of the room began to toll the hour of twelve. Mechanically I counted, under my breath, the strokes: "One, two, three," on through "twelve," and the silent room echoed with the low vibration of the last stroke. . . .

Quickly Woodrow Wilson, now the private citizen, turned to make his way to the elevator, leaning on his cane, the ferrule striking sharply on the stone pavement as he walked; but his spirit was indomitable. . . . By the time we reached the elevator, the brief ceremony in the Senate Chamber had ended, and the multitude outside were cheering Mr. Harding as he appeared at the east front of the Capitol to deliver his inaugural address. We heard the United States Marine Band playing "Hail to the Chief." For a few seconds I looked toward the reviewing stand. The new President, Warren G. Harding, was taking his place on the stand amid the din and roar of applause. He was the focus of all eyes, the pivot around which all interest turned. Not one of the thousands turned to look back at the lonely figure laboriously climbing into the automobile. The words of Ibsen flashed into my mind:

"The strongest man in the world is he who stands most alone."

1. *1921–1923*—WARREN G. HARDING: HE LOVED
FELLOWSHIP

❨ *With the war over, the United States did its best to forget the nightmare it had gone through. The armies were demobilized as quickly as possible. First the Senate and then the country rejected the League of Nations, and almost every other measure for which Wilson had stood. In 1920 the voters elected a man as different from the stricken President as one human being could be different from another. Warren G. Harding, owner and editor of the Marion, Ohio, STAR, possessed no qualifications for the Presidency except an apprenticeship in Ohio politics, one term in the United States Senate, and an imposing appearance. Even his good friend, Senator James E. Watson of Indiana, candidly admitted Harding's*

510

*deficiencies and summarized the difficulties into which his easy-going
nature led him.*

I had a great affection for Warren G. Harding. We were born on the
same day and had been personal and political friends for many years.
He was about as handsome a man as I ever saw, and he had one of
those affidavit faces whose very appearance carries conviction, and
withal he was a magnificent figure. He just loved fellowship. He wanted
to have a crowd around and have a good time. He could smoke a cigarette, or a cigar, or a pipe, he could take a nip of liquor without ever
using it to excess, he liked to indulge in a game of poker whenever
an idle hour permitted, and he was exceedingly fond of golf. The truth
about it is that he was altogether too urbane, too good-natured, too
generous-hearted, and too fond of having a good time for his own good.

The simple fact is that my dear old friend just did not like to work,
and he ought never to have taken upon himself the enormous burdens
incident to the presidency and entailed upon the president immediately
following the most titanic struggle that ever cursed the earth. He simply was not adapted to the place and daily shrank from its exacting and
gruelling toil. . . .

He never wanted to be nominated for president in the first place.
Many senators knew that, all of them being his friends, and they never
thought that he could be persuaded to lay aside his manifest disinclina-
tion and accept the nomination. And neither did Mrs. Harding want to
enter the White House.

Immediately after he had delivered his Inaugural Address, and
while we were coming from the front portico of the Capitol back to the
Senate chamber, I stepped up to Mrs. Harding and, speaking very in-
formally as I then could, said: "Well, my dear girl, how is it?"

She said to me, looking me squarely in the eye: "Jim, you naturally
suppose that I ought to be the happiest woman in the world, but the
truth is that I am not. Somehow or other, I am filled with a fear that I
shall walk into the White House but that they will carry me out." Almost with a shudder I left her, filled with the gloom of that thought. . . .

By all odds the most unfortunate incident that occurred in the administration of Warren G. Harding was the one commonly known as
the Teapot Dome oil scandal. It arose out of the long personal friendship of the Secretary of Interior, Albert B. Fall, with Edward Doheny
and his associates in the oil business. Fall and Doheny had been boy-
hood friends, had worked together in the mines from their youth, had
been associated in the development of various oil fields, and naturally
there existed between them a very warm personal friendship.

Secretary Fall had been a United States senator before Harding
took him into his Cabinet and was a man admired by his colleagues for

his straightforward manner of dealing with public questions and his ac-knowledged ability as a lawyer and a debater. It was therefore appro-priate that Harding, never dreaming of any unfortunate relationship or untoward incident, should put him in his Cabinet.

But, be that as it may, when Secretary Fall leased the Teapot Dome oil lands to Edward Doheny and his associates, and when it came to light that at the same time Fall had received a sizable sum of money, the public blamed Harding for the appointment of Fall, and the affair had a most blasting effect upon his administration. He was in no way re-sponsible for any peculation or fraud that might have been perpetrated by Fall, and of course he had no previous knowledge of any such scheme.

It was a terribly ill-smelling mess, given the widest publicity by the investigating ability of certain United States senators, many of whom delight in turning up foul matter of that kind with a double object in view: first, really to bring offenders to book, and second, to glorify themselves. For in most cases a man does not start out deliberately to besmirch and besmear and destroy other men simply for the public good. My wide experience teaches me that all too frequently back of such investigating there is a flaming desire for publicity that nothing can appease but the sight by the investigator of his name in startling head-lines every day. . . .

The day before President Harding started on his last trip, I called at the White House to see him and was at once ushered into his presence. Our conversation was very brief, and at its close I took hold of his right hand and, putting my left one on his shoulder and looking him in the face, said: "Warren," (the only time I ever addressed him as any-thing but "Mr. President" after his inauguration), "I am telling you good-by, and I think for the last time. I know about the condition of your heart and your general state of health, and I do not believe that you will ever survive this trip."

Looking me straight in the eye, he answered: "Well, Jim, you are mistaken about that, because I am feeling perfectly well and consider myself fit in all respects to make this trip."

"But you are going to many places over a mile high," I replied, "the weather is exceedingly hot, they will run you around from one place to another to have you make speeches and to exhibit you, as they always do a president when they get control of one, and, Warren, you simply cannot stand it, and in my judgment this is the last time I shall ever be permitted to shake hands with you or to look you in the face. I am mighty sorry to say this, old pal, but I think this is the most foolish trip a man ever started out to make, and I most keenly regret your going."

We wrung each other by the hand, and I departed, fully confident that I should never see him alive again. And I never did. Just as I predicted, they hurried and harried him on that western trip until his weakened heart gave way.

Mrs. Harding brought the body of the dead President across the country and everywhere it was greeted with every manifestation of deep sorrow and profound respect. She sat throughout the days and nights like a grim warrior guarding the body of her dead, and her conduct throughout was heroic and unflinching.

I was appointed on the committee to receive the remains at the station, but, strangely enough, Mrs. Harding requested that no senators attend the funeral at Marion and that no resolution be passed in the Senate.

2.   *1923–1929*—"SILENT CAL" COOLIDGE

❰ *It is unlikely that any President could have controlled the yeasty forces at work in the 1920's, but the dour and reticent New Englander who succeeded Harding gave no indication that he was even aware that the nation was undergoing a social and economic transformation. Thomas L. Stokes, Washington correspondent of the United Press, offers a characterization of Calvin Coolidge.*

The impression I had of Coolidge the person, and still have, is of a country fellow who had just come to town, a shrewd fellow, with a crude kind of rural humor that smacked of casual, cryptic barnyard chatter. This impression, as far as physical appearance contributed, was heightened by the fact that he always wore his hat gingerly on his head, not comfortably. It always seemed just a shade too small. It sat too far up on his head. He looked as I've seen the farmer look on Sunday. He was overly neat, stiff of manner, as if not quite accustomed to his position. . . .

He was a political accident, as, so far as the Presidency was concerned, was Warren Harding. He came up the political ladder because he would go along with the organization and keep his mouth shut. He did his job and got into no unnecessary controversies. He was projected into the national limelight for a time as Governor of Massachusetts by the Boston police strike, and largely through a one-sentence telegram he sent to Samuel Gompers, president of the American Federation of Labor: "There is no right to strike against the public safety by anybody, anywhere, any time." Republican leaders at the 1920 convention had selected Senator Irvine Lenroot of Wisconsin as the Vice Presidential nominee, in a hurried session after the wearing struggle over the Presidential nomination, but a delegate from Oregon, Wallace McCamant,

---

Thomas L. Stokes, *Chip Off My Shoulder* (Princeton University Press, 1940), 136–41. Reprinted by permission of the publisher.

jumped up on a chair, nominated Coolidge, and swept the convention along with him. Nobody knew anything much about him except that he was supposed to be safe and sane and in favor of law and order. . . .

Being President was something quite different from presiding over the United States Senate, attending dinners, and making an occasional, dry prosaic speech. He was a copybook maxim personified, shoved into a post which, properly occupied, requires imagination, feeling, large knowledge, and ability to grow with the office. He lacked these qualifications, though he might have made some effort to enlarge his knowledge, which he did not. He just sat, mostly. . . .

He preached economy in government. He did not cut very deeply, for the four and five billion dollar budgets which the country regarded as natural after the war continued; but tax returns were lucrative and the budget was kept balanced. He dramatized economy in the White House executive office staff by giving a prize of ten dollars—which he paid out of his own pocket!—to the employee who could suggest the best way to economize. A formula which included substitution of the old-fashioned drinking glass for paper cups and using notepaper on both sides and using pencils down to the bitter end won the award. Public health organizations screamed about the drinking glass. He decreed the economies nonetheless. . . .

The sudden thrust of the Presidential mantle about his thin shoulders staggered him for a time. He really was a timid person those first few days. He promised to carry on the Harding policies—whatever that might mean—and then lapsed into silence for a month.

During that month he was built into a myth. It was one of the greatest feats of newspaper propaganda that the modern world has seen. It really was a miracle. He said nothing. Newspapers must have copy. So we grasped at little incidents to build up human interest stories and we created a character. He kept his counsel. Therefore he was a strong and silent man. The editorial writers on newspapers which were satisfied with the status quo, the big Eastern journals, created the strong, silent man. Then, in time, as the country found out he was not a superman, neither strong nor silent, they emphasized his little witticisms, his dry wit, and we had a national character—Cal. Everybody spoke of him fondly as "Cal." He was one of us. He was the ordinary man incarnate.

"Did you hear what Cal said?"

He wouldn't rock the boat. He wouldn't interfere with business. He would live and let live.

Hurray for Cal!

We stood, twice a week at press conferences, and saw the man, not the myth. He was the same man who had sidled in and out of Cabinet meetings, but with more confidence. He talked, in his nasal twang, out of the corner of his mouth. Often he passed up important questions of national policy and expatiated at length about some trifle. I remember him talking on and on one day, when there were important matters we wanted him to discuss, about whether boys should be allowed to fish in the Tidal Basin. It was a purely local issue. The little sermon was good of its kind, whimsical and smalltownish.

There was the day, too, when someone asked him about a life of George Washington which Rupert Hughes had written and which the Daughters of the American Revolution, currently in annual session in Washington, were deploring. He turned about and looked out the window behind him.

"I see the monument is still standing," he said.

There were those moments.

They made the homely philosopher, but not the statesman.

It was impossible to destroy the legend of "Silent Cal" in the country, but he was, on occasion, garrulous as the old man who sits in front of the country store. He showed this occasionally at press conferences. He showed it to visitors who would find him interested in some particular subject, when they came to call about some government problem, and who would have to sit while he talked and talked.

He was lazy physically. Often of an afternoon when there were no engagements and no pressing business—and during the days of prosperity no one was concerned much about Washington or national affairs—he would rear his chair back, throw his spare legs on a corner of his desk, and take a nap. On Memorial Day I recall the grumbling among attachés who had to stay around merely because the President had come over to his office and spent the afternoon napping there. He kept Senator Smoot of Utah and the French debt-funding commission waiting for a long time one afternoon because he was taking a snooze after lunch. No one dared to disturb him. . . .

Figuratively, he slept through two administrations while the wrath to come was boiling underneath, a simple fellow asleep on a volcano. But he had waked up and slipped off down the hill and was not there when the lava started to boil forth. The "Wonder Boy" was full in its path. . . .

Warren Harding was the big, blundering human fellow who got mixed up in events and was pushed about by his friends.

Calvin Coolidge sat by and did not worry and said "No" when he didn't like what was going on.

During his occupancy, the White House might have been just any house along the highway of the world. To Calvin Coolidge it was just another home to live in, a bigger house, where you could give orders and somebody would run and fetch.

I recall a story one of the Secret Service men who is no longer at the White House told. It was in the first few days of the Coolidge régime.

515

He was shocked one afternoon to find the President sitting in a rocker on the front porch which faces on Pennsylvania Avenue.

"Mr. President," he said, "the other Presidents always use the back portico."

"I want to be out here where I can see the streetcars go by," came the reply.

3. *1927*—A VISITING GERMAN ENCOUNTERS PROHIBITION

⟦ *The movement to prohibit the manufacture and sale of intoxicating liquors had its origins before the Civil War, but made no real headway until the twentieth century. After 1900 a growing number of people came to the conclusion that the liquor interests were a corrupting influence in politics and that the unrestricted sale of liquor was inconsistent with the increasing mechanization of the country. By 1917 thirteen states were bone-dry, thirteen others had milder prohibitory laws. The spirit of self-denial which followed the entrance of the United States into the World War overcame all opposition to nation-wide prohibition. To conserve grain Congress forbade the sale of distilled spirits, wine, and beer from July 1, 1919 until the war should end. The Eighteenth Amendment to the Constitution, which went into effect on January 16, 1920, made the ban permanent.*

The national reaction against war-time measures and policies included prohibition. The Eighteenth Amendment had hardly gone into effect before evading it became popular. When Count von Luckner, the almost legendary commander of a German commerce raider, visited the United States in 1927, he found that the evasion of prohibition had become a game with many players.

I suppose I should set forth my investigations into the subject of prohibition. Here is a new experience, at a club's celebration. Each man appears with an impressive portfolio. Each receives his glass of pure water; above the table the law reigns supreme. The brief cases rest under the chairs. Soon they are drawn out, the merry noise of popping corks is heard, and the guzzling begins.

Or, I come to a banquet in a hotel dining room. On the table are the finest wines. I ask, "how come?" Answer: "Well, two of our members lived in the hotel for eight days and every day brought in cargoes of this costly stuff in their suitcases." My informant was madly overjoyed at this cunning.

Felix, Count von Luckner, *Seeteufel erobert Amerika*, in Oscar Handlin, *This Was America* (Harvard University Press, 1949), 495–97. Reprinted by permission of the Harvard University Press.

My first experience with the ways of prohibition came while we were being entertained by friends in New York. It was bitterly cold. My wife and I rode in the rumble seat of the car, while the American and his wife, bundled in furs, sat in front. Having wrapped my companion in pillows and blankets so thoroughly that only her nose showed, I came across another cushion that seemed to hang uselessly on the side. "Well," I thought, "this is a fine pillow; since everybody else is so warm and cozy, I might as well do something for my own comfort. This certainly does no one any good hanging on the wall." Sitting on it, I gradually noticed a dampness in the neighborhood, that soon mounted to a veritable flood. The odor of fine brandy told me I had burst my host's peculiar liquor flask.

In time, I learned that not everything in America was what it seemed to be. I discovered, for instance, that a spare tire could be filled with substances other than air, that one must not look too deeply into certain binoculars, and that the Teddy Bears that suddenly acquired tremendous popularity among the ladies very often had hollow metal stomachs.

"But," it might be asked, "where do all these people get the liquor?" Very simple. Prohibition has created a new, a universally respected, a well-beloved, and a very profitable occupation, that of the bootlegger who takes care of the importation of the forbidden liquor. Everyone knows this, even the powers of government. But this profession is beloved because it is essential, and it is respected because its pursuit is clothed with an element of danger and with a sporting risk. Now and then one is caught, that must happen *pro forma* and then he must do time or, if he is wealthy enough, get someone to do time for him.

Yet it is undeniable that prohibition has in some respects been signally successful. The filthy saloons, the gin mills which formerly flourished on every corner and in which the laborer once drank off half his wages, have disappeared. Now he can instead buy his own car, and ride off for a weekend or a few days with his wife and children in the country or at the sea. But, on the other hand, a great deal of poison and methyl alcohol has taken the place of the good old pure whiskey. The number of crimes and misdemeanors that originated in drunkenness has declined. But by contrast, a large part of the population has become accustomed to disregard and to violate the law without thinking. The worst is, that precisely as a consequence of the law, the taste for alcohol has spread ever more widely among the youth. The sporting attraction of the forbidden and the dangerous leads to violations. My observations have convinced me that many fewer would drink were it not illegal.

And how, it will be asked, did this law get onto the statute books? Through the war. In America there was long a well-developed temperance movement and many individual states already had prohibition laws. During the war it was not difficult to extend the force of those laws to the whole of the United States. Prohibition was at first introduced only for the period of the war. For the mass of the people it was very surprising when Congress in 1920 adopted the eighteenth amendment to the Constitution which made it a crime to manufacture, transport, or sell intoxicating liquor. The dry states had imposed their will on the whole Union.

4. *1920–1928*—THE HEMLINE RISES

❨ *During the 'twenties the revolution in attitudes extended to almost every phase of life. Women's fashions, and women's standards of conduct, changed more radically than they had in generations. Preston William Slosson of the University of Michigan, a historian who supplemented documentary sources with his own keen observation, described the progress of liberation.*

Women's fashions have always fluctuated—the waistline moving up and down anywhere between neck and knee; skirts ballooning out till they covered much of the ballroom floor, or again tucked in till they shackled movement, as in the "hobble skirt" so briefly popular about 1911 or 1912; hats towering like mountains or spreading out like pancakes. But usually the new styles came by degrees, so that people could get used to them; they "evolved" like the British constitution. But during and after the war a real sartorial revolution took place. The skirt, in the old sense of the word, disappeared altogether to be replaced by a sort of tunic or kilt barely reaching the knee. Conservative eyes were shocked by this, although the change was in the direction of common sense and, had it taken a century instead of five or six years to complete, would have provoked little comment. Skirts were already "short," ankle-length, in 1914, but the "very short" skirt, knee-length, hardly became general before 1920 and required about three years more to become the accepted mode for all sections, ages and classes. In 1929 clothing interests, impelled by Paris, made a desperate effort to restore the long skirt at least for evening wear and formal occasions. But many American women refused, for the first time in history, to obey the Parisian dictators of fashion.

With the shortening of the skirt went many other changes. Hampering petticoats were discarded, the corset was abandoned as a needless impediment to free movement, silk or "rayon" stockings became practically universal even among the poor and for a time were often rolled at the knee, sleeves shortened or vanished, and the whole costume became a sheer and simple structure, too light to be the slightest burden. H. G.

This selection from Preston William Slosson, *The Great Crusade and After, 1914–1928,* copyright 1930 by The Macmillan Company, is used with the publisher's permission. Pp. 151–57.

Wells, writing in war time, declared that his heroine "at fourteen already saw long skirts ahead of her, and hated them as a man might hate a swamp that he must presently cross knee-deep." But by the time Joan would have been old enough for the long skirts there were none for her to wear. These simplifications of costume started with the wealthier classes but were almost immediately copied everywhere. A survey in Milwaukee of more than thirteen hundred working girls showed that less than seventy wore corsets. The commercial effect of these changes of style was profound. Factories which specialized in petticoats, corsets or cotton stockings had to change their trade or go bankrupt, but the sale of silk and rayon hose more than doubled in four years, and the sale of bathing suits tripled in two.

During the sartorial revolution men proved to be, as usual, the conservative sex, making but minor changes in costume. A man who was well dressed for Roosevelt's inauguration would have provoked but little comment at Hoover's. What few alterations were made were usually in the direction of greater comfort. The soft hat replaced the derby for almost every occasion, warm weather permitted light tropical suitings, and softer shirts and collars passed muster for business wear in the daytime. But men still wore coat and collar in summer when women were comfortable in scanty one-piece frocks (unless they followed the fashion of summer furs). "Today our American women are in better physical condition than our men," declared Dr. Ephraim Mulford, president of the Medical Society of New Jersey. "And while there are many reasons, we might credit one to the fact that women do not wear too many clothes, especially in the summer. Their garments, light in weight and light in color, permit the ultraviolet ray of the sun to give its full benefit. Men, in their dark clothes which completely cover them from neck to ankle are denied this energy." The tailors and textile factories even had a certain revenge on the male sex for their losses on the skimpier female raiment. Small boys often wore long trousers, and at adolescence they adopted trousers not only long but wide—huge, baggy affairs that moved hardly a step to each two steps of their owner but were raised above criticism by the name of "Oxford." In swimming, both men and women wore the simplest possible one-piece suits, the woman's suit often having less coverage than the man's. On hot summer days many girls went stockingless everywhere.

When the public had scarcely recovered from the shock of the disappearing skirt, it received another. The girls began to cut their hair. The barber shop was the last refuge of masculinity in America, the only spot which had not become "coeducational." The saloon was gone; the polls were now open to women; swimming tanks were crowded with fair mermaids; the very prize ring had its lady guests, and nearly all men's clubs had their ladies' night. But in the barber shop the unshorn male could lean back at his ease in the great chair, unashamed in his suspenders, while the barber stuffed his mouth with lather and gave him the latest gossip of politics and baseball. This last trench was now taken. A fashion started for hair fitting compactly around the head and fluffed or banged over the ears; long tresses were out of style; hence occasional visits to the barber shop. Persons over thirty viewed the fad with some misgivings, but presently began to try cautious experiments in the same direction. The flapper grew bolder. The "boyish bob" appeared, and ears emerged once again from their retirement. Soon there was no difference between a man's hair cut and a woman's, unless the man were an artist or musician and wore his hair long as a professional asset. One Chicago barber shop had to advertise, "Men's custom ALSO welcomed!" The double prophecy made more than four hundred years ago had come true at last:

> Lo! yet before ye must do more, if ye will go with me,
> As cut your hair up by your ear, your kirtle by the knee.

The universalizing of the bob simplified the hat problem. Large, broad and unstably balanced hats were out of the question, as the hatpin found no anchorage. All the new hats took the form of a close-fitting, simple bonnet which a wind would not carry away. Birds and flowers on headgear largely disappeared, and the vanishing of the hatpin ended a major menace in crowded cars.

A third phase of the revolution in fashions, even more disturbing to the traditional than short skirts or short hair, was the freer use of cosmetics. In a way, this was a move in the opposite direction, as it represented a tendency not towards "naturalness" and freedom but towards artificiality and sophistication. If it be considered progress since the times of Victoria, when ladies got along with a little face cream and white powder, it might equally be considered a reversion to the days of Pompadour. Bright orange rouge and lipsticks advertised as "kissproof" were used by young ladies of the most unquestionable respectability. The fashionable "sun tan" was sometimes acquired at the drug store as well as on the beach. Like the other changes in fashion the cosmetic urge was democratic in the sense that it stopped at no class barrier. "Progress toward democracy," wrote a journalist,

has made amazing strides in this matter of personal decoration. Formerly it was the ladies of the court who used it most; today it is the serious concern and dearest pastime of all three estates. It was the spread of the use of furs, to take but one example, to all classes (and also to all seasons) which inspired the just description of woman as America's greatest fur-bearing animal. And nowadays no one can tell, either by the quantitative or the qualitative test, whether a given person lives on Riverside Drive or on East Fourth Street.

. . . "Beauty shoppes" blossomed on nearly every street of the shopping districts, their proprietors sometimes seeking to professionalize their status with the word "beauticians." Seven thousand kinds of cosmetics were on the market in 1927, a large majority of them being face creams. Fortunes were made in mud baths, labeled "beauty clay," in patent hair removers, in magic lotions to make the eyelashes long and sweeping, in soaps that claimed to nourish the skin, in hair dyes that "restored the natural color," in patent nostrums for "reducing," and in all the other half-fraudulent traps of the advertisers for the beauty seeker.

One manufacturer of dentifrice based a clever advertising campaign on the vogue of the feminine cigarette, with such headlines as "Why are Men so Unreasonable about Women Smoking?" and "Can a Girl Smoke and Still be Lovely?" arguing that since women were determined to smoke they should keep their teeth stainless by the daily use of tooth paste. Cigarette advertisers took a similar ingenious advantage of the craze for the "boyish form"—*e.g.,* "And now, women may enjoy a companionable smoke with their husbands and brothers—at the same time slenderizing in a sensible manner. . . . Reach for a *Lucky* instead of a sweet." Thus one fad supported another. Earlier advertisers, not so bold, had usually depicted pretty girls not themselves indulging in a cigarette but in the company of young men so engaged, perhaps pleading, "Blow some my way!" The number of cigarettes sold in the period 1911–1915 averaged less than fifteen billion annually; for the period 1921–1925 sales averaged well over sixty-five billion, and in 1928 reached one hundred billion. As during the same period there was no greater sale of cigars and a much smaller sale of chewing tobacco, the increased vogue of the cigarette did not mean an increased tobacco hunger. Rather it meant the entrance of the American girl into the ranks of the smokers. A cigarette had about it a slim, feminine daintiness; it could be gracefully twirled and dandled like a fan between dances when a cigar or pipe would have been ridiculous. The war, too, had its effect. Y.M.C.A. secretaries who had spent years warning young men of the peril of the demon nicotine had perforce to hand out cigarettes by the thousand to the soldiers in France. Army life also convinced men who were sensitive about their masculinity that cigarettes and wrist watches were as suitable for "he-men" as the Pittsburgh stogie or the pocket Ingersoll. As for chewing tobacco—the nightmare of the European traveler since the days of Dickens—it had been very largely replaced by the increased use of chewing gum, perhaps another victory for feminism.

Thus the flapper of the 1920's stepped onto the stage of history, breezy, slangy and informal in manner; slim and boyish in form; covered with silk and fur that clung to her as close as onion skin; with carmined cheeks and lips, plucked eyebrows and close-fitting helmet of

521

hair; gay, plucky and confident. No wonder the house rang with applause; no wonder also that faint hisses sounded from the remoter boxes and galleries. But she cared little for approval or disapproval and went about her "act," whether it were a Marathon dancing contest, driving an automobile at seventy miles an hour, a Channel swim, a political campaign or a social-service settlement. Eventually she married her dancing partner, that absurdly serious young man with plastered hair, baby-smooth chin and enormous Oxford bags, and then they settled down in a four-room-kitchenette apartment to raise two children, another "younger generation" to thrust them back stage among the "old fogies."

5. *1927*—MOVIES AND TALKIES

❮ *The motion picture came into its own in the 1920's—through bigger theaters, through better pictures, and finally by adding sound to the silent film. Preston William Slosson describes the flowering of the industry.*

The motion picture as a factor in American life had an influence difficult to overestimate. It became during this period one of the most popular pastimes in all parts of the country, and one of the weekly habits of a large portion of the population. By the middle 1920's it had become the fourth largest industry in the country, representing a capital investment of more than one and a half billion dollars. By 1927 there were twenty thousand five hundred motion-picture theaters with a seating capacity of some eighteen million. In these were shown daily about twenty-five thousand miles of celluloid film, and to these resorted weekly about a hundred million of the American people, counting the many who habitually went more than once a week. About half of these theaters were in towns of less than five thousand inhabitants, and they extended about as far out into the suburban fringe of the cities as groceries and drug stores. Only the most remote localities were beyond easy reach of the movies and only the most exclusive individuals failed to patronize them occasionally.

The small, unattractive and often unsafe halls which served well enough in the earlier years of the century now developed into gorgeous and gigantic theaters designed especially for the purpose, equipped with pipe-organ and symphony-size orchestra, and providing elaborate divertissements involving soloists, ballet and chorus, in addition to the pictures, which, it must be confessed, did not improve in proportion to their setting, except in photographic technic. The turning point in this development of building and program may be dated as 1914 when Samuel L. Rothafel, known to millions as "Roxy," who not many years before in a little Pennsylvania mining town had had to give his show behind a barroom on such days as he could borrow chairs from an undertaker, opened the Strand Theater in New York and developed a form of entertainment more akin to the opera than to the old "nickelodeon."

Meantime the art of the silent drama was showing steady improvement. Those actors who possessed the peculiar power to impress their personality on the public through pantomime rose speedily to prominence and attained, what previously had been an exaggeration, worldwide celebrity. Among the first to become such popular favorites were three young girls: the Gish sisters, Lillian and Dorothy, and Gladys Smith (better known as Mary Pickford) in pathetic and sentimental rôles; and, among the men, Charlie Chaplin in comedy and Douglas Fairbanks in romantic drama.

In 1913 Charles Spencer Chaplin was an inconspicuous vaudeville actor, playing a character part that he had picked up as a boy from observing an old man who had been reduced to holding horses in front of a London public house. Michael Simm Sinnot (Mack Sennett) offered him $150 a week to play in his Keystone Comedies. Two years later another company was glad to take him over at $1250 a week, and the next year he was getting more than ten times that salary. Before he had been in the movies ten years Charlie Chaplin was known by name and sight to more of his contemporaries in all lands than any man who had ever lived. This unique position was due to the unprecedented opportunity afforded by the invention of the motion picture and to his being particularly clever in a field and in a rôle of perennial popularity. The slap-stick farce had been a favorite from the earliest ages of acting, and no plot in folk tales had made a wider appeal than that of the underdog who by some surprising turn came out on top. Charlie Chaplin's customary make-up, his tiny mustache, his ill-fitting shoes, suit and hat, his air of injured innocence under unmerited misfortunes, and his quick "comeback" aroused amusement and subconscious sympathy in all lands and classes.

The first photoplay to develop the dramatic capabilities of the film was "The Birth of a Nation," produced in 1915 by David Wark Griffith from *The Clansman* by the Reverend Thomas Dixon, a novel of Reconstruction days in which the Ku Klux Klan was presented as the defender of white supremacy and feminine virtue. Though the play aroused the bitter resentment of the Negroes and their Northern sympathizers, and though it was the first motion-picture show for which the full theater price of two dollars was charged, it was an immediate and long-continued popular success. It was perhaps no mere coincidence that a few years later the K. K. K. was revived and became an active factor in American politics. "The Birth of a Nation" was an epoch-making work in the history of the motion picture, because Griffith had the courage to cut loose from the conventions and limitations of the stage and to employ the technic peculiar to the screen, such as flight and pursuit, mobs and battles, distant views and close-ups, the fade-out and the switchback, and by the alternation of views of simultaneous events in distant places to keep the attention of the spectator on their interaction, as, in this case, the extremity of the besieged and the approach of the rescuers.

Griffith's production also demonstrated the value of the photoplay in the depiction of historical events, and established the supremacy of the feature film. The feature film ordinarily ran from one to two hours and cost to prepare from ten thousand dollars to several millions. Between seven and eight hundred feature films were produced in America annually. Among the most successful were: several of pioneer days, "The Covered Wagon," "The Iron Horse" and "The Pony Express"; war plays, "The Big Parade," "The Four Horsemen of the Apocalypse" from the story of Blasco Ibañez, and "What Price Glory"; religious dramas, "The Ten Commandments," "The King of Kings," "Quo Vadis" and "Ben Hur"; Griffith productions, "America" and "The Orphans of the Storm"; North African plays, such as "The Sheik" and "Beau Geste"; romantic dramas in which Douglas Fairbanks starred, such as "The Three Musketeers," "Robin Hood" and "The Thief of Bagdad."

Hollywood, California, as we have seen elsewhere, became the world center of motion-picture production on account of its brilliant sunshine, mild winter weather and diversified scenery. After the war American films largely monopolized the field in Europe, Asia and South America, often constituting from eighty-five to ninety per cent of the pictures exhibited. This aroused patriotic opposition which took the form of protests against the pernicious influence of the spread of American luxury, manners, morals and ideals as portrayed, oftentimes with great want of fidelity, in the pictures. Finally, France and other European governments imposed restrictions, requiring the exhibit of a certain quota of homemade films.

By the end of the period methods of synchronizing voice, music and other incidental sounds with the film were perfected so that dramas and operas were heard as a whole. The achievement was first demonstrated by the sudden success of "The Jazz Singer" in which Al Jolson, a Jewish black-face favorite, sang his characteristic "Mammy" songs. This was in October, 1927, and within two years the leading theaters of the country had remodeled their mechanism so as to use sound.

6. *1920–1927*—THE AUTOMOBILE CHANGES THE PATTERN OF LIVING

❲ *In the 1920's two social scientists, Robert S. Lynd and Helen M. Lynd, made a minute study of the way people lived in the typical, medium-sized city of Muncie, Indiana. Their findings, published in a book entitled* MIDDLETOWN, *highlighted new patterns of conduct of which most people had been no more than vaguely aware. One of the Lynds' most revealing passages had to do with the social effect of the automobile.*

The first real automobile appeared in Middletown in 1900. About 1906 it was estimated that "there are probably 200 in the city and county." At the close of 1923 there were 6,221 passenger cars in the city, one for every 6.1 persons, or roughly two for every three families. Of these 6,221 cars, 41 per cent. were Fords; 54 per cent. of the total were cars of models of 1920 or later, and 17 per cent. models earlier than 1917. These cars average a bit over 5,000 miles a year. For some of the workers and some of the business class, use of the automobile is a seasonal matter, but the increase in surfaced roads and in closed cars is rapidly making the car a year-round tool for leisure-time as well as getting-a-living activities. As, at the turn of the century, business class people began to feel apologetic if they did not have a telephone, so ownership of an automobile has now reached the point of being an accepted essential of normal living.

Into the equilibrium of habits which constitutes for each individual some integration in living has come this new habit, upsetting old adjustments, and blasting its way through such accustomed and unquestioned dicta as "Rain or shine, I never miss a Sunday morning at church"; "A high school boy does not need much spending money"; "I don't need exercise, walking to the office keeps me fit"; "I wouldn't think of moving out of town and being so far from my friends"; "Parents ought always to know where their children are." The newcomer is most quickly and amicably incorporated into those regions of behavior in which men are engaged in doing impersonal, matter-of-fact things; much more contested is its advent where emotionally charged sanctions and taboos are concerned. No one questions the use of the auto for transporting groceries, getting to one's place of work or to the golf course, or in place of the porch for "cooling off after supper" on a hot summer evening; however much the activities concerned with getting a living may be altered by the fact that a factory can draw from workmen within a radius of forty-five miles, or however much old labor union men resent the intrusion of this new alternate way of spending an evening, these things are hardly major issues. But when auto riding tends to replace the traditional call in the family parlor as a way of approach between the unmarried, "the home is endangered," and all-day Sunday motor trips are a "threat against the church"; it is in the activities concerned with the home and religion that the automobile occasions the greatest emotional conflicts. . . .

The automobile has apparently unsettled the habit of careful saving for some families. "Part of the money we spend on the car would go to the bank, I suppose," said more than one working class wife. A business man explained his recent inviting of social oblivion by selling his car by saying: "My car, counting depreciation and everything, was costing mighty nearly $100.00 a month, and my wife and I sat down together the other night and just figured that we're getting along, and if we're to have anything later on, we've just got to begin to save." The "moral" aspect of the competition between the automobile and certain accepted expenditures appears in the remark of another business man, "An automobile is a luxury, and no one has a right to one if he can't afford it. I haven't the slightest sympathy for any one who is out of work if he owns a car."

Men in the clothing industry are convinced that automobiles are bought at the expense of clothing, and the statements of a number of the working class wives bear this out:

"We'd rather do without clothes than give up the car," said one mother of nine children. "We used to go to his sister's to visit, but by the time we'd get the children shoed and dressed there wasn't any money left for carfare. Now no matter how they look, we just poke 'em in the car and take 'em along."

"We don't have no fancy clothes when we have the car to pay for," said another. "The car is the only pleasure we have."

Even food may suffer:

"I'll go without food before I'll see us give up the car," said one woman emphatically, and several who were out of work were apparently making precisely this adjustment.

Twenty-one of the twenty-six families owning a car for whom data on bathroom facilities happened to be secured live in homes without bathtubs. Here we obviously have a new habit cutting in ahead of an older one and slowing down the diffusion of the latter.

Meanwhile, advertisements pound away at Middletown people with the tempting advice to spend money for automobiles for the sake of their homes and families:

"Hit the trail to better times!" says one such advertisement.

Another depicts a gray-haired banker lending a young couple the money to buy a car and proffering the friendly advice: "Before you can save money, you first must make money. And to make it you must have health, contentment, and full command of all your resources. . . . I have often advised customers of mine to buy cars, as I felt that the increased stimulation and opportunity of observation would enable them to earn amounts equal to the cost of their cars."

Many families feel that an automobile is justified as an agency holding the family group together. "I never feel as close to my family as when we are all together in the car," said one business class mother, and one or two spoke of giving up Country Club membership or other recreations to get a car for this reason. "We don't spend anything on recreation except for the car. We save every place we can and put the money into the car. It keeps the family together," was an opinion voiced more than once. Sixty-one per cent. of 337 boys and 60 per cent. of 423 girls in the three upper years of the high school say that they motor more often with their parents than without them.

But this centralizing tendency of the automobile may be only a passing phase; sets in the other direction are almost equally prominent. "Our daughters [eighteen and fifteen] don't use our car much because they are always with somebody else in their car when we go out motoring," lamented one business class mother. And another said, "The two older children [eighteen and sixteen] never go out when the family motors. They always have something else on." "In the nineties we were all much more together," said another wife. "People brought chairs and cushions out of the house and sat on the lawn evenings. We rolled out a strip of carpet and put cushions on the porch step to take care of the unlimited overflow of neighbors that dropped by. We'd sit out so all evening. The younger couples perhaps would wander off for half an hour to get a soda but come back to join in the informal singing or listen while somebody strummed a mandolin or guitar." "What on earth *do* you want me to do? Just sit around home all evening!" retorted a popular high school girl of today when her father discouraged her going out motoring for the evening with a young blade in a rakish car waiting at the curb. The fact that 348 boys and 382 girls in the three upper years of the high school placed "use of the automobile" fifth and fourth respectively in a list of twelve possible sources of disagreement between them and their parents suggests that this may be an increasing decentralizing agent.

An earnest teacher in a Sunday School class of working class boys and girls in their late teens was winding up the lesson on the temptations of Jesus: "These three temptations summarize all the temptations we encounter today: physical comfort, fame, and wealth. Can you think of any temptation we have today that Jesus didn't have?" "Speed!" rejoined one boy. The unwanted interruption was quickly passed over. But the boy had mentioned a tendency underlying one of the four chief infringements of group laws in Middletown today, and the manifestations of Speed are not confined to "speeding." "Auto Polo next Sunday!!" shouts the display advertisement of an amusement park near the city. "It's motor insanity—too fast for the movies!" The boys who have cars "step on the gas," and those who haven't cars sometimes steal them: "The desire of youth to step on the gas when it has no machine of its own," said the local press, "is considered responsible for the theft of the greater part of the [154] automobiles stolen from [Middletown] during the past year."

The threat which the automobile presents to some anxious parents is suggested by the fact that of thirty girls brought before the juvenile court in the twelve months preceding September 1, 1924, charged with "sex crimes," for whom the place where the offense occurred was given in the records, nineteen were listed as having committed the offense in an automobile. Here again the automobile appears to some as an "enemy" of the home and society.

Sharp, also, is the resentment aroused by this elbowing new device when it interferes with old-established religious habits. The minister trying to change people's behavior in desired directions through the spoken word must compete against the strong pull of the open road strengthened by endless printed "copy" inciting to travel. Preaching to 200 people on a hot, sunny Sunday in midsummer on "The Supreme Need of To-day," a leading Middletown minister denounced "automobilitis—the thing those people have who go off motoring on Sunday instead of going to church. If you want to use your car on Sunday, take it out Sunday morning and bring some shut-ins to church and Sunday School; then in the afternoon, if you choose, go out and worship God in the beauty of nature—but don't neglect to worship Him indoors too." This same month there appeared in the *Saturday Evening Post,* reaching approximately one family in six in Middletown, a two-page spread on the automobile as an "enricher of life," quoting "a bank president in a Mid-Western city" as saying, "A man who works six days a week and spends the seventh on his own doorstep certainly will not pick up the extra dimes in the great thoroughfares of life." "Some sunny Sunday very soon," said another two-page spread in the *Post,* "just drive an Overland up to your door—tell the family to hurry the packing and get aboard—and be off with smiles down the nearest road—free, loose, and happy—bound for green wonderlands." Another such advertisement urged Middletown to "Increase Your Week-End Touring Radius." If we except the concentrated group pressure of war time, never perhaps since the days of the camp-meeting have the citizens of this community been subjected to such a powerfully focused stream of habit diffusion.

7. *1920–1927*—THE RADIO: A NEW NECESSITY

❡ *Though less fundamental in its influence than the automobile, the radio was also changing deep-grained habits and attitudes. Between 1920, when Station KDKA of Pittsburgh went on the air, and 1927, when the Lynds were completing the study that led to* MIDDLETOWN, *American radio stations increased in number from one to 732.*

Though less widely diffused as yet than automobile owning or movie attendance, the radio nevertheless is rapidly crowding its way in among the necessities in the family standard of living. Not the least remarkable feature of this new invention is its accessibility. Here skill and ingenuity can in part offset money as an open sesame to swift sharing of the enjoyments of the wealthy. With but little equipment one can call the life of the rest of the world from the air, and this equipment can be purchased piecemeal at the ten-cent store. Far from being simply one more means of passive enjoyment, the radio has given rise to much ingenious manipulative activity. In a count of representative sections of Middletown, it was found that, of 303 homes in twenty-eight blocks in the "best section" of town, inhabited almost entirely by the business class, 12 per cent. had radios; of 518 workers' homes in sixty-four blocks, 6 per cent. had radios.

As this new tool is rolling back the horizons of Middletown for the bank clerk or the mechanic sitting at home and listening to a Philharmonic concert or a sermon by Dr. Fosdick, or to President Coolidge bidding his father good night on the eve of election, and as it is wedging its way with the movie, the automobile, and other new tools into the twisted mass of habits that are living for the 38,000 people of Middletown, readjustments necessarily occur. Such comments as the following suggest their nature:

"I use time evenings listening in that I used to spend in reading."

"The radio is hurting movie going, especially Sunday evening." (From a leading movie exhibitor.)

"I don't use my car so much any more. The heavy traffic makes it less fun. But I spend seven nights a week on my radio. We hear fine music from Boston." (From a shabby man of fifty.)

"Sundays I take the boy to Sunday School and come straight home and tune in. I get first an eastern service, then a Cincinnati one. Then there's nothing doing till about two-thirty, when I pick up an eastern service again and follow 'em across the country till I wind up with California about ten-thirty. Last night I heard a ripping sermon from Westminster Church somewhere in California. We've no preachers here that can compare with any of them."

"One of the bad features of radio," according to a teacher, "is that children stay up late at night and are not fit for school next day."

"We've spent close to $100 on our radio, and we built it ourselves at that," commented one of the worker's wives. "Where'd we get the money? Oh, out of our savings, like everybody else."

In the flux of competing habits that are oscillating the members of the family now towards and now away from the home, radio occupies an intermediate position. Twenty-five per cent. of 337 high school boys and 22 per cent. of 423 high school girls said that they listen more often to the radio with their parents than without them, and, as pointed out above, 20 per cent. of 274 boys in the three upper years of the high school answered "radio" to the question, "In what thing that you are doing at home this fall are you most interested?"—more than gave any other answer. More than one mother said that her family used to scatter in the evening—"but now we all sit around and listen to the radio."

8. *1927*—LINDBERGH FLIES THE ATLANTIC

〔 *Airplane manufacturers and fliers made steady progress after the First World War, but it took a twenty-five-year-old aviator named Charles A. Lindbergh to dramatize the fact that the airplane had come of age. Backed by a group of St. Louis businessmen, Lindbergh supervised the construction of a Ryan monoplane with one 225-horsepower Wright Whirlwind motor which he proposed to fly non-stop from New York to Paris—a feat which no one had yet accomplished. He took off on the morning of May 20, 1927. Thirty-three hours and thirty-nine minutes later he landed at Paris. In that short time, as Frederick Lewis Allen, then editor of* HARPER'S MAGAZINE, *points out, Lindbergh gave new life to ideals in which a jaded people had almost lost faith.*

He was modest, he seemed to know his business, there was something particularly daring about his idea of making the perilous journey alone, and he was as attractive-looking a youngster as ever had faced a camera man. The reporters—to his annoyance—called him "Lucky Lindy" and the "Flying Fool." The spotlight of publicity was upon him. . . .

On the evening of May 19, 1927, Lindbergh decided that although it was drizzling on Long Island, the weather reports gave a chance of fair skies for his trip and he had better get ready. He spent the small hours of the next morning in sleepless preparations, went to Curtiss Field, received further weather news, had his plane trundled to Roosevelt Field and fueled, and a little before eight o'clock—on the morning of May 20th—climbed in and took off for Paris.

Then something very like a miracle took place.

No sooner had the word been flashed along the wires that Lindbergh had started than the whole population of the country became united in the exaltation of a common emotion. Young and old, rich and poor, farmer and stockbroker, Fundamentalist and skeptic, highbrow and low-brow, all with one accord fastened their hopes upon the young man in the *Spirit of St. Louis*. To give a single instance of the intensity of their mood: at the Yankee Stadium in New York, where the Maloney-Sharkey fight was held on the evening of the 20th, forty thousand hard-boiled boxing fans rose as one man and stood with bared heads in impressive silence when the announcer asked them to pray for Lindbergh. The next day came the successive reports of Lindbergh's success—he had reached the Irish coast, he was crossing over England, he was over the Channel, he had landed at Le Bourget to be enthusiastically mobbed by a vast crowd of Frenchmen—and the American people went almost mad with joy and relief. And when the reports of Lindbergh's first few days in Paris showed that he was behaving with charming modesty and courtesy, millions of his countrymen took him to their hearts as they had taken no other human being in living memory.

Every record for mass excitement and mass enthusiasm in the age of ballyhoo was smashed during the next few weeks. Nothing seemed to matter, either to the newspapers or to the people who read them, but Lindbergh and his story. On the day the flight was completed the *Washington Star* sold 16,000 extra copies, the *St. Louis Post-Dispatch* 40,000, the *New York Evening World* 114,000. The huge headlines which described Lindbergh's triumphal progress from day to day in newspapers from Maine to Oregon showed how thorough was public agreement with the somewhat extravagant dictum of the *Evening World* that Lindbergh had performed "the greatest feat of a solitary man in the records of the human race." Upon his return to the United States, a single Sunday issue of a single paper contained one hundred columns of text and pictures devoted to him. Nobody appeared to question the fitness of President Coolidge's action in sending a cruiser of the United States navy to bring this young private citizen and his plane back from France. He was greeted at Washington in a vast open-air gathering at which the President made—according to Charles Merz—"the longest and most impressive address since his annual message to Congress." The Western Union having provided form messages for telegrams of congratulations to Lindbergh on his arrival, 55,000 of them were sent to him—and were loaded on a truck and trundled after him in the parade through Washington. One telegram, from Minneapolis, was signed with 17,500 names and made up a scroll 520 feet long, under which ten messenger boys staggered. After the public welcome in New York, the Street Cleaning Department gathered up 1,800 tons as against a mere 155 tons swept up after the premature Armistice celebration of November 7, 1918!

Lindbergh was commissioned Colonel, and received the Distinguished Flying Cross, the Congressional Medal of Honor, and so many foreign decorations and honorary memberships that to repeat the list would be a weary task. He was offered two and a half million dollars for a tour of the world by air, and $700,000 to appear in the films; his signature was sold for $1,600; a Texas town was named for him, a thirteen-hundred-foot Lindbergh tower was proposed for the city of Chicago, "the largest dinner ever tendered to an individual in modern history" was consumed in his honor, and a staggering number of streets, schools, restaurants, and corporations sought to share the glory of his name. . . .

To appreciate how extraordinary was this universal outpouring of admiration and love—for the word love is hardly too strong—one must remind oneself of two or three facts.

Lindbergh's flight was not the first crossing of the Atlantic by air. Alcock and Brown had flown direct from Newfoundland to Ireland in 1919. That same year the N-C 4, with five men aboard, had crossed by way of the Azores, and the British dirigible R-34 had flown from Scotland to Long Island with 31 men aboard, and then had turned about and made a return flight to England. The German dirigible ZR-3 (later known as the *Los Angeles*) had flown from Friedrichshafen to Lakehurst, New Jersey, in 1924 with 32 people aboard. Two Round-the-World American army planes had crossed the North Atlantic by way of Iceland, Greenland, and Newfoundland in 1924. The novelty of Lindbergh's flight lay only in the fact that he went all the way from New York to Paris instead of jumping off from Newfoundland, that he reached his precise objective, and that he went alone.

Furthermore, there was little practical advantage in such an exploit. It brought about a boom in aviation, to be sure, but a not altogether healthy one, and it led many a flyer to hop off blindly for foreign shores in emulation of Lindbergh and be drowned. Looking back on the event after a lapse of years, and stripping it of its emotional connotations, one sees it simply as a daring stunt flight—the longest trip up to that time—by a man who did not claim to be anything but a stunt flyer. Why, then, this idolization of Lindbergh?

The explanation is simple. A disillusioned nation fed on cheap heroics and scandal and crime was revolting against the low estimate of human nature which it had allowed itself to entertain. For years the American people had been spiritually starved. They had seen their early ideals and illusions and hopes one by one worn away by the corrosive influence of events and ideas—by the disappointing aftermath of the war, by scientific doctrines and psychological theories which undermined their religion and ridiculed their sentimental notions, by the spectacle of graft in politics and crime on the city streets, and finally by their recent newspaper diet of smut and murder. Romance, chivalry, and self-dedication had been debunked; the heroes of history had been shown to have feet of clay, and the saints of history had been revealed as people with queer complexes. There was the god of business to worship—but a suspicion lingered that he was made of brass. Ballyhoo had given the public contemporary heroes to bow down before—but these contemporary heroes, with their fat profits from moving-picture contracts and ghost-written syndicated articles, were not wholly convincing. Something that people needed, if they were to live at peace with themselves and with the world, was missing from their lives. And all at once Lindbergh provided it. Romance, chivalry, self-dedication—here they were, embodied in a modern Galahad for a generation which had foresworn Galahads. Lindbergh did not accept the moving-picture offers that came his way, he did not sell testimonials, did not boast, did not get himself involved in scandal, conducted himself with unerring taste—and was handsome and brave withal. . . .

Pretty good, one reflects, for a stunt flyer. But also, one must add, pretty good for the American people. They had shown that they had better taste in heroes than anyone would have dared to predict during the years which immediately preceded the 20th of May, 1927.

9. *1928–1929*—THE BOOM

❨ *The spirit of change and adventure did not stop with inventions and manners and morals; it invaded the securities market. The feeling spread that the future of the country was unlimited. Every industry, every company in every industry, had golden days ahead. To enjoy certain wealth one needed only to buy stocks—which he could by paying only a fraction of the market price—and the expanding economy would do the rest. The result was the wildest boom in the country's history.*

Frederick Lewis Allen, keen observer of the American scene, described the boom before time had dimmed its incredible proportions.

Gradually the huge pyramid of capital rose. While supersalesmen of automobiles and radios and a hundred other gadgets were loading the ultimate consumer with new and shining wares, supersalesmen of securities were selling him shares of investment trusts which held stock in holding companies which owned the stock of banks which had affiliates which in turn controlled holding companies—and so on *ad infinitum*.

From *Only Yesterday*, by Frederick Lewis Allen; copyright, 1931, by Frederick Lewis Allen. Reprinted by permission of the publishers, Harper & Brothers. Pp. 314–16.

Though the shelves of manufacturing companies and jobbers and retailers were not overloaded, the shelves of the ultimate consumer and the shelves of the distributors of securities were groaning. Trouble was brewing—not the same sort of trouble which had visited the country in 1921, but trouble none the less. Still, however, the cloud in the summer sky looked no bigger than a man's hand.

How many Americans actually held stock on margin during the fabulous summer of 1929 there seems to be no way of computing, but it is probably safe to put the figure at more than a million. . . . The additional number of those who held common stock outright and followed the daily quotations with an interest nearly as absorbed as that of the margin trader was, of course, considerably larger. As one walked up the aisle of the 5:27 local, or found one's seat in the trolley car, two out of three newspapers that one saw were open to the page of stock-market quotations. Branch offices of the big Wall Street houses blossomed in every city and in numerous suburban villages. In 1919 there had been five hundred such offices; by October, 1928, there were 1,192; and throughout most of 1929 they appeared in increasing numbers. The broker found himself regarded with a new wonder and esteem. Ordinary people, less intimate with the mysteries of Wall Street than he was supposed to be, hung upon his every word. Let him but drop a hint of a possible split-up in General Industries Associates and his neighbor was off hot-foot the next morning to place a buying order.

The rich man's chauffeur drove with his ears laid back to catch the news of an impending move in Bethlehem Steel; he held fifty shares himself on a twenty-point margin. The window-cleaner at the broker's office paused to watch the ticker, for he was thinking of converting his laboriously accumulated savings into a few shares of Simmons. Edwin Lefèvre told of a broker's valet who had made nearly a quarter of a million in the market, of a trained nurse who cleaned up thirty thousand following the tips given her by grateful patients; and of a Wyoming cattleman, thirty miles from the nearest railroad, who bought or sold a thousand shares a day,—getting his market returns by radio and telephoning his orders to the nearest large town to be transmitted to New York by telegram. An ex-actress in New York fitted up her Park Avenue apartment as an office and surrounded herself with charts, graphs, and financial reports, playing the market by telephone on an increasing scale and with increasing abandon. Across the dinner table one heard fantastic stories of sudden fortunes; a young banker had put every dollar of his small capital into Niles-Bement-Pond and now was fixed for life; a widow had been able to buy a large country house with her winnings in Kennecott. Thousands speculated—and won, too—without the slightest knowledge of the nature of the company upon whose fortunes they were relying, like the people who bought Seaboard Air

Line under the impression that it was an aviation stock. Grocers, motormen, plumbers, seamstresses, and speakeasy waiters were in the market. Even the revolting intellectuals were there: loudly as they might lament the depressing effects of standardization and mass production upon American life, they found themselves quite ready to reap the fruits thereof. Literary editors whose hopes were wrapped about American Cyanamid B lunched with poets who swore by Cities Service, and as they left the table, stopped a moment in the crowd at the broker's branch office to catch the latest quotations; and the artist who had once been eloquent only about Gauguin laid aside his brushes to proclaim the merits of National Bellas Hess. The Big Bull Market had become a national mania.

In September the market reached its ultimate glittering peak.

10. *1929*—THE CRASH

❰ *The boom could not last. Stock market prices broke in March, 1929, but recovered to rise to new heights despite signs of trouble in various industries. On Thursday, October 24, the market crashed with a suddenness and severity that gave notice of the end of the bull market. The days that followed were even worse. Jonathan Norton Leonard, a journalist and historian of the contemporary, describes the financial turn of fate that impoverished millions.*

That Saturday and Sunday Wall Street hummed with week-day activity. The great buildings were ablaze with lights all night as sleepy clerks fought desperately to get the accounts in shape for the Monday opening. Horrified brokers watched the selling orders accumulate. It wasn't a flood; it was a deluge. Everybody wanted to sell—the man with five shares and the man with ten thousand. Evidently the week-end cheer barrage had not hit its mark.

Monday was a rout for the banking pool, which was still supposed to be "on guard." If it did any net buying at all, which is doubtful, the market paid little attention. Leading stocks broke through the support levels as soon as trading started and kept sinking all day. Periodically the news would circulate that the banks were about to turn the tide as they had done on Thursday, but it didn't happen. A certain cynicism developed in the board rooms as the day wore on. Obviously the big financial interests had abandoned the market to its fate, probably intending to pick up the fragments cheap when the wreck hit the final bottom. "Very well," said the little man, "I shall do the same."

When the market finally closed, 9,212,800 shares had been sold. The

From *Three Years Down* by Jonathan Norton Leonard. Copyright, 1944 by J. B. Lippincott Company. Published by J. B. Lippincott Company. Pp. 80–82.

Times index of 25 industrials fell from 367.42 to 318.29. The whole list showed alarming losses, and margin calls were on their way to those speculators who had not already sold out.

That night Wall Street was lit up like a Christmas tree. Restaurants, barber shops, and speakeasies were open and doing a roaring business. Messenger boys and runners raced through the streets whooping and singing at the tops of their lungs. Slum children invaded the district to play with balls of ticker tape. Well-dressed gentlemen fell asleep in lunch counters. All the downtown hotels, rooming houses, even flop-houses were full of financial employees who usually slept in the Bronx. It was probably Wall Street's worst night. Not only had the day been bad, but everybody down to the youngest office boy had a pretty good idea of what was going to happen tomorrow.

The morning papers were black with the story of the Monday smash. Except for rather feeble hopes that the great banks would step into the gap they had no heart for cheerful headlines. In the inside pages, how-ever, the sunshine chorus continued as merry as ever. Bankers said that heavy buying had been sighted on the horizon. Brokers were loud with "technical" reasons why the decline could not continue.

It wasn't only the financial bigwigs who spoke up. Even the outriders of the New Era felt that if everybody pretended to be happy, their phoney smiles would blow the trouble away. Jimmy Walker, for ex-ample, asked the movie houses to show only cheerful pictures. *True Story Magazine,* currently suffering from delusions of grandeur, ran full page advertisements in many papers urging all wage earners to buy luxuries on credit. That would fix things right up. McGraw-Hill Com-pany, another publishing house with boom-time megalomania, told the public to avert its eyes from the obscene spectacle in Wall Street. What they did not observe would not affect their state of mind and good times could continue as before.

These noble but childish dabbles in mass psychology failed as utterly as might have been expected. Even the more substantial contributions of U.S. Steel and American Can in the shape of $1 extra dividends had the same fate. Ordinarily such action would have sent the respective stocks shooting upward, but in the present mood of the public it created not the slightest ripple of interest. Steel and Can plunged down as steeply as if they had canceled their dividends entirely. The next day, Tuesday, the 29th of October, was the worst of all. In the first half hour 3,259,800 shares were traded, almost a full day's work for the laboring machinery of the Exchange. The selling pressure was wholly without precedent. It was coming from everywhere. The wires to other cities were jammed with frantic orders to sell. So were the cables, radio and telephones to Europe and the rest of the world. Buyers were few, sometimes wholly absent. Often the specialists stood baffled at their posts, sellers pressing around them and not a single buyer at any price.

This was real panic. It was what the banks had prevented on Thursday, had slowed on Monday. Now they were helpless. Reportedly they were trying to force their associated corporations to toss their buying power into the whirlpool, but they were getting no results. Albert Conway, New York State Superintendent of Insurance, took the dubious step of urging the companies under his jurisdiction to buy common stocks. If they did so, their buying was insufficient to halt the rout.

When the closing bell rang, the great bull market was dead and buried. 16,410,000 shares had changed hands. Leading stocks had lost as much as 77% of their peak value. The Dow Jones index was off 40% since September 3. Not only the little speculators, but the lordly, experienced big traders had been wiped out by the violence of the crash and the whole financial structure of the nation had been shaken to its foundations. Many bankers and brokers were doubtful about their own solvency, for their accounting systems had broken down. The truth was buried beneath a mountain of scribbled paper which would require several days of solid work to clear away.

11. *1930–1937*—THE DEPRESSION

❨ *After the market crash, industry slowed down. Billions in purchasing power had disappeared almost overnight. What purpose could there be in producing cars and radios and automatic washing machines when millions were wondering where they could find next month's rent? With decreased production men and women were laid off; potential buyers became fewer and fewer. By 1932 the United States found itself in the grip of want and suffering. Frederick Lewis Allen, surveying the American scene for a sequel to* ONLY YESTERDAY, *cited examples of human tragedy.*

Walking through an American city, you might find few signs of the depression visible—or at least conspicuous—to the casual eye. You might notice that a great many shops were untenanted, with dusty plate-glass windows and signs indicating that they were ready to lease; that few factory chimneys were smoking; that the streets were not so crowded with trucks as in earlier years, that there was no uproar of riveters to assail the ear, that beggars and panhandlers were on the sidewalks in unprecedented numbers (in the Park Avenue district of New York a man might be asked for money four or five times in a ten-block walk). Traveling by railroad, you might notice that the trains were shorter, the Pullman cars fewer—and that fewer freight trains were

From *Since Yesterday* by Frederick Lewis Allen. Copyright, 1939, 1940, by Harper & Brothers. Reprinted by permission. Pp. 59–64.

on the line. Traveling overnight, you might find only two or three other passengers in your sleeping car. (By contrast, there were more filling stations by the motor highways than ever before, and of all the retail businesses in "Middletown" only the filling stations showed no large drop in business during the black years; for although few new automobiles were being bought, those which would still stand up were being used more than ever—to the dismay of the railroads.)

Otherwise things might seem to you to be going on much as usual. The major phenomena of the depression were mostly negative and did not assail the eye.

But if you knew where to look, some of them would begin to appear. First, the breadlines in the poorer districts. Second, those bleak settlements ironically known as "Hoovervilles" in the outskirts of the cities and on vacant lots—groups of makeshift shacks constructed out of packing boxes, scrap iron, anything that could be picked up free in a diligent combing of the city dumps: shacks in which men and sometimes whole families of evicted people were sleeping on automobile seats carried from auto-graveyards, warming themselves before fires of rubbish in grease drums. Third, the homeless people sleeping in doorways or on park benches, and going the rounds of the restaurants for leftover half-eaten biscuits, piecrusts, anything to keep the fires of life burning. Fourth, the vastly increased number of thumbers on the highways, and particularly of freight-car transients on the railroads: a huge army of drifters ever on the move, searching half-aimlessly for a place where there might be a job. . . . It was estimated that by the beginning of 1933, the country over, there were a million of these transients on the move. . . .

Among the comparatively well-to-do people of the country (those, let us say, whose pre-depression incomes had been over $5,000 a year) the great majority were living on a reduced scale, for salary cuts had been extensive, especially since 1931, and dividends were dwindling. These people were discharging servants, or cutting servants' wages to a minimum, or in some cases "letting" a servant stay on without other compensation than board and lodging. In many pretty houses, wives who had never before—in the revealing current phrase—"done their own work" were cooking and scrubbing. Husbands were wearing the old suit longer, resigning from the golf club, deciding, perhaps, that this year the family couldn't afford to go to the beach for the summer, paying seventy-five cents for lunch instead of a dollar at the restaurant or thirty-five instead of fifty at the lunch counter. When those who had flown high with the stock market in 1929 looked at the stock-market page of the newspapers nowadays their only consoling thought (if they still had any stock left) was that a judicious sale or two would result in such a capital loss that they need pay no income tax at all this year.

Alongside these men and women of the well-to-do classes whose fortunes had been merely reduced by the depression were others whose fortunes had been shattered. The crowd of men waiting for the 8:14 train at the prosperous suburb included many who had lost their jobs, and were going to town as usual not merely to look stubbornly and almost hopelessly for other work but also to keep up a bold front of activity. (In this latter effort they usually succeeded: one would never have guessed, seeing them chatting with their friends as train-time approached, how close to desperation some of them had come.) There were architects and engineers bound for offices to which no clients had come in weeks. There were doctors who thought themselves lucky when a patient paid a bill. Mrs. Jones, who went daily to her stenographic job, was now the economic mainstay of her family, for Mr. Jones was jobless and was doing the cooking and looking after the children (with singular distaste and inefficiency). Next door to the Joneses lived Mrs. Smith, the widow of a successful lawyer: she had always had a comfortable income, she prided herself on her "nice things," she was pathetically unfitted to earn a dollar even if jobs were to be had; her capital had been invested in South American bonds and United Founders stock and other similarly misnamed "securities," and now she was completely dependent upon hand-outs from her relatives, and didn't even have carfare in her imported pocketbook. . . .

Further down in the economic scale, particularly in those industrial communities in which the factories were running at twenty per cent of capacity or had closed down altogether, conditions were infinitely worse. . . . In every American city, quantities of families were being evicted from their inadequate apartments; moving in with other families till ten or twelve people would be sharing three or four rooms; or shivering through the winter in heatless houses because they could afford no coal, eating meat once a week or not at all. If employers sometimes found that former employees who had been discharged did not seem eager for re-employment ("They won't take a job if you offer them one!"), often the reason was panic: a dreadful fear of inadequacy which was one of the depression's commonest psychopathological results. A woman clerk, offered piecework after being jobless for a year, confessed that she almost had not dared to come to the office, she had been in such terror lest she wouldn't know where to hang her coat, wouldn't know how to find the washroom, wouldn't understand the boss's directions for her job. . . .

At the very bottom of the economic scale the conditions may perhaps best be suggested by two brief quotations. The first, from Jonathan Norton Leonard's *Three Years Down*, describes the plight of Pennsylvania miners who had been put out of company villages after a blind and hopeless strike in 1931: "Reporters from the more liberal metropolitan papers found thousands of them huddled on the mountainsides, crowded three or four families together in one-room shacks, living on dandelions and wild weed-roots. Half of them were sick, but no local doctor would care for the evicted strikers. All of them were hungry and many of them were dying of those providential diseases which enable welfare authorities to claim that no one has starved." The other quotation is from Louise V. Armstrong's *We Too Are the People,* and the scene is Chicago in the late spring of 1932:—

"One vivid, gruesome moment of those dark days we shall never forget. We saw a crowd of some fifty men fighting over a barrel of garbage outside the back door of a restaurant. American citizens fighting for scraps of food like animals!"

1. *1933*—ROOSEVELT TAKES OVER

❨ *With the country in the grip of the worst depression in its history, a change of administration was inevitable. The Democratic nomination fell on Franklin Delano Roosevelt, Assistant Secretary of the Navy in Wilson's Cabinet, and now, in 1932, approaching the end of his second term as Governor of New York.*

Roosevelt swept the country, winning by a popular majority of almost 6,000,000 in a total vote of 39,747,000, and carrying the electoral college by 472 to 59. In an atmosphere vibrant with the prospect of change the newly-elected President took the oath of office. The reporter is Thomas L. Stokes of the United Press.

I can never forget the man who stood, high above, on the platform at the East Front of the Capitol on March 4, 1933.

Thomas L. Stokes, *Chip Off My Shoulder* (Princeton University Press, 1940), 309–12. Reprinted by permission of the publisher.

541

The day was dark and drear. Clouds hung heavily as if ready at any moment to open their funnels and pour a torrent upon the huge crowd below.

He stood, bareheaded, as the raw wind pecked at his hair.

He spoke and his voice had an electric, vibrant quality that magnetized the multitudes before him.

"This nation asks for action and action now," he cried.

The crowd thundered back its acclaim. Little boys, hanging from trees and lamp posts, unknowing, clapped their hands and whistled shrilly.

His face was stern. Tightly he gripped the sides of the reading stand. He knew—as those before him could not know—the gigantic task which had been imposed upon him a few minutes before he took the oath of office.

To millions of Americans in despair his voice was the symbol of hope. As we listened, it seemed that the pall of gloom was lifting a bit. It was an overwhelming gloom. The newspapers brought word of banks closing all over the country. The structure seemed to be giving away at every point. Desolate men, even now as he spoke, trailed in gaunt lines about windy corners to get a bowl of soup and a piece of bread. Farmers looked out across their acres and wondered how they would meet the mortgage. Families in financial straits watched neighbors evicted and wondered how long before they would be on the streets. Businessmen scanned their balance sheets and knew not how they would survive. America was in panic.

This *must* be the Deliverer from the troubles which encompassed us on every side.

Certainly it was a complete change of management. The old order had been swept out in the election the previous November.

Standing behind the new President, when he took the oath of office, pulling their cloaks tightly about them against the wind, looking drearily into the future, were the apostles of the old order, the key men of the delirious decade which began with Harding and wound so merrily for a time through that wild dance that had ended so disastrously.

Back whence they came to power now went Senator Reed Smoot of Utah, the high priest of tariff protection; Senator George H. Moses of New Hampshire who had given the revolution now manifest a push with his quip about "the sons of the wild jackass"; Representative Willis C. Hawley of Oregon, the school teacher become statesman for a time, who as chairman of the House Ways and Means Committee was co-author of the Smoot-Hawley Tariff Act; Senator Jim Watson of Indiana who had flapped his long arms so cheerily in his fashion and proclaimed that passage of the Smoot-Hawley Tariff meant "happy days are here again."

Ironically, the bands played "Happy Days Are Here Again" on this occasion—but not for Jim Watson, or for any of his like.

Herbert Hoover's round face was like the mound of dough before it goes into the oven, drab and puffy and expressionless. I watched him as he sat on the front row of the Senate during the ceremonies of swearing in Vice President Garner. He looked as if only vaguely conscious of what went on here and not the least bit interested. I wondered what he was thinking as I wrote a running descriptive story of the scene. He vouchsafed no smile. Mrs. Hoover, on the front row of the gallery to my left, likewise was grim and glum. This, perhaps, was one of the most trying ordeals in the lives of this couple who had dined with kings and potentates and realized now that so many millions of their own countrymen only prayed for this hour when they would be shuffled out of the White House.

They wanted to forget the name Hoover and everything it connoted.

There was no mention of him, except derisively, that night in the buzz of conversation about Washington. Franklin D. Roosevelt was the man of the hour, his name the charmed sesame to open the door of hope and new life. Washington trembled with excitement. It still vibrated to the voice from the front of the Capitol. People read his speech again and recited sentences and phrases and speculated avidly what he would do. There was general agreement that he would begin to act. Washington is cynical and blasé; it had been unusually so in the closing months of the Hoover administration. But little doubt crept into the conversation that night. Washington was ready to believe, to have faith. It looked forward, too, to a great adventure. That was in the air. And the adventure would occur right here, in its sight and hearing. If Washington reacted thus to a man and a voice, what must be happening out in the country where people were crushed and desperate? Washington still was above the storm by its very nature. Depression touches but lightly the capital, a city with no industry except the industry of government and its only business that of the entrepreneur who sells food and clothing and the necessities to a stable population with a steady income supplied by the taxpayer. Washington was ready for the drama. Eagerly it waited for the play to begin.

It did not have long to wait.

Action began dizzily on every front.

The hope of a nation was crystallized in this man.

But no one knew exactly what to expect of him.

His triumph had been easy. The nation had revolted—the biggest electoral revolt thus far in its history—against a system under which it had suffered. The election sweep was negative in character. People were voting more "agin" than for. Anything, they felt, would be better than Hoover.

2. *1933*—HOOVER IN SHADOW

❲ *Franklin D. Roosevelt succeeded a man who had taken over the presidency amid almost universal applause only to leave it burdened with the blame for an economic collapse which no one could have prevented. It was natural that Herbert Hoover should have been disgruntled during the first months of his successor's administration. Yet Nicholas Roosevelt—diplomat, journalist, and member of the Republican branch of the family—found a generous heart under the gruff exterior.*

In the autumn of 1933, Jay Darling (better known as the cartoonist "Ding") and I joined Herbert Hoover as guests of Milton H. Esberg to fish for steelhead on the Klamath River in northern California. I had never been a member of the little group of Hoover intimates, but from my first contact with him in 1919 I was an admirer of his. In the early twenties I had met him numerous times, largely through the intercession of friends of his, such as Mrs. William Brown Meloney, the editor of *This Week,* and George Barr Baker. I had shared their enthusiasm for him as a presidential candidate when the 1928 convention approached. We felt that his firsthand knowledge of Europe would be of great value and that his demonstrated ability as an efficient executive would stand him in good stead in the presidency. Furthermore, we were eager to see in the White House a man of action, unafraid of responsibility, and experienced as an engineer and a promoter of great enterprises. He seemed the ideal man—as the country obviously believed when it elected him by an overwhelming majority in November of 1928.

It was Hoover's misfortune to have come to power only a few months before the world plunged into the worst depression of modern times. The dislocations in the European economy caused by World War I had begun to make themselves felt here in 1928. Our own machinery of production, overstimulated by the war demands and by the needs of postwar Europe, continued to turn out goods of all kinds, agricultural as well as industrial, in increasing quantities. Businessmen and farmers were convinced that there would be no end to prosperity. They did not realize that Europe's capacity to buy from us had reached a saturation point, and that this would cause a piling up of goods in America in larger quantities than we could consume. No man in the White House—or elsewhere—could have checked the ensuing economic paralysis. Because Mr. Hoover was no wiser than anyone else in foreseeing the depression or in anticipating its intensity, and yet was head of the nation, people began to blame him for their troubles. By 1932, his name

---

Reprinted from *A Front Row Seat*, by Nicholas Roosevelt, copyright 1953, by University of Oklahoma Press. Used by permission. Pp. 235–38.

had become synonymous in the public mind with hunger, unemployment, and financial disaster.

Mr. Hoover's lack of political experience made his four years in the White House more difficult and burdensome for himself. A president's every act, and even his every hope, is conditioned by politics and by his past, present, or future relations with politicians. If he by-passes or ignores a senator, or shows his impatience with a congressman, he is laying up potential trouble for himself when next he needs congressional support. To an expert administrator like Hoover it must often have been exasperating to be hampered or thwarted or delayed at every move by the need for considering the feelings or political ambitions of a legislator.

During this fishing expedition Mr. Hoover told us about his experiences with F. D. R. in February, 1933, in connection with the growing banking and gold panic. . . . Mr. Hoover was doing his utmost to avert the nationwide closing of the banks. His sole concern was to try to steer the ship of state through the ever worsening storms to avert disaster. Rightly or wrongly, he believed that assurances from the President-elect that there would be no tinkering with the currency and that the budget would be balanced would stem the incipient panic. He wrote a personal longhand letter to F. D. R. urging him to make such a statement, and sent it by the head of the Secret Service to be delivered personally into the hands of the President-elect. This was February 17, 1933.

Common courtesy, let alone concern for the fate of the country, justified Mr. Hoover's expectation that Mr. Roosevelt would give this extremely urgent appeal from the President of the United States prompt attention. Mr. Roosevelt did not even acknowledge receipt of it for twelve days, and then expressed regrets that the intended reply, which had been dictated a week earlier, by an oversight had not been sent. It proved to be an evasive rejection of Mr. Hoover's plea. During these critical twelve days the panic had been growing. Mr. Hoover therefore made a new appeal to the President-elect for some sort of reassurance about credit and currency and offered to work with him in any way possible to try to stem the tide of disaster. But F. D. R. took the constitutionally correct position that he could do nothing until noon, March 4, and that, until then, to use Ray Moley's phrase, "the baby was Hoover's, anyway."

. . . While we were fishing for steelhead on the Klamath River an incident occurred which dramatized the conflicting elements in Mr. Hoover's character. On the third afternoon, while he was in the river and the rest of us were at the Esbergs' camp, the local schoolteacher called to ask if Mr. Hoover would visit her one-room school the next morning, saying that it would mean a lot to the children to be able to see and meet a former president of the United States. Mr. Esberg, who knew his Hoover well, said that he thought it could be arranged. Accordingly, when Mr. Hoover returned and had had a good supper, Mr. Esberg remarked casually: "By the way, Chief, I've ordered the car tomorrow morning and thought we might go upstream a bit."

"What for?" Mr. Hoover interrupted gruffly and suspiciously.

"I thought we might have better fishing up there, and it would give us a chance to stop off at a school," said Mr. Esberg.

"I won't do it," Mr. Hoover snapped.

"It would mean a lot to the children," Mr. Esberg explained soothingly, "and would only take five minutes of our time."

"I won't do it," Mr. Hoover repeated stubbornly.

"Ding" interposed with a plea that the children would greatly appreciate it, and I remarked that such things were a part of the role of a former president. None of us made any impression, so the matter was dropped until the next morning, when, after breakfast, Mr. Esberg announced that the car was waiting. Mr. Hoover growled but got in, and in a few minutes we arrived at the little schoolhouse near the river.

Not knowing him as well as did Mr. Esberg, I had misgivings. They proved unfounded, for not only did Mr. Hoover speak gracefully and graciously and show a deep personal interest in each of the children and in the teacher, but when he left the school he turned to Mr. Esberg and said: "Do you know that nearly all the children in this school are undernourished, and that the teacher is taking five dollars a month out of her own small salary to furnish them an extra snack at lunch?" Mr. Esberg had not been aware of it. But Mr. Hoover was not content to let the matter drop. "It would only take about a hundred dollars to provide a decent meal for the kids for the rest of this year," he said. "If you and your friends will help out, I'll underwrite the balance." There spoke the real Hoover. Few other people visiting that school would at once have discovered the need. It was typical of him that, having discovered it, he at once took steps to meet it appropriately and effectively.

3.   *1933*—"THE FIRST HUNDRED DAYS"

❴ *Thomas L. Stokes describes the buoyant approach of the new administration to its first and most pressing problem: the restoration of the country's banking system.*

One night in that early, hectic, breathless era of the New Deal which my friend Ernest K. Lindley has called "The First Hundred Days," a group of us kept our vigil in front of the White House, waiting for

Thomas L. Stokes, *Chip Off My Shoulder* (Princeton University Press, 1940), 361–69. Reprinted by permission of the publisher.

one of the innumerable conferences to break up. They came in dizzy succession, those meetings in which the President, his Cabinet and his experts drafted plans, first to salvage the banks and get the nation's financial system back into some sort of order, and later for other legislative measures to patch up the weakened structure of the American economy and to reform some of the abuses revealed.

It began to rain and, by the grace of a kindly police officer, we herded ourselves on the front portico. Marvin McIntyre, one of the President's secretaries whom we all had known for many years about Washington as a newspaperman, came out and joined us. Mac is never so happy as when he is "harmonizing." He loves to assemble a quick quartet. It is as important to him in his leisure moments—and he had very few in those days and the years afterward—to harmonize a bit as it was for those baseball players whom Ring Lardner has left us as merry minstrels of the washroom on the train as they went from one city to another. Mac drew us about him and we struck up the White House favorite "Home on the Range." Rich and strong and slightly raucous, it filled the rain-drenched air as we huddled together, arms across each other's shoulders, on the front porch of the White House. We finished. Then, suddenly, we all looked at each other and laughed.

"Imagine doing this in the Hoover administration!" someone said.

He spoke the thought of all of us.

That scene is typical to me of the carefree bravado of those days. The gloom, the tenseness, the fear of the closing months of the Hoover administration had vanished. It seemed for a time that the country had gone to hell. But, what the hell, said we, we are going to build it over again! We were so confident and cocksure.

So, too, were the young men who descended upon Washington from college cloisters and lawyers' offices and quickly found themselves places behind hundreds of desks and began to explore every cranny of the national economy, to probe its faults and to draw diagrams and blueprints of a new world. They were going to make the world over. We talked then of a planned economy. We learned new nomenclature. In time there were agencies with initials which gave the whole task the aspects of revolution. We spoke of "The Roosevelt Revolution."

They were exciting, exhilarating days. It was one of the most joyous periods of my life. We came alive, we were eager.

We were infected with a gay spirit of adventure, for something concrete and constructive finally was being done about the chaos which confronted the nation. The buoyancy and informality of the New Deal, the roll-up-your-sleeves and go-to-it attitude, percolated out from the conferences at the White House, from conferences in other government buildings, from conferences at the Capitol where Congressmen were caught up in the enthusiasm.

We achieved a national unity that was glorious to see. A little sadly I look back upon it. It was good that we were able to get together in that time, for otherwise we might have lost our democracy. But it is good, too, I suppose, that when we acquired a certain health again we began to quarrel and question, for otherwise we might have lost the resiliency necessary for democracy and might have set up a system that later would have been available for something other than democracy. Franklin D. Roosevelt, however, never would have been party to anything else than democracy. Of that I am convinced. . . .

Roosevelt could have become a dictator in 1933. He did not. . . . His first job was to do something, and do it quickly to save the nation's banking structure. The banks were cracking all about us on that March 4. One of his objectives throughout his administration has been to harness financial power, to move the financial capital from New York to Washington, to turn the control of money and credit back to the people through their elected representatives. This he could have accomplished in one bold stroke by taking over the banks at the time and nationalizing them. But he did not take this way, though he was urged to. Instead he turned the banks back to their owners and operators and tried to realize his ends by the slow process of reform of the system through law. How hard that has been, how it was resisted, I myself can testify; for I covered the tedious course through Congress of the securities act, the stock market act, and the banking acts of the administration designed to give Washington regulatory powers over the operations of private finance.

Roosevelt in those early days was the confident commander, blithe of spirit, resourceful.

One night I walked away from one of the general legislative conferences with a Republican leader. We strolled along the White House driveway.

"My, that man is refreshing after Hoover!" he said.

"Like a nice, cool highball after drinking stale, flat beer. It is interesting, too, to watch him operate. I sat there tonight, sort of back in a corner—after all, I'm a Republican, you know."

He smiled.

"He was courteous. He deferred here and there. He was good-humored. But all the way through he kept a straight line toward what he wanted. When it was all over, he had got his way. He's smart!"

In his voice was the admiration of one politician for another.

Roosevelt's calm and optimism carried us through those trying days, so that we could joke about our individual plights as he closed the banks. That was ordered in a proclamation issued at the White House at one o'clock in the morning of Monday, March 6, less than two days after he had been in the White House. Most of the banks were shut down already. The bank holiday he proclaimed stopped all financial transactions. Working day and night, he and his experts drew up a plan for their reopening. He called in the heads of the press associations and explained the plan to them. Ray Clapper represented us, the United Press. I was on the night service at that time. I was in the office standing by, ready at the telephone to take the story when Ray called. His voice had a tense quality and he sounded far away. He explained he was calling from within the White House. He dictated his lead, which was pulled from my typewriter and rushed to the wire. Take by take the story went out.

The next night the President talked to the people in their homes about the radio in the first of his "fireside chats." He explained the banking dilemma in simple language and told what was being done about it. It was a masterpiece of exposition. His voice inspired confidence. The effect was just as if he were sitting in the room with the family. He displayed in that talk the insight into public psychology which made him the idol of the masses. . . .

My endeavor is to recapture the fine frenzy of that period, to recapture my own enthusiasm and zest. For it had an important influence upon my thinking. New hope filled me. I saw that something could be done about lots of things. Those who had been so long in the minority, crying in the wilderness, now became a militant majority. A new period of education began for me. I went back to school. We reporters all went back to school—we have commented on it often since. We had to in order to turn out our daily copy, for the administration was probing into the whole economic structure. The classrooms were government offices, headquarters for the new agencies which sprang up over night in Washington. . . .

As I look back upon myself in those days I see that I was pretty naive in some respects. I was so eager, so hopeful. I don't regret it. I regret none of my enthusiasms. Some of them died away, but I still retain others. Some heroes developed bad cases of clay feet. Some have worn well. I am glad that I could have faith again in something.

I learned to know my country, then, and I learned to love it, and I knew that it could be saved.

4.   *1933–1939*—HARRY HOPKINS AND THE FEDERAL RELIEF PROGRAM

❲ *With millions out of work, and with the states, cities, and counties nearing the end of their resources, the federal government undertook to provide relief. Frances Perkins, Secretary of Labor and the first woman to hold a cabinet position, describes the relief program of Harry Hopkins, one of the most controversial figures of the New Deal.*

Shortly after Inauguration Day Harry Hopkins and William Hodson came down from New York to see me. Hopkins was chairman of the New York State Temporary Emergency Relief Administration, which had been established by Roosevelt when he had been Governor. Hodson was director of the Welfare Council of New York City. Hopkins was not then a close friend of the President's. He had been appointed to his New York job because he had been recommended by people Roosevelt trusted. . . .

Hopkins, Hodson, and I met at the Women's University Club, which was jammed. We found a hole under the stairs, and there, in cramped, unlovely quarters, they laid out their plan. It was a plan for the immediate appropriation by the Federal Government of grants-in-aid to the states for unemployment relief. I was impressed by the exactness of their knowledge and the practicability of their plan.

They told me they had not been able to get to the President to present their program. I knew that Secretary Marvin McIntyre was almost frantic trying to arrange appointments for people with political influence, for old friends, job seekers, congressmen, as well as a few people with ideas. Feeling certain of my ground, I cut across the usual formalities and made an appointment for Hopkins and Hodson to see the President immediately, telling McIntyre that these people knew how to operate and had a concrete proposal.

Roosevelt heard their views with interest. He knew about Hopkins's work as relief administrator in New York. In his conversations that day and in later conferences Roosevelt showed that he intended to incorporate some of New York's experience in handling relief into the federal program. After a series of preliminary talks Roosevelt called in Senators Wagner, La Follette, and Costigan, and asked them to draw a bill to establish the Federal Emergency Relief Administration. The three Senators were good enough to consult me, chiefly on the New York experience, and the measure was drawn up and approved by the President. Congressional committees conducted hearings on the bill in April, and the Congress passed it early in May. The President signed the measure on May 12, 1933, and appointed Harry Hopkins as Federal Emergency Relief administrator. FERA opened for business on May 22 with a working capital of $500,000,000. . . .

The fortunes of the unemployed took a turn for the better the day FERA began to operate. The original appropriation and an additional $850,000,000 were expended by March 1934, including the Civil Works program. Congress, surveying the results at that time, was generous with FERA.

In its brief span of life FERA received and spent $4,000,000,000 on all projects. It was the first step in the economic pump priming that was to break the back of the depression. FERA spent money for many things, all necessities of life—food, clothing, fuel, shelter, medicine. In an analysis of how the money was spent, Harry Hopkins said, "We can only say that out of every dollar entrusted to us for lessening of distress, the maximum amount humanly possible was put into the people's hands. The money, spent honestly and with constant remembrance of its purpose, bought more of courage than it ever bought of goods."

. . . Very early in the program Hopkins and his assistants, Aubrey Williams and David K. Niles, began to explain to those of us who would listen how degrading and humiliating was a program of handouts when Americans wanted, above everything, to work and contribute. There was the story, not lost on Roosevelt, of the elderly man who had been the support of a large family and who was getting fifteen dollars a week on relief. He went out regularly, without being asked, to sweep the streets of his village. "I want to do something in return for what I get," he said.

When Hopkins proposed in the autumn of 1933 that we launch a program which gave work rather than cash relief to the unemployed, he met with a sympathetic response from the President. Roosevelt asked him to come to a cabinet meeting and describe what he had in mind. He had in mind a program, which we called "made work" in New York, of finding useful things for people to do.

The Civil Works Program was intended originally to give employment to about four million unemployed, anticipating that others in distress would have help through direct relief. It was never intended that Civil Works would offer permanent employment. For many families, however, it was the sole source of occupation and income for a considerable period of time. Brief experience with it convinced most observers that it should be continued with careful attention and planning. The effect upon people of having their own money to spend rather than having it doled out to them was good, and their ingenuity in making ends meet was better than that of any social work adviser in a vast majority of cases.

Hopkins handled this program with extraordinary skill in selecting projects, securing the co-operation of local agencies, and managing so that real work was accomplished and people were truly rehabilitated. He was also skillful in his management of the political phases, which were numerous and difficult. When money is to be spent, politicians come into the picture and tensions develop between the adherents of the governor and the senator. Hopkins was wise enough to make allowances for the facts of life, to do the job with honesty and to make friends with politicians at the same time. He did not alienate them from the project and the President. Moreover, he gave the President not only bulk statistics but examples of how a family had been rehabilitated, how a project had resulted in a playground or a swimming pool for a poor community that had never thought of having such a thing; how it brought the cataloguing of a gift of books to a library in a small town so that they became available to readers.

Projects to give work to unemployed teachers, artists, and theatrical people needed enlightened understanding and courage to be endorsed and developed. The President hadn't realized, as perhaps none of us had, the degree to which professional people and artists failed to sustain themselves when the national income had shrunk to the lowest level. People out of work do not give music or dancing lessons to their children nor buy tickets to the theater. The President had a keen feeling for the sensibilities of recipients of this relief.

Thousands of the most respectable groups had to accept it and were deeply grateful for the opportunity to maintain their self-respect. An almost deaf, elderly lawyer, a Harvard graduate, unable to find clients, got a WPA job as assistant caretaker at a small seaside park. He did double the work anyone could have expected of him. He made little extra plantings, arranged charming paths and walks, acted as guide to visitors, supervised children's play, and made himself useful and agreeable to the whole community. I had occasion to see him from time to time, and he would always ask me to take a message to the President— a message of gratitude for a job which paid him fifteen dollars a week and kept him from starving to death. It was an honorable occupation that made him feel useful and not like a bum and derelict, he would say with tears in his eyes. . . .

Roosevelt supported the Civil Works Administration and later became a great advocate of the Works Progress Administration which grew out of it. The Works Progress Administration, at its peak in the fiscal year July 1938/ July 1939, took care of 3,325,000 people, and in the fiscal year 1939, its largest year of expenditure, spent $2,067,972,-000 in both federal and sponsors' funds.

The President was always annoyed that so much complaint was made about the WPA. It is granted that there were ridiculous aspects to some of the enterprises and that some parts of the program got out of control. The freedom encouraged in this country led to the selection of some strange plays by local groups, and some congressmen and other citizens protested that the public money was being used to circulate subversive propaganda or to challenge the moral code. Roosevelt bore these accusations without being too disturbed. It amused him that there should be so much protest over play acting, even if supported by public funds. He liked people to have a good time in their own ways. Using unemployed musicians to play at community celebrations and in railroad stations at the rush hours, the existence of little WPA orchestras in almost every community, struck him as modern versions of the town band which bred so many American music lovers. . . .

As times grew better the relief projects were gradually slowed down and closed off. WPA became unpopular in Congress and there was constant protest against further relief appropriations. There remained in this country, however, a core of people, not too many in number, who did better on WPA than ever before in their lives and perhaps better than they are ever likely to. Among these were the handicapped, and it was not until the war years that they were again used to advantage. . . . One of the items which most interested Roosevelt in reports on labor supply for the war industries was that blind, deaf, and semi-crippled people were being given opportunity to work and were doing well. He was particularly pleased that people in their seventies and eighties were holding jobs, and that no longer did one hear the cry that a man of fifty is too old for industry. . . .

The President, I repeat, never regretted the relief program. He never apologized for it. He was proud of what it had done.

5. *1933–1935*—GENERAL JOHNSON AND THE NATIONAL RECOVERY ADMINISTRATION

[*In June, 1933, the Roosevelt Administration set up the National Recovery Administration (NRA), an emergency agency designed to eliminate unfair competition, increase purchasing power, and improve the status of labor. As administrator the President chose General Hugh S. Johnson, a retired army officer with a flair for the spectacular. From the vantage point of the Department of Labor, Miss Perkins reviews the achievements of the agency, which the United States Supreme Court would eventually terminate by an adverse decision on the code system.*

Roosevelt counted greatly on NRA to act as a shot in the arm for industry, and it did. At the President's request, and also at General Johnson's, I kept close to NRA and made great efforts to promote its success. The President appointed a committee of cabinet officers to be general advisers to General Johnson and to insure that the NRA kept within bounds and did not take over all government functions, since Johnson had a tendency to think in large controlling terms.

General Johnson didn't like this advisory committee. It chafed him. He hated to explain himself. Most of the members stopped coming to meetings because it seemed futile. I stuck because the necessity of getting the country onto a program of short hours and wages above subsistence seemed paramount to any administrative difficulties.

Before the bill was through Congress and Johnson began operating, he and Mrs. Johnson used to come to see me often in the evenings, and I realized that his ideas included "codes of fair practice" for each industry. He planned to give his personal approval to each code. Then he would recommend it to the President, who would sign it. It would become the over-all pattern for that industry, entitling those who signed the agreement to be exempted from the more difficult sections of the anti-trust law. He expected to have his own legal counsel, economists, and statisticians, and to make up his mind and proceed to the President without advice or approval of the other, older government agencies or without public hearings or publication of proposed codes in advance.

When this was reported to the President, he saw the hazard of such procedure. He persuaded rather than directed General Johnson to utilize the economic and statistic bureaus of the Departments of Commerce and Labor and to consult the Attorney General systematically on the ground of economy and integration of government activities. Incidentally, this process gave two cabinet officers knowledge of what was going on before it was too late to check monopolistic or undemocratic trends and to inform the President of dangers and problems ahead. The President's final suggestion, which really appealed to Johnson, was that the publicity attendant upon public hearings would, in fact, be a great educational feature for securing understanding, confidence, and support of the people throughout the country. . . .

The NRA became . . . one of the most vital causes of the revival of the American spirit, and signalized emergence from the industrial depression. Industry after industry, beginning with textiles—often regarded as a model code—set up codes of fair practice. These provided for fair competition and honorable practices in industry, and every code called for limitation of hours, minimum wage regulations, limitation or abolition of child labor, and other labor standards. The code proposed by the code authority of an industry was referred to the Labor, Employer, and Consumers' Advisory Committees, which discussed it and suggested changes. The administrator then held public hearings and, after considering the objections and support so brought out, recommended the amended code and took it to the President as the President's Re-employment Agreement. On signature it became effective.

After a few months of experience with NRA, it was evident that its operation had led to improvements in working conditions and the status of labor. Through NRA the regulation of hours of labor of men and women alike were undertaken for the first time in our history. Whereas state laws regulated only the hours of labor of women, some permitting women to work as many as ten hours a day, under NRA most of the codes prescribed forty hours a week as the standard, and about twenty-five per cent required a limit of eight hours or less as the hours to be worked any one day. Thus we came practically to a five-day, forty-hour week as standard in the United States. . . .

NRA was enormously popular. The Blue Eagle spread everywhere, and in some people's minds the New Deal and NRA were almost the same thing. As a matter of fact, other programs which had been inaugurated were also operating to improve conditions. But there was a great lift in the spirit of the people as they marched in parades, proudly displayed the Blue Eagle in their windows, and listened to Roosevelt explaining it on the radio. They began to have faith in themselves, and they determined to make it work. . . .

The President regarded the NRA purely as an emergency agency. He hoped that out of this experience would come a pattern of hours and wages and operating practices which might be embodied in law when the emergency was past, or adopted, without law, as part of the permanent way of our industrial life. He conceived of less administrative improvisations and more reliance on simple statute and administration lodged in the regular already established agencies of government.

Looking back on those days, I wonder how we ever lived through them. I cannot, even now, evaluate the situation. One thing I do see—it was dynamic. It was as though the community rose from the dead; despair was replaced by hope. Certainly an enormous number of good enterprises grew out of NRA whether or not it was itself successful. They were not only new enterprises in governing but new attitudes among businessmen. The laissez-faire and stick-in-the-mud type began to disappear from the leadership of business thinking, and younger, better educated, and more informed men came to have influence. Organized labor took a new lease on life. And what is perhaps of most importance to the future, business and labor began to participate with public officers in developing a sound, socially just economic and industrial pattern.

6. *1931–1933*—THE PLIGHT OF THE FARMER

❮ *One day in 1933 I, the writer of these sentences, met a friend in a bank in Springfield, Illinois, in the center of the corn belt. He was a hog buyer, much concerned with farm prosperity, much depressed by prevailing prices. During our conversation he took a fifty-cent piece from his pocket and threw it on one of the bank's glass-topped writing tables. "Paul Angle," he exclaimed, "you're a sturdy fellow, but you can't carry out of this bank all the corn that half-dollar will buy!" He was right: there are fifty-six pounds in a bushel of corn, and the price was then ten cents a bushel.*

What such prices meant to individual farmers is made clear by

---

Remley J. Glass, "Gentlemen, The Corn Belt!" *Harper's Monthly Magazine*, July, 1933, 201–02, 204–06.

Remley J. Glass, who described himself as a "country lawyer" in an Iowa county seat.

During the year after the great debacle of 1929 the flood of fore-closure actions did not reach any great peak, but in the years 1931 and 1932 the tidal wave was upon us. Insurance companies and large investors had not as yet realized (and in some instances do not yet realize) that, with the low price of farm commodities and the gradual exhaustion of savings and reserves, the formerly safe and sane investments in farm mortgages could not be worked out, taxes and interest could not be paid, and liquidation could not be made. With an utter disregard of the possibilities of payment or refinancing, the large loan companies plunged ahead to make the Iowa farmer pay his loans in full or turn over the real estate to the mortgage holder. . . .

Men who had sunk every dollar they possessed in the purchase, up-keep, and improvement of their home places were turned out with small amounts of personal property as their only assets. Landowners who had regarded farm land as the ultimate in safety, after using their outside resources in vain attempts to hold their lands, saw these assets go under the sheriff's hammer on the courthouse steps. . . .

Take, if you please, what seems to me to have been a typical case of the tenant farmer, one Johannes Schmidt, a client of mine. Johannes was descended from farming stock in Germany, came to this country as a boy, became a citizen, went over seas in the 88th Division, and on his return married the daughter of a retired farmer. He rented one hundred and twenty acres from his father-in-law and one hundred and sixty acres from the town banker. His live stock and equipment, purchased in the early twenties, were well bought, for his judgment was good, and the next eight years marked a gradual increase in his live stock and reductions in his bank indebtedness. During these years two youngsters came to the young couple and all seemed rosy.

In the year 1931 a drought in this part of the Corn Belt practically eliminated his crops, while what little he did raise was insufficient to pay his rent, and he went into 1932 with increased indebtedness for feed, back taxes, and back rent. While the crops in 1932 were wonderful . . . prices were so low as not to pay the cost of seed and labor in production without regard to taxes and rent.

Times were hard and the reverberations of October, 1929, had definitely reached the Corn Belt. The county seat bank which held Johannes' paper was in hard shape. Much of its reserve had been invested in bonds recommended by Eastern bankers upon which default of interest and principal had occurred. When the bottom dropped out of the bond market the banking departments and examiners insisted upon immediate collection of slow farm loans. . . . When Johannes sought to renew his bank loan, payment or else security on all his personal property was demanded without regard to the needs of wife and family. Prices of farm products had fallen to almost nothing, oats were ten cents a bushel, corn twelve cents a bushel, while hogs, the chief cash crop in the Corn Belt, were selling at less than two and one half cents a pound. In the fall of 1932 a wagon load of oats would not pay for a pair of shoes; a truck load of hogs, which in other days would have paid all a tenant's cash rent, did not then pay the interest on a thousand dollars.

This man Schmidt had struggled and contrived as long as possible under the prodding of landlord and banker, and as a last resort came to see me about bankruptcy. We talked it over and with regret reached the conclusion it was the only road for him to take. He did not have even enough cash on hand to pay the thirty-dollar filing fee which I had to send to the Federal Court but finally borrowed it from his brother-in-law. The time of hearing came, and he and his wife and children sat before the Referee in Bankruptcy, while the banker and the landlord struggled over priorities of liens and rights to crops and cattle. When the day was over this family went out from the office the owner of an old team of horses, a wagon, a couple of cows and five hogs, together with their few sticks of furniture and no place to go.

George Warner, aged seventy-four, who had for years operated one hundred and sixty acres in the northeast corner of the county and in the early boom days had purchased an additional quarter section, is typical of hundreds in the Corn Belt. He had retired and with his wife was living comfortably in his square white house in town a few blocks from my home. Sober, industrious, pillars of the church and active in good works, he and his wife may well be considered typical retired farmers. Their three boys wanted to get started in business after they were graduated from high school, and George, to finance their endeavors, put a mortgage, reasonable in amount, on his two places. Last fall a son out of a job brought his family and came home to live with the old people. The tenants on the farms could not pay their rent, and George could not pay his interest and taxes. George's land was sold at tax sale and a foreclosure action was brought against the farms by the insurance company which held the mortgage. I did the best I could for him in the settlement, but to escape a deficiency judgment he surrendered the places beginning on March 1st of this year, and a few days ago I saw a mortgage recorded on his home in town. As he told me of it, the next day, tears came to his eyes and his lips trembled, and he and I both thought of the years he had spent in building up that estate and making those acres bear fruit abundantly. Like another Job, he murmured "The Lord gave and the Lord hath taken away"; but I wondered if it was proper to place the responsibility for the breakdown of a faulty human economic system on the shoulders of the Lord. . . .

557

I have represented bankrupt farmers and holders of claims for rent, notes, and mortgages against such farmers in dozens of bankruptcy hearings and court actions, and the most discouraging, disheartening experiences of my legal life have occurred when men of middle age, with families, go out of the bankruptcy court with furniture, team of horses and a wagon, and a little stock as all that is left from twenty-five years of work, to try once more—not to build up an estate—for that is usually impossible—but to provide clothing and food and shelter for the wife and children. And the powers that be seem to demand that these not only accept this situation but shall like it.

7. *1933–1937*—THE CIVILIAN CONSERVATION CORPS

⟦ *Many of the New Deal measures were attacked as wasteful, visionary, or socialistic, but one venture—the Civilian Conservation Corps (CCC)—drew almost universal praise. Under this program unemployed young men were recruited to work on public parks, forests, and other natural resources. They were paid $30 a month and lived under semi-military discipline in camps administered by the army.*

Harold L. Ickes, Secretary of the Interior, describes an inspection tour he made with the President; Louis McHenry Howe, the President's Secretary; and Henry A. Wallace, Secretary of Agriculture.

Saturday, August 12, 1933

I got up at five o'clock this morning and was at the White House just before six to pick up Colonel Howe for our trip to Harrisonburg, Virginia, to meet the President, who went there by train from Hyde Park. . . .

The President's train got into Harrisonburg about half past nine, about twenty minutes after we arrived, and we started to inspect some of the CCC camps in the Shenandoah Park and neighborhood. Leaving Harrisonburg, Secretary Wallace and I were in the President's car. He drives in an open car, just as old T. R. used to do, and it is not only good politics but good public policy, because it gives people a chance to have a much more intimate contact with him than if he drove in a closed car. Everyone was out en route, especially at Harrisonburg, which is a fair-sized town of ancient lineage. Everyone seemed cordial and glad to see the President, and he has the happy way of waving and smiling which I think makes people feel that they are in intimate contact with him.

From *The Secret Diary of Harold L. Ickes: The First Thousand Days*, © 1953, by Simon and Schuster, Inc. Reprinted by permission of Simon and Schuster, Inc. Pp. 79–81.

The first camp we visited was in course of construction. The second was up in the Blue Ridge Mountains along the new Skyline Drive. This was a well-established camp. In all the camps the men seemed fit, and we were told by the commander of this corps area that the average gain in weight had been fifteen pounds per man. The average age is about nineteen years.

At the third camp, which was still farther up on the Skyline Drive, we stopped for lunch. We had steak, mashed potatoes, green beans, a salad, iced tea, and a so-called apple pie, which, while it was made of dough and apples, was not the conventional apple pie. All of the food was good and it was all that anyone wanted. The general in charge told us that this was a typical meal, and that the food supplied the men cost the Government an average of thirty-five cents a day.

The camps are well set up, sanitary, comfortable, and clean. Army officers are in charge. Of course, it is impossible to say whether there is too much of an Army atmosphere, but I suppose it may be granted that some sort of discipline is necessary. Moving pictures galore and still pictures innumerable were taken from the beginning of the day to the end of the day. I often wonder what becomes of the thousands of feet of film that are used on public men, especially the President, who can't go anywhere without being photographed continuously.

We stopped at two more camps on our way to Washington. Secretary Wallace and I left the President's car at our first stop, but at the last stop, which was just shortly after we left the mountains, the President sent word back to my car that he wanted Colonel Howe, Secretary Wallace, and myself to join him. So we rode all the way into Washington with him and we had a most delightful time.

The President is a fine companion to be out with. He is highly intelligent, quick-witted, and he can both receive and give a good thrust. He has a wide range of interests and is exceedingly human.

We reached the White House shortly after four o'clock and there I transferred to my own car and went home to a bath, to dinner, and to early bed.

There is one incident that I must record because it was so amusing, and the President on the way back, when I brought it up, laughingly said that I ought to include it in my memoirs but he couldn't. The commanding general, while probably a very good officer, is just a little pompous and doesn't want to be left out of any conversation. He hasn't a very wide range of subjects he can talk upon so he keeps repeating the same thing over and over again and he speaks with quite a bit of *empressement*. At the camp where we were having luncheon he began to tell what the Army is going to do in the way of educating the CCC boys while they were in camp. Apparently he didn't know, or chose to ignore the fact, that we are going to assign teachers to these camps, not on invitation of the Army but in spite of the Army. At any rate, he is the type of man that is ready to adopt and claim credit for anything for which credit can be claimed. It gave him great pleasure to assure the President and all within hearing of his voice that any CCC boy could receive instruction on any subject. He told how someone was teaching trigonometry to one of the boys, how another was learning French, and he concluded with this gem: "There won't none of these boys leave these camps illiterate."

8.   *1935*—THE TVA IN PROGRESS

❨ *In the Tennessee Valley Authority the New Deal embarked on a project unique in the history of the federal government. The Authority was authorized to build a series of dams on the Tennessee River and its tributaries for the purpose of furthering navigation, controlling floods, and generating power, but it was also charged with promoting agricultural and industrial expansion. Legislation for much narrower objectives had been vetoed by President Coolidge and President Hoover; the sweeping program of President Roosevelt encountered violent but powerless opposition. Some of the opposition, as the Pearson brothers explain, came from those who stood to benefit most from the development of the Valley.*

The TVA is committed to doing vastly more than merely pouring concrete into forms until the Norris and Wheeler dams have risen. When, shortly after his inauguration, President Roosevelt summoned President Arthur E. Morgan of Antioch College to the White House and asked him to undertake direction of the new Authority there was scarcely a word said about power. He talked chiefly about a designed and planned social and economic order. He revealed that he was thinking less in terms of the Tennessee River and its wasted electric energy than in terms of the Tennessee Valley and its wasted human energy. The latter ideals have lost no fervor in being passed from one mind to the other. Though Chairman Morgan in his discussion of the work reveals that he was an engineer before he became a college president, he is interested not so much in the material manifestations of TVA, so largely publicized, as in "lives that are rusting away, the hopes that are fading."

In short, he commits himself and the Authority to a program for changing the lives of people who want to be let alone.

If this "uplift" work were merely a charitable afterthought that could be dropped by the wayside if it did not work, the independent

Drew and Leon Pearson, "The Tennessee Valley Experiment," *Harper's Monthly Magazine,* May, 1953, 703–07. Reprinted by permission of Drew Pearson.

spirit of the Valley folk would be little cause for concern. But it is not. It is the nubbin of the problem of TVA. The capacity of generating facilities which exist in this area already exceeds by more than one hundred per cent the present demand and consumption. Therefore, without a revolution in the lives of the people of the Tennessee Valley, the South faces a flood of kilowatt hours even less useful than the bales of cotton with which it once depressed the world market.

An easy escape from this impasse would be to lure existing industries with cheap power and cheap labor to leave Northern communities, which would create worker unemployment in one place and worker exploitation in another. But TVA directors close that avenue of escape, undertaking not to steal an existing market but to build a new one. They are rubbing hard on a modern sixty-watt Aladdin's lamp to make miracles happen in the Valley. They have assigned to themselves the stupendous task of introducing not only electric lights but also electric appliances to people who scratch their fields with handmade plows, card their cotton for homemade quilts, and sit in the sunny doorway making tobacco "twisties."

Already the campaign is on. Rural mail carriers have grown accustomed to the sight of the big brown envelope from the Chattanooga office, which they know contains the bright colored folder telling about Electric Home and Farm Authority and its wares. For the first time in the history of the United States Government, advertisements are going out in franked envelopes. Uncle Sam is a drummer with a commercial line to sell. He has sold Liberty Bonds before, but never refrigerators. And in the settled communities of the South he has been making sales. . . .

TVA agents cannot, no matter how tactful, how deferential, take the pain out of the impact with which the new social order strikes the old. A heritage of individualism cries out against the inexorable new force, cries out either in a wilful or pathetic strain.

On good bottom land in Elbow Hollow, Widow Ridenour stands in the doorway of her log house. The neatness of the place, the dignity of her speech and bearing suggest a refinement rare in the ridge country.

"This has been my home for a long time now," she says sadly. "And it's been a good home too. I've educated all my children, school and college, and I'd aimed to round out my life here. I declare it hurts worse than death to move."

Several miles beyond, Hester Robbins is carrying pieces of wood from her partly demolished woodshed. "My mammy used to stock wood in this building," she laments, "and now I'm tearin' it down piece by piece."

. . . On Cedar Creek lives Isabel Brantley.

"I was born in this house and so was my pappy before me, and here

561

I've lived and here I'll die, even if I have to bolt the door and let the flood come—but there hain't a-goin' to be no flood!"

This was her greeting to the TVA appraiser, prepared to offer twelve hundred dollars for her log cabin and eroded acres. In the end she was won over by the generosity of TVA's laborers, who offered to move the house in their spare time, without cost to her, to a site below the dam. Persuaded but not softened, she declared, "You got to find me a place with a spring or a well. I don't want none of this newfangled pipe water runnin' into my house."

Such is the sales resistance encountered by Government agents.

When Ezra Hill saw the plans for the home which was to replace his old one in the flood area, he pointed to the place on the print showing the circles and oval of bathroom fixtures. "What's all this? . . . I won't have it! I guess a privy is still good enough for me."

. . . TVA's soundest hope lies in what is going on at Norris. Here a new social order has sprung from an uncut tract of oak and pine, an order which may spread its beneficent contagion even to the older homes of the Valley. The homes that have grown at Norris are new; those who live within them are young. Old social habits have largely been left behind. Four miles from the site of the dam, this community is the antithesis of what it might have been—a construction camp.

Art Lipscomb drops from the rear end of a truck which has brought him and a score of others from the "graveyard shift" to the community center. The sun is just rising over the hills, and his "day" of work is done. For five and a half hours he and his "bulldozer" have been scraping stone into handy piles for the big jaw of the electric shovel. In his dormitory room he pulls off his work clothes, goes down the hall for a shower, and returns to dress for breakfast. At the cafeteria he gets a generous *table d'hote* meal for a quarter, with seconds thrown in. He sits with his hat on his head and has no compunction about the toothpick at the end of the meal. Strolling out, he stops at the bulletin board. Movies . . . . wrestling match. . . . A notice: "If the party that found that black kid glove with the rabbit skin lining for the right hand will call at Room 227 Dormitory 5, I will gladly give them the one for the left hand to make a pair." . . . There are courses in shorthand, English, parliamentary government; trades training in wood-working; automotive, general metal, electrical, radio courses; vocational courses, dairying, poultry farming, farm management, bee culture.

Work is over for the day. He has earned five dollars and a half. He faces ten waking hours of leisure. Shying at English and shorthand, he thinks radio might be worthwhile. It doesn't cost anything. He draws some money from the credit union, buys a chocolate bar, and signs up.

Art Lipscomb is one of thirty-eight thousand men who competed under civil service for jobs under the new "Authority"; one of five thousand who left their homes to take those jobs, left their habits of work, habits of diet, habits of leisure. They are the potential leaders of the new Valley, the men whom A. E. Morgan is urging to be the stockholders of the future.

"If you fellows put something aside," he says, "you can be the owners; you can stay on living here, building up after the dam is finished. The country is working toward a decentralization of industry. There are many articles that can be made—better made—in the small independent shop; and industry is better off if its workers can live on the land, making a living partly from the soil, partly from the pay check."

It is in the soil of the Tennessee Valley lowlands that the seeds of the new social order may grow. The ridge country will not change. Its mountaineers will hire their teams to the Government, send their sons to pour concrete, sell their land when they can get sufficient price; but the underlying sentiment will continue to be approximately that of the farmer on Big Barren Creek who warned, "I'll take my hog rifle, and the first one of them TVA fellers come onto my land, I'll shoot him before he can show his hind quarters."

It is in the open country that the dream of the President and Chairman Morgan may come true. Driving a car here with a TVA license, one is greeted with friendly gestures on every hand. Here a forester can win converts for his gospel of taking an eroded hillside out of corn to replant with fruit-bearing trees and bushes. And here youth's achievements and spirits may slowly, year by year, take the irony out of the headlines of a Tennessee newspaper which announced:

"BRIGHT FUTURE FOR CAREYVILLE—
WILL BE FLOODED WITH WATER."

9.   *1935—FEUDING IN THE NEW DEAL*

❮ *The New Deal seemed to attract men liberally endowed with temperament. As a result, more than the usual amount of jealousy and distrust characterized relations between high government officials. One of the better known feuds was that between Secretary of the Interior Harold L. Ickes and Harry Hopkins, head of the Works Progress Administration. The fundamental difference between the two agencies contributed to the friction: PWA made grants to states and municipalities for such durable projects as the construction of schools, highways, and subways; WPA favored undertakings, often "made work," in which most of the money spent went for labor.*

From *The Secret Diary of Harold L. Ickes: The First Thousand Days*, © 1953, by Simon and Schuster, Inc. Reprinted by permission of Simon and Schuster, Inc. Pp. 337–38, 424–26.

Entries which Ickes made in his diary in the spring and summer of 1935 reveal the infighting that often marked official life.

Monday, April 1, 1935

. . . Harry Hopkins has come back to Washington. He called up and asked if he might come over and lunch with me at one o'clock. He brought with him a rough draft of an Executive Order that the President has been considering in connection with setting up an administration under the Work Relief Bill when it should pass. The President has put himself down as chairman of the committee to allocate the funds and next in line appears my name. However, this is a big committee, with practically everyone on it, including Henry Wallace, Rex Tugwell, Harry Hopkins, Admiral Peoples, General Markham, Dr. Mead, and two or three others. Then there is the committee the President has discussed with me, which is to receive applications and interview those presenting them. The other committee, of which Hopkins is to be chairman, has, it seems to me, been given the real power. While on the face of it, it is not given final authority or even complete executive authority, the setup is such that I haven't the slightest doubt that before long Hopkins would emerge as cock of the walk. After reading this, I haven't the slightest doubt that Hopkins or McIntyre gave out the story that came from Miami last week to the effect that Hopkins was to be the big man in the new work-relief organization.

Hopkins said that the President wanted this redrafted and then sent down to him so that after he has signed the bill, he can announce the setup from Miami. I told Harry Hopkins that I preferred not to be in the organization at all and that I hoped the President would not make any announcement from Florida. Hopkins said that I had better write to the President telling him how I felt. I noted that he did not even intimate that he hoped that I would go along as part of this organization. It is clear as day to me, both from what he said and from what he didn't say, that he is not averse to looming large and with as few rivals as possible in the new setup.

This afternoon I went over to see Steve Early. I was much more outspoken with him. I told him very flatly that I would not go along on this organization. I said that two or three months ago I had talked with Louie Howe about the matter, telling him that I was perfectly willing to step aside as Public Works Administrator, that I didn't relish the thought of reading one day in the newspapers that I had been set aside. I remarked to Early that this was just what had happened, in view of the story that came out of Miami last week. I assured Early, as I had assured Louie Howe, that I really wanted to step aside, but I added that there was nothing in the situation that justified my getting a slap in the face. Early understood my point of view and sympathized with it. He asked me whether the Interior Department might become involved and I told him very frankly that, if necessary, that would have to go too, but that I would not take a window-dressing position in the new organization. Then he remarked: "You're Public Works Administrator, you're Secretary of the Interior, and Oil Administrator. I believe the President will work it out." . . .

Tuesday, August 27, 1935

. . . Monday at noon I had an appointment with the President. Late in the afternoon a letter from him, dated August 22, was placed on my desk. This letter contained the following opening paragraph:

I am writing to inform you that, with respect to public works funds available for carrying out the purposes of The National Industrial Recovery Act, as amended, I desire that all future applications for allocations and all cancellations, rescissions, and modifications of previous allocations be submitted to the Advisory Committee on Allotments, to be acted upon in the same manner and to the same extent as that committee acts with respect to allocations made under the Emergency Relief Appropriation Act of 1935.

When I read this I went right up into the air, and I didn't feel any better when I discovered later that the noon edition of the *Washington Star* had carried a news release on this letter, the headline of which was: ICKES IS SHORN OF PWA POWER. This headline was sustained by the story itself and the story was a perfectly justified interpretation of the President's letter as practically doing away with the PWA.

I must admit that I was very angry. I resented PWA being put out of business in this manner, and I particularly took exception to my being advised of such an important action affecting me personally appearing in the newspapers before I had any knowledge of it. Slattery and Burlew went home to dinner with me and the more I considered the matter and the more we discussed it, the madder I got. I made up my mind that there was nothing left for me to do except to resign as Public Works Administrator and member and Chairman of the Advisory Committee on Allotments of the work-relief fund. Accordingly, right after dinner, the three of us came back to my office, I in the meantime having called Mike Straus to join me here.

I called Hiram Johnson to the telephone from the floor of the Senate. The Senate at that time was in its final session but was thoroughly tied up by a filibuster by Senator Long. I told Hiram about the President's letter, the newspaper publicity, and my purpose to resign. He agreed with me that this way of handling it constituted an affront which I was justified in resenting. He sympathized fully with my attitude and said he would feel himself just as I expressed myself as feeling if he were in my place. He told me, however, that he thought I ought to go and face the President and have it out with him before resigning. He said there might be some explanation after all, although he said he didn't see what explanation there could be. He was kind enough to say that he would regret my resigning because the President needed me and the country needed me. He said there were too few men of my kind in the Administration. He commented on the cunning way in which the President had done this, and I remarked that it was customary for him to deal with men on the basis of a *fait accompli.*

I was reluctant to do so, but I called the President after my talk with Hiram shortly before nine o'clock. I told him I hoped he would let me come over to see him and he asked me what it was all about. Of course, I had no option except to discuss it with him over the telephone. He told me that the newspaper story was not justified. I told him it was, that it was the only inference that could legitimately be drawn from that paragraph of his letter. He said he had had no intention of changing my status as PWA Administrator. I replied that he had in effect put PWA out of business. He said the newspapers were cockeyed and that I mustn't be childish. I told him I wasn't being childish and that I had good reason to take exception to learning first from a newspaper about a matter vitally affecting my administration.

I was pretty angry and I showed it. I never thought I would talk to a President of the United States the way I talked to President Roosevelt last night. I think I made it pretty clear that I wasn't going to stand for much more of the same kind of medicine. I reminded him that I had had occasion to complain before that Executive Orders affecting my Department had been issued without my being advised of them, and that more than once the first information of important news affecting myself I had gotten from the newspapers. He kept insisting that the interpretation of the *Star* was not justified, and I was equally obstinate in saying that it was and that no other interpretation was justified. Then he said that Steve Early was with him and he would have Steve give out a statement saying that his letter had been misinterpreted and that there was no change intended in my status as PWA Administrator. Finally we ended the conversation but with very poor grace on my part. Subsequently Steve called me up to read a statement which he said the President had dictated. The statement was as good as was possible in the circumstances. It did categorically deny that there was any intention to change my status as Administrator of Public Works. The statement sounded fishy to me, but I couldn't suggest any improvement.

I talked again with Steve over the telephone this morning. He said he hoped that I had noticed that his press release was not interpretive but merely narrative. I told him he need never have any fear that I would misunderstand his attitude, and that I did notice that his release was just as he stated. He asked me who I thought had written the letter of the President. I told him I believed it had come from the Treasury. He said he suspected that also, although he had no facts on which to base his suspicion. He told me he had taken it on the chin last night because he took exception to the President's saying that the newspapers were a thousand per cent wrong and that their interpretation of his letter was not justified. He volunteered with me that I was exactly right when I said it was justified. I said to Steve that I wasn't going to stand very much more of this sort of thing and he said he understood and sympathized with me in many things.

The reason I wanted to send in my resignation right away was because I was afraid the President would do just what he did do. He sidetracked me. It is almost impossible to come to grips with him. I could have done that if I had sent him my resignation, but now I will have to go along, at least for the time being.

10.   *1933–1945*—SHE LED HER OWN LIFE

⟦ *Before Mrs. Franklin D. Roosevelt, wives of Presidents had remained in the background. But this vital woman, interested in a myriad of causes, refused to allow her life to be changed by her sudden rise to eminence. Throughout the Roosevelt regime, she was a public personality second only to her husband. Raymond Clapper, Washington newspaperman, offers a characterization.*

You have to think of Mrs. Roosevelt as you would about the strong man at the circus. She simply has several times the physical energy of the average person.

I never realized that until long after Mrs. Roosevelt had moved into the White House. It was the time she drafted several of us brokendown, flat-footed newspaper correspondents into one of her Virginia reels.

None of us had done the Virginia reel since we were kids. We all knew it was too late to start in again. But when Mrs. Roosevelt decides it would be nice to do the Virginia reel, you do the Virginia reel. She may be gentle and humble, always eager to understand the other person's problems. But when it comes to dancing, she is a woman of iron will. You dance.

Well, a dozen of us were rounded up at the White House one night to rehearse. Mrs. Roosevelt decided to put us into bright-colored satin colonial breeches, with tail jackets and lace ruffles on the cuffs, so we could do a really old-fashioned Virginia reel, Mount Vernon style, at the White House newspaper party that year.

Rehearsal night found Mrs. Roosevelt all ready to go. She had returned to Washington that morning about 5 A.M. from one of her trips

With permission of McGraw-Hill Book Co., Inc. from *Watching the World* by Raymond Clapper. Copyright, 1944, McGraw-Hill Book Co., Inc. Pp. 121–25.

down into a West Virginia coal mine. She had written her column, entertained guests at luncheon, seen half a dozen people by appointment, taken a horseback ride, finished off an early dinner, and when we arrived in the East Room, there she was, waltzing around the empty floor with her brother, the late Hall Roosevelt.

We lined up and for half an hour swung our partners until we were gasping. We couldn't go on any longer, so Mrs. Roosevelt gave us a 10-minute recess. We dropped exhausted to the floor, but Mrs. Roosevelt took her son Elliott around the East Room in a fast waltz while we recovered our breath. Then we went back at the rehearsal for another half hour. As we dragged ourselves out of the East Room that night, Mrs. Roosevelt was still waltzing around the floor, waving good-by to us over the sagging shoulder of brother Hall.

After that I knew it was no use to try to judge Mrs. Roosevelt by what you would expect of an ordinary person.

And on the night of the party, Mrs. Roosevelt swung us around so heartily that several of us were tossed halfway out of our bright satin minstrel jackets, so that we barely escaped disastrous exposure, as it was a hot night and we had stripped down to nothing underneath our satin clothes and lace ruffles.

Mrs. Roosevelt's triumph was complete. She had put a troupe of spavined old fire horses through what no doubt seemed to her the gay and light-footed spirit of the dance. She was sure that it did our souls good, as it had done hers.

Sweet, gentle, and kind—yes. But don't fool yourself. There's a core of iron, too. There wasn't any more chance of our escaping that Virginia reel at the White House than there was of electing Alf Landon President.

Most of Mrs. Roosevelt's troubles flow from a really good heart. She can be perverse and headstrong and she can blunder into unfortunate controversies. Yet, if these incidents are studied from her point of view, it will be seen that usually they are the eggs which, in spite of the mother instinct, hatch out into ugly ducklings instead of into the expected adorable little cotton-ball chicks. These cruel tricks of nature leave Mrs. Roosevelt baffled but unshaken in her maternal loyalty to her brood. She mothers each and every one, for better or for worse.

Mrs. Roosevelt's belief in people and their good intentions often overpowers her judgment. During her years in the White House, Mrs. Roosevelt has been exposed to all of the scheming, selfish, grasping, clawing side of human nature that storms so fiercely around that throne of power. Still, Mrs. Roosevelt sees no evil, hears no evil, thinks no evil. Some call that being plain gullible. But she goes on, looking for sorrow and trouble to heal, telephoning the State Department to ask if they won't please get a visa for some poor victim who wants to get out of Europe, never realizing that she is thereby shoving a favorite case in ahead of hundreds of others, all possibly equally heart-rending. She does not seem to realize—or does she?—that her slightest word, spoken ever so softly to an official appointed by her husband, has the impact on his mind of an executive order.

Once Mrs. Roosevelt was invited to visit a charity institution. She found a delicious hot lunch, with meat balls and everything that those housed in the institution could want. But she was suspicious, and returned a few days later unannounced. That time she found the regular luncheon was weak, watery soup. She was able to thus prod the management of the institution.

As a newspaper columnist Mrs. Roosevelt is able to bring to public attention many conditions which need airing and which can be corrected by simply giving them publicity. True, she has been criticized for writing professionally, and for her hopping about the country, some 40,000 miles a year, often driving her own car, but the criticism never really took hold. After all, she had always led her own life. Although some criticized her, they had to agree in the end that, even though she was the wife of the President, she had a right to conduct her personal affairs as she pleased.

Sometimes Mrs. Roosevelt seems so naive that you wonder whether it isn't something just a little more subtle. When anyone who has spent a lifetime in politics seems naive, watch out. It is the most baffling technique in the business, and so completely disarming that I have never understood why the ordinary politician didn't make more use of it, since politicians try every other crafty trick they can think of.

Mrs. Roosevelt may be gullible and naive, but when she throws her heart into a cause she works at it with persistent skill. She is a most effective and formidable propagandist.

She was one of the first to take an interest in the Okies of California, long before *The Grapes of Wrath* was published. She visited the miserable Okie camps and called the attention of the nation to them.

Mrs. Roosevelt did the same kind of work in behalf of Negro share croppers who were evicted by landlords wishing to avoid sharing A.A.A. benefit payments with them. Out of that experience grew her great interest in Negro problems.

Her mother instinct led her to listen sympathetically to the problems of youth. Mrs. Roosevelt was largely responsible for creating the National Youth Administration. She has had a long series of embarrassing experiences with the American Youth Congress, which has been at times under fire by Congress.

Mrs. Roosevelt has given the shelter of the White House to the leaders of these and other movements. She opened her summer home at Campobello Island for a seminar of youth leaders. She invites them to tea, to discussion dinners, and sometimes to remain as house guests. When they seem to be wandering too far off in their views, Mrs. Roosevelt argues with them. Often they have argued back, as on one night when her son Franklin said they didn't seem to have very good manners. Mrs. Roosevelt excused them by saying they had not had the opportunities he had. Always she remains loyal and tolerant.

11.   *1940*—THE THIRD TERM

❪ *The Second World War broke out when Germany invaded Poland on September 1, 1939. By the summer of 1940 France had collapsed, and Great Britain was being pressed to the limit. The situation, which threatened to involve the United States at any time, induced Roosevelt to break tradition and seek a third term. Robert E. Sherwood, a dramatist who would write a revealing biography of Harry Hopkins, analyzes the influences which led the President to his decision.*

On January 22, 1940, Hopkins told me he was virtually certain that Roosevelt would decide to run for a third term, but three months later, April 23, he expressed grave doubts about it. He said then that the President seemed disinclined to do anything about the nomination or to permit any of his friends to do anything, which would have meant that it would go to the Farley faction by default. . . . Hopkins asked me if I really believed Roosevelt should run. I answered that I considered it was his duty to run. He then asked me what were my reasons for this conviction, and I made the obvious answers: the United States was the only power that could prevent the world from going to hell, and Roosevelt was the only man with the personal strength and prestige as well as intelligence to lead the United States in the way it should go. Hopkins then said to me, "I wish you'd sit down and write all of that to the President, emphasizing the 'duty' part of it."

"But," I said, "he'd pay no attention to a letter from me. He wouldn't even read it."

"You'd be surprised," said Hopkins, "how many letters from private citizens he does read and how seriously he takes some of them."

Hopkins urged me to persuade the greatest possible number of my friends who felt as I did to write similar letters to the President, and I did so. Those letters were not acknowledged, even by the customary note from a secretary saying, "The President has directed me to express his appreciation . . ." etc. I doubt that any or all of them exerted the slightest influence on Roosevelt's final decision. . . . Pending the appearance of further evidence . . . it may be assumed that it was Hitler and Mussolini—and also Churchill—who made up Roosevelt's mind for him. Had the Phony War still continued, with no sign of a break, had

From *Roosevelt and Hopkins* by Robert E. Sherwood. Copyright, 1948, by Robert E. Sherwood. Vol. I, pp. 172–76. With permission of Harper & Brothers and Eyre & Spottiswoode.

the British Government advised the White House that it must sue for peace in the event of the fall of France—then nothing but over-inflated personal vanity could have induced Roosevelt to seek a third term. Granted that Roosevelt had his full share of personal vanity—no man would run for President of the United States in the first place without it—he also had the ability to form a highly realistic estimate of the odds against him and, taking the most cynical view of the prospect, and leaving all questions of patriotic duty out of it, he would best serve the interests of his own present prestige and his ultimate place in history by retiring gracefully before the storm broke and thereby leaving the reaping of the whirlwind to his successor. However, as long as Britain held out, and as long as there remained a chance that German victory might be prevented, Roosevelt wanted to stay in the fight and sincerely believed that there was none among all the available candidates as well qualified to aid in the prevention as he. . . .

Willkie's nomination at the Republican Convention had represented an extraordinary triumph by a group of suddenly organized amateur zealots over the steam-rolling political bosses of the Republican party. These bosses distrusted Willkie, despite the fact that, as president of the Commonwealth and Southern Corporation, he was one of the few businessmen who had ever fought against a New Deal agency (the Tennessee Valley Authority) and won at least a moral victory in his fight. For one thing, he was deeply suspect because he had formerly been a Democrat. For another thing, the isolationist fetish was so strong in the Republican hierarchy that anyone who opposed it must, they felt, be tainted in some sinister way with the poison of Rooseveltism. Furthermore, they did not know whether Willkie would prove to be the kind of amenable, controllable time-server that they preferred to have in public office. . . .

Roosevelt considered Willkie the most formidable opponent for himself that the Republicans could have named. Willkie had the glamor which previous Republicans had so conspicuously lacked. What is more, Willkie had no previous political record to attack as did those who, for isolationist reasons, had opposed every move toward national defense. Nevertheless, despite Roosevelt's respect for Willkie as a dangerous competitor, he considered this nomination "a Godsend to the country," for it tended to remove the isolationist-interventionist issue from the campaign (at least, until the final days) and thereby prevented the splitting of the people into two embittered factions. It guaranteed to the rest of the world—and particularly to the warring nations—a continuity of American foreign policy regardless of the outcome of the election. The importance of this consideration could hardly be overestimated. To begin with, Willkie came out in favor of Selective Service, thereby eliminating that extremely controversial issue.

Another important issue came up—the destroyers deal. . . . Churchill had first told Roosevelt of Britain's desperate need for destroyers in a cable written five days after he became Prime Minister. After the fall of France, Joseph Alsop, the Washington columnist, urged Benjamin Cohen to use all his influence in support of the transfer of fifty or sixty U. S. destroyers of First World War vintage to the British, saying that without such naval reinforcement Britain might not be able to hold the Channel against invasion. Cohen conveyed this to his chief Harold Ickes, who took it up with the President. Ickes noted: "I spent a lot of time arguing with the President that, by hook or by crook, we ought to accede to England's request. He said that . . . we could not send these destroyers to England unless the Navy could certify that they were useless to us for defense purposes."

. . . Various suggestions were made to the President for new legislation to be asked of Congress to free his hands—but he was having none of that. He was determined to find a way to circumvent Congress on this problem, and he found it. There were concurrent negotiations for the granting of leases for American bases on eight British possessions in the Western Atlantic. Roosevelt decided that these could be used as a *quid pro quo* for the destroyers, thereby enabling [Admiral] Stark to certify that the total measure would strengthen rather than weaken America's defense, which was of course the truth. Churchill at first resisted this. He wanted the transfer of the bases to be a spontaneous gesture by His Majesty's Government—an expression of British gratitude for American aid—and not merely part of a sordid "deal." He had to yield on this, but he insisted that the two most important bases, Bermuda and Newfoundland, should remain free gifts, apart from the deal, "generously given and gladly received"—an academic point, as it turned out.

The progress of these secret negotiations—announced to the Congress as an accomplished fact on September 3—was known to Wendell Willkie, who had privately approved of it (through William Allen White) and agreed not to make a campaign issue of Roosevelt's action. Indeed, Willkie's main criticism was on the ground that the transfer of fifty over-age destroyers was not nearly enough aid for Britain, which was very different from the criticisms which might have been heard had the Republican nominee been, for instance, Senator Taft. As it was, isolationists accused Roosevelt of having taken the first, long, treasonous step toward delivering the United States back into the British Empire, but the American people as a whole were not greatly interested, for by the time the deal was announced, the air Battle of Britain had started and the swapping of a few old destroyers for a few dots on the map seemed a relatively trivial matter.

The agreements between Roosevelt and Willkie on foreign affairs were strictly circumscribed and even those went by the board before

the campaign ended. Otherwise, Willkie was loudly and vigorously o.
for the kill. Even before his nomination, he had challenged Roosevelt
to run for a third term, saying that he wanted the privilege of meeting
and beating the toughest opponent the Democrats could name. His cry
was, "Bring on The Champ!" A shrewder politician would not have
said that. The people interpreted Willkie literally as saying, "The hell
with the third term tradition. Let's make this a *real* fight!" That dramatized the contest—made it an exciting sporting event—and the more
popular excitement there was in a campaign, the better it always was
for Roosevelt. When Roosevelt agreed to run, people took it not so
much as violation of a tradition as acceptance of a challenge to an old-
fashioned, bare-knuckled slugfest.

12. *1940*—ELECTION NIGHT

❲ *Robert E. Sherwood describes election night at Hyde Park,
Roosevelt's home on the Hudson.*

On Sunday evening, the President and Hopkins were to go by train
to Hyde Park and Rosenman and I were flying back to New York. Before we left, we offered somewhat self-conscious best wishes. "It has
been grand fun, hasn't it!" said Roosevelt, with more warmth than
accuracy. "And, don't forget—the Missus is expecting you and Dorothy
and Madeline [Mrs. Rosenman and Mrs. Hopkins] for supper Tuesday
evening."

. . . I suppose that, on the day before every Presidential election
in American history, each rival camp has been nerve-racked with rumors
that, at the fifty-ninth minute of the eleventh hour, the opposition would
come out with some unspeakable charges of corruption or personal
scandal which could not possibly be answered or exposed until too late.
I do not know whether this has ever actually happened, but it will
probably always be expected, making for that much extra tension. I
know I sat constantly at the radio that election eve. I heard a transcribed
Republican broadcast that was bloodcurdling. It was addressed to that
overworked audience, the Mothers of America, and delivered in the
ominous, insidious tones of a murder mystery program: "When your
boy is dying on some battlefield in Europe—or maybe in *Martinique*—
and he's crying out, 'Mother! Mother!'—don't blame Franklin D.
Roosevelt because he sent your boy to war—blame YOURSELF, because YOU sent Franklin D. Roosevelt back to the White House!"
There was nothing new in that, however; that sort of threat had been
uttered many times. (Martinique was mentioned because it was then

From *Roosevelt and Hopkins* by Robert E. Sherwood. Copyright, 1948, by Robert E. Sherwood.
Vol. I, pp. 198–200.

the strongest Vichy outpost in the Western Hemisphere and there were rumors, not entirely baseless, that American troops might be sent to seize it.)

The Democrats had possession of the election eve airwaves from 10:00 P.M. to midnight and devoted these two hours to short speeches by Roosevelt, Hull, Carl Sandburg, Alexander Woollcott and Dorothy Thompson mixed in with a great deal of entertainment from Broadway and Hollywood. The Republicans had the radio from midnight to 2:00 A.M. There were no shocking last-minute surprises, and the next day 49,815,312 people went to the polls and voted—most of them, in all probability, having made up their minds before a single word of oratory had been uttered by either candidate. . . .

On election night, after a stand-up supper at Mrs. Roosevelt's cottage, we drove through the Hyde Park woods, beloved by Franklin Roosevelt, to the big house to listen to the election returns. In a little room to the left off the front hall sat the President's mother with several old lady friends. They were sewing or knitting and chatting. A radio was on, softly, but they seemed to be paying little attention to it. In the big living room there was another radio going and a large gathering of weirdly assorted guests. The President was in the dining room in his shirtsleeves, with his sons and his Uncle Fred Delano and members of his staff. Large charts were littered on the dining table and news tickers were clattering in the pantry. The Roosevelt boys were excited, but not their father. Mrs. Eleanor Roosevelt moved about from one room to another, seeing to the wants of the guests, apparently never pausing to listen to the returns. If you asked her how she thought things were going she would reply, impersonally, "I heard someone say that Willkie was doing quite well in Michigan," in exactly the tone of one saying, "The gardener tells me the marigolds are apt to be a bit late this year."

My wife and George Backer and I joined Hopkins in his bedroom. He had a small, $15 radio, similar to the one he later gave Churchill. He had a chart and had been noting down a few returns, but most of it was covered with doodles. The first returns early in the evening indicated that Willkie was showing unexpected strength and Hopkins for a time seemed really worried; I have been told that early in the evening even Roosevelt himself was doubtful of the outcome, but I saw no signs of that. After ten o'clock, the sweep of Roosevelt's victory was so complete that there was no point in trying to keep the exact score. Later, the President and all the guests went out on the front porch to greet a parade of Hyde Park townspeople, one of whom carried a hastily improvised placard bearing the legend, "SAFE ON 3RD." Roosevelt was particularly elated because he had carried his own home district, normally solid Republican, by a vote of 376 to 302. This was the best he ever did on election day in Hyde Park.

CHAPTER XXIII

WORLD WAR II

1941 – 1945

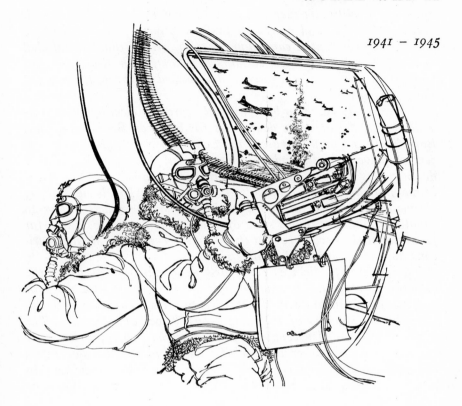

1. *1941*—PEARL HARBOR

❲ *For months after the outbreak of World War II the American people hoped that the United States would keep out of a conflict which it had had no part in bringing on. Many who remembered World War I had come to believe that American participation had been a tragic mistake. Many others were simply isolationist, convinced that the nation could live in safety if it would only mind its own business. To make certain that it would, Congress had passed, in the thirties, a series of Neutrality Acts forbidding American firms to sell arms and ammunition to nations at war.*

When Hitler occupied Austria in the spring of 1938, American sentiment began to change. Successive aggressions—Hitler's occupation of Czechoslovakia, Mussolini's invasion of Albania, the German attack on Poland which provoked Great Britain and France

From *Battle Report, Pearl Harbor to Coral Sea*, Prepared from Official Sources by Commander Walter Karig and Lieut. Welbourn Kelley. Copyright, 1944, by Rinehart & Company, Inc. Reprinted by permission of Rinehart & Company, Inc., New York, Publishers. Pp. 44–46.

*to war—hastened the shift of opinion and brought about the repeal
of the Neutrality Act then in force. The country armed itself with
desperate purpose and passed its first peacetime draft law. Still, as
late as the presidential campaign of 1940, after France had fallen
and Great Britain seemed certain to follow, both Roosevelt and
Willkie insisted that they were determined to keep the United
States out of war.*

*But we had ceased to be neutral. Before the election the Presi-
dent had traded over-age destroyers for bases on British territory.
Early in 1941 Congress passed the Lend-Lease Act, giving the Executive power to sell, lend, or lease war supplies to nations whose
defense was vital to our security. By late summer the Navy was
convoying supplies to England, American ships had been sunk by
German planes and torpedoes, and naval gunners had orders to
shoot on sight. But if this state of affairs was not peace, it was far
from the kind of warfare that raged on the continent. Most Americans hoped that it would become no worse.*

*The general public was concerned with Europe and paid little
attention to Japan. That nation had incurred American disfavor
by invading Manchuria in the thirties, and its occupation of Indo-
China in the summer of 1941 had aroused deep apprehension. The
United States applied economic sanctions; the two countries made
demands on each other that neither would meet. But that Japan
should suddenly strike, confident in her ability to crush the world's
strongest power, was a possibility that few Americans took seriously.*

*Unfortunately, the naval and military commanders at Pearl
Harbor, the powerful Pacific naval base, were as incredulous as the
people at large.*

*When the unexpected happened, one naval officer—Rear Admiral
William R. Furlong, commander of minecraft in the Pacific Fleet—
had presence of mind enough to dictate an account of the catastrophe three hours after the first Japanese bomb exploded. The*
OGLALA *was Admiral Furlong's flagship.*

At about 0800 this morning, Sunday, December 7, 1941, I was on the
deck of my flagship and saw the first enemy bomb fall on the seaward
end of Ford Island close to the water. This one did not hit the planes
parked there. Another fell immediately afterwards in the same vicinity
and caused fires near the water. U. S. planes were on the ground nearby
and later flames flared up from the structures at the south end of the
island. The next bombs fell alongside or on board the seven battleships
moored on the east side of Ford Island.

Japanese planes flew within fifty and one hundred feet of the water and dropped three torpedoes or mines in the channel on a line between *Oglala* and the seaward end of Ford Island. A torpedo hit *Oglala* and *Helena,* which were moored abreast at Ten Ten Dock with *Oglala* outboard of *Helena.* Fire was opened by *Oglala* and *Helena* anti-aircraft battery.

I at once signalled Commander-in-Chief that these three objects mentioned above which had just been dropped might be mines because they were dropped in the middle of channel. They could have been torpedoes or mines because no plume went up from them; whereas plumes over one hundred feet high went up from bombs that hit close alongside of battleships.

I then hailed two small contractor tugs, which were working with dredges across the channel from *Oglala,* to give assistance to haul *Oglala* aft of the *Helena* in order that *Helena* could sortie. I obtained submersible pumps from the *Helena* but then discovered that there was no power in the *Oglala* because of the hit which flooded the fireroom, and she could not use her pumps.

One Japanese plane was shot down over the harbor and came down in flames to seaward of Ford Island but probably on land. There was no trouble distinguishing Japanese planes because the red Sun painted on the side showed plainly.

Meanwhile planes were strafing as well as bombing. Planes kept coming for quite some time, making it difficult to estimate numbers. I saw four battleships hit with bombs and fires broke out. I saw one battleship turn over. There were six to ten enemy planes visible at any one time over the harbor.

The *Nevada* got under way and passed out of channel near where I had seen the three mines or torpedoes fall. When she arrived in this vicinity her bow apparently hove up as if she had passed over a mine and about a minute later two bombs fell, one of which hit her starboard topside throwing up flame and smoke, and the other missed close along the port side, throwing up a plume of water.

During all of this, as these dive bombers flew within five hundred to a thousand feet of the *Oglala,* we were given an excellent opportunity to fire our anti-aircraft battery and did so for over an hour, the *Helena* firing over us.

The *Oglala* was got astern of the *Helena* with help of tugs mentioned, and was hauled and pushed into the pier and secured with many wires and manila lines. As all compartments were closed below she settled slowly.

At this time I ordered the two tugs which were assisting the *Oglala* to go to the assistance of the *Nevada,* which was then in the channel between the floating dry-dock and seaward end of Ford Island.

On the second attack I saw a bomb drop which hit the forward part

577

of the *Pennsylvania* or in the dry-dock ahead of the *Pennsylvania*. Two destroyers of Destroyer Division Five were in the dock ahead of the *Pennsylvania,* and flames went up from them.

Another Japanese plane was hit and fell in flames seaward of 1010 dock, possibly falling near the entrance of the channel. It went down in a streak of flame as did the first one mentioned. Of the two planes that I saw shot down in this part of the harbor one was in flames after passing over the battleships from north to south about 2,000 feet altitude; the other plane shot down flew over the harbor at about 2,000 feet in the same general direction but closer to 1010 dock and pier, and was engaged by vessels on this side of the harbor. Guns operable by hand proved particularly advantageous, especially where power was knocked out of the steaming firerooms by torpedoes.

Following the bombing of the *Pennsylvania,* I saw a bomb fall near or on the destroyer *Shaw* in the floating dry-dock. This destroyer was later in flames.

Meanwhile the *Oglala* had taken a list of about 40 degrees. The wire lines to the deck parted and her port upper deck rail was so far under that she might sink suddenly at any moment. I ordered all hands to abandon the ship shortly after 9:00 A.M., the only ones remaining being the guns' crews and myself. The *Oglala* kept up the anti-aircraft fire until the ship's list was at such an angle that the men on the machine guns were sliding off the deck and the angle was too steep to longer stick on the deck and serve the 3″ gun. During this last period the Japanese planes were strafing us, not bombing. As the ship was about to turn over, I ordered the guns' crews to leave the ship, and left with them. The machine guns were slid off the top of deckhouse to the pier as the ship went over and were set up on the pier.

The guns' crews manned their battle stations promptly and stood to their guns during bombing and strafing as if at target practice, keeping up a continuous fire at enemy planes during the bombing and strafing. The signal force manned their bridge stations and sent signals during the action; one to sortie and one to the *Nevada* warning her of mines, during which time the bridge was struck by machine gun bullets. The men on the fires when the fireroom was flooding very promptly turned off the oil fires and no one suffered oil burns. . . .

Above dictated at 11:00 A.M.

William R. Furlong.

2. *1941*—"SO HELP US GOD!"

❡ *News of the attack on Pearl Harbor, detailed enough to make certain that the United States had suffered a major disaster,*

From *F. D. R. My Boss* by Grace Tully, copyright 1949 by Grace Tully. Reprinted by permission of Charles Scribner's Sons. Pp. 254–56.

reached Washington almost immediately. (Morning in Hawaii is mid-afternoon in Washington.) Grace Tully, one of the President's private secretaries, describes the shocked unbelief and then the grim resolution which greeted the reports.

On Sunday afternoon I was resting, trying to relax from the grind of the past weeks and to free my mind from the concern caused by the very grave tones in which the President dictated that Saturday night message. I was rather abstractedly looking at a Sunday paper when the telephone rang and Louise Hackmeister said sharply:

"The President wants you right away. There's a car on the way to pick you up. The Japs just bombed Pearl Harbor!"

With no more words and without time for me to make a single remark, she cut off the connection. She had a long list of people to notify. In twenty minutes I was drawing into the White House driveway, already swarming with extra police and an added detail of Secret Service men, with news and radio reporters beginning to stream into the Executive Office wing and State, War and Navy officials hurrying into the House. Hopkins, Knox and Stimson already were with the Boss in his second floor study; Hull and General Marshall arrived a few minutes later.

Most of the news on the Jap attack was then coming to the White House by telephone from Admiral Stark, Chief of Naval Operations, at the Navy Department. It was my job to take these fragmentary and shocking reports from him by shorthand, type them up and relay them to the Boss. I started taking the calls on a telephone in the second floor hall but the noise and confusion were such that I moved into the President's bedroom.

General Watson, Admiral McIntire, Captain Beardall, the Naval Aide, and Marvin McIntyre were on top of me as I picked up each phone call and they followed me as I rushed into Malvina Thompson's tiny office to type each message. All of them crowded over my shoulders as I transcribed each note. The news was shattering. I hope I shall never again experience the anguish and near hysteria of that afternoon.

Coding and decoding operations in Hawaii and in Washington slowed up the transmission. But the news continued to come in, each report more terrible than the last, and I could hear the shocked unbelief in Admiral Stark's voice as he talked to me. At first the men around the President were incredulous; that changed to angry acceptance as new messages supported and amplified the previous ones. The Boss maintained greater outward calm than anybody else but there was rage in his very calmness. With each new message he shook his head grimly and tightened the expression of his mouth.

Within the first thirty or forty minutes a telephone circuit was opened from the White House to Governor Joseph B. Poindexter in Honolulu. The Governor confirmed the disastrous news insofar as he had learned it. In the middle of the conversation he almost shrieked into the phone and the President turned to the group around him to bark grimly:

"My God, there's another wave of Jap planes over Hawaii right this minute."

Mr. Hull, his face as white as his hair, reported to the Boss that Nomura and Kurusu were waiting to see him at the exact moment the President called to tell him of the bombing. In a tone as cold as ice he repeated what he had told the enemy envoys and there was nothing cold or diplomatic in the words he used. Knox, whose Navy had suffered the worst damage, and Stimson were cross-examined closely on what had happened, on why they believed it could have happened, on what might happen next and on what they could do to repair to some degree the disaster.

Within the first hour it was evident that the Navy was dangerously crippled, that the Army and Air Force were not fully prepared to guarantee safety from further shattering setbacks in the Pacific. It was easy to speculate that a Jap invasion force might be following their air strike at Hawaii—or that the West Coast itself might be marked for similar assault.

Orders were sent to the full Cabinet to assemble at the White House at 8:30 that evening and for Congressional leaders of both parties to be on hand by 9:00 for a joint conference with the Executive group.

Shortly before 5:00 o'clock the Boss called me to his study. He was alone, seated before his desk on which were two or three neat piles of notes containing the information of the past two hours. The telephone was close by his hand. He was wearing a gray sack jacket and was lighting a cigarette as I entered the room. He took a deep drag and addressed me calmly:

"Sit down, Grace. I'm going before Congress tomorrow. I'd like to dictate my message. It will be short."

I sat down without a word; it was no time for words other than those to become part of the war effort.

Once more he inhaled deeply, then he began in the same calm tone in which he dictated his mail. Only his diction was a little different as he spoke each word incisively and slowly, carefully specifying each punctuation mark and paragraph.

"Yesterday comma December 7 comma 1941 dash a day which will live in infamy dash the United States of America was suddenly and deliberately attacked by naval and air forces of the Empire of Japan period paragraph."

The entire message ran under 500 words, a cold-blooded indictment of Japanese treachery and aggression, delivered to me without hesitation, interruption or second thoughts.

"I ask," he concluded, "that the Congress declare that since the unprovoked and dastardly attack by Japan on Sunday comma December 7 comma a state of war has existed between the United States and the Japanese Empire period end."

As soon as I transcribed it, the President called Hull back to the White House and went over the draft. The Secretary brought with him an alternative message drafted by Sumner Welles, longer and more comprehensive in its review of the circumstances leading to the state of war. It was rejected by the Boss and hardly a word of his own historic declaration was altered. Harry Hopkins added the next to the last sentence: "With confidence in our armed forces—with the unbounded determination of our people—we will gain the inevitable triumph—so help us God."

3.   1942—AN ARMY NURSE AT BATAAN AND CORREGIDOR

❢ *The destruction of the American fleet and air force at Pearl Harbor made the loss of the Philippines inevitable. On December 8 Japanese bombers caught most of the army planes based at Manila on the ground and destroyed more than half of them. Two days later another attack put Cavite Naval Yard out of commission. Japanese ground forces landed simultaneously. General Douglas MacArthur, commanding U.S. and Filipino troops, withdrew to Bataan peninsula on the west side of Manila Bay. No supplies could be brought in, no reinforcements landed, but the stubborn defense lasted until April 9. General Jonathan M. Wainwright, now commanding—General MacArthur had been ordered to Australia— moved the remnant of his troops to Corregidor Island, and there held out until May 6, when he was forced to surrender.*

An army nurse describes the hopeless, heroic resistance.

Conditions at Hospital Number 1 were not too good during the last few weeks we spent there. Patients were flooding in. We increased from 400 to 1,500 cases in two weeks' time. Most were bad shrapnel wounds, but nine out of ten patients had malaria or dysentery besides. One night we admitted 400 patients, most in worse condition than usual. They'd been left at first-aid stations near the front because of the shortage of gasoline.

We were out of quinine. There were hundreds of gas gangrene cases,

"An Army Nurse at Bataan and Corregidor," As Told to Annalee Jacoby. From *History in the Writing,* by Gordon Carroll; copyright 1945 by Time, Inc., by permission of Duell, Sloan & Pearce, Inc. Pp. 84–87.

and our supply of vaccine had gone months before. There was no more sulfapyridine or sulfanilimide. There weren't nearly enough cots so triple-decker beds were built from bamboo, with a ladder at one end so we could climb up to take care of the patients, who were without blankets or mattresses.

There was almost no food but carabao. We had all thought we couldn't go carabao, but we did. Then came mule, which seemed worse, but we ate that too. Most of the nurses were wearing Government-issue heavy-laced men's shoes. We had to keep our feet taped up to walk in them. Our uniforms had been gone for a long time, so we mostly wore size 32 Air Corps coveralls. We carried steel helmets and gas masks even in the wards, but it was an automatic gesture. We didn't expect to use them.

We went about our work feeling perfectly safe because of the Red Cross roof markings. When bombers came overhead on April 4, we hardly noticed them. Then suddenly incendiary bombs dropped. They hit the receiving wards, mess hall, doctors' and officers' quarters, and the steps of the nurses' dormitory, setting fire to all buildings but luckily not hitting the wards. One officer had been confined to quarters with malaria; he was walking outside for the first time when the planes came over. A bomb hit near his bed. Several enlisted personnel wandering outside were killed. The patients were terrified, of course, but behaved well. The Japanese prisoners were perhaps the most frightened of all. Everything was a blur of taking care of patients, putting out fires, straightening overturned equipment.

We remained frightened until two hours later when someone heard the Jap radio in Manila announce that the bombings had been an accident and wouldn't happen again. So after that, we wouldn't even leave the hospital for a short drive. We felt safe there and nowhere else.

Life at the hospital went on just the same, perhaps even busier. There was no time off except 30 minutes for two meals a day. Commanding Officer Col. James Duckworth was fine. He announced calmly that no matter how long we had to work, we weren't working as hard as the boys in the front lines. "We're all in the Army. Let's carry on!" he said.

The morning of April 7 we were all on duty when a wave of bombers came over. The first bomb hit by the Filipino mess hall and knocked us down before we even knew planes were overhead. An ammunition truck was passing the hospital entrance. It got a direct hit. The boys on guard at the gate were shell-shocked, smothered in the dirt thrown up by the explosion.

Convalescent patients picked us up and we began caring for men hurt by shrapnel. Everything was terror and confusion. Patients, even amputation cases, were falling and rolling out of the triple-decker beds to run. Suddenly a chaplain, Father Cummings, came into the ward, threw up his hands for silence and said: "All right, boys, everything's all right. Just stay quietly in bed, or lie still on the floor. Let us pray." The screams stopped instantly. He began the prayer just as a second wave of planes came over.

The first bomb hit near the officers' quarters, the next struck the patients' mess just a few yards away. The concussion bounced us three feet off the cement floor and threw us down again. Beds were tumbling down. Flashes of heat and smoke burned our eyes. But through it all we could hear Father Cummings' voice reciting the Lord's Prayer. He never faltered, never even fell to the ground, and the patients never moved. Father Cummings' clear voice went through to the end. Then he turned quietly and said: "All right, you take over. Put a tourniquet on my arm, will you?" And we saw for the first time that he'd been badly hit by shrapnel.

The next few hours were a nightmare, except for the way everyone behaved. We were afraid to move, but realized we had to get to work. One little Filipino with both legs amputated—he'd never gotten out of bed before by himself—rolled onto the ground and said: "Miss, are you all right, are you all right?" The ward boys all told us, "You go on outside—don't stay here any longer. We'll take care of everything." We tried to care first for the patients most seriously hurt. A great many all over the hospital were bleeding badly. We went to where the bomb had hit the ward and began pulling patients from the crater. I saw Rosemary Hogan, head ward nurse, and thought for a moment her face had been torn off. She wiped herself with a sheet, smiled and said: "It's nothing, don't bother about me. Just a nose bleed.' But she had three shrapnel wounds.

It would be hard to believe the bravery after that bombing if you hadn't seen it. An enlisted man had risked his life by going directly to the traction wards where patients were tied to beds by wires. He thought it was better to hurt the men temporarily than to leave them tied helpless above ground where they'd surely be hit by shrapnel, so he cut all tractions and told the patients: "Get under the bed, Joe."

We began immediately to evacuate patients to another hospital. We were so afraid the Japanese would be back again the next day that even the most serious cases were moved, because giving them any chance was better than none. Everyone went—orthopedic, surgical, medical cases. There were only 100 left the next morning and every patient was clean and comfortable. We worked all that day making up beds to admit new patients. It never occurred to anyone that we wouldn't go on as usual. Suddenly, after dark, we were told we were leaving in 15 minutes— that we should pack only what we could carry. Then we heard the Japanese had broken through and Battle of Bataan was over. The doctors all decided to stay with the patients, even doctors who had been told to go to Corregidor.

We left the hospital at 9 that night—got to Corregidor at 3 in the morning. The trip usually took a little over an hour. As we drove down to the docks, the roads were jammed. Soldiers were tired, aimless, frightened. Cars were overturned; there were bodies in the road. Clouds of dust made it hard to breathe. At midnight on the docks we heard the Japs had burned our hospital to the ground.

Bombers were overhead, but we were too tired to care. We waited on the docks while the Navy tunnel and ammunition dump at Mariveles were blown up. Blasting explosions, blue flares, red flares, shrapnel, tracers, gasoline exploding—it was like a hundred Fourths of July and Christmases all at once, but we were too frightened to be impressed. As we crossed the water with Corregidor's big guns firing over our heads and shells from somewhere landing close by, the boat suddenly shivered and the whole ocean seemed to rock. We thought a big shell had hit the water in front of us—it wasn't until we landed that we found an earthquake had come just as Bataan fell.

Corregidor seemed like heaven that night. They fed us and we slept, two to an Army cot. We went to work the following morning. Everyone was thoughtful, wonderful. Col. Chester Elmes of the Quartermaster's Corps called us in and said: "I'm going to dress you up. Woo Lee, bring the tape measure." For the first time we had tailor-made overalls that fit.

Months before, patients on Corregidor had filled a few laterals only. Now they were in double-decker beds all along the halls and in the main tunnel. There was constant bombing and shelling—sometimes concussion from a bomb outside would knock people down at the opposite end of the tunnel. Emperor Hirohito's birthday, April 29th, was a specially bad day. The bombing began at 7:30 a.m. and never stopped. Shelling was heavy; soldiers counted over 100 explosions per minute. Dive bombers were going after the gun on the hill directly above our heads and the concussion inside was terrific.

Most of the patients were shrapnel cases, but many had malaria and dysentery too. One night 250 patients passed through the hospital for treatment of meat poisoning—they were deathly ill but soon recovered. There were two in each bed, vomiting everywhere. But the worst night on Corregidor was when a bomb lit outside the tunnel entrance on the China Sea side. A crowd had gone outside for a cigarette and many were sleeping on the ground at the foot of the cliff. When the first shell hit nearby, they all ran for the tunnel, but the iron gate was shut and it opened outward. As more shells landed, they smashed men against the gate and twisted off arms and legs. All nurses got up and went back to work—the surgery was overflowing until 5:30 in the morning. There were many amputations.

Through all those weeks on Corregidor everyone was grand. At 6 o'clock one evening, after the usual bombing and shelling, 21 of us were told we were leaving Corregidor by plane with 10 pounds of luggage apiece. We don't know how we were selected. Everyone wanted to leave, of course, but morale was splendid. Everyone realized the end was getting close, but none gave up hope.

All Corregidor was under shell fire. We waited for an hour on the dock while medical supplies were unloaded from two seaplanes. Then we went out to the planes in motorboats. The pilot hustled us aboard— said to pile in quickly, not to bother to find seats. He was anxious to get off because we were between Cavite and Corregidor, directly in the range of artillery. On that trip we almost skimmed the water.

There was so much fog over Mindanao that we had to make a forced landing. A hole broke in the bottom of the ship and water came through. But we did reach the scheduled lake when the fog lifted. They had breakfast ready for us there on Mindanao. Some of us had champagne for the first time since the war started, but scrambled eggs, pineapple and pancakes were also the first we had seen since December. People on Mindanao were just as courageous as those on Corregidor and Bataan. They knew they would be trapped but cheerfully wished us a good trip and happy landings.

At dusk we left for Australia. We had to throw all our luggage overboard, and even then the plane barely got off. There is no joy in escaping when all one's best friends are prisoners or dead. But we reached Australia dirty, tired, dressed in overalls we'd worn for four days.

Now we're safe, but the only reaction we notice is wanting to make up somehow, anyhow, for those who didn't get away.

4. *1942*—THE BATTLE OF THE CORAL SEA

⟨ *The Coral Sea washes the northeast coast of Australia and the eastern tip of the island of New Guinea. In that warm body of water, only a few hundred miles south of the equator, Japanese and American carrier groups hunted for each other in the first week of May. On the 5th the planes of both groups found targets. A correspondent on the* YORKTOWN *describes the action that followed.*

To the United States, the loss of two carriers was serious, but the Japanese suffered almost as heavily, and were forced to abandon their attempt to occupy Port Moresby, a position which would have threatened Australia.

The Coral Sea fighting was just beginning. On May 5 the *Yorktown*

John Field in *History in the Writing*, by Gordon Carroll; copyright 1945 by Time, Inc., by permission of Duell, Sloan & Pearce, Inc. Pp. 182–85.

joined forces with the carrier *Lexington,* and on the afternoon of the 7th came the ominous news: "Two Jap carriers in immediate area." They were less than 130 miles away. Together the *Yorktown* and the *Lexington* launched their planes and together attacked a Jap carrier. Back on the *Yorktown,* as in other battles, the ship's crew waited for news. To them was relayed the *Lexington's* historic "Scratch one flat top," and cheers rolled out across the water.

Later at dusk the planes started coming back, swung into their landing circle around the carrier. Suddenly one of them began firing at the plane in front. Three Jap Zeros by mistake had got into the *Yorktown's* landing circle. Immediately anti-aircraft, tracer bullets, machine guns opened up in a steady stream. All the U. S. planes ducked into the clouds and the Japs winged off toward their own ship. One or two of them may have been shot down.

A few minutes later the *Yorktown's* planes again began coming in, but two of them had disappeared. The last heard of them, they radioed they were circling the ship. Unfortunately, they were not circling the *Yorktown.* Fellow pilots thought they might have made the same mistake the Japs had made . . . landing on an enemy carrier.

The night was tense. The *Yorktown* and *Lexington* knew that at least two more Jap carriers were in the vicinity, and that with dawn the fight would be renewed. On the *Yorktown,* reserves of chocolate bars, kept for such an emergency, were broken out. The mess boys got out their razors, ready to repel "a land attack."

At 8:30 in the morning came the announcement, "Two Jap carriers sighted." Before 10 a.m. the attacks were launched from both the *Lexington* and *Yorktown.* On the way to the Jap carriers, the fliers passed Jap bombers en route to attack the U. S. ships. The planes paid no attention to each other but continued on their way.

Far down inside the *Yorktown,* four decks below the hangar deck, Chief Carpenter McKenzie looked at his men of Repair Party 4. With the galley compartment doors secured, it was hot and the men were sweating. They were all good men, experienced, ready: this was what they had been trained for—to control any damage done in battle.

Over the loudspeaker came the calm announcement, "Large groups of enemy planes approaching ship 30 miles distant." Then later, "Air department take cover. Gunnery department take over." The ship's engines began to hum faster and faster. The ship began to zigzag in tight turns. "Stand by for torpedo attack on port bow." Everybody at Repair 4 braced himself.

Suddenly the anti-aircraft let loose, a crashing crescendo. "Stand by for torpedo attack on starboard beam." "Stand by for torpedo attack on port quarter." The ship heeled from side to side, dodging the torpedoes.

"We've dodged them all," said the battle telephone. "Torpedo planes are falling like leaves." Everybody grinned. But then came another announcement. "Stand by for dive-bombing attack."

"Boom" . . . a near miss. "Boom." "Boom." The deck in the galley compartment jumped three feet. The ship lurched sideways. Another bomb and another. The engines kept on roaring, the ship dodging, the AA firing. The men's stomachs drew up in knots. Suddenly there was a terrific bang in the adjoining compartment, the door flew open and a bloody sailor staggered in.

His face and hands were burned, one leg dangled. "We've been hit," he said. "I'm blind. They've been blasted to hell." From the next compartment rolled black smoke. The *Yorktown* had received a direct hit.

Said the battle telephone, "The *Lexington* is hit badly." But the battle was over.

The repair party moved into the bombed compartment. The smoke was strangling and water sloshed over their shoes. Bodies were pulled from the debris. They were placed in orderly rows.

The *Yorktown* had been hit and the *Lexington* was sinking, but the Japs had had trouble too. One carrier had been almost certainly sunk, another hit. There were heroes both among the fliers and the ship's crew. For instance, Bill Ott of the *Lexington*. On the way back, Ott was attacked by Japs and shot up. Running out of gas, he called the *Yorktown*, said he could fly only 15 minutes more. His radioman was dead, he himself had only one good arm and one good leg. Finally his last report came, "I am out of gas. That is all. Good luck and God be with you."

That night, after dark, the *Lexington* sank. The *Yorktown*'s crew watched her go down and it saddened them. But there is no time for sentiment in war. After the sinking the "Y" picked up speed and, accompanied by the *Lexington*'s cruisers and destroyers as well as her own, went south. She was leaking oil badly. In all, 44 of her crew had been killed. . . .

During the night of June 3-4 the *Yorktown* parted from the other carriers. Before dawn the scouts took off, thundering across the flight deck and zooming into the west. Shortly after dawn the first battle reports came in. Midway was under attack. One Jap battleship was being bombed. Two Jap carriers had been spotted. Then later, after the *Yorktown*'s own attack group had been launched, the reports said, "One enemy carrier in flames" and "Another carrier hit, damaged." The Japs were beginning to turn and run.

At 11:45 came the announcement everybody expected: "Stand by to repel enemy air attack." Down below, the repair parties lay down. The only noise was the noise of the engines, but the ship began heeling over from side to side. She was already dodging enemy planes.

587

"Stand by to repel dive-bombing attack." A deafening blast bounced the decks upward. The ship lurched sideways. Another and another. Then again the deck bounced and there was the crash of flying debris. The ship had been hit. Hell broke loose. The bombs dropped on all sides, one right after the other, uncountable in number. Another hit forward and one amidships. The engines began to whine and their volume diminished. The ship slowed down. More hits and near misses. There was the crashing of metal and the dim cries of wounded men. The AA guns stopped firing. From below, it was difficult to tell whether they had been put out of action. The ship was dead in the water.

The repair crew opened the door, climbed up to the hangar deck. All was shambles. The decks were a mass of twisted metal and debris. Dead and wounded lay everywhere. Five parties fought the fires and gradually brought them under control. Electricians rigged up portable lights to illuminate the dark, smoke-filled holes. Engineers worked on the engines. Other men patched the flight deck and began landing the *Yorktown*'s planes. Gradually the *Yorktown* got up to 15 knots, but she was still not safe.

Suddenly the loudspeaker, temporarily repaired, went into action again: "Stand by to repel air attack." Below decks, there was a tight feeling in stomachs. Then the AA's broke loose and the Japs were on the *Yorktown* again, this time with torpedo bombers. But the high, satisfying whine of the main engines could no longer be heard. The ship struggled into a starboard turn, but two torpedoes caught her forward. All lights went out. The ship listed rapidly and water ran gurgling across the decks. Another torpedo smacked amidships and again the decks lurched. Remember the Jap ship which sank in seven minutes? The engines stopped. The ship was dead, apparently capsizing. The guns were silent.

Then followed a conference between officers, who decided nothing could be done below decks. "All right, let's get out." On the hangar deck there was daylight but the port side was awash. Up forward men climbed down ropes into the water. The wounded went down in wire stretchers. The sea was a mass of bobbing heads. There was little conversation, no hysteria. Destroyers pulled the survivors aboard. Almost everybody was rescued. That night the American battle fleet went on to the west, leaving the mighty "Y" a ghostly hulk on the horizon.

But the ship did not sink. In the morning it was decided to put a salvage party aboard to tow her into Pearl Harbor. In the afternoon 141 enlisted men and 31 officers were sent back to the *Yorktown*. Soon three to four degrees of list had been taken off her. Then suddenly at 3 p.m. the Japs struck again. This time with torpedoes from submarines. One hit the carrier. Two more hit the destroyer *Hammann*, tied up alongside. The *Hammann* started going down, and its crew and the carrier crew started abandoning ship.

Aboard the carrier two carpenter's mates and a petty officer were trapped below decks. The telephones still worked. Somebody called down, "Do you know what a fix you're in?" Came back the answer, "Sure, but what a hell of an acey-deucey game we're having down here right now."

That night, the destroyers chased Jap subs. On the decks of the destroyers, underneath the stars, were piled dead and wounded bodies. Survivors of the *Yorktown* watched the hulk of their ship still floating through the night. Perhaps she could still be saved? But at dawn, salvage was impossible. The ship had a terrible list to port. Said Captain Buckmaster, "Her flight deck was in the water. Her battle flags were still flying. We hadn't taken them down."

At 6:30 a.m. all hands on the destroyers were called on deck. Gradually the *Yorktown* was settling. There was no commotion, no fire. Nobody said anything. Taps sounded out across the water. Sailors, lining the rails, raised their hands in salute. At 7:01 a.m. the *Yorktown* sank. It was June 7, six months to the hour after the first shot at Pearl Harbor.

5. *1942*—ON THE RUN TO MURMANSK

❨ *The story runs that a newspaper correspondent found an American Negro merchant sailor on the docks at Casablanca. The correspondent learned that the sailor had been on a ship that was torpedoed but that he had been rescued and brought to North Africa. When asked whether he would sign up again the sailor replied: "Well, sah, that depends. When you signs up for Liverpool, or Southampton, or Casablanca, you either gets there or you don't, but when you signs up for Murmansk, you don't!"*

The stranded sailor expressed a truth: the run to Murmansk, Russia's all-year-round ice-free port, was little short of suicide. Fred Herman, seaman on a Liberty ship loaded with high explosives, tells the story of his first trip in a convoy bound for Murmansk. The JASON *had a U. S. Navy gun crew; the escorting ships were British. Before the convoy reached Murmansk the ships were torpedoed, but Herman and most of her crew were taken off by a British minesweeper and eventually landed at a Russian port.*

Russian-bound convoys in those days followed a circuitous route and put into Murmansk or, as we intended, into the White Sea and Archangel.

We sighted land broad off our starboard beam. The sinking northern sun had transformed an ice-sheathed coast into towering glass moun-

Reprinted by permission of the publishers, The Vanguard Press, from *Dynamite Cargo*, by Fred Herman. Copyright, 1943, by Vanguard Press, Inc. Pp. 47–59.

tains of pink, yellow, orange, blue and blue-green. Preston Nickerson, one of the Gloucestermen, spat a streak of tobacco juice over the rail and informed me: "Thrifty sort of place. Not any colder'n New York, or nohow Boston. Come Christmas or New Year's, I won't say. Right now it ain't anyway cold to speak of."

It was as cold as I wanted that September evening. I took a look at the ocean which had picked up some colors of the sunset. It still looked cold. I had heard about men jumping overboard from sinking ships into the Arctic Ocean. Sixty minutes was as long as you could expect to survive, even clothed in one of the special rubber suits we had, which were lined with wool and cotton insulation. Some people said a man could last an hour and a half, but I think they were optimists. You wouldn't stay conscious even sixty minutes. But if you were picked up inside of that time you might be brought around. . . .

Nickerson slacked off his jaw and brushed his chin with the back of his hand. "Any day now we'll get ours. There ain't been much about it in the papers, but I figger no more'n a ninth or tenth of the stuff we're sendin' the Rooshians gets there."

I didn't believe him. I was sure that the percentage was a lot higher than that. I said to Nickerson: "Where do you get your information?"

"I figger it out. The way wars are run nowadays, that percentage is all right. Right nice percentage."

He was too damn lugubrious. I moved on. "We'll get it any day now," he shouted after me.

Two days went by and we hadn't got it yet. We had daily drills and practice alerts. . . . We zigzagged constantly on a prearranged course, taking our cues from the escort vessels. We were blacked out. We felt most secure during the hours of darkness, but they only lasted from about 11 P.M. to around two or three in the morning at this time of year.

It was a Saturday evening. I went below and stretched out on my berth. I had the steering trick at midnight and I thought I would grab a little nap. But I couldn't sleep. I was reading Sandburg's Lincoln when Scotty came down and began moving his gear around, whistling through his teeth. "Pipe down," I snapped at him.

He quit whistling and said we had received the signal that we were to fire on anything that looked irregular.

Scotty kept puttering about. "For God's sake, light somewhere," I snarled at him, and tried to concentrate on Sandburg.

Scotty began snarling back, "This place would look like a monkey house—" and stopped. We both heard it—the bark of a gun.

Scotty straightened up from stowing a bag under his berth. We looked at each other. I got up and followed Scotty onto the deck, both of us listening and hearing nothing but the thud-thud of the engines and the familiar creaks and groans which the *Jason* made when she was under way. Then another gun spoke, and another. We headed for the deck.

We were in time to see two bright flashes away up at the head of our formation. Then, from one of the navy ships, an anti-aircraft cut loose in a prolonged rattle. There was silence again.

Nickerson had been out on deck when the first cannon sounded. He told me without excitement that he had heard the drum of a single plane and then the rumble of a number of them. "Scoutin', I reckon. But there's no use in losin' sleep over it. They won't be back before daylight."

He was probably right. They wouldn't attack before there was some light on the sea. They were just checking our position. They would come back tomorrow.

The Old Man and the First and Second were all on the bridge. "Mind your steering," the Old Man said to me. He had a pair of night glasses and he kept moving from one side to another, staring out. I kept my eyes on the only spot of light in the wheelhouse, the glowing compass card in the blue-lit binnacle.

It was a long trick but I was sorry when it was over. From now on there would be nothing to do but wait around in idleness. Having nothing to do was the worst part of it. I went back below. Scotty was asleep. I lay down in my berth and, believe it or not, I went right to sleep.

It was around six o'clock, as I remember, when the bells began to jangle like all the bells in hell.

We had been through this before in practice. We went to our stations automatically, beating our hands together and lifting our rigid faces to the sky. An icy wind whipped our breaths away. Spread across the leaden ocean were the ships of our convoy, some of them hull down on the horizon.

From a plane, the merchantmen in our convoy would be seen plodding along in six or seven long columns, with the stream of destroyers and corvettes on the parade's flanks. The flagship *Scylla* was in the center of the whole formation, with two of the cargo ships just astern of her, two just ahead. The small aircraft carrier was in the rear of our vast convoy. There she would have room to maneuver and put her nose in the wind when she wanted to get her planes off. Now the destroyers and corvettes were breaking their alignment, fanning out, closing in, flipping the water in high-flying spray. We were all zigzagging, so that you never had the same ship off your beam for very long.

My station was at one of the 20-mm. cannon on the starboard side, in the bow, standing by, ready to move in if needed. It was a gray day with an overcast, a ceiling, I judged, of about 2,000 feet. I was calculating this when I heard the explosion.

Most of us had expected an air attack. It was mostly wishful thinking —if they came by air the merchantmen would have a chance of cracking back at them. We thought at first that the explosion was from the cannon of a cruiser off to the southwest. Then we saw the ship, which was astern of us and in the same column, belch smoke from her hull. She was a Russian, a big girl with a high, broad bow. Ensign Hawley had just appeared to check up on the green crew. "She's been torpedoed, I think," he said. "We're being attacked by U-boats."

Already, incredibly, she was listing. We could see people running along her decks. They looked orderly enough but in a great hurry. They were lowering their boats, which filled with people almost the instant they hit the water. She was settling visibly. Thick, white steam gushed out of her stack. The ocean around her was covered with boats, debris, men. Women too, probably. We had seen women sailors among the Russian crews when we were waiting at the rendezvous in the bleak harbor.

All we could do was watch in fascination. We held our course, getting farther and farther away from the stricken vessel. The merchantmen in a convoy cannot stop. Rescue work, if it is possible, is left to the warships. Several destroyers were racing for the spot. A corvette crossed our bows, lurching through the sea and dropping depth charges as she went. We rocked with their detonations.

Then another ship got it.

This one was an American. She was astern of the sinking Russian. We knew she had been hit by the way she lurched to port, then rolled back again, listing heavily to the starboard. She stayed afloat. But her engines must have been knocked out because she lost way almost immediately. For all practical purposes she was as dead as the Russian. . . .

There were several miles of ocean by now between the *Jason* and the two casualties. All we could see, without glasses, was a foregathering of vessels and over it all a black and gray cloud that rolled away southwards. Presently we could see that the Russian had vanished.

It had all happened inside of a few minutes. I found out later how the U-boats had got past the destroyers. The submarines must have been waiting for us with engines shut off so they wouldn't be picked up by detectors. When the escort screen had passed over them they got the merchantmen in their periscopes or on their sound apparatus, and let go with torpedoes. We hoped to God that the British got some of them. Destroyers and corvettes were still racing around, dropping depth charges. We zigzagged on.

Swanson the Navy kid had the 20-mm. gun to which I was assigned. He leaned back against the strap, nervously beating his hands against his legs. I lighted a cigarette and noted that my hands were steady, pretty steady. . . . Hawley walked aft. The Old Man came out on the flying bridge, his nose blue, his shoulders hunched up, his head in a knitted cap, turning first one way then another.

It was at that moment that the signal came that we were being attacked by planes.

We heard the drum-beat of a plane, possibly several planes. They were out of sight, way up above the overcast. But abruptly an eruption of water off our port bow showed where one of them had let go a bomb, plopping it down through the clouds.

Swanson's hands fumbled with the mechanism and his child-like face lifted to the sky with an expression of frustration. The Germans were headed away from us, the direction of their attack marked by the sprouting of huge black and white cabbages across the surface of the gray ocean.

This was high-level bombing. It made us sore. They were yellow. Why didn't they come down, the bastards, where we could see them? Several of the warships opened up with futile ack-ack fire. The bombing, though nerve-wracking, was just as futile. Minute after minute went by as the cabbages continued to sprout. No ships were struck. Finally the bombers were gone. From the flagship came the all-clear.

We learned later what their idea was. They were trying to split us up, scare some of our cargo ships out of the convoy, then run them down later. They had worked that trick on another convoy. Nazi surface raiders took a terrible toll after the planes had broken up the parade. But we stuck together, like kittens in a basket, and zigzagged along according to orders.

It was not a question of the Nazis being yellow either. We found that out almost immediately. The high-level bombers had scarcely drummed out of hearing when we heard more aircraft approaching from another quarter. Their racket became a roar.

They broke out of the overcast, half a hundred Heinkel 111's fanning out across the convoy. But only two interested us. One trailing the other, they had plummeted down, come out of their dives, and were heading straight for the *Jason*. They were scarcely higher than our deck, until the leader abruptly lifted his nose and thundered over us. I saw one torpedo drop.

It must have missed us. But we scarcely had time to note it. No. 2 plane was on us. I ducked down on the deck beside Swanson. I realized for the first time that he had the 20-mm. in action. The kid's face was as white as a sheet. The gun's orange tracers caught the German. Bursting shells ripped the plane's wing. It swerved away from us, wabbling crazily, while Swanson's 20-mm. and the other 20-mm. in the *Jason*'s bow followed and held it, and a stream of fire chewed up its belly and literally tore it to pieces in midair. What was left of the Heinkel flopped and crashed into the sea.

Swanson kept on firing. His gun was pointed at the empty sky. Hawley came running. "Cut it," he yelled above the din. "You're wasting ammunition."

Swanson paid no attention. His hands were frozen to the gun's action and he hung there bucking up and down with the gun's recoil.

The preacher grabbed his hands and yanked them loose. "Unstrap him," he ordered me. "He's gone off his head."

"He's doing all right," I told Hawley.

"Unstrap him and take over."

I did as the preacher ordered. . . .

Hawley asked one of the Cape Verde Negroes to take the kid down to his quarters. The Negro took the little soda jerk under the arm, half lifted him from his feet and dragged him away.

I got in behind the gun. But the Germans were departing. They were ducking up into the overcast again, making tracks for the coast of Norway. We had gotten a number of them. I saw their wreckage. They had gotten a number of us, too. How many I am not allowed to say. But the smoke of their fires raised a black pall that marked our slow and terrible course across the northern sea.

6. *1942*—THE FIRST ATOMIC REACTION

❨ *The armies and navies and air forces grappled in a combat the like of which the world had never seen. Yet it was a group of scientists, working in the utmost secrecy at the University of Chicago, who were really changing the course of history. The leader of the group was Enrico Fermi, an Italian scientist who had come to this country in 1939 to escape Fascist tyranny.*[1] *Mrs. Fermi had to wait two and a half years to learn that she had given a party on the day of the first atomic reaction.*

The period of great secrecy in our life started when we moved to Chicago. Enrico walked to work every morning. Not to the physics building, nor simply to the "lab," but to the "Met. Lab.," the Metallurgical Laboratory. Everything was top secret there. I was told one single secret: there were no metallurgists at the Metallurgical Laboratory. Even this piece of information was not to be divulged. As a matter of fact, the less I talked, the better; the fewer people I saw outside the group working at the Met. Lab., the wiser I would be. . . .

Willingly we accepted the hint and confined our social activities to

From *Atoms in the Family: My Life with Enrico Fermi*, by Laura Fermi. Copyright, 1954, by the University of Chicago Press. Pp. 176–80.
[1] Dr. Fermi died of cancer on November 28, 1954. He was then fifty-three years old.

the group of "metallurgists." Its always expanding size provided ample opportunities of choice; besides, most of them were congenial, as was to be expected, for they were scientists. . . .

Early in December, 1942, I gave a large party for the metallurgists who worked with Enrico and for their wives. As the first bell rang shortly after eight in the evening, Enrico went to open the door, and I kept a few steps behind him in the hall. Walter Zinn and his wife Jean walked in, bringing along the icy-cold air that clung to their clothes. Their teeth chattered. They shook the snow from their shoulders and stamped their feet heavily on the floor to reactivate the circulation in limbs made numb by the subzero weather. Walter extended his hand to Enrico and said:

"Congratulations."

"Congratulations?" I asked, puzzled. "What for?" Nobody took any notice of me.

Enrico was busy hanging Jean's coat in the closet, and both the Zinns were fumbling at their snow boots with sluggish fingers.

"Nasty weather," Jean said, getting up from her bent position to put her boots in a corner. Walter again stamped his feet noisily on the floor.

"Won't you come into the living room?" Enrico asked. Before we had time to sit down, the bell rang again; again Enrico went to open the door, and amid repeated stamping of feet and complaints about the extraordinarily cold weather I again heard a man's voice:

"Congratulations."

It went on this way until all our guests had arrived. Every single man congratulated Enrico. He accepted the congratulations readily, with no embarrassment or show of modesty, with no words, but with a steady grin on his face.

My inquiries received either no answer at all or such evasive replies as: "Ask your husband," or: "Nothing special. He is a smart guy. That's all," or: "Don't get excited. You'll find out sometime."

I had nothing to help me guess. Enrico had mentioned nothing worthy of notice, and nothing unusual had happened, except, of course, the preparations for the party. And those did not involve Enrico and provided no ground for congratulating. . . .

I went up to Leona Woods, a tall young girl built like an athlete, who could do a man's job and do it well. She was the only woman physicist in Enrico's group. At that time her mother, who was also endowed with inexhaustible energy, was running a small farm near Chicago almost by herself. To relieve Mrs. Woods of some work, Leona divided her time and her allegiance between atoms and potatoes. Because I refused either to smash atoms or to dig potatoes, she looked down on me. I had been at the Woods's farm, however, and had helped with picking apples. Leona, I thought, owed me some friendliness.

"Leona, be kind. Tell me what Enrico did to earn these congratulations."

Leona bent her head, covered with short, deep-black hair, toward me, and from her lips came a whisper:

"He has sunk a Japanese admiral."

"You are making fun of me," I protested.

But Herbert Anderson came to join forces with Leona. Herbert, the boy who had been a graduate student at Columbia University when we arrived in the United States, had taken his Ph.D. with Enrico and was still working with him. He had come to Chicago a few months before I did.

"Do you think anything is impossible for Enrico?" he asked me with an earnest, almost chiding face.

No matter how firmly the logical part of my mind did disbelieve, there still was another, way back, almost in the subconscious, that was fighting for acceptance of Leona's and Herbert's words. Herbert was Enrico's mentor. Leona, who was young enough to have submitted to intelligence tests in her recent school days, was said to have a spectacular I.Q. They should know. To sink a ship in the Pacific from Chicago . . . perhaps power rays were discovered. . . .

When a struggle between two parts of one's mind is not promptly resolved with clear outcome, doubt results. My doubt was to last a long time.

That evening no more was said about admirals. The party proceeded as most parties do, with a great deal of small talk around the punch bowl in the dining-room; with comments on the war in the living-room; with games of ping-pong and shuffleboard on the third floor, because Enrico has always enjoyed playing games, and most of our guests were young.

In the days that followed I made vain efforts to clear my doubts.

"Enrico, did you really sink a Japanese admiral?"

"Did I?" Enrico would answer with a candid expression.

"So you did not sink a Japanese admiral!"

"Didn't I?" His expression would not change.

Two years and a half elapsed. One evening, shortly after the end of the war in Japan, Enrico brought home a mimeographed, paper-bound volume.

"It may interest you to see the Smyth report," he said, "It contains all declassified information on atomic energy. It was just released for publication, and this is an advance copy."

It was not easy reading. I struggled with its technical language and its difficult content until slowly, painfully, I worked my way through it. When I reached the middle of the book, I found the reason for the congratulations Enrico had received at our party. On the afternoon of that day, December 2, 1942, the first chain reaction was achieved and the first atomic pile operated successfully, under Enrico's direction. Young Leona Woods had considered this feat equivalent to the sinking of an admiral's ship with the admiral inside. The atomic bomb still lay in the womb of the future, and Leona could not foresee Hiroshima.

7. *1943*—A TANK DRIVER AT BIZERTE

❲ *By the fall of 1942 the United States was strong enough to move into the European theater of the war. The target was North Africa. If successful, the movement would clear the Mediterranean and provide bases for an attack on Italy, the weakest member of the Axis.*

The landings succeeded, but six months of hard fighting ensued before the American forces in North Africa reached their objective: Bizerte, the northernmost point in Tunisia. Sergeant Samuel Allen, Jr., of Hudson, Ohio, describes the capture of the town.

(AFRICA)
May 15, 1943

DEAR FAMILY:

. . . . It's an awfully funny feeling, sitting there on top of your tank just waiting. You knew that not everybody was coming back and as I sat there I looked over each tank and hoped that it was all a bad dream. After you've been in an outfit ever since it was formed and lived with the fellows as long as I have, you get to feel like one big family. You know all about each man, his wife, kids, or his girl friend; maybe you've met his family, any way we've shared each others packages from home and things like that. I know, that as a tank commander you know the other five men in your crew better than your own family and it's sort of your job to see that they all come back. That's the way we feel about it, it's just your job!

Mount up! That's the call and I guess we were all glad, I know I was, you'd go nuts if you had to sit there any longer. The minute you are in the Tank you become part of a machine, you have your certain job to do and hold your end up. You stop thinking about yourself and think of your job.

We moved out into the valley travelling in two inverted wedges VV with our platoon in support *VV.* B company was to be in the same position on our left. But as we later saw they jumped off after we did and then did not go up to the objective. As we got to the hill we (our platoon) was to swing in an arc up the valley to the right of the hill,

From Mina Curtiss, Ed., *Letters Home* (Boston: Little Brown & Co., 1944). Reprinted by permission of Mrs. Mina Kirstein Curtiss. Pp. 59–65.
Sergeant Allen was killed in the Italian campaign a few months after he wrote this letter.

between the hill and the mountains on the right. I was to take my section up into the valley as far as I could to get at the artillery that was behind the hill.

As we moved through a large cactus patch they opened up on us with everything they had. It seemed to me that one gun picked my tank out because there were always four shell bursts after me. The German 76.2 MM gun shoots four shots, one in the chamber and three in a clip. From then on it was just a question of outguessing them. The valley had a lot of small bunkers in it and we sort of jumped from behind one to another—if it hadn't been for those little hill-cocks we never would have made it. First they would drop four about fifty yards behind me and then four right in front of me, then it was time to move on. About this time the other tank in my section ran into a land mine and blew one track off. When that happens they are usually in a mine field and you can't help them because you'd hit one yourself. But I saw the boys bail out so I knew they could make it on foot. Now the infantry came out of the waddie on our left and swung across the valley, among us. It's not very nice to watch those boys out there running in all that flying hell, but you can't watch them, you have a job to do. You can't see the guns because they are dug in and in concrete implacements, then all at once you spot one and lay your guns on it. Over to my left I could see two tanks burning and on my right two more in the mine field. The hill was getting closer now and then I could see the road up ahead; there's a tall cactus fence between us and the road and a large ditch also, boy, it's no time to get stuck now. Just then somebody stood up in the ditch—Our Infantry! They grinned, waved, and one of them pointed to a spot where I could get through. Thank God for the Infantry! Across the road and my friend who is shooting at me stops. I guess he can't depress his gun far enough; just then I saw a gun on my right, just next to an Arab hut, so here we go—and then I've got to get up that valley all alone now; wonder how Toth is making out in the mine field. Dam it that gun sees me and is swinging over on me, gosh it has a barrel about 15 feet long. But just up there ahead is another bunker, we've got to get there fast. Safe for a minute but then Waitman phones up that our 75 mm. gun is jammed. Pawling has that 37 going like a machine gun and we are in one hell of a position. If we move from behind this bunker we'll get it sure because it's only 200 yards over to that gun. Just then Lieut. Maloney called on the radio "Let's get the hell out of here, let's go home." So we back around and pull out just enough so I can see, the gun isn't there any more. It must be our lucky day!

As we ran back across the road I look again and see that somebody put one right on it. The place is lousy with German machine gun nests and we tear them up on the way back.

Then my friend opens up on me again and we play games until I'm out of range. But we knew that we took the "objective" and our infantry was up there laying in with mortars and cleaning up in general. The gun that is on me must be up in the mountains on the right because he is still after me.

On the way back I stopped as close to Toth as I could but I could see that I couldn't do him any good so off we go again. One of Christison's crew comes running up and tells me that I'm in the mine field also. You can see where mines are planted if you look close enough so I got out of the tank and brought my tank through on foot, those shells were awfully close at times but we made it.

Back to our area to gas and ammu. up. We knew that we had lost some friends and equipment out on that field. But we have found that it is best to forget all about those friends, not to talk about them—they didn't even exist.

But it is gratifying to know that we opened the way and the British are on the way to Kairouan.

I'm a great believer in luck now, some one got that gun—and later I learned that after I crossed the road I was in one of their mine fields all the way. Luck—I travelled 600 yards on it!

That is what I did in my first real action and those were some of my thoughts. Scared? Not for one minute. I was too busy to be scared. . . .

Then on May 7 at 7:10 A.M. we jumped off. They hadn't told us just what our objective was so we proceeded very cautiously around hill 609 and along the lake, and then we cut North up through a valley and over some steep hills. We stopped once in the valley and because I was the tank on the up slope of the hill, I dismounted and ran up for a look see. Our infantry had an O P up there and I could see Bizerte off to my right. What a thrill that was!

The valley ahead looked clear and peaceful. But they had an anti-tank gun up there banging away. I don't think they knew just what they were shooting at but all the same "reconnaisance by fire" is valuable. You may make them mad enough to shoot back and then you know where they are. I reported back to Lieut. Maloney and we moved out down into the valley. Two platoons crossed the valley and rolled over the hills to our left and rear. Then we got together and moved slowly up the valley toward Bizerte.

Way back in our rear we could see the two companies of Tank Destroyers moving up to support us, but no infantry.

We had only gone about a mile or two when the captain called all tanks and told us that we were ordered to take Bizerte and hold it until the Infantry moved in. My heart jumped right out I think. Take Bizerte, one of the last strongpoints in Tunisia, what are they talking about! We hit the road and rolled full speed ahead. We passed the great Army and

Naval Air Station and then through the main gate into Town. That was the greatest thrill yet for me.

Instructions over the radio to cruise around, go in town and knock out the snipers so down one street we went. We ran the length of the street and out through the gate (the city has a stone wall around it). There as I turned the tank around to go back in a bunch of Frenchmen came running out of some houses, jumped up on the tank and started kissing me. You see we tank commanders always have our heads out because you can see much better and you are the eyes of the tank when you are buttoned up. I finally got away from them and back into town. This time I turned down a street that ran to the water front.

In Bizerte there is a large Channel running from the bay to Lake Bizerte, on this channel is the water front docks, etc. I had no sooner gotten started down the street when machine gun fire started flying around and then we could see across the channel up on a hill behind it, gun flashes. So I stopped right in the middle of the street and started shelling the gun positions. By this time they were giving it to us hot and heavy, but we were giving plenty back. Each tank was down a street and shelling the hill. While all this was going on there were snipers in the buildings near us and they kept things from getting dull. George Waitman, my gunner, knocked out the two guns that were bothering us the most and we moved over to another street looking for some targets.

Pulled down a side street and started again. This was a nice quiet street without snipers or machinegun nests. After we were there for a while an old lady and four men came up. There we were sitting in the middle of the street, motor cut, shooting away. It's sort of funny now that you think back to it. The town itself was deserted and had been heavily bombed, and to sit there everything sort of quiet and deserted, ruined buildings all around you, shutters banging in the breeze. By this time it was getting very hot and stuffy in the tank so we climbed out and took a smoke, cleaned the brass up in the tank and stuff. Then one of the Frenchmen comes up with a bottle of wine and we all had a smoke and drank the bottle of wine. A shell lands behind the tank and sort of makes us mad so we get back in and start shooting away again. And the people just standing there on the sidewalk. Every time George would shoot the 75, plaster would fall down from all the buildings around but they didn't seem to mind that, they were so glad to see us.

I was running short of ammunition and my radio went out so we drove back to the center of town. There we ate supper and then went back for some more shooting. I don't know what happened to the Infantry but it was getting dark and we all were worrying because we knew we couldn't hold the town at night with tanks. Then at 9:00 P.M. we moved out of town. We captured the town at 3:55 P.M. and held it to 9:00 P.M. and still no Infantry.

We drove back out to the Air Station and stayed all night out on the field. I was the first one up in the morning and what a sight it was. Picture an airport as large as Cleveland's. The channel across the field, hangars at both ends of the field and hangars behind you. Long concrete runways stretching out in every direction and airplanes all over the field. Some they had burned themselves and some were all set to take off. Evidently they had seen us coming way back in the valley and moved out. You should have seen us running around that field picking up souvenirs. Some of the hangars were full of planes and engines, wings, spare parts and everything imaginable. In their quarters beds were made up, they had left but fast. Bill Bolich had a Folk Wolf 190 out taxiing it around and things were like a mad-house. At the Naval Air station end of the field we found two four man submarines, a motor torpedo boat and sea planes. That was a morning I'll never forget. We got parachutes, helmets, life rafts, rubber boats, tools, rifles, machine guns, radios, tables, chairs, anything you wanted you could have because WE took it, it was ours until G 2 air corps came and took it off our hands.

We filled up and ammunitioned up and at 1 :00 P.M. we moved back into town. The Infantry still hadn't arrived and the snipers had moved in again and were holding things up. We used the same plan that we used the day before and had lots of fun hunting them down. Once when we were sitting, trying to locate a machine gun that had been bothering us, I heard singing. Looking across the park on my left I could see a native soldier come weaving down the street. He was drunk, had his shoes off, battle dress open, no tin hat, and brandishing a long knife. I knew that the minute he hit the corner the machine gun would open up on him, but there wasn't anything I could do to stop him. When he came to the corner the lead just flew all around him, and he danced around in the middle of it, waving his knife, cursing at them, then staggered off down the street again. We did locate the gun and put it out of action.

The Infantry showed up and at 7 :00 P.M. we pulled out again. . . .

Loads of love,

DUKE

P.S. My company has the credit for taking Bizerte and the Airport and some five hundred planes and equipment there. No other company holds such a record!

8. *1943*—THE INVASION OF ITALY

❲ *With North Africa in their possession, the Allies began the second phase of their offensive: the invasion of Italy. Their first target was Sicily, the large island off the toe of the Italian boot. Early in July,*

From Mina Curtiss, Ed., *Letters Home* (Boston: Little, Brown & Co., 1944). Reprinted by permission of Mrs. Mina Kirstein Curtiss. Pp. 90–94.

*after weeks of pounding from the air, British and American troops
dropped from gliders and hit the beaches in landing craft. By mid-
August, they had captured or driven out the Axis defenders.*

*The Italian mainland came next. In September invading forces
consisting of British, American, French, Canadian, and Polish contingents landed at several points in the lower part of the peninsula.
The American Fifth Army, going ashore in the Gulf of Salerno
near Naples, found the Germans alert and well prepared. A month
later Private Eric Golub, an engineer, described his experiences in
a letter to his wife in Brooklyn.*

ITALY

October 16, 1943

BABY DEAR,

I'm writing this now but have no idea as to when I may mail it. As
soon as the censorship lifts then you shall have it. I'll attempt to bring
you up to date on my Italian experiences.

Unlike the Sicilian invasion the crossing was very nice. We had the
fortunate luck of having a perfect sea all the way over. The Jerries
made sure of giving us a very warm reception all the way over! It was
the most sustained bombing we ever saw them do. They were over every
night and stayed plenty long. As far as I could see they didn't hit a
thing. Four of them came over in daylight once and one of them got
shot down pretty fast. He came down like a comet from about 10,000
feet and landed about 400 yards in front of our ship. There was absolutely nothing left of him but a big circle of oil. We saw something else
drop way off our port bow but we could not tell whether it was a plane
or a bomb. What a terrific feeling of power it gave all of us, when, at
one time the convoy changed its course and in swinging out we could
see ships stretched out to the horizon and far beyond it. There were
other convoys coming from other directions also. After seeing all these
ships you wonder how in hell Hitler ever dreams that he is going to
beat us.

As you probably know from newspaper reports the Jerries expected
us and made a very excellent guess at to where we would land. Therefore they had their artillery and mortars trained on the beaches. We
had much heavier guns than they did and our battleships and cruisers
could easily outrange anything that they had ashore. We were sitting
out in the harbor watching a U. S. cruiser throw broadside after broadside into some enemy shore positions. They were letting go with six
6 inch guns at one time, what a racket. This was in broad daylight. On
the beach we could see various explosions occurring every few minutes but couldn't make out the cause. During all this the little mine
sweepers were quickly going about their business and they really blew

up plenty of mines. There would be a dull boom and a great geyser of water would shoot into the air. Finally we were signaled to come into shore, we came in slowly and gradually could make out figures on the beach and see some of the doings. When we hit the beach the vehicles went off first (and a beautiful job it was too, there wasn't a moment's delay). While they were going off we were waiting on the deck and were watching a ship further down the beach. She was disembarking her troops and they had to come off running and crouched down. The ship was under mortar and artillery fire. A smoke pot was covering the men as they came off (a smoke pot lays a smoke screen). A destroyer was laying offshore some 8 or 9 hundred yards and pouring hell into the Jerries position that was shelling the ship. After a few minutes we disembarked. No one had to say "Hurry" either. Everyone took off for all he was worth. We assembled on the beach and quickly marched right off it. We marched to the road and then proceeded to our appointed rendezvous area. Just before we turned off the road we passed a 105 mm Howitzer and further down the road were some beautifully smashed and burned Jerry tanks, one was still burning brightly. We got to our area, threw down our packs, ate some tomatoes that were growing right there and rested briefly.

After this we just moved around here and there for a few days and did odd jobs. One day we did nothing for a whole day, just lazyied around. Everybody smelled a rat. That night about 8 o'clock an announcement came through, "Get into O.D.'s, full field equipment with light pack, come with ammunition and hand grenades, we're going up to the front." It was the most peculiar moment we ever experienced. I got a peculiar gripping feeling in the pit of stomach. It was hard to believe, yet here you were getting ready to go. After all preparations were ready we layed around for some time. Finally we got aboard our trucks and moved up. This of course was at night. We got to within a few miles of our line, got off the trucks and started to march. It was all so peculiar, here we were marching on a road, the moon was bright but overhanging trees and cliffs kept the road dark. There was great numbers of artillery pieces and tanks moving out to the back areas. We kept going forward until we were overlooking a valley. We took up positions on the side of the hill and stayed there all night. Nothing happened. Next morning we started moving down the road to take new positions when we noticed some tanks about 500 yards from us in the valley. We thought they were ours when suddenly shells started breaking all around them. Our artillery was firing at them. The Jerries spotted some of our boys in different places and opened with machine guns. Our bunch of boys got pinned down for five hours and couldn't move. They eventually got away. To shorten this part of it, we were there for a number of days and constantly had Jerry shells breaking around us. We suffered casualties. I found this pen while on patrol in "No Man's Land". I also found a very lovely river or stream in which I took the nicest bath, also in No Man's Land.

When we were relieved the Jerries knew damn well that we were going out that night because they kept shelling the road leading out and came damn near hitting a whole squad once. I've learned from being out there that you can believe anything vile and bestial about the Nazis. Certain things that have happened have shown that. (By the way, one of our heavy weapons squads knocked out a Nazi tank and killed four Jerries including a Major and captured another Jerry officer who was in the tank.) One of our boys, while going back in an ambulance from the front, was shot at by a Jerry machine gun. This tank deliberately aimed at the ambulance. Another of our boys while waiting on a chow line at a hospital was strafed by a Nazi plane. Now all hospitals are very plainly marked with a very large cross so that it couldn't be a mistake. Infantry men coming back from an engagement, told stories of how the Jerries would have one or two men surrounded and would call to them to surrender. The men would throw down their rifles and come forward with their hands up and the Nazi bastards would shoot them.

After this we started a series of moves doing our regular engineer work. It was at all times interesting. Let me say without qualification that Italy is by far one of the most beautiful countries in the world. Talk about fruit and nuts, we've been bivouaced in an apple orchard, grape orchard, nut orchard, what more could one ask. They have excellent wine also. It really was a thrill to bite into my first apple in months. The oranges aren't ripe as yet. The women are really all right too. Some of them are so damn buxom. Anyone who has the idea that Italians are dark is sadly mistaken. I've seen more blonds here than I ever dreamed of. Some of the children are amazingly good looking, and the people look absolutely no different from any other race on earth. They have their short and tall and light and dark, fat and thin, rich and poor.

Some of their poor are really miserable. They wear rags as torn as the Arabs. Some of the Fascists were filthy rich. I've seen apartments that were so richly furnished that your eyes would pop out. Certain cities have some of the most beautiful houses that you have ever seen. And the people are very well dressed. There seems to be a town every few miles in Italy. You can't travel any distance without running into a house or town. Some of the towns perched on the side of the hills command views that are awe inspiring and they have been there for hundreds of years also. Certain other towns have been horribly smashed by both artillery and bombs. It's almost beyond the imagination to go through a town and see not one house standing. Everything smashed flat. I've seen Bizerte in North Africa but that didn't compare with one particular town that I saw in Italy. There is nothing left of the town but the name and that's a long one. Other towns have been fortunate enough not to have been touched. The worst part of all is the fact that civilians get killed and sometimes hundreds get buried under the rubble. It's something to come into a town newly captured and smell the bodies. Many of them are lying in the streets just decomposing. Many times groups of people are to be seen digging in the ruins of their homes looking for relatives. I have seen women in the worst stage of grief standing by while their husbands dug in the wreckage for some child that was buried underneath. At the same time they salvaged what few belongings they could from all the rubble. It's a tremendous experience to see the people coming back from the hills to town. They're carrying all kinds of furniture and bedding on their heads. Most of them have no shoes and slosh around in the mud barefooted.

Let that suffice as a small picture of war as it has hit Italy. I'm just tremendously thankful that it has never hit America.

Love,

ERIC

9. 1943—CAPTAIN WASKOW

❲ *The war saw no more stubborn fighting than that which followed the Allied landings in Italy. Even though Italy had surrendered, leaving the Germans to defend the country unaided, the conquest of the peninsula was not completed until the very end of the war. The cost, to the Allies, was heavy—350,000 in killed, wounded, and missing. The cost in agony and sorrow cannot be measured. There were thousands like Ernie Pyle's Captain Waskow.*

In this war I have known a lot of officers who were loved and respected by the soldiers under them. But never have I crossed the trail of any man as beloved as Captain Henry T. Waskow, of Belton, Texas.

Captain Waskow was a company commander in the Thirty-sixth Division. He had led his company since long before it left the States. He was very young, only in his middle twenties, but he carried in him a sincerity and a gentleness that made people want to be guided by him.

"After my father, he came next," a sergeant told me.

"He always looked after us," a soldier said. "He'd go to bat for us every time."

"I've never known him to do anything unfair," another said.

I was at the foot of the mule trail the night they brought Captain

From *Brave Men* by Ernie Pyle. Copyright, 1943, 1944, by Scripps-Howard Newspaper Alliance. Copyright, 1944, by Henry Holt and Company, Inc. Reprinted by permission of the book publishers. Pp. 106–07.

Later, Ernest Taylor Pyle reported the war in France and in the Pacific. He was killed by Japanese machine-gun fire on April 18, 1945.

Waskow down. The moon was nearly full, and you could see far up the trail, and even partway across the valley below.

Dead men had been coming down the mountain all evening, lashed onto the backs of mules. They came lying belly-down across the wooden pack-saddles, their heads hanging down on one side, their stiffened legs sticking out awkwardly from the other, bobbing up and down as the mules walked.

The Italian mule skinners were afraid to walk beside dead men, so Americans had to lead the mules down that night. Even the Americans were reluctant to unlash and lift off the bodies when they got to the bottom, so an officer had to do it himself and ask others to help.

I don't know who that first one was. You feel small in the presence of dead men, and you don't ask silly questions.

They slid him down from the mule, and stood him on his feet for a moment. In the half-light he might have been merely a sick man standing there leaning on the others. Then they laid him on the ground in the shadow of the stone wall alongside the road. We left him there beside the road, that first one, and we all went back into the cowshed and sat on water cans or lay on the straw, waiting for the next batch of mules.

Somebody said the dead soldier had been dead for four days, and then nobody said anything more about it. We talked soldier talk for an hour or more; the dead man lay all alone, outside in the shadow of the wall.

Then a soldier came into the cowshed and said there were some more bodies outside. We went out into the road. Four mules stood there in the moonlight, in the road where the trail came down off the mountain. The soldiers who led them stood there waiting.

"This one is Captain Waskow," one of them said quietly.

Two men unlashed his body from the mule and lifted it off and laid it in the shadow beside the stone wall. Other men took the other bodies off. Finally, there were five lying end to end in a long row. You don't cover up dead men in the combat zones. They just lie there in the shadows until somebody comes after them.

The unburdened mules moved off to their olive grove. The men in the road seemed reluctant to leave. They stood around, and gradually I could sense them moving, one by one, close to Captain Waskow's body. Not so much to look, I think, as to say something in finality to him and to themselves. I stood close by and I could hear.

One soldier came and looked down, and he said out loud, "God damn it!"

That's all he said, and then he walked away.

Another one came, and he said, "God damn it to hell anyway!" He looked down for a few last moments and then turned and left.

Another man came. I think he was an officer. It was hard to tell officers from men in the dim light, for everybody was bearded and grimy. The man looked down into the dead captain's face and then spoke directly to him, as though he were alive, "I'm sorry, old man."

Then a soldier came and stood beside the officer and bent over, and he too spoke to his dead captain, not in a whisper but awfully tenderly, and he said, "I sure am sorry, sir."

Then the first man squatted down, and he reached down and took the captain's hand, and he sat there for a full five minutes holding the dead hand in his own and looking intently into the dead face. And he never uttered a sound all the time he sat there.

Finally he put the hand down. He reached over and gently straightened the points of the captain's shirt collar, and then he sort of rearranged the tattered edges of the uniform around the wound, and then he got up and walked away down the road in the moonlight, all alone.

The rest of us went back into the cowshed, leaving the five dead men lying in a line end to end in the shadow of the low stone wall. We lay down on the straw in the cowshed, and pretty soon we were all asleep.

10.   *1943*—ROOSEVELT AT THE TEHERAN CONFERENCE

❨ *As the war progressed, the Allied heads of state met every few months to decide on joint policy. At Casablanca, early in 1943, Roosevelt and Churchill agreed on the invasion of Sicily and Italy. In late November of the same year these two statesmen met Chiang Kai-shek at Cairo, and then moved on to Teheran in Iran, where they had their first joint meeting with Stalin. The result was an agreement that the British and Americans would open a new front in Europe in May, 1944. Elliott Roosevelt gives his impressions of the Russians and his father's relations with them.*

After lunch, Father met with the American chiefs of staff to hear what progress had been made that morning. They were short and snappy: in a fast fifteen minutes Leahy, Marshall, and others told of the conversations, chiefly concerned with OVERLORD [the Normandy invasion], its time, its weight, its command.

And when they had left to resume their talks with their British opposites and the slender Soviet staff, I joined Father, in some excitement, to be with him when Stalin and Molotov came by appointment. Punctual to the minute, the Soviet leaders arrived with slender Pavlov. I was introduced. We pulled up chairs in front of Father's couch, and I sat back to collect my thoughts.

In spite of the fact that I had been told Stalin was shorter than aver-

From *As He Saw It*, by Elliott Roosevelt; copyright 1946 by Elliott Roosevelt, by permission of Duell, Sloan & Pearce, Inc. Pp. 178–80, 193–94.

age, I was surprised. I was also feeling pretty good, for I had received a very friendly greeting, together with a twinkle in the eye which invited me to smile. As he spoke—first offering Father and me each a Russian cigarette, two or three puffs of strong, black tobacco at the end of a two-inch cardboard holder—I realized something else about him: that his quiet, deep, measured voice and his short stature notwithstanding, he had a tremendously dynamic quality; inside him there seemed to be great reserves of patience and of assurance. Beside him, his Foreign Commissar, Molotov, was gray and colorless, a sort of carbon copy of my Uncle Theodore Roosevelt as I remember him. Listening to Stalin's quiet words, watching his quick, flashing smile, I sensed the determination that is in his name: Steel.

In the forty-five minutes that followed, Father and he did most of the talking. At first I paid most attention to our visitor—noting his beige uniform—well made and well cut. But after a time I listened to their words: they were discussing the Far East, China, the things that Father had already discussed with Generalissimo Chiang. Father was explaining Chiang's anxiety to end Britain's extraterritorial rights in Shanghai and Hong Kong and Canton, his anxiety about Manchuria, and the need for the Soviets' respecting the Manchurian frontier. Stalin made the point that world recognition of the sovereignty of the Soviet Union was a cardinal point with him, that most certainly he would respect, in turn, the sovereignty of other countries, large or small. Father went on to the other aspects of his conversation with Chiang, the promise that the Chinese Communists would be taken into the Government *before* any national Chinese elections, that these elections would take place as soon as possible after the war had been won. Stalin punctuated his remarks, as they were translated, with nods: he seemed in complete agreement.

This was the only phase of policy that the two discussed during this interview. For the rest, it was completely informal and relaxed, until, when it was nearly half-past three, Pa Watson looked in the door and announced that everything was ready. We got up and moved into the board room. . . .

The final meeting of the American, British, and Russian chiefs of staff was scheduled for four o'clock, and Father, the P. M., and Uncle Joe all attended. For a few minutes, while their discussions were going on, I stepped out on the balcony which overlooked the high room with its round table; constantly, around this balcony, Russian guard officers moved about, quietly and watchfully. Below, spread before me, was the proof of our united effort and our combined might: the same twelve Americans, the same eleven Britishers, the same five Russians as at the last plenary session, talking quietly, forcefully, meeting each other's arguments, coming to final agreement.

When they adjourned at six-fifteen I joined Father again, while he rested before Churchill's projected birthday party.

"It's settled at last," Father said, happily. "And," he added wrily, "for the fourth time. The western invasion is set. Even the date."

"The spring?" I asked.

"The first of May. Auspicious for the Russians: that's their big holiday, you know." Father was vastly relieved that this—as he hoped and thought—final decision had been reached, and the weight and timing of the all-out Allied effort finally buttoned up. Only the question of command was still in the air, but Father and the P. M. had promised Stalin that even this last detail would be decided upon in the extremely near future—they meant within the fortnight, if possible before they left Cairo the second time.

"And we agreed, too, that there should be a thrust up from the Mediterranean," Father added.

"Through the Balkans after all?" I asked, incredulous.

"No. Through southern France. Everything will be timed simultaneously—from the west, from the south, and the Russians from the east. I will say the end of 1944 will see the end of the war in Europe. Nobody can see how—with a really concerted drive from all sides—the Nazis can hold out much over nine months after we hit 'em."

11.   *1944*—EISENHOWER MAKES AN EPOCHAL DECISION

❨ *Immediately after the Teheran Conference, General Dwight D. Eisenhower, supreme commander of the Allied expeditionary forces, established his headquarters in England and began preparations for the cross-Channel attack. Because of the shortage of landing craft, D-day was postponed from May to June. Success depended on a favorable combination of tides, moonlight, and daylight; only on June 5, 6, and 7 could this combination be expected. June 5 was selected as the date, and the infinitely complicated machinery of invasion put in motion. When the weather turned bad, Eisenhower faced a decision of epoch-making importance. The account is his own.*

A number of other details remained to be ironed out during the days at Portsmouth preceding D-day, but the big question mark always before us was the weather that would prevail during the only period of early June that we could use, the fifth, six, and seventh.

All southern England was one vast military camp, crowded with soldiers awaiting final word to go, and piled high with supplies and equip-

From: *Crusade in Europe* by Dwight D. Eisenhower. Copyright 1948 by Doubleday & Co., Inc. Reprinted by permission of the publishers. Pp. 248–50.

ment awaiting transport to the far shore of the Channel. The whole area was cut off from the rest of England. The government had established a deadline, across which no unauthorized person was allowed to go in either direction. Every separate encampment, barrack, vehicle park, and every unit was carefully charted on our master maps. The scheduled movement of each unit had been so worked out that it would reach the embarkation point at the exact time the vessels would be ready to receive it. The southernmost camps where assault troops were assembled were all surrounded by barbed-wire entanglements to prevent any soldier leaving the camp after he had once been briefed as to his part in the attack. The mighty host was tense as a coiled spring, and indeed that is exactly what it was—a great human spring, coiled for the moment when its energy should be released and it would vault the English Channel in the greatest amphibious assault ever attempted.

We met with the Meteorologic Committee twice daily, once at nine-thirty in the evening and once at four in the morning. The committee, comprising both British and American personnel, was headed by a dour but canny Scot, Group Captain J. M. Stagg. At these meetings every bit of evidence was carefully presented, carefully analyzed by the experts, and carefully studied by the assembled commanders. With the approach of the critical period the tension continued to mount as prospects for decent weather became worse and worse.

The final conference for determining the feasibility of attacking on the tentatively selected day, June 5, was scheduled for 4:00 a.m. on June 4. However, some of the attacking contingents had already been ordered to sea, because if the entire force was to land on June 5, then some of the important elements stationed in northern parts of the United Kingdom could not wait for final decision on the morning of June 4.

When the commanders assembled on the morning of June 4 the report we received was discouraging. Low clouds, high winds, and formidable wave action were predicted to make landing a most hazardous affair. The meteorologists said that air support would be impossible, naval gunfire would be inefficient, and even the handling of small boats would be rendered difficult. Admiral Ramsay thought that the mechanics of landing could be handled, but agreed with the estimate of the difficulty in adjusting gunfire. His position was mainly neutral. General Montgomery, properly concerned with the great disadvantages of delay, believed that we should go. Tedder disagreed.

Weighing all factors, I decided that the attack would have to be postponed. This decision necessitated the immediate dispatch of orders to the vessels and troops already at sea and created some doubt as to whether they could be ready twenty-four hours later in case the next day should prove favorable for the assault. Actually the maneuver of the ships in the Irish Sea proved most difficult by reason of the storm. That they succeeded in gaining ports, refueling, and readying themselves to resume the movement a day later represented the utmost in seamanship and in brilliant command and staff work.

The conference on the evening of June 4 presented little, if any, added brightness to the picture of the morning, and tension mounted even higher because the inescapable consequences of postponement were almost too bitter to contemplate.

At three-thirty the next morning our little camp was shaking and shuddering under a wind of almost hurricane proportions and the accompanying rain seemed to be traveling in horizontal streaks. The mile-long trip through muddy roads to the naval headquarters was anything but a cheerful one, since it seemed impossible that in such conditions there was any reason for even discussing the situation.

When the conference started the first report given us by Group Captain Stagg and the Meteorologic Staff was that the bad conditions predicted the day before for the coast of France were actually prevailing there and that if we had persisted in the attempt to land on June 5 a major disaster would almost surely have resulted. This they probably told us to inspire more confidence in their next astonishing declaration, which was that by the following morning a period of relatively good weather, heretofore completely unexpected, would ensue, lasting probably thirty-six hours. The long-term prediction was not good but they did give us assurance that this short period of calm weather would intervene between the exhaustion of the storm we were then experiencing and the beginning of the next spell of really bad weather.

The prospect was not bright because of the possibility that we might land the first several waves successfully and then find later build-up impracticable, and so have to leave the isolated original attacking forces easy prey to German counteraction. However, the consequences of the delay justified great risk and I quickly announced the decision to go ahead with the attack on June 6. The time was then 4:15 a.m., June 5. No one present disagreed and there was a definite brightening of faces as, without a further word, each went off to his respective post of duty to flash out to his command the messages that would set the whole host in motion.

12. *1944*—WE TAKE THE NORMANDY BEACHES

⟨ *The assault waves struck along a hundred miles of Normandy beach on June 6. Ernie Pyle, going ashore the next day, assesses*

From *Brave Men* by Ernie Pyle. Copyright, 1943, 1944, by Scripps-Howard Newspaper Alliance. Copyright, 1944, by Henry Holt and Company, Inc. Reprinted by permission of the book publishers. Pp. 246–48, 250–53.

1 THE AMERICAN READER

*the awful wreckage, in men and material, that was the price of
success.*

Owing to a last-minute alteration in the arrangements, I didn't arrive on the beachhead until the morning after D-day, after our first
wave of assault troops had hit the shore.

By the time we got there the beaches had been taken and the fighting
had moved a couple of miles inland. All that remained on the beach
was some sniping and artillery fire, and the occasional startling blast
of a mine geysering brown sand into the air. That plus a gigantic and
pitiful litter of wreckage along miles of shore line.

Submerged tanks and overturned boats and burned trucks and shell-
shattered jeeps and sad little personal belongings were strewn all over
those bitter sands. That plus the bodies of soldiers lying in rows covered
with blankets, the toes of their shoes sticking up in a line as though on
drill. And other bodies, uncollected, still sprawling grotesquely in the
sand or half hidden by the high grass beyond the beach. That plus an
intense, grim determination of work-weary men to get that chaotic
beach organized and get all the vital supplies and the reinforcements
moving more rapidly over it from the stacked-up ships standing in
droves out to sea.

After it was over it seemed to me a pure miracle that we ever took
the beach at all. For some of our units it was easy, but in the special
sector where I landed our troops faced such odds that our getting ashore
was like my whipping Joe Louis down to a pulp. The men who did it
on that beach were men of the First and Twenty-ninth Divisions. . . .

Ashore, facing us, were more enemy troops than we had in our
assault waves. The advantages were all theirs, the disadvantages all
ours. The Germans were dug into positions they had been working on
for months, although they were not entirely complete. A 100-foot bluff
a couple of hundred yards back from the beach had great concrete gun
emplacements built right into the hilltop. These opened to the sides
instead of to the front, thus making it hard for naval fire from the
sea to reach them. They could shoot parallel with the shore and cover
every foot of it for miles with artillery fire.

Then they had hidden machine-gun nests on the forward slopes, with
crossfire taking in every inch of the beach. These nests were connected
by networks of trenches, so that the German gunners could move about
without exposing themselves.

Throughout the length of the beach, running zigzag a couple of
hundred yards back from the shore line, was an immense V-shaped
ditch fifteen feet deep. Nothing could cross it, not even men on foot,
until fills had been made. And in other places at the far end of the
beach, where the ground was flatter, they had great concrete walls.

These were blasted by our naval gunfire or by explosives set by hand after we got ashore.

Our only exits from the beach were several swales or valleys, each about a hundred yards wide. The Germans made the most of those funnellike traps, sowing them with buried mines. They also contained barbed-wire entanglements with mines attached, hidden ditches, and machine guns firing from the slopes.

All this was on the shore. But our men had to go through a maze nearly as deadly before they even got ashore. Underwater obstacles were terrific. Under the water the Germans had whole fields of evil devices to catch our boats. Several days after the landing we had cleared only channels through them and still could not approach the whole length of the beach with our ships. Even then some ship or boat would hit one of those mines and be knocked out of commission.

The Germans had masses of great six-pronged spiders—made of railroad iron and standing shoulder-high—just beneath the surface of the water, for our landing craft to run into. They had huge logs buried in the sand, pointing upward and outward, their tops just below the water. Attached to the logs were mines.

In addition to these obstacles they had floating mines offshore, land mines buried in the sand of the beach, and more mines in checkerboard rows in the tall grass beyond the sand. And the enemy had four men on shore for every three men we had approaching the shore.

And yet we got on. . . .

The first crack in the beach defenses was finally accomplished by terrific and wonderful naval gunfire, which knocked out the big emplacements. Epic stories have been told of destroyers that ran right up into shallow water and had it out point-blank with the big guns in those concrete emplacements ashore.

When the heavy fire stopped, our men were organized by their officers and pushed on inland, circling machine-gun nests and taking them from the rear.

As one officer said, the only way to take a beach is to face it and keep going. It is costly at first, but it's the only way. If the men are pinned down on the beach, dug in and out of action, they might as well not be there at all. They hold up the waves behind them, and nothing is being gained.

Our men were pinned down for a while, but finally they stood up and went through, and so we took that beach and accomplished our landing. In the light of a couple of days of retrospection, we sat and talked and called it a miracle that our men ever got on at all or were able to stay on.

They suffered casualties. And yet considering the entire beachhead assault, including other units that had a much easier time, our total casualties in driving that wedge into the Continent of Europe were remarkably low—only a fraction, in fact, of what our commanders had been prepared to accept.

And those units that were so battered and went through such hell pushed on inland without rest, their spirits high, their egotism in victory almost reaching the smart-alecky stage.

Their tails were up. "We've done it again," they said. They figured that the rest of the Army wasn't needed at all. Which proves that, while their judgment in this respect was bad, they certainly had the spirit that wins battles, and eventually wars. . . .

I walked for a mile and a half along the water's edge of our many-miled invasion beach. I walked slowly, for the detail on that beach was infinite.

The wreckage was vast and startling. The awful waste and destruction of war, even aside from the loss of human life, has always been one of its outstanding features to those who are in it. Anything and everything is expendable. And we did expend on our beachhead in Normandy during those first few hours.

For a mile out from the beach there were scores of tanks and trucks and boats that were not visible, for they were at the bottom of the water—swamped by overloading, or hit by shells, or sunk by mines. Most of their crews were lost.

There were trucks tipped half over and swamped, partly sunken barges, and the angled-up corners of jeeps, and small landing craft half submerged. And at low tide you could still see those vicious six-pronged iron snares that helped snag and wreck them.

On the beach itself, high and dry, were all kinds of wrecked vehicles. There were tanks that had only just made the beach before being knocked out. There were jeeps that had burned to a dull gray. There were big derricks on caterpillar treads that didn't quite make it. There were halftracks carrying office equipment that had been made into a shambles by a single shell hit, their interiors still holding the useless equipage of smashed typewriters, telephones, office files.

There were LCT's turned completely upside down, and lying on their backs, and how they got that way I don't know. There were boats stacked on top of each other, their sides caved in, their suspension doors knocked off.

In this shore-line museum of carnage there were abandoned rolls of barbed wire and smashed bulldozers and big stacks of thrown-away life belts and piles of shells still waiting to be moved. In the water floated empty life rafts and soldiers' packs and ration boxes, and mysterious oranges. On the beach lay snarled rolls of telephone wire and big rolls of steel matting and stacks of broken, rusting rifles.

On the beach lay, expended, sufficient men and mechanism for a small war. . . .

The strong, swirling tides of the Normandy coast line shifted the contours of the sandy beach as they moved in and out. They carried soldiers' bodies out to sea, and later they returned them. They covered the corpses of heroes with sand, and then in their whims they uncovered them.

As I plowed out over the wet sand, I walked around what seemed to be a couple of pieces of driftwood sticking out of the sand. But they weren't driftwood. They were a soldier's two feet. He was completely covered except for his feet; the toes of his GI shoes pointed toward the land he had come so far to see, and which he saw so briefly.

A few hundred yards back on the beach was a high bluff. Up there we had a tent hospital, and a barbed-wire enclosure for prisoners of war. From up there you could see far up and down the beach, in a spectacular crow's-nest view, and far out to sea.

And standing out there on the water beyond all this wreckage was the greatest armada man has ever seen. You simply could not believe the gigantic collection of ships that lay out there waiting to unload. Looking from the bluff, it lay thick and clear to the far horizon of the sea and on beyond, and it spread out to the sides and was miles wide.

As I stood up there I noticed a group of freshly taken German prisoners standing nearby. They had not yet been put in the prison cage. They were just standing there, a couple of doughboys leisurely guarding them with tommy guns.

The prisoners too were looking out to sea—the same bit of sea that for months and years had been so safely empty before their gaze. Now they stood staring almost as if in a trance. They didn't say a word to each other. They didn't need to. The expression on their faces was something forever unforgettable. In it was the final, horrified acceptance of their doom.

13.   *1944*—THE NORMANDY BREAK-OUT

❲ In six weeks of gruelling fighting the Allies enlarged the area they held on the coast of Normandy and built up their forces for a break-out. By the end of July they were ready. With the British and Canadians at the eastern end of the line pressing hard on Caen, the American forces, commanded by General Omar N. Bradley, penetrated the German defenses at St. Lô on the west. Bradley describes the battle as he saw it from the headquarters of General J. L. Collins, commanding the VII Corps.

All morning long on July 25 the air throbbed with heavy bombers

From *A Soldier's Story* by Omar N. Bradley. Copyright, 1951, by Henry Holt and Company, Inc. By permission of the publishers. Pp. 348–49, 358, 369–71, 379–80.

while I fidgeted in Collins' CP within easy reach of the telephone. Once again Eisenhower had come across the Channel to be with us on the breakout. After three days of postponement and the previous day's bad bombing, our nerves were tight and stringy.

The thunder had scarcely rolled away when casualty reports began trickling in.

Thorson handed me a TWX. "They've done it again," he said.

"Oh Christ," I cried, "not another short drop?"

He nodded and sifted the messages he still held in his hand. Air had hit the 9th and 30th Divisions a punishing blow. Both units had been rocked off balance and as the bombers floated serenely away, reserves were rushed into the gaps.

Later that afternoon Collins called to report that McNair had been killed in the short bombing. As in Tunisia where he had been seriously wounded while probing about the front, McNair had joined a battalion in the attack to view the results of stateside training. A direct hit on his foxhole had killed him. . . .

When Eisenhower took off for England that evening, the fate of COBRA still hung in doubt. Several hundred U. S. troops had been killed and wounded in the air bombing. It had dislocated Collins' advance and there was little reason to believe we stood at the brink of a breakthrough. . . .

Just as soon as Collins reorganized his line where it had been lacerated by our own bombing, and closed the gap in front to the Périers-St.-Lô road, he picked up speed through the smoking carpet. The dejection that had settled over us like a wet fog the day of the jump-off was soon burned off by preliminary reports of the destruction that greeted him there. For though air had pummeled us, it had pulverized the enemy in the carpet to litter the torn fields and roads with the black hulls of burned-out tanks, the mutilated bodies of soldiers, and the carcasses of bloated, stiff-legged cattle. By noon on July 26, a bare 24 hours after the jump-off, we sensed that the initial crisis had passed, and that the time had come for bold exploitation of the breakthrough. . . .

COBRA had caught the enemy dangerously off balance with six of his eight panzer divisions concentrated on Montgomery's front. As we splintered the line at St.-Lô, the enemy turned to shift his armor toward the breakthrough. But then as Middleton's advance down the Coutances road unhooked the German line from where it reached to the sea on the west Cotentin coast, the enemy suddenly found his left flank dangling loosely and in distress. And now as Patton pointed his tanks toward the Seine-Orléans gap, and Hodges wheeled against the loose end of that enemy line, the German command was faced with a perplexing decision. For it involved the choice as to where he would seek a showdown on the Western front. *Either* he could withdraw that loose left flank, straighten his north-south line, and hold it intact for an orderly retreat to the Seine, *or* he could gamble an Army by striking for Avranches in an effort to close our gap and peg the loose end of his line back on the sea. . . .

While strategically an attack against the Avranches hinge could have netted the German a bonanza, tactically it lay quite beyond his means. Had this choice been left to the enemy field commanders, they undoubtedly would have chosen to forego the attack in favor of a safe withdrawal across the Seine. They were aware of the vacuum that opened behind them, mindful that disaster on the Normandy front could break a path all the way to the Reich. And far better than Hitler's yes-men in Berlin, they knew how completely outclassed they were on the Normandy front. But it was characteristic of the Nazi regime that even such fateful field decisions as these be divined by the Fuehrer. Thus from his far-off command post on the Eastern front, Hitler peremptorily ordered von Kluge to stand his ground in Normandy and counterattack through the hinge with the objective of re-establishing his line at Avranches. That decision, more than any other, was to cost the enemy the Battle for France.

It was not until 1 A.M. on the morning of August 7 that the enemy collected sufficient strength to launch that fatal attack. He struck toward Mortain, just 20 miles east of the shallow Bay of Mont St. Michel. Five panzer and SS divisions formed the hammerhead of this attack, the German's first great offensive in France, his last until the Bulge. . . .

On August 19, 12 days after the enemy attacked us at Mortain, six days after Patton reached Argentan, Montgomery closed the trap at Chambois, 15 miles to the southeast of Falaise. More than 70,000 demoralized Germans were killed or captured in that pocket. . . . The bulk of 19 German divisions had been chewed up . . . ; only their mobile remnants escaped and they slipped through in broken pieces. The enemy west of the Seine had been destroyed and as he fell, the liberation of France lay only days away.

14. *1944*—BOMBERS OVER GERMANY

❨ *From 1942 until the end of the war American bombers, based on England, pounded German cities and industries. The "Flying Fortresses" specialized in pin-point daylight bombing, leaving to the Royal Air Force the nighttime saturation raids. Day or night, bombing missions made extreme demands on crews. Joseph Theodore Hallock, a bombardier from Portland, Oregon, and a First*

Brendan Gill, "Young Man Behind Plexiglas," in *The New Yorker Book of War Pieces*, pp. 286–90. By permission of the author, © 1944 The New Yorker Magazine, Inc.

Lieutenant at the age of twenty-two, tells the story of his thirty missions.

My first raid was on December thirty-first, over Ludwigshaven. Naturally, not knowing what it was going to be like, I didn't feel scared. A little sick, maybe, but not scared. That comes later, when you begin to understand what your chances of survival are. Once we'd crossed into Germany, we spotted some flak, but it was a good long distance below us and looked pretty and not dangerous: different-colored puffs making a soft, cushiony-looking pattern under our plane. A bombardier sits right in the plexiglas nose of a Fort, so he sees everything neatly laid out in front of him, like a living-room rug. It seemed to me at first that I'd simply moved in on a wonderful show. I got over feeling sick, there was so much to watch. We made our run over the target, got our bombs away, and apparently did a good job. Maybe it was the autopilot and bomb sight that saw to that, but I'm sure I was cool enough on that first raid to do my job without thinking too much about it. Then, on the way home, some Focke-Wulfs showed up, armed with rockets, and I saw three B-17s in the different groups around us suddenly blow up and drop through the sky. Just simply blow up and drop through the sky. Nowadays, if you come across something awful happening, you always think, "My God, it's just like a movie," and that's what I thought. I had a feeling that the planes weren't really falling and burning, the men inside them weren't really dying, and everything would turn out happily in the end. Then, very quietly through the interphone, our tail gunner said, "I'm sorry, sir, I've been hit."

I crawled back to him and found that he'd been wounded in the side of the head—not deeply but enough so he was bleeding pretty bad. Also, he'd got a lot of the plexiglas dust from his shattered turret in his eyes, so he was, at least for the time being, blind. The blood that would have bothered me back in California a few months before didn't bother me at all then. The Army had trained me in a given job and I went ahead and did what I was trained to do, bandaging the gunner well enough to last him back to our base. Though he was blind, he was still able to use his hands, and I ordered him to fire his guns whenever he heard from me. I figured that a few bursts every so often from his fifties would keep the Germans off our tail, and I also figured that it would give the kid something to think about besides the fact that he'd been hit. When I got back to the nose, the pilot told me that our No. 4 engine had been shot out. Gradually we lost our place in the formation and flew nearly alone over France. That's about the most dangerous thing that can happen to a lame Fort, but the German fighters had luckily given up and we skimmed over the top of the flak all the way to the Channel.

Our second raid was on Lille, and it was an easy one. Our third was on Frankfurt. France was the milk-run, Germany the bad news. On the day of a raid, we'd get up in the morning, eat breakfast, be briefed, check our equipment, crawl into the plane, maybe catch some more sleep. Then the raid, easy or tough, and we'd come back bushed, everybody sore and excited, everybody talking, hashing over the raid. Then we'd take lighted candles and write the date and place of the raid in smoke on our barracks ceiling. Maybe we wouldn't go out again for a week or ten days. Then we'd go out for four or five days in a row, taking chances, waiting for the Germans to come up and give us hell. They have a saying that nobody's afraid on his first five raids, and he's only moderately afraid on his next ten raids, but that he really sweats out all the rest of them, and that's the way it worked with me and the men I knew.

When we started our missions, we were told that after twenty-five we would probably be sent home for a rest, so that was how we kept figuring things—so many missions accomplished, so many missions still to go. We worked it all out on a mathematical basis, or on what we pretended was a mathematical basis—how many months it would take us to finish our stint, how many missions we'd have to make over Germany proper, what our chances of getting shot down were. Then, at about the halfway mark, the number of missions we would have to make was raised from twenty-five to thirty. That was one hell of a heartbreaker. Supposedly, they changed the rules of the game because flying had got that much safer, but you couldn't make us think in terms of being safer. Those five extra raids might as well have been fifty.

The pressure kept building up from raid to raid more than ever after that. The nearer we got to the end of the thirty missions, the narrower we made our odds on surviving. Those odds acted on different guys in different ways. One fellow I knew never once mentioned any member of his family, never wore a trinket, never showed us any pictures, and when he got a letter from home he read it through once and tore it up. He said he didn't trust himself to do anything else, but still it took guts. Most of the rest of us would lug a letter around and read it over and over, and show our family pictures to each other until they got cracked and dirty. There was also a difference in the way we faked our feelings. Some of the guys would say, "Well, if I managed to get through that raid, it stands to reason they'll never get me," but they didn't mean it. They were knocking on wood. Some of the other guys would say, "I'm getting it this time. I'll be meeting you in Stalag Luft tonight," but they were knocking on wood, too. We were all about equally scared all the time.

My best friend over there was an ardent Catholic. He used to pray and go to confession and Mass whenever he could. I kept telling him,

"What's the use? The whole business is written down in a book some-place. Praying won't make any difference." But whenever I got caught in a tight spot over Germany, I'd find myself whispering, "God, you gotta. You gotta get me back. God, listen, you gotta." Some of the guys prayed harder than that. They promised God a lot of stuff, like swearing off liquor and women, if He'd pull them through. I never tried to promise Him anything, because I figured that if God was really God he'd be bound to understand how men feel about liquor and women. I was lucky, anyhow, because I had something to fall back on, and that was music. I went up to London several times between missions and visited some of those Rhythm Clubs that are scattered all over the country. I listened to some good hot records and a few times I even delivered lectures on jazz. The nearest town to our base had its own Rhythm Club, and I spoke there to about a hundred and fifty people on Duke Ellington and Louis Armstrong. Now and then I got a chance to play drums in a band. That helped a lot and made it seem less like a million years ago that I'd been leading Ted Hallock's Band out at Oregon.

The missions went on and on, and the pressure kept on building. Guys I knew and liked would disappear. Somebody I'd be playing ping-pong with one day would be dead the next. It began to look as if I didn't have a chance of getting through, but I tried to take it easy. The worst raid we were ever on was one over Augsburg. That was our twenty-sixth, the one after what we expected to be our last mission. When we were briefed that morning and warned that we might be heading for trouble, I couldn't help thinking, "By God, I'm getting rooked, I ought to be heading home to Muriel and New York and Nick's this very minute."

There was never any predicting which targets the Germans would come up to fight for. I was over Berlin five times, over Frankfurt four times, over Saarbrücken, Hamm, Münster, Leipzig, Wilhelmshaven, and I had it both ways, easy and hard. We had a feeling, though, that this Augsburg show was bound to be tough, and it was. We made our runs and got off our bombs in the midst of one hell of a dogfight. Our group leader was shot down and about a hundred and fifty or two hundred German fighters swarmed over us as we headed for home. Then, screaming in from someplace, a twenty-millimetre cannon shell exploded in the nose of our Fort. It shattered the plexiglas, broke my interphone and oxygen connections, and a fragment of it cut through my heated suit and flak suit. I could feel it burning into my right shoulder and arm. My first reaction was to disconnect my heated suit. I had some idea that I might get electrocuted if I didn't.

I crawled back in the plane, wondering if anyone else needed first aid. I couldn't communicate with them, you see, with my phone dead.

I found that two shells had hit in the waist of the plane, exploding the cartridge belts stored there, and that one waist gunner had been hit in the forehead and the other in the jugular vein. I thought, "I'm wounded, but I'm the only man on the ship who can do this job right." I placed my finger against the gunner's jugular vein, applied pressure bandages, and injected morphine into him. Then I sprinkled the other man's wound with sulfa powder. We had no plasma aboard, so there wasn't much of anything else I could do. When I told the pilot that my head set had been blown off, the tail gunner thought he heard someone say that my head had been blown off, and he yelled that he wanted to jump. The pilot assured him that I was only wounded. Then I crawled back to the nose of the ship to handle my gun, fussing with my wounds when I could and making use of an emergency bottle of oxygen.

The German fighters chased us for about forty-five minutes. They came so close that I could see the pilots' faces, and I fired so fast that my gun jammed. I went back to the left nose gun and fired that gun till *it* jammed. By that time we'd fallen behind the rest of the group, but the Germans were beginning to slack off. It was turning into a question of whether we could sneak home without having to bail out. The plane was pretty well shot up and the whole oxygen system had been cut to pieces. The pilot told us we had the choice of trying to get back to England, which would be next to impossible, or of flying to Switzerland and being interned, which would be fairly easy. He asked us what we wanted to do. I would have voted for Switzerland, but I was so busy handing out bottles of oxygen that before I had a chance to say anything the other men said, "What the hell, let's try for England." After a while, with the emergency oxygen running out, we had to come down to ten thousand feet, which is dangerously low. We saw four fighters dead ahead of us, somewhere over France, and we thought we were licked. After a minute or two we discovered that they were P-47s, more beautiful than any woman who ever lived. I said, "I think now's the time for a short prayer, men. Thanks, God, for what you've done for us."

When we got back to our base, I found a batch of nineteen letters waiting for me, but I couldn't read a single one of them. I just walked up and down babbling and shaking and listening to the other guys babble. I had my wounds looked at, but they weren't serious. The scars are already beginning to fade a little, and the wounds didn't hurt me much at the time. Still, I never wanted to go up again. I felt sure I couldn't go up again. On the day after the raid, I didn't feel any better, and on the second day after the raid I went to my squadron commander and told him that I had better be sent up at once or I'd never be of any use to him again. So he sent me up in another plane on what he must have known would be a fairly easy raid over France, the milk run, and that helped.

That was my twenty-seventh mission. The twenty-eighth was on Berlin, and I was scared damn near to death. It was getting close to the end and my luck was bound to be running out faster and faster. The raid wasn't too bad, though, and we got back safe. The twenty-ninth mission was to Thionville, in France, and all I thought about on that run was "One more, one more, one more." My last mission was to Saarbrücken. One of the waist gunners was new, a young kid like the kid I'd been six months before. He wasn't a bit scared—just cocky and excited. Over Saarbrücken he was wounded in the foot by a shell, and I had to give him first aid. He acted more surprised than hurt. He had a look on his face like a child who's been cheated by grownups.

That was only the beginning for him, but it was the end for me. I couldn't believe it when I got back to the base. I kept thinking, "Maybe they'll change the rules again, maybe I won't be going home, maybe I'll be going up with that kid again, maybe I'll have another five missions, another ten, another twenty." I kept thinking those things, but I wasn't especially bitter about them. I knew then, even when I was most scared, that fliers have to be expendable, that that's what Eaker and Doolittle had us trained for. That's what war is. The hell with pampering us. We're supposed to be used up. If the Army worried one way or another about our feelings, it'd never get any of us out of Santa Ana or Deming.

15.   1945—THE DEATH OF ROOSEVELT

❨ *In spite of signs of failing health, President Roosevelt was nominated and re-elected in 1944. In early April, 1945, he went to Warm Springs, Georgia, to rest. There, on the afternoon of April 12, he died. Grace Tully describes the end.*

Dewey Long talked to F.D.R. a few minutes that morning in connection with the proposed trip to San Francisco. Long proposed a scenic route through Colorado but the Boss instructed him to set up the most direct itinerary between Washington, Chicago, and San Francisco.

Meanwhile, in company with Toi, Hacky and Dorothy, I had gone to the pool for a swim. Dr. Bruenn was there also and when we left shortly before 1:00 o'clock, he was dressing for lunch.

I proposed to the other girls that we go directly to Georgia Hall for our own lunch but as we neared our cottage, Hacky said she wanted to check her own switchboard and speak to the Foundation operator. As soon as she got on the line the Georgia Hall operator asked if she knew the whereabouts of Dr. Bruenn.

"Who wants him?" Hacky asked in her businesslike voice. "We just left him at the pool."

From *F. D. R. My Boss* by Grace Tully, copyright 1949 by Grace Tully. Reprinted by permission of Charles Scribner's Sons. Pp. 361–65.

"The Little White House," the other operator answered.

Hacky plugged in at once to the President's cottage. Daisy, the cook, answered and confirmed the inquiry for Dr. Bruenn.

"Does the President want him for lunch?" Hacky asked.

"No, he's sick," Daisy replied. "The President's sick."

"I'll get him right away," Hacky said and her voice crackled with efficiency. "The President's sick," she said to us as she jammed the plug in and rang the pool dressing room.

"The President's sick," she repeated as soon as Dr. Bruenn came to the phone. "They want you right away."

She listened for a moment, then plugged in on another connection to get George Fox.

"George, the President's sick. Dr. Bruenn wants you to go to his cottage, pick up his bag and meet him just as soon as possible at the Little White House."

I could feel a chill in my heart, a sense that this was something different from another complaint about his sinus acting up or his tummy being out of whack. I decided to go at once to the President's cottage.

By the time I reached the house, both Bruenn and Fox were with the President in his bedroom. Miss Suckley was in the living room, Miss Delano entered from the bedroom as I walked in. There were sounds of tortured breathing from the bedroom and low voices of the two men attending him. Miss Delano and Miss Suckley looked shocked and frightened; the former told me the President had finished some work with Mr. Hassett and was sitting for Madame Shoumatoff. At 1:00 o'clock the President remarked to the artist, "We have only fifteen minutes." At 1:15 he put his hand to his head and slumped backward in a coma. Prettyman and a Filipino house boy had carried him from his chair to his bedroom.

Hacky already had gotten Dr. McIntire on the phone in Washington and had put Bruenn on the line with him. At McIntire's instruction, Dr. James E. Paullin, a heart specialist in Atlanta, had been summoned. Dr. Paullin made a desperately fast automobile trip to Warm Springs and arrived while we were waiting anxiously in the living room.

Almost within seconds of Paullin's arrival, Bruenn was called again by Dr. McIntire. While on the phone he was summoned back to the bedroom. Bruenn left the line open as he disappeared into the Boss's room. In a minute or so he was back. With a tragically expressive gesture of his hands he picked up the phone again. I knew what his message was before he spoke. The President was dead.

My reaction of the moment was one of complete lack of emotion. It was as if my whole mind and sense of feeling had been swept away. The shock was unexpected and the actuality of the event was outside belief. Without a word or a glance toward the others present, I walked into the bedroom, leaned over and kissed the President lightly on the forehead. Then I walked out on the porch and stood wordless and tearless. In my heart were prayers and, finally, in my mind came thoughts, a flood of them drawn from seventeen years of acquaintance, close association and reverent admiration. Through them, one recurred constantly—that the Boss had always shunned emotionalism and that I must, for the immediate present at least, behave in his pattern. I did, for a matter of hours.

The death of a President cannot be accepted with inertia. His life, for more than twelve years, had belonged to the people of the United States and, in fact, to the free peoples of the world. His death must, in a sense, be shared with them. . . .

Eventually—it was not as long as it seemed—Steve Early was back on the line from Washington. Mrs. Roosevelt had finished her speech and was told what had happened by Steve. Hassett told Hacky to call the correspondents back and ask them to meet him at his cottage. Dr. Bruenn and I rode with Bill to his cottage to wait for them.

From the circumstances of the summons the three reporters knew that there was urgency and importance in their recall. They arrived quickly, driven in an Army car by a Communications Sergeant. From the expressions on our faces they probably knew what the announcement was to be; they were not kept waiting.

Hassett was standing near the center of the living room.

"Gentlemen," he said quietly, "It is my sad duty to inform you that the President of the United States is dead. He died at 3:35 o'clock this afternoon, Central Standard Time."

There were three separate telephone lines into the cottage, one in the living room and one in each of two adjoining bedrooms. Frantically, the three scrambled for the phones, put in calls to their Washington offices through Hacky's switchboard. They were through in three or four minutes, by which time Steve Early was making a simultaneous announcement in Washington. It was shortly after 5 o'clock.

Still on their phones, the correspondents next fired a barrage of questions at Hassett and Bruenn.

"What was the cause of death?"

"A massive cerebral hemorrhage," Dr. Bruenn replied.

"Had you seen the President today, Bill?"

"Yes, at about noon. He signed some bills and some mail."

"Was he ill then, or in good spirits?"

"He seemed to be fine. He joked about all the 'laundry' I had to dry."

The term "laundry" was applied to bills which the President signed and which Mr. Hassett then laid out individually until the signature had dried without blotting.

"Who was with him when he was stricken?"

"Madame Shoumatoff was working on her portrait of him."

"Did he have any warning of the attack, or know it was coming?"

"Madame Shoumatoff says that he had reminded her that 'we have just fifteen minutes'."

Those were the last words he spoke. It had been exactly fifteen minutes after those words that he collapsed.

The questioning went on in this manner at some length, hurriedly but with a grim solemnity. No one broke but the strain was biting deeper into each of us. One of his last official actions had been to approve the design of a United Nations stamp, and an approval that had been given over the telephone to Postmaster General Frank Walker after the Boss had studied several alternative samples. And on his bedside table was a paper-covered detective story with a page turned down at a chapter headed: "Six Feet of Earth."

16. *1945—"it's all over"*: the war ends in europe

❨ *After a serious but temporary setback in December, 1944 (the Battle of the Bulge), the Allied forces drove the German armies relentlessly. In late March American troops crossed the Rhine. With Russia pressing in from the east, Allied forces moving up in northern Italy and others in Austria, Germany collapsed. Hitler committed suicide, and the commanders of the German army and navy signed articles of surrender.*

General Omar N. Bradley, in the West German town of Bad Wildungen, relates how he received and relayed the news of victory.

While Alexander accepted the surrender of Kesselring's forces in Italy and Montgomery denied terms to Admiral Hans Friedeburg on the Luneberg Heath, we continued to press on into Austria, killing those Germans who still resisted, capturing those who had given up.

Reports reached us of a surrender mission that was rumored en route to SHAEF but Eisenhower had not called to confirm them. On May 6, I went to bed shortly before midnight after writing a letter home to my wife.

It was not yet 4 A.M. when the telephone rang on my bedside table in the Fürstenhof Hotel. I sat up and switched on a lamp. It was Eisenhower calling from Reims.

"Brad," he said, "it's all over. A TWX is on the way."

Jodl had signed for the German army; Friedeburg for the navy. The surrender had taken place at 2:41 that morning in the schoolhouse

From *A Soldier's Story* by Omar N. Bradley. Copyright, 1951, by Henry Holt and Company, Inc. By permission of the publishers. Pp. 553-54.

SHAEF had requisitioned near the marshaling yards of Reims.

I buzzed the operator for LUCKY SIX and roused Patton from his trailer in Regensberg. "Ike just called me, George. The Germans have surrendered. It takes effect at midnight, May 8. We're to hold in place everywhere up and down the line. There's no sense in taking any more casualties now."

Hodges was asleep in the ornate home he had requisitioned in Weimar. Simpson occupied the commandant's quarters of a Luftwaffe headquarters at Brunswick. I repeated the message to both. By the time I had reached Gerow, then in bed with a cold near Bonn, it was almost 6:30. I could hear the mess kits rattling in the chow line outside the hotel. I crawled out of bed and dressed.

A canvas map case lay under my helmet with its four silver stars. Only five years before on May 7, as a lieutenant colonel in civilian clothes, I had ridden a bus down Connecticut Avenue to my desk in the old Munitions Building.

I opened the mapboard and smoothed out the tabs of the 43 U. S. divisions now under my command. They stretched across a 640-mile front of the 12th Army Group.

With a china-marking pencil, I wrote in the new date: D plus 335.

I walked to the window and ripped open the blackout blinds. Outside the sun was climbing into the sky. The war in Europe had ended.

17.   *1945—D-DAY, IWO JIMA*

⟨ Early in 1945 the United States began to prepare for the invasion of Japan. A necessary step was the occupation of Iwo Jima, one of the Bonin Islands about 750 miles south of Tokyo. Iwo Jima was essential to the preparatory aerial attack: it would offer a base for fighter planes protecting bombers raiding Japan, and provide an emergency landing field for the bombers themselves.

The Marines took Iwo Jima. The Fourth and Fifth Divisions swarmed ashore on February 19; the Third Division landed later in the month. John Lardner, war correspondent, describes the stubborn Japanese defense, which inflicted more than 21,000 casualties before the island was completely occupied.

D Day was Monday, February 19th, and H Hour was 0900. On D-minus-one, the regimental surgeon reported a hundred and twenty-five cases of diarrhea among the men and officers aboard. This had come from something they ate, but that evening the Navy cooks did better and served everyone a turkey dinner with ice cream. At the last

John Lardner, "D Day, Iwo Jima," in *The New Yorker Book of War Pieces*, pp. 464–71. By permission of the author, © 1945 The New Yorker Magazine, Inc.

meal, breakfast at 0500 the morning of the nineteenth, there were steak and eggs. Everyone had dressed in his green combat blouse and trousers and had strapped on his pistol belt, with a long knife, ammunition, a bandage roll, and one or two canteens attached, and had checked his carbine. After breakfast, everyone put on his helmet, which had a camouflage cover simulating sand, and went out on deck and over to the ladder nets. The sun was just coming up, so Iwo Jima was visible from our line of debarkation, which was several miles out at sea. There the larger transports halted, to keep beyond the range of shore batteries, and put off their cargoes of Marines into small boats. On Suribachi, the volcano at the south end of the island, we could see bursts of fire and smoke from our naval shelling, which continued till H Hour. Some of the men stared at the island. Others remarked that the wind was running in our favor, from the northwest, and that the sea was calmer than it had been, though still difficult. Many could think of nothing but the immediate necessity of climbing the slick, flaccid web of rope down the ship's side without looking silly or getting killed. Even young Marines have been killed on these descents when the sea has been rough, and for those over thirty-five the endless sequence of nets, Jacob's ladders, bouncing gangways, and lurching boats is a hazard and nightmare which can occupy their minds to the exclusion of all other dangers. Admirals and generals can look ridiculous in these circumstances. They are well aware of it, and their tempers during amphibious operations are correspondingly short.

I got into a small boat with Colonel Thomas Wornham, regimental commander, and some of his staff, his messengers, and his radio operators. We chopped and splashed through the ocean swells to Wornham's control ship, which was anchored nearer the shore, at the line at which the first assault troops formed up in their amtracks and began their long, slow, bobbing run for the beach. They went in in ragged waves, which left the departure line at intervals of a few minutes, coached hoarsely by a loudspeaker from the bridge of the control ship. The men in the amtracks were a fierce and stirring sight as they passed us to disappear in the valleys of water between us and the beach. I stood watching them as well as I could from the rail of the control ship beside a regimental messenger, a Navajo Indian named Galeagon, and we spoke of how most of the shock troops we could see, their hands and faces greased dead white for protection against possible flame barriers, sat up very straight and looked intently ahead. The first wave struck the beach approximately at the appointed hour of nine, and simultaneously the Navy shellfire, which had been raking the shoreline, jumped its range to the ridges and pillboxes farther inland. The central ridge was in our sector of the island. We could see the wreckage of Japanese planes piled at one edge of the plateau. We knew that an airfield lay just beyond this junk—one of the two airfields for which the Marines were beginning the dogged battle of Iwo Jima. . . .

Wornham's Higgins boat, a rectangular little launch with a hinged landing ramp in the bow, pulled up on the starboard quarter of our ship, and those of us who were going ashore with the Colonel climbed down a ladder and jumped in. It was exactly 1100, or two hours after the first landings, and this was the fourteenth wave. I should say that we were the fourteenth wave. As far as I could see, no other boat was moving shoreward at that moment. As we cast off, Galeagon came to the ship's rail and yelled something at us through a megaphone. Wornham, a short, stocky career Marine of about forty, smiling and convivial on our voyage north but now very taut and serious, leaned precariously over the stern of the boat, clutching at the rail, and cupped a hand to one ear. "Red One now under heavy mortar fire!" shouted the messenger. The Fifth Division's share of the beaches was Green Beach and Red Beaches One and Two. To the north, the Fourth Division had landed on Yellow One and Two and Blue One and Two. We were fifty feet from the control ship when Galeagon yelled another message. "Red Two under mortar fire," he said, the sound of his voice seeming to bounce across the waves. "Heavy mortar fire on both Red beaches." The others in the boat looked with expressionless faces at Wornham, who smiled wryly. "Head for a point about a hundred feet to the right of the line between Red One and Two," he told the coxswain. Then he turned to the rest of us and said, "All right, be ready to bail out of here goddam fast when we touch that beach. . . ."

We saw puffs of smoke—white, gray, and black—pluming from the beach as our boat came closer. Most of the men in the boat, whose first task was to set up a regimental command post somewhere between the beach and the front lines, were burdened with radio equipment. Alwyn Lee, an Australian war correspondent, and I were also fairly cumbrously loaded. A pack in three light pieces is more trouble than a single heavy pack, and I had, in addition to my Army musette bag, a typewriter and a blanket roll containing a poncho and a small spade, or entrenching tool. I also had a sash-type life belt buckled around my waist, in conformance a few hours earlier with a transport regulation. This belt dropped off and vanished that day on Iwo Jima, I don't know when or where.

The landing ramp slapped down on the beach and the passengers bustled out with their loads and disappeared behind the first low hummock in the sand. I was on the point of disembarking, second to last, just ahead of the Colonel, when I realized that I had forgotten my gear, and in the moment it took to turn and pick it up piecemeal, Wornham whizzed by me and was gone. I slogged up the beach across one wind-made ridge and trench and then another. Loose, dark sand came up to the tops of my high combat boots at each step, and my breathing was sharp and painful. I made it to the third and deepest trench, some thirty yards in from the shore, and fell to my face there alongside Lee and several men of the command-post detail. When you stopped running or slogging, you became conscious of the whine and bang of mortar shells dropping and bursting near you. All up and down Red Beaches One and Two, men were lying in trenches like ours, listening to shells and digging or pressing their bodies closer into the sand around them. . . .

Lee and I, by agreement, finally left our gear in a trench near the shore (we planned to salvage it later, if possible) and worked our way up the beach in the wake of Wornham and his men. There were Marines on all sides of us doing the same thing. Each man had a different method of progress. One, carbine in hand, walked along steadily, pausing and dropping to one knee only when something about the sound of the shells seemed to confuse him. Another made a high-hurdling jump into every trench or hole he used. At one point I listened to a frail Nisei interpreter arguing with an officer who wanted to help carry his pack. Again, at a moment when Lee and I were catching our breath, something stirred beside the dune just behind us. A wounded man, his face blackened by sand and powder, had roused himself from the lethargy in which he lay and noticed us. Shell fragments had hit him in one arm, one leg, the buttocks, and one eye. His eye, a red circle in his dark-stained face, worried him most. He wanted to know if there were any medical corpsmen with a litter nearby. He had been so deafened by the explosion of the shell that I had to go very close to make him hear me. There were no corpsmen or litters about. In fact, the enemy fire on the beach made it hard to get help to wounded men for the first two days, and then the process of evacuating them in boats, which had to bump their way through a high surf, was incredibly rough and painful. I promised this man to report him and get him help as soon as possible.

The next Marine we passed was dead, and so were a number of others on our diagonal course over the beach to the upland, but I didn't see a dead Japanese soldier until we got near the edge of the plateau. "That's the third one we've found on Red beaches today so far," said a soldier who sat near the mouth of a Jap concrete pillbox, which gave off a faint, foul smell. This pillbox, with walls three feet thick and built on a frame of metal tubing, was a good specimen of the Jap defenses on Iwo Jima, but in the days that followed I saw others even more substantial, with walls four to five feet thick, revolving gun turrets, and two or more approaches lined with neat stairs.

It seemed clear, by the time we reached Wornham's command post, now at least several minutes old, in a broad shellhole above the beach, that the Japs had quickly abandoned the beaches, after losing a few men, and had taken most of their dead with them. This worried Wornham, because he figured that it meant heavy counterattacks in the next night or two, and he was also worried, as regimental commanders are everywhere in battle, by the problem of keeping his combat battalions in communication with each other and with him. Sitting in his shellhole, along with a couple of dozen staff men, medical officers, messengers, radio operators, and stray visitors who just wanted to be in a hole with other people, we followed, by radio and courier, the adventures of three battalions a few hundred yards away. The battalions were known in Wornham's shellhole by their commanders' names—Robbie, Tony, and Butler. "Tony says he's ready to make his turn up the west beach," Wornham said fretfully, looking at a message in his hand. "I gotta get him." Now and then he looked around his hole and said plaintively, "Come on, let's break this up. Let's have some room here." At these words, a few of the strays would drift away in one direction or another, and a few minutes later others would take their places. The shells dropped more rarely in that neighborhood, but they were close enough. Tanks began to rumble up from the beach, at long intervals, and angle and stutter their way through a gap at the top of the ridge nearby. Purple Heart Louis came to the edge of the command post and had his right arm bandaged by a doctor to whom we had already reported the position of the wounded Marine on the beach. "I knew Louis would get it again," said a young captain. "Right where he deals the cards, too. I hope it will be a lesson to him."

By the time we reached a hole by the water's edge, near where we had landed, we had lost our sense of urgency and entered the stage, which comes after a certain amount of time in a shelled area, when you can no longer bring yourself to duck and run constantly, even when you are moving in the open. But the men in the boats along the shoreline immediately aroused us. Since they came into the fire zone only at intervals and remained as briefly as possible, they had no time to lose their awareness of danger. It suddenly seemed to us a matter of desperate importance to get out of there at once. An ammunition dump was beginning to grow up around us, and the shelling did not abate. . . .

It was getting dark and our clothes and equipment were nearly dry again when we finally boarded an LCT bound for the general neighborhood of the flagship. Five sailors returning from a shore job were grouped in a corner of the hold aft, where the boat's sides rose above their heads. As the vessel pulled out, we saw that four of them were trying vaguely to soothe the fifth, who was in the throes of shock from a near miss by a shell. He was a small young man with an underslung lower jaw. His head lolled back against the bulwark and his eyes rolled violently. "They can't get you here," said one of his colleagues, pointing at the boat's high sides. "Look. They can't even see you." By the time we were a couple of miles out, the sailor had recovered to the point of asking questions about the battle, but these and the answers he himself supplied only had the effect of returning him to a state of shock. The four others stopped looking at him and talked listlessly among themselves. . . .

The nature of the Iwo Jima battle did not change much in the days that immediately followed. The Marines made slow and costly gains in ground as they fought northward—gains that struck me then, and still do, as very little short of miraculous. A week or so after D Day, in a little scrub grove halfway across the island, I recognized, behind his whiskers, a staff officer in our transport group who used to surprise me a little by the passion and complete engrossment with which he could discuss for two or three hours at a time such a question as whether or not certain items of battalion equipment should be distributed divisionally, or whether a brother officer of his named Logan, thirty-five hundred miles away, stood eighty-sixth or eighty-seventh on the promotion list. It now seemed to me that such preoccupations were useful indeed if they contributed to the professional doggedness with which this man and the troops of his unit moved forward against such overpowering intimations of mortality. "I hear that the mortar fire is easing up on the beaches," he said seriously. "That's good. There's no reason why everybody on the island should get killed."

18. *1945*—TRUMAN DECIDES TO USE THE ATOM BOMB

❲ *In the end the atom bomb rather than invasion would force Japan to surrender. President Truman, who succeeded Roosevelt on April 12, recounts the steps by which he came to a momentous decision.*

[April 12.] That first meeting of the Cabinet was short, and when it adjourned, the members rose and silently made their way from the room —except for Secretary Stimson.

He asked to speak to me about a most urgent matter. Stimson told me that he wanted me to know about an immense project that was under way—a project looking to the development of a new explosive of almost unbelievable destructive power. That was all he felt free to say at the time, and his statement left me puzzled. It was the first bit of information that had come to me about the atomic bomb, but he gave me no details. It was not until the next day that I was told enough to give me some understanding of the almost incredible developments that were under way and the awful power that might soon be placed in our hands. . . .

[April 24] During the day I received from Secretary of War Stimson the following communication:

"Dear Mr. President, I think it is very important that I should have a talk with you as soon as possible on a highly secret matter. I mentioned it to you shortly after you took office but have not urged it since on account of the pressure you have been under. It, however, has such a bearing on our present foreign relations and has such an important effect upon all my thinking in this field that I think you ought to know about it without much further delay."

I knew he was referring to our secret atomic project, and I instructed Matt Connelley, my appointment secretary, to arrange for the Secretary to come in the next day. . . .

[April 25] At noon I saw Secretary of War Stimson in connection with the urgent letter he had written.

Stimson was one of the very few men responsible for the setting up of the atomic bomb project. He had taken a keen and active interest in every stage of its development. He said he wanted specifically to talk to me today about the effect the atomic bomb might likely have on our future foreign relations.

He explained that he thought it necessary for him to share his thoughts with me about the revolutionary changes in warfare that might result from the atomic bomb and the possible effects of such a weapon on our civilization.

I listened with absorbed interest, for Stimson was a man of great wisdom and foresight. He went into considerable detail in describing the nature and power of the projected weapon. If expectations were to be realized, he told me, the atomic bomb would be certain to have a decisive influence on our relations with other countries. And if it worked, the bomb, in all probability, would shorten the war.

Byrnes had already told me that the weapon might be so powerful as to be potentially capable of wiping out entire cities and killing people on an unprecedented scale. And he had added that in his belief the bomb might well put us in a position to dictate our own terms at the end of the war. Stimson, on the other hand, seemed at least as much concerned with the role of the atomic bomb in the shaping of history as in its capacity to shorten this war. As yet, of course, no one could positively know that all the gigantic effort that was being made would be successful. Nevertheless, the Secretary appeared confident of the outcome and told me that in all probability success would be attained within the next few months. He also suggested that I designate a committee to study and advise me of the implications of this new force. . . .

[June 1] The conclusions reached by these men, both in the advisory committee of scientists and in the larger committee, were brought to me by Secretary Stimson on June 1.

It was their recommendation that the bomb be used against the enemy as soon as it could be done. They recommended further that it should be used without specific warning and against a target that would clearly show its devastating strength. I had realized, of course, that an atomic bomb explosion would inflict damage and casualties beyond imagination. On the other hand, the scientific advisers of the committee reported, "We can propose no technical demonstration likely to bring an end to the war; we see no acceptable alternative to direct military use." It was their conclusion that no technical demonstration they might propose, such as over a deserted island, would be likely to bring the war to an end. It had to be used against an enemy target.

The final decision of where and when to use the atomic bomb was up to me. Let there be no mistake about it. I regarded the bomb as a military weapon and never had any doubt that it should be used. The top military advisers to the President recommended its use, and when I talked to Churchill he unhesitatingly told me that he favored the use of the atomic bomb if it might aid to end the war.

In deciding to use this bomb I wanted to make sure that it would be used as a weapon of war in the manner prescribed by the laws of war. That meant that I wanted it dropped on a military target. I had told Stimson that the bomb should be dropped as nearly as possible upon a war production center of prime military importance. . . . Four cities were finally recommended as targets: Hiroshima, Kokura, Niigata, and Nagasaki. . . .

19.   *1945*—HIROSHIMA

❮ *By early August the bomb was ready. On the 6th a B29 dropped it on Hiroshima, an important Japanese industrial city of 380,000. The effect was devastating beyond anything the mind of man had been able to imagine. The classic account is that of John Hersey, who interviewed many of the survivors.*

The Reverend Mr. Tanimoto got up at five o'clock that morning. He was alone in the parsonage, because for some time his wife had been commuting with their year-old baby to spend nights with a friend in Ushida, a suburb to the north. Of all the important cities of Japan, only two, Kyoto and Hiroshima, had not been visited in strength by *B-san*, or Mr. B, as the Japanese, with a mixture of respect and unhappy familiarity, called the B-29; and Mr. Tanimoto, like all his neighbors and friends, was almost sick with anxiety. He had heard uncomfortably detailed accounts of mass raids on Kure, Iwakuni, Tokuyama, and other

John Hersey, "Hiroshima," in *The New Yorker Book of War Pieces*, pp. 507-12, 514-17. By permission of the author, © 1946 The New Yorker Magazine, Inc.

nearby towns; he was sure Hiroshima's turn would come soon. He had slept badly the night before, because there had been several air-raid warnings. Hiroshima had been getting such warnings almost every night for weeks, for at that time the B-29s were using Lake Biwa, northeast of Hiroshima, as a rendezvous point, and no matter what city the Americans planned to hit, the Superfortresses streamed in over the coast near Hiroshima. The frequency of the warnings and the continued abstinence of Mr. B with respect to Hiroshima had made its citizens jittery; a rumor was going around that the Americans were saving something special for the city.

Mr. Tanimoto is a small man, quick to talk, laugh, and cry. He wears his black hair parted in the middle and rather long; the prominence of the frontal bones just above his eyebrows and the smallness of his mustache, mouth, and chin give him a strange, old-young look, boyish and yet wise, weak and yet fiery. He moves nervously and fast, but with a restraint which suggests that he is a cautious, thoughtful man. He showed, indeed, just those qualities in the uneasy days before the bomb fell. Besides having his wife spend the nights in Ushida, Mr. Tanimoto had been carrying all the portable things from his church, in the close-packed residential district called Nagaragawa, to a house that belonged to a rayon manufacturer in Koi, two miles from the center of town. The rayon man, a Mr. Matsui, had opened his then unoccupied estate to a large number of his friends and acquaintances, so that they might evacuate whatever they wished to a safe distance from the probable target area. Mr. Tanimoto had had no difficulty in moving chairs, hymnals, Bibles, altar gear, and church records by pushcart himself, but the organ console and an upright piano required some aid. A friend of his named Matsuo had, the day before, helped him get the piano out to Koi; in return, he had promised this day to assist Mr. Matsuo in hauling out a daughter's belongings. That is why he had risen so early.

Mr. Tanimoto cooked his own breakfast. He felt awfully tired. The effort of moving the piano the day before, a sleepless night, weeks of worry and unbalanced diet, the cares of his parish—all combined to make him feel hardly adequate to the new day's work. There was another thing, too: Mr. Tanimoto had studied theology at Emory University, in Atlanta, Georgia; he had graduated in 1940; he spoke excellent English; he dressed in American clothes; he had corresponded with many American friends right up to the time the war began; and among a people obsessed with a fear of being spied upon—perhaps almost obsessed himself—he found himself growing increasingly uneasy. The police had questioned him several times, and just a few days before he had heard that an influential acquaintance, a Mr. Tanaka, a retired officer of the Toyo Kisen Kaisha steamship line, an anti-Christian, a man famous in Hiroshima for his showy philanthropies and notorious for his personal tyrannies, had been telling people that Tanimoto should not be trusted. In compensation, to show himself publicly a good Japanese, Mr. Tanimoto had taken on the chairmanship of his local *tonarigumi,* or Neighborhood Association, and to his other duties and concerns this position had added the business of organizing air-raid defense for about twenty families.

Before six o'clock that morning, Mr. Tanimoto started for Mr. Matsuo's house. There he found that their burden was to be a *tansu,* a large Japanese cabinet, full of clothing and household goods. The two men set out. The morning was perfectly clear and so warm that the day promised to be uncomfortable. A few minutes after they started, the air-raid siren went off—a minute-long blast that warned of approaching planes but indicated to the people of Hiroshima only a slight degree of danger, since it sounded every morning at this time, when an American weather plane came over. The two men pulled and pushed the handcart through the city streets. Hiroshima was a fan-shaped city, lying mostly on the six islands formed by the seven estuarial rivers that branch out from the Ota River; its main commercial and residential districts, covering about four square miles in the center of the city, contained three-quarters of its population, which had been reduced by several evacuation programs from a wartime peak of 380,000 to about 245,000. Factories and other residential districts, or suburbs, lay compactly around the edges of the city. To the south were the docks, an airport, and the island-studded Inland Sea. A rim of mountains runs around the other three sides of the delta. Mr. Tanimoto and Mr. Matsuo took their way through the shopping center, already full of people, and across two of the rivers to the sloping streets of Koi, and up them to the outskirts and foothills. As they started up a valley away from the tight-ranked houses, the all-clear sounded. (The Japanese radar operators, detecting only three planes, supposed that they comprised a reconnaissance.) Pushing the handcart up to the rayon man's house was tiring, and the men, after they had maneuvered their load into the driveway and to the front steps, paused to rest awhile. They stood with a wing of the house between them and the city. Like most homes in this part of Japan, the house consisted of a wooden frame and wooden walls supporting a heavy tile roof. Its front hall, packed with rolls of bedding and clothing, looked like a cool cave full of fat cushions. Opposite the house, to the right of the front door, there was a large, finicky rock garden. There was no sound of planes. The morning was still; the place was cool and pleasant.

Then a tremendous flash of light cut across the sky. Mr. Tanimoto had a distinct recollection that it travelled from east to west, from the city toward the hills. It seemed a sheet of sun. Both he and Mr. Matsuo reacted in terror—and both had time to react (for they were 3,500 yards, or two miles, from the center of the explosion). Mr. Matsuo dashed up the front steps into the house and dived among the bedrolls and buried himself there. Mr. Tanimoto took four or five steps and threw himself between two big rocks in the garden. He bellied up very hard against one of them. As his face was against the stone, he did not see what happened. He felt a sudden pressure, and then splinters and pieces of board and fragments of tile fell on him. He heard no roar. (Almost no one in Hiroshima recalls hearing any noise of the bomb. But a fisherman in his sampan on the Inland Sea near Tsuzu, the man with whom Mr. Tanimoto's mother-in-law and sister-in-law were living, saw the flash and heard a tremendous explosion; he was nearly twenty miles from Hiroshima, but the thunder was greater than when the B-29s hit Iwakuni, only five miles away.)

When he dared, Mr. Tanimoto raised his head and saw that the rayon man's house had collapsed. He thought a bomb had fallen directly on it. Such clouds of dust had risen that there was a sort of twilight around. In panic, not thinking for the moment of Mr. Matsuo under the ruins, he dashed out into the street. He noticed as he ran that the concrete wall of the estate had fallen over—toward the house rather than away from it. In the street, the first thing he saw was a squad of soldiers who had been burrowing into the hillside opposite, making one of the thousands of dugouts in which the Japanese apparently intended to re- sist invasion, hill by hill, life for life; the soldiers were coming out of the hole, where they should have been safe, and blood was running from their heads, chests, and backs. They were silent and dazed.

Under what seemed to be a local dust cloud, the day grew darker and darker.

At nearly midnight, the night before the bomb was dropped, an an- nouncer on the city's radio station said that about two hundred B-29s were approaching southern Honshu and advised the population of Hiro- shima to evacuate to their designated "safe areas." Mrs. Hatsuyo Naka- mura, the tailor's widow, who lived in the section called Nobori-cho and who had long had a habit of doing as she was told, got her three children—a ten-year-old boy, Toshio, an eight-year-old girl, Yaeko, and a five-year-old girl, Myeko—out of bed and dressed them and walked with them to the military area known as the East Parade Ground, on the northeast edge of the city. There she unrolled some mats and the children lay down on them. They slept until about two, when they were awakened by the roar of the planes going over Hiroshima.

As soon as the planes had passed, Mrs. Nakamura started back with her children. They reached home a little after two-thirty and she imme- diately turned on the radio, which, to her distress, was just then broad- casting a fresh warning. When she looked at the children and saw how tired they were, and when she thought of the number of trips they had made in past weeks, all to no purpose, to the East Parade Grounds, she decided that in spite of the instructions on the radio, she simply could not face starting out all over again. She put the children in their bedrolls on the floor, lay down herself at three o'clock, and fell asleep at once, so soundly that when planes passed over later, she did not waken to their sound.

The siren jarred her awake at about seven. She arose, dressed quickly, and hurried to the house of Mr. Nakamoto, the head of her Neighborhood Association, and asked him what she should do. He said that she should remain at home unless an urgent warning—a series of intermittent blasts of the siren—was sounded. She returned home, lit the stove in the kitchen, set some rice to cook, and sat down to read that morning's Hiroshima *Chugoku*. To her relief, the all-clear sounded at eight o'clock. She heard the children stirring, so she went and gave each of them a handful of peanuts and told them to stay on their bedrolls, because they were tired from the night's walk. She had hoped that they would go back to sleep, but the man in the house directly to the south began to make a terrible hullabaloo of hammering, wedging, ripping, and splitting. The prefectural government, convinced, as everyone in Hiroshima was, that the city would be attacked soon, had begun to press with threats and warnings for the completion of wide fire lanes, which, it was hoped, might act in conjunction with the rivers to localize any fires started by an incendiary raid; and the neighbor was reluctantly sacrificing his home to the city's safety. Just the day before, the prefecture had ordered all able-bodied girls from the secondary schools to spend a few days helping to clear these lanes, and they started work soon after the all-clear sounded.

Mrs. Nakamura went back to the kitchen, looked at the rice, and began watching the man next door. At first, she was annoyed with him for making so much noise, but then she was moved almost to tears by pity. Her emotion was specifically directed toward her neighbor, tearing down his home, board by board, at a time when there was so much unavoidable destruction, but undoubtedly she also felt a generalized, community pity, to say nothing of self-pity. She had not had an easy time. Her husband, Isawa, had gone into the Army just after Myeko was born, and she had heard nothing from or of him for a long time, until, on March 5, 1942, she received a seven-word telegram: "Isawa died an honorable death at Singapore." She learned later that he had died on February 15th, the day Singapore fell, and that he had been a corporal. Isawa had been a not particularly prosperous tailor, and his only capital was a Sankoku sewing machine. After his death, when his allotments stopped coming, Mrs. Nakamura got out the machine and began to take in piecework herself, and since then had supported the children, but poorly, by sewing.

As Mrs. Nakamura stood watching her neighbor, everything flashed whiter than any white she had ever seen. She did not notice what happened to the man next door; the reflex of a mother set her in motion toward her children. She had taken a single step (the house was 1,350 yards, or three-quarters of a mile, from the center of the explosion) when something picked her up and she seemed to fly into the next room over the raised sleeping platform, pursued by parts of her house.

Timbers fell around her as she landed, and a shower of tiles pommelled her; everything became dark, for she was buried. The debris did not cover her deeply. She rose up and freed herself. She heard a child cry, "Mother, help me!," and saw her youngest—Myeko, the five-year-old—buried up to her breast and unable to move. As Mrs. Nakamura started frantically to claw her way toward the baby, she could see or hear nothing of her other children. . . .

On the train on the way into Hiroshima from the country, where he lived with his mother, Dr. Terufumi Sasaki, the Red Cross Hospital surgeon, thought over an unpleasant nightmare he had had the night before. His mother's home was in Mukaihara, thirty miles from the city, and it took him two hours by train and tram to reach the hospital. He had slept uneasily all night and had wakened an hour earlier than usual, and, feeling sluggish and slightly feverish, had debated whether to go to the hospital at all; his sense of duty finally forced him to go, and he had started out on an earlier train than he took most mornings. The dream had particularly frightened him because it was so closely associated, on the surface at least, with a disturbing actuality. He was only twenty-five years old and had just completed his training at the Eastern Medical University, in Tsingtao, China. He was something of an idealist and was much distressed by the inadequacy of medical facilities in the country town where his mother lived. Quite on his own, and without a permit, he had begun visiting a few sick people out there in the evenings, after his eight hours at the hospital and four hours' commuting. He had recently learned that the penalty for practicing without a permit was severe; a fellow-doctor whom he had asked about it had given him a serious scolding. Nevertheless, he had continued to practice. In his dream, he had been at the bedside of a country patient when the police and the doctor he had consulted burst into the room, seized him, dragged him outside, and beat him up cruelly. On the train, he just about decided to give up the work in Mukaihara, since he felt it would be impossible to get a permit, because the authorities would hold that it would conflict with his duties at the Red Cross Hospital.

At the terminus, he caught a streetcar at once. (He later calculated that if he had taken his customary train that morning, and if he had had to wait a few minutes for the streetcar, as often happened, he would have been close to the center at the time of the explosion and would surely have perished.) He arrived at the hospital at seven-forty and reported to the chief surgeon. A few minutes later, he went to a room on the first floor and drew blood from the arm of a man in order to perform a Wassermann test. The laboratory containing the incubators for the test was on the third floor. With the blood specimen in his left hand, walking in a kind of distraction he had felt all morning, probably because of the dream and his restless night, he started along the main corridor on his way toward the stairs. He was one step beyond an open window when the light of the bomb was reflected, like a gigantic photographic flash, in the corridor. He ducked down on one knee and said to himself, as only a Japanese would, "Sasaki, *gambare!* Be brave!" Just then (the building was 1,650 yards from the center), the blast ripped through the hospital. The glasses he was wearing flew off his face; the bottle of blood crashed against one wall; his Japanese slippers zipped out from under his feet—but otherwise, thanks to where he stood, he was untouched.

Dr. Sasaki shouted the name of the chief surgeon and rushed around to the man's office and found him terribly cut by glass. The hospital was in horrible confusion: heavy partitions and ceilings had fallen on patients, beds had overturned, windows had blown in and cut people, blood was spattered on the walls and floors, instruments were everywhere, many of the patients were running about screaming, many more lay dead. (A colleague working in the laboratory to which Dr. Sasaki had been walking was dead; Dr. Sasaki's patient, whom he had just left and who a few moments before had been dreadfully afraid of syphilis, was also dead.) Dr. Sasaki found himself the only doctor in the hospital who was unhurt.

Dr. Sasaki, who believed that the enemy had hit only the building he was in, got bandages and began to bind the wounds of those inside the hospital; while outside, all over Hiroshima, maimed and dying citizens turned their unsteady steps toward the Red Cross Hospital to begin an invasion that was to make Dr. Sasaki forget his private nightmare for a long, long time.

Miss Toshiko Sasaki, the East Asia Tin Works clerk, who is not related to Dr. Sasaki, got up at three o'clock in the morning on the day the bomb fell. There was extra housework to do. Her eleven-month-old brother, Akio, had come down the day before with a serious stomach upset; her mother had taken him to the Tamura Pediatric Hospital and was staying there with him. Miss Sasaki, who was about twenty, had to cook breakfast for her father, a brother, a sister, and herself, and— since the hospital, because of the war, was unable to provide food—to prepare a whole day's meals for her mother and the baby, in time for her father, who worked in a factory making rubber ear-plugs for artillery crews, to take the food by on his way to the plant. When she had finished and had cleaned and put away the cooking things, it was nearly seven. The family lived in Koi, and she had a forty-five-minute trip to the tin works, in the section of town called Kannon-machi. She was in charge of the personnel records in the factory. She left Koi at seven, and as soon as she reached the plant, she went with some of the other girls from the personnel department to the factory auditorium. A prominent local Navy man, a former employee, had committed suicide the day before by throwing himself under a train—a death considered honorable enough to warrant a memorial service, which was to be held at the tin works at ten o'clock that morning. In the large hall, Miss Sasaki and the others made suitable preparations for the meeting. This work took about twenty minutes.

Miss Sasaki went back to her office and sat down at her desk. She was quite far from the windows, which were off to her left, and behind her were a couple of tall bookcases containing all the books of the factory library, which the personnel department had organized. She settled herself at her desk, put some things in a drawer, and shifted papers. She thought that before she began to make entries in her lists of new employees, discharges, and departures for the Army, she would chat for a moment with the girl at her right. Just as she turned her head away from the windows, the room was filled with a blinding light. She was paralyzed by fear, fixed still in her chair for a long moment (the plant was 1,600 yards from the center).

Everything fell, and Miss Sasaki lost consciousness. The ceiling dropped suddenly and the wooden floor above collapsed in splinters and the people up there came down and the roof above them gave way; but principally and first of all, the bookcases right behind her swooped forward and the contents threw her down, with her left leg horribly twisted and breaking underneath her. There, in the tin factory, in the first moment of the atomic age, a human being was crushed by books.

20. *1945—*JAPAN SURRENDERS

⟨ *Three days after Hiroshima a second atom bomb was dropped, this time on Nagasaki. Japan saw that her only alternative to surrender was annihilation. On August 10 she sued for peace. The formal surrender took place on the battleship* MISSOURI *at 9:08* A.M. *(Tokyo time), September 2. The brief account is one sent out by the Associated Press.*

Associated Press Dispatch in *Chicago Tribune,* Sept. 2, 1945.

U. S. S. Missouri, Tokyo Bay, Sept. 2 (Sunday)

Two nervous Japanese formally and unconditionally surrendered all remnants of their smashed empire to the allies today, restoring peace to the world.

Surrender hour was cool and cloudy, but the sun broke through the overcast 20 minutes later as Gen. MacArthur intoned, "These proceedings are closed. The entire world is quietly at peace. A new era is upon us."

Foreign Minister Mamoru Shigemitsu, who signed for the Japanese government, doffed his top hat and nervously fingered his fountain pen before he firmly signed the two copies of the surrender document—one for Japan, one for the allies.

Gen. Yoshijiro Umezu, for the imperial staff, signed hurriedly and quickly stepped aside. A Japanese colonel wiped his eyes. All of the Nipponese present were tense and drawn.

Then MacArthur signed, deliberately, using five pens. The first two —silverplated especially for the occasion—he handed in turn to Lt. Gen. Jonathan M. Wainwright and to British Gen. Arthur Ernest Percival, who were forced to surrender Corregidor and Singapore, respectively, in the war's darkest hours. Wainwright and Percival smiled; saluted snappily. They had been rescued only a few days ago from Japanese prisoner of war camps. . . .

The 45,000 ton *Missouri*, which less than a month ago was blasting war industries with her 16 inch guns, had those rifles pointed skyward and her bow pointed toward the heart of Japan for the ceremony. Flags of the United States, the United Kingdom, China, and Russia fluttered from the veranda deck. . . .

CHAPTER XXIV

THE UNITED STATES
IN AN UNEASY WORLD

1945 – 1958

1. *1945*—TRUMAN SUCCEEDS ROOSEVELT

❰ *The death of Franklin D. Roosevelt put Harry S. Truman, former Senator from Missouri who had been elected Vice President in 1944, in the Presidency. Truman tells how he learned of Roosevelt's death and took the oath of office as his successor.*

Shortly before five o'clock in the afternoon of Thursday, April 12, 1945, after the Senate adjourned, I went to the office of House Speaker Sam Rayburn. I went there to get an agreement between the Speaker and the Vice-President on certain legislation and to discuss the domestic and world situation generally. As I entered, the Speaker told me that

From *Memoirs of Harry S. Truman: Year of Decisions* (Doubleday & Co., 1955). Reprinted by permission of Time Inc., copyright owner. Pp. 1, 4–8.

Steve Early, the President's press secretary, had just telephoned, requesting me to call the White House.

I returned the call and was immediately connected with Early.

"Please come right over," he told me in a strained voice, "and come in through the main Pennsylvania Avenue entrance."

I turned to Rayburn, explaining that I had been summoned to the White House and would be back shortly. I did not know why I had been called, but I asked that no mention be made of the matter. The President, I thought, must have returned to Washington for the funeral of his friend, Bishop Atwood, the former Episcopal Bishop of Arizona, and I imagined that he wanted me to go over some matters with him before his return to Warm Springs.

On previous occasions when the President had called me to the White House for private talks he had asked me to keep the visits confidential. At such times I had used the east entrance to the White House, and in this way the meetings were kept off the official caller list. Now, however, I told Tom Harty, my government chauffeur, to drive me to the main entrance.

We rode alone, without the usual guards. The Secret Service had assigned three men to work in shifts when I became Vice-President. However, this guard was reinforced, as a routine practice, during the time President Roosevelt was away on his trip to Yalta and again when he went to Warm Springs. A guard had been placed on duty at my Connecticut Avenue apartment, where I had lived as Senator and continued to live as Vice-President, and another accompanied me wherever I went. These men were capable, efficient, self-effacing, and usually the guard who was on duty met me at my office after the Senate had adjourned. But on this one occasion I slipped away from all of them. Instead of returning from Speaker Rayburn's office to my own before going to the car that was waiting for me, I ran through the basement of the Capitol Building and lost them. This was the only time in eight years that I enjoyed the luxury of privacy by escaping from the ever-present vigil of official protection.

I reached the White House about 5:25 P.M. and was immediately taken in the elevator to the second floor and ushered into Mrs. Roosevelt's study. Mrs. Roosevelt herself, together with Colonel John and Mrs. Anna Roosevelt Boettiger and Mr. Early, were in the room as I entered, and I knew at once that something unusual had taken place. Mrs. Roosevelt seemed calm in her characteristic, graceful dignity. She stepped forward and placed her arm gently about my shoulder.

"Harry," she said quietly, "the President is dead."

For a moment I could not bring myself to speak.

The last news we had had from Warm Springs was that Mr. Roosevelt was recuperating nicely. In fact, he was apparently doing so well that no member of his immediate family, and not even his personal physician, was with him. All this flashed through my mind before I found my voice.

"Is there anything I can do for you?" I asked at last.

I shall never forget her deeply understanding reply.

"Is there anything *we* can do for *you?*" she asked. "For you are the one in trouble now. . . ."

It seems to me that for a few minutes we stood silent, and then there was a knock on the study door. Secretary of State Stettinius entered. He was in tears, his handsome face sad and drawn. He had been among the first to be notified, for as Secretary of State, who is the keeper of the Great Seal of the United States and all official state papers, it was his official duty to ascertain and to proclaim the passing of the President.

I asked Steve Early, Secretary Stettinius, and Les Biffle, who now had also joined us, to call all the members of the Cabinet to a meeting as quickly as possible. Then I turned to Mrs. Roosevelt and asked if there was anything she needed to have done. She replied that she would like to go to Warm Springs at once, and asked whether it would be proper for her to make use of a government plane. I assured her that the use of such a plane was right and proper, and I made certain that one would be placed at her disposal, knowing that a grateful nation would insist on it.

But now a whole series of arrangements had to be made. I went to the President's office at the west end of the White House. I asked Les Biffle to arrange to have a car sent for Mrs. Truman and Margaret, and I called them on the phone myself, telling them what had happened— telling them, too, to come to the White House. I also called Chief Justice Harlan Fiske Stone, and having given him the news, I asked him to come as soon as possible so that he might swear me in. He said that he would come at once. And that is what he did, for he arrived within hardly more than fifteen or twenty minutes.

Others were arriving by now. Speaker Rayburn, House Majority Leader John W. McCormack, and House Minority Leader Joseph W. Martin were among them. I tried personally to reach Senator Alben W. Barkley, Senate majority leader, but I could not locate him. I learned later that word of the President's death had reached him promptly and that he had gone at once to see Mrs. Roosevelt. In fact, he was with her in the White House while the group about me was gathering in the Cabinet Room.

There was no time for formalities and protocol. Among the people there were a score or so of officials and members of Congress. Only three women were present—Mrs. Truman and Margaret and Secretary Frances Perkins.

The Cabinet Room in the White House is not extensive. It is dominated by the huge and odd-shaped table, presented to the President by Jesse Jones, at which the President and the members of the Cabinet sit, and by the leather-upholstered armchairs that are arranged around it.

Steve Early, Jonathan Daniels, and others of the President's secretarial staff were searching for a Bible for me to hold when Chief Justice Stone administered the oath of office.

We were in the final days of the greatest war in history—a war so vast that few corners of the world had been able to escape being engulfed by it. There were none who did not feel its effects. In that war the United States had created military forces so enormous as to defy description, yet now, when the nation's greatest leader in that war lay dead, and a simple ceremony was about to acknowledge the presence of his successor in the nation's greatest office, only two uniforms were present. These were worn by Fleet Admiral Leahy and General Fleming, who, as Public Works Administrator, had been given duties that were much more civilian in character than military.

So far as I know, this passed unnoticed at the time, and the very fact that no thought was given to it demonstrates convincingly how firmly the concept of the supremacy of the civil authority is accepted in our land.

By now a Bible had been found. It was placed near where I stood at the end of the great table. Mrs. Truman and Margaret had not joined me for over an hour after I had called them, having gone first to see Mrs. Roosevelt. They were standing side by side now, at my left, while Chief Justice Stone had taken his place before me at the end of the table. Clustered about me and behind were nine members of the Cabinet, while Speaker Rayburn and a few other members of Congress took positions behind Chief Justice Stone. There were others present, but not many.

I picked up the Bible and held it in my left hand. Chief Justice Stone raised his right hand and gave the oath as it is written in the Constitution.

With my right hand raised, I repeated it after him:

"I, Harry S. Truman, do solemnly swear that I will faithfully execute the office of President of the United States, and will to the best of my ability, preserve, protect and defend the Constitution of the United States."

I dropped my hand.

The clock beneath Woodrow Wilson's portrait marked the time at 7:09.

Less than two hours before, I had come to see the President of the United States, and now, having repeated that simply worded oath, I myself was President.

645

2. *1945*—SHAPING THE UNITED NATIONS

⟨ *The death of Roosevelt was a matter of deep concern to the members of the U. S. delegation to the San Francisco conference out of which it was hoped that a United Nations organization would emerge. In diary entries and letters Arthur H. Vandenberg, Senator from Michigan and member of the delegation, expressed his initial misgivings, followed the course of the conference, and recorded the ratification of the Charter by the Senate.*

April 13, 1945

. . . With 15 others, I had lunch with Truman this noon. He told me he was *not* going to Frisco personally (as F. D. R. had intended to do) and that he expects to "leave Frisco to our Delegation." Unquestionably we will have greater freedom—but also greater responsibility.

I am puzzled. Stettinius is now Secretary of State in *fact*. Up to now he has been only the presidential messenger. He does *not* have the background and experience for such a job at such a critical time—altho he is a *grand person* with every good intention and high honesty of purpose. *Now* we have *both* an inexperienced President *and* an inexperienced Secretary (in re foreign affairs). . . .

But I liked the *first* decision Truman made—namely, that Frisco should *go on.* Senator Connally immediately prophesied, after F. D. R. died, that Frisco would be postponed. . . . Truman promptly stopped *that* mistake (which would have confessed to the world that there *is an* "indispensable man" who was bigger than America). . . .

May 13, 1945

There is much underground chatter about Stettinius. Unfortunately he pretty generally has the press against him. There is increasing gossip about a successor, when this Conference is ended. I agree that there is no longer any strong hand on our foreign policy rudder—neither Truman nor Stettinius nor Grew. I agree that it is a tragic situation in these difficult times. Stettinius does *not* have a seasoned grasp of foreign affairs. He rarely contributes to our policy decisions. We improvise as we go along. Stettinius is not *really* Secretary of State. He is *really* "General Manager" of the State Department (which is a totally different thing). Incidentally, he is the *best* "General Manager" I ever saw. He *gets things done.* But I am afraid that is his chief idea—just to "get things done." He does *not* take the same firm stand in respect to *policy*

From *The Private Papers of Senator Vandenberg*, Arthur H. Vandenberg, Jr., Ed. (Boston: Houghton Mifflin Company, 1952). Reprinted by permission of the publishers. Pp. 167–68, 191, 197, 215–17, 218–19.

that he does in "getting things done." President Truman sadly needs a real Secretary of State in the realm of *policy*. . . .

May 23, 1945

Yesterday our Sub-committee unanimously o.k.'ed the final Regional draft. This afternoon, the full Committee did the same. There followed about 20 speeches lauding the results and very generously applauding my part in them. I made a brief acknowledgment at the end.

I am deeply impressed by what has happened. . . . At the outset many of the Nations were far, very far, apart. Our own Delegation was not wholly united. The subject itself was difficult—how to *save* legitimate regionalism (like Pan-Am) and yet not destroy the essential over-all authority of the International Organization. By hammering it out vis-à-vis, we have found an answer which satisfies practically everybody. In my view, that is the great hope for the new League itself. If we do nothing more than create a constant forum where nations must *face* each other and *debate* their differences and strive for common ground, we shall have done infinitely much. . . .

June 23, 1945

We had our final meeting of the American Delegation this morning. . . .

Now that we are at the end of our labors and our tensions are relaxed, I look back upon what I believe to be a remarkable performance not only by our Delegation but by the Conference as a whole. To have attained virtual unanimity under such complex circumstances is a little short of a miracle.

I think Stettinius has done a magnificent job. Without his "drive" we should have been here for two more months.

I think the most valuable man in our entire American setup has been John Foster Dulles. Nominally just an "advisor," he has been at the core of every crisis. His advice and his labors have been indispensable. I do not know what we should have done without him. He is not only an acute lawyer but he also has a great facility for dealing with diplomatic matters of this nature. He knows more of the foreigners here personally than any other American. Incidentally, he has perfect poise and patience and good nature. He would make a very great Secretary of State.

I want to add a word about the work of Assistant Secretary Nelson Rockefeller. He has been responsible for our Pan-American contacts. I never realized before how important the work of his department is in keeping our "good neighbors" united with us. . . . I do not see how anyone could be more efficient. But it is invidious to try to call this roll. We really have had remarkable team ball. The whole Secretariat has done a stupendous mechanical task with superlative efficiency. . . .

I have made some critical observations about Stassen. . . . But, in retrospect, I want to put him down as one of the ablest young men I have ever known; with not only a tremendous capacity for hard work but also with an equal facility for going to the heart of difficult and complex problems; with a fine personality and a superb earnestness in pursuing the highly important assignments which he has carried here; and with the greatest tenacity in his fidelity to his ideals.

We have finished our job. I am proud of it. It has been the crowning privilege of my life to have been an author of the San Francisco Charter. It has an excellent chance to save the peace of the world *if* America and Russia can learn to live together and *if* Russia learns to keep her word.

[To Mrs. Vandenberg]

[Undated]

The flight back from Frisco was o.k. We had a very distinguished "load" aboard—including Stettinius, Halifax (Ed!), Velosso, Padilla, etc. . . . We were met at the airport by the Foreign Relations Committee and a band. From that hour to this there has been terrific momentum behind the Frisco Charter. I begin to believe that we did a real job. Later that afternoon Connally and I arranged to appear in the Senate at the same time. There was an immediate "explosion." They took a 15-minute recess while we had a "reception." Connally spoke the next day and was noisily received. I spoke the following day. . . . The galleries were packed and there were 78 Senators in their seats. You could have heard a pin drop all the way through my speech; and at the finish the whole place broke out in a roar.

[To Mrs. Vandenberg]

[Undated]

Well—the battle is over. . . . 89 to 2! Only Shipstead and Langer in opposition! Hi Johnson couldn't vote because he is in the Naval Hospital again. . . . It really was an amazing outcome. . . . Everybody now seems to agree that I could have beaten the Charter if I had taken the opposition tack. I must confess, now that it's all over, that I am very proud to have been at least one of its fathers. It has stood up amazingly under every possible scrutiny. The things we did at Frisco to remove potential Senate opposition have paid rich dividends.

Heaven only knows whether the Charter will "work." I *think* it will. If not, *nothing* would. Everything, in the final analysis, depends on Russia (and whether we have *guts* enough to make her behave). At any rate, I have "done my bit" for the peace of the world—and I guess that justifies my senatorial existence.

3. 1947—ANNOUNCING THE TRUMAN DOCTRINE

❡ *Soon after the end of World War II Soviet Russia made it clear that she had no intention of abating her ambition to dominate Europe and Asia. Contrary to earlier promises, she turned Poland into a communist satellite. She obstructed any solution of the problem of divided Germany, gave unstinted aid to the Chinese Communists, and in general strove to bring every faltering nation within her power by instituting communist regimes which would take orders from Moscow.*

The first counter-move by the United States came when President Truman, alarmed by the prospect that Greece might fall into the Soviet sphere, announced that military and financial help would be extended to "free peoples who are resisting subjugation by armed minorities or by outside pressures." The announcement of this policy is generally considered to mark the beginning of the "Cold War."

Truman describes the reasons which led to the vital decision.

On Monday, February 24, Secretary Marshall brought me the official copy of the note which he had received formally that morning from the British Ambassador. This note set forth the difficulties confronting the United Kingdom in the fulfillment of her overseas commitments and advised us that as of March 30, 1947, it would be necessary for the United Kingdom to withdraw all support to Greece.

General Marshall and I discussed the impending crisis with Secretaries Forrestal and Patterson, and the three departments pressed their study of all aspects of the situation. In his talk with the British Ambassador, Secretary Marshall learned that the British were planning to take their troops out of Greece as soon as this could be conveniently done.

The urgency of the situation was emphasized by dispatches from our representatives in Athens and Moscow. General Smith recorded his belief that only the presence of British troops had so far saved Greece from being swallowed into the Soviet orbit. From Athens, Ambassador MacVeagh sent a picture of deep depression and even resignation among Greek leaders; their feeling seemed to be that only aid given at once would be of use. Time, MacVeagh urged, was of the essence.

At three o'clock on Wednesday, February 26, Marshall and Acheson brought me the result of the studies of our experts. The State-War-Navy Coordinating Committee had met that morning in an extended session and had agreed on a general policy recommendation. General Eisenhower furnished a memorandum from the Joint Chiefs of Staff supporting the conclusion reached from a military point of view.

From *Memoirs of Harry S. Truman: Years of Trial and Hope* (Doubleday & Co., 1956). Reprinted by permission of Time Inc., copyright owner. Pp. 100–01, 103–06.

Under Secretary Acheson made the presentation of the study, and I listened to it with great care. The diplomatic and military experts had drawn the picture in greater detail, but essentially their conclusions were the same as those to which I had come in the weeks just passed as the messages and reports went across my desk.

Greece needed aid, and needed it quickly and in substantial amounts. The alternative was the loss of Greece and the extension of the iron curtain across the eastern Mediterranean. If Greece was lost, Turkey would become an untenable outpost in a sea of Communism. Similarly, if Turkey yielded to Soviet demands, the position of Greece would be extremely endangered.

But the situation had even wider implications. Poland, Rumania, and the other satellite nations of eastern Europe had been turned into Communist camps because, in the course of the war, they had been occupied by the Russian Army. We had tried, vainly, to persuade the Soviets to permit political freedom in these countries, but we had no means to compel them to relinquish their control, unless we were prepared to wage war.

Greece and Turkey were still free countries being challenged by Communist threats both from within and without. These free peoples were now engaged in a valiant struggle to preserve their liberties and their independence.

America could not, and should not, let these free countries stand unaided. To do so would carry the clearest implications in the Middle East and in Italy, Germany, and France. The ideals and the traditions of our nation demanded that we come to the aid of Greece and Turkey and that we put the world on notice that it would be our policy to support the cause of freedom wherever it was threatened.

The risks which such a course might entail were risks which a great nation had to take if it cherished freedom at all. The studies which Marshall and Acheson brought to me and which we examined together made it plain that serious risks would be involved. But the alternative would be disastrous to our security and to the security of free nations everywhere. . . .

The vital decision that I was about to make was complicated by the fact that Congress was no longer controlled by the Democratic party. While expecting the help of such fine supporters of the idea of bipartisanship in foreign affairs as Senator Vandenberg and Congressman Eaton of New Jersey, I realized the situation was more precarious than it would have been with a preponderantly Democratic Congress. It seemed desirable, therefore, to advise the congressional leadership as soon as possible of the gravity of the situation and of the nature of the decision which I had to make. I asked Secretary Marshall and Acheson to return the following day at ten, when I would have the congressional leaders present. At ten o'clock on the morning of February 27 Senators

Bridges, Vandenberg, Barkley, and Connally, Speaker Martin, and Representatives Eaton, Bloom, and Rayburn took their seats in my office. Congressman Taber had been invited but was not able to be present. He called later in the day, and I discussed the situation with him.

I explained to them the position in which the British note on Greece had placed us. The decision of the British Cabinet to withdraw from Greece had not yet been made public, and none of the legislators knew, therefore, how serious a crisis we were suddenly facing. I told the group that I had decided to extend aid to Greece and Turkey and that I hoped Congress would provide the means to make this aid timely and sufficient.

General Marshall then reviewed the diplomatic exchanges and the details of the situation. He made it quite plain that our choice was either to act or to lose by default, and I expressed my emphatic agreement to this. I answered congressional questions and finally explained to them what course we had to take.

The congressional leaders appeared deeply impressed. Some in the group were men who would have preferred to avoid spending funds on any aid program abroad. Some had, not so long ago, been outspoken isolationists. But at this meeting in my office there was no voice of dissent when I stated the position which I was convinced our country had to take. . . .

On Wednesday, March 12, 1947, at one o'clock in the afternoon, I stepped to the rostrum in the hall of the House of Representatives and addressed a joint session of the Congress. I had asked the senators and representatives to meet together so that I might place before them what I believed was an extremely critical situation.

To cope with this situation, I recommended immediate action by the Congress. But I also wished to state, for all the world to know, what the position of the United States was in the face of the new totalitarian challenge. This declaration of policy soon began to be referred to as the "Truman Doctrine." This was, I believe, the turning point in America's foreign policy, which now declared that wherever aggression, direct or indirect, threatened the peace, the security of the United States was involved. . . .

When I ended my address, the congressmen rose as one man and applauded. Vito Marcantonio, the American Labor party representative from New York, was the only person in the hall who remained seated.

4.   *1947*—JACKIE ROBINSON BREAKS THE COLOR LINE

❲ *The post-war decade saw the American Negro make tremendous progress toward social and economic equality. The decision of the United States Supreme Court, on May 17, 1954, holding segregated*

Arthur Mann, *Branch Rickey, American in Action,* (Boston: Houghton Mifflin Company, 1957), pp. 220–23. Reprinted by permission of the publishers.

651

schools unconstitutional, climaxed the trend. Yet it could be contended that this decision only recognized what "Jackie" Robinson had accomplished seven years earlier when he broke major-league baseball's ancient color line.

Arthur Mann, biographer of Branch Rickey, who signed Robinson for the Brooklyn Dodgers, tells the story.

Jackie Robinson remembers only patches of his three dramatic hours in the office of Branch Rickey on Tuesday morning, August 28, 1945. He recalls the illuminated goldfish tank and how much like a fish he felt. He remembers Rickey's bushy brows, and the large, gnarled fingers lighting a cigar, and the heavyset figure rocking back and forth in a large leather swivel chair behind a massive walnut desk. Rickey's voice, emphasis and the mounting tension in the opening seconds were overpowering. The interview began with salutations and inquiry about his game and whether or not he had a girl, then, "Are you under contract to the Kansas City Monarchs?"

"No, sir," Robinson replied quickly. "We don't have contracts."

"Do you have any agreements—written or oral—about how long you will play for them?"

"No, sir, none at all. I just work from payday to payday."

Rickey nodded and his bushy brows mashed into a scowl. He toyed with the ever-present cigar, seeking the right words, "Do you know why you were brought here?"

"Not exactly. I heard something about a colored team at Ebbets Field. That it?"

"No . . . that isn't it." Rickey studied the dark face, the half-open mouth, the widened and worried eyes. Then he said, "You were brought here, Jackie, to play for the Brooklyn organization. Perhaps on Montreal to start with—"

"Me? Play for Montreal?" the player gasped.

Rickey nodded. "If you can make it, yes. Later on—also if you can make it—you'll have a chance with the Brooklyn Dodgers."

Robinson could only nod at this point.

"I want to win pennants and we need ballplayers!" Rickey whacked the desk. He sketched the efforts and the scope of his two-year search for players of promise. "Do *you* think you can do it? Make good in organized baseball?"

Robinson shifted to relieve his mounting tension.

"If . . . if I got the chance," he stammered.

"There's more here than just *playing*, Jackie," Rickey warned. "I wish it meant only hits, runs and errors—things you can see in a box score. . . ."

Rickey produced Papini's *Life of Christ* from the drawer of his desk. He often read the book himself as a guide to humility. It seemed appropriate to read aloud from it to a Negro baseball player who might become the first of his race to enter organized baseball.

"Can you do it? Can you do it?" Rickey asked over and over.

Shifting nervously, Robinson looked from Rickey to Sukeforth as they talked of his arms and legs and swing and courage. Did he have the guts to play the game no matter what happened? Rickey pointed out the enormity of the responsibility for all concerned: owners of the club, Rickey, Robinson and all baseball. The opposition would shout insults, come in spikes first, throw at his head.

"Mr. Rickey," Robinson said, "they've been throwing at my head for a long time."

Rickey's voice rose. "Suppose I'm a player . . . in the heat of an important ball game." He drew back as if to charge at Robinson. "Suppose I collide with you at second base. When I get up, I yell, 'You dirty, black son of a —' " He finished the castigation and added calmly, "What do you do?"

Robinson blinked. He licked his lips and swallowed.

"Mr. Rickey," he murmured, "do you want a ballplayer who's afraid to fight back?"

"I want a ballplayer with guts enough *not* to fight back!" Rickey exclaimed almost savagely. He paced across the floor and returned with finger pointing. "You've got to do this job with base hits and stolen bases and fielding ground balls, Jackie. *Nothing else!*"

He moved behind his big desk again and faced the cornered Robinson. He posed as a cynical clerk in a southern hotel who not only refused him a room, but cursed him as he did so. What would Robinson do? He posed as a prejudiced sportswriter, ordered to turn in a twisted story, full of bias and racial animosity. How would Robinson answer the sportswriter? He ordered the player from imaginary dining rooms. He jostled him in imaginary hotel lobbies, railroad stations. What would Robinson do?

"Now I'm playing against you in a World Series!" Rickey stormed and removed his jacket for greater freedom. Robinson's hands clenched, trembled from the rising tension. "I'm a hotheaded player. I want to win that game, so I go into you spikes first, but you don't give ground. You stand there and you jab the ball into my ribs and the umpire yells, 'Out!' I flare up—all I see is your face—that black face right on top of me—"

Rickey's bespectacled face, glistening with sweat, was inches from Robinson's at this point. He yelled into the motionless mask, "So I haul off and punch you right in the cheek!"

An oversized fist swung through the air and barely missed Robinson's face. He blinked, but his head didn't move.

"What do you do?" Rickey roared.

"Mr. Rickey," he whispered, "I've got two cheeks. That it?"

5.   *1950*—WE DECIDE TO FIGHT IN KOREA

([*Before the end of World War II the great powers had agreed that Korea, originally a part of China but occupied by the Japanese since 1910, would be given her independence. But it was also agreed that for the time being Russia would administer the northern part of the country (above the thirty-eighth parallel) and the United States would be responsible for the southern part. Two radically different regimes developed, and the "Cold War" thwarted efforts at unification. In 1948 the southern part proclaimed itself the Republic of Korea; the north the People's Democratic Republic. Shortly afterward the Soviet Union announced that it was withdrawing its forces; the United States followed suit except for a small group of military advisers.*

On June 24, 1950, North Korean troops suddenly crossed the thirty-eighth parallel. Truman, who had been re-elected in 1948, describes the shocked reaction of the American government.

On Saturday, June 24, 1950, I was in Independence, Missouri, to spend the weekend with my family and to attend to some personal family business.

It was a little after ten in the evening, and we were sitting in the library of our home on North Delaware Street when the telephone rang. It was the Secretary of State calling from his home in Maryland.

"Mr. President," said Dean Acheson, "I have very serious news. The North Koreans have invaded South Korea."

My first reaction was that I must get back to the capital, and I told Acheson so. He explained, however, that details were not yet available and that he thought I need not rush back until he called me again with further information. In the meantime, he suggested to me that we should ask the United Nations Security Council to hold a meeting at once and declare that an act of aggression had been committed against the Republic of Korea. I told him that I agreed and asked him to request immediately a special meeting of the Security Council, and he said he would call me to report again the following morning, or sooner if there was more information on the events in Korea.

Acheson's next call came through around eleven-thirty Sunday morning, just as we were getting ready to sit down to an early Sunday dinner. Acheson reported that the U. N. Security Council had been called into

From *Memoirs of Harry S. Truman: Years of Trial and Hope* (Doubleday & Co., 1956). Reprinted by permission of Time Inc., copyright owner. Pp. 331–35.

emergency session. Additional reports had been received from Korea, and there was no doubt that an all-out invasion was under way there. The Security Council, Acheson said, would probably call for a cease-fire, but in view of the complete disregard the North Koreans and their big allies had shown for the U.N. in the past, we had to expect that the U.N. order would be ignored. Some decision would have to be made at once as to the degree of aid or encouragement which our government was willing to extend to the Republic of Korea.

I asked Acheson to get together with the Service Secretaries and the Chiefs of Staff and start working on recommendations for me when I got back. Defense Secretary Louis Johnson and Chairman of the Chiefs of Staff General Omar Bradley were on their way back from an inspection tour of the Far East. I informed the Secretary of State that I was returning to Washington at once.

The crew of the presidential plane *Independence* did a wonderful job. They had the plane ready to fly in less than an hour from the time they were alerted, and my return trip got under way so fast that two of my aides were left behind. They could not be notified in time to reach the airport.

The plane left the Kansas City Municipal Airport at two o'clock, and it took just a little over three hours to make the trip to Washington. I had time to think aboard the plane. In my generation, this was not the first occasion when the strong had attacked the weak. I recalled some earlier instances: Manchuria, Ethiopia, Austria. I remembered how each time that the democracies failed to act it had encouraged the aggressors to keep going ahead. Communism was acting in Korea just as Hitler, Mussolini, and the Japanese had acted ten, fifteen, and twenty years earlier. I felt certain that if South Korea was allowed to fall Communist leaders would be emboldened to override nations closer to our own shores. If the Communists were permitted to force their way into the Republic of Korea without opposition from the free world, no small nation would have the courage to resist threats and aggression by stronger Communist neighbors. If this was allowed to go unchallenged it would mean a third world war, just as similar incidents had brought on the second world war. It was also clear to me that the foundations and the principles of the United Nations were at stake unless this unprovoked attack on Korea could be stopped.

I had the plane's radio operator send a message to Dean Acheson asking him and his immediate advisers and the top defense chiefs to come to Blair House for a dinner conference.

When the *Independence* landed, Secretary of State Acheson was waiting for me at the airport, as was Secretary of Defense Johnson, who himself had arrived only a short while before. We hurried to Blair House, where we were joined by the other conferees. Present were the three service Secretaries, Secretary of the Army Frank Pace, Secretary of the Navy Francis Matthews, and Secretary of the Air Force Thomas Finletter. There were the Joint Chiefs of Staff, General of the Army Omar N. Bradley, the Army Chief General Collins, the Air Force Chief General Vandenberg, and Admiral Forrest Sherman, Chief of Naval Operations. Dean Acheson was accompanied by Under Secretary Webb, Deputy Under Secretary Dean Rusk and Assistant Under Secretary John Hickerson, and Ambassador-at-Large Philip Jessup.

It was late, and we went at once to the dining room for dinner. I asked that no discussion take place until dinner was served and over and the Blair House staff had withdrawn. I called on Dean Acheson first to give us a detailed picture of the situation. . . .

I then called on Acheson to present the recommendations which the State and Defense Departments had prepared. He presented the following recommendations for immediate action:

1. That MacArthur should evacuate the Americans from Korea—including the dependents of the Military Mission—and, in order to do so, should keep open the Kimpo and other airports, repelling all hostile attacks thereon. In doing this, his air forces should stay south of the 38th parallel.

2. That MacArthur should be instructed to get ammunition and supplies to the Korean army by airdrop and otherwise.

3. That the Seventh Fleet should be ordered into the Formosa Strait to prevent the conflict from spreading to that area. The Seventh Fleet should be ordered from Cavite north at once. We should make a statement that the fleet would repel any attack on Formosa and that no attacks should be made from Formosa on the mainland. . . .

As we continued our discussion, I stated that I did not expect the North Koreans to pay any attention to the United Nations. This, I said, would mean that the United Nations would have to apply force if it wanted its order obeyed.

6. *1950*—KOREA: THE FIRST MONTHS

❨ *The day after the invasion, the Security Council of the United Nations demanded that North Korea withdraw her forces. Two days later the Council asked the members of the United Nations to furnish aid to the Republic of Korea. The United States had already committed its air force; it would soon send in ground troops. Other nations—principally Great Britain, Australia, Canada, New Zealand, and Turkey—supplied troops in appreciable numbers; eventually the South Korean army would be reorganized and play an important part.*

From *War in Korea* by Marguerite Higgins. Copyright © 1951 by Time, Inc., Copyright © 1951 by Marguerite Higgins. Reprinted by permission of Doubleday & Co., Inc. Pp. 116–22.

In the beginning, the United Nations forces were pushed back until they occupied only a small area around Pusan in the southeastern part of the Korean peninsula. This was the situation when Marguerite Higgins, correspondent of the New York HERALD TRIBUNE, visited the headquarters of the 27th Regiment of the 25th Division. The action she described was typical of much of the fighting in Korea.

I reached the southwest front in time for the 25th's first big battle after the "stand or die" order. By luck, I happened to be the only daily newspaperman on the scene. The rest of the correspondents were at Pusan covering the debarkation of the United States Marines. My colleague on the *Herald Tribune* had selected the marine landing for his own. So I left Pusan and hitchhiked my way west.

At Masan, I borrowed a jeep from the 724th Ordnance and drove in the dusk over the beautiful mountains that wind west and overlook the deep blue waters of Masan Bay. The jewel-bright rice paddies in the long, steep-sided valley held a soft sheen and the war seemed far away. But only a few nights later the sharp blue and orange tracer bullets were flicking across the valley's mouth until dawn.

The valley leads to Chindongni, where the 27th (Wolfhound) Infantry Regiment had established its headquarters in a battered schoolhouse under the brow of a high hill. Windows of the schoolhouse were jagged fragments, and glass powdered the floor. For our big 155-millimeter artillery guns were emplaced in the schoolhouse yard, and each blast shivered the frail wooden building and its windows. The terrific effect of these guns is rivaled only by the infernal explosions of aerial rockets and napalm bombs, which seem to make the sky quake and shudder.

I had been looking forward with great interest to seeing the 27th in action. Other correspondents had praised both the regiment's commander, Colonel John ("Mike") Michaelis, Eisenhower's onetime aide, and the professional hard-fighting spirit of his officers and men. . . .

On that first night at Chindongni, I found Colonel Michaelis in a state of tension. Mike Michaelis is a high-strung, good-looking officer with much of the cockiness of an ex-paratrooper. His ambition and drive have not yet been broken by the army system.

He has inherited from his onetime boss, "'Ike"—or perhaps he just had it naturally—the key to the art of good public relations: complete honesty, even about his mistakes.

That night Mike Michaelis felt he had made a bad one. His very presence in Chindongni was technically against orders. He had turned his troops around and rushed them away from assigned positions when he heard the Reds had seized the road junction pointing along the southern coast straight at Masan and Pusan. There was nothing in their path to stop them. But, reaching Chindongni, his patrols could find no enemy. There were only swarms of refugees pumping down the road. And at the very point Michaelis had left, heavy enemy attacks were reported.

Miserably, Michaelis had told his officers: "I gambled and lost. I brought you to the wrong place."

But depression could not subdue him for long. He decided he would find the enemy by attacking in battalion strength. If the road really was empty, his men might recapture the critical road junction some twenty miles to the east.

Michaelis asked the 35th Regiment some miles to the north to send a spearhead to link up with his troops approaching the junction on the coastal route, and ordered Colonel Gilbert Check to push forward the twenty miles. The advance turned into the first major counterattack of the Korean campaign.

Michaelis told me about it in the lamplit headquarters room where conversation was punctuated by roars from the 155 guns. Again he was unhappily belaboring himself for having made a bad gamble.

It appeared that the Reds had been on the coastal road after all. Disguised in the broad white hats and white linen garb of the Korean farmer, they had filtered unhindered in the refugee surge toward Chindongni. Then, singly or in small groups, they had streamed to collecting points in the hills, some to change into uniform and others simply to get weapons.

From their mountainous hiding places they had watched Colonel Check's battalion plunge down the road. Then they had struck from the rear. Mortars and machine guns were brought down to ridges dominating the road. This screen of fire—sometimes called a roadblock— cut the road at half a dozen points between Michaelis's headquarters and Colonel Check's attacking battalion. Rescue engineer combat teams had battered all day at the hills and roads to sweep them clean of enemy, but had failed. The worst had seemingly happened. The regiment was split in two; the line of supply cut. The 35th Regiment to the north had been unable to fight its way to the road junction.

The fate of Colonel Check's battalion showed that the enemy was here in force and proved that Michaelis had been right to wheel his forces south to block this vital pathway to Pusan. But he felt he had bungled in ordering the battalion to advance so far.

"I overcommitted myself," Michaelis said miserably. "Now Check's men are stranded eighteen miles deep in enemy territory. From early reports, they've got a lot of wounded. But we've lost all contact. I sent a liaison plane to drop them a message to beat their way back here. I'm afraid we've lost the tanks."

Colonel Check's tanks took a pummeling, all right, from enemy anti-tank guns. But the tanks got back. Colonel Check himself told us the remarkable story as his weary battalion funneled into Chindongni at one o'clock in the morning.

"Antitank guns caught us on a curve several miles short of our objective," Check said. "Troops riding on the tanks yelled when they saw the flash, but they were too late. The tanks caught partially afire and the crews were wounded. But three of the tanks were still operable. I was damned if I was going to let several hundred thousand dollars' worth of American equipment sit back there on the road. I yelled, 'Who around here thinks he can drive a tank?' A couple of ex-bulldozer operators and an ex-mason volunteered. They got about three minutes' checking out and off they went."

One of the ex-bulldozer operators was Private Ray Roberts. His partly disabled tank led Check's column through ambush after ambush back to safety. Men were piled all over the tanks, and the gunners—also volunteers—had plenty of practice shooting back at Reds harassing them from ridges. Once the tank-led column was halted by a washout in the road. Another time Colonel Check ordered a halt of the whole column so that a medic could administer plasma.

"It might have been a damn-fool thing to do," Colonel Check said, "and the kids at the back of the column kept yelling they were under fire and to hurry up. But—well, we had some good men killed today. I didn't want to lose any more."

That night I found ex-bulldozer operator Roberts in the darkness still sitting on the tank. He was very pleased to show me every dent and hole in it. But he dismissed his feat with, "I fiddled around with the tank a few minutes. It's really easier to drive than a bulldozer. You just feel sort of funny lookin' in that darn periscope all the time."

I was amused after the roadside interview when Roberts and several of the other volunteers came up and said, "Ma'am, if you happen to think of it, you might tell the colonel that we're hoping he won't take that tank away from us. We're plannin' to git ordnance to help fix it up in the mornin'." Private Roberts and company graduated from dogfeet to tankmen that night, but no special pleas were necessary. There were no other replacements for the wounded crews.

The battalion at final count had lost thirty men. In their biggest scrap, just two miles short of the road junction, the battalion artillery had killed two hundred and fifty enemy soldiers. . . .

When Check had gone, Michaelis turned to Harold Martin of the *Saturday Evening Post* and myself. We had been scribbling steadily as the colonel told of the breakout from the trap.

"Well, is it a story?" Michaelis asked. "You've seen how it is. You've seen how an officer has to make a decision on the spur of the moment and without knowing whether it's right or wrong. You've seen how something that looks wrong at first proves to be right. F'rinstance, coming down here against orders. And you've seen how a decision that seems to be right proves to be wrong—like sending Check's column up that road without knowing for sure what it would face. And then you've seen how a bunch of men with skill and brains and guts, like Check and the kids who drove the tanks, can turn a wrong decision into a right one. But is it a story?"

I said it was a honey and that I'd head back to Pusan first thing in the morning to file it.

7. 1953—ONLY ORDINARY MEN

❴ *In mid-September, 1950, General Douglas MacArthur, commanding the United Nations forces, began a counter-offensive. Marines and army units landed at Inchon, on the west coast of Korea deep in enemy territory; at the same time strong forces broke out from the Pusan area and slugged northward. The movement was a brilliant success. By the end of October nearly all of South Korea had been reoccupied, more than half of the North Korean army had been captured and the remainder scattered in disorganized retreat.*

At this point Communist China threw in its massive weight. In a few weeks, by expending men heartlessly, the Chinese drove the United Nations south of the Han River. Many American units retreated in bitter cold, under terrible hardship, and with heavy losses. Almost 200,000 troops and Korean civilians were evacuated from the port of Hungnam, far to the north. The withdrawal, however, was orderly, resistance stiffened, and in the spring of 1951 the line was stabilized along the thirty-eighth parallel.

For more than two years the armies faced each other, but not passively. Patrols probed at the opposing lines, small battles for small posts took place constantly. Casualties brought sorrow to thousands of American homes. The mood of the people changed from determination to frustration and weariness. Corporal Martin Russ of the First Marine Division expressed the attitude of the nation when he described memorial services held by his regiment.

May 8th, CAMP GUYOL

Memorial services were held yesterday at the regimental parade ground. There were thirteen companies of marines present. A four-mile walk. General Ballard made a speech, a typical droning, platitudinous, meaningless speech. I doubt that anyone listened. A chaplain and

From *The Last Parallel: A Marine's War Journal*, by Martin Russ. Copyright, 1957, by Martin Russ. Reprinted by permission of Rinehart & Company, Inc., New York, Publishers. Pp. 293–94.

a rabbi spoke. Isolated phrases that I remember. ". . . in glory . . . that they will not have died in vain . . . not forgotten," etc. None of those men died gloriously. Only the ones that died while saving the lives of others did not die in vain. The most disturbing thing of all is that not one of them knew why they were dying. I still have a book called *The Greek Way* by Edith Hamilton. I have underlined a sentence or two. "Why is the death of an ordinary man a wretched, chilling thing, which we turn from, while the death of a hero, always tragic, warms us with the sense of quickened life?" I don't know, Miss Hamilton. You tell me. You're the one who felt that sense of quickened life. I never felt it.

The roll of the dead was read off. Many, many names, some familiar. Edward Guyol. John Riley. Willy Mayfield. Waldron, Carlough. All ordinary men, no heroes.

8. *1953*—KOREA: THE END

⟦ *Corporal Russ records his activities, and his emotions, in the last hours of the Korean War.*

July 1st, 1953

We are occupying a hill not far behind the lines. The ——— squad, accompanied by a machine-gun crew, are responsible for it, although we have no grenades and little ammunition. But it makes little difference. The Korean war is over. No one will bother us up here.

Last night we sat around a couple of Coleman stoves and drank coffee. In the distance far to the north we could see numerous small fires like ours, in the Chinese sector. No Man's Land is deserted. New Bunker, Old Bunker, Hedy, East Berlin, Little Rock, the Pentagon, the Fan—all deserted and quiet except for the rats.

The truce was signed at ten in the morning, on June 27th, 1953. The news was relayed at once to all unit commanders. After 10 P.M. no one was to fire his weapon. Even an accidental discharge, we were told, would mean a court-martial. Throughout the hot sunny afternoon the Chinese sent over barrage after barrage of propaganda pamphlets. The projectiles exploded hundreds of feet in the air; the cannisters would open and the papers would flutter down to earth like snow. The papers would sometimes fail to separate and an entire packet would streak downward, landing hard. Judging from the height of the trajectory and the angle of the smoke trails, the projectiles were probably artillery. The smaller ones—mortars—made a peculiar noise before they detonated, like a loon. Sometimes they went WHOOP-WHOOP in a kind of falsetto. These harmless barrages were mingled with ac-

From *The Last Parallel: A Marine's War Journal,* by Martin Russ. Copyright, 1957, by Martin Russ. Reprinted by permission of Rinehart & Company, Inc., New York, Publishers. Pp. 317-20.

curate artillery and mortar bombardments. No one was interested in chasing around the paddies looking for pamphlets. It seemed as though the Chinese were merely trying to expend all of their heavy ammunition and pamphlets before the cease-fire went into effect.

The tank road, a segment of which was under direct enemy observation, was bombarded continually through the day. Troops were forced to use this road, however, in order to carry equipment back to the supply point for withdrawal. (One of the agreements of the truce was that all troops and equipment of both sides must be withdrawn from the MLR within seventy-two hours after the signing of the truce.) Fortunately there were many old bunkers along the tank road to provide cover during the sudden barrages. Van Horn and I, working together, were nearly annihilated by incoming shells that seemed to walk back and forth along the road. Some of them were 76mm. recoilless rifle projectiles. By nightfall the exposed segment of the tank road was pockmarked with small craters. . . .

UN spotter planes droned above No Man's Land and the Chinese hills during the day, checking enemy activity. Enemy antiaircraft crews sent up intensive but inaccurate fire. The gunners might have knocked down several of our planes had they put a little more range on their fields of fire. In most cases, the little white puffs of smoke following each flash red explosion—barely discernible—seemed to follow the Piper Cub in a neat, harmless line. Twice a shell exploded near a plane; one under the belly, the other beside the tail section.

One large patrol was scheduled to go out after dark, returning before 10 P.M. Van Horn and I volunteered for it, but they had room for only one extra man; we threw fingers and Van Horn won. So I asked the lieutenant (7th Marines) if I could go out on listening post, and was turned down. By 8:30 it was fully dark and the patrol members were lined up behind Green gate, ready to move out. Van Horn and I talked for awhile; I was bitching because I couldn't go along. Several rounds of 60mm. exploded nearby and everyone scurried for cover. The light barrage continued and gradually increased in intensity; 82mm. projectiles and occasional rounds of 120mm. Our reverse slopes were then under continual bombardment until 10 o'clock. The patrol leader, the 7th Marine lieutenant, had seen that everyone was inside a bunker. Van Horn and I had found a deserted ammo bunker and we sat in it. This would have been a hell of a time to get hit, an hour before the long-awaited cease-fire. Five men, including the 7th Marine lieutenant were caught by shrapnel in the ———— Platoon sector. Two men on outpost Ava—in front of Green gate—were wounded. As far as we know, none died. . . .

The barrage subsided momentarily and we went outside. A projectile—we believe it was a 120mm.—thundered into a gully nearby and blasted it. We went back inside. A quarter to ten we went outside again and raced around looking for a feeder trench, found one, and rushed up to the MLR. We huddled in the bottom of the trench and waited.

We could not be certain, but it seemed as though the marine artillery and the company mortars had stopped firing.

At 10 P.M. the hills were illuminated by the light of many flares; white star clusters, red flares, yellow flares and other pyrotechnics signifying the end of a thirty-seven-month battle that nobody won and which both sides lost. The brilliant descending lights were probably visible all along the 150-mile front, from the Yellow Sea to the Sea of Japan. The last group of shells exploded in the distance, an 82mm. landed nearby, the echoes rumbled back and forth along the Changdan Valley and died out.

A beautiful full moon hung low in the sky like a Chinese lantern. Men appeared along the trench, some of them had shed their helmets and flak jackets. The first sound that we heard was a shrill group of voices, calling from the Chinese positions behind the cemetery on Chogum-ni. The Chinese were singing. A hundred yards or so down the trench, someone began shouting the Marine Corps hymn at the top of his lungs. Others joined in, bellowing the words. Everyone was singing in a different key, and phrases apart. Across the wide paddy, in goonyland, matches were lit. We all smoked for the first time in the MLR trench. The men from outpost Ava began to straggle back, carrying heavy loads. Later in the night a group of Chinese strolled over to the base of Ava and left candy and handkerchiefs as gifts. The men that were still on Ava stared, nothing more. So ends the Korean conflict, after some 140,000 American casualties—25,000 dead, 13,000 missing or captured.[1]

9. *1955—HEART ATTACK*

⟨ *Between 1948, when General Dwight D. Eisenhower had stated that he would not contend for the Presidency under any circumstances, and 1952, a movement to nominate him as the Republican candidate gained irresistible force. The intelligence, wit, and devotion to the public welfare of Adlai E. Stevenson, the Democratic nominee, stirred the enthusiasm of millions, but in the end dissatisfaction with the Truman administration and Eisenhower's unprecedented personal popularity gave the Republicans an easy victory.*

Eisenhower brought the Korean War to an end, though without

---

[1] According to the figures of the U. S. Department of Defense: 33,629 battle deaths; 20,617 other deaths; 103,284 wounds not mortal.

From *Eisenhower: The Inside Story* by Robert J. Donovan. Copyright 1956 by New York Herald Tribune, Inc. Reprinted by permission of the publishers, Harper & Brothers, New York. Pp. 362–66.

victory, and shaped an administration that suited the increasingly conservative temper of the American people. The nation purred with prosperity, and except for the "cold war," the future seemed serene.

On the early afternoon of September 25, 1955, I was standing on the platform of a railroad station in Montreux, Switzerland, waiting for a train to Geneva. The words, "Eisenhower...Coup de Coeur" flashed at me in big type from a bundle of papers that had just been delivered. The waiting travelers, all Swiss, snatched at the pile as eagerly as I did. For the next few days, which I spent in Switzerland and Italy, the health of the American President took precedence over all other news. I doubt that the pulse-beats of any one man have ever been of as much concern to as many people as were those of Dwight D. Eisenhower at that time.

Robert J. Donovan, Washington correspondent of the New York HERALD TRIBUNE, *describes the onset of the illness that startled the world.*

Shortly after 2:30 on the morning of September 24 Mrs. Eisenhower, whose bedroom was across the hall from the President's on the second floor, heard her husband tossing about in bed. She went into his quarters to see what was disturbing him. The plain, comfortable room was familiar. On her left as she entered was a round table with a lamp. On one side of the table was a small straight chair and on the other a large overstuffed upholstered chair and ottoman. In the far wall opposite the door was a fireplace flanked by windows. To Mrs. Eisenhower's immediate right stood a shoulder-high chest of drawers and just beyond, parallel to the windows looking out on the elm-shaded street, was the large old-fashioned double bed her husband slept in. At the foot of it, completing the furnishings, was a low dresser.

Mrs. Eisenhower stepped over and found the President asleep, but because he was very restless, she woke him up.

"What's the matter, Ike?" she asked. "Are you having a nightmare or something?"

Rousing himself, the President replied that he was feeling all right, and with this assurance Mrs. Eisenhower returned to her room. The President did not drop right back to sleep, however, and within a very short time he was assailed by a pain in his chest of a kind he had never experienced before. He went into Mrs. Eisenhower's room and put his hand on his chest to show where he was suffering. On the assumption that it might be a recurrence of the indigestion of the afternoon before, she gave him a dose of milk of magnesia and sent him back to bed. But not satisfied that this was sufficient, she telephoned General Snyder, who was living at the bachelor officers' quarters at Lowry four miles away.

"Ike has a pain in his chest," she said, as her words have since been recalled. "You'd better come over."

Snyder called the air-base dispatcher for a car and instructed him also to pick up a medical kit in his office on the second floor of the administration building. Without wasting a minute, the handsome, seventy-four-year-old physician, who had been Eisenhower's doctor for ten years, slipped on his clothes over his pajamas and was waiting on the steps with his bag when the car arrived, driven by Airman 2/c Jacob Judis.

"Seven hundred fifty Lafayette Street and step on it," Snyder said.

Speeding through the overcast night without paying attention to traffic lights, Judis wheeled Snyder up to the Doud house at 3:11 A.M., and the general went at once to the President's room. Eisenhower was lying in bed restless, tormented by the severe pain in his chest. He was perspiring and flushed, though the flush was slowly giving way to pallor.

Snyder listened to Eisenhower's chest with a stethoscope and took his pulse and tested his blood pressure with a band on his arm. The pressure had gone up and the pulse was rapid. It took only two or three minutes for Snyder to come to the grave conclusion that the President of the United States was suffering from a coronary thrombosis. The extent of damage to the heart he could not, of course, determine immediately.

Quickly Snyder broke an ampoule of amyl nitrate and told the President to sniff it. Following this he gave him an injection of papaverine hydrochloride to dilate the arteries in the heart and then a shot of morphine to ease the pain and shock. A little later he prepared a hypodermic of heparin, which tends to increase the liquidity of the blood and to prevent clotting, and injected it in his arm.

A tall, straight, gray-haired, bespectacled man with unbounded affection for Eisenhower, Snyder stood tensely by the bedside observing his patient. He did not tell him what his diagnosis was, but the President knew he was very ill. His pain continued. About 3:45 A.M. Snyder gave him a second shot of morphine. As it pried loose the grip of pain, the President began sliding into a deep sleep. This was a profound relief to Snyder. The President was passing through a crisis, and the physician believed that sleep was the best thing for him.

To avert shock to Mrs. Eisenhower, who has long suffered from valvular heart disease herself, Snyder sent her back to bed without telling her the President's true condition. Also, he put aside the idea of a public announcement because he feared that it would cause great excitement which inevitably would permeate the Doud house and might possibly kill the President. Sitting alone in the dead of night with his slumbering patient, therefore, Howard Snyder was the only man in the world who knew that the President was stricken with a damaged heart.

All night long and through the morning, Snyder remained in the room with the President. He left the band on Eisenhower's arm to keep check of the blood pressure. Gradually the pressure came down and his pulse slowed to a steady beat. Although the President's condition was precarious and the future inscrutable, these encouraging signs were the faint beginnings of a remarkable recovery.

Shortly before 7 A.M. when the Presidential staff began stirring at Lowry, Snyder called Mrs. Whitman, the President's secretary, and informed her that the President was not feeling well and would not come to his office for appointments. Still holding back the truth about Eisenhower's condition, he told her that he was suffering from digestive upset. Soon afterward Murray Snyder (no kin to the general) got him on the phone and the doctor repeated this description of the illness. At 10:30 A.M. Murray Snyder, whose handling of the story in the next twelve hours won the deep admiration of the reporters in Denver, announced the President's condition as it had been told to him by Dr. Snyder.

Meanwhile Dr. Snyder calmly informed Mrs. Eisenhower of her husband's condition and telephoned Colonel Byron E. Pollock, chief of cardiology service at Fitzsimons General Hospital on the outskirts of Denver and told him to bring an electrocardiograph to the Doud house. The President began stirring about 11:45 A.M. When he was fully awake but still very weak, Dr. Snyder told him that he had summoned Dr. Pollock to take an electrocardiogram. Pollock arrived with Major General Martin E. Griffin, commanding general of the hospital, and they and Snyder made a tracing of the President's heart impulses.

The doctors took the tracing downstairs and laid it out on the dining-room table. It confirmed Snyder's diagnosis. A blood clot had blocked an artery in the front wall of the President's heart, cutting off the supply of blood from that part of the heart muscle. Snyder and Pollock returned to the President's bedroom. Snyder told Eisenhower that his heart had suffered an injury.

"We would like to take you to Fitzsimons," Snyder said.

The news did not seem to shock the President in the least, but, of course, he was still somewhat numbed from morphine.

"We're not going to get an ambulance," Snyder said.

"All right, Howard," the President replied, "call Jim"—James J. Rowley, chief of the White House Secret Service detail—"and get my car and let's go out."

Sergeant Moaney, his valet, helped the President into a bathrobe, and the three doctors supported him walking down the stairs, taking as much of his weight on their shoulders as they could manage. They had decided that it would be less of a strain on the President to walk down in this fashion than to be strapped to a stretcher and tipped in the air at the sharp angle that would have been required to carry him down the steep and narrow stairs, rounding the small halfway landing.

A limousine had been backed into the driveway, and on the porch two sturdy Secret Service men, Rowley and Deeter B. Flohr, Eisenhower's chauffeur, took over from the doctors and supported the President down the steps and into the rear of the car. Snyder sat on one side of the President and Pollock on the other. General Griffin slipped into a jump seat. With Flohr at the wheel and Rowley beside him they pulled away from the Doud house and made the nine-mile drive to the hospital at moderate speed. At Fitzsimons the car rolled up under a rear portico where a wheel chair was waiting to carry the President to the elevator. He smiled at the attendants in the corridor and had a friendly word for Charles Adams, the elevator operator who brought him up to the eighth floor to a special suite with cream-colored walls, light-green furniture and green drapes. As soon as he slipped into bed, an oxygen tent was placed over the upper half of his body.

Then the news was broken to the world. Shortly after 2:30 P.M. Murray Snyder turned the press room at Lowry into bedlam with the announcement: "The President has just a mild anterior—let's cut out the word 'anterior'—the President has just had a mild coronary thrombosis. He has just been taken to Fitzsimons General Hospital. He was taken to the hospital in his own car and walked from the house to the car."

10.   *1956—*"POSITIVE, THAT IS, AFFIRMATIVE"

❲ *After the President's recovery the question, "Will he run again?" absorbed the country. Robert J. Donovan, who was given access to all the confidential material of the first Eisenhower administration, tells the inside story of the decision.*

One of the critical moments leading up to the decision came on February 11 at Walter Reed Hospital when the President's doctors took two X-ray pictures and placed one upon the other. The one on the bottom was a picture of Eisenhower's heart before his attack. Superimposed upon it was an up-to-date picture. Everything hinged on whether the damaged heart had enlarged since he had resumed more or less normal activity in January. Because the President had been under a doctor's eye every day, this question was the only one on which his physicians needed to be reassured. With the X-rays in front of them they bent forward to see if the outlines of one heart were contiguous to those of

From *Eisenhower: The Inside Story* by Robert J. Donovan. Copyright 1956 by New York Herald Tribune, Inc. Reprinted by permission of the publishers, Harper & Brothers, New York. Pp. 402–07.

the other. When the pictures were fitted together, the two hearts matched almost precisely. This was decisive. It was the green light to the President to run again.

On February 14 the doctors announced at a press conference that "the President's health continues to be satisfactory."

"Medically," Dr. White[1] said in answer to a question, "I think we would agree that his present condition and the favorable chances in the future should enable him to be able to carry on his present active life satisfactorily for this period, as I have said, for five to ten years, knowing full well, as we have just emphasized, the hazards and uncertainties of the future."

When asked if he would vote for Eisenhower if he should run again, White said that he would.

From this day forward all signs pointed toward Eisenhower's running. The next day he went to Secretary Humphrey's plantation at Thomasville, Georgia, where he tested his strength playing golf and hunting.

"He plunged into it with what you might call an I'll-show-'em attitude," one of his companions recalled later.

After a strenuous walk through waist-high grass hunting quail one day, the President returned to the house, saying proudly, "Well, I'm feeling pretty good. I didn't get tired out. It didn't bother me."

The reassurance that this exercise at Thomasville gave him was the final brick that went into the making of his decision. He flew back to Washington on Saturday, February 25, and began preparing secretly with Hagerty for announcing on Wednesday, the 29th, first at a press conference and later on a broadcast, that he would run. Mrs. Eisenhower, it appears, did not try to influence his decision one way or another. Some of those best acquainted with the family believe that in the gloomy November and December days at Gettysburg she had come to the conclusion that her husband was not ready for retirement.

At his celebrated press conference on Wednesday Eisenhower said that he had still been arguing with himself the day before as to whether he should run. But he was speaking in the sense that since his decision had not yet been announced, he could still change his mind. By the time he had returned from Thomasville on Saturday he was clear as to his decision.

On Tuesday afternoon he began passing the word to a few close associates like Nixon, Hall, Adams and Persons, who saw him individually (for Adams and Persons this was a formality because they knew what he had decided almost as soon as he had made up his mind),

---

[1] Paul Dudley White, Boston heart specialist, who had been called in on the President's case soon after his heart attack.

and he telephoned his brother at Penn State and invited him to Washington for the broadcast Wednesday evening. But even on Wednesday before the press conference, which was scheduled for 10:30 A.M., most of the White House staff did not know for sure that he was going to run. They did not know, but they sensed it as Hagerty, presiding as he always does at staff meetings on the mornings of press conferences, went through the order of business without saying a word about the question that was on everyone's mind. All knew that Hagerty was privy to the secret, but no one could quite get up nerve to ask him. Many of the staff felt, however, that if the President had decided not to run, Hagerty would have dropped a hint at this last minute. When he did not, they were confident that Eisenhower was going to announce his candidacy. One of the chief reasons the secret was held so tightly was that the President wanted to ward off any charges that the administration was a party to manipulation of the stock market.

Early in the morning, reporters had begun lining up for the press conference outside the Indian Treaty Room on the fourth floor of the Executive Offices Building, across the street from the west wing of the White House. Three hundred and eleven of them had jammed into the ornate room when at 10:31 the President walked in, dressed in a tan suit and vest, white shirt and brown tie. His head was bowed slightly as if in thought.

Great suspense filled the high-ceilinged room as he began to speak. In a circumstance like this, Presidents seem to experience an irresistible temptation to tantalize reporters. Eisenhower began by calling upon the people to support the Red Cross drive. Next he told of his pleasure over the visit of President Giovanni Gronchi, of Italy, who had just arrived in Washington. Then he voiced his opposition to the rigid price supports which had been written into the farm bill pending in the Senate. From there he dragged his impatient audience into the subject of the Upper Colorado River Basin project, which was then up for consideration before the House. He hoped it would be approved. Seven minutes had passed. Unconsciously he unbuttoned his coat. He thrust his left hand into the pocket of his trousers.

"Now my next announcement," he said, "involves something more personal, but I think it will be of interest to you because you have asked me so many questions about it.

"I have promised this body that when I reached a decision as to my own attitude toward my own personal future, I would let you know as soon as I reached such a decision. Now I have reached a decision. But I have found, as I did so, that there were so many factors and considerations involved that I saw the answer could not be expressed just in the simple terms of yes and no. Some full explanation to the American people is not only necessary, but I would never consent to go before them unless I were assured that they did understand these things, these influences, these possibilities."

The reporters groped for the meaning of all this. Was the President saying that he was or was not going to run? He continued:

"Moreover, I would not allow my name to go before the Republican convention unless they, all the Republicans, understood, so that they would not be nominating some individual other than they thought they were nominating."

This could only have one meaning—yes. But the President went on talking. He said:

"So for both reasons, because I don't know, certainly for certain, that the Republican convention, after hearing the entire story, want me, I don't know whether the people want me, but I am—I will say this:

"I am asking as quickly as this conference is over, I am asking for time on television and radio. I am going directly to the American people and tell them the full facts and my answer within the limits I have so sketchily observed; but which I will explain in detail tonight so as to get the story out in one continuous narrative—my answer will be positive; that is, affirmative. . . ."

Twelve hours after his press conference the President spoke by television from his office. While he was waiting to go on the air, someone called attention to the motto on his desk: *Suaviter in modo fortiter in re.*

"That proves I'm an egghead," he chuckled.

Launching into his speech, he said:

I have decided that if the Republican Party chooses to renominate me, I shall accept. Thereafter, if the people of this country should elect me, I shall continue to serve them in the office I now hold.

He discussed the problem of his health very frankly. He said:

Aside from all other considerations, I have been faced with the fact that I am classed as a recovered heart patient. This means that to some undetermined extent, I may possibly be a greater risk than is the normal person of my age. My doctors assure me that this increased percentage of risk is not great.

So far as my own personal sense of well being is concerned, I am as well as before the attack occurred. It is, however, true that the opinions and conclusions of the doctors that I can continue to carry the burdens of the Presidency contemplate for me a regime of ordered work activity, interspersed with regular amounts of exercise, recreation and rest. . . .

But let me make one thing clear. As of this moment, there is not the slightest doubt that I can now perform as well as I ever have all of the important duties of the Presidency. . . .

He said that he would have to eliminate many of the social and ceremonial functions of his office and that he would not stump the country during the campaign.

He then cited his political reasons for running again, concluding:

The work that I set out four years ago to do has not yet reached the state of development and fruition that I then hoped could be accomplished within the period of a single term in this office.

When his half-hour talk was ended, the President joined his wife and Major and Mrs. Eisenhower and other members of his family who had come into the office for the broadcast. Throughout the day he had not shown any of the elation that was sweeping through the Republican ranks all over the country as a result of his decision. Rather, his feeling seemed to be one of profound relief that he had at last made up his mind and had put the matter behind him. Before leaving his office he bade members of his staff goodnight.

"I'm glad to get *that* off my chest," he told them.

The Eisenhowers strolled back to the White House proper and took an elevator to the second floor. It had been a long day for the President and in a little while he went to bed.

11. *1957—*LITTLE ROCK

⟦ *In May, 1954, the United States Supreme Court handed down one of the most momentous decisions in its history. Speaking for a united court, Chief Justice Warren held separate schools for white and Negro children to be unconstitutional, and directed that segregation be abolished "with all deliberate speed."*

The decision struck at a fundamental feature of life in the Southern states. That many communities would resist it was certain. Few observers, however, expected the most crucial test to come in Arkansas, a state where racial tension had not been marked. Nevertheless, when nine colored pupils attempted to attend Central High School at Little Rock at the opening of the term in September, 1957, violence was threatened. Governor Orval Faubus called out the National Guard—to maintain order, he asserted; to maintain segregation, his opponents charged. The Negro pupils did not attend school. Thus a direct issue was raised between the State of Arkansas and the Federal Government. After three weeks President Eisenhower ordered a strong detachment of the 101st Airborne Division to Little Rock and took the Arkansas National Guard into the federal service. The Negro children, under the protection of the troops, went back to school.[2]

In a press conference on October 3, 1957, a grave and troubled President explained his position.

Official Transcript, *U.S. News and World Report*, October 11, 1957.

[2] As this is written (February, 1958), federalized guardsmen are still on duty in Little Rock, although their number has been reduced.

Q: What prospects do you see for working out an agreement with Faubus at this stage, and what do you think the next step in this direction should be?

The President: Well, to that one there is—several things that could happen.

The Southern Governors' committee that visited me, while unquestionably, as they stated on the television, disappointed by what happened, nevertheless are not completely hopeless and are pursuing the purpose for which they were originally appointed by the Southern Governors Conference.

The two things—there are two different situations could justify the withdrawal of federal troops:

One, the satisfactory and unequivocal assurances that the orders of the federal court would not be obstructed, and that peace and order would be maintained in connection therewith.

The second would be that—an actual factual development of peaceful conditions to the extent where the local city police would say, "There will be no difficulty that we can't control in the carrying out of this court's orders."

I think, having answered your specific question, it is well to remember—to re-emphasize to ourselves—why the troops are there.

The problem grew out of the segregation problem, but the troops are not there as a part of the segregation problem.

They are there to uphold the courts of the land under a law that was passed in 1792, because it was early discovered that, unless we supported the courts—in whose hands are all our freedoms and our liberties, our protection against autocratic government—then the kind of government set up by our forefathers simply would not work. That is why they are there, and for no other purpose, and it is merely incidental that the problem grew out of the segregation problem. . . .

Q: Mr. President, do you feel that Governor Faubus really wants to put an end to the trouble in Little Rock?

The President: Well, I wouldn't want to answer that question specifically, for this reason: I make it a practice never to try to interpret the motives of a person who does something that I believe to be a mistaken action.

What his motives are I am not sure. I just believe that he is mistaken in what he is doing, and is doing a disservice to the city and to his State.

Q: Sir, should we interpret your statement of principles here, in which you say that you are obligated to use whatever means may be required, as meaning that, if a situation like this arises in any other part of the South, you will feel obligated to move in the federal troops?

The President: I don't want to be imitating the Supreme Court, but I don't think it is wise to try to answer hypothetical questions.

Each one of these cases is different. The National Guard, or the State Guard at that moment, was called out and given orders to do certain things which were a definite direct defiance of a federal court's order.

That put the issue squarely up to the executive part of the Government, and I would not, as I told you once before in a meeting—such as this—I couldn't conceive that anyone would so forget common sense and our common obligations of loyalty to the Constitution of America that force of this kind would ever have to be used for any purpose. But I just say this:

The courts must be sustained or it's not America. . . .

Q: Sir, you probably are aware that some of your critics feel you were too slow in asserting a vigorous leadership in this integration crisis. Do you feel, sir, that the results would be any different if you had acted sooner instead of, as your critics say, letting the thing drift?

The President: I am astonished how many people know exactly what the President of the United States should do.

To imply that this problem wasn't studied, not only from the time this particular one arose but from the time that that decision was passed by the Supreme Court in 1954—the question has been discussed privately or at least within the inner circles of the Administration time and time again, and it's been discussed publicly.

Now, you will recall that I have here stated a belief that is the very core of my political thinking, which is that it has got to be the sentiment, the good will, the good sense of a whole citizenry that enforces law. In other words, you have got to win the hearts and minds of men to the logic and the decency of a situation before you are finally going to get real compliance.

Law alone, as we found out in the prohibition experiment, does not cure some of the things it set out to cure. . . .

Q: Should this situation continue, do you have any practicable matter in mind or practicable system for insuring the continued attendance of these Negro children at Central High School, beyond the continued use of federal troops?

The President: Well, I don't know of any method that could be used —that is, you have to use the means that will make effective the orders of the court. Now, you want to make that as minimum as possible. Certainly, you want to interfere in local situations as little as possible.

No one can deplore more than I do the sending of federal troops anywhere. It is not good for the troops; it is not good for the locality; it is not really American, except as it becomes absolutely necessary for the support of the institutions that are vital to our form of government.

Q: Governor Clement told us yesterday that, in view of the gravity of the situation in Little Rock, if all negotiations break down he thought that perhaps you and Governor Faubus should meet again to settle this thing.

Would you comment on that suggestion, sir?

The President: No, I don't think I would comment on it at this time. I have met with him. I thought we had an understanding. I know that the four Governors thought that they had an understanding.

But I will say this: To bring back respect for the law, to clear our whole present scene of this unpleasant incident, I would do a lot. I will tell you that.

12.   *1957*—SPUTNIK I

❲ *The program of the International Geophysical Year, extending from July 1, 1957 to the end of 1958, called for the cooperative study, by scientists of more than forty nations, of many aspects of the earth and its environment: solar activity, the behavior of glaciers and the oceans, cosmic rays, the upper atmosphere. The United States willingly joined in the program, but the average American paid little attention except to note with pride the progress of an expedition to the South Pole and to look forward with confidence to the launching of a much-publicized American satellite.*

On October 4, 1957, the entire country was shocked by the announcement that Russia had projected a satellite into space and that it was circling the earth in a planned orbit. The achievement was taken as evidence that the Russians had outdistanced the United States in scientific progress and that this superiority constituted a mortal threat to our existence. Not a few leaders of opinion became almost hysterical in their demands for "crash programs," huge appropriations, and unlimited emphasis on the training of scientists. The report of Richard J. Davis, NEWSWEEK's Military Affairs correspondent, on the attitude of the Pentagon is relatively restrained.

The Pentagon feels there is still time to break the U. S. logjam and catch up. While the U. S. ICBM[1] has yet to fly, there are no doubts in the military that both the Atlas and the Titan will be successful, or that Thor, Jupiter, and Polaris, the intermediate range ballistic missiles (1,500 miles), will similarly succeed. Moreover, in the face of the Red triumph, there is complete outward confidence that in battlefield rockets, air-defense missiles, air-to-air missiles, and air-to-ground missiles, we are up to par.

In fact, our whole approach to satellites has been somewhat different from Russia's. No U.S. scientists would say so openly—first because

---

Newsweek, October 14, 1957.

[1] Inter-Continental Ballistic Missile.

674

it would sound like quibbling; second, because they are full of open admiration for the Soviet scientists. But they keep stressing the fact we are planning highly instrumented satellites, quite in contrast to the relatively simple, radio-signal-transmitting ball now rotating around the earth.

Nonetheless, whatever the confidence in Washington, it is inescapable that the Soviet satellite has been a stunning shock to the nation and is likely to bring heavy pressure on our military planners. The knowledge that a Soviet-made sphere is whirling over America many times a day will evoke a torrent of questions and there will have to be some solid answers.

Officials will parry as best they can, but behind the scenes they are surely going to work with greater dedication and speed to get the Atlas off on a good flight quickly. Economic and other restrictions on the missile programs will be lifted. Missilemen will now probably get what they want, even if their requests seem wasteful, or even if other parts of the defense program suffer.

The central fact that must be faced up to is this: As a scientific and engineering power, the Soviet Union has shown its mastery. The U. S. may have more cars and washing machines and toasters, but in terms of the stuff with which wars are won and ideologies imposed, the nation must now begin to view Russia as a power with a proven, frightening potential.

This is something our top scientists have known for some time, something the leaders of research and development have preached constantly within the military. They have urgently deplored the scarcity of youngsters going into science; they cry for more money for basic research; they cry for the kind of economic sacrifice that it takes to win an epic struggle in space.

But the Administration and Congress have been confronted with persistent demands for economy. Both will listen to the missilemen now. The harsh fact is that whatever we're doing is not enough.

13. *1958—*EXPLORER

⟦ *National apprehension deepened with the news that on November 3, 1957, Russia had launched Sputnik II, a giant satellite weighing 1,120 pounds as against the 184 pounds of Sputnik I. Apprehension approached panic when the U. S. Navy's Vanguard missile, carrying the first American satellite, failed to rise more than a few feet above its launching pad when it was fired on December 6. The foreign press made fun of the failure; American prestige dropped the world over.*

Associated Press Dispatch, Feb. 1, 1958, as printed in *Chicago Tribune*, Feb. 1, 1958.

But on the last day of January, 1958, the international balance was restored. An Associated Press dispatch from Cape Canaveral, Florida, reports the launching of Explorer.

The army fired a satellite into an orbit around the earth last night.

It completed its first orbit around the earth in 106 minutes.

A 70-foot long Jupiter-C launching vehicle sent a six-foot long tube of metal more than 200 miles into space and clusters of smaller rockets pushed it to orbital velocity of 19,400 miles an hour.

The Jupiter-C roared away from its launching pad into a starry sky at 8:48 P.M.

Two hours later President Eisenhower announced that America's first satellite was in orbit around the earth. . . .

The missile took off in a beautiful launching. It rose slowly at first in a huge splash of flame with a roar that could be heard for miles.

The missile, gleaming white in the searchlights, continued to climb upward with terrifically increasing pace into a sky dotted with a few white clouds. It soared on upward in the light of a pale moon. . . .

Newsmen watching the launching shouted and cheered as though at some exciting sports game.

Even before the missile was launched, its form, heretofore secret, could be easily made out in the searchlights.

It was tall and slender and snow white up to the stubby end of the Redstone first stage rocket. On top of that stage sat a round bucket which, about 11 minutes before the launching, was seen to start spinning.

Above the spinning bucket—containing a number of smaller size rockets—the slender satellite itself protruded several feet.

The satellite was a polished silver color, marked with parallel stripes of dark brown running barber-pole fashion down the sides. These stripes were layers of zirconium oxide applied to minimize reaction to temperature changes.

The Redstone first stage rocket was scheduled to burn out about two minutes after leaving the stand, and shortly thereafter would fall away. This separation, visible on some previous Jupiter-C launchings, was not discernible on this occasion.

The rocket vehicle on taking off demonstrated that it was one of the most powerful rockets ever launched here. Its red fiery blast extended far beneath it as it pushed its way up into the sky.

The missile became fully visible to watchers on the beaches some miles away about an hour before launching, when the crane surrounding it was rolled back.

It stood there with fumes of liquid oxygen drifting out like steam from a simmering kettle.

As minutes raced by and it appeared more and more likely that at last the United States would launch a satellite, tension grew among watching newsmen.

At the moment the rocket engine was started, there was a sharp flash of fire. Almost immediately this expanded to a huge orange balloon of flame accompanied by an earthshaking roar.

The thunder of the rocket engine was so terrific that observers had to shout at each other, and even then could not make themselves understood. Watchers waved their arms and pounded each other on the back as the missile surged skyward.

The Jupiter-C climbed vertically for what appeared to be an extremely long period in contrast to ballistic missiles fired here recently. . . .

Some moments after take-off sparks could be seen trailing back in the rocket's path. These were fragments of burned graphite, representing erosion of carbon vanes that provide means of guidance.

The Jupiter-C was launched slightly to the south of east. Its satellite nose thus would follow an orbit path over a considerable part of the densely populated areas of the earth.

Dana, Richard Henry, in Anthony Burns case, 290
Dane, Deliverance, recants, 38
Daniels, Jonathan, Jr., at Truman's succession, 645
Danport, Ensign, in Pequot War, 33
Danvers (Salem, Mass.), witchcraft in, 34–38
Darling, Jay ("Ding"), mentioned, 544
D'Autry, Sieur, witnesses prise de possession, 47
Davenport, John, mentioned, 142
Daviess, Joseph Hamilton, at Battle of Tippecanoe, 173
Davis, Sergeant, in Pequot War, 34
Davis, Abel, in Spanish-American War, 449
Davis, Isaac, killed at Concord, 89
Davis, Jefferson, demands surrender of Fort Sumter, 312
Davis, Matthew L., account of Burr-Hamilton duel, 143–44
Davis, Richard Harding, describes San Juan Hill, 442–44
Davis, Richard J., reports reaction to Russian satellite, 674–75
Dawes, William, warns minutemen, 86
Dayton, Jonathan, mentioned, 140
Dayton, William L., placed in nomination, 302; vote for, 304
Deberdt, Mrs., at First Continental Congress, 98
Declaration of Independence, adopted, 101–02; reception of, 102–03
Declaration of Rights, adopted, 99
Dehart, at First Continental Congress, 98
Delano, Miss, and death of Roosevelt, 623
Delano, Alonzo, describes gold rush, 253–55
Delano, Columbus, seconds nomination, 302
Delano, Frederick, at Hyde Park, 574
Delaplace, William, commands at Ticonderoga, 92
Delaware River, crossing of, 107–09
Democratic National Convention (1912), White describes, 475–78
Democratic Party, in Western country, 158–59
Dennis, Frank, cowboy, 361–62
Denton, John, in Donner party, 230, 231
Denver (Col.), described, 382
Depression (1930's), 537–40

Desegregation, Supreme Court decision, 651–52; trouble over, in Little Rock, 671–75
Detroit (Mich.), description of, 50; surrender of, 178–79; retaken, 182
Detroit (ship), in Battle of Lake Erie, 188
Dewey, George, wins Battle of Manila Bay, 438–42
Dickens, Charles, describes railroad travel, 205–07
Dickinson, Emily, describes life at Mount Holyoke, 271–73
Dickinson, John, at First Continental Congress, 96, 98
Digby, William, describes Burgoyne's surrender, 109–10
Dillon, Sidney, at completion of Union Pacific, 357–58
Discovery (ship), 22
Disease, in Spanish-American War, 448–49; in Canal Zone, 454–55
Dixey, friend of Edison, 385
Dixon, Mrs. E. L., at Lincoln's death, 341
Dixon, Thomas, author of The Clansman, 523
Doddridge, Ensign, at Manila Bay, 441
Dodge, Grenville M., at completion of Union Pacific, 357–58
Doheny, Edward, bribes Fall, 511–12
Dolphin (warship), at Guantanamo Bay, 445
Don Antonio de Ulloa (warship), at Manila Bay, 439–42
Don Juan de Austria (warship), at Manila Bay, 439–42
Donner, Jacob, in Donner party, 230
Donner party, hardships of, 229–31
Donovan, Robert J., describes Eisenhower's heart attack, 664–67; reports second term decision, 667–71
Dorsten, Rudolph Van, describes Washington's inauguration, 133–35
Doughty, John, warning from, 152
Douglas, Stephen A., defies anti-slavery crowd, 292–94; debates with Lincoln, 294–98
Douglass, Davis B., on Cass expedition, 167
Doyle, Major, tavern keeper, 264–66
Dring, Thomas, experiences of prison ship, 124–27
Drum, S. H., at Molino del Rey, 247
Duane, James, at First Continental Congress, 99

Duckworth, James, at Bataan, 582

Duddingston, William, commands *Gaspée,* 84–86

Dudley, Thomas H., nominates Dayton, 302

Duff, John R., at completion of Union Pacific, 357–58

Dulignon, Jean, witnesses prise de possession, 47

Dulles, John Foster, and United Nations, 647

Dunbar, Colonel, at Braddock's defeat, 71–72

Dunn, Benjamin, in capture of *Gaspée,* 85–86

Du Pratz, Le Page, describes New Orleans, 48–49

Duquesne, Ange de Menneville, Marquis de, fortifies frontier, 69

Duquesne, Fort, capture of, 69

Durant, Thomas C., at completion of Union Pacific, 357–58

Durham, Israel W., "boss" of Philadelphia, 405–07

Duryea, J. Frank, wins first automobile race, 417–18

Early, Stephen, and dissension in New Deal, 564–65; announces death of Roosevelt, 624; and succession of Truman, 643–45

Eaton, Charles A., and Truman Doctrine, 650–51

Eckert, Thomas T., at death of Lincoln, 340–42

Eddy, Mrs. Eleanor, in Donner party, 230, 231

Edison, Thomas A., character sketch, 383–86

Education, of women, 271–73

Edwards, Albert (Arthur Bullard), describes building of Panama Canal, 450–57

Eighteenth Amendment, imposes prohibition, 516–18

Eisenhower, Dwight D., narrative of, i; sets invasion date, 609–11; at Normandy breakout, 616; announces end of war in Europe, 625; suffers heart attack, 663–67; second term decision, 667–71; defends desegregation enforcement, 672–75; announces U.S. satellite, 676

Eisenhower, Mrs. Dwight D., and President's heart attack, 664–66; and second term decision, 668

El Caney (Cuba), Americans capture, 442–44

Elliott, Jesse Duncan, in Battle of Lake Erie, 186–87

Elliott, Milton, in Donner party, 230, 231

Ellsworth, Oliver, in selection of capital, 136–37

Elmes, Chester, at Corregidor, 584

Emancipation, Lincoln decides on, 320–22; in South Carolina, 343–49

Emerson, Ralph Waldo, characterized, 423–24

Emporia Gazette (Kansas), mentioned, 471

Engelmann, George, settles in Illinois, 263–65

Engelmann, Sophie, settles in Illinois, 263–65

Engelmann, Theodore Frederick, settles in Illinois, 263–65

Engineers, in World War II, 602–05

England, war with France, 65–79

Erickson, John, builds *Monitor,* 317

Erie Canal, travel on, 195–96

Erie, Fort, 182

Esberg, Milton H., host to Hoover, 544–46

Etherington, George, at Michilimackinac, 78

Europe, invasion of. *See* Normandy, invasion of

Evans, Major, at Alamo, 238

Evarts, William M., nominates Seward, 302; in impeachment trial, 353–54

Everett, Edward, and Webster, 212–14

Explorer, first U.S. satellite, 675–77

FERA, New Deal agency, 550–51

Fairbanks, Douglas, motion picture actor, 523

Fairchild, Charles, Iles employs, 209

Fairlie, Mary, letter to, 146

Falcon (ship), voyage on, to California, 251–53

Fall, Albert B., defection of, 511–12

Faneuil Hall (Boston), mentioned, 59

Fanning, Nathaniel, describes battle between *Bonhomme Richard* and *Serapis,* 120–24

Farm life, Norwegians in U.S., 366–69

Farmer, plight of, in depression, 555–58

Farmer, Captain, in Battle of New Orleans, 191

Fashions, men's, in 1920's, 519

Fashions, women's, in 1920's, 518–22

Faubus, Orval, and desegregation, 671–75

Fauquier, Francis, describes defiance of Stamp Act, 81–83

Federal Emergency Relief Administration, 550–51

Federalist Party, formed, 139; in Western country, 158–59

Feltham, Jocelyn, at Ticonderoga, 93

Ferdinand (of Spain), sponsors Columbus' voyage, 1–2

Fermi, Enrico, and first atomic reaction, 594–97

Fermi, Mrs. Enrico, story of first atomic reaction, 594–97

Few, William, in capital selection, 137

Fields, James T., on Nathaniel Hawthorne, 274–75

Finletter, Thomas, and Korean War, 656

Finley, John, accompanies Boone, 148

"Fireside chat," first, 549

"First Hundred Days," of New Deal, 546–49

Fithian, Philip Vickers, describes Virginians, 56–57

Flanders, Walter, Ford employee, 391

Fleming, Philip B., at Truman's succession, 645

Flint, Timothy, describes keelboat trip, 193–94

Florida, Spanish claim, 20–21

"Flying Fortresses," bomb Germany, 617–22

Foch, Ferdinand, Allied commander, 503–04

Folsom, Nathaniel, at First Continental Congress, 96

Fones, Daniel, at Louisbourg, 66–68

Football, development of, 413–14

Ford, Henry, manufacturing genius, 389–91

Ford Motor Company, early years, 389–92

Ford's Theatre, Lincoln's assassination, 338–40

Forrestal, James, and Truman Doctrine, 649

Forsyth, Robert A., on Cass expedition, 167

Forsyth, Thomas, ransoms captives, 177

Fort Dearborn Massacre, 174–77

Foster, Dwight, mentioned, 142

Foster, Theodore, mentioned, 140

"Four Horsemen of the Apocalypse," motion picture, 524

Fourth of July, celebrated, 152–53

Fowler, Joseph S., votes to acquit Johnson, 356

Fox, George, and death of Roosevelt, 623

France, war with England, 65–79

Francis Ferdinand, Archduke, assassination of, 483

Franklin, Benjamin, to draft Declaration, 101; urges adoption of Constitution, 130–33

Freedmen, 343–49

Freeman's Farm, Battle of, 109

Freeport (Ill.), debate at, 297

Fremont, John C., vote for, at Chicago convention, 304

French and Indian War, beginning of, 72

French army, in Yorktown campaign, 127–29

Frontier religion, 265–68

Frontiersmen, characterized, 155–56; cabins of, 156–57; Cuming describes, 157–59; political differences, 158–59

Fugitive slave law, enforcement of, 289–92

Fur trade, 220–26

Furlong, William R., describes Pearl Harbor, 576–78

Gadsden, Christopher, at First Continental Congress, 96

Gage, Thomas, at Braddock's defeat, 70–72; seizes colonists' powder, 87; attacks at Bunker Hill, 93–94

Galamb, Joseph, Ford employee, 389–90

Galesburg (Ill.), debate at, 297

Gallegos, Baltasar de, with De Soto, 12

Galloway, Joseph, at First Continental Congress, 97, 99

Gangs, in New York, 402–04

Garland, in Battle of Monterey, 240

Garner, John N., inauguration of, 543

Gaspé Bay, Cartier visits, 13–15

Gaspée (revenue cutter), burning of, 84–86

Geiger, Captain, at Battle of Tippecanoe, 173

General Gratiot (lake steamer), 198–99

General Lezo (warship), at Manila Bay, 439–42

"Gentleman of Elvas, The," quoted, 9–13

Genung, Charles Harvey, at Mark Twain dinner, 430

George III (of England), attempts to coerce colonies, 84; arms torn down, 102–03

Georgia, slavery in, 287–89

German army, defense of Normandy, 612–14, 616–17

Hansom cab, pleasure riding, 410
Hardin, John J., killed at Buena Vista, 243
Harding, Warren G., inauguration of, 507–09; characterized, 510–13
Harding, Mrs. Warren G., apprehensions, 511; grief, 513
Harmar, Josiah, at Marietta, 151
Harpers Ferry, John Brown's raid, 299
Harris, Clara H., at death of Lincoln, 341
Harrison, Benjamin, at First Continental Congress, 97, 98
Harrison, William Henry, at Battle of Tippecanoe, 172–74; report to, on Battle of Lake Erie, 186; Flint visits, 194
Harvard College, mentioned, 60
Harvey, Peter, describes Webster speech, 212–14
Haskell, Frank A., describes Pickett's charge, 323–25
Hassett, and death of Roosevelt, 623
Hawkins, Lieut., at Battle of Tippecanoe, 173
Hawkins, Hamilton S., at San Juan Hill, 443–44
Hawley, Willis C., at Roosevelt's inauguration, 542
Hawthorne, Nathaniel, characterized, 273–75
Hayne, Robert Y., speech of, 212–13
Heald, Nathan, in Fort Dearborn Massacre, 175–77
Helena (cruiser), at Pearl Harbor, 577
Helm, Leonard, in Vincennes expedition, 115–17
Helm, Linai T., describes Fort Dearborn Massacre, 175–77
Helm, Mrs. Linai T., in Fort Dearborn Massacre, 177
Henry, Alexander, adventures of, 72–79
Henry, Patrick, commissions Clark, 112
Herman, Fred, describes Murmansk convoy, 589–94
Hersey, John, describes devastation at Hiroshima, 633–40
Hessians, British employ, 101; at Trenton, 108–09
Heydon, in Pequot War, 32
Hickerson, John, and Korean War, 656
Higgins, Marguerite, reports Korean War, 657–60
Higginson, Henry Lee, founds Boston Symphony, 419
Hillhouse, James, mentioned, 142
Hiroshima (Japan), devastated, 633–40
Hitler, Adolph, aggressions of, 575–76

Hochelaga, Cartier visits, 15–19
Hodson, William, and federal relief program, 550
Hoffman, Charles Fenno, describes travel on National Road, 202–05
Holden, Joseph, accompanies Boone, 148
Hollywood (Cal.), emergence of, as film capital, 524
Holmes, Emma E., describes attack on Fort Sumter, 312–15
Holmes, Oliver Wendell, characterization of, 425–26
Homesteading, in Kansas, 370–71; in Oklahoma, 371–75
Hone, Philip, on Jenny Lind's triumph, 280–81
Hoover, Herbert, at Roosevelt's inauguration, 543; good will of, 544–46; vetoes TVA, 560
"Hoovervilles," of depression, 538
Hopeton (estate), slavery on, 287–89
Hopkins, Harry, and federal relief program, 549–53; feud with Ickes, 563–67; and third term, 570–74; receives news of Pearl Harbor, 579
Hopkins, John B., in capture of Gaspée, 85–86
Hopkins, Stephen, at First Continental Congress, 97
Horatio (ship), in China trade, 215–17
"House Divided" speech, 295
Howe, Louis McHenry, inspects CCC camps, 558–60
Howe, William, commands at Bunker Hill, 94
Howells, William Dean, describes New England writers, 423–27
Howes, Wright, U.S.-Iana, ii
Howland, John, narrow escape, 27
Huckleberry Finn, importance of, 429
Huffman, George, in Battle of New Orleans, 192
Hughes, Charles Evans, Wilson defeats, 480–82
Huguenots, in Florida, 20–21
Hull, Cordell, supports Roosevelt, 574; receives news of Pearl Harbor, 579
Hull, Isaac, reports on battle with Guerrière, 183–84
Hull, William, surrenders Detroit, 175, 178–79
Humphrey, Seth K., describes opening of Cherokee Strip, 371–75
Hunt, Henry J., at Gettysburg, 323
Huron (schooner), 197
Hurons (Indians), described, 13–14

Jolson, Al, in "The Jazz Singer," 524
Jones, John Paul, defeats *Serapis,* 119–24
Jones, William, report to, on Battle of Lake Erie, 186–87
Jonesboro (Ill.), debate at, 297
Judd, Norman B., nominates Lincoln, 302
Judson, Jacob, describes inefficiency in Spanish-American War, 448–49

KDKA, first radio station, 529
Kanorado (Kan. & Col.), described, 381
Kansas, John Brown in, 299; homesteading in, 370–71
Kansas-Nebraska Bill, passed, 292; effect of, 294
Kaskaskia (Great Village of the Illinois), Marquette visits, 44–45
Kaskaskia (Randolph Co., Ill.), capture of, 112–14
Keelboats, 193–94
Kellogg, Will Keep, founds cereal foods company, 388
Kelly, "King," and slide in baseball, 412
Kendall, George, Virginia colonist, 23
Kenly, John R., describes Battle of Monterey, 239–41
Kennelley, Arthur, and Edison, 384
Kent, J. L., at San Juan Hill, 442–44
Kentucky, Boone explores, 147–50; settlers characterized, 153–55
Keseberg, Lewis, in Donner party, 230, 231
King, Charles B., umpires automobile race, 418
King, Rufus, in selection of capital, 136–37
King George's War, 65–68
"King of Kings, The," motion picture, 524
Kinney, Mrs. Constance, at Lincoln's death, 341
Kinzie, John, in Fort Dearborn Massacre, 175–77
Kirkland, Joseph, 399–400
Knickerbocker's History of New York, 276
Knox, Doctor, at First Continental Congress, 96
Knox, Franklin, receives news of Pearl Harbor, 579
Knyphausen, Wilhelm von, Hessian commander, 108
Koerner, Gustave, describes German immigrants, 263–65; describes Lincoln-Douglas debates, 295–98

Kohlsaat, Herman H., sponsors automobile race, 417; describes McKinley's irresolution, 437–38
Korea, war in, 654–63

Labor, organized, 392–95; in Pullman strike, 395–99; in sweatshops, 399–400
Lacey, Mary, confesses to witchcraft, 35–37
Lacrosse, game of, 73
Lafayette, Marquis de, outmaneuvers Cornwallis, 127; tribute to, 493
La Follette, Robert M., in Republican Convention, 472
La Follette, Robert M., Jr., and federal relief, 550–51
Lake Borgne, Battle of, 188
Lake Erie, Battle of, 185–88
Lake Itasca, source of Mississippi River, 167
Lamberton, Benjamin P., at Manila Bay, 441
La Mothe, Guillaume, at Vincennes, 115
Lamp, incandescent, Edison develops, 383
Lane, Franklin K., describes home front, 497–99
Lane, Henry S., at Chicago convention, 303
Lane, James H., mentioned, 355
Lane, Mrs. Joseph, at ball, 56
Langlade, Charles, aids Alexander Henry, 74–77
Langlade, Mme. Charles, aids Alexander Henry, 75–77
Lansing, Robert, describes Wilson's speech for declaration of war, 485–89
Laramie River Valley, fur trade in, 223
Lardner, John, describes Iwo Jima fighting, 626–31
Larpenteur, Charles, describes fur trade, 221–23
La Salle, Nicholas de, witnesses prise de possession, 47
La Salle, Robert Cavelier, Sieur de, claims Mississippi Valley, 45–47
Lasker, Albert D., describes early advertising, 386–89
Latrobe, Charles J., describes river steamers, 199–202; describes Irish immigrants, 262–63
Laub, Midshipman, killed in Battle of Lake Erie, 187
Lawrence (warship), in Battle of Lake Erie, 186–88

690

Rusk, Dean, and Korean War, 656
Russ, Martin, recounts Korean War, 660–63
Russia, convoys to, 589–94; ambitions of, 649–51; launches first satellite, 674–75
Rutledge, Edward, at First Continental Congress, 96, 99
Rutledge, John, at First Continental Congress, 96, 97, 99

Sabin, James, in capture of *Gaspée,* 85–86
Sackville, Fort, capture of, 114–17
Sacramento (Cal.), described, 254–55
Safford, Governor, at completion of Union Pacific, 357–58
St. Augustine (Fla.), founding of, 19–21
St. Clair, Sir John, at Braddock's defeat, 70–72
St. Ignace (Mich.), mission, 38
St. Lawrence River, Cartier ascends, 15–19
St. Lô (France), Americans break through, 615–617
St. Louis (Mo.), corruption in, 406–07
St. Louis Fur Company, 224–26
St. Nicholas Magazine, Paine edits, 429
Salem (Danvers, Mass.), witchcraft in, 34–38
Salmagundi Papers, The, mentioned, 276
Sampson, William T., commands U.S. fleet, 442
San Francisco (Cal.), United Nations conference, 646–47
San Francisco Bay, description of, 253
San Juan Hill, Battle of, 442–44
San Vicente, Juan de, Spanish commander, 20
Sanchez, Rodrigo, sights land, 4
Sandburg, Carl, supports Roosevelt, 574
Sands, Joshua Ratoon, at Vera Cruz, 244
Sangamon Valley (Ill.), Iles settles in, 207–09
Santa Anna, Antonio López de, besieges Alamo, 235–38; defeated at Buena Vista, 241–43; defies Scott, 246
Santa Fe (N. Mex.), described, 234–35, 383
Santa Fe Railroad, effect of, 382–83
Santa Fe Trail, experiences on, 231–34
Santa Maria (Columbus' ship), 2
Santiago, Battle of, 442–48
Sarajevo (Austria-Hungary), and beginning of World War I, 483

Saratoga (N.Y.), surrender at, 109–10
Satellite, Russian, 674–75; U.S., 675–77
Sault Ste. Marie, mission at, 38
Scalawags, 346
Scammel, Alexander, at execution of André, 119
Scarlet Letter, The, publication of, 273–75
Schmidt, Johannes, distress of, 556–57
Schoolcraft, Henry R., expedition of, 167–70
Schurz, Carl, seconds nomination, 302
Scott, Winfield, takes Vera Cruz, 243–46; receives news of Bull Run, 315–16
Seafaring, 214–19
Secession, Ordinance of, passage, 308–11
Semmes, Raphael, describes capture of Vera Cruz, 243–46
Sennett, Mack (Michael S. Sinnot), motion picture producer, 523
Serapis, defeated by *Bonhomme Richard,* 119–24
Seven Years' War, beginning of, 72; strengthens Great Britain, 80–81
Seward, Fanny, mentioned, 339
Seward, Frederick, assassination attempted, 339–40
Seward, William H., fails to win nomination, 301–04; receives news of Bull Run, 316; objects to Proclamation of Emancipation, 320; suggests change in Proclamation of Emancipation, 322; assassination attempted, 339–40
Seymour, S. A., at completion of Union Pacific, 357–58
Sezma, Ramirez, at Alamo, 236
Sharp, William G., welcomes Pershing, 491
Sheahan, James W., describes Douglas at anti-slavery meeting, 292–94
Sherman, Forrest, and Korean War, 656
Sherman, Roger, to draft Declaration, 101
Sherman, William Tecumseh, takes Atlanta, 333
Sherwood, Robert E., describes third-term campaign, 570–74
"Shiek, The," motion picture, 524
Shigemitsu, Mamoru, at Japanese surrender, 641
Shippen, William, at First Continental Congress, 96, 97
"Shirley, Dame," describes gold mining, 255–58

Shoemaker, Samuel, in Donner party, 230

Shoumatoff, Madame, paints Roosevelt's portrait, 623, 625

Sicily, U.S. attacks, 601–02

Sinnot, Michael S. (Mack Sennett), motion picture producer, 523

Sketch Book, The, mentioned, 276

Skinner, Otis, as theater manager, 420–23

Slaughter, Colonel, in Battle of New Orleans, 189

Slavery, described, 57–59; cause of colonial weakness, 62; unfavorable view, 283–87; favorable view, 287–89; and Proclamation of Emancipation, 320–22; fugitives from, 289–92. *See also* Anti-Slavery.

Slavs, as immigrants, 401–02

Sloan, James, criticizes Taft, 469–70

Slosson, Preston William, describes changes in manners and morals, 518–22; on history of movies 522–24

Slums, produce crime, 402–04

Smallpox, on *Jersey,* 126

Smiley, Colonel, in Battle of New Orleans, 189

Smith, Caleb, seconds nomination, 302

Smith, Colonel, attacks militia at Lexington, 88

Smith, Gladys (Mary Pickford), motion picture actress, 523

Smith, James, reports Lincoln's assassination, 339

Smith, John, at Jamestown, 21–24; and Pocahontas, 24–26

Smith, Jonathan B., at First Continental Congress, 96

Smith, Samuel, at Jackson's inauguration, 210

Smith, Mrs. Samuel Harrison, describes Jefferson's inauguration, 139–40

Smith, Thomas, at First Continental Congress, 98

Smith, William, at First Continental Congress, 97

Smith, William F., at Cold Harbor, 331

Smoking, by women, 521

Smoot, Reed, at Roosevelt's inauguration, 542

Snelling, Captain, at Battle of Tippecanoe, 173

Snyder, Howard M., attends Eisenhower, 664–67

Snyder, Murray, reports Eisenhower heart attack, 666–67

Social changes, 1920's, 525–30

Sod house, making of, 369–71

Solomons, Ezekiel, at Michilimackinac, 78

Sorensen, Charles E., early years with Ford, 389–92

Soto, Hernando de, explorations of, 9–11; death, 11–12

South, reconstruction in, 343–52

South Carolina, secedes, 308–11; reconstruction in, 343–49; "Black Parliament," 346–49

Spalding, Albert G., recounts baseball history, 411–13

Spanish-American War, 437–49; inefficiency in, 448–49

Speed, James, at death of Lincoln, 342

Spencer, Karl P., experiences at Belleau Wood, 500–03

Spillman, Henry, in Battle of New Orleans, 189

"Spirit of St. Louis" (airplane), 530–33

Spitfire (steamer), at Vera Cruz, 244

Spitzer, Augustus, in Donner party, 230

Sport, *see* individual sports

Springfield (Ill.), Iles settles in, 207–09; Lincoln speaks at, 295, 297; Douglas speaks at, 297

Sproat, David, commissary of prisoners, 125

Sprout, Rev. Mr., at First Continental Congress, 96

Sputniks, Russian satellites, 674–75. *See also* Explorer.

Square Deal, origin of term, 463–66

Stage, in U.S., 420–23

Stagg, Amos Alonzo, describes early football, 413–14

Stagg, J. M., meteorologist, 610–11

Stalin, Joseph Vissarionovich, at Teheran Conference, 607–09

Stamp Act, defied, 81; John Adams on, 83–84; repeal, 84

Standard Oil Company, Rockefeller defends, 378–80; first trust, 387n

Standish, Myles, Plymouth colonist, 30

Stanford, Leland, at completion of Union Pacific, 357–58

Stanton, C. F., in Donner party, 229, 230

Stanton, Edwin M., at death of Lincoln, 340–42

Stanton, Thomas, in Pequot War, 34

Stark, Harold R., and destroyer deal, 572

Stars and Stripes, first flown, 122

States' Rights, Hayne argues for, 212–13

Steel, Gadsden, in Klan trial, 349–52

Steevens, G. W., describes Bryan, 459–61; describes McKinley, 461–63

Steffens, Lincoln, describes corruption in Philadelphia, 405–07; on Roosevelt and Square Deal, 463–66

Steiner, Edward, describes Slavic immigrants, 401–02

Steptoe, Doctor, at First Continental Congress, 98

Sterling, Yates, commands *President Lincoln,* 493–97

Stetson, John, aids Skinner's troupe, 421

Stettinius, Edward R., Jr., at Truman's succession, 644; and United Nations, 646–48

Steuben, Friedrich Wilhelm, drills Continental army, 112

Stevens, Thaddeus, and Johnson impeachment trial, 356

Stevenson, Adlai E., defeated for Presidency, 663

Stewart, John, accompanies Boone, 148, 149

Stickney, Joseph L., describes Battle of Manila Bay, 438–42

Stimson, Henry L., receives news of Pearl Harbor, 579; reveals atom bomb project, 631–33

Stock market, boom in, 533–35; collapse, 535–37

Stokes, Thomas L., characterizes Coolidge, 513–16; describes Roosevelt's inauguration, 541–43; describes "First Hundred Days," 546–49

Stone, Harlan Fiske, at Truman's succession, 644–45

Storekeeping, Iles' experience, 207–09

Stoughton, Israel, in Pequot War, 33–34

Strike, at Pullman Company, 395–99

Strother, David Hunter, describes John Brown's execution, 299–301

Suckley, Miss, and death of Roosevelt, 623

Sugar Act, 81

Sullivan, John, at First Continental Congress, 96

Sullivan, John L., loses to Corbett, 414–17

Summerall, Charles P., commands troops on *President Lincoln,* 495

Sumner, Charles, vote for, at Chicago convention, 304; at death of Lincoln, 341

Sumter, Fort, attack on, 311–15

"Sunnyside" (Irving's home), 276–78

Supreme Court, U.S., ends NRA, 553

Susan Constant (ship), 22

Sutter, John Augustus, describes discovery of gold, 248–50

Svendson, Gro, describes life of Norwegian immigrants, 366–69

Sweatshops, in Chicago, 399–400

"Swedish Nightingale," American tour, 280–81

TVA, New Deal Agency, 560–63

Taft, William Howard, characterization of, 468–71; wins renomination, 471–74

Talking pictures, development of, 524

Tallmadge, Benjamin, mentioned, 142

Tank corps, in World War II, 597–601

Tarrying, described, 61

Tate, Alfred O., describes Edison, 383–86

Tattnall, Josiah, at Vera Cruz, 244

Taylor, Bayard, describes gold rush, 250–53; wins song contest, 280

Taylor, Zachary, Mexican War campaign, 238–43

Teapot Dome, scandal, 511–12

Tecumseh (chief), confederacy of, 172; in capture of Detroit, 178

Tedder, Sir Arthur William, and Normandy invasion, 610

Teheran Conference, 607–09

"Ten Commandments, The," motion picture, 524

Tennessee Valley, people of, 561–62

Tennessee Valley Authority, beginnings of, 560–63

Tenure of Office Act, and Johnson impeachment, 352

Texas, fights for independence, 235–38

Texas (battleship), at Guantanamo Bay, 445

Thacher, James, describes execution of André, 118–19; describes surrender of Cornwallis, 127–29

Thames, Battle of, 182

Thayer, Fred W., invents catcher's mask, 412

Theater, in U.S., 278–79; Skinner's experiences, 420–23

"Thief of Bagdad, The," motion picture, 524

Thomas, Theodore, rivalry with Damrosch, 419–20

Thomas Jefferson (lake steamer), 197

Thompson, Dorothy, supports Roosevelt, 574

Thompson, J. Walter, advertising agency, 387

Thomson, Charles, at First Continental Congress, 96, 97

"Three Musketeers, The," motion picture, 524

Ticonderoga, Fort, Allen captures, 91–93

Tiler, Hannah, recants, 38

Tiler, Mary, recants, 38

Tilghman, Edward, at First Continental Congress, 98

Tilghman, Matthew, at First Continental Congress, 98

Tippecanoe, Battle of, 172–74

Tobacco, use of, by women, 521

Tom Sawyer, importance of, 429

Tonty, Henry de, accompanies La Salle, 45–47

Toponce, Alexander, describes completion of Union Pacific, 357–58

Townshend Acts, passage of, 84

Towson, Nathan, at Jackson's inauguration, 210

Trade Union Advocate, 394

Transcendentalism, at Brook Farm, 268–71

Trask, William, in Pequot War, 34

Travel, *see* Keelboats, Canal boats, Railroads, etc.

Travis, William Barrett, commands at Alamo, 235–38

Treaty of Paris, recognizes American independence, 171

Trenton (N.J.), capture of, 107–09

Triana, Rodrigo de, sights land, 4

Trolley car, for pleasure riding, 409–10

Truckee Lake, Donner party at, 229–31

Truman, Harry S., succeeds Roosevelt, 642–45; decides to use atom bomb, 631–33; and United Nations, 646; decides to fight in Korea, 654–56

Truman, Mrs. Harry S., at Truman's succession, 644–45

Truman, Margaret, at Truman's succession, 644–45

Truman Doctrine, origin of, 649–51

Tugwell, Rexford G., and relief administration, 564

Tully, Grace, describes effect of Pearl Harbor, 579–81; recounts death of Roosevelt, 622–25

Tumulty, Joseph P., describes Wilson's inauguration, 478–80; describes Wilson's re-election, 480–82; describes Wilson's collapse, 505–06; describes Harding's inauguration, 507–09

Tunisia, capture of, 597–601

Turkey, threatened by Russia, 650; in Korean War, 656

Tuttle, Governor, at completion of Union Pacific, 357–58

Twain, Mark, authorizes biography, 429–31

Twice-Told Tales, sales of, 273–75

Tyng, James, wears catcher's mask, 412

Umezu, Yoshijiro, at Japanese surrender, 641

Underhill, John, in Pequot War, 31

Union Pacific Railroad, completed, 357–58

Unions, federation of, 392–95

United Nations, formation of, 646–48; condemns North Korean aggression, 654–55

United Press, correspondents of, 549

United States Supreme Court, desegregation decision, 651–52, 671–75

University of Chicago, and discovery of atomic fission, 594–97

Usher, John P., at death of Lincoln, 342

V-E Day, 625–26

V-J Day, 640–41

Vacuum tube, Edison's part in developing, 383–84

Valley Forge, hardships of, 110–12

Vandenberg, Arthur H., and founding of United Nations, 646–48; and Truman Doctrine, 650–51

Vandenberg, Mrs. Arthur H., letters to, 648

Vandenberg, Hoyt S., and Korean War, 656

Van Ness, W. P., at Burr-Hamilton duel, 144

Varnum, James Mitchell, at Marietta, 152, 153

Vasquez, Louis, fur trader, 221

Venable, C. S., describes Lee's surrender, 336–37

Vera Cruz, capture of, 243–46

Verdi, Doctor, attends Seward, 339–40

Versailles, Treaty of, 505

Vicksburg (Miss.), Ludlow in, 278–79; capture of, 325–28

Vincennes (Ind.), recapture of, 114–17

Virginia, first settlement, 21–26; described, 53–57; resists Stamp Act, 80–83

Virginia (Merrimack), 317

Virginia Company, sends out colony, 21

Viviani, René, welcomes Pershing, 491

Vixen (steamer), at Vera Cruz, 244

702

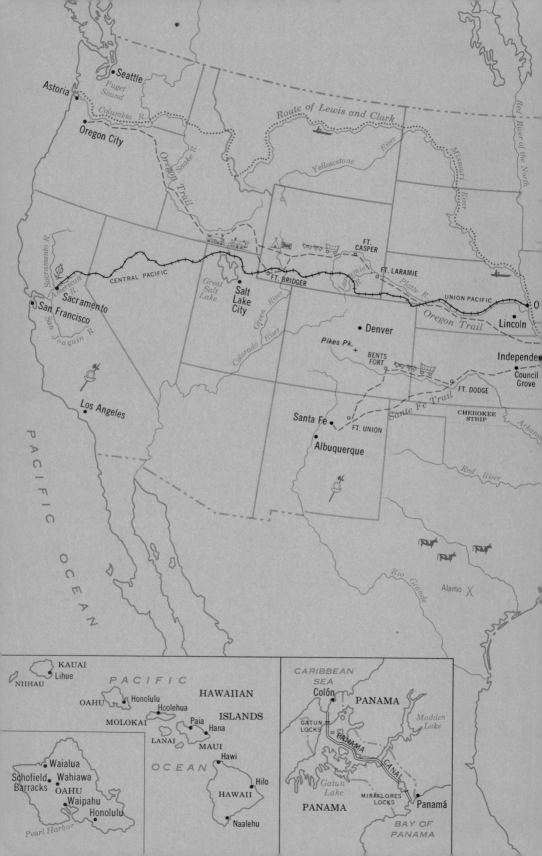